CURSED AND CROWNED

FAITH FRAY

Cursed and Crowned
Copyright © 2023 Faith Fray
All rights reserved.
No part of this book may be reproduced, distributed, or transmitted in any form or by any means, including photocopying, recording, or other electronic or mechanical methods, without written permission from the author, except for the use of brief quotations in reviews and other non-commercial uses permitted by U.S. copyright law.

For inquiries, contact faithfrayauthor@gmail.com

This is a work of fiction. The names, characters, places, and events portrayed in this book are products of the author's imagination or are used fictitiously. Any resemblance to actual persons, living or dead, events, organizations, or places is entirely coincidental.

First edition: May 2023

Cover Design by Rachel McEwan
www.rachelmcewandesigns.com
Editing by Stand Corrected Editing
www.standcorrectedediting.com

Identifiers:
ISBN: 979-8-9880762-0-9 (paperback)
ISBN: 979-8-9880762-1-6 (ebook)
LCCN: 2023908295

St. Lous, MO

www.faithfray.com

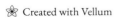 Created with Vellum

*To those who are dark yet delicate
and crave unconditional love*

CONTENT WARNINGS MAY CONTAIN SPOILERS

Cursed and Crowned is a dark fantasy book and therefore may contain triggering content for some. Please read the full list of content warnings below and take care of yourself while reading.

Blood and gore, depictions of violence, death of family, dead bodies, self-harm, suicidal thoughts, explicit sexual content, manipulative relationship tactics, traumatizing birth scene, postpartum depression (ending in the death of the affected character), death of children, murder, child abuse, off-page amputation, child soldiers, PTSD, verbal abuse, whipping, underaged drinking, kidnapping, religious abuse and indoctrination, social pressure to become pregnant, disturbing themes of childbearing, classism, sexism

CURSED AND CROWNED PLAYLIST

My Tears Ricochet – Taylor Swift
Beautiful Crime – Tamer
Only Love Can Hurt Like This – Paloma Faith
Don't Let Me Go – RAIGN
Give Us a Little Love – Fallulah
Arsonist's Lullaby – Hozier
Black Out Days – Phantogram
Love in the Dark – Adele
So Cold – Ben Cocks
In My Bones – The Score
Crossfire – Stephen
Easy on Me – Adele
Wait – M83
The Beach – The Neighbourhood
Dusk Till Dawn – ZAYN ft. Sia
Feel Something – Jaymes Young
Us – James Bay
Cardigan – Taylor Swift
Seven Devils – Florence + The Machine
Gilded Lily – Cults
Truce – Twenty One Pilots
Drowning – Vague003
Set Fire to the Rain – Adele
Wings – Birdy

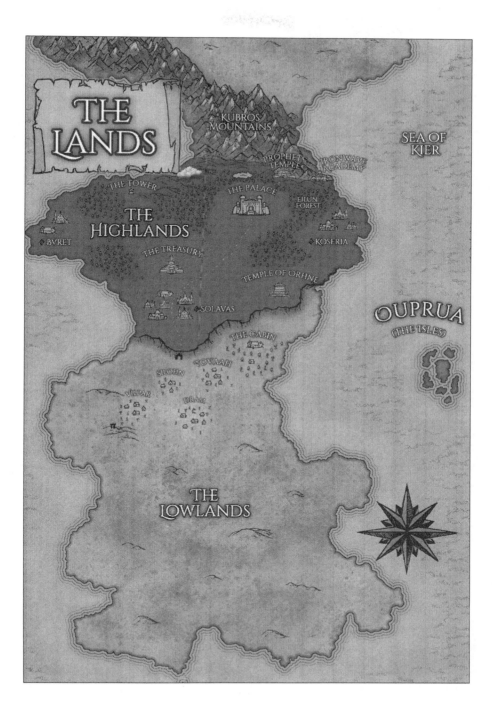

BEFORE
HER

"I love you," he breathed into her mouth as he rocked into her. His fingers threaded through hers and he pinned their locked hands against the pillows. "You're the only person I'll ever love. For all eternity." He pressed a searing kiss onto her lips. "Only you."

She gasped and writhed under him. Her free arm wrapped around his neck, bringing him closer even though there was barely an inch of space between them.

The inside of the tent was sweltering. Sweat dripped down their skin as their bodies slid together. She threw back her head and dug her nails into his shoulders as she reached her climax. He followed a moment later, groaning into her neck and then relaxing above her. Mindful of his weight, he rested his elbows on either side of her to make sure he didn't crush her, even though she'd told him many times that she didn't mind if he did.

After he caught his breath, he rolled away, collapsing on the bed next to her. She fit against his side easily, still panting. Her eyes traced the underside of the tent. He had put constellations above their bed—ordered men to find or make the fabric—because he knew she enjoyed looking at them. She could simply go outside if she wanted to see the stars, but he often said this was his way of keeping her in bed longer.

He absentmindedly ran his fingers through her hair. "They're different in other realms? You're sure?"

"You've seen them," she reminded him, pointing at the constellations. "Up there—the sky—doesn't change, but each realm has a different perspective of it. The sky is like . . . a map in that way. Most people go their whole lives only seeing it from the realm they were born in."

"Not me," he said. "Not us."

"No," she agreed. "We've been very fortunate. We've seen not only our realm, but many others as well."

Both grew silent then. The realms was a popular topic between the two of them, but also a sensitive one.

She sighed and went to roll away, but he pulled her back.

"Are you ready?" he asked. "You're sure you want this?"

She moved onto her stomach and stared down at him.

He was a confident man. A powerful one. He knew what he wanted, and he always took it. Stopping him from doing something he'd set his mind to was nearly impossible, so he had a great success record. But at moments like this, he reminded her that he was still very much mortal, no matter how many rumors circulated about his extraordinary power. He could be soft when he wanted to be.

She smoothed out the faint wrinkle between his brows. "I'm sure," she murmured, her heart full. "I choose you. Now and always."

It was a terrifying sensation—love to this degree. What they were doing couldn't be undone. It should frighten her scholar mind just as much as it intrigued her. Perhaps she would be more rational if love wasn't involved. Perhaps that was what had made her lose sight from the start. Even if there was an academy to go back to, they wouldn't take her now. She was too far gone. To him.

He smiled, full and bright and warm, and her heart expanded further. Yes, she would do this for him.

They got dressed and exited the tent. The generals were already waiting for them. Whatever they saw in Edynir's eyes got them moving.

She walked around the circular area formed by tents, observing it. The center had been dug out, leaving a small crater large enough to fit two people curled together. There were lines marked in the soil created with salt and water. It was a sigil. The one she had read about.

She and Edynir stood in the very center as the generals took their places around them. Words flowed from the generals' lips as blood coursed from the backs of their hands. Deep crimson trailed down the wet indents in the soil, reaching the two of them.

They repeated the arcane words, marking the beginning of something most would consider sinister.

She looked up at the spinning sky. The stars were dancing to the beat of the drum in her chest. A roar grew steadily in her ears, like the sound of waves crashing against the shore.

When she looked at Edynir, she could see him so clearly. She would see him again, but not like this. Her stare lingered, and she memorized every freckle and scar and shade of him for the last time in this lifetime.

He kissed her once more and rested his forehead against hers. "I will find you again. Whatever it takes, we will be together. I promise you that."

She nodded and unsheathed her dagger. They needed to do this at the same time. And they needed to look into each other's eyes as they did so. Their souls needed to see the soul they would be chasing for all eternity.

She pressed the tip of her dagger before his heart, and he did the same.

Something tightened in her gut, squirming, trying to break free. An energy surged through her body, breathing into her an essence of *life* she'd never experienced, but her limbs were heavy, her mind clouded. Not one drop of blood had spilled between them, but they were nearing their end, with or without the daggers.

The roar reached a crescendo.

"I love you," she murmured, her cheeks wet.

But he was too dangerous.

"And I love you." He brushed a tendril of hair from her face and wiped away her tears. "My Rhou."

They plunged the daggers forward and into each other's hearts, right where the soul resided. She gasped and his eyes widened. They fell to the ground together, wrapped in each other's arms.

The pain was unbearable, but it took her quickly. Within seconds, her soul was leaving and tugging on the other. But it would not go. Not yet. It was not finished.

Their blood stained the earth beneath them and ran over their clasped hands. They were joined as one. Nothing could ever tear them apart.

CURSED AND CROWNED
THE DIVINE TOUCH TRILOGY

BOOK 1

PROLOGUE

I'm too late.
     Rain was pouring down in torrents, flooding every inch of the land and creating a thick layer of sludge that sucked in her boots as she raced back to the palace. Her soaking wet clothes clung to her skin and weighed her down. She cursed herself again for wearing such rich and heavy fabric in the hope that it would make her fit in. She couldn't see where she was going; the sheets of rain were too thick. Cold too, meeting the warm earth and creating a layer of mist that surrounded her.
     Everything was working against her. She needed to hurry.
     Tuck had led her far from the palace, and she'd foolishly followed him. She knew something was wrong, something *worse* than a nasty joke, the moment he refused to let her leave. Tuck stood in front of her, impassive, his usual smirk nowhere to be found. The creeping sensation of dread prickled down her spine, causing bumps to rise across her skin in the cool air.
     Everything came together quickly in her mind. She'd expected this to happen, she realized. She'd always known that, sooner or later, they would turn on her.
     Thunder crackled in the sky and the rain began to pour.
     That was when his expression faltered. And this time, when she turned to leave, he let her go. The terror had coated her as quickly as the rain, addling her mind and sense of direction. But one thought had cut clean through the haze.
     I'm too late.
     She couldn't see the golden spires of the palace in the sky, and every tree looked the same. She couldn't hear anything past the roar of the rain.
     She held back a sob as she sprinted. Panic was a shard of glass nestled against her

heart, each footfall sending it closer to her soul. She needed to keep it together. She needed to get back to them.

A gate stood up ahead. She thanked the Numina as her fingers slipped over the wet iron, unlatching the lock and wrenching the door open. It slammed shut behind her as she soared through rows of drenched flowers and produce. She knew exactly where she was. Her family's personal garden. A door was—

—there.

It led to her family's private wing. She cried in relief when the door opened, but her relief was short-lived when she stepped inside and found no one guarding the door.

The heavy smell of iron hit her nose as she gasped for breath. Her trembling legs kept moving, stepping over fallen, unmoving bodies and avoiding pools of blood. But like the rain, blood was everywhere, nearly flooding the corridor. Her eyes widened as she caught glimpses of indigo uniforms belonging to the Sacred Guard, those sworn to protect her, the ruler. Were there any left?

The large doors to the drawing room were already open. A paralyzing cold enveloped her as she stepped into the room.

At first glance, the room appeared untouched by bloodshed. Flames crackled in the fireplace. The sofas and chairs surrounding the hearth weren't empty. The top of a head was visible over the back of an armchair. Someone sat on one of the sofas. They were still.

She crept closer to the furniture, each step sending prickles up her legs. When she stepped around the armchair to see who was slouched in it, a wail escaped her lips. She sealed her hands over her mouth as tears pooled in her eyes.

I'm too late.

Four people were artfully arranged on the furniture surrounding the fireplace. Her knees threatened to give out as she looked over each of their faces. Zehara. Torryn. Mother. Father.

They were all still, lips parted, eyes wide, faces frozen in a state of eternal shock and pain. Their chests had been punctured, and a gaping hole now replaced their hearts. Someone had taken their souls. So much blood stained their skin and clothes, the cushions and the floor.

A sob clawed its way out of her throat and she collapsed. Her fingers dug into the plush carpet, and she flinched when they touched something wet. Blood. Their blood was on her hands. She hadn't cut them down and ended their life, but she was the one who had brought them here, to the danger.

Tears dripped off her chin, mixing with blood as she continued to stare at her trembling hands. A noise came from behind her, but she didn't move. Her eyes slipped closed, and she waited for the bite of a blade.

But it never came.

A clash of steel rang out and then the unmistakable sound of flesh being severed.

It was a wet, squelching sound that made her cringe. A choked groan came after. A thud. Then silence.

Still, she did not move.

A hand grasped her shoulder and spun her around. A scream bubbled up, but it died as soon as she saw who stood before her.

"Kalena," Ezra gasped.

Ezra.

She sagged in relief. Her fingers inched forward to grab onto his indigo uniform, but she stopped at the sight of the blood covering it. Was any of it his? Her eyes trailed to the body behind him.

"*Kalena.*" He shook her, and her gaze snapped back to him. "Are you hurt?"

It took a moment for the question to register. She slowly shook her head. No, she wasn't injured.

Ezra let out a heavy breath and nodded. His eyes hardened when he looked past her, at her family. "You need to go. *Now.*"

Her brows furrowed and she shook her head again. Words caught in her throat. *Leave*? She couldn't leave. Where would she go?

Ezra huffed and pulled her to her feet.

"Wait!" She found her words then, but they came out weak and strained. "Ezra, *wait!*"

He ignored her. She dug her heels into the floor, yet he was still able to drag her out of the room, away from her family. She tripped over bodies and slipped in blood, but Ezra held her so she didn't fall. He brought her back to the door she'd entered through.

"You run," he instructed, gripping her shoulders and looking her squarely in the eye. His green eyes were frantic, but he was doing his best to conceal his alarm in front of her. "Don't stop. Don't look back. Don't trust anyone." He glanced over his shoulder.

She followed his gaze. No one was coming down the corridor. Not yet. Her mind was plagued by the scene in the drawing room. This was her fault.

"What's happening?" she said quickly. "Ira—"

"You don't have time!" Ezra shook her shoulders. He'd never handled her so roughly or raised his voice at her before.

A screeching roar echoed down the corridor. They froze. She recognized that sound. Once you heard it, you never forgot it. Or the immediate paralyzing fear that came with it.

Someone had set their Slayer loose.

The door opened and the pelting rain surrounded her once again.

"Run, Kalena!" Ezra shoved her outside, and he lingered for a moment, his face crumbling. "I'm sorry I wasn't able to keep my promise."

And then he was gone.

She stared at the door. For a moment, she considered tearing it open and going back inside, but that was foolish. And she was a coward. So she ran.

The gate smacked shut behind her with a terrible, grating cry. The low hanging tree branches cut into her skin as she sprinted through the forest. She pushed her wet hair out of her face, but it was no use. The visibility was worse than before.

Another bloodthirsty cry pierced through the thundering rain, but this one came from behind her near the palace. There was another Slayer in the forest. With her.

And it had caught her scent.

Lena swatted the underbrush and branches aside as she raced through them.

Slayers didn't need their eyesight to hunt. They relied on their sense of smell. She hoped the rain would somewhat throw it off. No one could survive a Slayer encounter on their own. Not even a Blessed in ideal circumstances. She was not a Blessed; she had no Slayer to call upon to defend herself. And these circumstances were less than ideal. She could be running toward the Slayer and not even know it.

Another shriek sounded. Even closer than before.

Lena sobbed as she dashed forward. The mud tugged her down with each step, unwilling to let her go. She couldn't go too fast or else she would fall. Hiding wasn't an option. And outrunning a Slayer was impossible, but she didn't have another choice. The adrenaline kept her moving. She couldn't stop even if she wanted to.

A green glow became visible through the mist.

She jerked to a halt and ducked behind a tree as the green grew brighter. The bark painfully dug into her skin as she pressed herself against the trunk, trying to make herself as small and quiet as possible. Her heart was too wild, too *loud*.

A coiling laugh permeated through the rain and sent chills across her skin. It was a giggle almost. Something anticipatory that slithered through the air. Slayers laughed like that when they were excited. When they were hunting.

She bit her lip and clasped a hand over her mouth, trembling against the tree. A stray tear trailed down her cheek as she squeezed her eyes shut.

Water splashed as the Slayer prowled toward her. The entire area was bathed in green. She felt the heat and the pure *power* that radiated from the Slayer. The air around it shifted, and its presence choked her.

The Slayer growled. Lena recoiled and held her breath. Not a sound could escape her. Blood filled her mouth.

It was close. *So close.*

Her muscles tensed in preparation for an attack. She expected claws to dig into her side or fangs to rip into her neck any second now. Maybe the heat and power of the Slayer would envelop her entirely and she would fry to a crisp. Slayer attacks were never pretty or painless. Would she suffer as much as her family had?

Then the glow disappeared.

It was there one moment and then gone the next.

The Slayer had left.

She didn't know why. It'd only been feet away from her. There was no way it hadn't smelled her, its prey, and yet it'd just . . . vanished.

It didn't make sense, but Lena didn't waste any more time dwelling on why. She pushed away from the tree and bolted in what she hoped was the opposite direction of the palace. The shrill roars faded the farther she ran, but her adrenaline remained high, lighting a fire under her heart.

She ran until she reached the Lowlands and then continued until air no longer reached her lungs. As soon as she stopped, her legs gave out.

Her knees sunk into the mud and she ducked her head, trying and failing to catch her breath. She dug her hands into the earth, needing something to hold on to. But it slipped through her fingers like everything else had. Tears filled her eyes as she curled in on herself. The noises she'd held back earlier came out, strangled and raw and agonizing.

No one heard. Her screams were drowned out by the rain.

PART ONE
THE REUNION

CHAPTER
ONE

L ena had to kill someone tonight.
She didn't particularly enjoy killing people, but her Slayer needed to eat, and she had learned the hard way not to get between a Slayer and its food.

However, while the matter of *if* she was going to kill someone tonight had already been decided, the question of *who* remained unanswered.

She peeked around the corner. The bright glow that came from the second-story window told her that he was still up.

Good. Perhaps she could kill two birds with one stone.

Two men were slumped near the side entrance on the first floor. One was lying down against the side of the house, covered in a large coat, and the other sat on a wooden box with a bottle in his hand. He hadn't taken one sip in the hour she had been there. To the untrained eye, they looked like homeless beggars, but she recognized them as hired muscle.

Midnight was approaching, and the three blood red moons rested high in the sky. One of them was a full moon. Prime time for Slayers to be released.

Dugell, the owner of the house across the alleyway, was a businessman who liked his money, but also his comfort. He would be calling it a night soon.

She had been following the path that led to Dugell for months now. It was a long one. He'd covered his tracks fairly well; she would give him that. She wasn't patient, but she was persistent, especially when it came to getting revenge.

But first, she needed answers. She had her suspicions about who'd been involved in her family's assassination. Certain Blessed had made their animosity toward her known. But she had to be *sure*.

People talked in the Lowlands; they relayed secrets and schemes. Some of them made a career out of it. Secret Sellers was the name they were given. It was dangerous, but high risk, high reward.

Law enforcement in the Lowlands was poor and sparse, but enforcers would come down from the Highlands if an issue grew large enough to warrant their intervention. You didn't want to be someone they were looking for. She knew that firsthand. Many people would sell someone out for a pretty coin.

Dugell was a Secret Seller, but he was more careful than the average fella, mostly because he could afford it. He had a vast network of people working for him. They couldn't sell him out if they were caught because they didn't know his true identity, which had been a pain for her. She'd had to sniff out his trail in other ways, jumping from informant to informant until she'd finally come across a merchant selling wine.

That was how Dugell did it. The wine. He was Cursed, but he had family who were Blessed. It was messy business—a Cursed being born into a predominantly Blessed family and vice versa—but it was inevitable. For the most part, Cursed resided in the Lowlands and Blessed in the Highlands, but Dugell still profited off his family's wealth.

They were winemakers and had fine orchards in the Highlands. He would make a trip up to them biweekly to collect the bottles made at the winery and then sell them for a high price in the Lowlands as a luxury item. Not many could afford them, but he still made decent money. However, the real coin came from the secrets he sold *with* the bottles.

Lena had found one herself, and the coded note on the inside had led her to a warehouse. A few months later, she'd found out who owned it. Dugell rarely visited. He had many figureheads put in place, but that was where his safeguards ended.

She'd tracked down his home a week ago and had been watching him since. He was a vain man. He thought he'd done enough to ensure his safety, so he had no guards inside his home, making it far too easy for anyone who hunted him down to reach him. He only contracted muscle to wait outside during certain times, so she merely had to wait for them to leave.

The door on the side of the house swung open and the hired muscle swiveled their heads. A dark figure stepped out and headed down the alleyway, away from her. They didn't spare the hired muscle a single glance. She was surprised to see Dugell entertaining clients at his home; she assumed he would do that elsewhere or have someone else meet with them. But then the figure moved to the side, revealing another shorter figure. A child. She knew Dugell had a family and that they came to visit him sometimes, but seeing them still made her pause.

After a few more minutes, the men slouched in the alleyway pushed themselves to their feet and stumbled away. Their shift was over.

Lena pulled away from the corner and tugged the hood farther over her head, making sure her face was properly covered. Heat spread from the Imprint on her chest, curling around her bones. She rested a hand over the warm mark.

Soon, she told it.

She pushed away from the corner and began to climb the house next to Dugell's. She'd climbed dozens of different surfaces dozens of times, so it was like second nature to her at this point.

Most houses in the Lowlands' towns had sturdier roofs than those in the countryside. They'd been built during the brief period when money had flowed from the Highlands to directly support infrastructure in the Lowlands. The towns might have better markets and dwellings, but they were more dangerous, which was why her parents had opted to reside in their quaint countryside house.

She pulled herself over the eave and scuttled across the top, keeping herself crouched low. Light still filled the window.

She slid down the other side of the roof. The soles of her boots hit the gutter and she used the force from the impact as momentum to leap across the alleyway. A dull thump sounded as she landed on top of Dugell's home. There was a small balcony near the back of his house that connected to his study. She dropped down to it and peered between the thick curtains that covered the doors. The chair Dugell was slouched in was turned away from the balcony. She grabbed the doorknob and twisted. It gave easily.

She smirked. *Idiot.*

She inched the door open just enough to slip through and made sure to lock it behind her.

Dugell hadn't noticed her presence, too busy counting the money in his hands. A bottle of wine sat on the desk next to him, half empty. Getting what she needed would be much easier if he were drunk.

Her footfalls were light as she moved around the edge of the study. She noticed only one other entry point, so she quietly locked that door too before unsheathing her dagger.

Lena moved behind his chair and placed the tip of the dagger against his neck. "Don't shout."

Dugell flinched when he felt the kiss of steel but stayed still and silent after that.

"Turn around."

He slowly swiveled his chair, conscious of the blade digging into his skin, until he was facing her.

She took in his features—the wrinkles next to his panicked eyes; the paleness of his clammy skin; his weak, trembling jaw.

Lena pulled down her hood. "Do you remember me?"

He squinted but shook his head, stopping when he remembered the dagger. "No."

She wasn't surprised by his answer. It had only been two years since she saw him in the pleasure house, but she'd kept a low profile while there. Though, she had seen him before then, across a crowd.

She cocked her head. "No? I suppose I wasn't your type then, was I?"

A spark of realization flashed across his eyes. "W-why are you here?" he said quickly, stumbling over his words but keeping them hushed. "You want money? Are you trying to blackmail me? My wife knows . . . about the pleasure houses. She doesn't care!"

He could be lying, but it didn't matter if he was. Polyamorous relationships were common in The Lands, and Dugell's trips to the pleasure houses were a weak substance for blackmail. She planned on using a more traditional method with a higher success rate.

The Imprint on her chest burned once again, and this time, she gave into it.

She released her Slayer.

A gust of wind blew out the lit candles scattered throughout the room. The air became heavier as a purple glow coated the otherwise dark study. The hairs along her arms stood as her Slayer's power crackled through the room, spreading heat along with it. Lena's vision changed—sharpened—and became almost layered. She could close her eyes and still see through the eyes of her Slayer. If she had a mirror, she would see the bright purple glow of her irises.

She had gotten used to her Slayer's presence in the past year and a half, but its appearance was still jarring.

Slayers varied in size and color, but they all looked similar. Like most, Lena's resembled a wolf, but that description wasn't quite right. For one, a Slayer was bigger than a wolf, standing six to nine feet at the shoulder. Hers stood at about seven feet. Its upper body was larger than its hind, and its head was narrow and long, perfect for sniffing out prey from a distance. The outline of its form shifted and blurred. A Slayer wasn't exactly corporeal as it was a manifestation of a Numen, a Divine entity, in this realm. The realm of the Divine wasn't on the same plane as the realm of The Lands. They overlapped. It was here but not. A veil separated the two, and supposedly only the prophets had the ability to find the veil and pull it aside.

When she'd first touched her Slayer, some resistance had met her fingers before they'd sunk into its form, but only by an inch or so. And if that Slayer had belonged to someone else, her fingers would've been incinerated.

Her Slayer's features were as indistinguishable as its outline, the dark pits of its eyes being the only distinct detail. Like all Slayers, hers matched the color of her Imprint. Bright, sizzling wisps of indigo aura flame drifted over it and into the surrounding air, making her Slayer appear on fire. It was an apex predator of unadulterated energy.

A split second after her Slayer materialized, it bolted toward Dugell, all but a blur across the room, ravenous for his flesh and blood. She stopped it almost immediately. Her Slayer listened to her now, but it hadn't always. Controlling its bloodlust had been difficult at the beginning, which resulted in more than a few incidents where bodies had been left behind and she'd had to move locations quickly. It was said that Slayers craved blood so much because the pact between a Numen and a Blessed was made in blood. She'd eventually learned that supplying her Slayer with food was easier than letting it hunt for itself. She would pick the lowest of the low. The scumbags. Her Slayer wouldn't even consider animal meat, not that there was a plentiful supply of animals to choose from in the Lowlands. For the most part, the land down here was barren.

A low growl permeated through the air and Dugell jerked back. Whether or not he was her Slayer's next meal was up to him.

"You and I," she said, waving the dagger between the two of them, "are going to come to an understanding. You're going to tell me what you know about the assassination on the queen's family, and in return, I'm going to let you live." She gave him a tight smile. "Understand?"

Dugell swallowed roughly, his pupils dilated in fear. Beads of sweat were already trailing down his face. "I . . . " His voice came out weak. "I don't know anything about the assassin—"

A bang echoed through the room as she drove the blade of her dagger into the desk. Dugell winced and huddled against his chair as the dagger quivered back and forth before standing still and straight.

"Don't lie to me," she snapped. "I know you know something. I know you sell secrets for a living, and I know someone's been whispering in your ear in the Highlands."

Lena closed her eyes and took a deep breath, reminding herself that she was in control. Sometimes the bloodlust from the pact was quick to grab hold of her too. Her Slayer would inflame her emotions, constantly testing its limits.

"I thought you understood—you do what I say, or you die."

Her Slayer took a step forward to emphasize her threat, a growl escaping its throat again as it bared its fangs. The air crackled and buzzed around it and the floor creaked and sizzled. Her Slayer could easily burn through this floor if it wanted to, but it could also withhold parts of itself, including its heat, leaving it in the realm of the Divine and summoning it at a moment's notice. As of right now, Lena's goal *wasn't* to burn down Dugell's house, so she was keeping her Slayer at bay, but she could feel its impatience. It wanted to eat sooner rather than later.

An acrid smell met her nose and she grimaced. He'd pissed his pants.

"Look." She dug into the pocket of her skin-tight pants and pulled out a piece of paper. She unfolded it before slamming it onto the desk, moving carefully to avoid the puddle at his feet. "Here. I even made it easy for you. I made a list. All you have to do is tell me who was or wasn't involved. And if I missed anyone, tell me who and I'll add them."

Lena had spent a lot of time on that list. Every day for five years she had thought about her family's assassination, but grief had consumed her for most of that time. She hadn't been in the right headspace to properly come up with a plan until recently, after she gained a way to fight back.

Dugell still hesitated, trembling in his seat.

Lena rolled her eyes and plucked a pen from his desk. She pointed at the first name on the paper, waiting for him to say something.

His gaze flitted to her and then the Slayer again. He nodded.

The corners of her lips tilted upward, just slightly, and she moved to the next one.

Slowly but surely, they made their way through the list. She marked off and circled names until she had her culprits. Her targets.

She smirked and tucked the piece of paper back into her pocket. "This probably won't be the last time you'll see me, Dug. You seem like a resourceful man."

His face paled, but he wisely remained silent. He was learning.

She tugged her dagger out of the wood and grabbed the bottle of wine for good measure. She backpedaled to the balcony and lifted the bottle in a mock salute. "I see a promising future for the two of us, Dug."

Her Slayer moved across the study in the blink of an eye, pushing the desk aside and toppling the chair over. Dugell crashed onto the ground, right into his puddle of piss. Her Slayer leaned over him, growling and dripping molten wisps of aura flame onto Dugell's body. It burned right through his clothes, singeing his skin. Dugell cried out and curled onto his side, shaking like a leaf. Her Slayer's teeth were only inches away from his skull.

"Look at me," she snapped, and he did as he was told. "You don't tell anyone about this visit. If you talk, I guarantee I'll find you before your people find me." She narrowed her eyes, jerking her chin to the Slayer above him. "And then you'll be dead."

Dugell nodded rapidly. She didn't believe in his word, but she believed in his fear.

She tugged her hood back up and recalled her Slayer as she slipped through the balcony doors. Its displeasure seeped through her chest as it returned to its realm.

I know, she said, trying to pacify it as she scaled the house and disappeared into the night. *It's hunting time.*

For both of them.

CHAPTER TWO

"You are here to repent for your sins."
     The prophet's voice echoed through the lecture hall, reaching all the way up to the ceiling and, unfortunately, all the way back to Atreus' ears. He stared straight ahead, trying to, at the very least, appear like he wasn't bored out of his mind. He'd heard a variation of this speech at least a hundred times before.

Enforcers lined the walls of the room. They stood still and tall at nine feet, every inch of them covered in armor. The helmet they wore was an elongated trapezoid, pinched at the top and wider at the bottom. He had never heard them speak, but they were always watching the firstborns through the dark vertical slits on the front of their helmet. They were the prophets' lackeys, carrying out their every order.

" . . . us mortals have made many mistakes, the War of Krashing being the most notable. Some mortals allowed greed to rule them, and they defied the Numina. They lost, of course, but rather than the Numina showing the full extent of their power and wiping those traitors out, they extended mercy and taught them a lesson. The Numina showed them that they weren't worthy. Not yet, but they could work toward it. Perhaps one day, in a new life, they would become Blessed and worthy of the Divine Touch. The unity after the war was remarkable. We strove for a better realm, one without sin, but we couldn't eliminate evil. Not completely. So, the Numina *contained* it in every firstborn child.

"It is a sacrifice every family has to make for the betterment of the realm, and it serves as a stark reminder of the greed that once came close to destroying us all. We cannot let it win. For the sake of our realm and our society, the firstborns and the evil they carry must remain hidden. Evil cannot be destroyed, but perhaps it can be altered. However, change cannot take place until one acknowledges their wickedness. I urge you to reflect on your sins and do penance. Write your regrets in your journal. Prophets are available to anyone who would like to talk rather than write."

The prophet stepped away from the podium at the front and returned to the line of prophets standing behind him. A shuffling noise sounded as some of the firstborns picked up their pencils and began to write.

The prophets made it sound like they were patients in some rehabilitation facility, but that was far from the truth. They were prisoners. These speeches, these prophets, these stiff uniforms, this place—it was all bullshit.

He was aware of the eyes on him. Prophet Silas stood near the front, his gaze never leaving Atreus. Still, he didn't pick up his pencil.

~

"Prophet Silas was glaring at you earlier," Finn whispered in Atreus' ear as they were ushered toward the dining hall for dinner.

Atreus had seen his friend trying to catch his eye earlier after seminar, but they'd been separated on their way to work in the mines for the afternoon. They all operated on the same schedule every day. Wake up. Eat breakfast. Go to seminar. Work in the mines. Attend lessons. Eat lunch. Go to seminar. Work in the mines. Attend lessons. Eat dinner. Go to seminar. Sleep. It only differed when they were being sent out. And they were. Tonight.

For that reason, he couldn't bring himself to particularly care about anything other than the Outing. There was no way of knowing where they would be sent, but that didn't stop him from thinking about it.

"So?"

"*So* maybe you should try a little more not to piss him off."

Atreus snorted. "My mere existence pisses him off," he said. "If I make it to eighteen, I'm using my wish to transfer Institutes."

"Do you really think they'll allow that?"

Probably not. Prophet Silas seemed resolved to make Atreus' life here as miserable as possible, so if there was anything he wanted, any minimal improvement that would perhaps bring him the slightest bit of relief, the prophet would deny it. Within reason, of course. The prophets couldn't very well let them starve, and they had to provide the firstborns with medical attention when they inevitably came back from the Outings or the mines bruised and bleeding. The bare minimum felt like a luxury at times. So, a transfer was most likely out of the question. Atreus might not even survive long enough to make that wish.

The wish was some sort of twisted incentive, something the prophets could dangle in front of their faces and say, *See? If you repent and cleanse your wickedness, you could get good things. You survive and make a wish.* It was a lie, of course. No firstborn had made it to eighteen before, not in the Institute.

"It doesn't matter," Atreus said. "And you're being a bit hypocritical, don't you think? With all the . . . *thoughts* you write in your journal."

Stories was more accurate, but Atreus wouldn't say it aloud. He wouldn't risk it.

"No one knows. I don't draw attention to myself, unlike *someone* I know. The prophets think I'm atoning for—"

"It's dangerous, Finn." Atreus turned to his friend. It was dark in the corridor, but he could still count the freckles that dusted Finn's cheeks, the shadows under his eyes, his torn-up lower lip. He still wasn't sleeping well. "What happens if one of the prophets or enforcers finds out you're writing those things?"

Nothing good. They both knew that.

The prophets' form of punishment often fell in the category of *rehabilitation*. They really kept pushing that agenda. However, the prophets would resort to physical violence if no other form of discipline worked. Execution was a form of punishment they never utilized. Not directly, that was.

"Well, I'm not going to stop," Finn protested. "I know the risks, but it's one of the only things that makes me feel—"

Atreus grabbed Finn's forearm and squeezed. Finn's mouth snapped shut right as a pair of enforcers appeared around the corner. The air in the corridor chilled as the two armored giants stopped, looked at them, and then continued. He always wondered what exactly they were and where they came from. It was possible they were of this realm, but he wouldn't know. Like every other firstborn, he had never left the Institute. It was a dangerous yet drab life here. For most of their life, they'd been told they were sinful, broken beings and their life in the Institute was their ordained punishment; that perhaps fate would be kinder to them in their next life if they behaved properly in this one; that the bad things that happened to them they deserved.

Their life underground was shit, but it was better than the realms they were sent to. And the bloodthirsty monsters that awaited them. *Te'Monai*, they called them. *Demon* in the old language. They knew that word because the prophets would sometimes call them that.

So Atreus understood. The small pieces of happiness one could find amidst their lousy life were treasured. He couldn't fault Finn for that.

"Just be careful." He let go of Finn's arm and bumped his shoulder against his.

Finn smiled. "I always am."

Their group filed into the dining hall. Like most of the rooms in the Institute, it was large and flat and dull. There were no windows in the Institute. No freshness or color. The room had likely been carved from stone and then smoothed to create flat surfaces. The Institute seemed dead, full of people who would soon be dead. The temperatures in nearly every room were freezing, but they'd grown somewhat accustomed to it.

A few dozen firstborns already had their food, and hundreds of others waited in line for their tray.

Usually, their meal was some form of glop that could hardly be classified as food, but on the days they were sent out, they were served meat. Receiving that meal before an Outing had made Atreus nauseous at the beginning, but he'd since gotten over his revulsion. The new arrivals always thought it was some grand last supper—a parting gift before being sent to the slaughter. But there was more to it.

Those who had their food were sitting at the tables, hunched over their trays as if they were worried someone would steal their rations, but Atreus knew that wasn't the case. Food was never worth fighting over, and he doubted anyone had that much of an appetite right now. Their minds were probably somewhere far away from this underground dining hall, much like his.

"*Move*," a voice hissed from behind him. "You're holding up the line."

Vanik shouldered past him and shot him a glare. Vanik normally wouldn't dare do something like that with the enforcers watching, but he was on edge like everyone else. And *normally*, Atreus would've snapped something back, but he kept his mouth shut. He was picking his battles. The enforcers didn't intervene.

The three members of Vanik's posse dutifully followed him. Harlow barely served them a glance, walking gracefully past with her chin up, appearing as unbothered as usual.

Weylin strolled past, a slight smirk on his lips. He dipped his head at them mockingly. He was gangly and slouched often, giving him an awkward appearance, but he was quick on his feet, which was resourceful.

Aspen came next. She was the smallest of the bunch with a soft, kind face that she used to her advantage.

Finn glared after them, but he also didn't say anything. The two of them got back in line and waited for their tray.

Mila had already secured their table in the corner. She gave them a terse smile when they sat but remained silent, which was fine. He didn't have much to say either. They had exhausted their *good luck*s and false promises long before.

Dinner was a quick and quiet ordeal. He ate as much of the meat as he could stomach, knowing he needed to keep his strength up if he wanted to survive this Outing. After he had his fill, he wrapped the knife in a napkin and slipped it into one of his boots. Mila and Finn did the same. No one said a word and no enforcers approached them.

The seminar after also passed by in a blur, and then they were all ushered to the familiar, dark cavity deep within the mines. It was the only room in the Institute that had been left in its original form. Jagged cuts of rocks jutted out from the walls. They probably hung from the ceiling too, but it was impossible to tell. The room was too large and dark for anyone to see the top. A strong draft of wind always blew through the space. Like every other room, there were sunstones on the walls that could provide light, but they were off when the firstborns shuffled inside.

The only source of light came from the floating portals on one side of the room.

They were pure white, so bright that they were blinding. They gave no glimpse of the realm beyond. No hint as to what waited for them.

Atreus watched as the firstborns in front of him walked forward and were enveloped by the white void. And then it was his turn. He took a deep breath and relaxed his muscles before stepping through.

CHAPTER
THREE

Lena stuck to the ravines, hidden by the shadows and stones as she moved north through the Lowlands. She kept her hood up and her head down. Since visiting Dugell, she'd traded her black cloak for a more practical brown one that blended in with the sepia monochrome landscape. The farther north she traveled, the more color and vegetation she saw. The cracks in the ground had shrunk from gaping rivers that could suck someone up to thin slivers that cut through the dry ground. The mounds of sand were completely gone.

She eventually had to cross over to the main roads. She ignored any calls her way and kept her pace brisk. Her Imprint flared on her chest; her Slayer could feel her apprehension.

She was finally going back after five years.

Going back. Not going home. She didn't have any home to return to. Her father had always said that *people* were home. He'd reminded her of this when they moved from the Lowlands to the palace in the Highlands when she was fourteen. She had just been told by the prophets that the Numina had chosen her, a Cursed girl, to be the next ruler of The Lands. Although her life had been uprooted then, she'd still had a home because she'd still had her people.

But it was different now. Her people had been killed.

She was going back to where she belonged because she had unfinished business with the Blessed. She could *do* things in the palace, as queen—things she wasn't able to do in another way. She had an agenda, and only one of the things on it happened to be revenge.

She slowed when she spotted the towering golden gates ahead. The gates leading to the Highlands were hard to miss, but they didn't receive much traffic since

Cursed were rarely allowed into the Highlands. It was even more unlikely that Blessed would come down to mingle with Cursed. The two were kept separate.

So, when she approached the gate, the two enforcers on duty took in her dirty, haggard form with disgust and then annoyance when she didn't immediately leave.

She cleared her throat and removed her hood. "Tell the High Council the queen has returned."

At first, neither of the enforcers moved. One rolled their eyes while the other guffawed, but when they saw that she was still standing tall and waiting expectantly, they sobered up. Their eyes raked over her carefully. No doubt they had been given a description of the runaway queen, and she obviously fit it.

After another thirty seconds of contemplation, one of the enforcers went up to relay her message. The enforcer returned with five others, four of which were members of the Sacred Guard. Their indigo uniforms gave them away, but she didn't recognize any of them. Her chest tightened, but she pushed down the guilt before she could dwell any more on the attack. She turned her attention to the fifth person who'd come down, someone she *did* recognize.

Avalon Vuukroma. One of Tuck's mothers. A member of one of the seven Blessed families that had the privilege and power to live in the palace and be given the title of a 'royal' family. She and her partners, Ophir and Celine, had been a part of the assassination of Lena's family.

All Blessed were beautiful, but Avalon was exceptionally so. She stood tall and graceful with her chin high. Her rich brown skin glowed under the sun and was complemented by the deep green dress she wore. Her long black hair was twisted away from her face and fell in curls down her back. Avalon had been cold to her from the beginning, but Lena had quickly learned that she wasn't necessarily warm to anyone.

Avalon's eyes lit up with recognition when they landed on her, and irritation quickly followed. "It's you."

The words sounded like a curse, and there was something else in Avalon's eyes. It was brief, but Lena still caught it. Something akin to fear.

The last time Avalon saw her, she'd been a useless, frightened, weak girl about to lose everything. Avalon, like everyone else involved in her family's assassination, had probably expected her to die in the Lowlands. But the Numina had never named a new ruler, so they knew she was alive. And now she was back, five years later, stronger than ever—like a dark spirit returning to haunt them.

"It's me," she confirmed, smiling tightly. She sounded a bit smug, but it was the only way to conceal her rage. She'd known it would be difficult to see them again, living their luxurious lives as usual as if they hadn't ruined hers. "Are you going to let your queen in?"

The enforcers gawked, no doubt not used to someone speaking to a Blessed of high status in this way.

Avalon's lips parted in outrage, but she caught herself and snapped her mouth shut. Her eyes narrowed and her mask of perfected poise returned. She turned and strode through the gates without a second glance, returning to where she'd come from.

The Sacred Guard didn't follow her. They waited for Lena. Once she stepped forward to follow Avalon, they positioned themselves into a loose formation around her. Instantly, her shoulders tensed, but she forced herself to relax. She would have to get used to this again—the constant supervision.

She eyed the Sacred Guard as they ascended. Members of the Sacred Guard were Blessed who had taken an oath to protect the ordained ruler, but a lot had changed over the past few years. She didn't know who she could trust, her own guards included. Her enemies in the palace had years to persuade the Sacred Guard to their side and convince them that she was a threat to order, and to The Lands. That they should kill her the first chance they got and protect the new, more deserving ruler who would be chosen next.

She had returned to the Highlands under the impression that she would have not one ally waiting for her. Her trump card was her Imprint. Perhaps people would support her because of it. Perhaps they would see her as one of *them*. Or maybe they would persecute her further. Maybe they would claim she'd used black magic, *sorcery*, to acquire an Imprint.

She was pulled out of her thoughts when they reached the end of the winding paths that hugged the cliffside.

The Highlands, as alluded to by its name, was *higher* in altitude than the Lowlands. And the increase wasn't gradual. Not everyone had the stomach to scale the cliffs, but some paths were less perilous than others.

The wind was stronger at the top, stinging her eyes and blowing back her short dark hair. Her breath caught at the sight of the Highlands after all these years.

It was the most beautiful place she had ever seen. Lush greenery and bright flowers covered the land, visible wherever one looked and layered over one another like streaks of watercolor on a canvas. Clear, full waterways cut through them, their surfaces reflecting the sky above.

The Highlands hugged the Lowlands, but the air quality up on the cliffs was better than the air quality down below. The sweet, refreshing aroma in the air was unlike the heavier, earthier smell of the Lowlands. A few hundred feet of elevation and there was such a drastic change, in more ways than one.

The paved streets leading through the capital city of Solavas were packed with people, who all stopped and stared. Their gazes first went to Avalon, then her, before finally moving to the indigo-swathed guards. The pieces connected and their eyes snapped back to her. After a few moments of shocked silence, the whispers began. They followed her through the city, clinging to her even as the golden spires of the palace came into view.

But one word in particular stuck out.

"*Arawn.*"

It slipped through the commotion to reach her. She looked to see if Avalon had heard it, but the royal's shoulders were no more tense than usual.

The palace was a huge structure made of stone and marble and other precious materials. It was as grand as could be. She would always get lost in its halls when she was younger, and one of her guards would then have to lead her back. The palace stretched deep and wide and tall, but even more impressive than the palace were the mountains behind it, which created a striking backdrop.

Their country was a peninsula. The Lowlands took up a majority of The Lands in the southern region and it was completely surrounded by water. The Highlands was the farthest inland, but it was cut off from the rest of the realm by the Kubros Mountains. Both routes, the water and the mountains, were near impossible to conquer. The Sea of Kier contained vicious riptides and jagged rocks hidden under dark waves. Raging storms were a common occurrence out at sea, which was part of the reason why the body of water had been named after the Numen of Wrath. The mountains nestled behind the palace were impractical to trek due to the violent weather and unstable paths; they even extended into the water, blocking the path for any sailor who hoped to travel north of The Lands without facing the rage of the deep sea. The wicked creatures that lurked in the mountain range also proved to be problematic, even for Slayers. It was almost like the country had been formed artfully and meticulously by the Numina they worshipped. The people of The Lands didn't have the resources to combat such things. To put it simply, they were all trapped here.

Lena's stride faltered when they reached another gate, this one golden and nearly fifty feet tall. An abstract symbol of the sun was centered at the top of the arched gateway, its golden rays stretching outward to meet another ring. At first glance, it could be mistaken for an eye, but everyone was familiar with the symbol of the Blessed; they knew it was a sun. But its similarity to an eye wasn't an accident. Blessed truly were full of themselves.

The symbol of the Cursed was the moons, but it was always presented as three waxing crescents because the full moon belonged to Slayers. She had always preferred the symbol of the Cursed. After all, there were three moons and only one sun.

The yard between the gate and the palace stretched on for miles. A wall wrapped around some of the yard but stopped when it reached the front of the palace, and that was one of the factors that had made it easier for her to sneak away at the start of her time in the palace. But her Sacred Guard had caught on quickly and ended her solo escapades. The palace wasn't a castle. It was meant to showcase the luxury of the Blessed, not protect those living inside it.

The green grass on either side of the gravel path was cut short and littered with small, precisely cut hedge statues and granite fountains. The grandeur was ridiculous. If this kind of effort and money was put elsewhere, to people who actually needed it . . .

She clenched her jaw and quickened her pace yet again, bypassing Avalon. She didn't need someone to lead her to the entrance, but the long stairwell at the front of the palace was just as intimidating now as it'd been six years ago when her family moved here. The sight of it made her pause.

Avalon stopped next to her and glanced over, waiting. There was an air of acuity about her, one that made Lena bristle and continue forward.

It was ridiculous what kinds of things scared her after being on the run for five years. This place was a different kind of nightmare than the Lowlands, but if she could survive out there, she could survive in here. She had to.

Her Imprint burned as she stepped foot inside the pristine walls of the palace. The whispers arose here too and would be quickly spread by servants. She sped up so she wouldn't lose Avalon, who strode through the halls like she had somewhere to be, moving faster than before.

"Why did you come down?" Lena asked. There were multiple questions tied into that. Why had the enforcer retrieved her of all people? And why had she agreed to go with?

"Not many people know what you look like," Avalon said curtly. "And anyone who does was otherwise occupied."

They took a turn down a long familiar hallway with tall double doors embellished in gold at the end. The High Council chamber. It was located at the back of the palace so the prophets could descend from their temple and home on the mountainside and take their seat on the council when a meeting was called.

The doors to the chamber were already being pushed open as they approached, and Avalon marched inside without preamble. The room was in uproar. Eighteen individuals were in varying states of disorder. Most of the council members were talking or shouting over one another, chairs forgotten. The room immediately quieted as she stepped inside. The doors fell shut behind her with a sharp bang. All eyes were on her.

The council had nineteen seats, the last one reserved for the ruler. Her seat was in the middle, directly in front of her. Empty, of course. There were five active prophets on the council. Seven seats were reserved for the royal families. And elected representatives made up the remaining six. Everyone was Blessed and from the Highlands. She recognized fewer than half the people in the room.

The questions began, but they faded into the background as her gaze caught onto a familiar face.

Ira.

It was Ira. Here, in this room, in front of her.

He had changed, which was to be expected. He'd been a boy of fifteen the last time she saw him. Now he was a man of twenty. But there were parts of him that were just as she remembered. The Tower had cut his hair close to his scalp when he was a prisoner there, and although it had grown out some before the attack, it was much longer now. His dark waves were full and healthy and in disarray as if he'd ran his fingers through it too many times, which she knew he had a habit of doing. His jaw was stronger, as were the rest of his features, like they had solidified over time, hardened and been carved out of stone. But he still had a softness to him, a beauty that had always been there. His skin had been fair before, but it had more color to it now, making him appear warmer. *Healthier.*

Lena looked over his form. He'd gained muscle and height. He dressed better and carried himself with more confidence. His fingers curled into fists at his side, and she raised her eyes to his.

Something soft and soundless escaped her lips. Ira's eyes drew her in like they always had. She thought of that exact shade of dark blue when picturing the deep ocean. His eyes were wide and almost shining, open and conveying so much without him having to utter a single word.

She wanted to go to him. She needed to touch him and see for herself that he was alive. That he was actually *here,* in the council chamber, and not a figment of her imagination, again.

Ira was a council member. *Ira was alive.*

"Kalena Skathor!" an irritated voice barked, stealing her focus away from Ira. Alkus Brendigar. Unfortunately, she remembered him. He looked as though he hadn't aged. One of the perks of being a Blessed was longevity; after thirty years, the aging process slowed. Alkus looked to be in his mid-thirties, but he was well into his fifties. There were a few pronounced wrinkles across his face, likely visible only because he was frowning at her. Fuming, really. It appeared his amiability also hadn't changed. "Where have you been?"

The words were blunt and accusatory, as if she was nothing more than a child who'd thrown a tantrum and run away, inconveniencing all of them.

Hiding, she wanted to snarl. *Running. So I could survive after you killed my family.*

Instead, she chose words that probably weren't any better. "I took a trip."

She watched in delight as Alkus' face reddened.

"Clearly," one of the women scoffed. Trynla Hybraeth. A bitch for lack of a better term. Her nose was always stuck up in the air. She exaggerated a sniff and directed her next words at Avalon. "You didn't take her for a bath first?"

Lena gritted her teeth, very aware of the grime that covered her and the tangles of hair around her head. "I didn't exactly have a place I could return to and bathe at every day when I was on the run."

"And you were on the run from what exactly?" Trynla challenged, her eyes gleaming, daring Lena to answer and say what the councilwoman already knew.

"Enough!" an older man called out.

His voice was weak with age, but everyone quieted when he spoke. He was the Grand Prophet, after all. Mikhail. These past few years had weighed on him. The Blessed's ability of elongated youth only lasted for so long. Time eventually caught up. If she remembered correctly, Mikhail was nearing 150 and still carried himself with the strength and agility of someone half his age. He had been nice enough to her when she was younger, but she thought he never quite viewed her as a person, as Kalena. He always saw the Numina's chosen when he looked at her.

"Seeing Her Majesty with our very eyes was more important." His milky eyes latched onto Lena's form, and if it wasn't for the intensity of his gaze, she would think he couldn't see at all. "Bless the Numina that you were safely returned to where you belong. I know you will carry on their will when you ascend the throne."

The air in the room grew heavier at Mikhail's words and everyone turned back to her. *Their will?* Would that be what she was doing?

"Well, you've seen her," another voice interjected after a few beats of tense silence. It was familiar yet foreign. Deeper and smoother than she remembered, but of course it was.

She easily found Ira's eyes when she turned.

He held her gaze as he said, "I'm sure Her Majesty is exhausted. Let her rest before we hound her with questions."

Her Majesty. It was strange to hear Ira call her that. It was strange to hear *anyone* call her that.

"Who's to say she won't run off again the moment we let her out of our sight?"

Lena nearly rolled her eyes. "I came back of my own volition. Why would I do that only to run away an hour later?"

If looks could kill, she would be well in her grave by now. How convenient that would be for them.

Alkus opened his mouth to snap something back, but Mikhail held up his hand, silencing Alkus before he could even begin. "We have important and timely matters to discuss with you, Your Majesty."

She'd expected that, and she would rather get it out of the way, but a moment to recoup would be nice. "I would appreciate a bath at the very least."

Mikhail sighed but agreed to let her wash up. She was to return right after. Rest could come later.

CHAPTER
FOUR

Avalon rid her hands of Lena as soon as they left the council room. It was the Sacred Guard who led her through the palace. She'd lost some of her familiarity with the twisting hallways, which gave rise to a bit of paranoia. The heat of her Imprint was a comfort and a reminder that she wasn't defenseless.

They eventually stopped in front of two cherry oak doors in a private corridor. "Your bedroom, Your Majesty," one of the guards said as they opened the doors.

She stepped into the room and the doors shut behind her. She was alone for approximately two seconds before another flock of individuals came upon her. All women. They were her assigned attendants. She didn't like that. She didn't need *attending* to, and if she was forced to have help, she would choose them herself.

"I do not require your assistance," she said before any of them could get a word in. "You're dismissed."

They gaped in shock and looked at one another, appearing unsure of what to do or say.

"Your Majesty," an older woman tried after a few moments of stilted silence, her smile weak and voice trembling. But the appalled look in her eyes gave her away. "I know you may not—"

"No," Lena interrupted sharply. "No, I don't want you here. Get out."

Her attendants shuffled and glanced around again, waiting, but she remained firm, both literally and figuratively, so after another wave of awkward silence, they left her room, shutting the doors behind them.

She took a deep breath and ventured from her antechamber into her actual bedroom. It was larger and more grand than necessary in true Blessed fashion. But it wasn't ostentatious, which she liked. A large four-poster bed was situated in the middle of the room and a fireplace sat farther down on the same wall. Doors to a balcony were on the far side of the room.

The spacious washroom was situated to her left, and the entire room was bright and crafted primarily from marble. A circular pool had been dug out of the center of the room, the edge of it rising about three feet from the ground. To the left was a large vanity in front of a mirrored wall. Dozens of bottles, jars, and containers littered the surface. The wall to her right had huge windows and another small balcony. The view was beautiful. She could see the beginning of the mountains and a stretch of the Highlands.

She went to the water spigot in the corner, but it controlled the shower, not the bath. There was only a thin waterproof screen that could be pulled forward if she wished for privacy, but it was transparent enough that someone could still see the outline of her body from the other side, which wasn't uncommon. Privacy and modesty were at the discretion of the individual. A body was a body. Everyone had one. In The Lands, one didn't hide it unless they wanted to.

Showering would be faster, but she loved baths. She chose the latter just to spite them. When she approached the pool, she noticed that it had its own small spigot attached to it. She messed with the handles until hot water gushed from the outlet. It stayed hot, unlike the water in the Lowlands.

She undressed quickly, setting her daggers aside and leaving her clothes in a heap on the floor as she stepped into the pool. A sigh of relief escaped her lips as the warm water soaked into her sore muscles and loosened the dirt on her skin. She submerged her entire body. Everything was muted and private under the water. It was nice—in more ways than one. She stayed under until she could no longer hold her breath.

A bar of soap and a sponge had been set along the edge of the pool, likely by one of her past attendants. She grabbed them and scrubbed the grime from her skin before turning her attention to her scalp and hair. She'd taken care of her hygiene as best she could in the Lowlands, so her hair wasn't too tangled.

By the time she was done, her skin was red and raw and her scalp tingled due to the force she'd used, but she felt divine.

Lena wandered back into the bedroom and spotted a huge dresser in the corner. She searched through it and then the wardrobe next to it. She even rummaged through the chest at the foot of her bed before she finally found a pair of pants.

She loved the soft, colorful dresses she could wear in the Highlands, but she also loved pants. They were comfortable and much more versatile, and she knew some Blessed would be irritated if she wore them to the council chamber instead of a dress. She slipped on the pants enthusiastically and hid her daggers before leaving her room.

Her guards escorted her back. The rest of the council members were present and seated as she walked in with dripping wet hair and slippers. Alkus and Trynla frowned at her. She realized just now that the latter was heavily pregnant.

The nineteen council seats were positioned in a line slightly curved at each end, like the cap of a circle, so everyone could see everyone.

Her eyes found Ira. He was already watching her, something akin to disbelief and amazement dancing in his eyes. Did she look the same, lost yet found, when staring at him? He gave her a slight nod of encouragement, but his face was pinched, his hair still wild.

She sat, grasped the cold golden knobs at the end of the armrests, and exhaled. The room remained silent, but it felt so loud.

"Your Majesty," Mikhail whispered from the seat directly on her left. Alkus was directly to her right. "You have to commence the meeting."

Right.

"Uh, let the meeting begin."

There was a snicker to her right.

Thankfully, they didn't waste any time on small talk.

"While we are glad you've returned in good health," Alkus began, not looking glad about anything, *especially* that, "there are many issues that have arisen because of your . . . excursion."

She bit her tongue.

"We all know your situation has never been quite ideal, but opposition against your rulership has grown while you were away. We need to fortify your presence as ruler if you don't want The Lands to split."

Alkus had also been involved in the killing of her family, so it was likely that the opposition had sprouted from him. He held influence on the council, as shown by his position next to her. He likely wanted nothing more than for her to lose support.

"You never did officially ascend the throne. The Ascension needs to happen soon. It's traditionally carried out in front of the entire country, so that should do something for your credibility, but that won't be enough. We've discussed other possibilities, and we believe if you get married, the people will be less skeptical about your true intentions and will stand in your support—"

"Married?" she blurted out. Her voice bounced off the confines of the domed ceiling.

"Yes," Alkus said, raising a brow as if daring her to protest further. "Is that an issue?"

She calmed her heart, telling herself she must've heard wrong. "What does getting married do for my credibility as ruler?"

"It's only natural for people to wonder what you did while you were absent. No contact for five years and then you suddenly show up at the gates—there's no telling what motives you have or who you could've aligned yourself with. Allowing someone in that situation to take the throne, even the ordained ruler, is understandably met with great apprehension. Your Ascension would be less worrisome if you had a trustworthy companion by your side. Someone in public light with influence. Someone who has been supporting this country while you weren't."

Her hands tightened on the arm rests. "What proof do you have that people find me untrustworthy?"

The look Alkus gave her was one of disbelief.

"There has been talk," Mikhail added.

"Fine," she said, "then give me a *companion*. An advisor. I don't need or want a spouse. I have the council and prophets. I'll be surrounded by others viewed as trustworthy—"

"If anything were to happen to you, your spouse would take the throne temporarily," Trynla chimed in.

Lena stilled.

So that was what this was about. It was another attempt at snatching the throne, but this time, they would put their pawn in place rather than leave it up to the Numina. Of course. Their best option wasn't to kill her, but to debilitate her until she was unable to rule but still alive. The Numina wouldn't pick a new ruler and their pawn could sit on the throne for as long as she lived.

She wasn't sure if it was her anger or her Imprint burning a path through her lungs. "I won't do it. I won't get married."

Alkus leaned toward her. "This isn't a decision for you to make."

"It's absolutely a decision for me to make!"

"This is not about what you want," he lectured. "This is about what The Lands *needs*. If you weren't ready to make sacrifices, you shouldn't have returned. As ruler, you act for others—you *exist* for others. That is your duty. It's no place for little girls who think of only themselves and—"

"Alkus!" a woman to her left scolded. A prophet, who Lena didn't recognize. "Watch how you speak to her."

"What? Did she truly think there would be no consequences for her actions?"

"My actions?" Lena hissed, nearly shaking in her seat. "What about the actions of those who murdered my family? Where are their consequences?"

The words were out of her mouth before her mind even registered them.

Silence again. No one seemed to have anything to say about that.

Mikhail cleared his throat. "I know this might not be what you want to hear, Your Majesty, but this is the best course of action. You need to marry—"

"I have yet to be convinced of that," she said tightly. "I can gain the people's trust in other ways. Surely I am not the first unliked ruler to ascend the throne. I will ascend one way or another, married or unmarried. You can't go against the Numina's wishes."

"But we can pull our support," a new voice said. It was very deep and belonged to a large man with dark brown skin and a piercing gaze, which his son had inherited. But while Ophir's eyes were brown, Tuck's were green. She had momentarily forgotten that Ophir resided in the seat reserved for the Vuukroma royal family. "It will be difficult for you to gain the people's trust if the royal families and the council don't back you."

She stared at him in outrage. He was what? Blackmailing her into marriage? And it would work. If what they said was true about the people doubting her, it would be very hard to win them over without the other influential Blessed at her side. They were never going to sing her praise. She knew that. They were her enemies. But being present and silent was enough. If they created a ruckus, well . . .

They were trying to make her see that this could benefit both of them. They would offer their passive support if she agreed to marry and give them a pawn they could replace her with and rule through. But she knew it wouldn't be that easy. Nothing ever was.

She pressed her lips together and glanced at Ira again. His eyes were sharp, his jaw clenched tightly.

"After this meeting," Mikhail said, "we planned to send word that there will be a ball held here tomorrow evening. We also would announce that you're looking for a partner to marry. The ball should be a great opportunity for you and potential partners."

She looked at Ophir, but he didn't falter under her gaze. Alkus was staring at her expectantly. They were probably looking for any reason to pull their support. If she gave them that reason now, she wouldn't be able to get far at all. She had so much to do. She hadn't even gotten started. She'd known she would have to pick her battles, but to be faced with something like this from the start . . .

"When would you need my choice by?" she asked, suddenly exhausted.

"A day after the ball. At most," Mikhail said regretfully. "I apologize for the pressing timeline, but you cannot ascend until you've married. I fear a revolt might break out otherwise."

She thought that was an exaggeration, but that wasn't her main concern. Ophir had made sure of that.

Her Imprint flared once again. Her hands itched to touch it, but she didn't want to draw any unnecessary attention to it. She would reveal her Imprint when the time was right.

"Fine," she said. "I'll do it. I'll go to the ball. Is that all? I have a headache and I'm tired."

"One more thing," Alkus jumped in. His voice was cutlery against dinner plates in her head. "We received word that you dismissed your attendants earlier?"

"Yes." *I dismissed them because I suspected they were your eyes and ears and you just proved me right.* "I don't need attending."

"A queen needs attendants—"

"Then I'll pick them myself." She turned to Mikhail this time. "Is there anything else that needs to be discussed?"

He shook his head.

"Then I call this meeting to a close," she said.

She didn't want to linger in the council's company, but she didn't want to dash out of the room like she was a child who hadn't gotten her way either. She distanced herself from the chairs and recalled the bed in her room, thinking about how soft it would feel. The fatigue was weighing down on her, and she was just about to exit the chamber when she felt a presence behind her.

She tensed right as someone said her name. Her shoulders dropped and she turned to find Ira behind her. She knew he was tall, but up close she could see that he was several inches taller than her now, easily past six feet.

"Can we talk?" he asked quietly, and dare she say, hopefully. His head was ducked as if to keep the words private, away from the others' ears.

She was somewhat caught off guard by this, but she did want to talk. Unable to find words at the moment, she nodded.

Ira straightened, a look of relief passing across his face.

When he left the council chamber, she followed.

CHAPTER
FIVE

They didn't talk as they made their way through the halls. Lena had so much to say, but all the words kept tumbling over one another, leaving her mind a jumbled mess that exhausted her further. But at the same time, she was wide awake. A current of adrenaline coursed through her, pulling her taut, and reminding her that *Ira was here, Ira was alive.*

She trailed after him like she had when seeing his spirit walking the streets in the Lowlands. She was suspended in some form of disbelief. After years on the road, she'd accepted the fact that good things didn't happen to her. And when they did, they were taken away quickly. She kept her eyes fixed on his back as if she expected him to disappear the moment she looked away.

They stopped in front of a familiar window. Members of the Sacred Guard halted a few feet away, and she threw them a look over her shoulder, one that clearly said *stay there.*

Ira gave her a small smile before slipping through the window and balancing on the cornice that wrapped around the perimeter of the courtyard. He inched to the side, and she followed suit, stepping over the window frame and onto the small six-inch ledge. She shuffled to the right after Ira, much surer of herself now with all her climbing experience. They only had to move a few feet before they reached a trellis wrapped around the top of a patio, hiding the space from anyone outside of it. Ira peeled back a piece of the wooden lattice and ducked inside. She followed once again.

They'd been here many times before. This had been their spot when they were younger. Well, it had been Ira's first. When he first came to the palace from the Tower, he kept to himself. He hardly left his room during the first few weeks, so meals were left outside of his door. She tried her hardest to make him feel welcomed without smothering him. One day she just happened to be passing by his door when he stepped out of it. They both froze when they spotted each other.

"... *Hi*," she offered up after a few moments of awkward silence, smiling after.

Ira stared back at her, giving nothing away.

The smile slowly slipped off her face. "*Um . . . do you want to join us for dinner*—?"

"*No, thank you*," he muttered before quickly turning on his heel and walking away.

She remembered feeling rejected.

She returned to that spot around the same time every day and always saw him slipping out of his room and going down the hall. One day she decided to follow him after sneaking away from her Sacred Guard and it resulted in her getting pinned to the wall by Ira. His lips were curled back in a snarl and his eyes were hostile as he stared down at her. She froze in surprise and fear. The coldness that greeted her was drastically different from the indifference she usually faced.

"*Why are you following me?*"

"*I'm sorry*," she blurted out. "*I just wanted to see where you were going.*" It was a rather lame explanation and it sounded worse when she said it aloud. "*You never leave your room, so I was just . . . surprised, I guess.*"

Ira ended up releasing her after she made a fool of herself for a few more minutes and he walked away. She wasn't stupid enough to try following him again.

She actually came across his spot by accident. She was in the courtyard—it was one of her favorites in the palace because of the giant oak tree in the middle—when she heard a noise coming from somewhere close by. Her head jerked up and she happened to catch sight of a boot disappearing through a window.

As Ira began to trust her and her family and the two of them grew closer, he finally took her to his spot above the courtyard. Cool, dark, and private, but one could still peek through the tiny holes and enjoy what the scenery had to offer. It had been nice, admittedly—the secret spot *and* spending time with him. But it hadn't lasted long before everything crumbled apart.

For the most part, the hidden space looked the same. Ira had decorated it somewhat and stashed some items within it. A thick quilt covered in blankets and pillows was spread out near the far wall, and in the corner was a short chest with small folded paper figures on top of it. After finding out he had a hard time sitting still and calming his mind, she'd suggested a handful of hobbies to him. This one had stuck.

"You've improved," she remarked as she looked over the figures. There was a horse, an animal that looked like a lion, and a bird of some sort. She could see the dozens of folds on each one.

"I'd hope so," he said. "It's been five years."

Silence fell between them.

It had been five years.

Krashing, five years.

She sat carefully on the quilt with her knees drawn up to her chest, her gaze fixed pointedly on the tips of her slippers.

"I can't believe you're here," Ira breathed out next to her.

"Me neither," she muttered, turning to him.

Beams of sunlight filtered through the lattice and illuminated parts of his face.

She lifted her hand. Ira's gaze cut to it, but he didn't stop it or say anything as her fingers neared his face. She needed to make sure he was real.

Her fingers touched his illuminated cheekbone. His skin was so smooth. And warm. He always ran hot while she ran cold. She trailed her fingers down his cheek, across his jaw and the stubble he'd missed. His gaze stayed locked with hers. He memorized her face with his eyes while she memorized his with her fingers. He was real.

She surged forward and wrapped her arms around him, dropping her head to his neck. His arms twined around her back a second later, clutching her just as tightly. No discomfort prickled across her skin as usual when someone else touched her. She sunk into his embrace.

"How are you here?" she asked as she pulled back. "I hoped that you made it out unscathed, but I didn't know. I couldn't! We were outnumbered—and young. You had your Slayer, I know, but still—"

She snapped her mouth shut, realizing that she was rambling. She had a habit of dissolving into a mess around him, but her emotions were particularly unbridled right now.

"When I came back," she said slowly, the weight of her words dragging her down, "I thought I'd have no one."

"And yet you still came back?"

"I had to."

The silence returned, heavy and wrought with tension.

She wanted to ask what had happened, what he'd been through, but it wasn't an easy thing to ask. Or answer. He likely wanted to know the same thing, and she wasn't sure if she could tell him everything she'd gone through in the Lowlands.

Trust wasn't the issue. She trusted Ira, even after all this time apart. It should scare her or at least worry her how much she openly trusted him, but it didn't. She'd been drawn to him from the moment she saw him being pulled back to the Tower by those guards all those years ago.

"You can ask."

She raised her gaze to his. "What happened?"

"I wasn't in my room when the commotion started. I didn't realize what was happening at first . . . but I suspected it. Ever since I arrived here from the Tower, I thought it was only a matter of time before this all came crashing down." He had subconsciously began picking at the loose threads of the quilt. There was a distant look in his eyes, and his face twisted at whatever memory he was recalling. "They hit your private wing first from what I understand. I saw it, but I couldn't go in and find you. I wanted to, but then they all turned on me. I ran and I fought."

His voice broke on the last word and he swallowed thickly. "I had my Slayer. I knew how to use it well, so I survived the initial attack, but I didn't know if you had. I stayed hidden in the forest surrounding the palace for days. I debated running and never looking back, but I couldn't. I needed to know what had happened to you.

"When I returned, Ezra told me he'd told you to run. And when the prophets announced that the Numina were quiet, I knew you were still out there somewhere."

His eyes were almost haunted when he looked at her, but he also somehow appeared relieved.

"Ezra," she cut in. "Is he okay? What about the others?"

She had left him alone, in the middle of a bloodbath, to face a Slayer. He had his own, but after seeing all the fallen, who'd been left on her side to fight with him?

Ira's face twisted again. "Lena . . . I'm sorry. He was exiled. He took the blame for everything. Said he was negligent. He was sent away days after the attack and no one has seen him since. The only one left is Cowen. He's in charge now."

Her chest ached.

Ezra was gone. Alive, but gone. Maeve hadn't made it. Cowen was the only one still here. The three of them had been the closest to her, though Cowen had been the youngest and meanest member of the Sacred Guard when she came to the Highlands. He'd poked fun at her but at least *talked* to her, which counted for something. The Sacred Guard was supposed to keep their relationship with the ruler professional; no personal relationships were to be had. But Ezra, Cowen, and Maeve had ignored that rule, and it had made her time in the Highlands somewhat brighter.

"Okay," she croaked. She had expected the worst. "Where is Cowen now? Why haven't I seen him?"

"He's been out looking for you. Sometimes he's gone for days on end. He's been doing it since you left. The council allowed him to search for you, but only him." Ira clenched his jaw and shook his head. "It was shit," he all but growled out. "Things were a mess."

"Then why didn't you leave?"

"I couldn't. And I didn't want to. Not really," he confessed. "I stayed because I finally had something here. I stayed because I didn't want you to come back and have no one. And I think I stayed because I was too scared to leave. I wanted to be the first to know if something happened to you. I had trouble sleeping. Every night I wondered where you were and if you were safe. I worried that when I woke, the prophets would declare that the Numina had chosen a new ruler. I would flinch when the bell at the top of the palace rang. I would count the gongs, and every time three sounded, I prayed that the bell would keep going."

Lena's parents had taught her what message was being relayed according to the number of times the bell rang. A single gong told people that the next hour had come around. Two gongs meant there was a trial of particular importance being held. Three gongs meant the previous ruler had died and the Numina had chosen a new one. Four was for danger. Five was for the funeral of a powerful figure. And six signified a celebration.

"Once I came back, news about the attack on your family and you fleeing had spread. Those behind the assassination couldn't outright kill me. It would be too risky, especially because I'm Blessed. So, they hurt me in any way they could . . . including Slayer duels."

Her breath caught in her throat.

Duels between Blessed were dangerous and brutal because their Slayers were allowed to participate. Death was also allowed if agreed upon beforehand. Ira had been fifteen and likely going up against people three or four times his age. He sat before her, so he'd survived, but at what price? How many had he fought? She knew not all scars were visible. Most of them ran deep.

He gave her a tight smile. "I'm fine."

"Don't say that," she shot back. "Don't write it off like that. That's horrible."

He shrugged. "I've come to terms with it, but I haven't forgotten it. Or what it felt like. How I felt."

"Good." She hadn't forgotten either. "Who were they?"

"You can probably guess."

Alkus. Ophir. She went through the faces of those on the council. There were dozens if not hundreds more who wanted her gone and were willing to do anything to make that happen. Ira had been attacked because he was associated with her. It wasn't her fault. Not really. She knew that. But that didn't stop her from feeling like she was to blame.

"I want to kill them," she said simply. She looked at the bright diamonds on the lattice wall instead of Ira. "I want revenge for me and my family. I know who was involved. I have proof now. And I intend to make them pay. That's one of the reasons I came back." She dug her chin into her knees. "They took so much from me. From *you*. They've taken so much from thousands before us, and they will continue to take from thousands after us."

"So, you'd be doing the people a favor then by killing them?"

"Yes," she said with absolute certainty.

"You can't say those things," he said after a moment.

She snorted. "What are they going to do? Kill me? Keep me from ascending?"

"You know they can do worse things than that. Don't bait them."

She gritted her teeth. "I want them to *hurt*. I want them to be *afraid*. Like I was . . . I didn't know if you had survived either. And even if you made it through the first day, there was still the second and the third and the fourth—five *years'* worth of days I worried for you. I had no sign to console me." Her words came out bitter, and she realized it was perhaps the wrong thing to say. Her resentment should not be directed at him. "Sorry—"

"No, it's okay. Don't apologize. I thought about that too—how you had no way of knowing."

It'd been haunting, thinking about Ira and the others day in and day out. She'd stayed sane by pushing it down, locking it behind a door, and never opening it.

"With my family, I at least had closure. It was hard for me to accept for a while, but I know what I saw."

Flashes of their bodies and their ripped-opened chests still flooded her mind often.

"They were killed, ripped apart, and then laid out like they were part of a display. It was *sick*. And *they* did that, so tell me why they don't deserve pain."

"I can't," he said, his voice thick and rough. "And I won't. It's horrible what they did. I could never love your family as much as you, but they were special to me. Not many people would give someone like me a chance, but they did. They were good people who didn't deserve that. But you won't be able to avenge them if you act recklessly."

She glared at him, but he didn't fold under it.

"I'm on your side, Lena," he said softly. "Us against them, alright?"

She hesitated. Then nodded.

"They think they're smart," he continued, "but they're blind. Use their rules against them."

"And how do you propose I do that?"

Ira smirked. "Are you asking for my advice?"

Lena rolled her eyes and lied, "Yes. Only this once."

"You have to be strategic with how you retaliate. Make small moves. They won't notice what you're doing at first and they won't protest too much. Agree with them. Make them think they're winning. When they realize what's happening, it'll be too late. The scales will be tipped against them and in your favor."

She let out a coarse laugh. "I don't know about that. I'm awfully outnumbered."

"So form allies. You're the queen. You have the influence and power . . ."

"Well, I'm not the queen yet *apparently*," she muttered dryly. "I have to get married first."

The only marriage she had to look to for guidance was her parents'. But they were gone now, and their marriage had been the result of love. They hadn't been rushed into it. Her situation was nothing like theirs. And she had two days to decide. That wasn't enough time.

Less than an hour had passed since the council meeting, so she hadn't had a lot of time to think about it. But someone had come to mind when a spouse was mentioned.

She rubbed her cheek, hoping to cover or erase the redness that might be there.

"That's ridiculous," Ira said gruffly. "I argued against it, but not many are willing to go against Alkus."

She'd suspected as much, but it was still worrisome. "They'd rather back him than back the queen?"

"The people are confused. They don't know everything, and Alkus took advantage of your absence and rallied. Discreetly, of course."

"He wants the throne?" she guessed.

"But he can't have it."

"Now that I'm back."

"No, he could never. He's not chosen. The people wouldn't accept him as ruler. He'd have to give himself another title."

She sighed and gnawed on her lower lip. There were so many variables. So many people, most of who were enemies, she had to keep an eye out for.

She would do that later.

"I'm tired," she exhaled as she leaned back against the pillows. The muscles along her back sang as they finally got to relax against something soft. Her eyes slipped closed for a moment. "I don't want to talk about these things anymore."

"Okay," Ira said easily.

She heard rustling next to her and felt the heat emanating from his body, but she didn't feel him. Part of her wanted to lean over and press herself against his side. Take in this moment.

Things had changed between them. *They* had changed. He acted different. He was less angry, or maybe just better at hiding it. He was surer of himself, but maybe he was just good at acting. She supposed he had to be. He'd always been smart. For the most part, she'd been able to evade the Blessed's wrath in the Lowlands. Ira had been in the very middle of it. He had to learn to adapt, to act, to do all the things he'd told her to do just minutes before. His position on the council was likely part of that act. It was another way he could fight. It was much harder to take someone out once they were in the public eye.

Her stomach chose that moment to growl loudly. A laugh tumbled from her lips, and once she began, she couldn't stop. She rolled onto her side and laughed into the blankets, her stomach cramping with the force of it. *Krashing*, she *was* tired. And hungry.

Ira's laugh quickly joined hers. "Here. I have some food stored in this thing."

She peeled her eyes open just in time to see Ira push himself up onto one elbow and lean over her to reach for the chest in the corner. She stared up at him, tracing his shape once again, marking his features and committing them to memory.

He grabbed what he was looking for and caught her gaze. A smile crept onto his face as he sat back. "What?"

"Nothing," she said, mirroring his smile. She couldn't help it. It was the fatigue, she told herself. She looked at the basket in his hands. "What's that?"

"Food."

He opened it and brought out containers of nuts, cheese, fruits, crackers, dried meat, and chocolate. The sight of it all made her mouth water.

"I know it's not much, but . . ."

But it was enough. Ira knew as well as her that when starved, nearly anything sounded delicious.

"I'll cook for you one day soon. I've been practicing,"

That stole her attention away from the food. She stared at him, lips parted in surprise. He hadn't been the best cook when he first arrived, and he hadn't been interested in attending her family dinners. But cooking had been special to her family; a fun bonding activity. They would often turn away the meals made by palace chefs to cook their own food from the ingredients in their garden. Ira had eventually joined them at the dinner table, and then in the kitchen. To know that Ira had continued to build his cooking skills despite everything filled her with warmth.

"I'd like that."

He nodded, but it was somewhat delayed, almost as if he was surprised by her answer. But his mouth was soft and curled up ever so slightly at the ends. She felt the urge to dig her finger into one of his dimples, but she refrained and distracted herself with food.

She quickly dug in and moaned when the flavors hit her tongue. Ira didn't laugh at her. He cut up a fresh pomegranate and picked out the seeds. It still appeared to be his favorite food. They snatched the bottle of water from the chest as well and passed it between them as they ate. She made sure to not stuff her stomach too much, less she wanted to be sick later.

As soon as she fell back onto the pillows again, her body and eyelids grew heavy. She was so comfortable and warm and sated.

Before she could think about getting up and going back to her bedroom, Ira collapsed beside her. He let out a heavy sigh and rested his hands on his stomach. She was only inches away from him. She could very easily shift her shoulder and touch his.

Instead, she gave in to her body and allowed herself to fully relax. Her head drooped to the side before landing on a pillow. She snuggled into it and let out a contented sigh.

Ira laughed softly. "You can rest," he whispered. "You're safe now."

She slipped under within seconds.

CHAPTER
SIX

Ira let her sleep until he could no longer. When she woke up, she immediately reached for her daggers, which weren't there. She relaxed only when she realized where exactly she was and who lay in front of her.

"Cowen's waiting for you in the hall," Ira said softly. "He's here to bring you to your room so you can get ready for the ball."

The sleepiness was still draining from her mind, so the implications of Ira's words hit her a few seconds later than they should have. Her eyes widened and she scrambled to her feet.

"The ball? That's tomorrow!"

"It is tomorrow."

Her lips parted. "How long was I asleep?"

Ira grinned "About twelve hours."

Her first reaction was to deny that. It couldn't be true. She usually had a hard time falling asleep because it took a while for her body and mind to relax. *Good* sleep was a luxury someone on the run could not afford. But her bladder told her that she had, in fact, slept for that long.

"*Shit.*"

She moved toward the exit and Ira followed her.

"You were properly asleep, draped over me and drooling on my shirt—"

She spun around before she stepped out onto the cornice and swatted Ira's arm, but he danced away from her, his grin blinding.

"Stop it." But there was a small smile creeping onto her face too.

The two of them slid along the side of the palace before slipping through the window and into the corridor.

In the light, she noticed the dark smudges under Ira's eyes. "Did you sleep?"

"Of course I did." His eyes moved past her.

She turned and froze when she set her eyes on Cowen.

His blond hair was longer, and he was tanner than before. She remembered what Ira had said about Cowen searching for her in the Lowlands. The sun was brutal down there, especially if you didn't cover up properly, and judging by the reddish burns on Cowen's cheeks, he hadn't. But the kiss of the sun only seemed to reach so deep. There was a paleness that shined through. Was he nervous to see her? Nauseous? Maybe he was just tired from his travels. He looked like he'd come to get her the moment he returned. That would also explain the bags under his eyes, but not the streaks of gray running through his hair. If she remembered correctly, he was forty this year, twice her age. So why did he look so much older?

"Cowen," she breathed out.

Part of her wanted to lunge forward and embrace him. Another part of her was wary. The latter won out.

He gave her an exhausted smile. "Kalena," he said warmly, dipping his head. "I'm glad you found your way back."

She nodded stiffly.

"I've come to escort you back to your room."

Ira moved in front of her, snatching her attention for a moment. "I'll see you at the ball."

"Yeah," she murmured absently.

She and Cowen made their way to her room, and she was grateful that the trip was short. Cowen didn't say a word, and she was grateful for that as well.

Two members of the Sacred Guard stood in front of her doors. She vaguely recognized them as the guards who had been with her yesterday.

"Your Majesty." The red-haired man dipped his head in her direction before turning to Cowen. "Sir."

She raised a brow at that.

"Kalena, this is Benji and Andra. They're the newest additions to the Sacred Guard. They will serve you well."

"Nice to meet you." She attempted to smile at them, but it came across as more of a grimace.

"Councilman Alkus and Grand Prophet Mikhail requested that Her Majesty be brought to choose her new attendants," Andra said.

Her eyes widened. "Now?"

"Who's going to help you prepare for the ball?" Cowen pointed out.

"I don't need help."

Cowen snorted in amusement. "Really?" He scanned her body, or more specifically, her outfit. "I heard you arrived at the council chamber like that yesterday."

Her shoulders tensed. There was the Cowen she knew. Though, his jest wasn't entirely unwelcomed.

"Yes," she said a bit defensively.

Now it was his turn to raise a brow.

She let out a heavy breath. "Fine, whatever. But I need to relieve myself first."

She would go ahead and get this over with. A few hours wasn't enough time to properly evaluate someone, but at least she got to choose this time.

After emptying her bladder, she was taken to a room filled with well over a hundred women. Alkus and Mikhail were in the room as well. While she wasn't surprised to see them together, it didn't bring her any comfort. Quite the opposite actually.

"How much time do I have?" she asked as she looked over the crowd of women.

Mikhail blinked slowly. "I beg your pardon?"

"How much time do I have to choose my attendants?"

"Three hours," Alkus answered brusquely.

"Very well." She crossed her arms and nodded toward the door. "You can leave now."

A muscle in Alkus' cheek twitched while Mikhail leaned forward on the cushioned chair he was sitting on. "Your Majesty, I don't think—"

"I want to make this decision on my own. There's no need for you to supervise." She raised her chin.

"We just think—"

"I won't start with you in the room," she said frankly, her eyes locked with Alkus'. "So please . . . " She swept her hand toward the door.

After a few seconds of silence, they rose to their feet and headed for the door, much like her attendants had. Alkus kept his eyes on her as he passed, his shoulder nearly brushing hers.

Once they left, she thought about how to approach this and decided upon asking all the women questions and having them write down their responses. Benji and Andra ran to get supplies.

She kept the questions simple. Some were more serious; she asked where they were from, how they got into this line of work, how long they had been in this line of work, how well they knew the palace. Some questions were lighter and more fun. She asked about their dreams and hobbies, their favorite place to visit, a secret about them. Her final question was what they thought about her.

She took the papers into another room to read through them once they were collected. She skimmed over most of them, only slowing when something caught her eye.

"Alkus is becoming impatient," Benji informed her, almost regrettably, upon returning to the room. Mikhail had left entirely after Lena's dismissal, but Alkus had stayed in the lounge at the end of the hall.

She read even slower. Going through all the papers took her nearly two hours, but in the end, she was pretty confident of the six women she'd picked. She announced her choices and the other women left.

"What are your names?" she asked the remaining six in front of her. "I want to know the names of the women who will be attending me every day."

She paid attention to the details—however much or little they decided to give her. Her father had always told her names were important, so she made a promise to herself to memorize them quickly.

Eloise. Louelle. Odette. Devla. Jhai. Renetta.

"Thank you," she said once they had finished. "You may call me Kalena or Lena. It only feels right for you to call me by my name since I have a feeling we will become rather close."

In more ways than one.

Based on some of the women's reactions, it was safe to say the name thing was going to be a work in progress.

She ignored Alkus on the way back to her room. Cowen, Benji, and Andra stayed outside her doors while Lena and her attendants slipped inside to get ready for the ball. It was almost noon, which apparently was cutting it far too close, even though Mikhail had told her the ball didn't start until three. The parties in The Lands always started during the day and went into the night.

"Oh, you don't need to do that," she said when she saw Louelle going over to draw a bath. "I can do it."

A puzzled expression came across Louelle's face, but she moved on to something else. The others were moving around the washroom and bedroom like they knew the space well.

"Could we measure you, Your Maj—er, Kalena?" Eloise asked. She appeared friendly with her big cheeks and dimples. Her hair was a wave of copper curls, which complimented her tan skin and hazel eyes. In her hand was a length of soft measuring tape.

"Uh, sure."

"It's for your dress," Eloise explained as she wrapped the tape around Lena's hips and then her bust. She listed off the numbers to Odette nearby.

"Of course."

Surely they weren't going to make a whole new dress in three hours.

Once Eloise finished her measurements, she and Odette disappeared.

Devla took their spot a moment later and ushered Lena into the washroom. The pool spigot remained untouched, but dozens of jars had been transferred from the vanity to the edge of the pool. Candles had been lit and incense was burning, filling the room with a pleasant aroma.

"You all really don't need to . . . do this." She faltered toward the end when she saw the perplexed and anxious looks thrown her way.

"We're your attendants," Devla said. "Our job is to attend to you."

"Yes, but . . . " There was no way for her to put this without sounding like an utter fool. "I really don't need it. You can all . . . rest—if you wish."

Her remaining four attendants exchanged glances, all of them looking lost in various degrees.

"You only returned yesterday, Your Majesty," Renetta said. She and Devla were the oldest of the bunch, but while Devla was all kind eyes and curves, Renetta was all stiff-lipped and bones. "Forgive me if I misspeak, but things haven't been easy for you. It is you, not us, who needs rest. And you may not need or even want our help, but that is our job. We will do everything we can to make you comfortable, but please let us do what you chose us for."

She couldn't see Devla, but Jhai and Louelle were gaping at Renetta like she'd let out the most execrable string of curse words to exist.

Renetta, however, did not seem panicked at all. She raised her chin. "May I draw you a bath, Your Majesty?"

Lena's lips parted. She too had been taken aback by Renetta's words, but she wasn't insulted. Very far from that actually. ". . . Sure."

Everyone in the room let out a visible exhale and resumed whatever they were doing.

Renetta was right. It didn't make much sense for Lena to have them stand by and do nothing when this was what they were here for. She truly didn't need the help, but this was another thing she would have to get used to now that she was back.

Eloise and Odette returned as the pool filled, platters of food and drinks in their hands.

Lena thanked them before undressing and stepping into the bath. Another groan of relief left her lips and her eyes slipped closed as the hot water worked at her aches and pains. Now *this* was something she could easily get used to again.

The room around her had gone silent. She didn't quite notice it at first, but when she opened her eyes, she saw everyone frozen, staring at her, or more specifically, her chest, where her Imprint rested between her breasts. They looked away when they realized they were caught.

"I-I'm sorry, Your Majesty—"

"It's fine."

She had mulled over Ira's advice earlier after seeing Alkus. She was willing to act cooperative, to play nice. She would marry and gain the people's favor. She would show them that she had power now. That she was a *true Blessed deserving of the throne*, whatever that meant. She was willing to bet that her Imprint would win her more allies than enemies if she played it carefully as Ira had advised. Anyone who wanted to be her enemy was already her enemy. The rest were looking for a reason to be swayed. So, she wasn't going to hide her Imprint any longer.

Her attendants probably had questions, but they didn't ask them. They poured salts and liquids into the pool that made the water and room smell even better.

She preferred to bathe herself, but she didn't want to insult them any more than she already had by further denying their help. They compromised. She would wash her body and they would wash her hair. She knew their touch was coming, but she still told them to announce themselves beforehand, now and in the future. After so many years of living on the run, she didn't . . . respond well to sudden touches.

She winced as they focused their attention on the remaining tangles. Various pastes and soaps were applied to her hair, some of which were washed out and others left in.

Once she finished her bath, she wrapped herself in a robe and sat on the stool in front of the large vanity. Her reflection surprised her. This was the first time she'd looked at herself since returning. This was probably the first time she'd looked at herself in well over a week. She tried to avoid it—avoid *her*. She looked . . . fresh but gaunt, even after the sleep and food.

Her thoughts must've been displayed on her face because Devla leaned forward, smiling kindly, and said, "Don't worry, Your Majesty. A few weeks of good sleep and hot meals will bring some color back to your skin and some meat on your bones."

Lena hummed and gave Devla what she hoped was a polite smile. She looked at her reflection again. Her tawny brown skin appeared almost sickly and leached of some of its pigment despite all the time she spent in the sun. Her cheeks and eyes were sunken, her collarbones stuck out too much, and her dark brown hair was brittle and dull, barely brushing her shoulders.

"You're naturally very beautiful, Kalena. Truly," Louelle murmured. Her warm brown skin and eyes were familiar in a way Lena refused to explore deeper. "Anyone at this ball would be lucky to have you."

Her chest tightened. Right. The ball. She'd almost had the pleasure of forgetting about it. Almost.

They set to work trimming, combing, and drying her hair, once again rubbing various oils into her roots and ends. While they did this, she found herself staring at her Imprint. It was still mostly visible, the branches of it disappearing in the *V* of the front of her robe.

The Imprint looked brutal—they all did. The thin, oval-like shape in the center resembled a wound, like a sword had been shoved into the skin and twisted. Fine, jagged lines stretched from it, like a sickness, a poison, that was spreading. The reason the center looked the way it did was because the Numen shoved its presence into one's body viciously. It was fast and painful. Most Blessed didn't recall this moment because the pact was almost always made during infancy, but she hadn't been so fortunate. She remembered every second of it, the excruciating pain and the burning essence that had flooded her veins, smothering her until she couldn't *breathe*.

An Imprint was supposed to be a blessing. An Imprint was the mark *of* the Divine Touch, but it wasn't all good. Nothing this gruesome could be.

She didn't know what to call herself now. She was born Cursed, but by all definitions of the term, she was now Blessed. Yet she knew some people in the palace wouldn't see it that way. *She* didn't even see it that way.

Labels were sometimes restrictive. The realm would be so different if labels like *Cursed* and *Blessed* weren't used.

"Are you alright?"

She jerked out of her thoughts and looked down at Jhai, who knelt next to her. "Yes, sorry. I guess I'm still kind of out of it."

Jhai appeared to be the youngest of the bunch, maybe around Lena's age, with rich black skin and glossy coils that were gathered out of her face. Her eyes were so dark you couldn't make out the pupil from the iris, and perhaps that was what gave her a doe-eyed look that made Lena's muscles relax.

Jhai nodded in understanding and resumed working on her nails. "Nervous?"

Lena took a deep breath. "I just . . . am ready for tonight to be over."

"You're the queen," Jhai said. "People will always be looking at you."

Always. This position was a life-long job. The previous ruler had reigned for nearly a century. She couldn't imagine doing this for that long.

Eloise and Odette left the washroom again while the rest of her attendants finished waxing and applying all sorts of powders and pastes to her skin. She dug her nails into the armrests, bearing it all. She was thankful when it was over. They moved on to makeup next, and they kept it light as she'd requested.

As the ball approached, a knot of tension tightened in the pit of her stomach. She really hated social events, especially when she was the center of attention.

But all of her anxiety fled her mind the moment she stepped into her bedroom and laid eyes on her gown for the ball.

"Oh . . . " Her breath escaped her at the sight of it. *It was very . . .* "Gold?" she questioned, turning to Odette and Eloise.

Odette smiled, showing the gap between her front teeth. She was the slightest in the group and quite soft-spoken. "Yes, the color of the Numina. It's appropriate for your first public appearance since returning, don't you think? And it goes lovely with your complexion, Queen Kalena."

Lena circled the dress. It was on a dress form that kept its fit. "Isn't it a bit . . . much?"

Renetta clucked her tongue. "Of course not. The eye of every person in that room will be on you."

Lena grumbled under her breath at the additional reminder. "Maybe we should go with something less flashy."

She immediately felt bad for suggesting it when she saw Eloise and Odette's faces fall, so she agreed to put it on. The others secured it onto her with practiced hands, and she held her breath as she stood still through all the tugs. When they stepped back, they motioned toward the tall mirror propped up next to the dresser. She hesitated before stepping in front of it.

She didn't recognize her reflection. She looked so different from the woman she'd seen in the mirror less than an hour ago. Her attendants had somehow returned the deep golden color to her skin. Her hair appeared shiny and lush, and even though it was short, they'd managed to style it in a way that made her look like she had much more hair than she did. Her eyes were outlined in black, and her eyelids shimmered. So did her cheekbones. A simple gloss covered her lips, making them appear lush and full. And the dress . . .

Seeing it on her was completely different from seeing it on the stand. The dress was made of a soft, dark fabric. She'd thought it was black at first, but the dress changed colors slightly as she shifted. It was a midnight violet color—darker even. Intricate gold embroidery trailed across the dress, focused around the seams. It was stunning. And revealing. She had seen how low-cut the front of the dress was on the stand; the draping fabric dipped down between her breasts, leaving her Imprint on full display.

"Oh," Eloise began when she noticed what had caught Lena's attention, "when we picked out the dress, we didn't know . . ."

"No, it's perfect actually." She brushed her fingers over her Imprint. "I think it's time I display it."

They surrounded her to put on the finishing touches, adorning her with jewelry and making sure her hair was just right. She slipped on low heels, which she had agreed to after seeing the optimistic look on Eloise's face, but she knew she would regret her choice after about a few dozen dances. Truthfully, she was already regretting it.

When her attendants gave her the mark of approval, Lena left her room and stepped into the hall. Cowen, Andra, and Benji took in her appearance.

"You look beautiful, Kalena," Cowen said.

She avoided his kind eyes and smiled. It was weird—seeing him like that. Seeing him *at all*. She brushed her hands over the skirt of her dress. It had been a long time since she'd worn one of these.

"Let's go find me a spouse," she muttered under her breath.

The palace had four ballrooms, and the event tonight was being hosted in the largest one situated in the middle of the palace.

The ball was in full swing when she arrived. Dozens of guests littered the halls surrounding the ballroom, and she could hear the commotion through the large double doors, yet the guards on either side didn't let her in.

"We've been instructed to announce your presence when you arrive."

"Oh, no," she blurted out. She looked between the guards. "No, that, um, won't be necessary." She didn't want any more attention than she was already set to get.

Luckily, they didn't push back against her wishes.

As soon as she entered the ballroom, conversations paused and dancing halted as people turned to look at her. She was thankful the orchestra continued to play because that would've only made matters worse.

It didn't take long for people's gazes to drop to her Imprint. She took in the various expressions before her—disbelief, fear, confusion, anger, awe, relief. It was the reaction she had anticipated.

Her eyes searched for Alkus in the crowd, and by coincidence alone, she was able to spot him. He stood toward the back of the room, leaning against the railing of a second-floor balcony. Even so far away, she could tell he was fuming.

She smirked. *Sorry to soil your plans.*

Hushed whispers sailed over the crowd. There must've been *thousands* of guests in this ballroom, which seemed like too many. But the dance room was ginormous and more than capable of holding that many people.

There were three levels to the ballroom. The top two levels were more like spacious balconies that wrapped around the edge of the room, extending out a bit but not enough that they covered the dance floor. The third level was smaller than the second, pulled back closer to the wall. Someone at the very top could see people on the second and first floor, but those people could not see them. The design of the room was like an upside-down cone with the dance floor being the tip and the large, tinted glass ceiling being the base. It was an elaborate, grandeur arrangement that left her in awe.

A throat cleared. "Your Majesty."

She turned to face a young man standing at the foot of the steps, his hand slightly extended. He appeared nervous, but she gave him credit for being the first to approach her.

"May I have this dance?"

And let the game begin.

CHAPTER
SEVEN

    Lena had lost count of how many people she'd danced with and how long she had been twirling around on the dance floor. But she knew one thing: she was not having a good time.

The whole event consisted of tight smiles and small talk. She hated small talk. She hated talking in general—at least to these people. None of them were even remotely interesting. She really didn't give a damn about their finances or hunting prowess or where they got their gowns made. But she remained cordial, even though she had no intention of pursuing a relationship with any of them.

Some were insulted by her lack of enthusiasm. Others were too busy talking about themselves to notice that she wasn't really paying attention. She considered leaving a handful of them on the dance floor when their hands strayed too low or they uttered a backhanded compliment, but she swore she could feel Alkus' gaze burning into the back of her skull, reminding her of her duty.

Ira's advice ran through her head again, so she endured the agony that was this event and continued dancing.

She was eventually able to peel herself away from the dance floor for the first time in what felt like hours. She didn't know the time; she'd lost track of how many times the bell had rung since her arrival. All she knew was that her feet were covered in blisters and half of the people she'd talked to were more interested in her Imprint than in her.

She paused at a refreshment table, picking up the first glass she saw and taking a sip. Alcohol. She flagged down a server and asked for water instead. While alcohol might make the evening more bearable, she didn't want to do anything that would lower her defenses around these people.

She was surprised that no one from the council had sought her out and asked about her Imprint. Though, she had been rather busy in the last few hours.

She had yet to spot Ira among the crowd, but she *had* seen her so-called childhood friends gathered together. Cressida. Vix. Crane. Leythi. Greer. Alden. Tuck and Xavien had been the only two missing. It was cute they all still hung out together.

Vix came over to ask her for a dance, then Crane five minutes later. She rejected both of them. They'd clearly approached her with the intention of mocking and humiliating her—she could see their sharp grins and pointed stares from dozens of feet away—but even if they hadn't, she still would've refused them. They had all stabbed her in the back.

The anger that arose within her when they went back to their little group, snickering and making snide comments that she couldn't hear but knew were about her, was *scorching*. Her Imprint burned alongside it and the heat traveled down her arms, collecting at her palms, begging to be let out, but she couldn't cause a scene here. Not this soon. Her anger wasn't only directed at them. She had played herself. When they were younger, at best, they would forget about their prejudices and tolerate her. At worst, they would target her in their cruel games. And she'd kept going back. Truly, what had she expected to happen? She had been so *stupid*. At least she'd finally come to her senses. Some good that did her family.

Cressida tested Lena's restraint earlier when she sauntered by her in between dances. "*Nice to see you back,* Your Majesty," she said under her breath, her words twisted and too sweet to be genuine. "*You look as out of place now as you did back then.*"

And then the bitch spilled wine on Lena's dress. She was discreet about it, Lena would give her that, but it still made her blood boil.

Cressida had been quiet when she was younger. She hadn't been the main instigator, but she'd always found pleasure in the ways others had ripped Lena apart. It seemed that she had grown into her cruelty.

Lena could still see Cressida through the gaps in the crowd. She was dancing now. The group had dispersed some time ago to partake in the ball's activities.

Lena set her glass down and pushed herself away from the table. She didn't know where she was going, but she had to move. Maybe she would seek out Ira.

A body stepped in front of her before she could get far.

"Your Majesty."

The title was spoken in a condescending tone. It was a familiar voice—one that sent warning bells off in her head.

She frowned when she saw who it was.

Krashing, she couldn't get rid of these people.

"Xavien," she greeted flatly.

He wore an arrogant smirk on his face. He was much larger than her now, which made her stomach twist with discomfort. But she could tell from one glance that he was still the same boy who would invite her places only to torment her and remind her of how much she didn't belong. His words were always laced with amusement. *I was just teasing,* he would say, lying through his teeth. No one had ever scolded him for it. He was Blessed, after all.

Xavien took a step forward, causing her to take a step back. She pressed her hands on top of the table and curled her fingers around another glass. She'd hurl it at him if she had to. No, if she *wanted* to.

He moved to stand next to her instead. A few people had been watching her, likely mustering up the nerve to come over and ask her for a dance, but they looked away when they spotted Xavien.

"You look like you're not enjoying yourself."

She was unwilling to keep the pretense with him. "I was enjoying myself just fine until you came over."

A partial lie.

Xavien laughed and turned his body toward her.

She stared straight ahead, eyes raking over the crowd, hoping to find Ira or even someone from the Sacred Guard. She glanced at the entryway, wondering when she'd be able to leave.

"So, that's how this is going to be. I'm assuming your mood will only worsen if I ask you for a dance."

She scoffed. She hoped Alkus was witnessing this exchange. In a way, telling Xavien off was like telling Alkus off since Xavien was his' nephew. "You're serious?"

"Deadly."

She clenched her jaw and carefully released the glass before she decided to smash it over his head. She turned to face Xavien. The bastard was still smirking down at her. It was vicious, just like before, and it made her skin crawl.

"Your sense of humor is shit."

"You know you could be insulting me *while* we're dancing."

"I could," she agreed. "But I'm not the same stupid girl I was before."

She had admired him once upon a time. She saw how all the other young Blessed looked at him, but she quickly got over that worship once she realized how nasty he was. How he would go out of his way to humiliate and torture her. She still had the scars he'd caused when he pushed her down a hillside and she crashed into an amberthorn bush at the bottom. But her desire to fit in, to impress them, had lasted much too long. She'd given them chance after chance when they'd never given her one.

She took a step closer and lowered her voice. "You haven't changed one bit. The only reasons you would approach me, asking for a dance, are if you wanted to humiliate me or if your parents told you to make nice, so maybe, just *maybe,* I would let bygones be bygones and consider you as a possibility when the council asks for my answer on who I wish to marry. And that, Xavien, will *never happen.*"

His smirk had fallen away. "You're still holding on to things in the past—"

Her Imprint burned and she spun around to leave, but a hand snatched her wrist.

She whirled, lips peeled back. "Get your hand off me."

He didn't. In fact, his grip only tightened as he leaned in. The civil facade he'd put up earlier had disappeared. His eyes were blazing. He couldn't even handle a taste of his own medicine.

"You stroll back in here after five years with this proud attitude, acting like you're better than everyone else," he hissed.

"I think you have me confused with yourself," she shot back as she tried to pull herself from his grasp. The only reason she hadn't rammed her fist into his throat was because she didn't want to make a scene if she didn't have to.

"You think you're so special now that you have one of *those*." His gaze dipped for a split second. "You're not. You're still Cursed. That Imprint is probably fake."

He reached his other hand out, and that was when she acted. She stomped on his toes as hard as she could with the heel of her shoe. Xavien cursed and his grip weakened just enough for her to slip out of it. She stumbled back, trying to regain her balance, but her back hit something first, stopping her momentum. Not something. Some*one*.

"Excuse me," a smooth, familiar voice said from just over her shoulder. There was an edge to his words. "Am I interrupting something?"

Xavien's eyes raised to meet the person behind her, and his scowl deepened. "Yes, actually, you were—"

"No," she said. She stepped forward and turned toward Ira. His dark glare melted away as he looked at her. "No, you weren't interrupting anything."

His lips twitched with amusement. "Well, then, if that's the case . . . " He raised his palm. " . . . May I have this next dance?"

Xavien made a sound of protest as she placed her hand in Ira's and allowed him to lead her to the dance floor. The heat in her chest dissipated the farther they got from Xavien.

She took a deep breath and muttered, "I fucking hate that guy."

Her words startled a laugh out of Ira. "For a second, I really thought you were going to punch him."

"I thought about it, but I have also been thinking about what you said."

Ira perked up, glancing at her out of the corner of his eye. "Oh?"

She squeezed his hand and knocked her elbow into his side. "You're so full of yourself."

He leaned in close to her so she felt his body heat all along her side. "Mhm, you like me that way."

She tripped.

She would've face-planted right there in front of the entire ballroom if Ira hadn't caught her. He wrapped his arm around her waist and pulled her up so her back was pressed against his front. She could feel the muscles in his forearm shifting against her abdomen, and her stomach tightened in response. She placed her arm over his and squeezed his wrist, silently telling him she was alright and he could let go, but part of her didn't want him to. She wasn't sure where that thought came from, yet it wasn't unwelcomed.

"Falling for me, are you?"

Whatever trance she had been in shattered.

She let out a groan of disgust.

"That"—she shoved his arm off her waist and spun to face him—"is *horrible*—"

"Lena," he breathed out her name softly. *Secretively*. Warmth filled her chest, a different kind. He gazed at her, his dark eyes uncertain. "I don't—"

A figure stepped up next to them, and Ira's face closed up in a flash. It was a drastic change and reminded her of how he'd been after the Tower. Over time, he'd slowly begun to show his true colors, but he'd always been able to pull that mask over his face at a moment's notice.

"Kalena."

If Alkus' tone was any indication, he was displeased.

"Yes?"

"You caused a scene back there. This is your *first* public sighting as Ruler since you've returned. Is it too much to ask—?"

"Your nephew was harassing her," Ira cut in, his voice cold.

"Really? Because from where I was standing, it looked like he was asking her for a dance."

She bit back the response that maybe he needed to get his eyes checked. "He was. I turned him down."

Alkus' eyes were ablaze, much like his nephew's only minutes earlier, but he kept his composure. "And why, pray tell, did you do that?"

"I've already made my choice," she said before she could think better of it.

She could see Ira looking at her out of the corner of her eye, but she kept her gaze on Alkus.

"Is that so?"

"Yes." And then before he could say anything else, she started leading Ira away. "Now if you'll excuse us, Ira and I are going to dance."

"Ira is needed somewhere else."

She paused.

Ira appeared just as surprised as she was. "I thought I was needed here."

"You were," Alkus said, "and now you're needed somewhere else. Prophet Nya called for you."

Ira's hand loosened in hers and she knew then that he would leave. Her shoulders slumped, but she tried to hide her disappointment.

"Very well." Ira nodded at Alkus, and then without any other formalities, he walked away. One of his hands was still intertwined with Lena's, so she moved with him.

"Wait." Alkus stepped in front of them. His face was cold as he looked at her revealed chest. "That mark on your skin—care to explain?"

"It's an Imprint," she corrected. "I didn't think I'd have to explain what that was to you?"

Ira's hand squeezed hers.

Alkus narrowed his eyes. "I don't know what you're trying to do—coming back and putting on this grand entrance while wearing that fake mark on your chest—"

"It's not fake. And I returned to take my *rightful* place as ruler of The Lands. This ball was not my idea, neither was any grand entrance."

Ira swooped in then. "Perhaps now is not the time to discuss such matters."

At first, Alkus looked like he wanted to argue, but when he realized they'd gained some attention, he stepped back. "The council will want an explanation."

She was sure they would.

Ira quickly pulled her away after that. There was no privacy in the ballroom, especially not for her, but Ira found them an idle spot away from the clusters of people.

"I'm sorry," he said, his eyes showing that, "but I do have to go."

She nodded. "I understand. You have responsibilities." But her words fell flat.

He squeezed her hand again. "Promise to save me a dance at the next ball?"

"I promise."

Silence fell between them, but the music and chatter helped to fill it. She realized this would be the last time she would see Ira today. And possibly before she had to give the council her answer. He hadn't asked her about what she'd told Alkus—just like he hadn't asked about her Imprint—and she didn't know if he would.

"You're not going to ask?" she said hurriedly. "About anything?"

He pressed his lips together, eyes soft as he gazed at her. "Do you want me to?"

She didn't know how to respond to that. A sudden urgency gripped her. "Ira—"

"Not here," he said in a hushed tone. His eyes darted around the room before he sent her one last apologetic look. His fingers fell from hers and he stepped back, still looking at her before finally turning and disappearing into the crowd.

It wasn't long before someone else came up to her and asked for a dance. As she spun around the ballroom floor, Ira's parting words replayed in her mind.

Not here.

She knew that wasn't a promise, but it sounded like one. She held onto it for the rest of the night.

CHAPTER
EIGHT

The realm they were sent to was dark. It smelled wet and earthy, like rot. A breeze sailed through the air, which told Atreus they were outside in an open space. It must've been night. A sudden flash of light nearly blinded him, and he jerked back, raising his arms to cover his eyes. He squeezed them shut, trying to get rid of the burning sensation that lingered.

What the fuck was that?

More flashes of light cut through his eyelids. Each one came with a harsh, snapping sound, like a whip. It was deafening. A complete sensory overload. He could barely think. Could barely see or hear.

But he knew they weren't alone.

The *Te'Monai* came onto them fast.

His ears popped from the blasting sound. There was a ghastly snarl next to him and then a scream pierced the air.

He didn't know where Finn or Mila was, but he knew that standing still was a death sentence, so he took off running before the bloodbath began.

If he tried calling out to Finn or Mila, his voice would be swallowed by the ear-splitting cracks around him. He kept his feet high, avoiding underbrush that could trip him up. He forced his eyes to stay open with each bright flash. They adjusted enough for him to slightly make out the terrain.

They had been dropped in the woods. Gnarled, tall trees littered the area, devoid of any leaves. Their crooked branches reached in all directions. The silhouettes were there one moment, gone the next. It looked like the trees were moving. Amongst the chaos, he couldn't tell if what he was seeing were trees or monsters.

Another flash illuminated the entire area. He stumbled to the side to avoid crashing into a younger boy. His palms hit rough tree bark. It was good that he'd stayed on his feet.

He turned around to yell at the frozen, wide-eyed boy. "If you stop moving, you're as good as dead!"

That was the first rule.

A moment later, there was a blur, and the boy was gone. His upper half was anyway. Most of his legs were still in front of Atreus, standing straight for another second or two as if they hadn't registered that they'd lost the rest of their body. And then they collapsed. An inhuman screech filled the air and then a very much human one.

He reached down to pull the knife out of his boot before running. His ears rang and his eyes burned, both of which badly affected his balance. The screams ate their way past any and all noise. The crazed howls and snarls joined them. The *Te'Monai* were hungry and excited that their meal had arrived.

He didn't stop when he saw a grotesque, slender figure sprinting in his direction out of the corner of his eye.

He didn't stop when he heard someone scream for help.

He didn't stop when he tripped over a body and his hands landed inside someone's shredded-open stomach. Intestines slipped between his fingers and the acrid smell of blood and flesh infiltrated his nose. His hands hit bone when he pulled them out. He swallowed the bile that crawled up his throat and grasped the knife with slippery hands. He kept running.

He couldn't stop.

The cries and the begging and the bloody images stuck with him—even when he was back in the Institute. This was how it always was. It didn't get easier. You just got used to it. Or you died.

None of them knew why they were sent out. Maybe there was no true reason. Maybe this really was just a form of punishment. The prophets could wash the blame and blood off their hands because they had left it up to fate. Whatever happened was meant to happen and there was no one for the firstborns to blame other than themselves. It wasn't the Numina's fault. It wasn't the prophets' fault. The firstborns were sinful. They had this coming.

Something rammed into him, and he crashed to the ground. He gasped in leaves and dirt, his side aching.

Get up. Get up!

Hands gripped his shirt as soon as he was on his feet again.

"Please! Please, you have to help me!"

He stared down at the girl. She was young, much too young. This was probably her first time out of the Institute. She was hysterical, covered in dirt and blood and tears. If he gave her his knife, he would be defenseless. He doubted she would even use it. And if he brought her along, she would only slow him down. But she was just a kid.

He swallowed. This wasn't his fault. This wasn't his responsibility.

She tugged at his shirt again. "Please!" she wailed.

A screech sounded nearby, and the girl screamed, bringing her hands up to cover her ears as she sobbed.

His chest tightened. "Stick close to me!"

Unsurprisingly, she didn't run fast. He grabbed one of her hands so he could haul her along. Her cries of terror grated on his ears and more than once he had to pull her to her feet when she tripped. He doubted she could even see where they were going. She was a nuisance, slowing him down and drawing attention to them. He wanted to shake her and scream in her face, '*Do you even want to survive?*'

Another flash revealed a large form running in front of them. It was the wrong shape to be a tree. It stopped, and he dug his heels into the ground, diving behind a tree and yanking the girl with him.

"Quiet!" he hissed, but of course, she didn't listen.

Another flash showed him that the *Te'Monai* lingered nearby. It slowly shifted its pointed, deformed head from side to side, trying to sniff them out. Its nose was smashed in, so he hoped it couldn't smell all that well.

Te'Monai were different in every realm. These ones were horribly ugly and tall, nearly ten feet. It had a hunched back with spikes protruding from it, bulbous legs, and a whip-like tail. Its nine-inch, razor sharp claws were already covered in blood. A chattering noise escaped its mouth, causing a chill to race down his spine.

"*Shut up!*" he snapped at the girl, so violently that she drew back and stopped crying. Good. "Stay here."

He let go of her hand and slid around the trunk, keeping himself crouched low to the ground. The blood on his hands had dried, so he could actually get a solid grip on his knife.

He willed his hands to stop shaking as he peeked around the trunk to make sure the *Te'Monai* wasn't looking in his direction. When he saw that it wasn't, he dashed behind another tree. The *Te'Monai* whipped its head around, chattering still.

He held his breath and leaned his head against the bark.

Think. Think. Think.

It knew they were here. He couldn't run. Not with the girl.

Between the flashes and the booms, the land was eerily dark and quiet.

When he turned around again, he saw another *Te'Monai* step out from behind the dying trees. This one was much closer to where he'd left the girl.

"Shit," he breathed out.

Don't do it. Don't—

A scream cut through the air. The little girl appeared from behind the tree, running from the reaching hands of another *Te'Monai*. The other two immediately began chasing after her, as if drawn to the scent of fear.

He closed his eyes and sagged against the tree. It was always the same. He lifted his hands, rubbing his palms over his eyes. Flakes of blood fell into his lap. Nothing changed.

He opened his eyes and pushed himself to his feet, only to stumble back when he found himself face to face with a *Te'Monai*. One must've circled back, knowing he was there.

It smiled at him with its long bloody teeth. Empty eye sockets stared at him, and its rancid breath rolled over his face.

A cry of surprise caught in his throat and he lurched away. His back hit the tree and he spun to the side, forcing his legs to move and put distance between him and the *Te'Monai*. A shriek sounded so close to him that it left his ears ringing.

A moment of silence occurred between booms and he heard a *schwing* behind him. He ducked behind another tree, feeling a *whoosh* of air sail over his skin. The top half of the tree he was behind fell to the ground.

He stared at it, chest heaving, imagining himself in its place. He took off.

The jarring screech followed him as he weaved through the trees. There was nowhere to hide. It was gaining on him.

His eyes darted around, trying to find *something* he could use. A knife fight was his last resort. He spotted a cave formation up ahead—or something that looked like it. Making out anything in this environment was difficult. He could only hope he wasn't running toward some other kind of *Te'Monai*.

He hit the rock. The *Te'Monai* scuttled behind him, but he couldn't see anything. He had to wait.

Come on. Come on. Come on.

A blinding white filled the space and—*there!* Atreus saw an opening and dove for it right as the *Te'Monai* crashed into the rock. Debris littered down from above and claws reached after him. One snagged on his pants, ripping the fabric apart and digging into his flesh. He screamed and leaned forward to stab his knife into the *Te'Monai*'s outstretched hand. It howled and retracted its claws. He scrambled farther into the tunnel and sagged against the wall. His leg bumped against the jagged floor, and he cried out as a pulse of pain spread up it.

He couldn't see his wound, but he hoped it wasn't that bad. He could still move his leg and probably put weight on it, but he couldn't afford to lose a lot of blood.

He ripped his pants below the knee on his injured leg, using the fabric to create a makeshift tourniquet to slow the bleeding. He tightened the knot until he couldn't distinguish the pressure from pain and the lower half of his leg became numb.

A screech sounded from outside.

"I'm coming for you, you bastard," he muttered. "I haven't forgotten about you."

It was as dark in the tunnel as it was outside, so his eyes didn't need to adjust at all. He continued crawling and stopped when he saw a flash of light ahead of him. The other end.

A lump a few feet in front of him made him pause. He crept closer, knife extended and ready. His shoulders sagged when he figured out what it was. A body. The firstborn had dragged themselves into the tunnel before bleeding out. One of their arms was missing.

Another inhuman shriek echoed down the tunnel. It was waiting for him.

He clenched his jaw, staring down at the body while he made up his mind.

They were dead. He wasn't. It was a corpse. He was still fighting and breathing.

"I'm sorry," he whispered as he brushed his hand over its face, closing its eyes. He then lugged the body over his shoulder and dragged it toward the exit.

When he reached the end of the tunnel, he paused to catch his breath before he called out to gain the *Te'Monai*'s attention. It roared and approached. He counted its footsteps and threw the body out of the opening, and the *Te'Monai* pounced on it not even a split second later.

He wasted no time. He slipped out of the tunnel, shifting to avoid the *Te'Monai*'s swinging limbs as it feasted. The body wouldn't keep it distracted for long. *Te'Monai* only seemed interested in fresh prey. They killed for fun, not for food. They quickly grew bored of game once they realized it was dead.

He ran around the side of the rock structure, but he didn't make it far before he was being yanked back. His head bounced off the stone and he saw stars for a moment.

The *Te'Monai* screeched in his face, the force of it blowing back his hair. Its claws had pierced his shirt—*only* his shirt thankfully—pinning him against the rock.

The limb he'd stabbed hung limp at the *Te'Monai*'s side, not appearing to work anymore. The *Te'Monai* attacked, its gaping jaws open and bloody. He darted to the side, his boot finding footing on the rock. He boosted himself up as he brought his arm down, driving his knife into one of the *Te'Monai*'s eyes. It screamed and whipped itself back, threatening to take him and his knife with it. He yanked the blade out, making sure he kept a hold of it. If he dropped it, he was done for.

He continued to climb up the rock structure and move away from the *Te'Monai*. His leg ached, but his adrenaline kept him going.

The distinct sound of scraping stone came from behind him.

He was close to the top where the formation flattened out. He could see over the trees from up here. That was all he could see—trees and bodies and *Te'Monai*.

He spun around to face the *Te'Monai* that was tailing him right as it pulled itself to the top. Inky blood streamed down the side of its face, one arm still limp against its side. It was twitching too. On its last leg.

He held the knife out in front of him, waiting, his heart pounding in his chest, his leg numb, his hearing distorted.

The *Te'Monai* moved first, swiping out with its good arm. He jumped to the side as sparks arched into the air when its claws raked over stone. He turned to a face full of teeth. Out of instinct and panic, he held the knife out. It pierced through the roof of the *Te'Monai*'s mouth as one of its fangs sliced open the back of his hand.

The *Te'Monai* let out another horrible noise as he flinched. He tried to pull his hand back before the *Te'Monai* bit down, but he couldn't dislodge his knife.

Fuck. I'm fucked.

The *Te'Monai* shook its head wildly, throwing him to the side. The breath was knocked out of him when he hit the rock. His leg *screamed* in tandem with him.

Light pulsed through the sky, and the snarling creature turned on him. Then he saw it.

Sitting there on the rock was a pearl-colored stone. It wasn't entirely round or opaque or stunning, but something about it stole his attention. It sang to him. And without thinking, he lunged for it, diving past the long limbs and sharp claws. Time seemed to slow, and then, as soon as his hand closed around the stone, everything disappeared.

CHAPTER
NINE

When Lena stepped into her bedroom after the ball, her feet were numb and her lower back ached.

Her attendants were already waiting for her. They helped her out of the dress and removed any of the pins from her hair before wiping off her makeup. The relief she felt when she stepped out of her heels was unparalleled. She wanted to take a bath. Alone. Thankfully, her attendants didn't push back when she dismissed them for the night.

When she finished washing away the lingering scents and touches, she wrapped herself in a soft robe and went back into her bedroom.

It was storming outside. The rumbles of thunder and patter of the rain might be soothing to some, but it brought back unwanted memories for her. Still, she walked over to the balcony doors and cracked them open, staring out into the darkness. She had tried to get over her fear of thunderstorms many times, but she'd been unsuccessful. It aggravated her—that rain and thunder were enough to weaken her.

There was a knock at her door. She frowned and went to open it. Cowen stood on the other side, appearing regretful, a letter in his hand.

"It's from Mikhail," he said.

She could guess what it was about. And she was sure Cowen knew too.

She took the letter from him, closed the door, and split the wax seal. Mikhail was reminding her that she needed to have her decision ready by tomorrow afternoon. She tossed the letter aside onto a wooden desk.

The room was a bit warmer now. The hot air from outside had flowed into the room from the cracked balcony doors. She walked over to shut them and clicked the lock but then paused and looked down. There were drops of water on the floor.

She stiffened and became faintly aware of all the sounds in the surrounding space. Her heart picked up in her chest. Her daggers were on the other side of the room under the bedside table, so she likely wouldn't be able to get there in time. She glanced out of the corner of her eye for something else she could use as a weapon and spotted the fire iron. She lunged for it.

Her fingers wrapped around the end right as a noise sounded behind her. Her Imprint flared alongside her instincts. She pulled the fire iron off the rack and swung it around.

The figure behind her stepped back, avoiding the arching iron rod. She advanced, not giving them a moment to recover, but they were quick and armed. The next time she swung the fire iron, it met a dagger.

She snarled and twisted her hips, throwing one of her elbows at the intruder's face. They slipped aside and she jabbed the fire iron toward their unguarded ribcage. They managed to deflect the strike, but just barely. She knew the hit had to sting their hand.

They went back and forth, trading blows. The intruder never went on the offensive, only blocking her attacks. She took the next potential opening she saw, lunging at her attacker. This time they easily moved with her, allowing her to pin them to the wall. The dagger clattered to the floor as she knocked it aside.

"What the *fuck*," she snarled, pressing the fire iron firmly over his chest, "are you doing here?"

Tuck smiled down at her. "I came to see you. Do I need another reason?"

"Cut the shit." He winced when she pushed the fire iron harder against him. "You had a dagger. Planning to get rid of me this quickly, then? Did someone send you?"

"I wasn't trying to kill you," he said in amusement. "Lena, ease up—"

"*Don't* call me that."

"What?" he challenged. He tilted his head to the side, his eyelids drooping as he appraised her. "Do you prefer *Your Majesty* now? So soon?"

She clenched her jaw but didn't rise to the bait. He likely had other daggers on him. She'd heard rumors about him while she was on the run. Evidently, he didn't favor the luxurious, lax lifestyle of a royal Blessed. He was away on tasks frequently. Spying. Scouting. Assassinating. Daggers were his weapon of choice. He'd even made a name for himself.

The Wraith of the Veils.

Tuck was apparently able to travel swiftly from place to place, making people believe he was somehow using the veils. It didn't make any sense. It was all a bit dramatic. And pretentious. It suited him perfectly.

"Take out your other daggers," she ordered.

"I don't have any."

He hissed when she shoved the fire iron against his lungs again. "Do you think I'm stupid? Take them out. *Now.*"

"You can do it," he said, a charming grin on his face. "I can't really reach them at the moment." He wiggled his fingers to show he couldn't do much with his arms pinned against the wall.

She scowled. She could call for her guards and have them deal with Tuck, but she didn't. Not yet.

She had been friends with him too once. He'd been the most tolerable of the bunch but not nice by any means. Charismatic and rebellious, yet sometimes withdrawn. He was an observer. He would never make any particularly nasty comments toward her, even when incited by the others, but he wouldn't defend her either. He would just watch the scene unfold with those steady green eyes of his, always appearing amused by something. Aside from the dagger throwing lessons, she didn't quite understand why they'd spent time together, just the two of them. He'd distanced himself first, and a few months later, she'd understood why.

Her family's assassination. Tuck's name was on the list and had been confirmed. He'd led her away while the rest of her family was slaughtered, and she would never forgive him for it.

She saw him as her problem to get rid of. No one else's.

Her lips curled back, and she raised the fire iron to jab him in the stomach. His flesh hardly gave, but he still hunched over and groaned. She shot toward the bedside table and finally got her own daggers in her hands.

Tuck raised himself to his full height again, wincing as he did so. His stomach and chest were likely bruised, but he was Blessed; it would heal quickly.

She took the time to appraise him now that she was a safe distance away. Had he been at the ball? He certainly wasn't dressed for it. His clothing was dark and full—something one would wear if they were sneaking around. Maybe he'd just gotten back from some assignment. His short, black hair was wet, and water dripped down his bronze skin. He'd slipped in so easily from the balcony. She hadn't even noticed, and she'd trained herself to notice such things over the past few years. He easily blended into the shadows. His body was strong and lithe. He had always been cunning, quick, and able to sneak up on people.

She had not. Learning to travel in the shadows, scale buildings, and slip through entryways like a sound spirit hadn't come naturally to her.

"Your daggers."

Tuck rolled his eyes but reached down to pluck three daggers from under his clothes. He tossed them onto the floor next to the first.

"The rest."

"That's all."

She didn't believe him, but then again, she would call him a liar even if he stated the obvious. But she let it be. She knew he enjoyed getting her riled up. She was confident in her ability to disarm and injure him if he made any sort of move to attack again.

"Great. Now get out."

"Your hospitality could use some work."

"Hypocritical, don't you think? Considering that *you* broke into *my* room?"

"You left your door open."

"And so you invited yourself in? And tracked mud all over my floor?"

"If only you had someone to clean that up for you."

She thought about throwing a dagger at him, but that would leave her with only two while he had five nearby. It was very possible that he was baiting her in the hope that she would lose her cool and leave herself defenseless.

"What the fuck do you want, Tuck?" she said between gritted teeth, waving one of her daggers around. "Why did you come here? And don't give me some bullshit answer about wanting to see me."

"What a dirty mouth Her Majesty has." Tuck's chin lowered as he stared at her from across the room. "You think you know me so well?"

She almost laughed. "I know *everything* I need to know about you."

The playful expression on his face was wiped away. A sort of distant neutrality replaced it. He moved and she stiffened, but he didn't even spare her a glance as he *strolled* through her room, looking around and taking it all in. His shoulders were relaxed, hands loose at his sides. He seemed so comfortable here, in *her* space. Rain roared in the background as he ambled over to her desk and picked up one of the candles to smell. The letter was right there. A crack of thunder sounded throughout the room, and she flinched.

"I came to congratulate you," he said. "Getting married is no small occasion."

"I'm not married yet."

"Right," he said drily as he set down the candle. He looked at the letter and tilted his head to the side. "Do you know what they're saying about you?"

He passed up the letter and plucked one of the flowers from the vase sitting on the corner of the desk. He brought it to his nose. "The prophets think you're the one they've been waiting for. The one the prophecy foretells. The one who will cut down the mountains and unite all the lands of the realm. *Heal* them. Bring us *prosperity.*"

She had heard about the prophecy plenty of times while growing up, but she hadn't learned the details of it until she was brought to the palace. That was also when she'd learned that the prophets believed she was this *savior* the prophecy talked about. Of course, most of the Blessed disagreed, but Mikhail was adamant. She'd heard more whispers about it after she left.

"Your Cursed status was one sign," Tuck continued, "but as soon as you came back with that Imprint on your chest, they became so certain. Some of the Blessed agree with the prophets now. Others still think you're an imposter."

"I'm well aware."

Maybe he *had* been at the ball. She'd only revealed her Imprint to the public a few hours ago. There hadn't been much time for talk to circulate.

"I heard other things while traveling. Some interesting things. I wonder if you also heard them during your time in the Lowlands." Tuck looked at her closely. "Does the term *Arawn* sound familiar?"

"No. It doesn't," she said curtly, her gaze and tone flat, clearly showcasing her impatience.

Tuck remained ignorant to her displeasure. "Really? All those years you never—?"

"What did I just say?" she interrupted. "I don't know what you're trying to get at, but I'm done entertaining you. Get out!"

He stared at her. The air between them bloomed with tension, and she imagined the thunderclouds expanding inside her room, filling it with a humidity and heaviness that made her skin itch. Tuck turned away first. "Extend my congratulations to Ira, would you? I wanted to stop by to give my felicitations before the wedding day. But I should be going now. Something tells me your husband wouldn't appreciate me being here when he stops by."

She tightened her grip on the daggers. There were a few implications in that last line, but she chose to only address one. "Ira is not . . . We're not getting married."

A fine brow arched. "Really?" he drawled out, clearly not believing a single word she'd said.

"It doesn't matter. It's none of your business." She was aware that sounded somewhat childish, but it was the truth. "And it doesn't matter what anyone else *appreciates. I* say you're not welcome in my room. So get out."

"No?" Tuck twirled the flower between his fingertips. "Never?"

She glowered. "Get out."

He sighed and set the flower down on the surface of her desk, not back in the vase. "You're colder."

A cruel laugh bubbled up her throat. "And that surprises you?"

He ran his slender pointer finger along the polished wood. "Not really, no."

"If you sneak up on me again," she said as he turned to leave, picking up his daggers as he passed them, "a few bruises will be the least of your worries. Consider tonight a warning."

Blood would spill next time.

Tuck grinned as he reached the doors to her balcony. "Looking forward to whatever you can give me."

"Tuck—"

But he was already gone, slipping through the shadows like he was a part of them.

Lena growled in annoyance and dropped her daggers onto the bed before raking her hands through her wet hair. She marched across her room and shut the balcony doors, flipping the latch so they were locked again. Then she trailed around her room and washroom, checking to make sure all her windows and doors were locked too. But she knew if someone really wanted to get in, locks wouldn't stop them. They were typically easy to pick.

She collapsed onto her bed and hunched forward, digging her elbows into her thighs as she scrubbed her face. She tasted blood inside her mouth and unclenched her jaw, prodding her cut cheek with her tongue.

She couldn't let him get to her. That was what he wanted. That was what they all wanted—her to cave under the pressure.

You've been through worse, she reminded herself. *And you're stronger now.*

She was heeding Ira's words, trying to play their game, but she wasn't patient. She couldn't shut off her emotions. If they pushed her too far, she'd snap. She wasn't naïve or arrogant enough to believe she was stronger than them all. They'd had a lifetime with their Imprints and decades to establish connections and learn about politics. They beat her in nearly every category, but what she had that they didn't was a deep-seated rage that had been festering for years. She wasn't about forgiveness. She doubted they felt any remorse, though she did wonder if later they would beg.

There was a knock at her door again. She sat up straight and debated ignoring it —she was far too exhausted, mentally and physically, to deal with anyone else tonight—but she ended up opening the door.

Cowen, once again, appeared contrite, but before he could say anything, she snapped at him, "Where were you?"

He blinked, clearly taken aback by her anger. "Here, Kalena. I've been here."

The exchange between her and Tuck hadn't been quiet. Cowen and the others should've heard.

She turned on her heel and walked back into her room. Cowen followed her, and as soon as the door clicked shut, she rounded on him again.

"Can I trust you, Cowen?" Her voice was quiet, careful, and cold.

His brows furrowed. He appeared confused, almost hurt. She didn't know why. Her question was simple.

"With your life, Kalena," he said just as softly, but there was a gravity to his words.

Cowen almost always said her name. Not *Your Majesty.* Even before he'd rarely used her title, despite being scolded by Maeve and Ezra for it. He wasn't protecting the ruler. He was protecting *her.* Her title was an accessory, not the focus.

She wanted to believe him. She did.

"I do not need a shoulder to cry on. I do not need a friend. I need a guard I can trust. A captain who others will follow. I need to rely on you, your protection, and your word."

"You can," Cowen said, his voice hoarse. "I searched for you. For years. I didn't give up and I didn't come back when the council urged me to stop. I knew you were out there. Ezra wanted me to find you."

Her eyes burned at the mention of the Sacred Guard's previous captain. She'd trusted Ezra, and he had taken the fall for the attack—something he should've never had to do. If what Cowen said was true, Ezra trusted Cowen. Or at least he had. Time had changed things for more than just her.

"Tuck Vuukroma was here," she said. "He broke in. I handled it."

Cowen's eyes widened. "What—?"

"The balcony," she continued. "I left the doors open for not even a minute. He must have been waiting—"

"I'll send Benji and Andra out to search the perimeter," Cowen said gruffly, already turning to the hall.

"He's gone," she said with certainty. "He got what he wanted."

"Which was what?"

When Cowen faced her again, she was startled by the animosity in his eyes. But it wasn't directed at her.

She sighed. There was too much to explain. Even *she* didn't fully understand why Tuck had come here. To kill her? To mess with her head? To talk about her relation to the prophecy? All three?

"That doesn't matter," she said, suddenly exhausted again. The aches from dancing for hours in heels returned. Her head felt disconnected from the rest of her, heavy and filled with disjointed thoughts. She didn't even know why she was upset with Cowen anymore. She'd been looking out for herself for five years and expected that to continue when she returned.

Cowen's face softened. "I'll still have them search the perimeter. This won't happen again, Kalena."

She nodded, but she couldn't believe him.

Not even two minutes after Cowen left, there was another knock at her door. A groan escaped her throat as she marched over.

"What?" she snarled as soon as she flung the door open, but she immediately snapped her mouth shut when she saw who was waiting in the hall for her.

Ira.

"I know it's late, but I had to speak to you. Tonight."

She froze in the doorway for a moment, just staring at him. Then she nodded.

She was astutely aware of Ira's presence when he followed her into her room. Her eyes landed on her daggers on the bed. She put them back under her bedside table, not caring if Ira saw.

"What's that?"

At first, she thought he was referring to her daggers, but when she turned and followed his gaze, she spotted the silver dagger sitting on her desk, right next to the flower. *Tuck's* dagger. It was small and sleek but not at all ordinary. The hilt had two emeralds in it, almost the exact shade of Tuck's eyes.

A white noise grew in her ears. She was suddenly in front of the desk, grabbing the dagger and storming over to the balcony doors. She fully intended on chucking the dagger out into the night and letting Tuck scour for it later.

"Hey, wait. Lena, wait!"

Ira was close behind her, his hand hovering over her shoulder, but he didn't touch her.

She stopped before the balcony doors and exhaled heavily. Her hands trembled slightly. She cursed Tuck and cursed herself for allowing him to affect her this way when he wasn't even present.

"Give it to me." Ira spoke gently as he uncurled her fingers from around the weapon. "Give me the knife."

She turned to face him. Anger simmered in his eyes, but it was much more subdued than her own. The dagger slipped from her fingers, and he pulled it back.

"I hate him," she seethed, pushing away from Ira and Tuck's dagger and the balcony. "I'm going to kill him."

Ira didn't chide her this time. "Tuck was here?"

"Yes, he snuck in."

"Did he hurt you?"

She wasn't so blinded by rage that she didn't detect the careful way Ira pieced together his words, the weight he put behind them.

"Lena, are you hurt?"

"No, it's fine." He looked like he was about to argue, so she changed the topic. "You said you had to speak to me?"

He pressed his lips together, and thankfully, took her diversion. "You told Alkus you'd already made your choice."

She knew what he was asking. "I . . . lied."

He nodded as if he expected that answer. "And now? Do you have anyone in mind?"

She was just as lost now as she'd been at the ball a few hours ago. One dance and a five-minute conversation wasn't enough to determine if you wanted to marry someone. But this wasn't about *want*, was it? Alkus had pointed that out.

But maybe . . . it could be.

She had thought about Ira after he left the ball, thought about him as an option, allowing herself to dwell on the musings from yesterday. It didn't scare her—being with Ira. But confessing what that might mean, her feelings toward him—did. The last people she'd held close to her heart had been killed because of her.

So she swallowed the truth and said, "No."

Ira's face was blank, the anger having slipped away, but he was still watching her carefully. "I have a proposal."

" . . . Okay."

He took a deep breath. "We should get married."

Her eyes widened.

"Wait—just . . . " Ira sighed and ran a hand through his hair—the one *not* holding the dagger. His cheeks were red. She didn't think she'd ever seen him this flustered.

"You don't have anyone in mind. Regardless, Alkus and the others will demand you give them a name tomorrow. And you know as well as I that whoever you choose will be given significant power, but more than that, they will be a constant part of your life. I don't want you to end up with some random person you met at the ball tonight who you interacted with for only a few minutes. They could be horrible to you. You could be miserable, and I don't want that for you. I know I have no right making decisions for you, but I'm offering . . . if you'll have me."

She continued to stare at him, wide-eyed.

"You would have someone you trust by your side. To be completely candid, now that you're back, I don't intend to stay separated from you for long, so marriage would suit us fine I think. And you'd be doing what the council wanted without *giving* them what they wanted."

He was right. About everything. As usual. The council wouldn't have a pawn if she married Ira.

He quickly wet his lips and stepped forward. "I know it's . . . probably not what you wanted, but—"

"Stop."

He did.

The floor was caving in underneath her, so she took a step to the side and collapsed onto the bed, her mind racing.

Ira was proposing they get married.

Yes, she had been thinking about it—them . . . *married*—not in detail, just entertaining the idea, but that was wildly different than said idea being proposed to her by someone, by *Ira* of all people. It made sense; she couldn't deny that, but . . .

She wanted Ira close because then she could better control a situation if anything bad occurred. She would know what happened to him, where he was. She could protect him. She knew security wasn't that easy, but still, she wanted him close. For her peace of mind at least.

Yet another part of her feared being that close to someone again. She was scared of losing them, yes, but also terrified of being let down. She had been hurt too many times by people close to her, by people she'd thought she could trust. These incidents haunted her. They affected everything.

She scrubbed at her face again until her eyes stopped stinging.

"None of this is what I wanted," she began. "Nevertheless, I have to go through with it. But you don't have to be dragged into this mess, too."

"*Dragged into this mess*?" Ira repeated. His steps were quick as he rounded the bed so he could face her. There was nothing between them now. "I'm not being *dragged* into anything. I'm choosing this—"

"*Why*?"

"Because I care about you." He parted his lips as if he was going to say more, but he didn't.

"What if there's someone else?"

She tried not to think about the very real possibility that Ira could've had relationships with other people while she was gone. It wasn't like the two of them had been romantically involved. And Ira wasn't unattractive. Quite the opposite really.

But if there was someone else, now or in the future, it wasn't a deal breaker per se since polyamory was commonplace in The Lands. Ira would be marrying her as a favor. If he wanted someone else, she wouldn't stand in his way. But she had to know.

"There's no one else," he said fiercely, his voice quiet. "There's no one."

Those statements were very different.

"But if there was—"

"There won't be."

"You can't know that—"

"I can." He sat on the bed next to her, only inches away, and rested his hand on top of his leg, palm facing up, open. "Us against them, alright?"

She stared at his hand. This was a bad idea. But also a good idea. Bad and good. If she removed her feelings from the situation, it was perfect. Feelings complicated things. And it would be harder to ignore those feelings if they got married. Things would change whether she wanted to admit it—at least they would for her.

The marriage between her parents had been genuine. They'd truly loved each other and been open about their affection, kissing and flirting right in front of their children's eyes. For a moment, she thought of her and Ira doing those same things. She thought about *more*.

Her gut tightened and she shook the thoughts from her head.

It's not like that, she reminded herself. *He's doing you a favor.*

This was what she needed if she wanted to complete her agenda. Ira would understand. He had to.

"Yeah," she murmured. She set her hand on top of his, threading their fingers together. "Us against them."

He brought their linked hands up, and her heart skipped a beat when he pressed his lips against the back of her hand. It wasn't a kiss, not really, but he lingered. Her eyes began to sting again.

When he lowered their locked hands back to his lap, she said once more, "Are you going to ask? About the other thing?"

"Your Imprint?"

She hummed.

"No. You can tell me what you want when you want. And if you don't want to tell me anything, ever . . . well then that's okay too. You didn't pressure me to talk about my past before the Tower. I won't ask for things you're unwilling to give."

It was a simple thing, but it broke her open.

She rubbed her other hand across her eyes before any tears could sprout. *Krashing, I'm fucking tired.*

She wanted to ask him to stay, but she thought of the last words he'd uttered. She wouldn't be cruel. To him or herself. Not right now.

So she pulled her hand away. "I'm exhausted."

He didn't appear upset. He seemed to understand that she was done for the night and all she wanted was peace and quiet, alone. He knew. She didn't know how he always knew.

He untangled his fingers from hers and laid her hand on the bed before standing. She felt his gaze on the side of her face, but when she didn't turn to meet it, he simply left.

She curled up on her bed, her knees to her chest. She was so cold.

CHAPTER TEN

Lena called for a council meeting early the next day so she could tell them her decision.

Her eyes found Ira when she stepped into the council chamber. He was smiling and speaking with two council members she didn't recognize. She needed to memorize everyone who sat on the council, as well as those in the Sacred Guard. There were a lot of things she needed to get caught up on.

The council members Ira was speaking with noticed her enter, and he turned to follow their gaze. There was a tenderness in his eyes when he looked at her that made her heart swell.

She sat in her seat and others followed suit. As soon as she commenced the meeting, she made her announcement.

"I'm going to marry Ira."

There were mixed reactions from the council, but none of them could truly protest. She had done what they'd asked. Still, Alkus made his displeasure known.

"Surely there are better options. This marriage is supposed to improve your image, make the public trust you."

Alkus didn't say it, but she knew he was referring to Ira's criminal background. She had brought him here from the Tower six years ago. And while she didn't know what he'd done to get in there, she didn't believe that he'd deserved to be in that prison in the first place. Alkus and others on this council had likely committed more crimes than Ira. They just hadn't been caught and convicted.

"If the public didn't deem Ira trustworthy, they wouldn't have elected him to the council," she bit out, carefully choosing her words. "You asked me to make a choice. I did."

Alkus opened his mouth to argue further, but Mikhail cut him off. "She is right, Alkus. Ira will do just fine." He looked at her, then Ira. "Congratulations, Your Majesty, Ira. I wish you a successful union. The wedding and Ascension ceremony are scheduled three days from now."

Her heart skipped a beat. She'd known it would be soon, but *three days?*

"You will both be assigned instructors who will run you through the proceedings of those ceremonies and teach you your duties. Your Majesty, your schedule will be considerably busier because your duties are more extensive. We apologize in advance. Most rulers have months to prepare."

She didn't think he meant it as an insult, but it still came across as one.

"If I may say something," Trynla interjected and then continued before anyone handed her the floor. "I think it's safe to say that everyone was surprised by the . . . spectacle you made last night. You didn't think to tell the council about the Imprint you gained?"

Everyone turned to Lena. Alkus made a quiet noise of agreement next to her. She was surprised he hadn't been the one to bring it up, but knowing him and Trynla's mutual aversion toward her, she wouldn't be surprised if they had gathered before the meeting to discuss how to bring up the matter of her Imprint.

Lena knew she had to tread carefully. "A lot happened the day I returned. I didn't think revealing that I had an Imprint was necessary then."

"You didn't think it necessary?" Trynla let out a grating laugh. "Telling us you had acquired a great power reserved for Blessed wasn't necessary?"

Alkus then said, "Maybe she didn't want us to know."

"I didn't hide it," Lena snapped. "And if I didn't want you to know, I certainly wouldn't have revealed it at the ball. You're clearly trying to get at something, so just come out and say it instead of wasting more of my time."

"Your Majesty—"

"As a council member, I am well within my rights to be concerned about The Lands' safety," Alkus said arrogantly, raising his chin. "I think the Imprint brings your loyalty into question again. Disregarding the fact that you didn't bring it to our attention immediately, I am also curious as to *how* exactly you got it. You're Cursed."

The slightest bit of distaste accompanied his last word. She knew Alkus' type, and there were many more like him. They believed they were superior to the Cursed. That they were meant to rule and live lavishly because they had been gifted the Divine Touch. He believed in the order of things, which was why he had hated her so passionately when fourteen-year-old her arrived at the palace.

She was Cursed. She couldn't be ruler . . . but the Numina had chosen her. And now the Imprint. A Cursed gaining an Imprint, a pact, a Slayer—it was unheard of . . . until her. She was breaking apart their order, their reasoning, the history they'd been taught for centuries. And Alkus, like many others, clearly felt threatened. If she, a Cursed, could attain these things, then what was it that made Cursed and Blessed so different?

"What does my Imprint have to do with my loyalty?"

"It makes you a bigger threat, for one, if your allegiance isn't entirely with The Lands. And I'm unconvinced that you managed to get an Imprint without some sort of sorcery involved."

A bark of laughter escaped her throat. She caught the warning look Ira sent her way, but she ignored it. She had anticipated the council's pushback. Some members, like Alkus, would think of every possible alternative rather than accept the truth. Sorcery was a bold accusation, but it was the only possibility that made sense to them. It was magic that wasn't derived from the Numina. Anyone could practice it, Blessed and Cursed alike, which was probably the main reason why so many Blessed detested it and declared it illegal. Sorcery put Blessed and Cursed on a more even playing field. The practice of learning sorcery was dangerous and arduous, but there was always someone desperate enough to try it.

She'd been desperate then, but she hadn't resorted to sorcery. She'd had no way to learn it and bigger problems to deal with—like staying alive. If she were being honest, she didn't know what had made that Numen extend a pact to her and form the Imprint on her skin.

"How do we even know it's real?" Trynla asked, leaning forward in her own chair.

"It's real," Lena said once again.

"I'm sorry," Ira all but scoffed, drawing all the attention to himself. "But you should know you can't fake something like that. I don't see the point of any of this. If you're saying she attained her Imprint through some means of sorcery, do you also believe she attained rulership in the same way? Do you not trust the Numina's reasoning?"

Trynla's face pinched. "Of course I do, but—"

"It seems like you second-guess their decisions, especially when it comes to Kalena. And you're not the only one." Ira's gaze cut to Alkus. "She was the first ever Cursed chosen to take the throne, so it makes sense that she was the first ever Cursed chosen to take an Imprint. We won't understand the Numina's reasoning behind everything they do."

"I don't remember the floor being given to you, Ira," Alkus said crossly.

"I could say the same to you."

"I just hope this recent announcement isn't clouding your judgment."

Ira's eyes narrowed. "Careful, Alkus. I have proved my loyalty and earned a spot on this council just as you have. Do not diminish my opinion because it goes against yours."

"That's enough," Mikhail said. "No more of this squabbling. But . . . what Ira said holds some truth. The Numina have spoken of someone like Her Majesty for decades now. While her situation is abnormal, perhaps it is a sign of prosperous times to come."

Lena recalled Tuck's words. *"The prophets think you're the one they've been waiting for."*

The *Arawn* that had been whispered in the street upon her return still sat at the forefront of her mind. *Savior.*

"I'd like to know how she acquired her Imprint at the very least," Ophir said.

A paralyzing fear snaked through her at the request. She wanted to say no. Many things had happened on the road that she didn't wish to share. Gaining her Imprint had been a particularly excruciating experience. It would reveal too much; it would force her to relive things she'd tried to push to the back of her mind and bury.

But everyone was already looking at her in interest. She knew this would be another sacrifice she would have to make.

"Fine," she rasped. "Then we'll be done with this conversation, yes?"

Everyone agreed rather easily. They wanted the story. They wanted to see if it would hold up or reveal her as a fake.

She didn't look at Ira as she dove into her past.

∽

Her stomach cramped with hunger pangs and her muscles ached under her skin, exhausted after days of running and hiding with little to no food or water to sustain herself.

She'd escaped from the caravan a few days ago and stumbled upon the town of Vilpar, but she was still running. She was always running. The dirtyhands were on her tail. She didn't know why. They usually didn't spend this much effort retrieving a runaway, which only made her insides further twist with discomfort. Did they know her true identity?

Thunder bellowed across the land the day they caught up with her. Rain poured down in sheets and lightning illuminated the sky.

She gulped down as much water as her stomach would hold from a leaking gutter, and then promptly threw up five minutes later. She quivered from the exertion, fear, and hunger.

Each pellet of rain felt like a tiny weight that threatened to push her to her knees where the mud would suck her up. She was reminded of the day her family was murdered. Her chest heaved with restrained sobs and her breaths were coming out much too fast, too short, too shallow. She could hardly see anything, but the tears in her eyes were as much to blame as the rain.

When she fell against the side of a building, she was unwilling to detach herself from it and get lost in the downpour again, but then she saw the dirtyhands. And they saw her a few seconds later. Their shouts cut through the rain as they hurried in her direction. She wanted to believe that her eyes were playing tricks on her, but she couldn't afford to be wrong.

She bolted.

Her survival outweighed the fatigue and fear. She moved on instinct, her legs taking her out of town and into the sparse woods beyond it, heading in the direction of the colossal hill.

One of the things she'd heard around town was that the abandoned shrine on the hillside was haunted. Some still trailed up to leave offerings, worried that if they didn't, great misfortune would befall the town. Some believed a Numen didn't even occupy it anymore.

Whatever people's exact thoughts on it were, they all agreed it was dangerous, but she had nowhere else to go. She couldn't think of another option, not when she was exhausted, panicked, and sprinting from the people she'd escaped.

Their shouts followed her as she raced through the rain. Even with the adrenaline streaming through her, she was slow and weak. The mud pulled her down numerous times and her heart stuttered when she heard the dirtyhands' voices get closer. But she couldn't see them. They could reach their hands through the sheets of rain at any moment and snag her again. This time, she was too frail to fight back, and they wouldn't give her another chance to escape.

She had mud in her hair, her mouth, her nose, and under her fingernails. Her hair was pasted to her head, covering her eyes and making her vision even worse. Why wouldn't they leave her alone? Why did these kinds of people keep coming back?

She ran and ran and ran, caught up in her pounding heart and the roaring rain. She was back in the Highlands. Back to that horrible day when she'd lost everything.

And then she was at the shrine.

She fell to her knees in front of the blood red gate. The rain had let up only slightly. She looked behind her; there were no more shouts. Had she lost them? How far had she run?

When she faced the shrine, the rain and thunder became muffled, and a slight whistling noise came from the darkness beyond the gate. She pushed herself to her feet and walked toward the shrine. She noticed that the rain stopped a few feet away from the entrance; there was a clear line on the dirt. Not a single spot on the gate was wet.

She hesitated, but only for a second. She needed shelter. She needed a place to hide and rest.

The shrine was dark and cold on the inside. Quiet too. Almost immediately, she spotted a gold statue with baskets of riches and food sitting at its feet. It must've been fake gold. If it were real, bandits would've already stripped it from the shrine.

She dropped to her knees and dug through the baskets of food. There was plenty left. It appeared that the animals hadn't ventured inside to take any yet. That should've alerted her more than it did. But she made yet another mistake and stayed. She stuffed food into her mouth and didn't think of slowing until she reminded herself *of what had happened earlier with the water. She paced herself and eventually fell asleep.*

Her dreams were odd. She frequently had nightmares, but nothing like what she experienced in that shrine.

She saw flashes of memories. Not hers, but they were so vivid . . . They had to be someone's. She saw glimpses of war and blight. Famines and floods and fears of all kinds. Screams filled her mind. She could see everyone's faces so clearly, and they all turned to her for help.

"I . . . I'm sorry," she said. "I can't help you. I don't know what to do. I'm sorry."

But they didn't turn away. Hands grabbed at her clothes, yanking at them and pulling her down.

"Please, help us!" those horrible voices cried.

"I can't! I'm sorry! But I can't! I . . ."

She couldn't help them because she could barely help herself. She was weak. But she didn't want to be weak anymore.

She woke with a scream caught in her throat and jerked up from her position on the floor. The air was colder now, and she was deeper in the shrine. She couldn't see the entrance. The only source of light was a lit torch on the wall.

She pushed herself to her feet and looked around for any signs of someone else. The light the torch provided only made the shadows appear more ominous. Someone could be hiding in here along with her and she wouldn't even know.

Or something.

Her heart pressed against the confines of her chest and the food she had consumed earlier threatened to come back up.

Was it the bandits? Had they managed to follow her trail and venture inside?

A shrill whistle sounded behind her and she spun around. The scream from earlier resurfaced, but her breath was stolen before a shred of sound could leave her lips.

In front of her was a dark figure that resembled a snake in shape, but it was much larger, at least five times her size. At the front of the snake-like form wasn't a reptilian head, but a human's body from the waist up. Its outline was blurred around the edges and the figure was so dark that she couldn't make out any features. As she stared at it, she could only think of the dark spirits her parents had warned her to stay away from.

Terror grasped her in its iron claws, but it was the heavy presence surrounding her that kept her still.

"You come into my home."

The voice was booming, heavy and powerful in a way that made her bones rattle and her head ache, yet it was low-spoken and drawled out.

"You eat my food and sleep on my floor."

She trembled from the pressure and pure power surrounding her, stretching and squeezing her form.

I'm sorry, she wanted to say, but her mouth remained sewed shut.

"You came from the town. I'm sure you've heard the stories surrounding this place. Why did you come?"

The invisible force clamping her mouth shut disappeared and she took a shuddering breath. "I . . . I was running from people. Bad people," she choked out. The words were pulled out of her. "I needed a place to hide. Food and shelter."

The pressure returned and increased tenfold. She dropped to her knees and cried out, but it was muffled between her closed lips.

"Try again. Why did you come?"

The voice filled every crevice of her mind, ripping it apart and making it impossible to think.

"Answer carefully. I'm growing bored."

"I . . . " Tears dripped from her face as words fell from her mouth. "I'm tired of being weak," she admitted. "I . . . want to be strong."

The dark spirit hummed and then laughed. It was a low chuckle that curled around her spine and dug its thorns into her skin. Nothing like the shrill laugh of a Slayer, but it had the same effect.

"Yes, I can see that. You're shaking like a leaf in my presence. Though, all you humans do."

A force suddenly pulled her to her feet, and she cried out again. She stood bolt upright, her chin up in the air and her toes barely touching the stone floor.

"I knew you were coming to me," the voice said. "I've been waiting for some excitement."

She bit her lip, feeling her salty tears burn her wind-scorched face.

"What am I? Take a guess."

She had thought a dark spirit, but that was completely wiped from her mind. The truth materialized from the depths of her subconscious. ". . . You're a Numen. A God."

"That's right. Now what's my title?"

That answer didn't come to her as easily.

"I don't . . . I don't know."

There was silence, and then, "You want power?"

She thought of the murder of her family. She thought of the Blessed who had pretended to be her friends only to turn on her in the end. She thought of the bandits on the road and the horrible people who took advantage of weak and desperate people like her. She thought of all the nights she'd gone without the comfort of safety and stability. The nights she'd cried herself to sleep or patched up her wounds or gone to bed without food in her belly. She thought of the hundreds of thousands of others in a position like hers because they had been dealt a shitty hand in this life. She thought of how different things would be if she had been born Blessed rather than Cursed.

"Yes," she whispered. "I want power. I want it more than anything."

"I can give it to you." The voice was but a whisper now, brushing her cheeks and combing back her hair. A tantalizing thing. "All you have to do is say yes."

It was the easiest yes she'd ever spoken.

The first touch of power was a breath of the freshest air she'd ever breathed. She felt like she was floating on top of the realm, untouchable and all-knowing. All of her anguish was alleviated. Her mind was expanded. Life couldn't get better than this. It was ethereal and addictive. And then, a second later, it all came crashing down. And that was when the excruciating pain took hold.

It split her open, diving in relentlessly and tearing her apart until she was a pile of flesh and blood on the stone floor. Screams tore from her throat, scraping it raw. Her muscles seized and ripped. Her bones splintered and broke. Her heart was beating a mile a minute—too fast, too hard. She couldn't get a breath in. Her chest was going to explode. Her senses had been amplified a hundred times over. Every brush of air and scratch of stone brought the pain of a million daggers being driven into her. She cried for help and forgiveness as her skin stitched itself back together, as her bones mended, as her muscles reformed. The blood from her eyes cleared and her lungs expanded.

The first breath in her new body was like inhaling shards of glass. She leaned over and coughed and gasped, but the sensation remained. Blood dribbled from her mouth, joining the puddle beneath her. The fire coursing through her body wouldn't stop.

"What did you do to me?" she sobbed.

"I did exactly what you asked. I gave you power."

She cried and trembled on the floor as her new body finished coming together. Her chest continued to burn, and there in the center was a spot that seared, *oozing blood and power. She could* feel *it.*

"As for my title—many know me as the Numen of Calamity, or Oberus. But you may call me something else."

∽

LENA STUCK to the main points, keeping the story short. The town, the bandits, the shrine, and then the Numen that extended her a pact. She kept the details to herself, as well as the name of the Numen she'd met in that shrine.

When they asked for its title, she told them it was the Numen of Fortune. After all, it had certainly changed her fate.

CHAPTER
ELEVEN

Atreus had never been so glad to be back in the Institute.
His cheek was pressed against cool rock. It took him a minute to realize he was sprawled across the floor of the cavern, like he'd been promptly deposited there.

He reached his hand out—the one that wasn't holding the stone—and slapped it against the floor. It was real. He was back.

He waited until the trembling subsided and then pushed himself up. He rotated his body, lifting his hips so he wouldn't scrape his leg against the rock as he sat. A sharp gasp left his lips as the fiery pain engulfed his leg. He looked at the wound now that he could see it. Only a bit of blood was visible through the fabric he'd tied around it. His body had already begun to heal. That was good, even if it didn't necessarily *feel* that way.

Some firstborns stood in the cavern, dazed and frozen, save for their shaking limbs. Others were hunched over like him, their head in their hands. Some were writhing and moaning on the ground, having lost entire limbs during the Outing.

Portals took them *to* the realm, but not from it. No, they had always just . . . left. There one moment and in the cavern the next. He'd never known what exactly brought them back. He'd assumed the prophets ran some sort of clock. When they decided the firstborns had been punished long enough, they yanked them back. But now he knew that wasn't the case.

He looked down at his lap, uncurling his fingers to reveal the stone. It was smeared with his blood.

He supposed it could've been a coincidence—him grabbing the stone at the same time the prophets pulled them back—but something in his gut told him it wasn't. The stone *sang* to him. It was a hum, really. One that was low and soothing to the ear. It blocked out the groans of pain and the hysterical cries. He narrowed his eyes at the stone and rolled it between his fingers. It was hot.

A pair of boots stopped in front of him. Prophet Silas stared down at him, his face giving nothing away, but his eyes dipped to the stone.

"Come with me," he said. *Ordered.*

Atreus closed his hand and hauled himself to his feet, gritting his teeth when his blood rushed down and unpleasant tingles spread throughout his leg.

Prophet Silas noticed his injuries. "Miss Anya will patch you up." He took a few steps forward, clearly waiting for Atreus to follow.

Atreus' eyes swept over the cavern, looking for two people in particular. The knot in his chest tightened as his gaze darted from firstborn to firstborn. He let out a heavy breath when he finally spotted Finn, dirty and bloody, but standing on his feet. He saw Mila a moment later, appearing better off than the majority. They were okay. They were all okay.

"Let's go," Prophet Silas said again, a trace of annoyance in his voice.

Atreus limped after him, growing more skeptical as the prophet led him out of the cavern and down a series of long, dark corridors. All of the paths in the Institute looked the same—there were no telling decorations or designs—so it was nearly impossible to memorize this place, but he had a suspicion he'd never been in these particular corridors before. And his hunch was confirmed when they ended up in front of a pristine white door.

He was breathing hard and sweating profusely; his leg was *throbbing*. Prophet Silas hadn't slowed once, even when Atreus had faltered. One of the enforcers left to get Miss Anya, the singular physician in the Institute.

The room beyond the white door was the nicest he'd ever seen. The floor matched the door and was smooth and polished. A large black desk stood near the back of the room with a sitting area composed of three black sofas and a low-sitting table in front of it. Six enforcers were present at the walls. On the other side of the room were two doors, both of them black.

"Got a color scheme going on?" he huffed out.

Prophet Silas' boots clicked against the floor as he walked ahead. "Sit."

Atreus collapsed onto one of the sofas, not caring if he got blood, sweat, and dirt all over it. He leaned his head back, allowing his muscles to relax against the soft cushions.

"The knife?"

He raised his head to find Prophet Silas looking at him expectantly, his hand outstretched.

"I lost it."

The prophet raised a blond brow.

Atreus was forced to take off his boots, roll down his waistband, and shake out his shirt before the prophet took his word for it.

There was a knock at the door and then Miss Anya entered. She was young and pretty, he supposed, with dark curls and russet skin. Her eyes were a lighter brown, like honey, which made her appear more approachable than any of the hardened prophets. Other firstborns had said that, but he wasn't stupid enough to go spilling his secrets to her. No doubt she'd relay them directly to the prophets.

She flashed him a small smile that he didn't return as she walked over to him, eyes trailing over his form to survey his injuries. She set down her medic kit and hovered her hands over the makeshift tourniquet on his leg.

"May I?"

He nodded and clenched his hands against the sofa as she unwrapped the fabric. He hissed when she peeled the material away from his bloodied skin and it pulled at his flesh, causing blood to trickle down his shin.

"Oh, that's not pretty, but it doesn't look too worrisome. You will probably need stitches, but your body was able to clot the blood and repair the cells quickly. That's good, Atreus. Let me clean it before I dress it."

Blessed firstborns had their Imprints sealed from a young age. It was reversible, but typically only by those who had created it. A seal was like a signature, a complex personalized puzzle, a code. For another to unravel it without a key . . . It was very difficult, nearly impossible. The prophets had told them this to quash any hopes they might've had about finding a way to break it themselves. This seal cut them off from their Slayer and prohibited them from using their Flair, if they had one. All the other enhancements like healing, speed, and strength they still had access to, but sometimes, because of the disconnect the seal created, those enhancements didn't quite work properly. He was supposed to be grateful they worked for him. At least for now.

Miss Anya moved to his hand next, which was in much better shape than his leg.

"You'll be on garden duty for the next few days until your injuries heal and I say you can return to work in the mines," Miss Anya said as she finished bandaging his hand. "Come to me before each meal for your pain medicine."

Firstborns weren't allowed to hold or distribute their own medicine.

As soon as she stepped away, Prophet Silas stepped forward.

"You did well," he said, offering up a rare bit of praise, which immediately sent off alarm bells in Atreus' head. "That realm appeared to be quite challenging."

How would you know? he wanted to bite back, but he held his tongue.

Prophet Silas nodded toward Atreus' closed hand. "What did you find?"

Atreus didn't want to show it to him, mostly out of spite, but he knew he wasn't going to be allowed to leave until he did, so he opened his hand.

Prophet Silas inhaled sharply. "Where did you find it?"

"On top of a rock."

The prophet's eyes cut to his, narrowing. But rather than scolding Atreus for his attitude, he let it go. Like he had before.

It was Atreus' turn to narrow his eyes as soon as the prophet looked away.

Prophet Silas held out his hand, waiting. Atreus must've taken too long to hand it over because he said, "Atreus, give it to me."

Reluctantly, he handed it over. It still sung to him even in the prophet's hand, but a cold feeling coursed through him, a faint *thung!* ringing in his head when he let it go.

Prophet Silas rolled the stone between his fingers before holding it up and scrutinizing it.

"You did well," he said again, still staring at the stone. He closed his fist and dropped his hand. "You will be compensated for your efforts."

Miss Anya led Atreus out of the room. She'd forgotten to lock one of the latches on her kit, so part of it swung open and some of her supplies spilt across the floor. She knelt down and hastily scooped up the medical tape, vials, and pastes. Rather than help her, he peeked through the gap in the doorway that had yet to be sealed.

Prophet Silas opened one of the black doors in the back of the room and a man stepped through. They immediately began to discuss something, but Atreus couldn't make out what they were saying.

His eyes lingered on the stranger. The man was younger than the prophet, and tan. *Warm.* There was a certain *life* to his skin that those down here didn't have. It was like . . . he lived in the sun.

∼

ATREUS WOKE TO CRIES.

It wasn't a peaceful wake-up call. As soon as he identified the sound, he jerked up in bed, heart pounding and eyes adjusting to the darkness to identify the threat. His first thought was that he was still in that realm, that the *Te'Monai* were here.

But a second later, he recognized his surroundings and who the cries were coming from. He was still in the Institute. Those cries were Finn's. He was having another night terror.

"Shut him the fuck up," someone grumbled.

Atreus jumped down from the top bunk and threw a glare into the darkness. Finn wasn't the only one making noise. Not everyone chose to sleep once they were locked inside, so there was always a constant background hum.

Atreus sat on the edge of Finn's thin mattress, his eyes drifting over his friend's trembling form. He was careful not to touch him.

"Finn. Hey, Finn. Wake up. It's just a dream. You're safe. It's Atreus. I'm here with you. Wake up, Finn. Come on."

He continued to repeat those things until he lured his friend out of his night terror. Finn woke up with a strangled cry and suddenly grew quiet, as if his voice had been taken from him. The sunstones scattered around the room provided just enough light for Atreus to see the terror in Finn's large eyes. Finn reached for him, and Atreus grabbed his hand, holding it tightly until his friend's tremors let up. Finn moved over, and Atreus took his spot next to him. They didn't talk about it. Everyone had night terrors about the same things. And no one wanted to relive them more than they already had to. He would have to get Finn more sleep elixir.

They stayed like that, awake and curled around one another, for the rest of the night.

Atreus thought of the man he'd seen talking to Prophet Silas. He was from above. A sunwalker. Atreus knew the prophets interacted with people from above, but why? Why had prophet Silas met with this sunwalker? What had they talked about? Maybe the Institute would be getting a new shipment of kids soon to replace the ones they'd lost.

He squeezed his eyes shut and tried not to think any more about what he'd witnessed in that monochrome room. Not tonight.

Morning came and the enforcers wrenched open the door to their sleeping hall. The firstborns trudged to breakfast together and then seminar. The core lecture alternated with the opening and closing always being the same. Today, the prophet leading seminar talked about Edynir Akonah, the original sinner who thought he could challenge the Numina and ended up shattering the realms.

It was said that greed had consumed him and he'd started preaching these crazy ideas of rebellion and promises of power to anyone who would listen. He was ambitious, charismatic, and cunning, so people naturally followed him, spurred on by their own greed. His army grew, and with it he conquered towns, cities, kingdoms, and nations across the realms. His thirst for power became insatiable and he decided to move against the Numina in what became known as the War of Krashing.

It was a giant bloody mess. Edynir Akonah lost, put down by his childhood friend, Kerrick Ludoh. His friend realized how corrupted he had become and began to move against him, converting half of Edynir Akonah's army to his side.

For his service, Kerrick Ludoh was named the first prophet and the first Blessed. All those who had joined his side were also deemed Blessed by the Numina, whereas those left on Edynir Akonah's side were declared Cursed. In the end, they'd all had to share the burden and sacrifice their firstborns.

If you looked at it in a certain way, the firstborns sounded like heroes, didn't they? *They* took the burden, the evil, so everyone else was free of it. But the prophets would say they didn't *take* anything. They *were* it. Their very essence was evil.

The prophet went on, explaining that Kerrick Ludoh had continued his selfless streak and pledged himself to the Numina, giving up his opportunity to have a normal, mortal life. The prophets were closer to the immortals than anyone else, which was why they could *allegedly* pull aside the veils.

Kerrick Ludoh had also given up some of the gifts he'd been blessed with. Prophets only had the enhancements. They gave up their Imprint and Slayer. They couldn't have a Flair either. The Numina only gave certain Blessed a Flair of unique and great power. It was an honor to receive one, but an even greater honor to serve as a prophet, *said the prophets*. Kerrick Ludoh had sworn off violence, and every prophet that followed him did the same.

Atreus always fought the urge to roll his eyes at that part because *really?*

But Finn enjoyed hearing about Edynir Akonah, so he was in better spirits after seminar. The prophets painted Edynir Akonah as a villain, but Finn didn't buy it. He said it didn't add up. He had a theory—a *story*—that Mila and Atreus tried to keep him from talking too much about.

"Do you think he would've won the war if Kerrick Ludoh hadn't stepped in?" Finn asked as they walked down the corridors.

Atreus gave Mila a look behind Finn's back.

"It's hard to say," Mila responded easily. She was better at changing the focus of the conversation. "But there's no use wondering, Finnian. You know that. This line of thinking can get you in trouble."

In more ways than one. The prophets wouldn't like it, but this kind of hope was dangerous even if it remained in your head. *Especially* then. *Dreaming* for a different outcome, an impossible one, would only hurt you.

"There *is* a use to it. To wondering. It can drive you crazy, sure, but it keeps some of us sane too," Finn grumbled. "And if he had won, maybe we wouldn't be here? Maybe we would be out living normal lives—whatever that means. Is it so bad that I want to think about that?"

Atreus' heart clenched. *Ah, there*. Finn believed in Edynir Akonah, wanted him to have been the triumphant hero, because he, like the rest of them, was resentful. They knew the outcome of the war if Edynir Akonah was defeated. They were living it.

But it was upsetting to Atreus to see Finn like this. Bitter and dejected.

"Yes, and you know why," Mila said sternly yet not unkindly.

"What if—"

"What if," Mila cut in with a sing-song voice, "you tell me about that game you came up with the other day? The one with the person who steals something. Atreus told me about it."

They had limited forms of entertainment down here and Finn's mind was always full of new, creative ideas. He was too big for this small place.

They went on with the rest of the day, splitting up again when Mila and Finn went to work in the mines and Atreus went to the garden. It was a large room full of healthy produce despite being underground. Slabs of sunstone were hung over the gardens, giving the plants the light and heat they needed to grow.

Later in their shift, a firstborn on a latter burned himself on one of the slabs as he was pulling his hand back. He fell to the ground and immediately started screaming as the skin on his arm bubbled up. The enforcers had Atreus help him to the infirmary since he had to collect his meds before dinner anyway.

Miss Anya told the kid he had a nasty second-degree burn. When she unwrapped the cloth that the others in the garden had secured around his elbow in their haste, the kid turned green in the face at the sight of his bloody, melted skin. Miss Anya had to give him a bit of sleep elixir to keep him from panicking and making the burn worse. He slipped under quickly.

It was then that Miss Anya remembered why Atreus was there. When she turned to retrieve his dose of medicine, he snagged the half-empty bottle of sleep elixir she'd returned to the shelf and slipped it into his pants. There was a tear along the seam that made a little pocket. His uniform was loose and dark enough that the outline of the vial wasn't noticeable.

"Here you are," Miss Anya said, turning and dropping two small pills into his hand. She watched him swallow them and made him lift his tongue to ensure there was nothing left in his mouth. A kind smile stretched across her face again and she told him he could go.

After dinner and seminar, when all of them were settling for the night, he pressed the vial into Finn's hands before climbing up to his bed. He stayed awake for another hour, staring up at the dark abyss and thinking, once again, about the stone and the sunwalker he'd seen speaking to Prophet Silas.

CHAPTER
TWELVE

Lena knew she had little time before the wedding and Ascension, but each passing day made that all the more apparent. Her schedule, as Mikhail had warned her, was packed. She had to attend daily lessons to catch up and refresh herself on the history, politics, and economic and social matters of The Lands.

When she first came to the Highlands, she'd started intensive schooling that would teach her all of these things and more, but her instructors had sabotaged her lessons in many ways. They would give her the wrong time or information, or be vague with their lessons. They would torment her, making snide comments and slapping her hands with their wooden pointers. She'd eventually stopped going, so most of what she knew about The Lands she had learned from her parents or while on the run. The extent of her knowledge was fair but far behind that of Blessed's living in the palace. She needed to know more if she wanted to even be a *contender* in their game.

Thankfully, her new instructors, Miss Tornell and Miss Orissa, were much more bearable than her last. She didn't know if they were simply better people or if her Imprint had changed their outlook. Regardless, they were thorough in their teachings about The Lands and didn't get annoyed at her questions. On top of the lessons about The Lands, she had to memorize what to do, when to do it, and what to say for two ceremonies. She was flooded with information and had a near constant headache because of it.

Cowen kept trying to talk with her, but she shut him down every time. Perhaps if she wasn't so stressed, she would feel guilty. She *had* largely ignored him since returning, but she couldn't help it. She was grateful he was here, *alive*—she really was—but she needed . . . space. Not necessarily physically, just . . . emotionally. He didn't take any of her dismissals personally. In fact, Cowen seemed to take them as a challenge and was around more often than usual. She suspected he was picking up shifts.

Ira, on the other hand, she hadn't seen since the council meeting days ago. He supposedly had a relatively busy schedule too. She'd told herself two days ago when the lessons grew too overwhelming that she was going to rely on Ira somewhat during the wedding. The Ascension she would be doing alone, so she had to have everything perfectly memorized for that. Her instructors told her not to fret. They said she had gone over it so many times that muscle memory would kick in even if her nerves got the best of her. She was counting on that.

In the days before the wedding, while she was away at lessons, presents from Blessed and Cursed alike were delivered to her room—after being thoroughly checked, of course. She stacked them all in a corner, too busy and anxious to open them, but they were accumulating and slowly beginning to take over her room. When would she and Ira find the time to open them? Was Ira also receiving gifts? He wasn't the ruler, but he was going to be the king consort as soon as she was crowned.

She thought about that the night before the wedding. She thought about a lot of things, but at the forefront of her mind was her and Ira's relationship and how it would change. Because it *would* change. And she would admit in the solitude of her room that it scared her.

She couldn't dwell on it. Not tonight. She was too tired and worried that she would forget everything if she overwhelmed herself and got little sleep.

Besides, thinking about something wouldn't change it.

Tomorrow she would be married. To Ira.

And tomorrow she would be queen.

～

HER PARENTS' wedding day had been special. Lena had thought hers would be too if she ever married. But it wasn't.

She just wanted this day to be over with.

She was woken up very early and taken to the temple a few miles away from the palace. This one wasn't often used by the prophets. It was more of a monument of sorts. Every Ascension took place there because of the temple's significance. And its location.

The temple sat at the edge of the Highlands and had a large terrace that extended over the edge of the cliffs. Both ceremonies would be carried out on this terrace so the inhabitants of the Lowlands could gather to watch. She only caught a glimpse of the large area before she was ushered into the temple and then down a labyrinth of halls.

She rubbed a hand over her chest as her attendants and a hired cast of a dozen more scrambled around the room to make sure everything was accounted for before getting her ready. She didn't understand why she needed more than her usual attendants, but she didn't push against it. She had very little energy to spend and was already on edge. There were the obvious reasons—marriage and finally being named queen—but her Imprint had been burning from the moment she awoke. She needed to let her Slayer out soon. The Night Run was coming up. Nearly every Blessed would be participating in the tradition and letting their Slayers run wild within the confines of the Eilun forest that surrounded the palace. She could wait until then. Right now, she just needed to get through today.

She was bathed and groomed until Vera, who she had learned was one of the women in charge of the temple and Ascension year after year, was satisfied. Her instructors entered the large suite and began to review the ceremonies with her as she sat down for hair and makeup. She focused on what they were saying as numerous hands moved her from station to station and told her to stand, sit, turn, raise her chin, close her eyes. Before she knew it, she was ready, and the wedding was set to start in thirty minutes.

Her appearance made her pause. She'd only been back in the Highlands for a little over a week, but her attendants had been fitting her into elaborate dresses and doing her makeup and hair every time she allowed them to, which had frankly been a shocking number of times. Though to be honest, she quite enjoyed the soft dresses, intricate hairstyles, and various makeup looks. So she'd thought she'd gotten used to how she could look when dressed up. Apparently not.

Her only request when picking decorations and styles for the ceremonies was that she didn't want to wear white. Any other color was fine. They had picked gold.

It was a brilliant gown, lush and long but not heavy. Embroidery and beading trailed all along the bodice. The neckline was low, leaving her Imprint uncovered. She could feel a slit in the skirt, though it wasn't visible through all the layers. The train of her gown extended back a good twenty feet from what she could see, but it was folded under itself, so she knew it was even longer. Ridiculously long. It was embroidered and beaded just like her bodice. Her sleeves were long and loose, trailing past her fingertips and pooling onto the floor alongside the train of her gown. A cape as long as the gown's train was attached at two points on her shoulder blades.

Dangling gold earrings hung from her ears. She'd gotten them pierced when she was younger, and again at the pleasure house. The holes had closed since then, but Devla had quickly re-pierced them with a clean needle days ago. The bottoms of the earrings brushed the tops of her shoulders. She wore a large necklace that splayed across her collarbones and the top of her chest. Thick golden bars of all sizes hung from it. The design matched the crown nestled on her head.

Her dark hair was pulled back and securely pinned, a tendril of hair left out on both sides of her face to frame it. Her attendants knew she preferred a light makeup look, but they'd negotiated with her today, saying a darker makeup look with a bold lip would make her more visible to the crowd. It would send a message. She didn't want to stand out, but she had still agreed.

She looked . . . powerful.

"Everything alright, Your Majesty?"

Her eyes met Jhai's in the mirror. The day had been hectic thus far, but her attendants had still announced themselves every time before touching her. It'd annoyed some of the others, but Lena didn't care. And it seemed her attendants didn't either.

She nodded and then they were moving again.

Vera pulled down the gold veil Lena's crown secured, and it tumbled down in front of her face.

"It's tradition for the people of The Lands to catch the first glimpse of their ruler after they've ascended," Vera explained.

Lena could point out that many of the people watching had probably already *seen* her, but she didn't.

Her head felt too light when she walked down the halls. The floor and walls tilted, but she managed to keep her balance. Since her dress was so long, she was able to wear flat shoes.

The walk through the temple passed by in a flash and she was suddenly standing before two large doors. They were already open, letting in the breeze from outside. It fluttered along her veil and through her loose-fitting sleeves.

Beyond the doors was the vast white terrace. It seemed to stretch out for hundreds of yards. Cracks of glittering gold snaked throughout the granite. A few dozen people were already standing on the terrace—the council and members of the royal families; those who worked at the temple and facilitated these ceremonies; Ira.

Vera motioned for her to step outside.

Lena wasn't sure she could breathe.

She felt the weight of everyone's stares as soon as she set foot on the terrace. She squinted her eyes to combat the sunlight reflecting off the granite. It was nearly blinding and caused her headache to flare.

Right. Left.

Right. Left.

Right. Left.

She placed one foot in front of the other, continuing forward, but the end of the terrace didn't appear any closer. It was silent yet loud. She thought she could hear screams in the distance, but it could've just been the wind playing tricks on her.

A few moments later, she realized the screams were very much real. But they weren't screams of fear. They were *cheers*. It was coming from below. From the Lowlands.

The wind snagged her dress, threatening to yank her back, or even worse, off the side.

She took a deep breath and tried to block out the screams.

Right. Left.

Right. Left.

Right. Left.

"Lena."

Ira was next to her, dressed in black. She'd reached the end. Nearly. The terrace tapered to a point, the final fifty or so feet forming a narrow triangle that extended from the cliff, nothing but air underneath it. And the people of the Lowlands.

She pitched forward and glanced at the tens of thousands of people who had gathered below. Their cheers were for her.

"Lena? Did you hear what he said?"

Ira was staring at her. Mikhail too.

"Are you ready for the ceremony to begin, Your Majesty?"

She nodded, not trusting her voice. Ira's hand found hers through the folds of fabric and squeezed it as they walked farther out onto the point. They stopped halfway down it and faced each other. Her other hand grabbed Ira's free one. The sun shined directly into her eyes from this angle.

"On the steps of the Temple of Orhne, before the people of The Lands, under the watchful eyes of the Numina we obey, stand Kalena Skathor and Ira Vaenyr who desire to strengthen their bond through a blessed union . . . "

Mikhail's voice slipped away. Lena stared at Ira to keep herself grounded. She remembered her attendants telling her not to lock her knees. A bead of sweat dripped down her back. The gown was itchy now, irritating her skin.

Recited words slipped from her lips when Mikhail prompted her. She saw Ira's lips move too, but the sound was lost in the wind.

The people of the Lowlands looked so small from up here. Was this how the Blessed always viewed them?

Ira dropped her hands and was given a dagger. She held her breath as he made a small cut in the center of his palm. Blood welled. He passed her the dagger, and she did the same to her hand. They clasped their injured palms together again, their blood smearing between them.

They were each given one end of a single, thick ribbon. As Mikhail spoke certain lines, each of them took their end and wrapped it in a specific way around their joined hands. They worked their way through the ribbon, creating an elaborate encasing that locked their hands together. Their blood seeped into the ribbon, signifying their fortified bond—their marriage.

There was no going back.

Her stomach was the Sea of Kier. She prayed to the Numina that she wouldn't throw up here.

More words escaped her mouth. Her veil was lifted just enough so that a chalice could be placed to her lips. She swallowed the bitter liquid, wincing as it coursed down her dry throat. Ira followed suit.

Mikhail said a few more words and then it was over. She felt the change in her chest. In how her Imprint flared. The string that had always been there, tying her and Ira together, was pulled taut, coursing with something *electric*.

The Grand Prophet unwrapped their hands. She didn't look at her palm, but she knew there would be a small mark in the center of it, right where she had cut herself. A mark that showed she was married, that she had formed a deeper bond with someone. She could feel it burning like her Imprint.

Ira lifted one side of her veil, making sure to keep her face hidden from spectators. His eyes searched hers, looking for something. Now they were supposed to kiss. The press of lips on lips. It would be nothing special.

She'd told herself that earlier and now when Ira found what he was looking for in her eyes and dipped his head. His lips touched hers, and it was not nothing.

Warmth spread from his touch and something electrifying zapped through her. The sensation emerged and vanished like a bolt of lightning.

The kiss didn't even last a second. Ira drew away and lowered her veil.

They immediately moved into the Ascension.

The dread that had been kept at bay by Ira's presence rushed over her now. She walked farther down the point, as rehearsed.

Mikhail reappeared with a large stone box in his hands. Symbols were etched into the sides, the top darkened with the dried blood of all the rulers before her. Lena's blood joined theirs as she repeated the words Mikhail chanted, promising to look out for The Lands' best interests and protect the people of it. She tied herself to this place for as long as her soul existed in these realms. Forever.

She drank from another chalice filled with bitter liquid, but this one was worse. It certainly wasn't wine. She forced it down, even when it made her eyes water and her skin burn.

The symbols glowed and the middle of the stone began to deteriorate at the top, creating a hole down to the middle. She pulled her arm clear of the gown and reached down the pocket. The air inside was so cold.

Her fingers touched an icy piece of metal, and she pulled it out. It was a gold ring with a purplish-white opaque gem secured in the middle.

The Ring of Rulers.

It was beautiful, even though it looked almost . . . messy, like the molten metal had been poured around the gem and left to cool that way. The ring looked much too big for her fingers, but she did what she'd been told to do and slipped it on her middle finger. The ring transformed before her eyes, shrinking to her exact size.

"*All the rulers of The Lands have worn this ring,*" her instructors had told her. "*It's a symbol of power, but it's also powerful in its own right. The ring is yours as long as you are ruler, and it will only respond to you.*"

The ring was no longer cold as it sat on her finger.

The crown was lifted off her head and the veil rose with it. Even though it was a near-sheer piece of fabric, she felt exposed with it gone. She took a deep breath as she felt the weight of another crown—*the crown; her* crown—being placed on her head. It settled, as did something in her chest. Her Imprint thrummed and the jagged pieces in her found their match. Only for a moment.

The cheers increased tenfold. She raised her head and stared down at the mass of people gathered below.

Now, she was queen.

CHAPTER
THIRTEEN

A small celebration succeeded the ceremonies, but it was mostly for the people, not for Lena.

Mikhail quickly found her. "Congratulations, Your Majesty. Wife and queen in one day. What an accomplishment."

She blinked at him, wondering if she'd heard him correctly. Surely not. But his elated expression hadn't faltered.

"Now, I don't want to . . . put a damper on such an exciting day, but I feel as though it is my duty to remind you of all the tasks you will soon need to complete." He spoke slowly and almost delicately, as if he expected her to lose it right then and there at the mere mention of governing duties. "You will need to review and approve pending legislation. And buy a house, of course; every ruler must have a proper house. That would be the perfect time for you to check the Ruler's Treasury. And have you started thinking about children . . . ?"

The longer he talked, the wider her eyes grew. Her Slayer could sense her waning patience and growing irritation and tried to push its boundaries. She shoved it back down and snapped, "You know, I think—"

Ira appeared at her side then, slightly out of breath. "Grand Prophet, thank you for your well wishes, but Her Majesty and I will be taking our leave now."

Mikhail frowned at the interruption, but he couldn't push back against it. Her and Ira's leave had been discussed earlier. Ira quickly swept her away without further comment.

Typically, a grand celebration took place after the Ascension, but since the ceremony had been so sudden, she and Ira were taking their honeymoon first while the celebration was being put in order. She didn't know what had to be arranged or why it took so long, but she was grateful for the break. She needed some distance from everyone.

Her Sacred Guard was accompanying her, of course, but they were staying at a place nearby in between shifts, so it was only her and Ira. Alone. In a house together. For three days.

"Close your eyes," Ira told her once they passed the palace. He had been leading her so far, refusing to answer any of her questions.

"Ira..."

"Humor me, Lena. Close your eyes. I won't let you fall."

She did, and Ira moved closer. His hands cupped her elbows, gently guiding her as they moved and telling her when to step up and down. They walked for a while. Ira had cleared their honeymoon destination with Cowen, but she couldn't imagine the head of her Sacred Guard letting them stray too far from the palace.

"We're going down a lot of stairs," Ira said. His grip on her tightened as they descended.

The wind was just as wild here as it'd been earlier, howling in her ears and whipping her hair around her head. She'd changed before leaving the temple, so she wore comfier and more practical clothing. Still, the wind made her doubt her balance, but she kept her eyes shut, trusting Ira to keep his word.

They returned to somewhat even ground and walked a bit more. Finally, Ira stopped and released her.

"You can open your eyes now."

In front of her stood the most beautiful house she'd ever seen. It was big—two stories—but not enormous like some of the houses in the Highlands, and it was made almost entirely of red wood. There was a rounded balcony above the front door and a wrap-around porch. Flat stones were laid out in a broken path that led to the front steps, and colorful flowers and draping trees surrounded the path and the house. A comforting orange glow seeped out from the windows, beckoning them inside.

She sucked in a breath, but her chest was already so full.

"It's beautiful," she gasped. The house had a considerable stretch of yard around it. Beyond that, all she could see were trees. There was a cliff behind them, but no mountains. "Where are we?"

"The Lowlands."

She spun around. "What? No, we're not."

But seconds after she said that she realized he was telling the truth. She could see it now. Smell it and feel it. The splash of color was certainly throwing her off, but she assumed the vegetation wasn't natural. They had been brought here—maybe the soil had too—and likely needed to be watered a few times a day to stay alive. Though, while most of the Lowlands was desolate, the land closest to the Highlands was somewhat fertile and therefore capable of producing something useful. She had been lucky enough to grow up around trees with leaves and grass that remained green during the warm season. But of course, every good thing came with a bad. Almost all Cursed wanted to live in the north, so it was crowded. And dangerous. But so was the south. In a different way, of course. Cursed had to pick their poison.

Ira held back a smile. "We are. It took some convincing, but Cowen agreed to it. We're close to the cliffs and have a private route up, so we could get back quickly if need be." Ira headed up the path toward the house. "Come on. Look at the inside."

She stared after him for a moment, and then snapped her mouth shut and followed. Well, alright then.

The inside of the house was just as cozy as the outside, and the fashion of the Highlands was nowhere to be found. Instead of a pristine, ornate look, the interior was busy with colors, furniture, and decorations that most Blessed would view as clutter. Red sofas and chairs were squished around a kindling stone fireplace, checkered quilts draped over the back and pillows overflowing on the cushions. Knitted rugs covered the wooden floors and a large, lacquered table stood to her right, big enough to fit ten people.

Behind the dining room was a well-equipped kitchen with a stove and a tall wooden prepping table. Utensils of all sorts hung over the table and sink. The stairs leading to the second floor were to her left. The area under them was cut out, creating a large arch through which she could see the other side of the house. She traveled through the arch and down the long hall to find a library with another fireplace and shelves lined with books. Attached to it was a small, personal study.

"How'd you find this place?" she asked as she ventured back to the main sitting room. She ran her hand over a crocheted blanket, threading her fingers through the loose holes of the yarn.

"I didn't find it. I built it."

She whirled on him once again. "No, you didn't."

"I did." He smiled, unable to hold this one back. "I've been working on it for a while, since before your return. It was a project of sorts. Something to keep me busy."

Right, because Ira didn't relax. He liked keeping himself busy, his mind and his hands.

"I didn't do this all by myself, though. I had an idea of what I wanted, but I recruited others. Engineers and general builders. A few volunteers. Cowen was one of them. He would help when he could." Ira glanced over his shoulder. "There's more I want to show you before the sun sets."

She followed him out the back door. There was a small but full garden behind the house that she intended to sift through tomorrow, and a decent-sized pond rested farther back.

Ira led her past all of it and into the woods. It was difficult to see amid the shade of the trees since the sun had almost disappeared under the horizon. The sunset was beautiful, though. The sky was bathed in hues of orange, pink, and purple.

"I came down here a few years ago after the turmoil in the Highlands settled. I needed some distance, and it was less suffocating here. I continued to return for that, but not only that."

They stepped out of the trees and into another, smaller clearing.

"I found this."

She stopped breathing.

The fading light made everything appear dark and blurred, taken over by shadows, but she recognized the structures in front of her. They were much smaller and more beat up than the house she and Ira had come from, but it was home. *Her home.* The place she had lived for the first fourteen years of her life. Her eyes passed over the well, the shed that had collapsed in on itself, and the modest garden that was now probably filled with nothing but weeds.

She was home.

Her eyes stung.

"I remember you telling me about it. Your home from before. When I stumbled across this place . . . I don't know. I just knew this was what you were talking about."

Memories of her childhood resurfaced. The day was brighter. The buildings cleaner. She saw her and her siblings playing in the backyard while their mother tried to get them to help her carry baskets of produce inside. She saw her father helping her befriend the stray cat that hunted for mice in their shed. During the warm season when it grew too hot and humid to cook anything, she, Zehara, and Torryn would sit at the table and help their parents cut up overripe fruits and eat leftover flatbread with cooked beans and cheese.

Here, she could see her family so clearly.

"I thought about fixing it up, but I didn't want to change it too much. Not without your permission. I've been trying to keep it somewhat clean. Keep the critters out. I wouldn't say it's livable, but it could be. If you wanted."

She spun and embraced Ira. She clung to him, her fingers digging into his back, his collarbone pressed against her cheek.

"Thank you," she said thickly.

Ira squeezed her tightly and his chin dropped to rest on her head. "I have one more thing to show you," he murmured into her hair.

Behind the collapsed shed, four stones stuck out of the ground. She knew what they were the moment she saw them, even with it now being too dark to read the names etched into them.

They were graves.

One for each member of her family she'd lost five years ago.

Ira stayed back while she approached the graves, her legs suddenly weak and unsteady. She all but dropped to her knees before them. Her eyes began to sting once again, and her throat closed up.

Mother.

Father.

Zehara.

Torryn.

They were all in front of her. Not *them*—she knew that wasn't possible even though she so badly wished it was—but the memory *of* them. Of before. Of home.

She reached out a hand and brushed the face of one of the graves. Her lips trembled, but she couldn't bring herself to speak the words aloud.

I'm sorry.

I'm sorry I was too late.

CHAPTER
FOURTEEN

The smell of cooked meat woke Lena up the following morning. Her stomach growled a few seconds after her nose picked up on the delicious aroma and she groaned, rolling over in bed.

She and Ira had immediately fallen asleep upon returning to the cabin last night. After visiting her family, she hadn't even had the energy to explore the second floor, but there were three rooms. One for her, one for Ira, and one for a guest. They'd both gone into their respective rooms and passed out.

Her stomach grumbled once again as a waft of freshly cooked food rolled into the room. She realized now that she'd hardly eaten anything yesterday. She had been too nervous to eat more than a few bites in the morning and at the celebration.

She cracked her eyes open and stretched. Another groan escaped her lips when the muscles in her back popped. She got up and didn't bother to make her bed. That could come later; so could scoping out the second floor. She was starving.

Ira stood at the stove wearing a loose shirt and pants. His hair stuck up in all directions and he was poking at something in front of him. She leaned against the wall behind him, crossing her arms as she took in the sight. It was almost . . . domestic.

"Should you be in the kitchen unsupervised?"

"I'm not unsupervised now, am I?" he said without turning around.

She smiled and walked over to him. "It smells good."

"That means I'm doing something right." He took his eyes off the ham he was cooking and smiled at her. "Good morning," he said warmly. His voice was like maple syrup, and it loosened her limbs.

Her smile turned sappy. "Good morning," she said back.

Ira glanced down at the pan. "It's almost ready."

She perched herself on the counter. "You didn't have to do this all by yourself. You could've woken me up."

"You needed the sleep."

She wasn't insulted by his comment. He'd spoken it plainly, but with softened words. She *had* needed the sleep. He wasn't coddling her. He just . . . knew.

Sometimes it frightened her, when she really thought about it, how well they knew each other. Especially considering how much time they'd actually spent together. Not even a full year. And they had been apart for the past five. Yet this—living with him, cooking with him, spending time with him—felt as natural as ever.

She had always wondered about this connection between them—the origins of it; the extent of it; the reason behind it. She hadn't looked into it yet. The odd bond between them hadn't been her top priority as of late, but she believed it had something to do with the ease in which she and Ira navigated each other. She wanted to know more about it. The connection wasn't a *bad* thing, but it was . . . unknown. Familiar but not understood.

"And I told you I'd cook for you sometime."

His words pulled her from her thoughts. Ira had finished cooking, the stove now turned off and two plates made. He was staring at her.

She slid down from the counter and took one of the plates, slightly embarrassed to have been caught inattentive, thinking about her and Ira.

"Well . . . thank you."

They ate breakfast on the back porch. She sat in a swinging chair that hung from above and Ira sat on the sofa next to her. She stared at the birds swooping over the pond while absently picking at her food. It was *very* good—he had certainly improved—but she was distracted. Still.

Her thoughts from a few minutes ago hadn't completely disappeared but had morphed into something else.

Her and Ira.

Them.

There had always been a *them*, but this *them* was different. They were husband and wife. And on their honeymoon.

She knew what married couples did on their honeymoon, or at least what people expected them to do. But there would be none of that with them.

He was doing this as a favor.

But she didn't quite know where marriage put them. There were legal ties between them now, but that didn't forbid extramarital relations. She could fulfill her desires elsewhere. And so could he.

"There's no one else . . . There's no one . . . There won't be."

The first two sentences had stuck with her, though she wished they hadn't.

Which was it? No one *else* or no one at all?

It mattered. Krashing, it mattered. Because if she knew his answer then maybe she would allow herself to feel—

"Hot?"

"What?" she said far too quickly. She jerked and her fork clattered against her plate, but she quickly grabbed it before it fell.

"Your food," Ira elaborated, smirking. "Or is it just bad?"

"No, um, no, it's not bad. Or hot. I'm just . . . thinking."

His head tilted to the side ever so slightly. His deep blue eyes swept over her face. "About?"

Krashing.

She could've lied, but she felt like he could see into her. She'd always had trouble lying to him, but for her sake, and probably his too, she needed to get over it.

She went for a less dangerous half-truth.

"You. Me. Us. How this is going to work." She looked back at the pond. "And don't say everything will be the same as before." She couldn't ignore the inevitable change. "Mikhail mentioned kids before we left the temple yesterday. I don't want them right now. Or any time soon." She added the last part before Ira could dwell any more on *that.*

People's relationships were their own. They could be with however many people they wanted. Her uncle had three partners. Kaini and Aber had been around for as long as Lena could remember. Willa had come later. Not every relationship had been on the same level, but that was normal. As far as she was concerned, they'd all been family. They'd lived under the same roof, loved one another, and taken care of their kids together. Until the very end. The Blessed had likely killed them too, even the kids. But she didn't have any proof. Maybe they weren't dead. Maybe they were just *gone.* She hoped that was the case. She hoped they were still raising their kids and tending to their relationships far away from this mess. Maybe they had added to the family. Maybe her family was still thriving and larger than she knew.

Having relationships outside of the established ones was socially acceptable and only considered infidelity if your other partners weren't okay with it. That matter was something to be discussed beforehand. For the most part, everything was left up to the individual. They were free to love.

Childbearing was the one aspect the prophets stuck their nose in. Having children was supposedly good for The Lands' economy and for people's relationships, but it was the firstborn child the prophets cared about. They were a sacrifice; a price that needed to be paid. Sin had once threatened to tear apart this realm and every other one. This evil couldn't be erased, but it could be contained—in every firstborn child. The Numina had made it so. Firstborns purged the realm—and, by extension, their parents—of sin. It kept things . . . relatively peaceful.

They were told absolute peace was unobtainable. They were flawed beings, even with the Divine Touch. Ruin would follow them, but they could limit this ruin, prevent something catastrophic like the War of Krashing from happening again, as long as children were being born. Firstborns' existence was essential, so the prophets tried to ensure as many as possible were being born. They wouldn't call it a burden, but she sometimes saw it as such, and the burden fell onto those who could bear children.

"You don't have to do anything you don't want to," Ira said. "I meant what I said that night in your room. I won't ask for anything you're not willing to give."

And she wouldn't ask that of him either.

But . . . others would.

Her silence spoke for itself.

"And you shouldn't let them do that either," he added.

She exhaled and set her plate aside. She pulled her knees up to her chest, wrapping her arms around them. "They did that with my marriage, didn't they? Who's to say they won't do it again?"

"Me," Ira said. "And you. You're queen now. They can't bar you from anything. They can threaten to, but you've already ascended. The people have seen you. Now you get to work. And if they demand something of you that you're not comfortable with, you tell them to fuck off. You know, subtly."

A short laugh tumbled from her lips, and she rubbed her face. "Subtly, yes. Of course. Thank you."

There was a beat of stillness between them.

"C'mere."

She pushed herself from the chair and collapsed onto the sofa next to Ira. He pulled her close, pressing his lips against the top of her head like he'd done last night.

She was selfish. And cruel. And a liar. She was using this moment. Using him. She turned her face farther into him, wishing this was happening under different circumstances. That they were upstairs in bed, rid of clothing, their bare skin touching. That this wasn't a friend comforting a friend.

"I hate them," she said again because she needed to say it again.

Ira was one of the only people she could tell this to. One of the only people who understood.

"I hate *them,* what they've done, how they treated my family. How they treat me. And *you.*" She tried to sit up so she could look at Ira, but he held her tight. She sighed and stayed put. "You made yourself an even bigger target—"

"Stop. We're not going to have this conversation again. I chose this." Then he said the words that barreled right past her defenses. She felt the impact in her chest. It added to the weight, drawing her throat closed. "I chose you."

She wanted to believe him when he said these things—that he chose her and there would be no one or no one *else.* Whichever it was. But she wouldn't *let* herself believe that. There would always be a voice in the back of her head telling her that those things weren't true—not because the other person was lying, but because she didn't deserve good things.

"You doubt me?"

She swallowed the lump in her throat and stayed silent.

"You saved me, but that's not why I stayed. Despite what you might think, I never felt indebted to you. I was going to get out eventually. But something compelled me to stay. Just for a while. And then you compelled me to *live*."

She squeezed her eyes shut.

"You gave me a chance when everyone else turned the other way."

"You deserved it." The moment she laid eyes on him, she'd realized that.

"I'm a criminal, Lena."

"So?" This time when she pushed away from him, he let her go. She frowned at him. "I hate the way you reduce yourself to that sometimes. We're all criminals. The Blessed are all criminals. I am." The innocent suffered one way or another. "The realm is shit, and because of that . . . you have to do bad things to survive it."

Ira stared at her carefully again, eyes open and honest, soaking her in. She internally squirmed under his gaze, but she didn't look away.

"Well, not everyone is as insightful and forgiving as you, Lena."

She laughed a bit brokenly. "I wouldn't say I'm the forgiving type anymore."

"You are," he murmured, his hand raking through her hair, pushing it from her face. "You have to be."

"Only on the outside, right?" She sighed and slouched against his side again. "Play nice, make them think things are going their way, and then stab them in the back."

Ira's fingers stopped at the base of her neck. "Just don't do it alone," he whispered. "I'm right here."

She nodded and tried to reel in the guilt. She knew, but . . .

She was selfish. And cruel. And a liar.

∽

LENA EVENTUALLY FINISHED HER BREAKFAST, and they went back inside. She was at a loss for what to do, but she had to keep herself busy or her mind would wander back to what had occupied it earlier—the bond, her and Ira, sex.

A loud, rattling noise sounded from the kitchen. She exited the library and looked down the hall. Through the arch she could see Ira picking up pans from the floor.

"You alright?"

"Yes," he said through gritted teeth. "I . . . I accidentally dropped them."

She ventured closer. "Do you need help?"

"No, I'm fine. I . . . I think I might go for a walk." He stood up, returned the pans to their rightful place, and headed for the back door.

"Oh . . . okay. Um, do you want—?"

"I'll be back in a bit," he said before shutting the door behind him.

And then she was alone.

She stared at the door for a while, brows drawn up in confusion. What was that? He'd seemed fine when they came inside minutes before.

She shook her head and walked toward the front of the house. He'd said he would be back, so there was nothing to worry about.

She finally explored the second floor. There were three bedrooms and three washrooms, including the one attached to her room. Ira's room had a washroom attached to it too, though it was devoid of a mirror. His room was pretty empty, with only a bed, a table, and a dresser. She assumed he wasn't done decorating his space. The third bedroom and washroom were separate. There were two more doorways in the hall, one leading to a small, private sitting room. More blankets and furniture pieces were scattered in here, and the balcony was connected to this room. A chessboard sat in the corner and part of the ceiling was a skylight. She didn't know what she expected the last door to be, but an armory wasn't it. Some might find it unsettling to have a weapons closet in their home, but she found it comforting.

She went to the garden next, taking count of the different kinds of produce and flowers. Now that it was daylight, she could see another building against the treeline about a hundred feet away. That must be where the Sacred Guard was staying. They were still close enough to keep an eye on her and help if need be but far enough away that she and Ira still had their privacy.

Two guards followed her as she explored the property, walking along the trees and through the grassy fields.

Her childhood home looked worn under the bright sun, like a shirt that had been washed too many times. She decided she was going to fix it up. There had been no time for her parents to sell it after the prophets came down, and it wasn't like they needed the money anymore. Their house was a decent distance from Tovaah, the closest town, so perhaps that was why no one had moved in since. Though it wasn't like houses were abundant down here, and this one was in a good spot. She was honestly surprised to find it vacant.

Lena stopped at the entryway, her feet stuck in the dirt. She grabbed the doorknob and twisted it. The door swung open easily. It was a new door. Ira must have replaced it.

From what she could see, the inside of her house was beaten up but not unsalvageable. It was dirty and lots of things were broken, but she didn't see any animal droppings or rot. But this was only the front of the house.

She couldn't bring herself to step inside.

It's fine, she told herself, legs trembling, her skin suddenly cold. She needed supplies before she could fix anything anyway, so she would come back once she got them.

She took a long way back to the cabin, weaving between the trees and fiddling with the ring on her finger. She stared at the diamond mark in the center of her palm. It signified marriage. Her and Ira both had one. It was physical as well as spiritual. She had felt the tug in her chest when they completed the wedding ceremony. Maybe her preexisting bond with Ira was some variation of the marriage bond. Maybe that was where she would start looking to get answers.

She veered off the path a bit to pass by the creek her family used to wash their clothes in when it wasn't dried up. They'd race to the creek with full baskets in their hands. Laundry day would always end in a water fight. While sitting on the rocks, scrubbing away, someone would inevitably sling a wet cloth at someone else. Father would try to get them back on task, but that would end as soon as Mother threw a wad of soaked clothing at him. They would go all in then and later trudge back to their house as wet as the laundry.

Lena smiled faintly and looked down at the water. She was so much older now. And more alone.

But not completely.

She had Ira. And Cowen.

Though she held them at a distance. She didn't want her emotions to control her, but they were, weren't they? It was just a matter of which she went with—love or fear?

When she got back to the cabin, it was mid-afternoon and her stomach was growling again. She went to the pantry, a small room to the right of the kitchen, and scanned the shelves. Her eyes lit up when she spotted chocolate. She grabbed a few squares and headed upstairs, stopping before entering her room when she noticed that the door to the sitting room was cracked open. She was sure she had closed it.

She inched toward the room and peeked behind the door. The light wasn't on, but the room wasn't empty.

Ira lay on the carpet, staring up at the skylight even though it was still daylight and the stars were tucked away. One of his arms was folded behind his head, the other at his side, his fingers threading through the carpet. His chest was bare. And *wet*. He must've just gotten out of the bath.

"I've been thinking about what you said earlier. About us. How we're going to work," Ira said, not moving an inch, his eyes still on the sky.

She slid into the room, her eyes following the drop of water that trailed down his side, soaking into the carpet.

"In marriage, that is," he added. "It is different. Than before."

A lot of things were.

She kept quiet, letting him talk.

"Everything I've said holds true. I'm by your side, *on* your side. Always. I . . . I want the best for you, but I worry because I care. And I don't want anything bad to happen to you, but I know I can't protect you from everything. And I know you don't *need* protection, but I still want to give it to you. I want . . . lots of things. But . . ." Ira removed the arm from behind his head and used it to prop himself up. She watched the muscles in his stomach contract, watched the water slide down the planes of his abdomen and disappear at the waistband of his pants. " . . . what do you want, Lena?"

Her mouth was dry, and her mind blanked momentarily. What the fuck. What was he saying? What was he *asking?*

Her mind immediately went to what she *wanted* him to be asking. To be clear, there were lots of things she wanted, but right now, it was only him. Her heart pounded in her chest, so loud she was afraid Ira could hear it.

"What do I want?" she repeated, her voice quiet and rough in the dim space.

Ira nodded, his dark eyes on her. "From me. For this relationship to work. I know it's . . . "

Not real, her mind supplied.

" . . . not ideal," he said, "but I want you to be comfortable. I need to know what you expect, what you need me to be. Now more than ever." His eyes narrowed slightly, assessing her. "You have a plan, don't you? Not for this, but for . . . ?"

Yes. She did.

"I just need honesty. And support." She pressed her lips together before she could say more.

"Okay," Ira said after a few seconds. "Okay, yeah. I think that'll work."

She found herself agreeing with him, absently nodding her head. Her gaze slipped down to his full lips and then the slope of his throat. His body was curved from his collarbone to his hipbones. The light only hit certain parts of his skin, defining the dip in his sides, on his abdomen, in his collarbones. Ira was handsome. No one could deny that. But only certain people could say that he was beautiful. Only certain people saw him like this.

Heat simmered in the pit of her stomach, slowly spreading through her, heading right to her face.

"Is that all?"

"What?" Her voice was breathless.

"Is that all you want? Honesty? Support?"

Her fingers twisted in the fabric of her shorts to keep her from reaching out. He was too far. She'd have to go closer.

"From you?" She needed to get a grip. "Yes."

Ira's face darkened and his head tilted to the side. Just barely, but it was enough. The beam of light that'd illuminated his hair cut across his face, leaving one side of it bright and sharp. The other side remained in the shadows. He scrutinized her, one eye a glittering, icy blue and the other nearly black. Waiting.

After gaining her Imprint, she'd told herself she would no longer be prey. She wouldn't feel intimidated by anyone else's gaze.

Until right now.

Ira swallowed and her eyes followed his throat as he did. "You don't . . . " He almost seemed hesitant. " . . . You don't have any other desires?"

Her ribcage grew tighter, pressing against her thumping heart.

"I am your husband."

The room was too small and dark. The heat built under her skin as the coil in her lower abdomen tightened. The chocolate slipped from her fingers.

"Ira—"

"If you have other desires, other needs . . . " The words rolled off his lips like silk and honey. " . . . you shouldn't be afraid to ask."

She hadn't taken her gaze off him since stepping into the room. He'd consumed her mind and her body. So quickly too. She didn't know what to think. She *couldn't* think. All she could do was react and he was lying there and saying those things and . . . and . . .

She wasn't sure who moved first.

They met in the middle, knees digging into the carpet. Her hands tangled in his hair, the wet strands slipping between her fingers. One of his arms wrapped around her waist while the other cupped the back of her head, her neck, pulling her hair, drawing her in.

Their mouths clashed and it was all passion and tongue and teeth. They didn't waste any time with pretenses. They knew each other. In soul and body.

When he angled his head down, kissing her harder, she nearly folded under him, but she didn't want to leave the heat of his body. There was no space between them. They were melded together from their knees to their chests. His bare skin seared through her thin shirt and his heart raced alongside hers. She clutched him closer, her hands slipping over his shoulder blades and the muscles of his back. He swallowed every gasp and groan that left her mouth.

It was hot and desperate and messy, but it wasn't enough. She needed *more*. She parted her legs and he immediately responded to her, one of his hands curling under her thighs and hauling her forward as he sat back. She landed in his lap, her legs spread on either side of his hips. The fabric of his pants brushed against her inner thighs as his hands smoothed over her bare skin, so close to where she wanted them. His touch made her soul sing and her blood thrum.

Their mouths found one another again. She kissed him until her lips were raw and her chest was tight. When they broke apart, he moved to her neck, biting, kissing, and licking his way down. Her eyes slipped closed, and her head unconsciously fell to the side, giving him more room.

She wanted him to leave bruises. To mark her.

His hands were so tight on her hips. The dark smudges were probably already there. And that thought sent another pulse of heat straight to her core.

She shifted her hips forward, desperate for some friction. Some pressure. She found it.

Her teeth dug into her bottom lip, stifling the noise that threatened to leave her throat. Iron filled her mouth. She cradled the back of his head and rotated her hips, grinding against his lap. Her eyes rolled to the back of her head as he groaned into her neck, his teeth nipping her sensitive skin.

She was high off of the pain and pleasure.

"*Fuck,*" he huffed against her skin. "*Lena.*"

His voice was like a bucket of cold water being tossed over her.

She froze and loosened her grip. What was she doing?

Ira tensed when she did and lifted his head. His eyes were dark and dilated, his lips swollen and red. That was all it took to send her scrambling off his lap.

"Lena, wait—!"

"I'm sorry, that . . . shouldn't have happened," she said quickly without looking at him before slipping out the door.

She ran down the hall and into her room, shutting the door behind her. Her heart was still beating wildly in her chest. Her lips were sore, and her throat and hips ached.

But she felt so *good*.

No.

Her face crumbled, but she pulled it together and stayed there, against the door, waiting.

About five minutes later, she heard Ira's footsteps in the hall. She held her breath when he paused in front of her door, but after a few beats, he continued to his room. Another door opened and then shut.

She exhaled and rested her head against the door.

"*What the fuck?*"

CHAPTER
FIFTEEN

Lena hadn't planned on sleeping much that night, which was good because sleep was no longer a possibility. Her mind was still racing with the events of earlier. And that gave her more of a reason to run away.

Her attendants had packed a chest of clothes for her. She'd left her wardrobe to their discretion for the most part, but she had requested a few items in particular. Comfortable clothes, for one, but also a cloak. And boots. She hadn't asked for daggers, thinking that would be too much. Luckily, there was an armory in the cabin. Sneaking into the hall and getting what she needed while being *very quiet* was tricky. She hoped that if Ira heard her in the hall, he would leave her be.

Slipping away from the cabin unnoticed was equally as tricky. Cowen was thorough, especially after the Tuck incident. But the Sacred Guard was looking for threats coming *in*. They weren't expecting anyone to bypass their established perimeter from the inside. Scaling trees was different from scaling buildings, but they were similar enough.

She let her Slayer out when she was a few miles away from the cabin. It darted ahead of her and she stopped, reaching out to tap into its senses. She looked through its eyes as it crashed through the trees to see if there were any threats she needed to look out for. It was an ability every Blessed could acquire if practiced. It had taken her months to master it, but it was worth it. Having another pair of eyes much sharper than her own was a very useful ability to have. *Her Slayer* was useful to have. After she recovered from her sickness, it'd taken her a few months to get a hold of her Slayer and understand it, in the practical and personal sense.

Each Slayer was different. They had their own personalities. They were sentient, of course. They were a Numen, but only a piece of it. That was all that could manifest in this realm, and she thought that was for the better. If they were too powerful, they could not be pacified by mortals. They would run rampant and whoever they were bonded to would quickly languish. That was still a risk even after a balance had been struck between a Blessed and a Slayer.

Once she reached an understanding with her Slayer and *learned* it, she'd used it to hunt down her enemies one by one. She'd made them feel as scared and helpless as they'd made her feel. Revenge had been sweet on her tongue. She wanted to taste it again. But not tonight. That wasn't her goal.

She'd been hearing rumors recently, in the Lowlands and the Highlands, about her and a prophecy. *The* prophecy. The one that coined the term *Arawn*—the savior who would bring the people out of ruin. That was what the Cursed thought anyway.

The Blessed's view wasn't as . . . liberating. Or it was, but in a different sense. The main difference was that the Blessed thought the prophesied one would expand their rule and lead them to greater things. The Cursed, on the other hand, waited for the day when the prophesied one would help them by changing the order that the Blessed held so near and dear to their hearts. It was a strange thing—many Cursed considered themselves wholly devoted to the Numina, yet they wanted change, and the type of change they were talking about went against the Numina's way. They were conflicted. And sometimes she would admit to herself that she was too.

The Blessed were well aware of what the Cursed whispered about, which was why talk of the prophecy was a dangerous thing in the Lowlands, but the mention of the *Arawn* . . . that could land someone in jail. Many debated if there was such a figure.

She didn't quite know where she stood, but the prophets weren't the only ones who whispered her name in the same sentence as the prophecy and that word —*Arawn*. And that was why she was doing this. She needed to hear what the people were saying. She needed to know what she was getting wrapped up in.

The journey to the town was short. Midnight was approaching. The moons were high, bathing the land in red. But the streets were still plenty busy, so she didn't have to worry about staying hidden. She kept her hood up, like many others, and chin down to avoid being recognized.

Her parents used to tell her there were three things the Lowlands had in abundance: temples, taverns, and amphitheaters. The latter two she had never visited as a child. Like every other citizen of The Lands, she'd visited temples occasionally. Her parents used to bring them to a small one in the woods, no taller than four feet tall. Most temples in the Lowlands weren't even big enough to fit a person.

The prophets said quantity was more important than size because it was the temples' presence and what they stood for—the people's past mistakes and sacrifices, history, and the Numina—that was important. By their logic, there was no need for large, lavish temples because it was the *essence* of these religious structures that mattered, yet the Highlands wouldn't be getting rid of their luxury temples anytime soon. In fact, they would probably build more while miniatures shrines continued to rise up in rural places down here. The Blessed had plenty of money to spare, but they were reluctant to spend it in the Lowlands.

As a child, she hadn't felt the urge to visit taverns, but she had wanted to see the amphitheaters. Artists of all kinds performed there—poets and musicians and dancers. The showcased art was always a beautiful form of entertainment, but sometimes it was more than just that. Sometimes artists slipped hidden messages inside their poems and songs, inside the notes of their music or the movements of their bodies. Art was used to tell stories and secrets, some of which weren't so legal, so it made sense that amphitheaters weren't rooted, physical places. They were more like a caravan. Most attendees were regulars, and they changed the location of their amphitheater frequently to prevent the enforcers from discovering it and lingering nearby. The enforcers knew what kind of ideas were spread at these amphitheaters and what happened there. Art. And treason.

She recalled her Slayer about a half-mile out from Tovaah, not wanting it to cause any trouble for her tonight. She wanted to get her answers and be in and out.

There was an amphitheater near here; its exact location was unknown to her, but she knew how to look for one. There was a trail hidden in the lanterns. Signals. She followed the crowds of people who avoided the taverns while taking note of the lights. She knew she made it when music trickled into her ears.

The amphitheater was tucked into the back of a building with a large overhang supported by two stilts. A small wooden platform sat under the cover, acting as a stage for the performance, and it was currently occupied by an older gentleman who was reciting a poem while a woman played a companion piece on the flute.

A crowd of about two dozen filled the space beyond the stage, lounging on the grass or leaning on a nearby building. Food, coins, alcohol, and notes passed between their fingers. There were no enforcers in sight.

She stayed near the back and listened. The woman's musical piece ended right as the final words of the poem were spoken:

"*The triad moons cast their reflection upon the earth,
and give way to the beginnings of a new birth.*"

They stepped off the stage and a trio took their place, wooden string instruments in their hands. The song they played was lovely, but it didn't contain anything she was looking for. The person who took the stage after them was draped in fabric, a large necklace resting on their collarbones, stones threaded through the leather string. A traveler.

Lena straightened. Maybe they would have something—

She caught the movement of a shadow in the corner of her eye. She turned, her gaze latching onto a figure at the mouth of an alleyway. Not an enforcer, but they were cloaked from head to toe, and watching her. Intently. Her hood was drawn up, so no one should have been able to recognize her. Before she could step forward, the person was gone, disappearing into the alley.

She didn't think. She moved.

The alleyway was empty when she entered it seconds later. She looked up, only because her years of running around in the Lowlands had taught her to do so, and spotted the figure disappearing over the edge of the rooftop.

She ran up a pile of stacked boxes and leaped for the lantern hook attached to the side of the building. It was sturdy, but the lantern swayed precariously as she heaved herself up and jumped onto the second-floor windowsill. She pulled herself up onto the roof and raced across the surface.

The figure was three buildings away and moving quickly, clearly used to traveling this way.

If she wanted to catch them, she needed to find a shortcut. She couldn't risk letting her Slayer out here. Not for this. It would garner too much attention.

The layout of the towns in the Lowlands was nothing like the careful city planning in the Highlands. The streets were crooked and impractical. Everything twisted around each other—the buildings, the people, the paths—which made it easy for her to spot an alternate route.

She bounded off to the right, jumping over a small wall and leaping down to the top of a smaller building.

Why was this person watching her? Had someone set them up to it? Alkus? Avalon? Trynla? How much had they seen? How long had they been trailing her?

She threw herself across the gap between two buildings and swung ninety degrees around the chimney on the next roof until she was heading in the direction the spy was coming from.

A flash of motion snagged her attention. The spy was not even twenty feet away. They saw her and skidded to a halt. She dashed toward them before they could take off again, pulling out one of her daggers.

The figure dropped off the side of the building, into another alleyway, and she followed. As soon as her feet hit the ground, she threw her dagger. The spy tried to dodge it but wasn't completely successful. It cut their arm. She was close enough to hear them hiss.

The spy spun around the corner of the building. Lena's boots thudded against the dry earth as she chased after them, turning the corner a few seconds later and—

They were gone.

She halted, whipping her head around and breathing hard. Nothing. She saw nothing. No movement. No person. Nothing.

It was like they had just . . . disappeared.

∽

Lena marched back to the cabin with a scowl on her face. Her mood had only soured since she'd lost the spy. She didn't know how it'd happened. She'd been *so* close—only *feet* away—and then they'd vanished. It didn't make any sense.

She had scoured the area after. Nothing in the vicinity gave them any *means* to disappear. No doors or drains. She had looked up too. Nothing.

It had to be magic—sorcery, or if they were Blessed, a Flair that allowed them to turn invisible. But it didn't matter *how* they'd escaped; it only mattered that they had. The spy was probably going to whoever had hired them right now.

She ground her teeth together. Another complication she would have to deal with. At least she had made them bleed.

A sudden pang in her chest made her stop. Her Slayer had spotted someone close by. She tensed and tapped into her Slayer's eyes, momentarily leaving her body. Another Slayer became visible through the trees. A larger blue one.

Her ears picked up on rustling near her. She snapped back to her body, gripping a dagger and spinning around.

Her attack was deflected, but rather than it being returned, she was shoved away.

She snarled, whipping back, ready to deliver another blow, but she stopped when she saw who it was.

"What the fuck are you doing?" Ira hissed, his blue eyes blazing.

CHAPTER SIXTEEN

Lena took her time washing the sweat, dirt, and smell of the Lowlands off her skin. She was still fuming, and she was sure Ira was as well for a completely different reason. He was probably busy downstairs talking to Cowen. While she had managed to sneak out without notifying her Sacred Guard, she hadn't been able to sneak back *in* just as discreetly, especially not with Ira.

The low murmurs stopped as soon as she stepped out of her room. Cowen held her gaze for a few seconds when she reached the foot of the stairs, his face giving nothing away. But before she could join them in the dining room, he strode past her and out of the house.

He was upset then.

She steeled herself and turned to Ira. "Well?"

His face was rather closed off as well. "So, I'm assuming you know how to use your Imprint and Slayer just fine."

"I manage."

The room fell into silence once again. She waited a whole minute, but Ira still had yet to say anything.

"If you're not going to speak what's on your mind then I'm going to go to bed—"

"Are you? For real this time?"

"Yes."

"See, that's the issue, Lena. I don't know if I can believe that." Ira stepped back from the table and ran a hand through his hair. "Not even six hours ago we had a conversation about expectations in our relationship. About what we needed from one another to make this work. You said you needed honesty and support. How can you ask that of me and then do what you did?"

She tried to look anywhere other than him but was unsuccessful. Her hands tightened into fists at her sides. "I only snuck out."

"You know what I mean."

Of course she did. It was the principle of the thing. Trust was fragile. Sometimes, one move was enough to topple it over. And once it shattered, it could never go back to the way it was before.

"I was never dishonest with you."

Ira knew just as much as she did how untrue that was. The anger from the woods had faded. He looked more upset than anything, and it made her chest ache.

"I thought I'd made it clear that I'm on your side," he said. "I want to help. I know . . . how lonely it can be. You were there for me, before. Let me be here for you, now."

She picked up on the unspoken words and wrapped her arms across her abdomen, fingers digging into her sides. She held herself close. Together.

"Lena." He drew out her name softly and almost fondly. *Lee-nah*. It was coaxing. "I won't ask. I said I wouldn't. But I know . . . The people who wronged me are dead or long gone. If they were in The Lands, I would've killed them by now." He made his way around the table, toward her. "I don't blame you. And I won't judge you—for anything you've done or anything you will do."

She took a deep breath and spun away before he could reach her, moving into the sitting room and putting the sofa between them when he followed.

"I know you understand. I know."

"Then what is it?" he asked a bit impatiently. "What is it that keeps this distance between us?"

Me.

She looked to the side, at the stairs, and debated disappearing again. Ira followed her gaze and shifted over as if to stop her if she tried. She wished she could answer him plainly and fully, but she couldn't. Still . . . she wanted to give him something. She wanted . . .

She wanted.

"Fear."

She looked anywhere but him, and this time, she succeeded.

"It's funny . . . so much of my life on the run was dictated by fear, and then I got the Imprint and Slayer and thought that would be over. And for the most part . . . it is. I don't fear people. I fear . . . *losing* people." She hid her trembling fingers behind her back and continued despite her tightening throat. "I fear . . . that one day you will leave, like everyone else. I'll tell you everything and let you in and you'll nestle further into my heart . . . and then leave."

It was too vulnerable. Too true. Too much. But she couldn't stop. She had to let it all go before the weight of it pulled her under. Ira could help her carry that weight. He could keep her adrift.

Just him, she told herself. *You can let him in.*

He walked around the sofa, and this time, she didn't run away. But she did step back when he reached for her. His hand froze, but it didn't drop. He held it in the air, inches away from her cheek.

"I wouldn't leave. Not ever. Someone would have to drag me away."

"Maybe they will," she said quietly. "My family didn't leave voluntarily. I don't care if they hurt me. I don't worry about that. I worry about them hurting those I care about."

"You should care if you're hurt—"

"Well, I don't," she snapped.

"Then I'll worry enough for the both of us." He leaned forward, staring at her intently. His eyes gave too much away. He gave *too much*. "I proposed this marriage between us because I care for you, and I knew it could help. I knew *I* could help. But I can't if you don't let me."

But you don't care for me like I care for you.

"I'm not asking you to tell me everything. I understand there are some matters you have to keep close to your heart, for your own sanity. You started it and you need to finish it. I understand. I just ask that you don't let yourself fall prey to that. I'm always here. I'm not going to leave."

She turned away, wiping at her eyes before a tear could fall.

"And don't run away." His words sounded as if they'd been pulled out of his chest, as if he was afraid that she would run right then if he didn't say it.

And she couldn't blame him. She ran a lot, didn't she? She'd run from here tonight, from *him*.

Heat flooded her cheeks.

The memory was fresh. She could still feel his touch, the heat of it. And rather than feeling panic or some sense of wrongness, she felt . . . comfortable and aroused. His touch hadn't been unwanted. She'd thought about it before tonight but only briefly before casting those thoughts aside. She'd never thought it was going to actually happen. He was doing this—marriage—as a favor to her, and she . . . she couldn't afford to be distracted.

But then it *had* happened, and she was *very* distracted. It wasn't some far-off, short-lived fantasy anymore. Ira had kissed her back. He had pulled her to him. He had left bruises on her skin. *And she liked it.*

She tried to save herself and rationalize their actions. They'd been confused and stressed. It had happened in the heat of the moment. It didn't mean anything.

But no matter what she told herself or how much she repeated it, it didn't stop her from wanting that moment again.

"Lena," Ira rasped. His voice was low and strangled. "Stop."

Shivers ran across her skin, and she turned back to him.

He appeared torn. Tormented. Ablaze. All of it. "While we're on the topic of honesty, there's something I should tell you. I've been unsure of what's exactly happening, but . . . since the wedding . . . I've been able to . . . *feel* you. Hear your thoughts—"

"*What?*" She reared back, feeling cold all over. "What did you say?"

Ira frowned. "Don't run," he said again, eyes flicking to the stairs.

"Ira, *what did you say?*"

"I think," he began slowly, "as a result of our marriage, the bond between us has strengthened. I've always been able to sense you to some extent, but nothing like I can now."

"So, what?" she asked impatiently. "You can read my mind now? Feel what I'm feeling? Can you see through my eyes too like you can with your Slayer?"

"What? Lena, no—" Ira reached forward, but she jerked out of his reach.

"Why didn't you tell me sooner?"

"Because I wasn't sure!" Ira exclaimed. "I was confused. I had another person's thoughts in my head. Another person's feelings." He paused and let out a dry laugh. "For a while, I thought everything was catching up to me and I was going mad."

She didn't laugh. Had she felt a change in their bond since their marriage?

"I don't quite know how to explain this," he continued. "I can't hear you clearly all the time. And it's not word for word what you're thinking, it's more . . . emotions, meanings, broken words. I *understand* you—even better now. It comes and goes. I don't quite know . . . why."

Well, she certainly didn't feel *that*. Not yet. So he could . . . read her but she couldn't read him? They had understood each other before, brought together by this string between them, but he had always been better at concealing himself than she had. It would have evened out the scales if *she* was the one better able to read and understand him as a result of this marriage bond.

"You're sure?" she breathed out.

"As sure as I can be."

She shook her head. "Why wouldn't they tell us about this? Mikhail didn't speak a word of it. No one did. Not my instructors or those in charge of the ceremonies."

"I suppose it's not common."

"Clearly," she snapped.

As someone who kept things close to her chest, it frightened her that someone could reach in and pry those things away. What solitude did she have if not her mind?

"I'm not able to see or hear or feel everything," he said quickly, no doubt picking up on the panic etched in her form and on her face. Maybe in her head too. "Only what's at the forefront of your mind when I'm close. And if I'm paying attention, reaching out."

It was meant to be a reassurance. Her secrets. Her memories. Her past. He couldn't get to them. Whatever this was . . . it was much more surface-level.

"Don't use it."

"I won't. I . . . Some things just come to me. I don't even realize I'm reaching for you, but I'll stop. I don't want to abuse this." He inched closer, appearing genuine. "We can speak to Mikhail when we get back. I knew you wouldn't like this. I didn't want to keep it from you, but I don't want you to worry either."

She nodded, but her mind was elsewhere, wrapping around the ramifications of this stronger bond between them. He wasn't able to hear and feel everything. Just a taste of what she was currently mulling over . . .

The cold was replaced with blistering heat. She was mortified. And her humiliation must've been obvious because Ira swooped in to reassure her once again.

"Lena, it's okay. You don't have to—"

She did what he'd warned her not to do and ran.

Well, she didn't actually *run*. That would only add to the embarrassment. She turned on her heel and briskly walked up the stairs. While she was still technically running, she told herself this was better, more dignified than actually sprinting away and hiding like she wanted to.

A hand clamped down on her arm and pulled her back.

"If you would just wait," Ira growled out.

"And let you embarrass me further?"

She spun with him, stepping back onto the second floor and putting a few feet between them.

"What?" His beautiful face twisted. "I'm not trying to embarrass you. I'm trying to talk to you—"

"Well, I don't want to talk right now." She turned toward her door and grabbed the handle.

"You're running away. You have nothing to be embarrassed about. Desire is something we all feel, in all sorts of capacities for all sorts of things. You shouldn't be ashamed of wanting—"

"I'm not," she said quickly. "I'm not ashamed, but some things I'd like to keep private."

Her sexual desire wasn't necessarily one of those things. She'd never been necessarily shy in that manner. But it was something she wanted to keep private from *Ira*.

"Okay, but you don't have to push them aside, or deal with them on your own," Ira said softly. He was closer behind her now.

Her brows furrowed. She might be overwhelmed at the moment, but she wasn't an idiot. She knew where this was going.

"Ira, leave it."

" . . . Do you really want me to?"

No.

"Yes!" she exclaimed, throwing her hands out and whirling around. Fire ignited in her veins and the pressure in her chest increased. Why couldn't he just *leave*?

Her eyes widened and the insult at her lips disappeared when she saw how close Ira was. Her forehead nearly bumped his chin, but still, he took a step forward, forcing her back against the door. The handle dug painfully into the small of her back.

"I don't believe you."

Of course he didn't. She wasn't even convincing herself.

Her heart stuttered when he placed one hand next to her on the door, boxing her in yet still leaving an opening for her to slip away if she wished. She stayed put, not wanting to leave, but wishing she was somewhere else, not wanting to face this, or him.

Ira didn't fold under her glare. In fact, he seemed to take it as a challenge. He cocked his head to the side and his eyes sharpened. "Stop it," he lightly scolded. "You're being a brat."

Her mouth dried up.

"Let me finish," Ira said, his eyes dark and fixated on her. "Then, if you still want, I'll leave." His gaze dipped to her hands, which were clenched at her sides. "What happened earlier, before you ran, if it made you truly uncomfortable, if you did not want it, I will apologize for that." His eyes rose, demanding and capturing her attention once again. "But I know that's not the case, so I won't apologize."

"Ira—"

"Stop interrupting."

She snapped her mouth shut and squeezed closer against the door, even with the handle at her back. She bit the inside of her cheek and tried to keep her heart steady, knowing he would pick up on it. There was still that opening, but she did not take it.

"You want things. And I . . . could give you those things. If you'd like. If you'd let me."

She wasn't sure if she was even breathing anymore. "Another *favor*?"

The acrid words spilled from her mouth before she could reel them back, staining the space between them like ink.

Ira did not flinch or pull back. "Not in the way you're thinking."

"I don't want to put any more strain on our relationship. You've already helped by marrying me. I can't ask—"

"More strain on our relationship?" he questioned incredulously. "And you're not asking! I'm—"

"Proposing, yes," she said between gritted teeth. "I know. But I almost wish you hadn't."

Then and now.

"Wish I hadn't what?" Ira challenged, his eyes lively and burning once again.

"Offered to marry you? You wish someone else was here in my place then? You act as if us being together is torturous. As if *you* are bad for *me*."

He let out a dark laugh as if that were the most ridiculous thing he'd heard.

It *was* torturous.

"Maybe I am—bad for you," she argued. When was the last time she was good for anyone? "Maybe I should have picked someone else to spare *you*."

That sobered him up, and he narrowed his eyes. "No one else would have worked," he said with such confidence that she was momentarily taken aback.

But she recovered quickly, lifting her chin. "You're wrong. I'm adaptable. There were plenty of people at that ball who were interested."

"In your power, not you."

True, but ouch.

"Does it matter?"

"Of course it matters. They would have used you—"

"And do you think of me as someone who's so easily manipulated?"

Ira pressed his lips together. "It would be one less thing you had to worry about."

Oh, but how ironic was that? Her marriage to Ira had solved one issue while creating another.

She smiled bitterly. "My hero."

Ira frowned and withdrew, only slightly. "You're being difficult, and while I often enjoy that, I find it especially irritating right now. This isn't just one-sided, Lena. You don't owe me. I don't owe you. It's an agreement. Mutually beneficial. If you want it."

A transaction then.

If you want it.

That was a dangerous, alluring invitation. *Want* was dangerous.

"You're thinking too hard," Ira said. "*Feel.* And if your heart still tells you no, I'll walk away and never bring this up again."

An unsteady breath left her lips. "You can still walk away."

He didn't immediately respond, and for a second, she thought he might just take up her suggestion. The disappointment that bloomed in her chest aggravated her.

"I don't want to," he replied simply as he leaned forward. "I'm your husband. I knew what I was agreeing to when I came to your bedroom that night and completed the wedding ceremony at the temple. You serve The Lands." His words danced in the air between them, tickling her ear. "Let me serve you."

"It doesn't mean anything," she said because she had to put it out there. She smoothed a hand over the front of Ira's shirt, staring at the fabric intently. "We . . . have an agreement. We'll sate each other's desires. Because we're comfortable with one another. That's all. This doesn't change anything."

You're a fool, some part of her spat.

"Yes. That's all," Ira repeated after a moment. "Nothing changes."

She had been the first to say it, but hearing Ira agree pulled her ribcage tighter. Her fingers tightened in the front of his shirt, and she yanked him down until their lips met.

Unlike before, their kiss started off soft and slow, but it quickly grew into something rough and desperate.

Ira shuffled closer, forcing her head back under the hot press of his mouth. She gasped when the door handle further dug into her back, and Ira pulled her to his chest, kissing her deeper, coaxing her mouth open with his tongue. She tried to match his fervor, but Ira was kissing her like he wanted to consume her, like he was afraid if he let up for one moment, she would run again. And maybe she would. One of his legs slipped between hers as he reached a hand back to push the door open. They stumbled into her room, still refusing to separate.

"How far . . . How much—"

"Whatever you want," Ira huffed, kissing the corner of her mouth, then her cheek. "Whatever you're comfortable with."

She pulled back and looked at him squarely. "What are *you* comfortable with?"

He met her gaze evenly and repeated, "Whatever you're comfortable with."

She traced his face with her eyes. She would never grow tired of it. He wasn't without flaws, but they made him all the more beautiful. It was unfair how handsome he was. How much she thought about him and how much of her he unknowingly controlled. She wished she was stronger. Maybe then she would've been able to brush him off like she had with Cowen. But she couldn't. She kept coming to that realization. She needed someone. Fate had introduced them, but she had chosen him.

"Lena," he murmured, resting his forehead against hers. "You're allowed to be selfish."

This was only her and Ira. It was a private matter between them. A transaction.

"Yeah," she said softly, more to herself than anything. She nodded. "Yeah."

She kissed him again, unrelenting and taking what she wanted, being selfish. Ira responded to her in kind, as he always did, molding himself against her. She moaned into his mouth. Their clothes were thin, so she could feel every curve and contour of his body, but that wasn't enough. She wanted to feel his *skin*. Feel it against her own.

She tugged at his shirt. "Off."

She stepped away, and he let her go. Her legs were unsteady and her eyes latched onto his as she backed up, only stopping when her legs hit the bed.

Ira reached behind his head and grabbed the collar of his shirt. In one swift motion, he pulled it over his head. Her eyes shamelessly roved over the flexing muscles along his side as he tossed his shirt somewhere in the room.

He followed her to the bed, and rather than return to her lips, his mouth latched on to the side of her neck. He left rough, open-mouthed kisses along her jugular, nipping occasionally to draw noises from her mouth. She tilted her head back, giving him more access to her bare skin as she ran her fingers through his hair. His kisses lingered at some spots, sucking until blood rose under her skin and it stung when he pulled away. She welcomed the new bruises he created.

But then he stopped and peppered soft kisses across her collarbones. She felt cared for and worshipped, but she didn't want slow and sweet and soft.

"You don't have to be gentle," she said. "I don't want you to be."

Right now, she wanted rough and heat and unbridled passion. She was desperate for some sense of control.

When Ira pressed himself against her, she waited for the panic to set in, but it never came. In its place was a burning, swelling desire.

Ira groaned and pulled away, pressing his mouth against her jaw. "Lena."

It was a question, an explanation, and a warning all at once. He was trembling, holding on to his threads of self-control just as she was. They should cut them together.

"Ira . . ." She placed a soft, tantalizing kiss under his ear and whispered, "Show me how much you've missed me."

They tumbled down to the bed together. He swallowed the breath that left her lips, and she became pliant in his hands. She tried to push herself up, but he knocked her arms aside, making her fall flat onto her back again.

He dipped himself over her so they were touching from knees to chest. She trailed her hands across his skin as his elbows rested on either side of her face, supporting his weight. Though, she didn't think she would mind if he crushed her. The lack of air added to the heat and the tightness and the desperation.

Favor. Proposal. Transaction.

She repeated those words to herself as their lips touched again and again. Sometimes feather-light. Sometimes bruising. Each one left her wanting more.

Ira pulled away and she chased him, but he evaded her lips.

"They didn't deserve to look at you that way," he said suddenly.

She blinked. It took her mind a few seconds longer than normal to process his words. "What?"

"The people at the ball. The ones who danced with you." His breath washed over her face, tickling her skin. "They didn't deserve to look at you like that."

"Like what?"

"Like they knew you. Like they knew what you wanted."

Ira dipped in, leaving a quick but searing kiss on her lips. She was dizzy with him so close to her.

"They don't know what you want." His voice was dark and smooth and so *sure* against the shell of her ear.

Perhaps his confidence bled into her because she parted her lips and said, "And you do?"

She could tell he was smirking even though she couldn't see it. But she did feel it when the corner of his mouth touched her ear.

"Absolutely."

She whispered, "Then show me."

Ira attacked her with a new fervor, his teeth scraping across her flesh. One of his hands twisted around her hair and pulled just enough so that the pain was too similar to pleasure. Heat spiraled downwards, threatening to pull her under and wash away any thought that wasn't him.

She closed her eyes. Her palms glided over every dip and jut of his skin, every raised scar. She memorized his body as if she were going to be asked to paint it later. She wanted to remember it. Remember this and him.

Ira's lips brushed the corner of her mouth, her jaw, her neck. Sighs of pleasure left her as she dug her fingers into his skin, pulling him closer. She widened her legs, allowing him to crawl in between. He pulled aside the collar of her shirt as he kissed down her shoulder. Her clothes were too itchy, too restraining. Her shirt had bunched up underneath her breasts, but it was still in the way.

"Take it off."

Ira lifted his head, his eyes dark and dangerous but not to her. Bumps rose across her skin as he slowly slid his hand up her bare side, his fingers tracing her ribs and testing her patience. He rested his thumb below her breast, and she took a deep, unsteady breath. His eyes stayed locked on to hers as he swiped his hand up, pushing her shirt up and revealing her breasts. He ducked down to take one of her nipples into his mouth, and she gasped at the heat and pressure it provided. Her entire body tensed, and her legs tangled with his, drawing him closer. In response, he sucked harder, and his tongue swirled around her nipple.

He sat up and pulled her with him. His lower half moved against her own and a choked groan left both of their lips. She could *feel* him. Hard and warm and pulsing against her upper thigh. She slid to the side and rocked against him as he grabbed her shirt and ripped it over her head. They collided again as soon as the thin piece of fabric was out of the way.

She reached down to his waistband, but Ira caught her hand in an iron grip.

"No," he murmured as he kissed her. He dug his teeth into her lower lip and then pulled back. His hair was a mess, his lips swollen and wet, and two splotches of red sat high on his cheekbones. She saw blood on his lip, and tasted it in her mouth. "Let me pleasure you."

She dropped her gaze from his eyes to his lips again. She nodded and leaned forward. Infernos raged inside of her when they kissed. Her mind roared, loud and overwhelming like the sea, but exceptionally focused. She knew exactly what she wanted. But it had never been up for debate, had it?

She angled her head, taking control of the kiss as his hand dipped below her waistband. The coils deep within her stomach stretched and turned. She all but squirmed on his lap as his fingers brushed over her sex.

"You're so wet," Ira breathed against her lips. "Wet for me. Isn't that right?"

She closed her eyes and nodded. Their next kiss was off center. Her lips landed on his cheek and a broken moan escaped her as one of his fingers dipped inside of her. She moved over his hand, rotating her hips, wanting him deeper.

"More."

"Shhh. I'll give you more. Always."

He slid a second finger into her and another noise tore from her throat as she shuddered. His fingers curled inside of her, rubbing against her innermost walls. He pressed his thumb over her clit and dragged.

"Ira!" she cried out as she tensed and ducked her face back into his shoulder. She trembled in his arms, her nails digging into his back. The coils in her lower stomach twisted with his fingers.

"Say my name again," he said as he drew back so he could see her face. "Let me see those pretty lips say my name again, Lena."

She threw her head back as his fingers reached deeper. "*Ira*," she whined, then cursed when his thumb moved over her clit again.

"There it is," he murmured.

Her slick skin slid against his as she moved higher onto his lap, almost trying to climb him, trying to fuse them together as one. Her skin burned and her limbs shook. She tasted the salt on Ira's skin when her lips slid across the curve of his neck.

He added a third finger as he ducked down to take one of her nipples into his mouth again. She moaned and the noises she was making seemed to spur him on because he curled his fingers while sucking, and he didn't stop as the heat and tension grew. And then that cord pulling her taut just *snapped*.

She cried out as her body locked and her vision whitened and a rush of ecstasy washed through her. And then she slumped against Ira, her body heavy and sated and exhausted. She continued to tremble, especially her legs, and her breaths were heavy, but they were full and light in her chest. She didn't want to detach herself from Ira. She couldn't if she tried. Her muscles were molten, and she was quite comfortable in his lap. Still, she shifted and brought her hand to his thigh.

"Let me—"

"No." Ira turned his head against hers. He was breathing just as heavily as she was. "No, it's fine. I'm—it's fine. Rest."

"I don't want to rest," she said even though the idea of it sounded lovely. Her mind was fuzzy, and her body felt like it was floating. Krashing, that felt nice.

Ira let out a short laugh, and she felt the puff of hot air along her cheek. He brushed her hair back and said again, "Rest."

She leaned back and smoothed her thumb over his brow bone. "Only if you stay with me."

His eyes dropped to her lips, but he didn't swoop in to kiss her. She wished he would. But she knew why he wouldn't.

Favor. Proposal. Transaction.

Their transaction was over. Ira didn't want to push the limits. And neither did she.

"Always."

He maneuvered them so they were lying down, her against his side. He grabbed her hand, his fingers twisting with hers. His thumb roved over her new ring. He was silent for a moment, studying it and shifting her fingers. "It's a fancy ring."

"It is," she agreed. "It's . . . heavy. Not the ring itself, but . . . what comes with it."

Ira hummed and laced his fingers through hers before resting their joined hands on his abdomen.

"You don't have to carry the burden by yourself."

She squeezed his hand, her heart full, and quickly slipped into a blissful sleep.

Chapter
Seventeen

The following morning, Lena told Ira about the spy she'd encountered in the village. He appeared to be just as troubled about it as she was, but there was nothing they could do about it. Not really. If something came up, they would deny it. She had Ira as her alibi. Cowen would lie for her as well. It was someone else's word against the queen and king consort's.

She cracked open a little bit more of herself and told him about her plan. She'd already told him about the list and that she wanted to kill them, but it was more than that. She *planned* on killing them. It was a matter of when, not if. Of course, she needed to be careful. If Blessed started dropping like flies, especially those in important positions of power, people would take notice and an investigation would begin. Her enemies were already watching her, and they would no doubt point the finger of blame at her once the search for the murder suspect began. That was inevitable. She had the information and the ability, but she needed allies and a cover. And that was where she would need help.

Admittedly, she didn't have all the details worked out. She didn't know in what order she was going to kill them all. She was waiting for an opportunity. If there was any death that could be written off as anything other than murder, she'd turn her focus toward that.

Ira listened to her carefully as she explained all of this while they sat at the dining room table eating the lunch they'd made together. "You'll need to leave Alkus last."

She set her jaw and stirred her soup. "I know."

She couldn't kill him now, but there were other ways to make him suffer.

"When they're all gone, then what?"

The killings needed to happen first before anything else on her agenda could be addressed. The current council wasn't going to agree with any of her suggested policies. She would need more council members on her side, and it was easier to start from scratch. Elected officials would be the easiest to convince—not easy, but the *easiest*. The royal families were typically rooted in their ways, and the prophets could go one way or another.

She realized that her plan—her *entire* plan—was extremely challenging. Most Blessed wouldn't approve of a law that would take things away from them, even if it was giving those things to people who needed them more. Most Blessed could be summed up in two words: ignorant and arrogant.

"Then we rebuild."

Ira smirked. "*We*, huh?"

She rolled her eyes. "Yes, *we*. What? Are *you* planning on running away before then?"

"No," he said fondly, a small, soft smile on his lips. "No, I'm here to stay."

They spent the rest of the day lazing around the house, cooking and reading and playing chess. Her skills were rusty, and Ira had been learning. He ended up winning half the time. They ventured downstairs when they grew tired of that, and she looked over the shelves in the library while Ira sat behind his desk in the study. She joined him once she found something to read, though he hardly looked up from the book he was writing in.

"I didn't take you for the type to journal," she commented as she sat in an armchair facing his desk. "What could you possibly be writing?"

A small smile crept onto Ira's face. He kept his gaze on the book for a few more seconds as he finished scribbling something. Amusement and fondness danced in his eyes when they met hers. "Who says I'm writing?"

She raised a brow, and Ira's eyes dipped to the book again as his pencil scratched against the paper.

"Are you *drawing?*"

The corners of Ira's lips curled up even more as his eyes flitted to hers again. "I record the moments I wish to remember," he said simply.

"Don't you have enough hobbies?" she huffed, but she was smiling. "What are you drawing? Can I see it?"

Ira looked back at the book again without giving her an answer, but there was still a playful curve to his lips, which told her this wasn't over. She would get a glimpse of those pages one day.

Her gaze returned to her own book, but she wasn't able to pick up any of the words her eyes skimmed over. Her heart was steady in her chest, making room for itself amidst the fullness residing there. She scratched her nose, hiding the smile she was unable to wipe away behind her hand.

Later that day, the two of them ended up making a mess of the kitchen after they decided to bake a chocolate cake. Ira wiped a stripe of chocolate down the bridge of her nose. Lena stared at him, aghast, and flicked flour in his direction. A battle broke out and they each grabbed ingredients, throwing them at each other until they and the entire kitchen were covered in eggs, flour, and chocolate.

They went to the backyard to wash off, which had resulted in some lustful glances and thoughts that led to making out on the sofa. Their hands roamed under shirts, but they didn't go further than that.

They were both still trying to find a balance in their little arrangement. There was a line not to be crossed. If one of them desired sex or getting off, the other was there. They were . . . helping one another. Giving each other a hand—sometimes literally. And this kind of relationship wasn't abnormal in The Lands, but sometimes the partners were at odds with one another. They wanted different things. They compromised or split. She couldn't split with Ira, not in law or otherwise, so she compromised. She took what he was willing to give and didn't ask for anything that he wasn't comfortable giving.

It was a dance of sorts they played around one another, but she couldn't read him in the same way he could read her.

She visited the library the following day in search of a book about bonds. She found a few and began to read up on and practice ways in which she could shield her mind from him. Ira hadn't been offended when she told him what she was looking for, which was both reassuring and maddening. Why was he so understanding and handsome and perfect?

She didn't act on her desires every time. She told herself that would be too intimate. But they *were* on their honeymoon. She was sure that once they returned to the Highlands, they would have far less time for sex of any sort because of their positions and duties. That was both a good and bad thing.

She was losing her mind. She needed something to do, so she decided to go for a walk. Ira didn't ask to join her, which made her wonder if he could tell that she didn't want company either from her body language or her mind. She'd thought this about a lot of things lately, even though Ira had reassured her repeatedly that this newly acquired ability of his didn't work like that.

She stopped by the garden shack on her way out and grabbed any helpful tools she could find before heading to her childhood house. Cowen followed her around the property and through the woods. He didn't try to talk to her and kept his distance, but she noticed him falter when he set his eyes upon her old home and the graves. He had been here once, six years ago when the prophets and Sacred Guard first came down to her home. That felt like eons ago.

She sat in front of her family and talked for an hour. About everything and nothing. And then, when her nerves settled as much as she thought was possible, she picked herself up and went to the front door of the house.

"Kalena," Cowen called out in apprehension.

She waved him off. It was fine. The structure wouldn't collapse on her. Ira had entered and left the house just fine. It was just a building.

She took a deep breath and then quickly, before she could talk herself out of it, stepped inside. The floorboards creaked under her feet, but they didn't break. The roof didn't cave in. She took a step farther and then another and another until she found herself in a deeper part of the house that she couldn't see from standing outside the entryway. This place was bruised, but it was salvageable.

"Kalena?" Cowen said again from somewhere behind her.

"In here."

Cowen appeared around the corner. His eyes swept over the room, taking in the space she used to live in before the palace. She felt the urge to pull his gaze away. She wasn't ashamed of her childhood home, but it was deeply personal.

"If you're going to stick around, you can at least help."

Cowen's eyes cut to hers and she extended a broom. An olive branch. He watched her for a moment before walking over and taking it.

And then they got to work.

Lena was quiet the evening before they left. She tried to enjoy her last night of serenity, but she kept thinking about what would happen tomorrow when they returned to the Highlands. She didn't want to leave.

"We'll come back," Ira assured her. "This place isn't going anywhere."

She held on to those words and spent the rest of her time committing the house and the property to memory so she could transport herself back whenever the Highlands became too much.

CHAPTER EIGHTEEN

They had a gift waiting for them when they returned to the Highlands.

There were five of them.

Five corpses had been strung up for her like banners.

The bodies hung from trees. Their arms were pinned together above their heads, stakes driven through their wrists. A cut tore through each of their stomachs, and rivulets of dried blood painted their lower halves almost entirely red. The shirts were ripped in the middle to reveal the large wound on their chests. And their hearts were missing.

Just like her family.

Lena's stomach rolled over itself as she approached.

Ira was by her side, rigid and silent. Mikhail and Alkus already stood in front of the tree, gazing up at the corpses. Palace guards and enforcers were littered around the area to make sure no one stumbled by and caught sight of the massacre. They didn't want panic to spread.

"They've been here for a few hours," one of the guards told her. "They were killed before being strung up. We haven't found where they were killed yet. There's no sign of struggle in the area, but there's no trail of blood either. It's almost like they just... appeared here."

"Keep searching," she ordered, her voice distorted and distant to her ears.

The guard nodded. "Of course, Your Majesty. We also don't think it was the *Ateisha*."

The *Ateisha*. The monsters of the mountains. She'd heard of them before—everyone had. And although she'd never seen one in person, she'd seen plenty of drawings. They were large, pale, and thick-skinned to survive the harsh mountain climate. Their eyes were a milky white and apparently so haunting that the memory of them drove some survivors mad. One glance was all it took for the vivid dreams and hallucinations to arise. They were tricky for even Slayers since *Ateisha* were pack creatures.

She returned her gaze to the bodies. It was a gruesome display. Was it a scare tactic? Was someone onto her? The timing couldn't be a coincidence.

"Take them down. Identify the bodies so we can reach out to their families," Ira said, his voice tight. "And give them a proper burial."

She eyed him out of the corner of her eye, noting his rigid stance.

"We'll add more guards to each rotation to look out for any suspicious activity," she added. "We don't want word of this getting out—not until we know exactly what's happening. But we don't want to put anyone in unnecessary danger. We'll have to cancel the celebrations—"

"We can't," Alkus interrupted.

Lena narrowed her eyes, turning on him. "Why not?"

Alkus sighed, looking up at the corpses as if they were nothing more than a nuisance. "We're expecting guests."

PART TWO
THE ROUSE

CHAPTER NINETEEN

A few days later, around five hundred kids arrived at the Institute, unaware of the night terror that awaited them here.

Atreus had learned the hard way that it was better to keep your distance from people—they were there one moment and gone the next—so he tried to stay away.

Finn and Mila had been an accident. They'd all come to the Institute in the same shipment. Night terrors had plagued him before he was sent to another realm and saw the *Te'Monai*. His bad dreams weren't frequent like Finn's, but when they did occur, they were terrifying. He would see . . . *horrible* things that left him paralyzed in bed and barely able to breathe. No one could wake him. He would hear them, sometimes even see them, but the images and the paralyzing fear didn't stop. It had to run its course.

Finn had noticed him having one of these night terrors, and instead of ignoring him like the others, he'd sat next to him and begun to tell a story. He didn't stop talking until the night terror ended.

Mila came shortly after. She befriended Finn first and then approached Atreus. He ignored her initially, even when she kept saving his skin in the mines, in lecture, during seminar. He would mess up and she would cover for him. He thought it was annoying until one day she got hurt doing it. She went to Miss Anya and came back with her arm in a splint. Her wrist was broken. He asked her why she did it, and she shrugged.

He didn't really know what'd happened after that, just that two became three, and he hadn't been able to shake off Mila or Finn since then. Though, he'd honestly stopped trying. Sometimes he thought he was only still sane because of them, but he truly had no intention of growing close to anyone else.

Finn, on the other hand, was a sucker for the new ones. Every time, without fail, he would swoop in when he saw them huddled together, alone and lost. He was too kind. Atreus would tell him that and Finn would snort and say, *"It takes one to know one."*

Most of the older firstborns avoided the unnecessary hassle of showing the new shipment the ropes. It was extra work, and they too didn't want to risk attachment. Everyone knew the younger kids were the bait; they took the hit so the others could get away. And because of that, everyone felt some relief. And then disgust. And guilt.

As soon as Finn went over to the kids, Mila followed. The kids latched on to Finn's enthusiasm and Mila's strong presence. Atreus stayed a few paces away, grimacing. Finn and Mila dragged him over eventually. He shifted on his feet and looked away when the kids' awed expressions transferred to him. It was like . . . hero worship. But none of them here, especially him, were heroes.

Miss Anya had finally cleared him to work in the mines again. It took him some time to orient himself to the altered layout. They always worked quickly, but he didn't know what they were digging so ardently for. No one did.

Mila told the kids to lug the smaller rocks back to the barrels. She and Finn didn't want them to get their hands on any picks or shovels and accidentally injure themselves. They didn't need any kids running around with pointy objects as big as them.

They went to seminar next, which, as expected, shook the kids.

Atreus didn't remember anything about his life before the Institute. Well, that wasn't entirely true. He remembered being told about his origins—about what it meant to be a firstborn. The sin. The punishment. The repentance. All of it. But that was it, and it'd been presented in a much less . . . abrasive manner than it was here.

When they stood to leave seminar, a little girl grabbed onto his pant leg. She was still staring at the prophets with horror.

"Uh, don't worry," he said awkwardly. She looked at him with her large eyes, flyaways surrounding her head like a lion's mane. "You won't be sent out. You're too small. You'll stay here."

He'd been sent out for the first time when he was eleven and arrived here when he was ten. These kids looked even younger than that.

"Promise?" she whispered.

He hesitated. He hated making promises, but he saw the kids peeking out from behind her, staring at him with hopeful eyes. He pinched his lips together. "I promise."

He told himself that he'd done a good thing, that seeing the tension ease from their shoulders and faces was worth it.

Every meal, the kids would squeeze themselves around the table that Mila, Finn, and Atreus had claimed for themselves. They were all pressed together, shoulder to shoulder. The kids stared at the three of them, waiting for their instructions. Today he gave up his seat and went to another table. Later, when they were going to the sleeping hall for the night, Finn materialized at his side.

"They're just looking for comfort," Finn said, his voice gentle.

Atreus shook his head. "I can't give it to them."

Whenever he looked at them, he saw the girl from their last Outing. He saw Eve. He saw the faces of all the other kids before them who hadn't made it. At least this shipment was too young to be sent out. The prophets were cruel, but they were also calculative. These kids were too young to be useful, or rather, they hadn't reached their prime usefulness. They would have a year or two of relative peace, but they should have more.

"You don't have to *give* anything," Finn said. "Just be there."

Atreus did better the next day, and then the next. His body and mind unwound as more time passed without them being sent out. The kids slowly acclimated to the schedule, but they still clearly looked at someone for guidance. The others turned their back, and he tried to do the same, but he was too slow.

One day a little boy caught his eye from across the lecture hall, and Atreus faltered, locking up as if a *Te'Monai* stared at him and not a visibly upset child. The kid's cheeks were red and blotchy, and his eyes were begging. Atreus sighed and cursed under his breath before walking across the room to the boy.

"What's wrong?" he asked bluntly, then winced right after. He wished Finn or Mila was here. They would be better at this. But they had probably gone ahead to guide the other kids to the mines.

"I . . . I don't know where to go," the boy sniffled. "Miss Anya told me I'm on garden duty from now on."

The boy shifted and Atreus saw his left arm. Or what remained of it. His arm was heavily bandaged and ended below the elbow. Atreus stared at the boy's amputated arm a bit too long. He yanked his gaze away, hoping he didn't look as horrified as he felt.

It was a new injury, one that had been caused by a situation in the mines. Accidents happened frequently. Explosions were the most common. They could usually tell when an explosion was coming due to the smell. Most of the time, there were only minor injuries, or none at all, but other times, rocks crushed people or pinned their limbs. Amputation was sometimes the only way to walk away. Lately there had been more explosions than usual because they had picked up their pace, but he hadn't heard of any injuries.

"I can take you there," he said. His voice sounded rough, so he cleared his throat. "Come on. Let's go."

The boy trailed after him dutifully. He kept reaching over like he wanted to wring his fingers together, but he would stop when he remembered that he didn't have another set of fingers anymore. Atreus walked faster, but not because he cared if he was late to his shift in the mines.

"What's your name?" the boy asked.

Atreus nearly tripped on a jutting piece of stone as his heart stuttered. "What?"

"Your name. What's your name?" And then before Atreus could change the subject, the boy said, "They told me my name is Judah."

Atreus tried to avoid names more than he tried to avoid people. Names were an attachment. But the boy had already shared his. Atreus felt like he couldn't leave him waiting.

"Mine is . . . Atreus."

"Atreus," the boy repeated in his small, wonder-filled voice. Atreus winced again. "That's a cool name."

He didn't know what to say to that.

But the kid moved on to a new topic quickly as kids do. "You're tall." He wasn't crying anymore, thankfully, but his eyes were still rimmed with red. "How tall are you?"

"Uh, I don't know."

"Miss Seila said I will grow strong and tall if I eat my fruit and vegetables. Is that true?"

"Um, yeah, for the most part."

If he hadn't worked in the garden for a short time, he wouldn't be so sure the firstborns were even fed fruits and vegetables. The prophets sure did their best to make the produce look as unappetizing as—

Wait.

"Miss Seila?" he asked, angling his head back so he could hear the boy's response. He didn't know anyone by that name here.

"Yeah! She was the nicest one from the place before. She would read us these bedtime stories about heroes and—"

"You can't repeat those here," Atreus said sternly, turning a corner. But he locked on to that one word: *before*. He didn't remember much of a *before*. And as far as he knew, neither did Mila or Finn or anyone else.

"Oh . . . okay." The kid stumbled forward, practically jogging to keep up. His breathing was loud and obnoxious. "Miss Seila told me those heroes ate fruits and vegetables to get strong and tall . . . They did other stuff too, but Miss Seila said I could get there some day. I just turned eight, so I have time . . ."

Atreus had been about to scold him for talking about those stories after he *just* told him not to, but all his thoughts were obliterated when the boy offered up his age. So innocently too. Atreus jerked back as if the boy's words had physically burnt him.

Eight? Newly eight too. How old are the others?

He spotted the door to the garden ahead and *thank fuck*. He dropped the kid off at the door, making sure he steered clear of touching him. Then Atreus was stumbling back down the corridors to the mines.

"Atreus!" the boy called out. He said it like *Uh-tray-ss* instead of *Uh-tray-us*. The kid couldn't even pronounce his name right. "Thank you for helping me!"

I didn't help you. I didn't do shit.

The trip to the mines passed by in a blur. He wasn't sure he got a single, good breath in. The caves were dark, and his spotted vision was little help.

Hands grabbed his shoulders, hauling him back and saving him from bashing his face against the rocks.

Mila shook him gently, her concerned face filling his narrowed vision. "Atreus? What is it? What's wrong?"

"He's eight," he gasped. "*He's eight.*"

Mila's face disappeared and Finn's came into view, drenched in sorrow. Of course he understood.

"He's eight. *They're kids.*"

Finn nodded. Atreus realized his friend's hands were on his cheeks.

"They are," Finn agreed solemnly. "We all were."

CHAPTER
TWENTY

Lena was furious.

When she found out what Alkus was talking about, she'd wanted to yell at him right there and release her Slayer, finally allowing herself to be rid of him. But Mikhail had intervened and directed them toward the council chamber. She started the meeting as soon as quorum was reached and turned on Alkus.

"How could you?" she hissed. Returning to the Highlands had already put her in a sour mood, but seeing those bodies and learning that Alkus had been keeping secrets—making plans behind the council's back—tipped her over the edge. "How could you think of inviting a large party of *foreign* guests without notifying me? Don't you think that's something important I should know? The council should know?"

Alkus watched her with undisguised irritation. "When I sent the letter, you hadn't yet returned—"

"I've been back for well over a week," she interjected. "There was plenty of time to tell me. Even so, you should've consulted with the council *before* you extended the invitation. Honestly, maybe we ought to be questioning *your* loyalty."

He had the gall to accuse her of treachery for keeping her Imprint from them for a day while he had kept things from her for a week and the council for much longer.

"I did . . . consult with some members of the council."

She scanned the room. She could probably guess who. "But you didn't call an official meeting?"

She turned to Mikhail for support, but he was staring at no one and nothing in particular as he contemplated something. She didn't know what there was to contemplate. Alkus had gone behind the council. He'd committed treason. And this time around, there was tangible proof.

Alkus saw the opportunity and took it. "Many things have happened while you were gone, Your Majesty. Until your Ascension, The Lands had been without a ruler for over *six years*. We weren't at liberty to discuss these matters with you in detail until you ascended, and we couldn't afford to wait until you decided to come back to take action." He turned his sharp gaze on Mikhail. "As the Grand Prophet, you're familiar with the challenges I speak of. The explosions in the distance are growing closer. The *Ateisha* are migrating down the mountains. And now this!" He flung his hand toward the doors, referring to the scene they'd just come from. "We need allies and aid. I acted because I care for The Lands and want to protect it and its people. And waiting for Her Majesty to make that realization on her own and come back to do her job was not a luxury we could afford!"

Her Imprint burned on her chest as her nails dug into the armrests, but she forced herself to remain composed, even when her Slayer's bloodlust spiked. She leaned forward to catch Alkus' gaze once again.

"You committed treason, Alkus," she said slowly in an attempt stifle her frustration. "It doesn't matter how you spin it, what you did was illegal." She could feel Ira through the bond, or what she assumed was Ira, trying to calm her down. She lowered her voice and added, "And this time, there is evidence."

Alkus narrowed his eyes.

"Your Majesty," Mikhail said. "Alkus will face consequences for his actions, but what he said does hold some truth."

"Then we'll address those issues," she said firmly. "Whether or not his words hold some truth doesn't change what he did. If he committed a crime, he will be dealt with accordingly. Just like everyone else would be. Blessed in power are not above the law."

The silence in the room made it clear that most did not agree with that.

"The Lands has been under great strain since your disappearance. Our unity wavers," Mikhail said.

The others wanted only to give Alkus a small slap on the wrist for what he'd done, but that could hardly be called a punishment at all, and it told Alkus that he could continue to break the law and get away with it.

"As Alkus said, explosions are growing nearer and more frequent in the west. The *Ateisha* are descending upon us from the north—"

"These guests," Ira interrupted. "Who are they? How do we know you haven't invited enemies into our land?"

"If they were our enemies, they would've already struck. They're open to an alliance. They've been having some difficulties of their own."

"Who are *they*?" a councilwoman pressed while eyeing Alkus distrustfully. Lena recognized her as the woman Ira had been speaking to the morning after the ball. A representative. Perhaps a potential ally.

"The people of the Isles."

The room took a collective breath.

"The people of the Isles?" another man questioned. The crest on his coat identified him as a royal. An Abaari. "The ones who ride the waves?"

It was a saying she'd heard before. The sea was a wild, raging beast. Everyone from The Lands who went out to conquer it never returned. But there were stories that circulated about people who lived on the ocean, past the wall of mist that appeared after the second sandbar. They were said to be people just as wild and raging as the waves and only they could master the waters. Some believed the stories, and some didn't. At the very least, they scared adventurous children away from the dangers of the coast.

If those stories were true, at least in some capacity, why were the people of the Isles coming *now*? Had they been as unaware of The Lands' presence as The Lands had been of theirs? And how had Alkus contacted them?

Various expressions of curiosity and concern came across the council members' faces. Alkus' betrayal had been forgotten now that the focus was on the Isles.

She turned to Mikhail. "I want a trial—"

The doors to the council chamber opened and a messenger stumbled in. His eyes swept over them, wide and disbelieving.

"The guests have arrived."

~

Lena had yet to see the throne room since getting back, but she remembered the grandeur of it clearly. A space that large and majestic wasn't easily forgotten. Still, she was taken aback when she entered the room.

The rectangular throne room was extensive just like the ballrooms and took up the entire height of the palace. A thick indigo and gold carpet ran through the middle of the room, from the entrance to the stairs that led to the throne. Pillars stood on either side of the room to create a private hall on the outer edges for spectators to gather.

But the most impressive sight in this space was the golden throne, which towered over everyone on a fifty-foot structure, its back fanning out in elegant curls and points across the glass wall that stood strong behind it. The carved symbol of the Blessed rested in the middle of the throne's back. Twin staircases flared out on either side of the structure, starting right before the carpet and ending on either side of the throne. Nine small balconies were attached to the outside of the staircases, each higher up than the last and housing a chair for a council member.

Huge banners displaying the Blessed's symbol hung on either side of the massive structure, tumbling down from the lofty ceiling and nearly brushing the floor. Some of the windowpanes on the glass wall behind the throne were cracked open, allowing the floral smell from the gardens to waft into the room, but the soothing scent of nature did little to calm her nerves.

"Your Majesty," Mikhail said quietly at her side.

She knew what he was going to say before he even opened his mouth.

"Perhaps someone else should—"

"No," she said tightly. "I can handle it."

The halls on either side of the throne room were already filled. She noticed Avalon and Celine, Tuck's other mother, and wondered if Tuck was hidden in the crowd. Perhaps he was with Xavien and the rest of her childhood friends.

She met Ira's gaze. His eyes were searching. She shook her head. *I'm fine.*

Cowen and Benji followed her up the steps to the throne. Only then did she realize the extent of its size. Five of her could sit on the cushioned seat and there would still probably be some room left. Up close she could see that various jewels were scattered throughout the back of the throne, winking in the rays of sunlight that rained down from the small skylights above.

The soft chatter in the room died down as she took her seat. The guards standing on the other side of the room by the doors were small specs, but she could see them clearly. They were waiting for her.

She cleared her throat. "Let them in."

Her voice rang out across the room. As did the knock the guards gave on the doors. A few seconds later, a bang sounded and then the doors opened.

Four guests filtered into the room, more guards following them. Two women and two men.

One of the men was quite possibly the largest person she'd ever seen. He had to be well over seven feet and was built like an ox. His skin was deeply tanned, as if he'd spent lots of time in the sun. Trinkets were weaved through his long hair, but his beard, which was equally as long, was devoid of any.

The second man was younger and slighter. He had alabaster skin and long blond hair that was neatly brushed and tied back. He wore a blue shawl that concealed most of his body, and earrings dangled from his ears. Out of everyone in the group, he looked the most relaxed, his bright blue eyes carelessly raking over the spectators on either side of the room.

One of the women was also relatively tall, around six feet. Her dark hair was cut short to her scalp and gloves covered her hands. Lena was tempted to mark her as the leader due to the way she carried herself. She had an ink marking across one sun-kissed cheek. A wave.

The last woman looked to be around Lena's age, maybe a little older, with golden skin. Her reddish-brown hair was long and full, twisted back into thick braids. She also wore gloves. Her dark gaze was already locked on Lena, a scowl shifting her face.

Lena frowned.

"We'd heard the queen of The Lands had returned home to her throne. We wondered if it was only a rumor," the leader said.

Funny, Lena thought, *I could say the same to you.*

"Clearly it wasn't," she replied. "Councilman Alkus tells us he's been in contact with you and that you've been experiencing some troubles of your own. That you possibly hope to strike an alliance with us."

The woman snorted. "You make it sound like we're crawling to you for aid. Do not forget it was *you* who reached out to *us*. We saw this as a good opportunity, but do not make the mistake of thinking we need you. We're perfectly capable of finding other solutions."

"Maybe you ought to speak to the queen with some respect," one of the prophets said.

"She is not *my* queen."

"But you are still guests here," Mikhail reminded them. "Please, we apologize for any insult we may have issued. We don't want to cause strife. That's not our goal here."

Lena eyed the prophet and took a deep breath. This was no time to be proud. She hadn't known this meeting was happening until an hour ago, but she didn't want their guests knowing that.

"Yes, I apologize. We are . . . adjusting." That was certainly one way of putting it. "Please, what are your names?"

Her words seemed to appease them enough. They each introduced themselves. The woman who had spoken was Sorrel. The large man was Von, and the other man was Kieryn. The woman around her age was still glaring and only offered up her name after Sorrel fixed her with a sharp look. She was Aquila.

"We received a message from The Lands that expressed an interest in an alliance. Ouprua . . . is also adjusting." Sorrel grinned sharply. "But we have other assets to offer."

Ouprua? That must be the official name of the Isles.

Lena raised a brow. "Such as?"

Sorrel laughed. "We're not going to show our cards until you've shown yours. But we do agree that an alliance between The Lands and Ouprua could be mutually advantageous. We'd like to discuss this potential partnership in further detail, but the means of securing the alliance must come first."

Lena hesitated and then cautiously said, "Yes, I agree. Did you have something in mind?"

"The customary means of safeguarding an alliance is through a union. The more important the people involved, the more successful."

It was clear what Sorrel was implying. Others picked up on the meaning and shuffled, looking in Lena's direction. She hoped her smile didn't give her away. "I'm already married."

"Yes—recently, we heard. Congratulations. But we also know polygamy is a common practice in The Lands. As the queen, shouldn't you live luxuriously?"

Murmurs rose, and Lena's smile tightened. She didn't look at Ira as she said, "I'm quite content with what I currently have, thank you."

"We can discuss marriage and other options for securing the alliance in the coming days. There's no need to make such a hasty decision," Mikhail added quickly.

Sorrel's eyes narrowed and she tilted her head. "Can your queen not speak for herself?"

"She can speak for herself just fine," Lena said pointedly.

"I must say it *is* a bit insulting when you're so quick to reject our proposal. It's like you don't even think it's worthy of consideration."

She nearly laughed at the word choice. "That's not—"

"Maybe she thinks now that she's acquired some fancy power, she doesn't need aid from anyone else," Aquila cut in, the sneer still on her face. Her eyes dipped to Lena's chest where her Imprint was visible.

"Aquila," Sorrel warned.

"What? I said what we were all thinking."

Lena pushed down the heat that came with her rising emotions. "I don't think that."

"No?" Aquila took a step forward so she was even with Sorrel, her dark eyes never leaving Lena. "Then prove it."

"*Aquila.*"

Lena squinted and leaned forward slightly. There was something about Aquila that she couldn't quite put her finger on, but it kept standing out to her.

"I advise you to watch your tongue when speaking to Her Majesty," one of the guards cautioned.

The other guards stiffened and took a half step forward, as if preparing for some sort of fight. Some of the spectators fidgeted. Below her, Mikhail gripped the arms of his chair tightly as if preparing to push himself to his feet and talk his way out of this conflict.

"I still don't understand why we came here," Aquila continued as if the air in the room hadn't grown heavier. "You said it yourself, Sorrel. We can make do without them. They should be showing *us* what *they* can offer."

Lena didn't know how dire The Lands' situation was. The council hadn't been able to go into detail before their guests arrived. So, she didn't know exactly how badly they needed aid. But it was clear that Ouprua was their only option. The Lands wasn't in contact with any other civilizations, at least as far as she knew, which she supposed didn't count for much. There were stories about other places—there were always stories—but how many more years would it be before they proved that those tales were true? Maybe it would never happen. And if it did, it could very well be too late if these threats were as large as Mikhail had made them sound. It was possible they had one shot to get this right and the reins were in her hands.

She needed to deescalate the situation. And the easiest way to do that was to tell them what they wanted to hear. Even if it wasn't what she wanted to say.

"This is not only about what you want. This is about what The Lands needs. If you didn't want to make sacrifices, you shouldn't have returned."

She had come back here willingly, knowing there would be difficulties. Sacrifices. But how many more?

"*You have to be strategic with how you retaliate,*" Ira had told her.

What was that saying? Lose the battle but win the war?

"I . . . will consider the offer."

That appeared to calm Sorrel for the time being, and she yanked Aquila back. Kieryn stepped up to Aquila's side and said something in her ear that made her shoulders relax, only slightly.

Mikhail looked over his shoulder, giving Lena an approving nod. "Excellent. Her Majesty will think on the matter. In the meantime, we will get you settled in your rooms."

"And the festivities?" Kieryn asked with a smirk on his lips. "We were told there was going to be a party."

CHAPTER
TWENTY-ONE

Lena stayed rooted on her throne after the guests left. Chatter rose quickly as soon as the doors slammed shut. People spilled from the side halls into the middle of the throne room, gathering in clumps and likely gossiping about what had just transpired. The council members stood from their seats and talked among one another. Everyone's gaze darted up to the throne where she still sat at least once.

She knew what they were thinking because she was thinking it herself.

Her first interaction with their guests had been less than ideal. It was hardly her fault, yet the blame lay entirely with her. She was the queen. She hadn't known about their existence or this meeting, but it'd been her job to make it work. Or she could have given that up, listened to Mikhail, and looked like a failure and figurehead in front of their guests and the people of The Lands, which was exactly what the latter wanted.

This is a battle. Not the war, she reminded herself.

She couldn't bring herself to move. Her mind raced with other information. The marriage. The party. The other threats The Lands faced. And her power, again, had been called into question. This time by people who had never even met her. Perhaps Ouprua shared prejudices with The Lands.

She watched Alkus converse with Trynla, Avalon, Ophir, and Celine. This was the first time she'd seen Tuck's other mother since returning. Like the others, she didn't look much different than before. She was beautiful, nearly as beautiful as Avalon, but while Avalon was dark-complexioned, Celine was light. Light skin. Light hair. Light eyes. Even her voice was light. Her darkness was deeper, hidden, which Lena thought was worse. Celine had never slipped up in front of her, but she still didn't trust her.

She hardly trusted anyone.

Everyone doubted her, and she had gained no new allies since returning. Now that she was back in the Highlands, she would have to work on that.

She looked over the crowd. It was clear that power swayed the people. Power and strength were not the same, but the people thought of them as such. She could be strong. She had the power, but she didn't have the people.

She felt their stares. Sitting on the throne, she was on display, at center stage, for everyone to critique. They weren't even trying to be discrete anymore. Their eyebrows raised and their mouths curled as they whispered about her.

The anger from earlier slowly seeped through her body. It was thick and warm and steady like syrup, and she let it run its course.

She *knew* she was powerful. She *knew* she was strong. Others didn't.

But they would.

"Kalena?" Cowen stepped forward, his brows drawn together.

Her Imprint burned and her ears popped. The voices that had blended into some unintelligible jumble separated and became clear. She could distinguish every conversation in the room, as well as who was saying what. Small details that she shouldn't be able to see at her distance were suddenly visible.

" . . . no idea what she's doing . . . "

" . . . lead The Lands to ruin . . . "

" . . . should've stayed away . . . "

" . . . would've been better if she died with her family . . . "

" . . . Imprint is probably fake . . . "

"Lena?" Ira's face and shoulders were rigid. He was frustrated. At her?

The audacity these people had to say these things about their queen *in front of her*.

" . . . not doing her duty at all. *Any* of them."

She latched onto this sickeningly sweet voice and pinpointed the culprit. Cressida. Of course. And the rest of the group surrounded her. Crane. Vix. Leythi. Alden. Greer. Xavien. Even Tuck was there this time, leaning against one of the pillars without a care in the realm. His gaze raked over the top of the crowd as Cressida went on.

"I mean, she just got married. I heard that Mikhail already asked about a child. She was gone for three days. She should be pregnant, but I doubt she is. She'll probably fail at that too."

Lena dug her nails into her palms.

"Cressida," Greer said. "Maybe you should keep your voice down."

Always the peacekeeper.

"Why? As that water witch said, I'm only saying what everyone is thinking."

Who knows what *Her Majesty* was doing in the Lowlands. She should've stayed there."

Lena's blood boiled, but she sat still, watching and listening.

"Lena," Ira said again, his voice urgent and low. "I think we should go. And talk."

Alkus looked over his shoulder, smirking, and Ophir's dark gaze was a weight upon her shoulders.

Her heartbeat was steady yet too loud. It filled her ears, muffling all conversations except for the one she wanted to hear the least.

"If she really wanted to help The Lands, she should go off herself. Then she could reunite with her pathetic family."

Lena stood abruptly and a hush fell over the room. The rage blistered her skin. Ira tried to grab her, but she brushed him off and took a step out of his reach. Her eyes locked with Cressida's.

Her, she picked.

Yes, a voice inside of her agreed gleefully.

"That's enough," she commanded as she looked over the crowd. There was a sharp ache behind her eyes, but she pushed it aside. "I'm tired of the jabs and the gossip. You question me? Your queen? The Numina?"

She knew Ira wouldn't approve of this. This wasn't playing nice and by their rules. But she didn't have his patience. Not with this.

"You question my power? You think this Imprint is fake?" She turned her gaze back to Cressida. "I'll prove to you that it's not."

"*Lena, no—*"

"Cressida." She raised her chin. "I challenge you to a Slayer duel."

CHAPTER
TWENTY-TWO

The next Outing approached quickly. They received but a day's notice and hardly anyone could sleep the night before. The day of the Outing was quiet and still as if they expected portals to appear out of nowhere and suck them away.

He'd been avoiding the kids, which led to him avoiding Finn and Mila as well. But he kept an eye out for Judah. Whenever Atreus did spot the boy, he was always looking over the crowd as if searching for someone in particular. Atreus would leave quickly to avoid getting caught under Judah's gaze again. He'd already shown the kid to the garden. What more did he need?

Atreus kept his head down and his stride long today. He let his mind shut down, his body running purely on instinct. He'd blocked out the prophet's self-righteous speech in seminar that morning and did the same in the afternoon. He was only snapped out of his stupor when he heard the commotion that suddenly swept across the room.

Some of the firstborns were frozen in their seats. Others were moving in every way, heads shaking, lips quivering, and hands waving out to catch the attention of a prophet. The kids were crying, and many looked like they wanted to flee from the room. A few enforcers took a step away from the wall. A warning.

What's going on?

Prophet Silas was the one speaking today. He cleared his throat and pushed back a lock of blond hair that had fallen out of place. "Calm down. Everyone, quiet! The Outing today is very important. That is why everyone is going. You should all understand..."

The rest of the words faded away, falling short of Atreus' ears.

Everyone is going.
Everyone.
Even the kids.
They're sending the kids.

He stood up. The legs of his chair scraped against the stone floor. Prophet Silas' eyes immediately cut to him.

"You can't do that," he said, but his voice was barely a mumble and easily lost amongst the disorder in the room.

He looked around, seeking out Finn and Mila. They wore identical expressions of panic and despair as if they'd already accepted it. They knew they couldn't change the prophets' minds.

~

THE TRIP to the cavern wasn't quiet tonight. It was filled with sobbing and screaming as the kids tried to go back. Some of them stopped walking altogether, collapsing and refusing to use their legs. Finn, Mila, and some of the other firstborns who took pity on the kids tried to pull them up, but they would only scream louder. The enforcers would step in soon.

Even though the kids were young, they understood what was happening. Finn and Mila had tried to get all of them to take their knives at dinner, but many of them had been inconsolable, crying and shoving the knives aside, or completely numb and unresponsive.

An ache was growing behind Atreus' temples, which wasn't ideal at this time. He went ahead, stepping past any kid who was throwing a tantrum. He couldn't afford to deal with it right now.

The first tug at the bottom of his shirt, he thought he imagined. The second he ignored. On the third insistent tug, he looked down, prepared to snap and release his pent-up emotions, but he stopped short when he saw who was next to him.

That boy. Judah.

He stared up at Atreus with wide, tear-filled eyes. "We're leaving?"

Atreus gulped, his hands trembling at his sides. He knew he should shake the kid off and lose him in the crowd. If he did, he'd likely never have to see him again, but he didn't. *Fuck.* Of course he didn't. He could keep his distance, but his conviction fell when they didn't keep theirs.

"Yes. We're all leaving."

"Why?" Judah's voice wavered. "Miss Seila said we were gonna stay here for a while."

Yeah, well she lied.
And so did I.

Atreus squeezed his eyes shut. The crowd was so tight that everyone was shuffling forward shoulder to shoulder. He was bumped along, but he never lost

Judah. It was some big joke. The hammering of his heart filled his ears, second only to the wails surrounding him. Chaos. And they hadn't even been sent out yet.

"You're shaking," Judah said, his one hand touching Atreus' arm.

He wasn't shaking because he was scared of stepping through that portal, though he didn't exactly welcome it. He was shaking because he'd come to a decision. It was quite possibly a shitty one, but this was a shitty situation.

He opened his eyes. "Did you keep your knife?"

The boy nodded. That was good. He possessed at least some survival instinct. And he could listen.

"Are you right or left-handed?" Atreus asked.

"Right."

That was also good. His left arm was the amputated one.

They filtered into the cavern. Atreus made a sweep around for Mila and Finn, but he didn't see them. Maybe they were behind him. He glanced at Judah, who still held his shirt and looked up at him, waiting.

He knelt down. "Give me your knife."

The boy reached behind him and pulled the knife from his pants. It was a miracle he hadn't cut himself with it.

Atreus fixed the knife in the boy's right hand, making sure his fingers were gripping the hilt correctly. "You don't let go of this. You hear me? You *never* let go of this. No matter how scared you are."

The boy nodded.

"Repeat it to me."

"I don't let go of this."

"No matter what?"

"No matter how scared I am."

"Right. And you stay close to me."

Since Judah only had one hand and he needed it to hold the knife, Atreus had to hold on to the kid. He hoped this realm's terrain wasn't too rough.

"Listen to me. If we happen to get split up, you need to keep moving. If any scary monsters come your way—*Te'Monai*—you run and don't stop. If you can't run, you fight. Understand?"

He knew there was no chance the kid would survive if they were separated, but he still had to say it.

Tears were building in Judah's eyes again, but he maintained eye contact, nodding at everything Atreus said.

He placed his hands on the boy's shoulders and gave him a firm shake. He lowered his voice. "You remember those heroes you used to hear stories about? They went through tough, terrifying situations like this. And they were scared, but they were also brave. So I need you to be brave, okay?"

"And then I'll be a hero?"

Atreus paused and then squeezed the kid's shoulders. "Yeah. Now remember what I told you."

He stood to his full height, berating himself mentally again and again. Mila and Finn had already caught sight of him and were heading over. Naturally, a group of kids followed them, trembling and looking scared out of their wits.

Mila looked at Judah. "You picked up a stray?"

That was exactly what had happened, but he didn't answer her question, not verbally at least. He instead looked between her and Finn and then their adopted group of kids to imply that they were just as guilty.

"What's the plan?" he asked. "You know we can't protect all of them."

"*I know*," Finn said quietly and pained. He wasn't responsible for the kids—none of them were—but it didn't lessen the guilt. "We . . . do what we can, but . . . "

"But we watch our own backs first," Mila finished somberly.

Atreus' eyes cut to hers.

Mila frowned at what she saw. "You know that, right?" she lightly scolded, her brows furrowing. "You have to watch your back, Atreus."

Her gaze moved to Judah and back to him. *It's you over him*, she was saying. *Remember that.*

"Yeah." He swallowed thickly. "Yeah, I know."

The portals appeared and the cries rose. The prophets stood unflinchingly on the far side of the cavern. Enforcers beckoned firstborns through the portals and shoved in the kids who refused to cooperate.

Atreus bent down to pull out his own knife, not wanting to waste any time retrieving it in the realm. He grabbed Judah's shirt with his other hand and they sunk into the milky white gateway.

~

THE REALM WAS bright and hot and smelled of salt. Atreus was relieved that they could at least see, but that relief was short-lived. The first scream rang out not even five seconds in.

He bolted before he saw a *Te'Monai*, hauling Judah along with him. He didn't check to see if Mila and Finn were doing the same. It was everyone for themselves. But they were survivors. They knew what to do. That was what he told himself every time.

The trees that surrounded them were tall and skinny with a bundle of large leaves blooming from the top. The leaves were easily as long as his body, and they swayed in the breeze.

He hesitated when he realized what he saw moving wasn't a leaf. The *Te'Monai* had already locked its eyes on to him. It blinked, the translucent membrane coming down to cover its eyes, yet he could still see its pupils dilate as it took in the smell of its next meal. The *Te'Monai* was covered in scales and slime. It was long, slick, and amphibious-looking with a flat head and rows of short, sharp teeth. The green-brown color of its body allowed it to easily blend in with the trees.

Judah let out a choked shout and huddled closer to Atreus.

"You have to be brave," Atreus reminded him as they ran. "Keep going. Don't look back."

The screams and roars were a cacophony in the air. He didn't know if Judah heard him over it. His grip on the kid's shirt and the knife were so tight, his fingers grew numb.

A *Te'Monai* skittered by in front of him, a small body locked between its jaws. Out of the corner of his eye, he saw others running through the canopy of trees alongside him. *Te'Monai* would drop from above, pouncing on the firstborns and cutting off their screams with a single chomp. The sounds of limbs tearing from bodies and heads crushing were layered on top of all the other horrible noises.

The truly sick thing was that the *Te'Monai* never finished the bodies. Some would be distracted for a while, but for others, a lethal blow was all they needed before leaving the corpse behind in search of their next victim. That was why the bodies piled up quickly.

He jerked to a stop when he saw a cliff ahead. Some firstborns were already climbing it, the *Te'Monai* chasing after them. The monsters were quick, but that was only part of the problem. He looked down at Judah, at what was left of his arm.

"*Shit.*"

He forced them to keep moving, skirting around the bottom of the cliff in search of some sort of incline. Eventually, he did find one. But right as he spotted it, a shadow fell over him. He yanked Judah back and dove aside just in time to avoid a *Te'Monai* dropping from the cliffside. Judah screamed and the *Te'Monai* cocked its head, its long, forked tongue slithering out. It stood between them and the incline.

Atreus moved to get the *Te'Monai*'s attention, then he shoved Judah to the side as he lunged in the other direction.

He dodged the *Te'Monai* when it jumped at him, but its long whip-like tail swung around and hit him in the chest, knocking him to the ground and stealing his breath. He regained his senses just in time to roll to the side to avoid being trampled by the *Te'Monai*'s feet.

He pushed himself up quickly and let out a cry as he threw himself at the *Te'Monai*. He landed on its back, his hand grappling for purchase against its slick skin, which became even more difficult when it began bucking and screaming. Its neck and legs were too short to allow it to reach him, so the tail was all he had to worry about.

He plunged his knife into the soft muscle of the *Te'Monai*'s neck. The creature screamed louder and bucked wilder, but Atreus held on tight, gritting his teeth and pushing the knife deeper, twisting. He then withdrew it and began stabbing the top of its head, again and again. The blade sunk into the flesh and bone so easily. Its skull crunched and blood splattered across him, but he didn't stop moving until the

Te'Monai did. When it slumped to the ground, he rolled off, his chest heaving and mouth tainted with blood. He spat it out and wiped the blood from his eyes.

"Judah? *Judah!*" he called as he stood and looked around.

He breathed a sigh of relief when he spotted the boy sitting on the ground nearby, right where he'd left him. Part of Atreus wanted to curse him for freezing— *'I told you to keep going! You have to be aware of your surroundings! Always!'*—but another part of him was glad the kid was still here and okay.

"Come on," he said as he hurried over. "Get up. We need to keep moving."

Judah hesitated before picking himself up. He jerked back when Atreus reached for him, making the older firstborn irritated. Atreus nearly snapped at him—they didn't have time for this—but he realized why Judah had hesitated. It was the blood.

"It's okay. It's not mine."

Judah still didn't come any closer.

A low noise of frustration left Atreus' throat, and he grabbed Judah's hand, turning and pulling him along . . . right as another *Te'Monai* strolled into view. Atreus pressed them back against the cliffside and shoved Judah up the incline. It hadn't seen them yet, but they had to worry more about its sense of smell. And unlike the *Te'Monai* in the last realm, these ones seemed to have perfectly functioning noses.

The new *Te'Monai* sniffed the one Atreus had just killed, nudged it with its nose, and then threw its head back and let out a low warble. It sounded . . . sad. The cry turned vicious and guttural, raising the hair along his arms. He tried to hurry Judah along, but it was too late. The *Te'Monai*'s gaze immediately cut to them.

Well, shit.

Something wet brushed Atreus' cheek and he flinched, looking up and coming nearly nose to nose with another *Te'Monai* hanging upside down on the cliffs. Its tongue struck out again. Judah screamed.

Atreus swung his arm, slicing off the end of the *Te'Monai*'s tongue. It fell to the rocks below, still squirming. The *Te'Monai* screeched and dropped down onto the incline. Atreus had nowhere to go on the narrow ledge. The *Te'Monai* hit him hard, ripping his hand from Judah's and pushing him over the side. The fall wasn't even ten feet, but the pain from the impact rattled his bones.

He struggled for a breath, but the *Te'Monai*'s weight on his chest was too great. It roared in his face, and saliva and blood coated his skin. He was vaguely aware of crying in the background as he wrestled with the *Te'Monai*, trying to keep its bloody jaws away from him. He didn't know where the other one was. He hoped Judah had listened to him this time and run, but the cries rang louder, telling him the kid had stayed put.

Atreus screamed and tried to shove the *Te'Monai* away, but it barely budged. Its severed tongue swiped out, surprisingly sharp, and cut his cheek.

There was a squelch, and the *Te'Monai* above him twitched and then stopped moving. It collapsed on top of him, and he panicked. His arms were trapped against his chest and his legs were pinned. He couldn't push it off. He couldn't *breathe*. His vision darkened and his chest grew painfully tight as air failed to reach where he needed it most.

Then, the pressure was relieved.

Atreus gasped and sat up, coughing when the air went down too quickly. He wiped away the tears, blood, and saliva and looked up.

"You owe me, asshole," a familiar voice sneered down at him.

He continued to blink until his vision returned to normal. In front of him, covered in carnage and sweat, stood Vanik. The *Te'Monai* that had tackled him was dead. The other one was too. They had both fallen by Vanik's knife.

Vanik had gone out of his way to help him, which was something that Atreus, admittedly, probably wouldn't have done for Vanik. Not here. He didn't ask why Vanik had stopped. And he didn't thank him.

A moment after pushing himself up, a force hit his legs and an arm wrapped around his waist. He groaned, stumbling back, but placed his free hand on top of the kid's head in an attempt to silence his cries.

"I'm fine. I'm okay," he huffed. "We need to keep moving."

He stepped toward the incline.

"*Don't*," Vanik hissed.

Atreus paused, looking back in question.

"Didn't you notice?" Vanik jerked his head skyward. "They're all going up."

Atreus backed away and followed Vanik's gaze. The *Te'Monai* crowded the cliffside now. They were crawling to the top, head to tail. In their mouths and wrapped in their tails were bodies. Sounds of hunting and death echoed from up on the cliffs, but down here, it was quiet.

Vanik and Atreus exchanged a wary glance and then silently moved back into the covering of the trees. They kept an eye out for *Te'Monai*, but none came. The screams in the distance faded. He expected the creatures to venture back down the cliff in search of more prey, but they didn't.

The three of them waited for the portals to appear to take them back. They waited . . . and waited.

He wasn't sure how much time had passed. He didn't know what the *Te'Monai* of this realm were doing or where they had gone. But one thing seemed abundantly clear as they stood among the trees in silence. He didn't want to believe it, but he didn't know what else to believe.

They had been left behind.

CHAPTER
TWENTY-THREE

Cressida couldn't back out of the challenge, not without embarrassing herself or bruising her ego. She seemed almost surprised that Lena would even issue such a challenge, but her face quickly morphed into something nasty again.

She laughed. "Do you even know how to use that thing?"

"You'll see, won't you?"

The rest of the crowd quietly watched the exchange. They couldn't interfere. Most of them were curious, waiting to see how things played out.

"Your Majesty, this is not a good idea," Cowen said in a low voice.

A duel, after all, was probably the only situation where her Sacred Guard wasn't allowed to interrupt. They had to stand by like everyone else.

She ignored Cowen like she'd ignored Ira and waited for Cressida's answer, but she knew what it would be.

They moved outside to a yard behind the palace, mostly made of loose gravel and dirt. Two palace wings extended from the main building to frame most of the space, but part of it was left open to the forest.

Mikhail had tried to pull her aside when they walked through the palace, but she'd shrugged him off. She hadn't seen Ira, but right now, she had eyes for no one but Cressida.

They would all see after this. They would understand that she wasn't that naive, weak Cursed girl anymore. People were already paying attention to her. Although her return was fairly recent, she'd ascended and gotten married, so she would use all that attention to her advantage and give them a show. She would prove that she was someone worth following. People were simple. When you couldn't convince them with words, kill them, or bribe them, you had to impress them.

The entirety of the throne room stood behind her, watching, waiting to be entertained. More people had come along when they heard the news of what was happening.

Cressida stood across from her in the yard. "Let's get on with it! I want to put Her Majesty in her place. Who's going to arbitrate?"

A few moments passed and then Alkus stepped forward. He stopped a few feet away and looked between them.

"Slayers?"

"Obviously," Cressida scoffed.

"Weapons?"

"No."

"Until what means?"

She and Cressida stared at one another. Lena kept her mouth shut, indicating that it was Cressida's choice. Noise rippled through the crowd. Death in Slayer duels was common enough, but no ruler had died in this way.

Cressida had an opportunity. A choice. But she said, "Until one of us forfeits or can no longer continue."

Lena smirked and ripped her dress so it stopped right at her knees. She tossed aside her shoes and dug her toes into the small gravel.

"Your seconds?" Alkus asked.

"Don't need one," they both said.

Anything else Alkus might have said, Lena didn't pick up. She was trembling with anticipation, and only part of that could be attributed to her Slayer. She felt its desires, its bloodlust, and its power spreading through her veins.

I hear you, she said. *We're going to make this quick.*

As soon as Alkus waved his hand and stepped back, she gave into the sensations, letting it all out.

It was both euphoric and disorienting, like she was breathing in the crispest air while also losing a limb. The essence that filled in the cracks of her being was pulled from her and she was left to reorient herself and find her balance.

Dealing with her Numen—her Slayer—had always been more mental than physical. With great power came the threat of great destruction. Slayers were finicky, deadly creatures, even with a fraction of their true power. Most Blessed couldn't call upon their Slayer until they were approaching their teen years because of the toll it took on their mind to summon and then control such a beast. But that meant they had over ten years to perfect the bond. She hadn't been afforded that time.

Through trial and error—and research made possible by breaking and entering—she'd learned to be aware of the risks but not scared of them. She wasn't her Slayer's master, but it couldn't be in this realm without her. There must be mutual respect but not worship. She couldn't falter when dealing with her Slayer. She needed to be firm with her intentions because it could sense her hesitation and choose to exploit it. If their connection became tainted, which could happen for a number of reasons, she could get Slayer Sickness, which was treatable but irritating, again, for a number of reasons. Being sick would be annoying enough, but losing access to her Slayer and potentially dying would also be a downside. The Numen she had a pact with would then have to find another Blessed if it wanted to explore this realm.

Her and her Slayer's interactions had become easier once their relationship stabilized, but it'd tried to test her many times in the beginning, and as a result, lots of blood, sweat, and tears had been shed. Her Slayer, like the Blessed, wanted her as a puppet more than it wanted her dead, but neither of them would get what they wanted.

Lena focused on Cressida and the power pulsing through her body. She was lighter. Her limbs were stronger, her eyesight clearer. She could fight and win.

Watch me. Watch.

Electricity and power crackled in the air. Heat radiated from her Slayer's form. Even in the daylight, the purple glow of her Slayer washed over their surroundings, as did the magenta hue of Cressida's. Both Slayers were curled low to the ground, growling and trembling, waiting for the moment to pounce. Sparks and wisps of pure energy fizzled around their skin, disappearing into thin air.

Lena's muscles relaxed as she let her instincts take over. She was back in the Lowlands, dealing with a dirtyhand. *Fast and brutal.* That was how she would handle them. And that was how she would handle Cressida.

When she moved, so did her Slayer. Cressida's sped forward. Flashes of indigo and magenta mixed as the two Slayers tangled with each other, clawing and snarling and biting.

Purple aura flame spread down Lena's arms, encasing them as she ran forward.

Most Blessed relied on their Slayer and aura flame to fight. The latter was what the former was made of, so it was also semi-corporeal and searing hot to anyone other than its user. Blessed sucked at simple hand to hand combat, so if she could slide in close, Cressida wouldn't stand a chance.

She shot her hand out and a misshapen sphere of aura flame flew toward Cressida, who deflected it easily, shielding herself with her own aura flame. She immediately shot an arrow back, which Lena dodged by sliding low to the ground. Still moving, she scooped up a handful of dirt. She was close enough now to throw a punch, but Cressida blocked it, leaving just enough of an opening for Lena to throw the dirt at Cressida's face. The blonde jerked back, sputtering as the dirt got into her eyes and mouth. She obviously wasn't expecting such a juvenile attack.

Lena landed a hit on her side, throwing Cressida off balance even more. She tried to get away and reorient herself, but Lena was already in. Cressida was sloppy. She had clearly underestimated Lena.

Cressida's aura flame shot back and latched onto the ground, keeping her from falling. Another stake of aura flame headed toward Lena. She didn't have time to dodge it entirely due to their close proximity, so it sliced through her dress sleeve and her skin, drawing first blood.

Cressida smirked.

Lena clenched her jaw and lunged. Her legs twisted around Cressida's, locking the Blessed in place, and her arm blocked the incoming hit. Their aura flames fizzled against one another. The heat was so intense it nearly singed Lena's hair. She steadied herself and then rotated her hips, bringing Cressida with her.

And then she roared.

Purple aura flame shot from the space in front of her mouth, heading right for Cressida's pristine face. The blonde's eyes widened as she jerked back. A thin wall of magenta aura flame tried to block it, and it managed to deflect Lena's attack at the expense of Cressida's focus and balance. And that was exactly what Lena wanted. She released Cressida, letting her fall to the ground.

When Cressida lost her *physical* balance, her mental balance went with it, causing her connection with her Slayer to waver. An opening was created, and Lena's Slayer took it, tackling Cressida's to the ground. It tried to fight back, but it was pinned, just like its bonded. When Lena's Slayer ripped into its neck, its form disappeared into the air.

Cressida scrambled to her feet, still disoriented. Her block was sloppy and one of Lena's aura flame-covered fists landed against her unprotected side. Lena didn't hold her hand there for long, but the smell of burning flesh was immediately noticeable. Cressida cried out and slouched over again. Lena kicked her to her knees and held a scorching hand next to her face.

"Move and I'll burn your face too." She would *gladly*. Cressida had saved herself by choosing to not fight 'till the death. "Forfeit."

Cressida gritted her teeth, and predictably, tried to attack Lena again. Her struggling stopped a split second later when Lena pressed one finger against Cressida's cheek.

"Stop! *Stop!*" she shrieked.

Lena did. She stepped back and Cressida slumped to the ground, holding her wounded side and gasping into the dirt. Lena's Slayer prowled off to the side, waiting for her to tell it to attack the writhing person it saw as food.

Not today, she told it before calling it back. Wisps of indigo were sucked away into the air as her Slayer faded much like Cressida's had.

The crowd shifted when she turned to them. They were quiet and staring at her with wide or wary eyes. Someone started slowly clapping. The spectators turned, trying to find the source, but she found it first. It was Sorrel.

Their guest was smirking, her eyes locked on Lena's as she clapped. Aquila stood behind her. Lena caught a glimpse of the startled expression on Aquila's face before it twisted into a scowl when she noticed Lena's gaze.

Someone moved behind the guests, temporarily snagging Lena's attention. She saw the side of his face before he turned and walked away. It was Ira.

She moved after him, her eyes on his back as he slipped through the crowd and toward the palace. He was tall, so she shouldn't have been able to lose him easily, but one moment he was there and the next he wasn't.

"Your Majesty, your wounds—"

"I'm fine," she insisted, stepping away from Mikhail.

She ran to the door. Cowen was already waiting for her there, but she motioned for him to stay. Though, he pushed back.

"I can't let you run off, especially after—"

"Stay *here*, Cowen."

She didn't give him time to respond. She hurried down the halls, hoping Ira hadn't completely disappeared yet. Blood dripped down her arm and onto the floor below, but she ignored her injury. It didn't hurt.

She turned a corner and saw Ira disappearing around another, so she picked up her speed.

"Ira!" She turned the next corner and saw him again. "Ira!"

He kept walking away, moving rather quickly himself. His steps were heavy and controlled.

She clenched her jaw in frustration. "Ira, *stop!*"

He halted in the middle of the hall, but he didn't turn. His shoulders were tense and noticeably rising and falling. It wasn't until she was a few steps away that Ira spun around. She paused, taken aback by the blaze in his eyes, but she recovered quickly, still running on the high of the victory.

"What's wrong? You just stormed off!"

"'*What's wrong?*'" Ira echoed. She frowned at the tone of his voice. "What's wrong with *me*? What's wrong with *you*?"

She flinched.

He flung his hand back, gesturing in the direction they'd just come from. "What the fuck was that?"

She hadn't seen him this angry in years. He'd always been more passive aggressive than not and more likely to avoid people altogether when frustrated instead of having an outburst. But that was exactly what he had been doing—*avoiding*—and she'd chased after him.

"What do you mean '*what the fuck was that?*' I challenged her to a duel because she was talking shit about me. Everyone was! They all doubted me, and now they don't. I won. You were there!"

"You shouldn't have done that," he said, taking a step back. His dark waves were wild again. "It was stupid. You're lucky your opponent underestimated you and you made it out easy. What happened to being agreeable? Making small moves—?"

"Not everyone can just sit by and allow people to spew shit about them and people they care about!"

Something flashed across Ira's face, and he stood up straighter, mouth in a tight line. "What? And you think it doesn't bother me when people say those things?"

She kept her mouth shut.

Ira scoffed. "They're baiting you, and you're falling for it. You haven't shown them anything—"

"I *have*."

"—except that you're still easy to manipulate."

She snapped her mouth shut and reeled back. The sting of his words cut straight into her heart. She'd known he wasn't going to be pleased but . . .

Silence sat between them.

Don't look at me like that, she wanted to say. *Not you.*

"I knew what I was doing," she said simply. She'd taken a gamble, and as far as she was concerned, it had paid off. "It'll be easier for me to gain allies now. For us."

"There was another way. There is always another way," Ira stressed. "But you were too impatient. You acted rashly and you could've gotten yourself killed."

"It wasn't until death. Only until one forfeited."

"But you left that choice up to her! It only takes one move, Lena! The difference between being cornered or injured and dead is just one blow. It happens so fast, and you can't take it back. Once it's done, it's done."

"I know that," she snapped. She'd seen her fair share of death.

"You have enemies here. You know how easy it would've been for one of them to tell Cressida to go in for the kill? Or for Cressida to make that decision herself? Rules be damned! A duel is the easiest and only legal way for them to kill you. An opportunity like that was what they were waiting for!"

"Well, they sure did fuck up then, didn't they? Because I'm still alive! I'm still standing!" She took a step forward, chest heaving. "Maybe I wanted to prove I'm not afraid of their games! That I'll play and *win*!"

Ira's laugh was short and cold, and his blue eyes were dark and burning. That ire was directed at *her*. She felt like she was fifteen again, stuttering over her words in his presence while he looked at her with nothing but contempt.

"This isn't how you do that," Ira said. "What about what we discussed at the cabin?"

"What about it?" she threw back. "I didn't lie. I *reacted*."

"You *chose* to duel! You weren't forced into it. You did it so you could show off."

The words were quiet and heavy, weighed down by something personal. She thought of the scars across Ira's skin and how young he'd been when forced into Slayer duels.

"You're wrong," she said firmly.

Even though she'd chosen to duel, she hadn't been showing off. Proving her power and capability wasn't showing off. For most of her life, she'd never had the privilege of doing something purely for those purposes. She'd needed to show them that she could be a threat. That she wasn't someone to be trifled with.

Ira stared at her, his eyes glossy. He looked away when he couldn't hold her gaze any longer and shook his head. And then he turned and walked away. Again.

She didn't chase after him this time, but words born from frustration and hurt left her mouth before she could think twice about them. "I thought you said you wouldn't run away!"

She immediately regretted the words, and then didn't when Ira kept walking. He hadn't even paused. Her words and feelings had bounced off his shields and fallen to the cold, marble floor.

There was a shift in the air a few seconds after Ira disappeared. She straightened right as she heard that grating, familiar voice.

"Trouble in paradise? And so soon after your honeymoon."

She grabbed the small dagger she'd secured at her wrist earlier and called on her Slayer as she turned on Tuck. Her Slayer began to form from her, the rough outline and details of its upper body rushing forward. And then she pulled it back before it could fully form. It was a useful distraction tactic she had learned months ago. A half-formed Slayer rushing at one's face was enough to send them stumbling back. Or, in Tuck's case, it was enough to make him hesitate, which was all she needed to swoop in and press him to the wall and her dagger against his neck.

"Cool trick."

"I told you if you snuck up on me again, I would make you bleed," she hissed, her hands already shaking.

"Actually, I don't think you got into the details," Tuck said. He looked far too comfortable for someone pinned with a dagger to their throat. "And I believe *I* told *you* that I'd be looking forward to whatever punishment you decided to give me."

"You get off on this, do you? On tormenting me?"

A bitter smile twisted his lips. "I have a feeling that you don't really want me to answer honestly."

She pressed the dagger deeper into his skin and watched the blood well up, but she still was insatiable. Long-lasting fury surged inside of her, burning away the lines she'd drawn for herself. Her recent interaction with Cressida and Ira only added to the fire. She wanted to make Tuck bleed, but she wanted to draw it out. Hurt him like he'd hurt her. He was on her list, and he was letting her dig her dagger into the delicate skin of his neck until it split and blood trailed down. He was just standing there. She imagined driving the blade farther and—

"Kalena."

She moved back. Only a little. But her dagger stayed against Tuck's neck. There was a wound, smaller than she'd envisioned, but it still bled steadily. Maybe if she was lucky, it would scar. Though Tuck hardly seemed bothered by it, much to her ire.

Cowen stood in the hall, staring at her apprehensively. She took a deep breath and pulled away from Tuck, taking several steps back as she put her dagger away.

He smoothly pushed himself off the wall and touched his neck. He stared at his bloodied fingers before touching them to his tongue. "I'm disappointed."

"Now you know what it's like."

The corner of Tuck's mouth twitched upward.

"Kalena," Cowen said again, but his voice was much less urgent this time.

Tuck didn't take his gaze off her, but he nodded in Cowen's direction. "Your knight in shining armor is here." He paused, folding his arms behind his back and contemplating something. "No, wait. That's Ira, isn't it? Or at least it was."

Her nails cut into her palms, but she forced herself to take another deep breath.

He's not worth it.

She walked past Tuck without saying another word and Cowen fell into step behind her.

CHAPTER
TWENTY-FOUR

Lena clapped politely when the next round of competitors stepped forward to present themselves to the crowd. The announcer read off their names, but she was barely paying attention. These festivities had been going on for hours now.

Despite everything that had happened, the celebration for her Ascension and marriage hadn't been canceled. She supposed the reasoning behind that decision was to save face in front of their guests and their own people. The celebration was supposed to go on for three days and three nights, which she thought was much too long, but she was required to attend. She was the one being celebrated, after all. Or so they said. The Blessed would take any opportunity to party.

Today was the first day and outdoor field games were on the agenda. So far, Lena had watched dozens of rounds of hammer throwing, horseshoes, wrestling, and now tug of war. There was still a lineup of games left to close out the day, but all she remembered from the schedule was that the last event was football.

She watched the competitors line up alongside the rope while fanning herself in the heavy heat. The air was dry, the wind absent, and the sun scorching. Her attendants had picked out a lighter dress for her today, one that was sleeveless and breathable, but the back of her neck continued to bead with sweat.

Along with the council members and their guests from Ouprua, she sat under a canopy that blocked the sun. Dozens of them littered the large green field next to the palace. Sorrel sat next to Lena; she was the only one of their guests who had stayed put.

Lena had seen Von competing in some of the games. Mikhail had been afraid of what would happen if he'd denied Von's request to participate in the festivities.

Now that she thought about it, it hadn't really been a request. Von smashed the competition and seemed to truly enjoy partaking in the events, but she wondered if Von's actions were calculated and his participation was a way for Ouprua to showcase their strength to the broader public of The Lands. After all, this celebration was one of the only times the Cursed were allowed to enter the Highlands.

Aquila and Kieryn had disappeared, Aquila first and then Kieryn about thirty minutes later. Sorrel didn't seem too concerned by their absence, even when council members would look back at their guests' empty seats.

"The games don't hold your interest?" Sorrel asked.

Lena continued to fan herself as she stared at the competition before her. "They're fine."

"But not entertaining?"

"Maybe they would be in different weather."

Sorrel laughed. "It is very hot and stagnant here. In Ouprua, there's a constant breeze that rolls in from the ocean. Keeps Ouprua bearable. The storms are a pain in the ass, though."

Lena hummed and moved her gaze from the field so she could look at the other stands. She had field glasses, but using those would make what she was doing quite obvious. She hadn't seen Ira since their fight in the hall the other day.

"Looking for someone?"

"No," Lena murmured as she dragged her eyes back to the game. "There's just . . . quite a lot of people here."

"Yes, well it's not every day that a new ruler is crowned. *And* married," Sorrel added as an afterthought. "Say, where is your spouse? I don't think I've met them."

Lena picked up her glass of water and took a sip. She had waved away the wine when the cupbearer offered it to her. Sorrel had not.

"He's been busy."

"Too busy for his wife?"

Lena's fingers clenched around the glass. "We've both been busy. We spent lots of uninterrupted time together during our honeymoon."

"Tired of him already?"

"No," she said, her voice hard. "That won't happen."

"He was the one you went chasing after the other day, wasn't he?" Sorrel took a sip from her chalice of wine. "He seemed upset."

"Yes, well, he was worried."

The spectators cheered when one team triumphed over the other. Another round of contenders took their place.

Sorrel shifted on her chair and crossed her legs. "Eh, you did what had to be done."

Lena hesitated before asking, "You think so?"

Sorrel snorted and leaned toward Lena. "Let me tell you something. When people give you shit, you gotta throw it back at 'em twice as hard and twice as large.

That's the only way they'll stop. Some people will tell you to fight with words or take the high route, whatever that shit means. But you know what's funny? They don't tell everyone that. They only tell those they wish to silence. I had a brother. My parents never told him those things."

Lena's parents had treated her and her siblings fairly and equally. They'd catered to each of their kids' needs and interests but taught all three of them the same lessons and discouraged them from fighting because, in their words, it often brought on more trouble than it resolved.

"Maybe they had good intentions," she murmured, still lost in thought. "Maybe they believed it would keep you safe."

"They didn't," Sorrel said before taking another swig from the chalice. "Maybe that's the case for others, but something I've learned over the past thirty years of my life is that people will always question those in power if their ideals don't match their own. Especially if they're young."

Lena cleared her throat and turned back to the field, deciding it was time to steer the conversation in another direction. "So, you're their leader?"

Sorrel shrugged and went with the change. "For this trip."

"But not back in the Isles—?" Lena caught herself. "Sorry. That's what we call it here. You're not the leader back in *Ouprua*?"

Sorrel smirked and fiddled with the rings on her fingers, but she didn't say anything about the mistake. "You ask a lot of questions."

"I'm a curious person."

"Insatiable?"

"Maybe."

"For every question I answer of yours, you have to answer one of mine."

Lena hesitated but nodded.

"Under our law, I'm not recognized as a leader. I don't have a title, and I won't ever have one because of my crimes. I killed two people when I was younger."

Another round of cheers filled the air as another game ended. Lena didn't care to know which team had won.

Sorrel continued as if she was describing the weather and not murder. "I don't regret it. They deserved it, but because of the law, I can't serve in government, which is fine by me. It's very tedious. Lots of paperwork and rules you have to follow." She gave Lena a sharp grin. "I like the freedom my current position allows."

"Which is? What's your current position?"

Sorrel waved her hand in the air as she searched for the right words. Her rings glittered, even in the shade. "I'm an . . . envoy? An opportunist? A voyager? Something along those lines. I find titles to be so constricting sometimes."

Lena understood that. "And Ouprua still chose to send you here?"

"Yes."

"Why?"

Her sharp grin returned. "Because I always deliver the best results."

Perhaps Sorrel meant to intimidate her, but Lena was more curious than anything.

"How?" she found herself asking. Her mind was elsewhere, thinking of other battles. "What you said before leads me to believe you're not too fond of fighting with words or taking the high route."

"Words are important up to a point. Then you have to take action."

"And how do you do that? Do you use your Numen?"

"Oh, no." Sorrel raised her hand to flag down a cupbearer. "I don't have an Imprint."

Lena fought to keep her reaction minimal.

Sorrel was Cursed. Like Lena has been. Maybe she still was. She didn't know what to call herself. But seeing another Cursed in a leadership position—even though the title wasn't officially recognized by Ouprua—was rare.

She must've failed in keeping her thoughts off her face because Sorrel said, "Don't make the mistake of thinking I'm Cursed. We don't go by that inane system in Ouprua."

Lena's brows rose and she looked around. Cowen stood behind her, so he'd heard what Sorrel had said, but it appeared that no one else had. The cheers that signified another game ending had likely covered her words. Lena thought the system was brutish too, but it was the way things had always been. She didn't agree with it though. She aimed to change what she could, but there were many people who didn't want that. And those same people would take issue with someone, especially an outsider, critiquing that system.

She pried a bit more. "But . . . surely you must have something like Imprints in Ouprua?"

Sorrel hummed and looked away, toward the far side of the field. "Sure we do," she said tonelessly.

Lena could tell from Sorrel's answer and body language that she didn't want to delve into this topic.

If Sorrel didn't have an Imprint, did that mean there were others in Ouprua who did? Or were Imprints not a thing there? How was that possible? *Everyone* should be Cursed or Blessed. Whatever the case, Lena doubted Ouprua would send people here who didn't have the ability to protect themselves. Did Sorrel have something else up her sleeve? Or did someone else? Von certainly could overpower people with pure strength alone, but he couldn't beat a Slayer. What about Aquila and Kieryn? Lena knew practically nothing about them, only that Aquila seemed to despise her despite them never having interacted, and Kieryn appeared to be completely uninterested in this whole trip aside from the party.

"I believe I answered more than enough of your questions," Sorrel said. "I'll only ask one now and take the rest as credit." She set her drink down. "Have you thought any more about the alliance and the marriage?'

Lena saw that one coming. "May I ask why you are so adamant that a marriage should be what seals the alliance?"

Sorrel's brows lowered. "I answered your questions, Your Majesty. Now it's time you answer mine."

"I have thought about it," Lena said carefully, "but I have yet to reach a decision. We haven't called a council meeting since the day you arrived."

"Well, I do hope you make a decision soon," Sorrel sighed. "We won't be here forever."

Lena nodded. "Of course. Just . . . another marriage would be a lot right now. The Lands has many matters to deal with—"

"We could postpone the actual ceremony. An engagement with an oath to marry in the future is all that would be needed to establish an alliance."

An oath was heavier than a promise. It was a public declaration overseen by the Numina. Breaking an oath had physical consequences, possibly even death.

"But making a decision now would still be binding, even if the ceremony was postponed," Lena gingerly pointed out. It was still a big choice to make. She considered the question resting on the tip of her tongue. Part of her didn't even want to entertain this idea, but she'd said she would think about it. If things got worse, she would have to agree. "Do I even know who I would be marrying?"

"Of course. I brought them along."

Lena once again fought to keep her expression neutral. "What?"

"Kieryn or Aquila," Sorrel supplied, shrugging. "Whoever holds your fancy."

She didn't fancy *either* of them.

"I don't think Kieryn has looked at me once since your arrival. Aquila, on the other hand, has looked at me with nothing but malice."

Sorrel essentially waved off her concern. "They're both a bit difficult, but you have nothing to fear."

"And they know that they could possibly be getting engaged?"

"They're aware of their duties," Sorrel said. "Are you?"

Before Lena could respond, cheers broke out again, louder than any time before. She winced and turned toward the field. The game had changed to dagger throwing, but the uproar had been caused by who was competing.

Tuck had made an appearance, leaving whatever canopy he'd been resting under to step onto the field. He waved gallantly at the crowd, a stupid smirk on his face. He accepted a flower from one spectator and kissed the back of another's hand. Lena rolled her eyes at his display.

Nine throwing daggers were placed in front of him. There were three targets about thirty, forty, and fifty-five feet away from where he stood. He picked up one of the daggers and kissed it before leveling it directly at her. She glared at him.

Tuck turned back toward the targets, found his footing, cocked his arm back, and then snapped it forward. His movements were smooth and quick, and the dagger sailed through the air, invisible until it lodged in the first target. Bullseye.

Tuck launched two other daggers in quick succession. They all hit their mark on the first target. And the crowd was eating it up. Tuck, in turn, thrived off their cheers.

Lena frowned. She turned back to Sorrel and simply said, "I am, but I will never blindly do what others want."

And then she pushed herself to her feet and strode down the stairs and across the grassy field before anyone could stop her. The crowd parted for her, and she halted right in front of the target range. Tuck watched her, green eyes glittering.

"Your Majesty," one of the staff members said hesitantly, "what are you—?"

"I want to compete."

The staff member balked. "Pardon?"

"I want to compete," she repeated firmly.

The man looked around like he expected someone to come and fire him on the spot. Or maybe for someone to come and tell him what to do in this situation.

"Sir Vuukroma is currently competing—"

"It's fine," Tuck intervened. His smirk only widened when she moved her gaze to him. "Her Majesty can step in. We'll take turns. Like a proper match."

Upon Tuck's approval, the man ran off to collect another set of daggers.

Lena turned, a noise of disgust leaving her. Now that she was this close to Tuck, she could see the cut she'd left on his throat. There was a bruise around it. He gestured toward the table in front of him. Six daggers remained.

She moved forward, running her gaze and fingers over each dagger. Some were more worn down than others, and natural grooves had formed along the hilt, their shape and depth a result of how often said dagger had been handled and by who.

Once she had her three daggers, she stepped up to the line and set her eyes on the first target. Tuck's daggers had been removed to leave space for hers. She let the first dagger fly.

Bullseye.

She did the same with the second and third dagger. Both of those were right in the center too. The crowd went wild.

"I like that dress," Tuck said as he stepped up to the line to take his turn again.

All three of his daggers hit the center of the second target.

The staff member from before had returned with nine more daggers. She picked hers and lined up again. She took a deep breath, blocking out the whistles and cheers of the crowd. They were enjoying this, but she wasn't doing it for them.

She let the daggers sail through the air. *One. Two. Three.*

She stepped back with a satisfied smile. Her confidence and adrenaline uplifted her mood. Only slightly.

"Didn't think to cover it up, did you?" Lena asked Tuck, tapping on the base of her neck.

"Now why would I cover up a mark you left on me?" He brushed past her, picking out his final three daggers.

"Does the bruising run deeper?" she asked. Tuck had always been frustratingly nonchalant. All Blessed had huge egos, but it was truly hard to tell with him. "For most, it does."

And maybe she imagined it, but she thought she saw Tuck glance to the side. Lena followed his gaze and found his parents. The three of them sat under a canopy, an empty chair among them.

Tuck threw his round and stepped back. Only two had hit the bullseye. One was slightly off.

She turned on him, prepared to accuse him of pulling his punches *again*, but when she saw the look on his face, she knew his misthrow had truly been a mistake.

Her daggers all landed in the center. The crowd cheered louder than ever.

She glanced back at Tuck, admittedly feeling a bit smug. The student had surpassed the master.

Not even a full minute had passed since Tuck's slip-up, but he had completely recovered. Lena had stepped up because she'd wanted to knock him down a peg, show him that he wasn't as great as he thought he was. She'd wanted to see just a *little* frustration simmering in his eyes, but much to her irritation, he looked more amused than anything.

"Nice throws," he said. "I wonder who taught you that."

Flashes of leaves and bloody nicks on her fingers and a treehouse filled her mind.

She sneered at Tuck before turning away and heading back to her seat. Sorrel smirked and looked at her with something akin to approval. She lifted her chalice as Lena approached as if to say *well played*.

CHAPTER
TWENTY-FIVE

Lena excused herself toward the end of the games, saying she wanted to look at the small marketplace that had been set up by vendors on the other side of the palace. Thankfully, no one tried to follow her. She was alone with her thoughts, save for Andra and Benji a few paces behind her. They'd stepped in for Cowen an hour ago.

For the first time since it was proposed, she truly thought about the marriage pact. At least now she knew her marriage options, though neither of them was really that great. She didn't know them, and they didn't seem to want to get to know her, but even if they did, there wasn't enough time for that to happen. She'd been in this same situation before her marriage to Ira, but instead of her position as Queen being on the line this time, it was a vital alliance that would strengthen their country.

She sighed and weaved through the stalls and tents, letting her mind wander as she took in the new sights, smells, and sounds. The marketplace was crowded and filled with booths of all shapes and sizes. Some were only a table, others were large tents. The items they sold varied greatly as well, from food to clothing to weapons to elixirs to household items to random little knickknacks that served no purpose other than entertainment. Music played from somewhere nearby. She heard the plucking of banjo strings, perhaps? And a flute? Countless delicious smells wafted through the air, blending with one another so she couldn't make out what was what.

Kids ran through the lanes, screeching and laughing as they chased each other. While watching the field games, she'd seen a few parents leave their seats with their squirming kids. She couldn't fault the children. Sitting through all of those games hadn't been fun for her either.

Some people tried to approach her, but she politely waved them aside. Thankfully, they didn't push, and neither did the vendors.

Benji and Andra were close behind her. They were paranoid, hands on their swords, even though they would use their Imprints to defend her first, and eyes darting about as if they expected someone to step out from between the stalls and attack her.

Lena caught sight of something that held her attention. Some*one*. They were ahead of her and in the row over, so she could only see their back, which wasn't much since they had a cloak on and their hood up. But something about them was familiar. She was taken back to that night in the Lowlands during her honeymoon. Someone had been spying on her then, and perhaps they still were.

She sped up her step, keeping her eyes on the cloaked person. Stalls would block her view momentarily, but she always found her target again. They weren't running, which meant they didn't know she was onto them, or they knew and were trying to lure her away. Lena moved to the side and slipped between two stalls, now in the same row as the spy.

"Your Majesty?" Andra questioned.

"I just want to go over here," she said absently as she maneuvered around the crowd.

She walked faster, nearly jogging. She didn't want to draw too much attention to herself and alert the spy if they weren't already aware they had a tail. Not to mention they were in public during the *day*. Lena tried to act like nothing was wrong and shot kind smiles to anyone who caught her eye. Her gaze never strayed from the spy for long.

They turned a corner and were suddenly in a maze of large, tall tents. Everywhere she turned, she saw giant stretches of fabric. Hidden from most onlookers, she picked up her pace, making sure she didn't trip over any stakes or ropes.

The spy sped up too. If they hadn't been aware of Lena before, they certainly were now, but she wasn't going to lose them again. She sprinted, pushing power into her muscles and gaining on the spy. If Lena lunged, there was a good chance she could grab their fluttering cloak, but she didn't want to risk it.

The Numina must've been looking down on her today or maybe her plethora of bad luck had finally tipped the scale in her favor. Whatever the case, the spy made a sloppy move and ended up tripping over a slim wire extending from one of the tents. They went down hard but, to their credit, were scrambling up seconds later, though Lena was already on them.

She shoved them back down, her legs pinning theirs to the ground and her hands locking around their wrists. Power still pulsed through her, adding to her strength. The spy bucked fiercely, trying to get away.

Lena gritted her teeth and channeled more power into her arms, giving another harsh shove that knocked the breath out of the spy. Quickly, Lena tugged back the hood, and then she froze, shock having taken hold of her completely.

"Aquila?"

The woman's eyes widened. All Lena could do was stare. Those eyes . . . She *knew* them.

Aquila lunged forward, and because Lena was too stunned to move, their heads collided.

She felt pain. And then nothing.

～

"Alright. Let me see you."

Lena took a deep breath and glanced at the cracked mirror one last time. She certainly looked different, and she felt it too. Her head was lighter than usual, and her shoulders were cold and bare with those several inches gone from her hair. She turned and surveyed her clothing. It really didn't matter what she thought. Julian had the final say.

She pushed the door open and stepped into the room. The squeaking hinges grated on her ears as the door swung back and forth behind her, the only sound reverberating through the room as Julian surveyed her from under the rim of his straw hat. He sat on a stool, facing her and leaning back against the bar. The pint of beer next to him was nearly empty. She knew that wasn't his first, but he still looked as alert as ever.

He squinted and scratched his stubbled chin. "Hmmm, your face is still too soft. It wouldn't be as much of an issue if you were younger but . . . just keep your chin down. And streak some more dirt across your face. Turn to the side."

She did.

"Lucky you're as skinny as a stick. Baggy clothin' and wrap is all it takes—Oh, don't give me that look! It's a good thing! More meat on your bones gives people more to grab on to."

"Is that why you eat and drink so much?" Lena grumbled as she turned to face him once again. Even though he did . . . indulge, he was in good shape.

"I can 'cause no one ever comes close to catchin' me." He winked at her. "Now give me a full spin."

She sighed but did as she was told.

"Let me hear your voice."

She cleared her throat and said something in the deeper tone she'd practiced for hours.

"Good, but just to be safe, try to limit your talkin'. And keep your voice down. What's your name?"

"Cal."

"And where'd you come from?"

"A small town in the east. My father caught a sickness and didn't make it. My mother and siblings take care of the house, but I go out and run errands for money."

Julian had taught her to keep the explanations vague and emphasize the emotions.

The delivery was more important than the words. Never let someone haggle you for more details. That was a red flag. Get out of there as quickly as possible without drawing attention to yourself.

Julian dragged the pint closer to him. "And you know what you're supposed to do?"

He kept his eyes locked on Lena's for a few moments longer than necessary. She nodded. Ever since telling her what the gig was, he'd also told her not to repeat it aloud.

"Good." He nodded and chugged the rest of the pint. He slammed it down and then raised his voice slightly. "Quil! You can come in here now."

Another door opened and Aquila—Quil—stepped into the room. She had already been checked by Julian, but he likely wanted to speak to them together before sending them off.

"Remember what I taught both of you, yeah?"

"All you've taught us is how to steal and cheat," Aquila said. Her frown was deep, and her downturned brows cut harsh lines across her face. "When are you going to teach us—?"

"Ah, ah, ah."

Julian held up a finger. His hands were gloved. They almost always were, even in the dreadful heat of the warm season. Lena and Aquila had seen him without gloves only twice. She'd expected to see horrible scars across his hands, but it wasn't an injury he was hiding. It was marks. Tattoos. *It didn't take a genius to connect the dots. They were important—the tattoos—and that was why he had to hide them. Those tattoos were connected to his sorcery.*

"How do you think you survive in a realm that forces you to resort to trickery?"

Aquila frowned. "You . . . have to be strong. Stronger than those you're up against."

Julian lowered his finger so that he was pointing at Aquila. "Wrong. You have to be smarter. It doesn't matter if you have all the strength in the realms. If you're reckless with it, you'll get caught. And soon as you're caught, your time is limited."

"So stealing and cheating is supposed to what? Make us smarter?" Aquila sneered.

Julian barely batted an eye. He leaned back, resting his elbows on the bar. "That's for you to figure out, kid. Now off you go. And don't mess up. I won't always be there to save you."

Aquila grumbled something else. Lena was still staring at his gloved hands as she headed for the door. Julian caught her gaze.

"And remember," he said before they left, "you're not my responsibility, you hear?"

∼

LENA WOKE up with tears and dried blood on her face.

"Your Majesty," Benji said, a note of relief in his voice as he knelt over her.

She was on the ground.

Why was she on the ground?

Her memories came back to her in pieces, their jagged edges violently searching for their match inside her head. She shifted and flinched at the sharp ache that went through her skull.

"Careful," Benji said. "You were hit pretty hard."

She was hit?

She squeezed her eyes shut, and when she opened them, the ringing in her ears disappeared, and the medley of background noise became audible once again.

Everything returned to her then. She was at the festival. In the booths. She'd seen the person from the Lowlands. The spy. And it was Aquila. Lena, like an amateur, had frozen and Aquila had gotten the upper hand.

"Fuck," she exhaled. She pulled herself straight up, ignoring Benji's concern and the throbbing in her head. "*Fuck*."

She'd been outside when Aquila knocked her out, but now she was in one of the tents. She prodded at her nose and hissed. Some of the blood flaked off and landed in her lap. Her eyes were sore and swollen too. She could imagine how she looked—a split and bloody nose and two black eyes. A great look for the ball tomorrow.

"Andra is getting Cowen and a physician. She should be back soon. We can report the assassination attempt once—"

"What?" Lena straightened. "No, no, no. There was no assassination attempt. Nothing will be reported."

Benji frowned. "Your Majesty . . . you were attacked. You are the queen. We need to—"

"You don't actually need to," she interrupted. "I'm telling you not to. It wasn't an assassination attempt. If it was, they would've finished the job as soon as I fell unconscious. But they didn't. It was a harmless attack."

"It wasn't harmless! You were bleeding!"

"It's stopped."

"And you could be concussed."

She had been concussed before, but this was not what it felt like. What was throwing her off was something else entirely; she was certain about that.

"You will not report it, do you understand? Your queen is telling you to leave it alone."

Benji didn't argue further, though she was sure Cowen would.

This wasn't the first time an incident had happened to her under the Sacred Guard's watch. There had now been two in about two weeks; three if you counted her sneaking out in the Lowlands. Lena should perhaps be more upset with her Sacred Guard, but she didn't rely on them for her protection. She didn't trust them —not really. She expected them to *not harm her* and that was about it. And their inadequacies made it easier for her to sneak away unnoticed when she wanted.

Benji stood up and grabbed a wet cloth from a bowl of water. He pressed it into her hands. "Did you see who attacked you?"

She looked at the small mirror on the table next to her. It reminded her of the one she'd seen in that vision . . . no, *memory*. Except this one was much nicer. " . . . No. I didn't."

Benji stared at her strangely, and she waited for him to call her out. She didn't know how close he and Andra had been behind her; they *should* have been right behind her, but for everyone's sake, she hoped they hadn't been. Because if they had, they would've seen her entanglement with the spy. They would know it was Aquila, and Benji would know she was lying. But he didn't say anything.

Lena washed the dried blood off her face and took in the damage. It wasn't as bad as she'd thought. Blessed truly did heal quickly, and they took less damage. There was a cut across the bridge of her nose and a bit of swelling, but hardly any discoloration. Perhaps it'd been worse but had faded to a yellow-green that wasn't as noticeable in the poor lighting.

"How long has it been?"

"Only about fifteen minutes, Your Majesty," Benji said. Then a moment later, he asked, "What were you chasing?"

"Nothing. It . . . I thought I saw something, but it was nothing."

She turned the mirror away, unable to look at her reflection.

"You can't run off like that, Your Majesty. This incident might not have been fatal, but another could easily be. We can't protect you if you keep running from us."

I don't need your protection, was at the tip of her tongue, but she knew that would only escalate the situation. And he wasn't *wrong*. She needed to be smart about when and where she ditched her Sacred Guard.

Benji inched closer and lowered his voice. "Cowen told Andra and I something when we were first brought on. He said it would be hard for you once you returned . . . that you would have enemies everywhere." Benji paused, contemplating something. "Even possibly in the Sacred Guard, and that we couldn't let that affect you. We had to be there to protect you from any threat, even ones you didn't know about."

So her suspicions were correct. Alkus had infiltrated the Sacred Guard with people loyal to him. Unlike her attendants, she wasn't easily able to replace members in the Sacred Guard. She had been around Benji, Andra, and Cowen the most, and now she knew why. Cowen had a select few he trusted.

"He didn't want to worry you with this, but he also said you'd probably have your doubts."

She did.

Lena took a moment to observe Benji. He appeared earnest, and perhaps that was what made him look so young even though he was closer to Cowen's age than her own. Benji had a certain kind of innocence about him. He was a free spirit. Andra balanced him out with her penchant for rules and schedules. They were both smart, Lena had noticed, but in different ways. Benji was more street smart while

Andra was book smart. They worked well together, and Lena found that she really didn't mind their company.

Someone entered the tent and Lena and Benji turned, expecting Andra and Cowen, but found a feeble old woman instead.

Benji stood. "I'm sorry, ma'am, but you can't be in here."

"This is my tent," the woman croaked. Her gray hair was pulled tight against her scalp and her face was lined with dozens of deep wrinkles. She continued to hobble farther inside.

Lena and Benji exchanged a look.

"I'm sorry," Benji repeated. "But we need it for a little bit longer. The queen is injured. We're waiting for guards and a physician."

The woman looked at Lena, squinting.

Lena smiled hesitantly. "I apologize for the inconvenience. Maybe we could buy some things from you. For your troubles." She pushed herself to her feet. "What are you selling?"

The old woman continued to stare at her. "Visions."

Lena blinked. "What?"

The woman smiled, showing her toothless gums. "I'm selling visions. Would you like one?"

"Oh." A weight plummeted to the depths of her stomach, twisting her insides. "No, thank you, actually—"

With the speed and strength of someone a quarter her age, the old lady rushed up to Lena and grabbed her shirt in an iron grip. Her eyes were wide and almost pleading, the blue of them too pale.

"You're in danger," the woman said, her voice hushed so no one else could hear. "You should have never come back."

Benji wrenched the woman off Lena and dragged her away. The lady cackled wildly.

Lena took a step forward, eyes wide and hands shaking. "Stop! Benji, *stop*!"

He released the old woman, but she didn't try to catch herself. She crumpled to the ground, her hysterical laughter filling the tent.

CHAPTER
TWENTY-SIX

After some debate, Atreus and Vanik decided to seek out high ground. They avoided the cliffs and headed in a different direction, knowing they ran the risk of coming across more *Te'Monai*. They didn't want to get stuck down in the trees where the *Te'Monai* could easily hide. Some elevation would give them a lay of the land, and then they could make a plan.

Judah's hysteria had calmed. He was numb but not in a state of shock, which was good for now. Atreus stayed close to the kid, ready to grab him and run if anything went amiss.

And he did just that—snagged Judah by his uniform collar—when he heard a noise to the right.

"Atreus?"

He froze, and the adrenaline slowly drained from his aching muscles. He untangled his fingers from Judah's jacket as Finn stepped out from behind a tree. His face and clothes were streaked with dirt and blood, but he was *alive*.

Atreus swept his gaze over his friend's body, watching him approach. "You're limping."

"I twisted my ankle. It's nothing serious," Finn assured him.

The two embraced. He gripped Finn's back tightly as the knot in his chest loosened. He looked over his friend's shoulder, waiting to see if anyone else was going to appear. No one did.

"Mila?" he asked as they stepped apart.

Finn's mouth twisted and he shook his head. "I don't know. We were separated."

She'll be alright, Atreus wanted to say, but there was no guaranteeing that. False promises of hope hurt more than accepting the worst fate, but that hadn't stopped him from making a promise to those kids.

The knot tightened once again.

Finn glanced at Judah and smiled. It was a small thing, the corners of his lips barely raising, his mouth trembling. There was pain in his eyes. Atreus understood. Finn, after all, had shown up alone.

It was then that Finn noticed someone else was nearby. His eyes widened and his voice came out a little choked. "Vanik?"

"Finnian," Vanik stated dryly. He stood off to the side, eyes lazily flicking between the two of them.

Finn's eyes went back to Atreus. "What are you doing with him?"

"I am right here," Vanik said in the same dry tone. "And for your information, I saved his sorry ass, so you're welcome."

Finn looked at Atreus differently now, but only for a moment. They didn't waste time thinking about *what-if*s.

"What's going on?"

"I don't know exactly, but I have a guess," Atreus said.

Vanik huffed and started walking away.

"And where are you going?" Finn called after him.

"High ground," Vanik replied without stopping or turning. "To get a look at the situation. That's where we were headed before you came along. You *can* walk and talk, right?" There was a pause. "Actually, it's better if you can't. How about you walk and don't talk at all."

Finn and Atreus exchanged a tired glance and trudged after Vanik. Atreus explained his hunch to Finn as they walked.

He had no proof that they'd been left behind, but he knew the prophets wouldn't harbor any guilt over leaving them here. And this Outing was different than all the others before. The kids were the first clue. The delayed return was the second. But there were still so many pieces that didn't make sense. The prophets needed them to continue running the Institute. Even if they wanted to wipe the firstborns out and start anew, they would need someone to show the new kids how things operated.

"Do you . . . know where Harlow, Weylin, and Aspen are?" Finn asked hesitantly.

Vanik's shoulders jerked in a shrug and he said curtly, "No. I'm not their keeper."

"Are the monsters gone?" a quiet voice asked.

"For now," Atreus told Judah.

"I can't believe you adopted a kid," Vanik groaned as he climbed over a rock. The ground was slowly beginning to slope upward.

Atreus ignored him and helped Judah over the rock, and then Finn when his ankle proved to be troublesome.

"You need help getting—?"

"I'm fine," Finn claimed.

The hill they were scaling wasn't too steep, but it was plenty tall. The grass disappeared a third of the way up and sandy soil and rocks made up the hillside for the rest of the journey. Atreus kept an eye on both Finn and Judah to make sure neither of them slipped. They walked slowly, taking careful but sturdy steps—which irritated Vanik to no end—and surveyed the hillside to make sure no *Te'Monai* were hiding nearby. The ascent took them a good thirty minutes because of how long the incline stretched.

"Well, I'll be damned," Vanik huffed when they reached the top.

Apparently, they hadn't been the only ones with the idea to get to high ground.

"You fuckers!" Vanik spat, but he had a grin on his face as he strode forward and nearly tackled Weylin to the ground.

But Weylin was ready for him and only staggered back under his weight, a slight smile of relief on his lips. Atreus didn't miss the way his fingers dug into Vanik's uniform, or the unusual paleness of his face.

"You survived," Weylin exhaled, his eyes a bit far away.

"You bet your ass I did. I'm guessing the *Te'Monai* didn't want a taste of your ugly self." Vanik pulled back then, and upon seeing the look on Weylin's face, the grin slipped off his. "What's wrong?"

Harlow came over then, and Vanik's eyes swept over her as he drew her in for a hug, too.

Atreus held back, watching the interaction.

Vanik was an asshole, but Atreus didn't hate him. That emotion was reserved for the prophets. He wouldn't befriend Vanik, but he recognized his abrasiveness as a sort of defense mechanism. They all had their methods and it helped keep them alive. It shielded them from their reality and the feelings that came with it, but pieces —*people*—always made it through the cracks.

A groan reached their ears. Aspen lay on the ground a few feet away. She gave Vanik a weak smile.

Vanik strode over to her and crouched down. "What happened?"

"Bitten in the side," Harlow said, her voice tight. "It didn't lock down on her, but . . . she's bleeding quite a bit."

"I'm fine," Aspen hissed. Her skin was unusually pale, and her breathing was ragged even when lying down. "I told them I was fine."

Vanik pressed his lips together but didn't argue with her. "Rest," he said simply before walking to the other side of the hilltop.

Weylin and Harlow followed him. Atreus turned away after seeing Weylin put a hand on Vanik's back.

Over the next thirty minutes, more people climbed to the top of the hill. Their injuries varied from minor to critical. Despite his own injury, Finn tried to go over and help, but Atreus pulled him back.

Mila showed up too, and the dread that had been building inside of him eased a bit when he saw her. She looked exhausted and had a deep cut on her forearm but that appeared to be the worst of it.

Finn gave her a weary but relieved smile and squeezed her hand when she sat down next to them.

Atreus looked over her closely, trying to see if he'd missed something. She caught his gaze, knowing what he was searching for, and shook her head. Her hand landed on his leg, a warm, comforting weight. *Real.*

"Fine," she said, her gaze unwavering.

And there it was again.

Fine.

It was the best term they had for their situation. It was relative. Because their fine wasn't actually fine.

Eventually, the flow of people stopped, and they knew no one else was coming.

Only the injured slept, dragged under by their pain. Grunts and cries filled the air as people tended to wounds. The ones who were unharmed or better off sat or stood silently to the side, lost in thought and shaken by the events they'd witnessed.

There were about a hundred of them on this hill. Fewer than ten of the kids.

"This can't be all of us . . . right?" Finn asked.

The four of them had claimed a spot a good distance away from everyone else. Finn had his injured foot propped up on Mila's lap, and Judah sat close to Atreus' side, not touching him but only a hair's breadth away. The kid's knees were curled under his chin and he stared pointedly at the ground, the knife still clutched in his hand.

Others across the hilltop had sat as time passed, but no one had dropped their guard since the last *Te'Monai* sighting two hours ago.

Atreus shrugged, tossing aside the false promise at his lips. "This is all we have."

The group sat in silence for another hour. The sun was setting and shadows rose, which only put them more on edge.

But as time ticked away, his muscles loosened and his eyes drew heavy, though the rest of him was awake and fighting to stay that way. Finn and Mila were likely battling the same sensation, but eventually, Mila's chin dipped to her chest and Finn's eyes gradually close. Judah had already slipped under.

Atreus let them rest because he couldn't. He rotated the knife in his hands and counted, his eyes flitting to the three often to make sure they were still there and safe. They looked younger when they slept, the lines of stress melting away when the night terrors were absent. Times like this reminded him of how young they all were. How unfair this all was.

There was an unspoken decision to set up camp on the hill. No one uttered a word about them being *stuck* here and what that could mean, but they did need to replenish their energy. They agreed to take turns on watch so others could sleep.

Vanik, Weylin, Harlow, and Aspen left. They weren't willing to put their safety in anyone's hands but their own. A few others trailed back down the hillside too. No one stopped them.

Atreus took the first watch, and before he knew it, someone tapped his shoulder. He went back to Mila, Finn, and Judah, and after being on lookout, his body and mind were spent. He was finally able to fall asleep.

But the *Te'Monai* crawled out in the dark.

The screams of the unlucky were what warned everyone else. Firstborns scrambled to their feet, trying to regain their bearings.

Atreus woke in an instant. The knife fit into his hand like it was an extension of his body, and he grabbed Judah.

Finn and Mila were already up. They hurried down the hill, Atreus hauling Judah along while Mila supported Finn. It was hard to see in the dark, so they slid on the loose rock more than once, but thankfully, never tumbled.

They ran and ran and ran. Until Finn's ankle proved to be an issue. Atreus passed Judah over to Mila while he took Finn, and they kept going, only stopping when Judah grew too tired and Atreus could no longer support Finn's weight.

Everything in him screamed against stopping, telling him to keep moving, but he couldn't leave them behind.

They found water and stole a few gulps before spitting it out when the salt burned their throat and chapped lips. The four of them coated themselves in a thick layer of mud in the hope that it would throw off the *Te'Monai*. And then they ran again until they found shelter in what looked to be a den.

He and Mila traded looks, likely thinking the same thing. There was no way to tell if it belonged to something else—something dangerous—but they were running out of options and energy. They placed Finn and Judah in the back of the small cave while the two of them sat at the entrance, knives at the ready.

But they never had to use them.

Just like before, the screams and roars eventually died down. The *Te'Monai* disappeared again. It was like they were attacking in waves.

The humidity of the realm had caused them all to sweat through the layers of their uniform, but Finn was sweating profusely when they left the den. His ankle was getting worse. They couldn't afford to go through another wave.

The four of them carefully walked through the trees, but as they suspected, the *Te'Monai* were nowhere to be found. They moved until the loose soil turned into sand. The smell of salt was stronger here.

Atreus saw miles upon miles of water ahead. It was a brilliant, sparkling blue that stretched to the horizon. The water seemed so inviting, but he knew better.

Judah gasped.

They jerked back under the safe cover of the trees. He followed Judah's gaze and stiffened when he saw *Te'Monai* in the distance.

About two dozen of them were lumped together at the shore, and more were appearing. All of the *Te'Monai* had at least one corpse, and with them, they waded into the water. Their giant tails swished back and forth as they swam deeper into the sea, in the direction of an island with a huge mountain. He could see small dots moving along the island's shore. Other *Te'Monai*.

"What are they doing?" Finn whispered.

Mila shook her head, eyes wide and locked on to the scene before them. "I don't know..."

Te'Monai typically didn't show any interest in dead bodies.

As Atreus stared at the mountain on the island, a ringing grew in his ears. He winced, but the pressure relieved itself quickly and turned into a hum. A hum he'd heard before during their previous Outing when he spotted the stone. He pulled his eyes away from the island and the humming stopped, like he'd been disconnected from the source. He looked back, and the pleasant, alluring hum filled his ears again. It was faint, carried by the wind, but he was sure it would get stronger the closer he went.

He took a step back. "Come on. Let's go find somewhere else to wash up and rest."

They had never needed to find a fresh water source in another realm before. Luckily, they came across a promising trail rather quickly. The good news was that the trail *did* lead them to fresh water. The bad news was that other people had found it first.

"Are you kidding me," Mila huffed when she saw who it was.

Vanik, Harlow, and Weylin had jumped to their feet when they heard someone approaching. Vanik lowered his knife, eyes narrowing as he identified their faces underneath the mud.

"What? Did they shit on you instead of eat you?" he sneered, even though he looked equally as worse for wear.

Atreus glanced past him at Harlow and Weylin. Their glares weren't as fierce as usual. There was another firstborn with them, but Aspen was nowhere to be seen. He felt a strange pang in his chest. He didn't say anything, but Vanik was watching him, waiting for him to slip.

"Aspen didn't make it through the second attack," Harlow bit out. Her eyes were a bit red, but it might have been from the dried blood coating her face.

No one apologized. It wasn't what anyone wanted to hear, and it wasn't any of their faults. Instead, Weylin held out a sunken stone filled with water. Finn strode forward to take it, and they all sat down and filled their stomachs with water in silence.

Harlow broke it a few minutes later. "We can't keep doing this. It'll kill all of us."

Vanik wiped the back of his hand across his mouth after taking a drink. "I think that's the point."

"No," Atreus said quietly while he contemplated something. "No, I don't think it is."

Everyone turned to him.

"What do you mean by that?" Weylin asked.

"Why get rid of all of us? The prophets have established an order in the Institute. If we all die, they would have to reteach everything to the new kids themselves. They'd be starting from square one."

"Square one?" Vanik questioned. "What? Like they have a plan? An agenda?"

"You think they don't?" Atreus shot back. He'd been thinking about this for a while, and he knew he wasn't alone. He was even more sure there was something bigger going on after visiting the black and white room. "What are we digging for in the mines? And these Outings . . . "

He hesitated, wondering how much he should tell them. Secrets were dangerous but resourceful. "Last time we were sent out, I grabbed a stone. I think . . . it's what sent all of us back to the Institute."

Weylin barked out a laugh and tipped his head back against the cliffside.

Atreus ignored him. "As soon as my hand closed around it, we were transported back. Prophet Silas brought me to this room and made me hand over the stone. He *knew* about it." He looked over everyone, Finn and Mila specifically. "Tell me why he would do that if the stone wasn't important?"

"Let me get this straight," Vanik said, leaning forward and resting his elbows on his knees. "You think a rock is our ticket out of here? That it's some . . . gateway between realms? And what? *That's* what the prophets have been sending us out for every time? A fucking rock?"

It sounded even more ridiculous when someone explained it to him.

"Maybe. Something like that." He shook his head. "I'm not saying they aren't sending us out as some twisted form of punishment, but I am saying I think there's more to it. And maybe it aligns with whatever we're digging for in the mines."

A heavy silence sat between them.

He looked at Finn and Mila again. Finn's brows were furrowed and eyes distant as he worked through Atreus' theory. Mila stared back at him, her face not giving anything away. Even his friends thought his theory was far-fetched.

"Did he hit his head?" Harlow asked genuinely.

He scowled. "No, I'm perfectly sound." Or at least reasonably. "*Think* about it. Have you seen one of the prophets pull someone aside after an Outing before?"

He hadn't, but he was only one person. The return and the moment after were always a blur to him. He was reorienting himself. Checking his injuries. Searching for his friends.

"I have."

They all turned to look at the firstborn sitting off to the side. His eyes dropped under the weight of their attention. "Maybe. A few Outings ago . . . I was injured and went to see Miss Anya. On my way back, I saw one of the prophets leading someone away. I didn't think much of it then, but maybe it had something to do with what you're talking about."

"Do you remember who it was?" Atreus asked.

The firstborn shook his head. "It looked like a girl. That's all I remember."

Well, that was something at least.

Atreus turned back to Vanik, raising a brow.

Vanik rolled his eyes. "This is ludicrous."

"Is it?" Atreus challenged. "Is it really?"

They had all been through so much. He didn't know what the outside realm was like, but he imagined it was better than *this*. On top of the shit they were put through daily, was this *really* too much to accept?

"Okay, fine. Let's say this crazy theory of yours is right," Vanik said. "How do we find this stone that's going to bring us back? There are probably a million fucking rocks here."

He threw his hand back toward the cliff to prove his point.

"I think I know where it is," Atreus admitted.

Harlow edged closer. "How?"

He opened his mouth, paused, and then decided to say it anyway, accepting the reaction he would get. "It sang to me before. Kind of like a hum. If I follow it, I can track down the stone."

Weylin laughed again.

"It sings to you?" Harlow verified, her voice full of skepticism.

Atreus rubbed the back of his head. "The point is, I can find it. But the problem is the *Te'Monai*." He looked back at Mila and Finn. "I think it's on that island."

"What island?"

"We saw an island in the distance when we were at the beach," Mila explained. "All the *Te'Monai* were heading toward it."

Harlow sighed through her nose, blowing bloodied strands of hair out of her face. "Of course the stone is there."

It was the least ideal situation. They needed to get the stone to go back, but retrieving it while the *Te'Monai* were on the island was a suicide mission. Assuming the *Te'Monai* had gone there after the first wave of attacks, they probably wouldn't leave until it was time to hunt again. A third wave *might* be less deadly than going to the island now, but neither option sounded inviting.

Vanik's face was blank as he stared off to the side, but he had an intense look in his eyes. He suddenly straightened and looked past Harlow.

"Hey, you!" Vanik called out to the other firstborn. "What were you mumbling about earlier?"

"About what?"

"About the *Te'Monai*," Vanik prompted impatiently. "What did you tell us?"

"Oh." The firstborn sat up straighter, his face twisted in confusion. "Earlier, during the break, the group I was with accidentally stumbled across some of the *Te'Monai*. We were about to run, but then we realized they weren't moving or reacting to us at all. They were sleeping."

Finn frowned. "Resting?"

"No, *sleeping*. They didn't move or anything when we walked past them. It was almost like they were temporarily shut down. One of the girls tripped and . . . *nothing*."

So they didn't *all* go to the island then. Some stayed behind. But *sleeping?* That was why the *Te'Monai* had been absent for hours before? Atreus had never thought about those things having to recuperate.

He pitched forward, snagging the firstborn's attention. "You're sure? You're absolutely certain they were sleeping?"

The firstborn nodded.

"You bet your life on it? Deep sleep?"

He hesitated, but still nodded. "Like they were hibernating."

Atreus sat back and let out a heavy sigh. He looked over his shoulder in the direction of the island. "I have an idea."

CHAPTER
TWENTY-SEVEN

Jhai lightly dabbed makeup under Lena's bruised eye as her other attendants readied her dress and selected the proper jewelry to match. Lena stared at her reflection while sitting at the vanity in the washroom. The poor lighting in the tent *had*, in fact, made her injury appear better than was. It still wasn't *bad*—the swelling and bruising had gone down overnight—but the color had deepened slightly. It was noticeable.

"It'll be gone tomorrow, Your Majesty," Jhai reassured her once more.

Lena realized she was frowning again, so she smoothed out her face and glanced at her attendant. "Call me Kalena."

Jhai bit her lip and nodded. "The makeup is covering it well."

"Yes," she agreed, "but I'll still know it's there."

Jhai hummed. She set down the sponge and picked up a brush with powder on it. "Close your eyes."

She did as told, and the bristles tickled her skin.

"You were lucky you weren't hurt worse, Kalena."

She had been told that *many* times. By Benji and then by the physician when they arrived, and then by Cowen. Even Mikhail had stopped by. Ira hadn't. Lena tried not to let that get to her.

But she couldn't stop thinking about what that old woman had said. Benji had told her not to worry about it, that the woman clearly hadn't been in her right mind, but Lena didn't quite buy that. The woman had looked at her with a startling clarity. Her words had been steady.

"You're in danger. You should have never come back."

She knew that, so the words shouldn't shake her. But they did.

And then there was Aquila . . .

"Kalena?"

She opened her eyes. Jhai was frowning at her, the skin between her brows wrinkled.

"Sorry . . . I have a lot on my mind."

"I can imagine," Jhai said. She asked Lena to close her eyes again. " . . . This question might come off too forward, so I apologize, but do you ever find yourself lonely here?"

The question *was* very forward. Personal. For a moment, Lena considered lying, but everyone knew how isolated she was, even as queen.

"Yes, but . . . I was much lonelier before I came back."

At least that was what she'd *thought*. After that memory yesterday, she found herself questioning her own mind. She *knew* Aquila—from before. But she hadn't *known* she knew her. Or Julian. It was like . . . part of her memories had been hidden from her.

"So you don't regret it? Returning?"

Jhai pulled away and Lena cracked her eyes open. Another rather forward question. She frowned at her attendant, but Jhai's back was to her as she sifted through the vanity.

Lena changed the topic. "Where are you from? How'd you end up working in the palace?"

"My aunt pulled some strings and called in a favor that got me into the Highlands." Jhai turned back to her with more products in her hands, appearing completely unphased by Lena's question. "I worked as a private attendant for a few weeks before I moved to the palace. I am quite fortunate."

Unlike the Sacred Guard, attendants didn't need to be Blessed. Most of Lena's attendants were from the Lowlands.

"And do you regret it?" Lena asked as Jhai applied the dark stain to her lashes. "Coming here?"

She could see Jhai's smile in the mirror.

"I miss the Lowlands if that's what you mean. I miss my home and my family. I try to go back whenever I can."

That wasn't what she'd meant, and she had a feeling Jhai knew that. But before she could say anything in response, Devla and Renetta came in to retrieve her.

The dress they had picked out for her was the sheerest one yet. It was light like her dress from the day before and fell in layers of periwinkle, lilac, and lavender. Her skin could be seen under the thin fabric almost everywhere but her chest and groin. The dress was very pretty. And fit the occasion.

The second day of the celebrations was more of a party than the first. It was a ball without all the grandeur and pleasantries one might expect from an event with that title. To be frank, it was a giant orgy.

Lena's attendants helped her slip into the dress and added the final touches to her look. They kept the makeup and jewelry simple today.

Cowen stepped into her room once Devla told him that Lena was ready. She stood in front of the open balcony doors, staring at the mountains in the distance as her attendants left the room.

"Do we have to go this early?" she sighed as she turned to face Cowen.

"You're expected to make a timely appearance at all of these events," he said. "They *are* celebrating your marriage."

Lena scoffed quietly. She didn't need the reminder.

Ira hadn't come to her room last night. Well, it was technically *their* room. After their marriage was announced, they'd been offered a larger room, but neither of them had really cared for it. They could have continued to live separately—many people in relationships did so—but they didn't want to appear divided before the council. They'd agreed during their honeymoon that Ira would move into Lena's room and they would share it. But they hadn't. Not once.

Cowen knew this, of course.

"They would celebrate anything if it meant they got to party." She walked over to her desk. The flowers were replaced regularly, swapped out the moment they began to wither. "Tell me . . . did they celebrate when my family died? When I fled?"

" . . . Not publicly."

She clenched her jaw. In a fit of rage, she thought about smashing the vase, but that would do nothing. She took a deep breath, lifted her chin, and strode past Cowen. "Let's go party."

He didn't follow. "Kalena . . . "

"What?" she snapped, spinning around.

She hated the way he was looking at her. Stern yet sad. Apologetic. Pitying.

"You need to stop," he said not unkindly. "This reckless streak—it's only going to get you hurt. I've allowed it long enough—"

"*Allowed?*" she echoed, her laugh hollow. "What? Am I your prisoner now? Do I have to ask you for permission if I want to do anything?"

Cowen frowned. "You know exactly what I mean. Our job—*my job*—is to keep you safe. It's already difficult, and you know why. I don't need you making it more difficult for me by running away and sneaking out all the time."

Lena glowered at him. "I can protect myself. I came back in one piece both times—"

"Yes, you got lucky," Cowen threw back. "One day you won't, and I don't need that on my conscience as well."

"Oh, well, sure," she drawled. "If it's for your conscience, I'll stop my bad behavior right away."

"Lena," Cowen groaned, sounding truly exasperated.

"I kept myself safe for *five years*," she said. "I was alone and young and powerless. I wasn't in control all the time, but I made it. On my own!"

"You shouldn't have had to!" he exclaimed.

Her throat closed up and she drew back. "Well, it happened, and I survived. And now I have an Imprint and a Slayer and all the money I could ever want and I live comfortably and I—"

"Do you think I don't know what you're doing?"

Lena snapped her mouth shut.

"You think I don't know you're being especially difficult to keep me at arm's length? I'm not arrogant enough to think you're doing this only to be a pain in my ass, not anymore, but I know pissing me off is a nice bonus, isn't it?"

She only stared.

Cowen shook his head and took a step forward. "You know, Alkus tried to get me to resign after Ezra was banished. Spouted some bullshit about how difficult this must be for me . . . the shame and guilt I must feel for failing at my job and being the only survivor. He offered me piles of money and an honorable discharge. I told him to shove it up his ass—in a much kinder way, of course. Even if Ezra hadn't told me to stay, I would have.

"Search parties were sent out for you, but the council called it quits after two weeks. I petitioned them to extend the search. They shot me down again and again, but I kept going back. I raised such a fuss that they eventually granted my request. I was given five enforcers—not even members of the Sacred Guard—to accompany me. I was out searching for you nearly every day. For five years." Cowen's face crumpled and he retreated into himself. "And I still didn't find you. But you came back on your own. You've been cold to me ever since you returned, and I thought maybe it was your way of punishing me for my failures. I saw that look on your face in the hall when I came to escort you back to your room for the ball. And then I saw you shove it away. But I didn't comment then, and I didn't comment when you snuck out of the cabin."

The muscles in Cowen's jaw flex. "When Andra came to get me yesterday, I imagined the worst. I thought, *'You failed again.'*"

Her first instinct was to say *you didn't*, but she couldn't bring herself to open her mouth. Not right now. She was worried what would come out of it.

"I know you're shutting me out because you're afraid." His voice was gentler now. "And I suppose part of me should be relieved you're able to be afraid. It means you still hold some things close to your heart. You still think some things are worth fighting for."

"Of course I do," she hissed.

"But not yourself?" he clarified. "Right? You don't think you're worth fighting for? Or else you wouldn't be punishing yourself in this way."

Lena opened her mouth to say that wasn't true. She was still fighting for herself. She had things she still wanted to do, people she wanted to avenge and help. But the air between them remained silent and stiff. Her lips trembled.

"Do you trust me?" Cowen asked.

Did she?

She searched for the truth, digging deep. She said what she felt, temporarily abandoning the rational side of her that fought for her self-preservation. " . . . Yes."

"Then why do you distance yourself?"

He knew. And so did she.

"Stop punishing yourself for something that was out of your control, Kalena. You can't live your life in fear. And you can't only fight for others. Fight for what *you* want."

Want. There was that word again.

"It doesn't matter what I want," she heard herself say. "The Numina don't care what we want."

"Fuck the Numina."

Lena gaped. A strangled laugh escaped her.

Cowen walked toward her and reached his hands out, hovering them over her shoulders. "If they don't care, then you *take* it. You're the fucking queen. They chose *you*. Now it's your turn to choose. But you *can* do that without being reckless."

She looked up at him, eyes searching his face. She cleared her throat and said, "You've grown."

One corner of his mouth quirked up. "So have you."

"I can't decide which Cowen is more annoying."

He scoffed and rolled his eyes. When he pulled her into a hug, she went willingly and sunk into his arms.

∽

Lena's private wing was untouched by the festivities, but as soon as she ventured past the private halls and into the part of the palace that was open to the public, a wall of perfume and smoke hit her. The entire space was hazy, which was honestly quite impressive.

She was torn between hurrying to the ballroom and keeping a leisurely pace. On the one hand, the ballroom was the peak of the party—the party she didn't want to go to at all. Public events weren't her strong suit, especially when she was surrounded by people who hated her. Alcohol could help her endure this nightmare, but she wasn't yet sure if she was willing to resort to that tonight.

On the other hand, the halls themselves were filled with people who would come up to her and try to start a conversation or invite her to join them off to the side on the cushioned benches with their drinks. After about twelve different people approached her in the stretch of a single hallway, she decided the ballroom was the lesser evil and picked up her pace.

The ballroom was loud and, despite it being early afternoon, dim. Curtains were drawn over the windows, and the staff had even managed to cover part of the glass ceiling with thick drapes. Sofas and chairs had been dragged into the room, as had rugs and tables covered with trays of snacks and cups of alcohol. The ballroom had been completely transformed into a large, fancy sitting room.

Lena summoned an agreeable smile and mingled with others until Mikhail pulled her away. She quickly found herself surrounded by unfriendly faces. Alkus. Ophir. Avalon. Trynla. Sorrel and Von were there too.

Trynla tilted her head and stared at Lena intently. "You can't even tell."

Lena pinched her lips together, immediately knowing what Trynla was pointing out. "Yes, well, despite what you might've heard from gossips, the injury is not that bad."

"But you were still injured," Ophir unhelpfully pointed out.

Lena's gaze moved to Sorrel. Did she know what Aquila was doing? Had Sorrel put her up to it? Aquila was the person who had been spying on Lena in the Lowlands, possibly on Sorrel's orders, which meant their guests had been in The Lands a few days before the council knew.

"Hm, unfortunately," she said. "Where's your other wife?"

That seemed to do the trick. Avalon's pleasant expression faltered. "Celine is currently hunting down my son."

"Still proving difficult?" a nameless face said.

Ophir grimaced before taking a sip of wine. "Tuck takes pleasure in being difficult. One can only hope he'll come to his senses one day soon and be ready for the council seat."

His voice was a growl near the end. Avalon placed her hand on his arm, and he quieted.

"I'm sure he will," Alkus said. "Some people are born to rule."

The sentiment *and other people are not*—Lena being *'other people'*—was left unsaid, but she picked up on it.

Mikhail nodded in agreement. "He shows promise. Give him another decade or so." His gaze moved over her shoulder, and he perked up. "Oh, Your Majesty, I believe I see Ira near the entrance. Come, you two should address the guests."

Lena was grateful for the distraction and allowed herself to be swept away. Her chest tightened as she took in the sight of her husband for the first time in days. He looked good. *Better* than good. She hesitated when Ira's cool blue eyes met her own. His face was impassive, and she still wasn't able to *feel* anything from him. Maybe he'd been blocking her out this entire time.

She had continued to read up on their strengthened bond, having books sent to her room late at night because that was the only free time she had lately. She hadn't mentioned it to Mikhail . . . not yet. But she'd been practicing her mental boundaries, though she had no idea how to check if they were working.

Mikhail led the two of them to the front of the ballroom. Lena moved on stiff legs. She'd been informed about the brief speech they would need to give, thanking everyone for attending, but public speaking *also* wasn't one of her strengths. And she felt even more off balance because of the rift between her and Ira.

Thankfully, her attendants had helped her rehearse her part last night and this morning, so she was able to get through it without stumbling. Ira said his piece, and then it was time for the marking.

It wasn't anything too serious. It was supposed to be an act of good faith that truly kicked off the party. People had the option of marking themselves with paint somewhere visible to display their relationship status. Open to a relationship or not. It was simple, and while displaying one's relationship status and sexual preferences used to be a tradition in The Lands, it wasn't a widespread practice anymore.

Green meant you were open to relationships, while red meant you were closed to relationships.

Usually people marked themselves, but Lena and Ira were marking each other, which did bring about some uncertainty in her. They had to choose for the other.

Two pots of paint were brought before her. Lena looked between them, her mind racing. If she picked red, she would essentially be claiming him publicly. He'd said there was no one else or that there was no one—she still didn't know—but he'd said a lot of things before their argument in the hall. She wasn't stupid enough to think that one disagreement would be what tore them apart. They had argued lots, but things were different now. She never wanted to hold him back, at any point, even if he tried to do that to her.

She dipped her thumb into the green paint and brushed it across his cheek. He held her gaze as she did so. Due to their proximity, she could see the flex of his jaw.

Now it was his turn.

Ira turned toward the pots, and when he faced her again, he grabbed her chin and drew her in for a heated kiss. His lips dragged across hers, hot and heavy, in front of the entire ballroom.

Her eyes widened, but like a fool, she folded under him, her eyes slipping closed and her lips moving with his. He pulled away much too soon, his teeth scraping against her bottom lip as he withdrew. His thumb followed, trailing down her lip and then her chin. She leaned into his touch, but he stepped back, releasing her entirely.

She was hot and cold all over. The spell between them shattered when Ira broke eye contact and disappeared into the crowd.

The people seemed satisfied with their exchange and quickly went back to enjoying the luxuries of the party. Some began to mark themselves. Even Mikhail had vanished. But Lena was frozen.

What the fuck was that? Ira hadn't talked to her in days. She hadn't *seen him* in days. And he did *that*? She realized then that Ira *still* hadn't talked to her. Not one word had been exchanged between the two of them during their speech.

A groan of vexation left her lips and she turned on her heel.

"I need a second," she said as she marched past Cowen.

She left the ballroom, Cowen hot on her heels, and hurried through the halls until she found a less populated area. She strode toward the first door she saw and wrenched it open. The room was big and somewhat lit, but it looked like no one else was inside. Good.

"Wait here," she told Cowen. "I'll be right out."

"Kalena, you can't—"

"I'm not running off. I promise. I just . . . I need a moment away from this all. Ten minutes is all I ask," she pleaded.

Cowen sighed and nodded. His gaze dropped to her chin.

She hesitated before slipping inside. "What . . . what color is it?"

She hadn't been able to see because Ira had drawn her into a kiss.

"Red."

Lena parted her lips, but she closed them abruptly. She nodded and shut the door behind her, pressing her back against it.

Ira had seen her reach for green and mark him, yet he'd still chosen red for her. In other words . . . she was taken. He wasn't sharing.

"What the *fuck*."

What was he playing at?

She let out a heavy breath and turned so her forehead was pressed against the door. The air in this room was noticeably cooler than it was in the halls and the noise from the festivities had been muffled entirely. When she shoved her worries aside, she turned to properly survey the room she'd walked into.

The palace had too many elegant rooms that served no true purpose. A row of pillars stood on either side of the space. The walls of the room were divided into tall panels, a painting on each one. They were muted murals of people, places, and things that filled the room with color.

Lena walked over to the side to study one closer. The lamp light cast shadows across the images, making them appear even more ominous.

As she moved down the wall, she realized that the panels told the story of Edynir Akonah. They spoke of his birth in a small village, his time at the academy, his rise to power and fame, and his defeat at the hands of his friend. She'd heard many stories about him. One of the lesser-known ones was that he was called the savior by some. *Arawn*. Much like Ouprua, Edynir Akonah's story was told to kids to warn them of the dangers of the realm, but this tale contained many more lessons, ones about evil and greed and sacrifice.

But there were parts here on this wall that she was unfamiliar with. People she didn't remember hearing or reading about.

The story didn't continue on the back wall. Instead, there was a large painting that tracked the lineage of the seven royal families. In addition to a seat on the council and a home in the palace, each royal family had a patron Numen that extended a pact to each family member.

She followed the intricate lines of each family tree. Some crossed over, which was unsurprising. The Lands was fixated on creating children, and strong ones at that. The firstborns were taken away, given up as a sacrifice. It was for the firstborns' safety as well as everyone else's, but the remaining children could better The Lands. It was believed stronger children attracted stronger Numina, but that wasn't proven.

A boom echoed throughout the room. Lena startled and turned, half-expecting to see Cowen. But instead, she saw one of the panels *rotating*, revealing a secret passage behind it. Three people came stumbling through, laughing and clearly intoxicated. And one of those people was Tuck.

He sensed her a moment later and turned, meeting her eyes. He looked thoroughly disheveled. His short curls were wild, and his eyes were bloodshot. He wore a loose, silk button-down shirt that matched his eyes. The top four buttons were undone, showing his sharp collarbones and the planes of his chest. He had several rings on his fingers, one being his family ring, and held a cup of what she presumed was alcohol, given his rumpled appearance and sloppy movements.

The other two people with him collapsed onto a sofa pushed against the wall. Tuck grinned at Lena before joining them, shoving himself in the middle. The three of them dissolved into laughter again.

She gritted her teeth and turned back around, glaring at the family trees. She debated leaving the room. There was nothing keeping her here.

She spun on her heel and walked back to the door, but she glanced at the trio out of the corner of her eye.

On one side of Tuck sat a woman around his age. She looked ruffled in her own right, hair unruly and lipstick smeared, but her eyes were only a little clouded. One of her dress straps had slipped off her shoulder, her neckline dangerously close to exposing her nipple.

Lena was surprised to find Kieryn on the other side of Tuck, slumped against the sofa. His long hair slid to the side, revealing his pale neck. Purple bruises littered it, some smeared with lipstick, some not. He wore a loose white shirt that draped across his lithe form. When he lifted his head to make a comment, his eyes were equally as glazed as the others. They were all tipsy but still sound of mind. Something told her they'd be less irritating if they were completely wasted.

The woman next to Tuck leaned forward to whisper something into his ear. She placed her hand on his chest and he tipped his head in her direction, but his eyes remained fixed on Lena.

However, it was Kieryn who beckoned her over. She went, but she told herself she only did because she had to talk with Kieryn. About Aquila. This alliance. The marriage. Not *here*, of course, but soon.

"Your Majesty," Kieryn drawled. There was a bit of a slur to his words, but he still managed to sound condescending. "I'm surprised to see you here, at this event."

Tuck laughed.

Lena's amiable smile was already slipping. "Well, it would be rude to not show up to your own party, wouldn't it?"

"So someone tells you to come and you come? Is that how it is?" Kieryn smirked at her as he pushed his fine hair out of his face.

Lena was keenly aware of Tuck's heavy gaze on her and the suggestion behind those words, though Kieryn hadn't said it in such a manner.

"I talked with Sorrel yesterday."

"Did you?" Kieryn leaned forward to pluck Tuck's glass from his hand. He took a sip and grimaced. "That's horrid," he choked, pushing it back in Tuck's direction.

Tuck grinned and tipped back the glass. His throat moved as he gulped down the rest of the wine like it was water. The bruise and cut had faded completely. No scar remained.

"Lena can rebel when she needs to," he said.

She didn't miss the implication behind those words either.

"Your Majesty," she corrected.

"Do you hold such an aversion to your given name that you prefer to be called other things, even in private amongst old friends?" Tuck flashed a sly smile, eyes roving over her. "I would've never thought you were into that sort of thing."

"Don't," she hissed.

"Don't what?" Tuck raised a brow. "You'll need to be more specific."

She scowled. No one managed to frustrate her more, and *quicker*, than Tuck did.

Kieryn pushed himself forward, placing one hand on the arm of the sofa and the other on Tuck's thigh for leverage. He plucked the bottle out of the woman's hands, a bottle that likely contained the liquid he'd just called horrid, and tipped it toward her. "Drink?"

"No thank you," Lena said tightly.

"Brrrrr," he said, bringing his shaking shoulders up to his ears and rubbing his arms as if to warm himself.

Krashing, these two together were a nightmare.

The woman giggled as if that was the funniest thing she'd ever heard and collapsed onto Tuck's lap. Her nipple was completely out now.

"So, what did you and Sorrel talk about? Me?" Kieryn blinked up at her from under his pale lashes. "I'm honored."

Lena's eyes flitted to Tuck, who watched this whole interaction with a slight smirk on his lips, his head back against the wall, and his eyes hooded.

"I want what's best for The Lands. And if that is an alliance with Ouprua, then I want it to work. Truly," she said. "So far, Sorrel is the only one from Ouprua who seems to share that sentiment. Von is hardly talkative. And you and Aquila run off before I even have the chance to speak with you."

"I'm speaking with you right now, aren't I?"

Lena pursed her lips and watched him take a swig of the bottle. Predictably, he gagged again. Tuck snorted.

"I imagined a different setting," she stated drily.

"Well, we can change that." Kieryn grinned and slouched into Tuck's side. The woman in Tuck's lap looked up at Lena, her lower lip caught between her teeth. "You say you want to get to know me. How do you mean?"

Lena smiled, slowly, but it was all spite. "Not in the way you may have hoped."

"She's off limits," Tuck said, His gaze dropped to her chin. "Red means she's not looking for any fun."

Lena had forgotten about the paint. She unconsciously reached for it, but then caught herself and dropped her hand.

"Unless . . . " Tuck's eyes raked down her form and then back up. " . . . this is one of those moments where Her Majesty chooses to rebel."

Lena smirked and leaned forward. "I can rebel plenty, but I will never do anything that brings you satisfaction."

"Oh, but you already have," Tuck countered, his eyes gleaming. "And we're not talking about my satisfaction. We're talking about yours. One night." His grin widened and his gaze dropped again. "Ira can learn to share."

Lena drew back, her muscles tight. "*Ira*? What does this have to do with him?"

Tuck's eyes flashed. The haze of the alcohol was beginning to fade, and the sharpness was coming back. Most Blessed had a high alcohol tolerance and didn't stay drunk for long. She didn't know if she preferred dealing with intoxicated Tuck or sober Tuck.

"You're telling me you put that mark on your chin?" he challenged.

Kieryn cut in before either of them could start a shouting match.

"Okay, that's enough. Tuck will stop being antagonistic. I will too. We'll be on our best behavior. Promise." He held up his hand, his pinky extended, but Lena didn't move. He dropped his hand and sighed. "Loosen up. This is *your* party, isn't it? Take a seat."

Kieryn shifted his legs to the side and patted the sliver of space he'd made between him and Tuck. Meanwhile, Tuck kept his legs splayed open, taking up more space than he needed.

She still didn't move an inch. "What's your schedule like the day after tomorrow?"

Tomorrow was the third and final day of the celebrations. There wasn't anything scheduled during the day—almost everyone would be nursing their hangover from today's party—but the Night Run began as soon as the sun set. Most larger celebrations ended with a Night Run. Everyone stayed indoors and Blessed released their Slayers so they could stretch their legs under the moons. It should give Kieryn plenty of time to recuperate.

He hummed. "I'm quite busy actually—"

"I'm sure you can make time for me."

Kieryn paused and raised his eyes to hers again. The corners of his lips curved up, only slightly. "If Her Majesty requires it."

Lena nodded and walked toward the door. "Two days from now. Make sure you don't drink too much."

CHAPTER
TWENTY-EIGHT

Lena had been at the party for only two hours and she was already tired of dealing with people. She thought about leaving early more than once since she already made her initial appearance, but each time she drifted near the exit, someone would approach and strike up a conversation with her. Cowen could tell when she had enough and would come up with an excuse that allowed her to cut the conversation short.

"I swear . . . ten more minutes and then I'm leaving," she grumbled to Cowen under her breath. "I don't care if Mikhail gets upset."

And then, of course, she caught sight of Aquila right before the Oupruan slipped out of the room. Lena moved after her without thinking.

"What are you doing? You're leaving now?" Cowen asked.

"No, uh, I saw someone who I need to talk to," she said distractedly as she stepped through the doorway.

Cowen followed. ". . . Really?"

She could hear the skepticism in his voice but chose to ignore it.

The halls close to the ballroom were even more crowded now, so Lena rose onto her toes to try to see over the waves of people, but she was still too short. She sighed and lowered herself before squeezing through the crowd. Thankfully, when people saw who she was, they began to make room for her.

Why was *she* always chasing after Aquila?

Lena only had that one memory to go by, but ever since it was restored, she'd felt a gap in her memories. No, *gap* wasn't the right word. She could *feel* something there, but she couldn't access or bypass it.

Was it the same for Aquila? Or did Aquila remember her? Lena suspected the latter was true. Why else would Aquila hate her so passionately? There had to be something else there. Something Aquila knew that she didn't, and she was going to find out what that was.

Lena spotted Aquila at the end of the hall when she shouldered through the thick of the crowd. Aquila's hair was captured in two long braids, and she wore flared pants, a tight top that showcased her toned arms, and gloves. Not at all dressed like someone wanting to be inconspicuous, but she hadn't run off yet.

"Aquila!" Lena called out when she was still a good distance away.

Aquila turned toward her, but so did dozens of Blessed. Lena smiled, and Aquila stood still and rigid, a scowl on her face. She couldn't run with so many eyes on her.

Lena stepped up next to her and said under her breath, "I need to talk to you."

"Oh, now you want to talk?" Aquila scoffed, not bothering to lower her voice.

Lena kept a polite smile on her face, aware of the eyes that lingered on them. "I haven't been able to talk with you because every time I try, you run away." Her eyes drilled into Aquila's own and she waved her hand down the hall. "Let's go somewhere more private so we can discuss . . . the alliance."

Aquila looked at her with nothing but contempt. However, she followed Lena around the corner. They didn't go too far. Lena wasn't patient enough, and the farther they went, the more likely it was that Aquila would make a run for it.

"I need to speak with her," she told Cowen when they stopped in front of a door. "Alone. Ten minutes."

"Again?"

She shrugged.

Cowen narrowed his eyes. "I'm getting really tired of waiting outside these doors."

Lena laughed, a bit nervous. "Trust me. I'm getting really tired of *having* you wait outside them. But I do need to speak with her." She glanced to the side to make sure Aquila was still there. She was, but she looked ready to bolt. "About the alliance."

His scowl deepened, but he agreed, "Ten minutes."

Lena nodded, and after Cowen swept the room, making sure it was indeed empty and safe, he left her and Aquila alone. Lena knew he would hold her to those ten minutes, especially because she'd gone a bit over earlier, so she didn't want to waste any time.

"Listen, I don't know what your problem with me is. I saw you for the first time a few days ago, at least that was what I thought. There was something familiar about you. Something I couldn't put my finger on."

Aquila stared at Lena, her eyes cold and face blank.

"Yesterday, I saw the cloak and I recognized it. I knew that whoever was wearing it was the person from the Lowlands. The person who had been spying on me. So imagine my surprise when I found out it was *you*. And then you knocked me out—thanks for that by the way—"

"You look fine," Aquila muttered.

"—and I had a vision. A memory came back to me. One I didn't have access to before."

A wave of emotions slowly unfurled across Aquila's face, and Lena saw what she needed to see. She was right. Aquila wasn't clueless. She remembered Lena.

"It was when we were younger. In the Lowlands. We were with a man named Julian. He called me Cal and you Quil."

A wrinkle appeared between Aquila's brows and her face fell. "Did you tell anyone about this?"

"No. Only you." Lena glanced toward the door and then back at Aquila. "In case it wasn't clear, I don't remember any of that. Any of you or him or even *me*. I know you do. You remember me, at least. That's why you've been glaring at me since you arrived. You probably thought I was ignoring you out of spite or—something! I don't fucking know. But in reality, there's this whole chunk of my memories that I can't access, and *you* are going to tell me *why*."

But she didn't. Aquila stood there, lost in her own thoughts. She looked as if someone had ripped the rug right out from under her feet, but unfortunately for her, Lena didn't quite care what crisis she might be having.

"*Krashing, say some—!*"

"Julian must've done something," Aquila whispered to herself.

"What?"

Aquila straightened and took a step toward Lena, but then she faltered and receded back into herself. She seemed almost . . . unsure. Upset. "You really . . . don't remember anything?"

"Nothing other than the memory I just told you about," Lena said. "Why? You said Julian must've done something. What do you mean?"

Aquila turned away and headed for the door.

"Hey!"

Lena lurched forward and wrapped her hand around Aquila's arm, but the Oupruan spun and knocked her aside. There was a flash of metal in the air. Lena caught Aquila's wrist, stopping the other's blade only inches away from her face.

"I don't think Sorrel would be happy to hear that one of her people tried to kill the queen and ruined this alliance before it could even begin," she snapped.

Aquila narrowed her eyes. "Is that blackmail?"

"It could be." She shoved Aquila away and took a step back. "We have the same reaction to . . . touch."

Aquila scoffed and tucked the dagger away. She had plenty of places to hide a weapon. "Julian taught us that. Anyone who grabs hold of you is a threat."

Lena swallowed thickly and crossed her arms. "Who is he?"

Aquila's face began to close up again, the cracks in her mask sealing.

"Please, I . . . I deserve to know, don't I? What happened to my memories? Why don't I remember anything from that time? If you know anything, you have to tell—"

"I don't have to tell you anything."

Lena paused, irritation sweeping through her. "I don't know why you would keep the truth from me . . . unless you have something to hide."

Aquila gave her nothing.

"You think Julian had something to do with taking away my memories." Lena didn't know how something like that was possible, but there really was only one sensible explanation. "Did he use . . . his sorcery?"

That got a reaction out of Aquila. "You know about that?"

"It was part of the memory. That's it, isn't it? Somehow, he locked away my memories with his sorcery. But why—?"

"Keep your voice down," Aquila hissed as she stepped forward, her hands twitching at her sides. Was she going to try to stab Lena again? Silence her? Both?

"Why?" Lena challenged. She motioned to Aquila's hands. "Worried someone might overhear and rumors might spread? Worried they might make you take off your gloves and check for tattoos underneath?"

Aquila shifted her hands, but there was no way to hide them.

Since their guests' arrival, both Aquila and Sorrel had worn gloves. Lena hadn't thought anything of it at first, but then Sorrel had mentioned that they didn't have Imprints in Ouprua, just something like it. Some sort of power they could use to fight. Sorcery was the only other known magic source outside of the Divine Touch. And then Lena had caught Aquila and that memory had unlocked . . . the gloves on Julian's hands, the sorcery tattoos underneath them, the gloves Aquila and Sorrel wore . . . it'd all made sense.

Heat slowly spread through her Imprint and out from it, reaching her fingertips.

"Was it Julian who hid my memories?" she asked softly, capturing Aquila's gaze. " . . . Or you?"

"Why would I erase your memories?" Aquila spat. She was tense, her hands curled into fists.

"That's what I'm trying to figure out. Why were you walking around the stalls like that, in a cloak? Did you *want* me to recognize you? *And* why were you following me that night in town? Did someone pay you to spy on me?"

A disbelieving laugh crept up Aquila's throat. The curve of her mouth was cruel. "A better question would be why were you even there?"

"I was on my honeymoon." Lena's smile was equally as sharp. Purple started to bleed into her eyes as it did when her Slayer was unleashed. Just slightly. "You just missed my husband. Lucky for you."

Aquila's face darkened and the lights in the room flickered.

Lena watched her, waiting, and part of her hoping. The only clear memory she had of Aquila was that one she'd regained yesterday, but a deeper part of her still remembered Aquila. There was affection there. She didn't know what else to call it. Something soft and calm. Comforting. She didn't know how much time they'd spent together in the Lowlands, but something told her that Aquila had been a friend then. Though she knew how quickly things could change. And if the glares and the dagger in her face was any indication, Aquila no longer thought of her as a friend. Lena wondered if they'd ended things badly and that was where the animosity and Aquila's reluctance to help her came from.

"Aquila," she said, trying one last time. "If there's any part of you that cares for me, *please . . . tell me*. Prove to me that you're not an enemy."

And for a second, she really thought Aquila would crack. Her eyes softened and her lips parted. Another scrap of familiarity hit Lena, bringing with it an ache that grew steadily behind her eyes. She winced. And then Cowen knocked on the door.

The trance between her and Aquila shattered. She could physically see Aquila's guard falling back into place, the crafted cold replacing the warmth she'd seen just seconds ago.

"Wait," she said as she rocked forward.

Aquila took a step back. She held up a finger and uttered a simple, "No."

The quiver in her voice made Lena stop in her tracks.

Aquila left the room.

INSTEAD OF LEAVING THE PARTY, Lena started drinking.

If she returned to her room, she would be alone with her racing thoughts, which didn't sound appealing, but she couldn't stay among the Blessed for another second while sober. So, she silenced her thoughts and heightened her geniality with alcohol while leaning on Cowen for support. Literally.

She wanted to forget all her problems and *duties*. Tonight, she could let that numbing feeling wash over her. After all, that was what everyone else seemed to be doing.

She stayed away from the main festivities and was pleased to find many ways to attain alcohol. Servers carried them down the halls on trays, and tables had been set up in empty rooms. Some of the party-goers, recognizing who she was, offered up their own half-empty glasses. Cowen declined for her and steered her away. Her worries faded, as did her anxiety, with each glass. Cowen tried to get her to slow down, but he was unsuccessful.

She ran off the high for an hour or so before she began to crash. She grew tired, sad, and angry—all things she wanted to avoid.

"Let's go back," she sighed.

The tension lining Cowen's form drained away at her words, and he guided her toward her room. Or at least she assumed so. Her ability to navigate properly had been one of the first things to go. Her vision was still blurry and her legs were wobbly. Cowen had one hand on her back to steady her, and she would clutch his arm occasionally when her knees thawed. The alcohol made her hot, which was nice.

"I'm sorry for making you wait outside those doors."

"It's alright, Kalena."

"No, nothing's alright. I—"

She stumbled when they turned a corner. Cowen reached out to grab her, but another set of arms got there first. Hands wrapped under her elbows, keeping her on her feet. Through the thin material of her sleeves, she could feel the cool press of metal against her heated skin.

Lena looked up, blinking the fuzz away from her vision. Her lips turned down and she tried to pull herself away.

"Ugh, it's you again."

Tuck's lips curled in the opposite direction as hers. "Try not to sound too excited to see me. People might get the wrong idea."

Lena scoffed. "Oh, I don't think so. You're just an ass. No, you're a double ass."

Tuck's brows rose as he stared down at her in amusement. "Pardon?"

"Assassin. *Ass-ass-in*. You're an asshole squared," she hissed, jabbing her finger at his stupidly firm chest. She wished her finger was a dagger instead.

Tuck laughed. "Shit, you're properly wasted, aren't you?"

"Yes, she is," Cowen cut in. His hands were on her shoulders. "Which is why Her Majesty should be retiring to bed."

"It's only six in the evening."

Lena noted that Tuck was more put together than earlier. He'd fastened two of his shirt buttons, leaving the top two open, and his hair was artfully messy. He'd washed the lipstick off, but the bruises remained.

"Don't *you* have somewhere to be?" she sneered. "Like sucking up to your parents and carrying out their wishes to get rid of some other unsuspecting souls who found themselves on your family's bad side. Is that what you were doing with Kieryn?"

Tuck's face shut down abruptly, like bars dropping down over a window.

"Kalena," Cowen hissed, pulling her back, but Lena struggled against him with her newfound strength.

"Are you angry?" she taunted. The alcohol gave her a rush of confidence. Or was it recklessness? She didn't care to differentiate the two. "Are you going for attempt number two right here in the halls? Or is this three? Does the night in my room count?"

"Kalena, *stop it!*"

Cowen let go of her with one hand to reach back for his sword—which was ridiculous because *Imprint*—and she took that as an opportunity to surge forward, ridding herself of his grip entirely.

Lena placed two hands against Tuck's chest and shoved him back. *Hard.* He barely budged, which made her even more annoyed. "Do you feel any guilt for what you did? For what you took from me? For what you continue to take from others?"

Tuck stared down at her impassively. His green eyes seemed so dull and unfeeling.

"When my family and I moved to the palace, I hoped everything would work out. I hoped we could live up here without being shamed or threatened. And you know why I hate you so much? Everyone else was so cold. I just needed *one* sign, *one person*, to convince me that maybe, just maybe, things would work. And that person was *you*." She jabbed her finger into his chest again, fighting Cowen's hands. Once she cracked open the floodgates, allowing herself to relive those moments again, the words didn't stop. "When you weren't giving me the cold shoulder or ignoring me completely, when we would talk in the treehouse, *you* gave me hope that things weren't as dangerous as I thought they were. And *you* were the one who stabbed me in the back."

Cowen managed to pull her away then, but Tuck followed her. Cowen held his arm out to force Tuck to keep his distance, but Tuck pushed it aside.

"Do not touch me," he all but snarled, his green eyes alight again.

The static in the air made Lena lightheaded. Was this what people felt when Tuck arrived to get rid of them? This paralyzing heaviness?

His eyes moved to Lena and only slightly let up in their intensity. "If you knew it would be dangerous up here, why did you come?"

Out of everything she'd said, *that* was what he'd latched on to?

"Sounds like exactly what a Blessed would say," she hissed. "You don't know what it's like down there. And I didn't have a choice! When someone tells you the Numina chose you as the next ruler of The Lands, you don't say no! You can't!"

Tuck took another step forward, ignoring Cowen's warning. Cowen was too busy holding Lena to do anything about Tuck. Her skin grew uncomfortably hot and itchy.

"Cowen, let go."

To his credit, he did almost immediately.

She took a large step away and a deep breath. Her hands trembled, and her head ached from raising her voice.

It always went back to that day. The images sprang back up and it *outraged* her that no one else was outraged at all. They didn't care. Meanwhile, she was screaming internally every day, and when she let some of it out, everyone looked at her as if *she* was the unreasonable one.

She strode forward and hit Tuck across the face.

He took it gracefully, standing his ground. Only his head turned with the force of her slap. He stayed that way for a moment, looking at the wall. Then, he rolled his jaw and turned back to her. "Did that make you feel better?"

Tears welled in her eyes. It didn't make her feel better. And she began to worry that nothing ever would. Maybe there was no remedy for the emptiness that consumed her.

"Your Majesty," Cowen said sternly. "It's time to go. You've attracted an audience."

And so they had. She grew more frustrated when she found that it was Ira who had stumbled upon them.

"Lena," Tuck said as she passed him. "Has it ever occurred to you that maybe I didn't have a choice either?"

She stopped but didn't turn back. She didn't want to see the look on his face.

"No," she said honestly. "No, it hasn't."

Lena didn't look at Ira either as she passed him. She tried to shove the panic down as she made her way to her room, but it was crippling at this point. She marched straight toward the washroom and promptly threw up.

CHAPTER
TWENTY-NINE

"So, we've got a little over an hour left?" Atreus confirmed, looking over at Nev again.

The other firstborn had told them his name after Vanik referred to him as *You!* for the third time.

Nev nodded. "If I've calculated it right."

He was smart enough to time the break.

Atreus wished they could be more certain, but they were working with limited time and information. They couldn't wait longer to test their theories. Therefore, their plan was built on quite a few assumptions, one of them being that each break was as long as the last. The only thing that Nev had to be absolutely certain of was that the *Te'Monai* were indeed in a deep sleep. Everything else would fall apart if that wasn't true. Nev swore several times that the *Te'Monai* were dead to the realm around them. Now Atreus just had to hope that they didn't wake up early.

He'd finished telling everyone the details of his plan thirty minutes ago. It'd been met with some resistance, but in the end, they'd all realized that there wasn't another option. If his hunch was right and the stone was what got them out of there, they needed to get their hands on it. And going over now as opposed to later when the *Te'Monai* were awake was preferable.

But the *Te'Monai* was only one issue. The first problem they faced was the stretch of water between the beach and the island.

Below the Institute in the mines, there was a deep reservoir in one of the caverns. Almost everyone knew about it. The prophets didn't care if the firstborns visited it in their free time, though they rarely had any of that. But a few firstborns had given in to their intrigue and gotten into the water. They'd learned the hard way that the reservoir drained quickly at regular intervals. A whirlpool would appear in the middle and a siphon of water would rush downward, the current so strong it swept away everything caught in it. No one stood a chance fighting against it. If you didn't get out quickly, you were a goner. Because of that, there had been a few drowning incidents at the beginning before they got the timing down and learned to swim.

Atreus was one of those who had given in. He found swimming relaxing, and sometimes he would push the limits, crawling out of the reservoir at the last available second and watching the water rapidly spin and disappear.

But it worked out—him being able to swim. He needed to go to the island since he was the only one who could sense the stone. Mila, Weylin, and Harlow were going with him while Finn, Judah, Vanik, and Nev were staying back on the mainland.

Bringing Finn and Judah along wasn't feasible, but he was nervous about leaving them behind, especially in their current condition. He felt better knowing they were with Vanik, who, as much as he hated to admit it, was one of the better fighters.

"What happens if you drown?" Vanik asked as the four of them took off their boots and uniform jacket on the beach.

Weylin clapped him on the back. "Then it's your turn."

Judah lurched forward from Finn's side and wrapped his arm around Atreus' waist, pressing his face into his abdomen as he had before. Everyone watched the interaction, looking a bit wide-eyed and unsure. Atreus too.

He hesitantly raised his hand and placed it atop Judah's dirty curls once again. "I'll be alright. Stay with Finn and listen to him."

Judah nodded into his stomach and his arm tightened. In the end, Finn had to gently pry him off.

They paced themselves as they swam to the island, alternating between swimming on their front and their back. This was not the time to hurry and exhaust themselves. The current made swimming more difficult and tiring.

Atreus kept his eyes closed most of the time, trying to avoid the burn of salt water and not think about what could be lurking under him. He opened them occasionally to check their progress and make sure they were still going in the right direction.

They all made it to the island, muscles aching and chests heaving. He crawled onto the rocky shore and pushed his wet hair out of his face, gazing up at the large mountain in front of him.

The four of them hurried through the trees and hiked up the rocks that made up the base of the mountain. They split up to find an entrance. Harlow and Weylin went in one direction while he and Mila went in another.

The rocks bit into his bare feet. Even though they had ditched their boots, they'd kept their knives in their hands as they swam. Every minuscule noise made him spin around and tighten his grip. He was beyond uneasy knowing the *Te'Monai* were here on this island. He wanted to go back to the relative safety of the mainland, but he *needed* to get back to the Institute.

Harlow came racing toward them. "Weylin found an opening."

They followed her around the mountain. The opening Weylin had discovered was so small that Atreus didn't know how he'd spotted it.

"Good thing none of us are claustrophobic," Harlow huffed as they crawled through the tunnel, one in front of the other.

"This can't be an entrance the *Te'Monai* use. It's too small," Mila said.

"We're getting closer," Atreus announced from the front. The humming had been growing in volume since they left the beach.

Thankfully, the tunnel widened the farther they traveled until they were able to stand. It wasn't a dead end either. The heat swelled as they moved deeper, and another layer of sweat coated their skin. This wasn't a mountain. With the heat came a horrible stench. Bodies didn't hold up well in high temperatures.

The tunnel fed into a cavity that stretched upward. He stopped abruptly at the edge of the tunnel. Mila nearly bumped into him, but he paid her no mind. His eyes were currently fixed on the lumps lying on the floor. None of them breathed a word and none of the *Te'Monai* moved.

He swallowed thickly and then took a step forward.

The humidity in the volcano made it difficult to breathe. Sweat dripped down his neck and back, and the grip he had on his knife kept slipping. The rocky floor was so hot that it nearly burned his feet and the jagged points dug into his soles, but he didn't so much as hiss as he weaved through the *Te'Monai*. And sure enough, none of them moved, not even the tiniest bit.

He sighed in relief when they reached the other side of the cavity. The huge wall in front of him had many openings—other tunnels. They led to another large space filled with more *Te'Monai* and another wall of gaping holes.

This place was like a hive.

"Come on, wonder boy," Harlow whispered. "Sniff out that stone."

Atreus ignored her, trying to focus on the humming that filled his skull. It was difficult to determine what path to take when they were all so close together.

As they crept from cavity to cavity, it became clear to him that they were heading toward the center of the volcano. The heat had nearly become unbearable. The rocks were too hot to walk on now, so they had to rip their shirt sleeves and wrap the fabric around their feet to provide an additional layer of protection.

Columns and piles of rock littered the interior of the volcano, so he hadn't realized that he'd come across a mound of corpses until he was right in front of it. The putrid smell intensified only a few steps away, right as his eyes recognized the limbs.

He stopped, and there was a sharp intake of breath behind him. The air was thick with blood and rot. They tried to avoid breathing it in, but it was inevitable. Gagging followed. His eyes stung, and the tears that escaped them mixed with his sweat.

His focus was captured yet again by the humming. It was more intense here. And coming from...

...right there.

His eyes latched on to an opening behind the pile of bodies about twenty feet up from the ground.

He gestured toward the aperture. "We need to get up there."

The wall was unusually flat, as were the floors. At a certain point, everything had smoothed. It was a drastic, almost unnatural change. He took that as a sign.

There were slight divots in the wall, too high up and far apart for them to use. He suspected that was how the *Te'Monai* climbed up into the tunnel.

A ripping noise came from behind him. He startled, worrying that the *Te'Monai* had awoken, but when he spun around, he realized that the noise had been Weylin tearing the bottom of his pants off. Weylin placed the handle of his knife into his mouth as he tied the fabric around his hands and began clambering up the pile of corpses. Weylin kept his eyes off the bodies, but Atreus couldn't look away. The poor lighting made it impossible for him to recognize any features, which was for the best.

When Weylin climbed high enough, he swung his arms and jumped. He landed lightly, his body easily absorbing the impact as if he was used to jumping from surface to surface. One of his hands gripped the ledge and he pulled himself up. He stared down at them expectantly as he tore off the hand wrappings and plucked the knife from his mouth.

At first, none of them moved, but then Harlow followed suit. When she jumped, she was a bit short, but Weylin was waiting at the edge and grabbed her hand.

Atreus tried to think of something else as he climbed the pile. This was just... loose soil. Sand, maybe. He held his breath and cringed when his hands or feet touched something wet.

He immediately ditched the bloody fabric around his hands once he was in the tunnel, but he couldn't afford to lose the foot wrappings.

Weylin stared at him with something akin to disapproval. "They're dead. We're not," he said. "If you want to keep things that way, you need to *move* and find that stone."

Of course. That was the first rule.

Weylin witnessed the myriad of emotions flashing across his face and scoffed. "Your bleeding heart is going to get you killed one day," Weylin said as he roughly brushed past him. "Wake up."

Atreus turned with Weylin's shove. He stared at the other's back, then shook his head. He needed to stay focused. They didn't know how much time they had.

The tunnel was sweltering—too hot now to feel like you were getting any real air—but they were so close to the stone. The humming had turned into a buzzing that he could feel along his skin.

This tunnel fed into another vast cavity, but this one was the biggest yet. Columns of rock at different heights littered the space before them. Between those columns was empty air.

Atreus leaned forward and peered down. The bottom of the cavity was visible, glowing a reddish-orange that looked inauspicious. The fall was long enough that no one would survive it. He could make out what looked like bodies lining the floor below them, which made him wonder how many people, if any, had tried this before.

But the stone *was* here. About a few hundred feet away in the middle of the cavity. He could see it, gleaming a bright aqua even in the dim light. His heart hammered wildly as he ran forward, his eyes on the prize. Once his hand closed around it, they would be back.

He was so focused on the stone ahead that he didn't notice the lumps that littered the outskirts of the space. Or how they began to stir.

Harlow's shout alerted him a few seconds later. The panic in her voice made him slow.

For a second, everything sat still.

When he turned, he was faced with a wall of darkness. Slowly, pairs of yellow eyes appeared, blinking lazily and fixing on him. The *Te'Monai* had awoken.

He bolted, pulling himself up onto columns and jumping down to others as fast as he could. He burned his hands on the rock and cursed himself for abandoning his hand wrappings earlier. But the panic trumped the pain.

Out of the corner of his eye, he saw dark blurs racing toward him. Toward the stone. They would disappear when he dropped to a new column and reappear even closer when he hauled himself up onto another one. It was like a warped game of hide and seek. But if he got caught, he was dead.

When he rose to the next column, one of the *Te'Monai* let out a cry and lunged at him. He dropped down right in time and the *Te'Monai* flew over him, crashing into one of the rock pillars with a yelp and falling to its demise. He stared after it, breathing hard, before urging his legs into motion again.

The stone was right *there*.

Sparks illuminated the space as another *Te'Monai* swung at him and its claws met rock instead of flesh. Another one chomped at empty space. He felt the force of its bite as air blew over his arm.

He leaped forward when he was only feet away from the stone, his hand outstretched. The humming was so loud it was nearly the only thing he could hear. He needed to get out of here. He needed to get everyone out.

A force slammed into his side.

He flew to the side and managed to stop himself before he tumbled over the edge. He coughed and spat on the rock before scrambling to his feet. The *Te'Monai* skulked across from him, circling the center of the column where the stone *had* been.

Atreus looked around and let out a sigh of relief when he saw that the stone hadn't gone over the edge. It was a few feet away, but closer to the *Te'Monai*.

He charged. The *Te'Monai* roared and swiped out. He dodged its hit and ran his knife along its side. Its screech echoed throughout the space.

They were still sluggish, he realized. His and the others' entrance had startled the *Te'Monai* awake, but they hadn't fully regained their senses yet.

He moved quickly, using every last bit of energy he had. The *Te'Monai* was off balance and attempted to use its tail to knock him away, but he ducked and drove his knife into its soft underbelly. He continued to drive it forward, pushing his bloodied feet against the hot rock until the creature was at the edge. And then he let go. He pitched forward, swinging his body around so he could catch the edge of the column. His shoulders *screamed* at the abrupt halt in momentum. He gasped for air as he pulled himself up.

His limbs were trembling as he looked back at the entrance where the others were fighting. One of the *Te'Monai* was going for Harlow's back while she fought off another. She couldn't stop the first one without leaving an opening for the second. He could see so clearly in his mind how the scene would play out. The *Te'Monai* would clamp its jaw around her neck and pull her head clean off.

"No!" he screamed. His eyes were locked onto Harlow, onto the *Te'Monai*. *NO!*

The *Te'Monai* soared over her. Atreus stared, bewildered. His heart skipped and he pushed himself to his hands and knees, scrambling forward and hurling himself at the stone. The rock sliced his skin open, but nothing mattered because a second later, his hand closed around the stone and the realm disappeared.

CHAPTER
THIRTY

When Lena woke up the next morning, she was burning. It wasn't from any fever or hangover. The burn came from somewhere deep inside of her. It was an ache. A desire. Her Slayer wanted blood. It wanted to be brutal. And right now, after everything that'd happened over the past few days —the alliance, Aquila, her memories, Ira, Tuck, the Blessed, *everything*—she wanted those things too.

It was a dangerous place to be in. If an Imprint bearer was somewhat unstable, the Slayer could challenge that and take advantage of their bonded's emotions. They didn't understand limits. Slayers, Numina, weren't moral beings. They didn't care about right and wrong. Everything for them—for immortal, all-powerful beings— was entertainment. Death, suffering, chaos . . .

Maybe that was why Oberus had offered her a pact. She supposed by its standards, she would be great entertainment.

She lay in bed, flat on her back, thinking about all of this. Her attendants had tried to get her up three times, but she'd ignored them every time they came. She was tired, and there wasn't anything important going on until later. She could mope and lose herself in her thoughts if she wanted to.

But her thoughts were so *loud*, and there were so many of them.

The burn remained deep in her chest, like a flame that just wouldn't go out.

She'd been in a situation like this before. Twice, actually. So she knew the burning wouldn't stop until she gave in. The first time she tried to ignore it, she'd ended up sick, sweating profusely and blacking out randomly for a week. She was lucky no one had picked her off. The second time she'd given in much sooner. And this time she actually wanted to give in.

She and her Slayer were on the same page.
It was about time for her to work on that list.

∼

The Slayers had been sent out about six hours ago. The night was coated in red and the howls of the bloodthirsty beasts echoed throughout the Highlands.

Lena mentally apologized to Cowen before slipping out through her balcony and locking it behind her. Cowen *had* surveillance around her room, but everyone was inside tonight, even the guards and enforcers.

This night belonged to the Slayers. Anyone foolish enough to be out tonight would find themselves as a snack for one of the roaming beasts, yet here she was, climbing down the side of the palace and running across the grounds.

She called her Slayer to her. If anyone else's Slayer decided to attack her, she needed her own nearby. For the most part, Slayers weren't pack creatures. They hunted on their own, and she was counting on that tonight. Her odds wouldn't be too great if some Slayers decided they were desperate enough to team up against her.

She stayed close to the palace as she jogged around the perimeter, suddenly reminded once again of the sheer size of the building. She'd traveled around a mile already and was still on the same side. It would be quicker, theoretically, to cut through the inside of the palace, but the building was currently swimming with enforcers.

Each royal family had their own wing in the palace, equipped with lots of bedrooms, a library, a study and a kitchen, but for some families, that wasn't enough. Therefore, houses had been built on palace grounds to give the royal families the option of more privacy. Well, *mansions*, not houses. The homes had two dozen bedrooms and sat vacant for most, if not all, of the year. It was a statement. And she hated it.

But lucky for her, and unlucky for her targets, one of the houses was occupied tonight. Lena thought it was rather stupid of the Covaylens to choose tonight of all nights to reside in their mansion rather than the palace. But she didn't have much room to talk. She *was* currently *outside*, making her way around the palace.

She picked up her pace when a human scream rang out in the distance. Her Slayer was still running alongside her just inside the treeline. She looked through its eyes for a moment and saw another Slayer in its peripheral. She sent her Slayer after it as she reached the Covaylens' mansion.

If she had her numbers right, twenty-three people were in this house.

If you were Blessed and tied to a royal family, either by blood or some other intimate relationship, you had a place to stay in the palace. Some families really took advantage of that, like the Covaylens. Other families weren't as close and distanced themselves.

For the Vuukromas, only the main line lived in the palace. Ophir. Avalon.

Celine. Tuck. And Alaric, Avalon's father. She was actually the one who had a claim to the council seat, but she hadn't wanted it, so Ophir sat there instead.

Lena was only killing Amos and Lyra Covaylen tonight. Lyra was on the council and Amos was one of her partners. They'd both had an active role in the death of her family. And they had made themselves easy targets. Well, *easier* targets. They were still Blessed, and there were two of them and one of her. She needed to be quick and quiet about this. She didn't want anyone else waking up and discovering her.

She climbed the side of the house that faced the forest to make sure no one looking out of the palace windows saw her. Lyra had a balcony connected to her room. No noise came from the other side of the door. Lena peeked around the curtain and peered into the dark room. She saw a lump under the covers. Lyra was sleeping.

The locks were easy to bypass. If the Numen of Luck was in her favor tonight, Amos would be sharing a bed with Lyra, and Lena would have to make fewer stops.

Before entering the room, she made sure her hood and mask were secured. Only her eyes were visible. They were bright purple now that her Slayer was out, which was a telling feature, one that *could* give her away. But there were many people with purple Slayers, and she wasn't planning on leaving any witnesses or survivors. She was skilled, but she couldn't fight two Blessed without the help of her Imprint.

She slipped inside the room and the smell of alcohol immediately reached her nose. Amos had also passed out on the bed, so it looked like luck *was* on her side tonight. She wondered if the Numen was watching her, looking forward to some entertainment.

She went for Amos first. It was too easy. Neither of them was a fighter.

Most Blessed were so conceited that it made them vulnerable. They thought no one would dare come after them because of their power, and for the most part, that was true. But those thoughts made them complacent and easier to take down when someone actually *did* come after them, especially since most Blessed had no real battle experience.

Lyra and Amos were out cold, but Lena didn't take her time. The alcohol had only numbed their senses, not shut them down completely.

Amos' eyes flew open when her dagger was a few inches from his chest, but he wasn't fast enough. Lena made sure she hit the heart. She really didn't want to create a bigger mess than she had to, but he didn't fall still immediately. She needed to move on before Lyra got away—the other royal's eyes were already fluttering open—so she sank her dagger into the side of Amos' neck too.

Lyra was up on her feet by the time Lena grabbed her. Aura flame covered Lyra's hands, but it was weak, and she was unsteady on her feet, clearly still somewhat intoxicated. They must've drunk *a lot* last night.

Lena called her Slayer back to her and then released it again, inside the room. Lyra stumbled back, a cry escaping her lips. Lena slapped her aura-flame-covered palm over Lyra's mouth, burning her face, and slid her dagger across her neck. She quickly threw the body toward the bed before any blood could spill onto the floor.

Breathing heavily, Lena looked at the two bodies. She'd acted so quickly—on instinct—but now that the threat was eliminated, she had time to fully process what she—

No, you need to keep moving.

She wiped the blood off her cheek and gathered up the corners of the sheets and quilts the bodies lay on, throwing it over them. Her Slayer growled behind her, and she stopped. It inched forward, its endless black eyes on the bodies. They were bloody and nearly bare. They had died disoriented from sleep and alcohol.

Lena waited to feel something else. Anything. But she didn't.

And that put her at ease in a way.

She stepped back and allowed her Slayer to deal with the bodies. It scooped both of them up in its jaws and dashed outside. Its large figure damaged the balcony entrance, breaking off one of the doors and cracking the frame. The wall was dented too, which was fine. Lena had planned to leave their bodies to the Slayers. She could just make it look like they'd been a bit too drunk and left their balcony doors open, inviting Slayers inside. Some people might not buy it, but they wouldn't have any other leads.

She pulled any bloody quilts and pillows closer to the balcony doors, making it look like the Slayers had dragged the bedding this way as they escaped with their victims. When she finished crafting the scene, it looked like a mess with a few streaks of blood along the floor and mattress. She left swiftly.

On her way back to her room, she was even more careful than before. She compromised speed for stealth. The Slayers were louder, howling and snarling in the distance. Maybe they smelled her Slayer's prizes.

When she crawled back into her room, she immediately readied herself for bed. She opted out of a bath or shower, worried it would raise questions if someone overheard the heavy running water. And she didn't need anyone asking her questions about tonight.

Instead, she turned on the sink just until the water trickled out and washed the blood off her hands. She removed her clothes and rinsed the rest of the blood and dirt off her body with a wet rag. She rubbed some paste under her armpits to remove any odor and sprayed some perfume around her. She then ducked her head under the sink, working out any gunk that might have gotten into her hair.

When she was clean and smelling fresh once again, she took her clothing and the washcloths to the fireplace and threw them into the flames.

And then, after another sweep around the room to make sure nothing was amiss, she went to bed.

CHAPTER
THIRTY-ONE

When Lena woke up again, her skin was cold and her Imprint was hot. Her mattress was too firm. Completely unyielding. Something tickled her cheek when she turned. A breeze washed over her, fluttering her loose hair and the bottom of her sleeping gown. But it was the low growl that crawled over her skin that made her jerk up.

It took her all of a second to make sense of what was going on.

She was outside. In the forest. During the Night Run.

A Slayer stood in front of her, larger than her own and yellow or orange in color, but the moons made it look darker. Bloodier.

Its mouth fell open, revealing long, pointed teeth. She tensed, her fingers digging into the grass. Despite the Slayer's heat, another wave of cold slithered under her skin, numbing her limbs. The heat from her Imprint worked to thaw them.

As soon as it lunged toward her, she was on her feet and kicking up dirt. Panic seized her, tightening her chest. She called her Slayer, and it tackled the orange one right before it snagged her.

Rocks dug into the soles of her feet and tree branches scraped her arms and face as she ran. She kept an eye out for large, bright figures in her peripheral, but the red glow of the moons made her doubt herself. She would see things and then they'd disappear a moment later.

She didn't dare stop.

Her heart pounded in tandem with her bare feet beating against the forest floor. She ran as fast as she could, hoping she'd see the golden spires of the palace. But she didn't. Step after step, all she saw were trees. Just how far out was she? How had she gotten out here?

Another Slayer was up ahead. It saw her the moment she spotted it.

She skidded to a halt and her heart jumped up to her throat. All she could think was, *A Blessed is no match for a Slayer.*

Her own Slayer was behind her, dealing with other Slayers that had caught on to her scent, but she was beginning to attract too much attention. Her Slayer would be overpowered within the next few minutes.

She braced herself. Aura flame shot across her arms and chest. Even if the odds were against her favor, she wouldn't go down without a fight.

But before either she or the other Slayer could move, another roar sounded through the trees. It was close. Lena cursed internally and shifted toward the noise.

The air crackled and grew heavy. The area around her was bathed in blue as a giant azure Slayer prowled through the trees. The heat radiating from its body reached her from several feet away, telling her just how strong it was.

She took a step back, her eyes wide, but the new Slayer didn't seem to care for her. Its gaze was solely fixed on the other Slayer ahead.

Lena glanced between the two while backing up. Neither of them was focused on her now. They growled at one another, their backs arched and teeth on display. A second of stillness passed. Then another. And then the Slayers charged toward each other. They crashed in midair and went rolling across the dirt, taking down trees.

She stared after them for split second before taking off again.

The wind cut straight through her thin sleeping gown and whipped past her cheeks, pulling tears from her eyes. Her feet were bleeding. She was sure of it. She looked up, trying to track the stars, but she was going too fast, and she wasn't as good at it as Ira.

A spark of hope filled her chest when she spotted a golden tower in the distance. A new surge of energy pushed her to go faster. The palace was just up ahead. She could make it.

A blur flashed to her left and she moved on instinct, dodging the strike that would've knocked her flat on her back. She spun on her heel and brought her knee up to her attacker's side. They blocked it easily and pushed her away with practiced hands, swinging at her again. Her balance was off, so all she could do to avoid the hit was stumble away.

Her back slammed into a tree. A grunt of pain escaped her lips as the rough bark dug into her skin.

Her attacker was a man close to her age. He had a slender frame and shoulder-length brown hair. The blood-red moons had painted his light skin slightly crimson, and the shade of his glowing, orange-red eyes matched the shade of the Slayer that had lunged at her. He looked like a dark spirit coming to enact his revenge.

Her attacker grinned, his gaze soaking her in. "You're her, huh?"

Lena squinted at him. "And who the fuck are you?"

His grin only widened. He took a step forward and she tensed further, pushing away from the tree. She debated running. She couldn't outrun a Slayer, though she might be able to outrun him. But before she could think any more about it, she sensed a familiar presence.

Her attacker stopped when the blade of a sword was placed against his neck.

"Don't move," a dark voice commanded.

Lena's eyes flickered over her attacker's shoulder to see Ira step out from the shadows. He was glaring at her attacker, eyes burning a brilliant blue.

The azure Slayer back there was his. She recognized it now.

Her attacker laughed and raised his hands, keeping the rest of his body very still. "Easy, easy. I wasn't going to hurt her."

"That's not what it looked like from where I was standing," Ira said as he slowly stepped around her attacker, keeping the blade flush against his neck.

"Well, you did have a bad vantage point."

"*Stop talking*," Ira said harshly, flicking the sword up so her attacker was forced to lift his chin. The sharp blade nicked his thin skin, but he didn't make a sound as blood seeped down his neck.

More rustling sounded behind her. She prepared herself for another Slayer, but it was Cowen who emerged from the trees, concern and anger etched across his face. He breathed out a sigh of relief when he spotted her and he ran over, his eyes a brilliant yellow. Andra and Benji were a few steps behind him, and they looked equally as relieved to see her unharmed. Cowen opened his mouth, but she cut him off.

"Back to the palace," she said, her voice strained. "Now."

Ira shoved her attacker forward, keeping the sword flush against his neck. "If you call your Slayer," he warned, "it'll be the last thing you do."

The six of them moved through the forest quickly, the roars and shrill laughs of the roaming Slayers urging them forward. With their pace and the help of their own Slayers, they made it back to the palace without any other run-ins.

No one else was outside, not tonight, but as soon as she stepped inside, the captain of the palace guard met her, and there went her wish to return straight to her room without any disruptions.

Palace staff members were scattered about, watching the scene warily. Some of the royal Blessed, people she didn't recognize, had woken up due to the commotion and were craning their necks, trying to see what was going on. She wanted to close her eyes and disappear.

Cowen seemed to understand that she didn't want to speak to anyone and stepped up.

Her Sacred Guard and the palace guard were two independent units. Cowen and Captain Haveers were the top of command in their respective divisions, so neither of them had any power over the other, nor did they have to answer to the other.

"Her Majesty has had a distressing night," Cowen said. "She wishes to return to her room."

Captain Haveers looked past Cowen at Lena. "Councilman Alkus said he'd like to speak with her."

Lena's nails dug into her palms. "Councilman Alkus can wait."

Ira moved forward, shoving her attacker toward the captain of the guard, but he kept a firm grip on the man's shirt. The blade was still all but attached to the man's neck. "He attacked your queen. Find out what he was doing out there and who he is. Bring him to the dungeon. Tell me everything you get out of him."

"And me," Lena said, throwing Ira a look, but he didn't so much as glance at her.

"I told you," the man drawled, "I wasn't going to hurt her."

Ira pulled the man back so violently that Lena swore she heard his neck crack. Her attacker winced and gritted his teeth.

"And I told you," Ira whispered darkly in his ear, "to stop talking."

She stared at Ira, at his face, his eyes, the prominent veins in his hands as he released the attacker and let guards take him. She'd never seen this side of him before. It was a crafted rage and power, one he hadn't had when he was younger and angry. And one he certainly didn't have when he was upset with her.

"Kalena," Cowen said softly, pulling her gaze toward him. He nodded his head down the hall.

Right. Her room.

The five of them got there without any more interruptions. They ran into people—guards, staff, and other Blessed—but everyone knew better than to stop and ask. Lena could guess how she looked: bare, dirty, and ruffled by more than just the wind.

Her attendants weren't in her room when she returned, and she was thankful for that. She really didn't want to see anyone else tonight.

She grabbed a candle and went into the washroom to draw herself a bath, leaving Ira and Cowen behind in her bedroom; Andra and Benji had stayed in the hall. Lena sat on the edge of the pool as water filled it. She pointedly kept her back to the washroom entrance, but she could feel their presence and the weight of their stares on her back.

"You can go."

They didn't.

Lena clenched her jaw and tapped her fingers against the marble. She picked up one of the vials and poured the liquid into the pool, watching as bubbles immediately began to form across the surface. She turned a few seconds later, her eyes settling on Ira. The light coming from her bedroom outlined his form. Cowen's too. Their faces were partly concealed by the shadows, but she could still make out the expressions that unfolded across them.

"I'm back safe and sound in my room, so you can leave now." She made a shooing gesture with her hand.

And go back to ignoring me.

Ira still didn't move. Not an inch. "This is our room—"

"Then why haven't you been staying in it?" she hissed. "Thank you very much for your assistance in the forest, but you don't get to come back and act like everything is fine and normal between us after ignoring me for days, so go back to wherever you've been staying. I need to speak with Cowen."

Ira turned to the captain of her Sacred Guard, his gaze icy once again. "Yes, well, as it turns out, I also need to speak with Cowen."

Her mouth fell open, but she abruptly snapped it shut. "Did you hear anything else I just said? Get out!"

Ira's demeanor thawed a bit under the heat of her words. His jaw relaxed and his eyes softened. "I heard, and you're right."

The words hung in the air between them. She waited for more, waited for a *'but'* that didn't come. She shifted on the edge of the pool and crossed her arms.

"... I am."

Ira took a step forward, his brow furrowing. "I—" He faltered and glanced at Cowen before returning his gaze to her. "Can we talk?"

She was very tempted to tell him no and make him wait like he'd made her wait. She could be petty. There was a large part of her that was cruel. She'd learned that over the years, and sometimes she leaned into it. But there was an equally large part of her that feared being alone. They were at ends with one another.

Still, she raised her chin and said, "No."

His jaw tightened and *oh, it felt good. Denying him something.* She smirked and Ira took a step forward. "Lena, please—"

"I want an apology. And an explanation."

Ira paused and then nodded a moment later. He wetted his lips, his eyes still latched with hers. "I can give you that."

"Fine." She turned to Cowen, dismissing Ira for the time being. "What happened?"

Cowen shook his head, his eyes shining with regret, irritation, and shame.

"I don't know." He spoke the words like they physically pained him, like they were the extension of his last breath. "You were just . . . gone. We checked on you a few hours after midnight. Since there were no guards outside at the perimeter, we wanted to make sure you were safe and sound, but you weren't. You weren't in bed. You hadn't left through the door and your attendants said you hadn't gone through their hall. None of the windows or balcony doors were open, but one was unlocked." He gestured over her shoulder toward the balcony doors in the washroom. "We locked it and then went in search of you."

She looked back at the rapidly filling pool and turned the knobs off. She thought about what would've happened if Cowen had come into her room a few hours earlier when she was out dealing with the Covaylens. That would have been messy.

"Someone took me?"

She tried to sound casual, but she was too tense. Her words were too stilted. The thought of someone creeping in here and taking her sent her skin crawling. But that was exactly what she'd done to Lyra and Amos, wasn't it? And she had made it out alive, whereas they had not.

"It seems so."

She nodded and checked the barriers in her mind, making sure they were still standing strong, making sure at least her thoughts were safe.

This is how the realm works, she reminded herself. *Be grateful you're still breathing.*

In a way, her kidnapping could benefit her. It could act as a cover-up. If the council didn't buy the Slayer attack, maybe they would assume that her kidnapper and the Covaylens' killer were one and the same. Rather than the talk of tonight just being about the murdered royals, it would also be about the kidnapped queen. Not that anyone had any reason to suspect her in the first place, but they certainly wouldn't after this. So she supposed, in some fucked up way, the Numen of Luck was still on her side.

She was startled out of her thoughts when Cowen suddenly dropped to his knees before her, his head hanging low.

"I take full responsibility for what happened tonight," he said, his voice grave and wrought with emotion. "I was negligent. *Again.* I—"

"Cowen, stop." She sighed. "Get up. Come on. *Get up.*"

He did.

"I know I should be upset with you, but I'm not," she said honestly. "The Night Run is the only time guards aren't doing rounds outside." She had used that to her advantage, and so had her kidnapper. "Whoever stole me away saw their chance and took it. I know it won't happen again."

Because there wouldn't be another Night Run for months at least, and Cowen would adjust the rotations accordingly. And she would be more on guard, but what bothered her the most . . .

"I'm more concerned about why I didn't wake up until I was in the forest. Surely I would have sensed an intruder. Or at the very least, I should have woken up as I was being carried away from the palace."

Had her kidnapper slipped something into her mouth? An elixir of sorts that kept her under? Was her kidnapper a sorcerer who knew a way to keep her from waking? She supposed that was possible. After all, Julian had blocked off an entire portion of her memories.

She turned back to Ira and Cowen to find them looking just as troubled as she felt.

"Magic," Cowen supplied.

"Or an elixir," Ira added.

"Do you feel . . . unusual?" Cowen asked. "Should we get a physician?"

She shook her head. "I feel fine."

Whatever her kidnapper had done, it didn't leave a trace.

She sighed again and dipped her hand into the water, which was growing tepid. "I'm tired. I want to take a bath before going to bed."

Cowen took that as a sign of dismissal and went to leave, but he paused and glanced back at Ira. Then Lena.

She shook her head. *It's fine.*

So Cowen left, and then it was just her and Ira.

She pulled her gown over her head and slipped into the water. A groan left her lips as the heat soothed her bruises and cuts. Her back was the most sensitive, so she rolled over, resting her arms on the edge of the pool and letting the rest of her body float. She hadn't realized her eyes had slipped closed, but when she opened them, Ira was standing closer.

"I'm sorry," he blurted out. "About my reaction to the duel. I'll admit I handled the situation poorly . . . as well as everything after that. I wasn't trying to undermine or insult you. I . . . I was scared of losing you. And I know that doesn't seem to make sense because after the duel I completely ignored you for *days*, but I needed time to think. I'm not trying to make up an excuse, but you said you wanted an explanation and I . . ."

Ira ran a hand through his hair and shifted forward like he wanted to come closer, but he didn't. There was a crease between his brows that she wanted to smooth, but he was too far away to touch. Maybe that was a good thing. It wasn't often that Ira was at a loss for words.

"It's unfair to you," he finally said. "How I react to some things, I mean. And I'm trying to change, but . . . sometimes it seems impossible." His voice faded into a whisper, but it sounded so loud in this dark room.

"Come here," she mumbled.

Ira edged forward and kneeled in front of her. He reached his hand out, leaving it inches from her own, and Lena moved her hand forward to twine their fingers together.

"I'm sorry too," she said as she fiddled with his fingers.

She kept her gaze fixed on their hands, her eyes tracing over the faint scars scattered across his skin. She too had done a lot of thinking since their argument in the hall, and he wasn't the only one at fault.

"I knew a Slayer duel was a bad idea before I even challenged her, but I was so *tired* of dealing with everything. I didn't care. I was upset and running off the high of winning. I'm used to fighting. I fought out there for five years. I'm still fighting here. I fought Cressida, and so it was so easy for me to fight you too right after. What you said . . . You weren't *wrong*."

It actually annoyed her how logical he always was, even when he let his emotions take control. But at the same time, she didn't regret what she'd done. She stood by her actions, but she also understood his perspective.

"I know," he murmured.

She glanced up at him, irritation written across her face.

His mouth softened, one corner drawing up. "But I understand where you were coming from too. Now I do. I didn't at the moment. The fear and hopelessness I felt while watching that duel transformed into anger once you won. I was relieved, of course, but you didn't even seem to realize or *care* how dangerous your actions were. I just . . . " Ira dropped his head, staring at their clasped hands. "I'm not used to having someone else I can rely upon. Someone else I can come back to. It's been just me for a long time. So when you came along . . . I treasured you. *Treasure*. And then you were taken away. I just got you back and then you volunteer yourself for something that could take you away again . . . "

Her hand went slack in his. "This realm is cruel. You know that just as well as I. Anything at any time can take away what you care about. I can't—I *won't* live my entire life in fear of that."

Cowen had reminded her that she couldn't, but she often found herself slipping back into that habit, holding those she cared about close to her heart and eliminating anything or anyone she saw as a threat in order to protect her peace and her people.

Ira tightened his fingers around hers, refusing to let her go. "There's a difference between acknowledging the dangers of the realm and throwing yourself into them," he said. "You can't fault me for wanting to keep you safe. Call me a hypocrite if you wish, but I won't apologize for that."

Lena raised her gaze to meet his. He stared at her steadily, the crease between his brows still there.

"I . . . care for you. So much. I know I've said it before, but I won't stop saying it. The Tower . . . " He hesitated, his lips trembling. " . . . The Tower wasn't great, but it was better than my life before. I've always had to fend for myself. If someone offered me their help, there were usually conditions that came with it. And that was why I was so confused when you pulled me out of the Tower and didn't demand anything of me. I thought it was a trick. I still have night terrors about . . . before. I can't sleep through the night most nights.

"I learned I would never have anything for myself," he rasped. "It took me a long time to accept it, but I did. And then *you* came along and changed everything and then you were gone. I'm not proud of what I did afterward to cope. All the animosity being directed at me gave me an excuse, I think. I don't like looking back on it, but I've revisited those moments over the past couple of days."

Ira lifted his other hand to wipe away a tear that had fallen to her cheek. "I will never blame you for how you react when you're hurt . . . but I was terrified when you issued that challenge."

Lena bit down on her lower lip until she was able to push down the emotions that threatened to crack her open and leave her bleeding and exposed on the marble. "I don't know what I am. Blessed. Cursed. Something entirely different. But after that duel . . . I didn't care. And neither did anyone else. For the first time since coming to the Highlands, the people gave me respect."

Ira clenched his jaw but didn't argue. Because he couldn't.

"You could have died," he said, his voice so fragile for one of the strongest people Lena knew.

Her ribcage was suffocating her, so she squeezed Ira's fingers tighter and brought their hands up, resting her forehead against them.

Death.

It was something she'd been close to many times but had evaded. She knew it was real. It had already taken so much from her. Maybe it was playing a game with her—coming close when she wanted nothing more than to live and staying away when she wanted nothing more than to die.

"I've had to do things I'm not proud of too. When I was on the road." She kept her eyes shut because she couldn't say this if she had to look at Ira's face. "Things . . . happened that I'm also not proud of. I hate it. I hate how shitty things are, and sometimes it feels like an endless cycle. Sometimes I wonder if it's even worth it."

Ira's grip on her hand strengthened. A wordless comfort.

"But I won't apologize for the things I've had to do to survive."

"I won't make you," Ira promised.

She squeezed her eyes shut tighter. "I'm sorry I made you."

Ira moved their hands and his forehead pressed against hers. She felt his warm breath across her face and she wanted to melt into him. She wanted him to hold her again. She hadn't realized how much she'd missed this—touch. *His* touch. Him.

"Promise me," he whispered. "Promise me no more. No more rash decisions."

He was extending his trust once again. She'd already broken it so many times since coming back. His and Cowen's, yet they had still chosen to stick around. They kept giving her chances.

She felt a pang in her chest once again. "Okay, but you have to do the same. Don't do anything reckless on your own. You have me now. You can't leave me behind."

She winced, thinking about the cruel words she'd thrown at him when he left her in the hallway after the duel.

His lips pressed against her forehead. "I promise."

They sat there until the bath water grew cold. And then Lena crawled out and wrapped herself in a robe. Ira had taken it upon himself to turn around to protect what was left of her modesty, so when she turned back toward him, she couldn't see his face and he couldn't see hers. Maybe that was for the best.

She debated telling him then how she felt. They'd poured out so much of themselves only minutes ago. What was one more line? Only three words. Maybe more because she tended to ramble when she was nervous.

Her time away from him had made her realize things, acknowledge feelings. The first time she lost him, she had no way of knowing if he was alive or dead. This second time, she knew he was alive and well, sharing the same space as her, yet he was still out of reach. It hurt, in a different way than before, to know he was *here* but not hers.

She'd convinced herself that all would be well as long as he was by her side. That those feelings of hers were only present because she finally had him back after years of thinking he'd been ripped away forever. She had thought perhaps they would settle back down to feelings that were appropriate to feel toward one's best friend.

But if anything, those feelings had only been heightened during their few days apart. What was that saying? You don't realize what you have until it's gone?

She didn't want it to be gone again. *Him* to be gone.

She opened her mouth, but the mess of letters crumbled in her throat, choking her. She was afraid of these words ruining things too.

Lena swallowed the lump in her throat, and like a coward, pushed everything aside.

Soon, she told herself. She didn't want to get into this tonight. It had already been hectic enough. *Soon.*

"Will you stay?" she dared to ask, hoping her voice didn't sound too pitiful.

Ira glanced over his shoulder. "Of course."

Despite the events of the night, her aching chest, and the voice in her head telling her to tell him how she truly felt, she fell asleep quickly in Ira's arms.

CHAPTER
THIRTY-TWO

Atreus glared at the blank piece of paper in front of him. He'd been scowling at it for the last thirty minutes. The pencil lay untouched next to it.

"If writing is still difficult, you can confess your regrets to me," Prophet Caysen said.

The burns on Atreus' hands hadn't been bad to begin with. Miss Anya had attended to them, and he healed quickly. Right now they were bearable but irritating and better than those on his feet. Writing would be uncomfortable, but he could do it. Probably. He wouldn't though. He had nothing to confess. He had plenty of regrets, but not the kinds the prophets wanted to hear.

He ignored Prophet Caysen and stayed silent.

When they returned from the realm, he'd refused to follow Prophet Silas out of the cavern. Enforcers had dragged him to the black and white room, and Prophet Silas had plucked the stone out of his hand with a dark look of disapproval before assigning him to restoration for the evening. The prophet had warned him about his defiance, but he'd pushed it aside.

Firstborns who were unlucky enough to catch a prophet's wrath were usually sent to restoration for a day or two. Their stay would extend each time they returned. The room was much smaller than the seminar hall and much darker. However, what firstborns did as a form of punishment—*restoration*—was similar to what they did in seminar. A prophet would preach, lay on the guilt, and ask you to apologize for things you'd never done. It was heavier than seminar, and crueler in some ways.

But Prophet Caysen seemed to be in a rather generous mood today. She didn't bother Atreus again for the rest of the session. Atreus left as soon as the prophet dismissed him, pushing himself out of his chair and bumping into the table. The pencil rolled off the edge and the blank paper fluttered to the ground, but he didn't pick them up.

He lifted his hands to stare at them as he limped through the Institute. Holding the pencil hadn't hurt, but he hadn't been able to *keep* hold of it for the life of him.

His hands were trembling. They had been ever since he got back.

∼

They put Atreus on garden duty until his hands and feet were completely healed. Judah practically lit up when he stepped into the room.

The kid had been having night terrors since returning, which wasn't abnormal. Atreus had heard Judah crying and whimpering in his sleep, but he'd stayed tucked under his covers, unmoving.

Not my problem, he'd told himself. *He's not my problem. I got him through that Outing. I did my part.*

But he kept an eye and an ear out in case anyone decided to smother Judah to get rid of the noise, but no one moved to do that. They let Judah and the other boys cry.

Eventually, Finn had taken pity on the others and climbed out of bed to help Judah like Atreus had helped him. Like Finn had helped Atreus. He had a suspicion that Finn was sharing the sleeping elixir with Judah, and maybe the others too.

Bleeding heart. Please, if anyone was one, it was Finn. He should have saved that medicine for himself. Facing their night terrors was probably the best thing for those kids to do right now. They needed to harden if they wanted to survive their introduction period.

Everyone, not only the kids, had been shaken up by their last Outing. The bloodbath was one thing, but the uncertainty was another. Everyone else was probably thinking the same thing he was. They'd thought they'd had this figured out, but there was more to the Outings now. More questions. And they needed answers quickly. Their lives were on the line, but that wasn't anything new.

He'd roughly counted their numbers when they returned. There had been thousands before. Now there were around five hundred. The cavern had never been so quiet.

"Come over and pick the wheat with me," Judah said after bounding up to him.

While Judah had night terrors, he seemed okay during the day. Atreus didn't know if this was the kid's mind boxing off the trauma or if he was putting up a front. It was probably a bit of both. But Judah had handled his first Outing better than Atreus.

He should really tell Judah no. This was his chance to put distance between them. The enforcers didn't allow socializing during working hours either, so he even had some sort of excuse. But Judah gazed up at him with wide, hopeful eyes, his feet shifting.

Atreus opened his mouth, but Judah's hand reached out to grab the bottom of his shirt. "Please."

His chest tightened and he berated himself over and over again. "Okay."

Bleeding heart. Bleeding heart. Bleeding heart.

⁓

ATREUS STUCK to the back of the crowd in the dining hall as they shuffled forward to return their trays. He moved up when the crowd did, but his mind was elsewhere, replaying the moments of their last Outing.

There was no way of telling if what had happened would be their new normal. Maybe all the *Te'Monai* attacked in waves, but they hadn't been in a realm long enough before to witness it. But now their Outings were longer . . . because the person who'd been getting the stones before now suddenly . . . wasn't? Had they died?

He kept going back to what Weylin had said to him.

"Your bleeding heart is going to get you killed one day. Wake up."

A laugh bubbled out of him. The firstborns in front of him turned to look at him oddly.

If only it were that easy.

He squeezed his tray tighter until his knuckles whitened. How long would this go on? How many realms were they going to be sent to and how many kids were going to be shipped in just to be sent to their death the next day?

"Hey."

Harlow stood next to him, a deep frown on her face. Atreus raised a brow.

"I want to talk about what happened during the last Outing. Under the mountain."

"It was a volcano."

She rolled her eyes. "Okay, *volcano*. Whatever. That's not the point."

"What *is* your point?" he asked, his patience waning by the second.

She glared at him and flicked her hair over her shoulder. "Never mind if you're going to be an ass about it."

He let out a huff of disbelief and turned so he was fully facing her.

"*You* came up to *me*." He looked over the crowd, seeking out two people in particular. "I'm surprised you would voluntarily talk to me outside of an Outing. Does Vanik know what you're doing?"

"He doesn't control me," Harlow snapped. "No one does. And I wouldn't be in your company if I didn't have to be, so why don't you stop being so defensive and just listen to me for a second?"

Atreus stared at her and made a gesture as if to say *go on*.

Her face twisted into something in between a glare and a grimace. "I want to preface this by saying I don't need your help. I don't need you to play hero, okay? But . . ." She swallowed thickly and moved her gaze anywhere but him. "When we were under the *volcano* in that room with the stone . . . when the *Te'Monai* woke and attacked, there were a lot of them and we were getting overrun. I felt that one behind me, you know? I could sense it. I knew there was no way for me to dodge it without leaving myself open to the one in front of me. I thought I was going to die. I was prepared to die." Her eyes returned to his. They were heavy with shadows smeared under them. "And then, it just . . . jumped over me."

He remembered. It was the last thing he'd seen in that realm.

"It doesn't make sense," she said. She was staring at his chest, but her eyes were unfocused. "The *Te'Monai's* main goal has always been to kill as many people as possible, so why would it bypass the opportunity to kill me?"

He clenched his jaw and moved up with the crowd. "I don't really know why you're telling me this."

Harlow glared at him again. "Because *you* are the only one who seems to have a clue about what the fuck is going on."

"I don't."

"Bull*shit*. The stones? That was all you."

"Keep your voice down," he hissed.

She laughed, but it was cold and short. "Why? What are you so afraid of? You *lived*."

"*So did you*." A creaking noise came from below and he looked down to see that he'd bent the metal tray. He squeezed his eyes shut and took a controlled breath. "Look, Harlow, I don't know what you want me to tell you. I don't know what happened, but you're alive. That's all that matters."

"Don't give me your righteous pep-talk," she spat. "*I should have died,* Atreus. And I didn't. I need to know why—"

"Well, I can't tell you that! You're wasting your time here. And mine. Why don't you go ask Weylin or Vanik?"

She looked at him coldly. Dare he say she appeared . . . disappointed?

"*Fuck you,*" she sneered before shouldering past him and disappearing into the crowd.

~

Later that night, he lay awake in bed yet again. His mind kept remembering that parting moment. He saw it clearly. The *Te'Monai* had changed direction at the last second.

It came as no shock when he gave into his exhaustion and slipped under only to be caught in a night terror for the first time in months.

He dreamed of *Te'Monai* and blood. Screams filled his ears and claws raked down his arms. He couldn't tell if they belonged to the *Te'Monai* or the firstborns.

He ran.

He ran away from everything, trying to escape.

And he did. For a moment. But the monsters always came crawling back.

His eyes were open, staring at the dark ceiling, but he couldn't move. His breath was caught in his chest and his limbs were immobile. Panic washed over him, but even that wasn't enough to get him to move. *Te'Monai* started to appear in the shadows, swarming him. He was frozen.

A strangled sound left him and his eyes widened.

"Atreus," Finn whispered, suddenly at his side. He knew better than to touch him. "Atreus, it's okay. It's just a dream. Nothing you're seeing is real. They can't hurt you."

Oh but they could. They could hurt him without touching him. Seeing the *Te'Monai* was enough to send his blood thrumming, his heart pounding, his mind *screaming*. He could feel their talons digging into him, wrapping around his neck, ripping into his sides. He could hear their shrill roars and the human cries that came afterward.

"What's wrong?"

Atreus faintly recognized the small voice and the panic that came with it.

"He's having a night terror. He's fine."

Their mouths were so big. Why were they taunting him? Why didn't they end it? His cheeks were wet, his hands bloody.

"Why aren't you waking him up?" the voice cried.

"We can't. He can't wake up. He's stuck. He'll be fine."

The *Te'Monai* were here. In the Institute. *How did they get into the Institute?* He didn't hear screams anymore. It was quiet. Was everyone dead?

". . . He doesn't look fine."

"He's strong," Finn said with conviction. "He'll be fine."

Atreus tried to say something else, but Finn gently shushed him and began another one of his stories.

CHAPTER
THIRTY-THREE

A council meeting was called the following morning. Lena was told she didn't have to be there, but she went to prove a point. And because she didn't want to be out of the know.

The entire council was tense as Captain Haveers read his report. Everyone had noticed the empty seat.

"There was an unusually large number of deaths last night. Forty-six bodies have been reported so far," Captain Haveers announced. "And that's only in the Highlands. Of this number . . . eight were found with their hearts missing. And these eight bodies were all relatively close to one another, a few miles out from the palace, and they weren't as badly mutilated as the others. All Blessed, as well. It could be a coincidence or mean nothing at all, but . . . with the recent killings, we found this detail worthy of being noted.

"Most of the remaining thirty-eight bodies were mauled beyond recognition, but we have identified some of them . . . including Lady Lyra Covaylen and Lord Amos Covaylen. They were staying in their palace-side manor last night. Upon visiting their home, it appears the lady and lord were taken from their room by Slayers. We suspect they were inebriated and perhaps left the balcony doors open or cracked, though no one else in the house heard any commotion or was harmed. It's unknown for sure what happened, but the Slayer activity last night was . . . odd. There hasn't been a death toll like this during a Night Run in over two decades."

The council sat in silence. Many of its members were, at the very least, stunned. Some might have been mourning two people they'd considered friends. Maybe they were trying to make sense of how this could happen.

Royal Blessed were supposed to be strong. Lyra and Amos had been royal

Blessed, yet they had been killed. It must've been a rude awakening for those on the council who'd thought themselves invincible. And while it would make her job harder, Lena wanted them to be afraid. To realize that someone could and would take them down.

She was also quiet and still, but her mind was on the other eight deaths. The ones with their hearts missing. Slayers weren't responsible for those bodies. A heart was too small. Taking one out and leaving the rest of the body in decent condition wasn't something a Slayer was capable of doing. They ate most, if not all, of their prey.

Another killer had been outside last night, other than her. And it must be the same person who had killed those five people and staked them up on trees.

But why last night of all nights? Why put yourself in danger to collect more victims? If they were trying to send her a message, it didn't make much sense either. Their victims were lost among the dozens of others who had fallen last night. What were they playing at?

The killer had to be Blessed. Cursed wouldn't dare go out during the Night Run. Right? Unless they were a sorcerer.

There were too many variables. Too many unknowns.

"Additionally, Her Majesty was found in the forest last night," Captain Haveers continued, his eyes flitting up to her. "After talking with the captain of the Sacred Guard, we believe someone took her from her room. Luckily, she was unharmed, but Councilman Ira did bring in a man attempting to harm her, likely the man who kidnapped her. He's Blessed, but he won't tell us his name. We've been interrogating him all night and morning . . . but he's being difficult. It's not that he doesn't talk—in fact, he sometimes talks *too* much—but he won't answer our questions about why he was out there and what his goals are."

Was he the killer? He could be, but there wasn't any substantial evidence behind that accusation. He'd been outside last night, same as she, and he *had* attacked her even though he *apparently* wasn't trying to hurt her. He could have taken her from her room and slipped her an elixir or used sorcery on her, but only if he was a sorcerer. He didn't wear gloves on his hands. His Slayer had been there when she woke up, just . . . staring at her. He was definitely hiding something, and he was a suspect, but then again, their evidence was coincidental at best.

Maybe he wasn't at all involved in the killings—or her kidnapping. Maybe he was a diversion and the real killer had set this all up to get the council off their back. Maybe there was more than one person they should be looking for.

And if the man in the dungeon *was* the killer, then why hadn't he finished her off when he had the chance? The fact that he hadn't only made her further believe that these deaths were some sort of message for her. An act of intimidation. But from who? And what did it mean?

Her first instinct was that this was another ploy set up by Alkus and the other

Blessed who wanted her out of her current position, but would they go so far as to kill other Blessed?

Yes. Of course they would.

The more she thought about it, the more obvious it became that some of the council members were connected to this killer. Or kill*ers*. There had to be more than one. She knew for certain that Alkus and the others hadn't been the ones to directly kill her family. They'd hired someone. And her family's bodies had been left in the same condition as these recent victims, with their hearts missing.

But at the same time, it seemed too obvious. Surely they must've known she would've immediately made the connection and they would be found out. Maybe they wanted her to know. She couldn't do anything without proof. And the Blessed ruled everything.

"Keep questioning him," she said. "And *make* him answer. In the meantime, identify the remaining victims. Alert their families and give a blessing on my behalf. Make sure they're getting a proper burial."

Captain Haveers nodded and then left with Lena's dismissal.

"What else is there to be discussed?" she asked as she rubbed one of her temples.

"... Your Majesty, if you're not up for—"

"I'm fine, Mikhail." She gave him a terse smile. "Just tired."

"I can imagine after the night you had," Ophir commented. "Where were your guards? Their only job is to protect you, yet they let you be kidnapped from your room?"

She took a deep breath and turned her head toward him. "Lord Vuukroma, while I appreciate your concern, I can assure you that my guards are taking every precaution necessary to ensure that this doesn't happen again. No one could have foreseen someone making a move such as this during the Night Run. Now we know to be prepared."

"Well, for your sake, I hope it doesn't happen again."

She summoned another tight smile. "What other current affairs are there to address?"

"Just one," Mikhail said after a moment.

"Enforcers in the Lowlands have reported a rise in talks of conspiracy and insurrection," Alkus continued. "The Cursed are aware of the prophecy just as we are. But they ... don't share our vision."

Lena frowned and turned to him. "And what is *our vision*, Councilman Alkus?" she asked, even though she already knew.

He stared back at her evenly. "It is one that does not involve overthrowing the order of things."

Order. The Blessed used it synonymously with law. The history books said law was supposed to be about fairness and justice, but the law of The Lands was flawed beyond measure. It was only natural, the prophets said, because the law was made by flawed beings. There was a clear hierarchy of things. Firstborns. Cursed. Blessed. Numina. But even the Numina were flawed. Corrupt.

Order was worse than law. Order meant control. And the Blessed thought there was nothing more important than staying in control.

Law. Order. Control. They all gave out power. Blessed were as hungry for power as Slayers were for flesh.

～

"Do you think Aquila will ever agree to meet with me?" Lena asked as she and Kieryn turned a corner in the hedge maze next to the palace.

They had met only about five minutes ago. She hadn't cut straight to this question, but she hadn't wasted much time with pleasantries either.

Kieryn possessed that gleam in his eyes that Tuck often did. It always put her on edge because when he wore that look, he was unpredictable. Tuck, that was. Lena couldn't speak for Kieryn. Not yet. But that was exactly why she was meeting with him—to get to know him better; and to hopefully get some of her questions answered.

He was dressed up again today. His long, light blond hair was pulled back and lay flat against his back. Only a few wisps of hair were free, artfully framing his face. His eyelashes were darkened and azure gems fell from his ears. His clothes were rich in color, matching his eyes yet again, and the fabric was thick, despite the heat. Though, he didn't appear uncomfortable in the slightest.

Lena, on the other hand, could feel sweat dripping down her neck and pooling in the small of her back. She was used to the heat but not immune to it.

Kieryn snorted at her question. "Subtle," he said, a grin on his lips. "And somewhat offensive. You ask me out only to ask about Aquila? I'm truly wounded."

Lena rolled her eyes.

"You fancy her?"

"No, I'm only trying to speak to her. She's run away from me twice."

Kieryn clicked his tongue. "Don't take it personally. She hardly talks to anyone but Sorrel. Not really a social bird, that one."

They entered one of the many courtyards interspersed throughout the maze. The grass under their feet turned into gravel as they approached the gazebo in the center of the space. Benji and Andra stood on the outskirts of the courtyard.

"Surely, this wasn't all you wanted to talk about."

"No, it's not." *But Aquila is a much easier topic to start on.*

Kieryn collapsed onto the bench inside the gazebo. "Ugh, it's so bloody hot here. Even the winds are scorching."

Lena raised a brow and raked her eyes over him. No sweat. No redness. "I wouldn't have guessed you were affected at all."

He winked at her. "Neat trick, isn't it?"

He was covered from head to toe, so it was impossible to tell if he had an Imprint. She thought it unlikely. It would make sense if he was a sorcerer like Sorrel and Aquila, but his hands were uncovered and free of tattoos.

"What's the trick?"

"I can't be telling you all my secrets now, can I, Your Majesty?"

"If The Lands is to form an alliance with Ouprua and we are to be married, I don't think keeping secrets from one another would do us any good."

Kieryn picked at something on his shoulder. "Now that's a big if."

"Not really."

With each passing day, it became clearer that this alliance and marriage was the only option she faced.

She sat next to him and lowered her voice. "Sorrel told me she doesn't have an Imprint. And she keeps her hands covered."

Kieryn's earrings jangled as he tilted his head in her direction. "Careful, Your Majesty. Your prejudice is beginning to show."

"*I* only recently gained my Imprint," she pointed out. "For most of my life, I didn't have one either. And I certainly never engaged in sorcery."

At least as far as she knew, which wasn't saying much with a chunk of her memories locked away.

"It's funny how one's mindset can so quickly shift when offered an opportunity once thought to be out of reach," Kieryn said loftily as he stretched his legs out in front of him.

Lena frowned and leaned forward so she could catch his eye.

"My mindset hasn't changed," she said firmly. "Blessed have always been stronger than Cursed. They have the power and the influence. That's just how it is here . . . Do you know how many times I wished it were different?"

"But now you're the one in power with an Imprint on your chest, so what will you do?"

She was a little caught off guard by the question. She answered honestly but *carefully*. While she thought she knew which way Ouprua's ideologies swung, she couldn't be certain.

"I want to be a good leader. I want to provide for my people. *All* of them. Under my reign, I want everyone to have their necessities met. I want to mitigate suffering . . . but I know that's easier said than done."

Wrongdoing could never be completely erased. That was what the prophets said.

Kieryn hummed in what she assumed was agreement. "And what if to do all those things, you need to enter into this alliance? And marriage is the only option? What will you do then?"

She pursed her lips. " . . . *If* marriage is the only option to achieve these things, then I'm willing to accept it. It's a big commitment, which is why I've been . . . hesitant. I'm trying to thoroughly understand just exactly what and who I'm saying yes to."

"Don't you think Sorrel is a better person to ask these questions to?"

She stayed silent.

Kieryn grinned and sat up straight. "Oh, did she not bite?"

"She answered some of my questions, but she wanted to know my decision about the marriage before answering any more," Lena grumbled.

She supposed she could go back to Sorrel now and tell her she'd made a decision, but she hadn't quite yet. There was a difference between thinking you were going to say yes and actually saying yes. That was where Lena was at the moment.

"She did tell me that if a marriage happened, I would be marrying you or Aquila."

"Yes, well, I must let you know that I'm terrible company."

Lena cracked a smile. "Is that self-sabotage I hear?"

"It's self-awareness, Your Majesty," he said. "And honesty."

She nodded. "Honorable qualities."

"Oh, no." Kieryn tried to backtrack. "I'm actually quite vain and honest to a fault. Ruthless, some might say."

"Well, if you claim to be so honest, then tell me. What's your trump card? Why come all the way out here, answer a call you've never answered before, for a country that you could apparently continue to survive without?"

He smirked slightly and spread his arms along the railing behind him. "You ask us to reveal our secrets to you when you're still keeping secrets from us, Your Majesty. How's that fair?"

"It's not," she answered. "Things hardly are. It's give and take. But I am *trying* to make this work. I sought out you *and* Aquila, even though you have both been avoiding me. Tell me, do *you* want this alliance to work?"

Kieryn scratched his chin. "Beautiful, ruthless, *and* smart."

She gave him a flat look. Flattery wasn't going to get him anywhere.

"I'll talk to the council and try to convince them to let you sit in on our meetings," she bargained.

Kieryn inclined his head. "That's a start."

"I'll tell you what I do know," she said. "Sorrel doesn't have an Imprint. I have a hunch that none of you do. Ouprua doesn't go by The Lands' system of Cursed and Blessed. I have a suspicion that Imprints don't even exist in Ouprua. I know Aquila and Sorrel practice sorcery, which is illegal here. You and Von have me stumped though. This realm is larger than just us. The Lands has known that for centuries, but we've been unable to make contact with anyone. Somehow. But then Ouprua answers our call. I don't know why you're here. I think you know more than we do. You can see the entire game board while we only see a fraction of it. And I hate that, but at the same time, I'm intrigued. I never thought . . ." Lena fought to find the right words. "I never thought people without the Numina's favor, without the Divine Touch, could triumph."

I want to know how you did it.

She doubted sorcery was the only answer, but perhaps that was why she'd been drawn to Julian. She hadn't possessed an Imprint then, and sorcery was another power source. Another way to fight.

"So, yes, I am suspicious of you. And if you want this alliance to start off on the right foot, I suggest you work with me."

Kieryn let out a whistle. "That was an impressive bout of honesty, Your Majesty."

"How about you give it a go? Show me how honest you can be."

"Hmm." He fiddled with an earring while staring off to the side. "No, I don't think I will."

She sunk back, momentarily at a loss for words but not exactly surprised by his response. It seemed this meet-up *was* helping her get to know him better. "You're infuriating, you know that?"

"Yes, I told you I'm terrible company." Kieryn grinned, but it slowly slipped away. He sobered up and leaned toward her. "*Some* of what you say is true, but I won't tell you what. What I *will* tell you is that we are not your enemy. I've seen how you act. How you interact with others. Aquila's the same. It's like you see everyone as your enemy, and I know we are not immune to that."

Lena scoffed and tossed her hair out of her face. "I don't know how much you know about me, but most of the people here *are* my enemy."

"So what I'm hearing is you need allies," Kieryn said smoothly. His mouth held no mischievous curve and his eyes held no gleam. "Have you ever thought that The Lands' way of life is strange? What kind of country allows half of their population to suffer because of something out of their control? What kind of country subjects their firstborns to some unknown fate as soon as they're out of the womb?"

"I never said I agree with it," she hissed. "I'm want to fix things, but I need—"

"You need support. An alliance," Kieryn supplied once again, nodding. "Ouprua's views align with yours more than they do the traditional beliefs of The Lands. The marriage would need to be in name only, and you wouldn't need to provide an heir. You need support *and* strength, and as you implied, you're not going to find a lot of that here. We would back you."

She knew very little about Ouprua. She had more questions than answers. Krashing, they could all be lying to her. Playing her like a fool. Taking advantage of her desperation and inexperience. Perhaps they had arrived in The Lands early to come up with this very plan. She wanted to trust them, to say yes and accept their aid, but she was also aware of her position. As queen, she couldn't afford to make decisions on a whim, yet she found herself doing that more times than what was proper.

"I have two questions that I need you to answer," she said as she met Kieryn's gaze again. "You're absolutely certain your country would support my cause?"

"Yes. There might be some pushback, but not because they think The Lands should remain how it is. War is costly. In a number of ways. Some people don't think getting involved in another country's affairs is worthwhile."

Lena frowned. "War?"

Kieryn laughed lightly. "How do you think change of this scale is accomplished? By asking nicely?"

Her cheeks warmed. "Of course not, but to propose immediately resorting to war—"

"I'm not proposing that, but it's inevitable." Kieryn lowered his voice and leaned in close. That gleam was back. "We have to be careful. We're speaking of a revolution. That's treason."

He didn't sound or look worried to be committing such a crime.

Lena pulled back. "*You* brought up war."

"But *you* brought up a revolution," he responded, far too coy for Lena's liking. "'*I want to fix things.*' You brought up the ideas of it. I just said what you were too afraid to admit."

She took a deep breath and went straight into the next question. He was trying to provoke her. And distract her. "You arrived in the Highlands five days ago, but I know you were in the Lowlands at least three days before that. And you were close to the cliffs too. You could've easily announced your arrival then, but you didn't. You stayed hidden for three more days. Why?"

Kieryn blinked slowly, his gaze still locked with hers. His eyes were clear and cold, but she didn't back down. His lips twitched. "We were strategizing."

"About?"

"I meant what I said. We're not your enemies."

"And I have trust issues—as you *also* said—so when you lie about something, I'm going to question your true intentions."

"Mhm, *was* it a lie though? And how many times have you lied to your council?"

Quite . . . a bit, but that was beside the point. This wasn't a morality issue. This was a trust issue. She couldn't trust people who lied to her, but she was at least *somewhat* self-aware, especially after the conversation with Ira in the cabin. If she wanted to receive honesty, she had to give it too.

She was startled out of her thoughts when Kieryn reached his hand toward her. His silver and blue rings glittered under the sunlight. His fingers grazed her temple as he pushed a lock of hair out of her face, tucking it behind her ear.

Lena was frozen. All her prior thoughts had been wiped away. His fingers lingered on the side of her neck, and one corner of his lips lifted. He looked over her shoulder, and she realized then what he'd done.

She jerked away from him and turned around. Ira stood next to Benji and Andra, glaring at them. No, glaring at *Kieryn*.

What is he doing here?

"You did that on purpose," she accused as she turned back to Kieryn.

He didn't deny it. "He's your husband, yes? The one who marked you as off limits at the party? I haven't seen much of him."

"He's been busy."

"Maybe I should introduce myself. Just in case you and I are wed. I'd imagine you'd want us to be on good terms with one another."

Kieryn started to stand, but Lena grabbed his sleeve and pulled him back down.

"Stop. You're trying to instigate something."

"I would never," he drawled.

She rolled her eyes.

"Does he know?" Kieryn asked. "About the marriage?"

She sat still, avoiding Kieryn's inquisitive gaze. She hadn't talked to Ira about it. They had just made up the other night.

"He was in the throne room when Sorrel proposed it," was the answer she settled for.

"Hmm, he doesn't seem like the friendly type. Or the sharing type. He'll probably tell you not to get married."

Lena knew that Ira could be a bit . . . *rude*, but he was also capable of being quite polite. He held more patience than she did, but sometimes he chose not to exercise it. He could be flippant and cold, and judging by the way he was looking at Kieryn, he would be exactly that if they ever spoke.

Still, she said, "How do you know what he's like? You said yourself you've never talked to him."

"Well, for one, he's glaring at me in a way that very clearly says *fuck off*. And if the mark he placed on you the other day was any indication of how well he plays with others, I'd say he doesn't. Play well, that is. I've heard some other things about him."

"Yeah? From who? *Tuck*?" Lena clenched her jaw. "You shouldn't believe everything he tells you. He has a habit of lying."

Kieryn's brows rose. "I sense some animosity."

She scoffed. *Some?* "Sure. You could say that."

She was honestly surprised she hadn't seen Tuck since the party—*surprised* but pleased. She seemed to have bad luck when it came to avoiding him.

"He's gone, if you were wondering," Kieryn said. "Tuck. He left this morning, apparently chasing the trail of that man you brought in last night."

Lena straightened and looked at Kieryn cautiously. "How do you know about that?"

"You told me."

"No, I didn't."

Kieryn smiled. The back of his hand brushed her face again.

"You did." Before she could question him further, he nodded over her shoulder. "You'd better hurry. Your husband looks like he's losing his patience."

Lena went to the dungeon after sunset, wearing a robe over her sleepwear, but now she wished she'd worn more, as the temperature difference between the palace and the dungeon was vast.

Two guards stood at the dungeon entrance. They straightened when she approached. "Your Majesty."

She nodded in greeting. "I'm here to speak to the prisoner."

The guards shifted and glanced at one another.

"Unfortunately, Your Majesty," the female guard said, appearing apologetic, "we've been ordered not to let anyone pass if they're not on the list we've been given."

Lena waited for them to realize their mistake and let her through. But they didn't. "I'm sorry? List?"

They nodded and still stood firm.

"I am the queen," she said.

There were no orders that trumped hers. None that were *supposed* to.

"Yes, Your Majesty, but you are not on the list."

Lena stared at them and then turned toward Benji and Andra, who looked just as astonished as she felt.

"I'd like to see this list," she told the guards.

The male guard reached into his pocket and pulled out a piece of paper. Lena snatched it from his hands, unfolded it, and read over the names.

Wes Haveers
Erin Lanta
Mikhail
Ira Vaenyr
Alkus Brendigar

"Only five people?"

"For now, Your Majesty."

She hastily folded the paper and shoved it back into awaiting hands. "Who gave you those orders and this list?"

"Your Majesty, please, don't be—"

"*Who?*" Her voice was ice. "Whose orders are you obeying over your queen's?"

For a second, she considered shoving them aside and breaking down the door herself.

The guards shared another glance, and she found something in their eyes that confirmed what she already knew.

"Alkus Brendigar."

CHAPTER
THIRTY-FOUR

Things took a turn for the worst.
    Cal and Quil were supposed to retrieve a scroll. Julian hadn't revealed what it contained, but its contents were obviously important. He'd told them everything they needed to know to find it—which ship and room it was in, what it looked like, the number of crew members on board, and when the ship would be docking and undocking—but when the Blessed showed up, everything was thrown off.
    Cal and Quil had found the room and acquired the scroll, but when they went to leave, a dozen enforcers from the Highlands intercepted them. Their shock wore off quickly. Julian had prepared them for everything, even the unexpected.
    They were armed and quick, but there was only so much they could do against a dozen fully trained and fully grown enforcers. And they still had the crew to worry about—pirates, Julian had called them. They sailed up and down the coasts, not venturing too far out into sea or else they would be lost, but sometimes they made their way down the shallow rivers in the short, wet season when the water was high enough to drop up or pick up treasures if the price was worth it.
    Cal hadn't asked how Julian got this information. She'd stopped questioning him a few weeks after finding herself under his tutelage. He never gave her answers, and he only disappeared the more she asked questions.
    Cal and Quil didn't like splitting up, but when the enforcers got between them while they were fighting, they had no choice. They were less powerful apart, but so were the enforcers.
    Cal ran along the ports of the river and headed for the roofs, scrambling up the side of the houses with practiced ease. The enforcers cursed behind her, and for a second, she

thought maybe they'd decided not to chase her. Enforcers could be lazy. If they did their job properly, crime rates would be a lot lower.

Both she and Quil had a bag that could contain the scroll, but the enforcers had no way of knowing which one of them actually had it. Perhaps, in the enforcers' minds, the price of the stolen scroll wasn't large enough to warrant their involvement. She would rather them leave her alone entirely, but if they were here for something in particular, she prayed that it wasn't her.

Her heart pounded in her chest as she ran over the rooftops. She was terrified of being caught and punished for stealing, but more than that, she was terrified of being discovered. She looked different, but not so different that she was unrecognizable.

A roar split through the air.

Cal hesitated, fear holding her in its iron grip.

The enforcers had stopped chasing her in favor of sending their Slayers after her. And that was far worse.

She'd been unsure if they would let their Slayers out with so many people around. The fact that they had only worried her further. They didn't want to lose her. They weren't treating her like another thief.

Cal forced her legs to move faster. She scaled down the building and slipped through a window. Slayers could fit into small spaces, but they didn't like to. She couldn't stay put. She had to keep moving. If she stayed on the rooftop, the Slayers would have her pinned in thirty seconds. At most.

Had the Slayers caught her scent yet? Maybe she could conceal it.

Cal moved from house to house, quickly yet quietly, trying not to draw more attention to herself. She doused herself in perfume and threw spices all over her body. She grabbed anything that looked like it might be useful and swapped it out when she found something better. But it wasn't enough. A Cursed was no match for a Slayer, let alone six.

A sword was in her hands when she was cornered.

Julian's voice echoed in her head.

"You're fighting for survival. There are no do-overs. You give them everything you've got."

She took down three enforcers before the rest of them shoved her to the ground. Her body was one giant bruise, aching and bleeding. She trembled as the adrenaline coursing through her screamed at her to get up and fight. To not let them take her.

She yelled and her mouth filled with blood and dirt. She couldn't see quite right and her head was foggy, but as the enforcers clipped the cuffs around her, one last thought crossed her mind before they knocked her out. It was strong and clear, so it cut through the haze. And she remembered it.

Julian betrayed us. He betrayed me.

Cal had always wondered if he knew who she truly was. She had a suspicion that he did, but she hadn't dared bring it up.

Had he sold her out because he'd decided that the price on her head was worth it?

· CHAPTER

THIRTY-FIVE

The next time they were sent out, they had a plan. The beginning bloodbath was inevitable, especially with the new shipments of kids that had arrived. There was another group every few days. It was sickening watching the prophets send the kids out alongside the rest of them without so much as batting an eye. Because in their mind, everything was justified. It was necessary for the larger cause.

Atreus focused on channeling all the rage and disgust he felt into power and concentration. He would need it if he wanted to make it out of the initial slaughter. It didn't matter how long he'd been there. One slip up was all it took. And he had Judah to look after. Since their last Outing he had come to terms with the fact that he was stuck with the kid. He couldn't turn away now. Thankfully, Judah was a fast learner. This time, he grabbed the steak knife without prompting from Atreus.

Once they stepped through the portal, Atreus ran, ignoring the confused cries and screams of the kids. They were bait. He hated it, but there was nothing the rest of them could do to change that, so they might as well use the given distraction.

Their plan revolved around him seeking out the stone once they distanced themselves from the *Te'Monai*, but that was easier said than done. The humming wasn't so clear among screams and roars and all the other horrible sounds that flooded the realm. He needed to go farther.

Judah struggled to keep up with him on his little legs, stumbling and tripping more than once, but Atreus hauled him up.

Atreus found high ground again to inspect the terrain below. It was colder here —not unbearable, but there was a brisk chill in the air that sank into his skin. The trees were tall and full of green needles. White powder clung to the top of the trees and the hills.

He spotted another hill in the distance and the humming intensified. Trees covered nearly every inch of its surface, save for a large circle on the hillside. In the middle of it was a dark hole that led deeper into the hill. The humming was coming from that pit.

Instead of immediately heading in that direction, he waited for three minutes as they had discussed. Staying still was dangerous, but they needed numbers if they wanted to pull this off. He remained on his toes, looking out for any *Te'Monai*. Thankfully, the other firstborns got to him first.

Weylin, Finn, and Harlow had arrived by the time the three minutes were up. Harlow glared at him, the dark circles under her eyes still very much visible.

They moved quickly and reached the pit right as the *Te'Monai* ran out of distractions and found them.

"Go!" Finn urged, and then ducked to avoid one of the *Te'Monai*'s arms.

Atreus gritted his teeth and raced inside the cave with Judah.

They had discussed his importance in this before. He was the only one who could sense the stone. If he died, so did their chances of returning to the Institute. That made him valuable. He hated that they were risking themselves for him, but Mila and Finn had said it wouldn't be much different from any previous Outing. They were always fighting to survive.

Yeah, but now you have to watch my back in addition to yours, he'd shot back.

But they hadn't budged. They were doing their part, so he was going to do his.

Where is it? Where is it?

His eyes adjusted to the darkness as he advanced deeper and deeper. The cold down here was crisp and cut straight through his uniform jacket, numbing his skin.

He spotted the stone.

But not a second later, a growl echoed through the cave. It came from close by. *Very* close by.

He spun, pulling Judah behind him. Red eyes floated in the shadows.

Time ticked slowly.

The *Te'Monai* rose on its hind legs and lunged, its jaw gaping and its white teeth cutting through the darkness. Atreus scrambled for his knife and held it out in front of him. Judah was screaming. Was there another *Te'Monai*? He couldn't afford to take his eyes off the one in front of him. It was too close. By the time his knife would enter its flesh, it would have already dug its teeth into his skull.

No. Stop. Stop! STOP!

And the *Te'Monai* did. It stopped only a foot away from him, teeth still visible but no longer diving toward his head.

Atreus stared at it with wide eyes, his entire body trembling, but he snapped out of it quickly and stumbled back, pulling Judah with him. The *Te'Monai* didn't move any closer. It just watched him, almost curiously.

His brows furrowed and he cocked his head to the side as he regarded the *Te'Monai* in front of him with fright, wonder, and disbelief.

It was almost like . . . it had listened to him. But that couldn't be. It wasn't . . . He couldn't . . .

His mind took him back to his conversation with Harlow a few days ago.

"I thought I was going to die. I was prepared to die. And then, it just . . . jumped over me."

It had abruptly changed direction. Just like this *Te'Monai* had abruptly stopped. Both had done so on his command. For it to happen once was a coincidence, but twice?

". . . Atreus," Judah whispered.

He ignored Judah and chased this ridiculous theory.

Walk away.

The *Te'Monai* stayed still. Atreus took a deep breath and focused. The song of the stone was strong. It floated through the air, wrapping around him.

Walk. Away.

He watched in amazement and horror as the *Te'Monai* turned its back on him —a *human*—and walked away. He stared after it, lips parted.

A scream sounded from outside the cave, reminding him of exactly where he was and what was happening.

The stone.

His eyes quickly found it again.

But before grabbing the stone, he picked up an ordinary piece of rock that was around the same size.

∽

Prophet Silas stopped in front of him again and waited expectantly.

"I don't have it."

The prophet didn't move. He continued to look at Atreus as if he hadn't said anything at all. Everyone was watching them. Finn. Mila. Judah. Vanik. Harlow. Weylin. They were all in the cavern. At least that weight could slide off his shoulders.

"I don't have it," he repeated.

It was a piss poor lie and he knew it. He had been the one to come back with the stone the last few times and his hands were curled into fists at his sides.

Prophet Silas called the enforcers over, and they dragged Atreus out of the cavern and to the black and white room again. The sound of the door shutting behind him, leaving him alone with the prophet, made him flinch.

The furniture in the room had been pushed against the walls. Only the desk remained untouched, alone in the middle of the space.

"I warned you that things were only going to get harder for you if you kept this attitude up," Prophet Silas said, standing in front of the desk with his hands folded behind his back.

Atreus stayed quiet, glaring back at the prophet.

"Mind your gaze," Prophet Silas snapped as he took a step forward. "You've never been an easy one, but you've been especially defiant lately."

Atreus let that sit in the air between them.

"Answer me when I'm speaking to you, boy."

"You didn't ask me a question," Atreus bit back.

Prophet Silas raised a brow. The firstborn could spy frustration in his body language, but his expression was so carefully crafted. Cool and collected, yet the cracks were starting to form.

"*What* are you planning?" Prophet Silas approached him, the click of his polished shoes echoing throughout the room.

"Nothing."

A crack rang out. His cheek stung, a hot prickling sensation spreading across it. His eyes were fixed on the wall, his lips parted.

"Do *not* lie to me. You think you're so *clever*, but I can see right through you."

"Then why ask me questions at all if you already know the answer? Some prophet you—"

The second hit he expected. And the third. He stumbled to the side, his cheek and jaw throbbing, but he stayed on his feet and didn't let go of the stone in his hand. He slowly turned his head straight.

Prophet Silas' face was carved in fury. He swooped forward, one of his hands clutching Atreus' jaw in an iron grip, and shoved him back. Atreus' face ached and he tripped over his feet. He would've toppled over if his back hadn't hit the wall.

"I've had *enough*!" the prophet hissed, his hand shaking Atreus with the intensity of his words.

Atreus' head throbbed as it hit the wall. His vision momentarily blackened before focusing on the enraged prophet in front of him.

"There will be no more rebelling from you! You may be able to take the form of a human, but I know what you are. You wicked, sinful creature! *Te'Monai!* Don't forget why you are here. Evil comes naturally to you. You *are* evil. You create it and you attract it, but I will not tolerate it here. Do you understand me?"

He shook Atreus again until stars filled his vision.

"Get these deluded fantasies out of your head! Things will never change," the prophet said slowly. "You will stay in the Institute, where you will work and go to the realms we send you to until you die. It's up to you whether you die as a sinner or an atoner. Though, I can already guess which you'll be."

Prophet Silas released his hold, throwing Atreus back. The crown of his head hit the wall again.

The prophet leaned in close, his hot breath washing over Atreus' face as he spoke slowly. "When I look at you, I see no potential. I only see a problem. You are a black hole. Nothing good will come out of you or with you. You're *nothing* and you will never have *anything*. You'll strive for it—for affection and wanting—but it will always be out of reach. Because no one could ever want something as broken and corrupt as *you*."

Atreus closed his eyes and turned his head to the side to break away from the prophet and his words. He kept his jaw locked and his lips pressed together. His eyes burned.

"You're throwing away your chance at redemption for *nothing*. So stop fighting. Whatever you're planning, it won't work."

Atreus felt the prophet retreat and let out a breath. Inhaled. Exhaled. Then again.

"Give me the stone."

He stared at the prophet, who was still close and looking at him with nothing but malice. Prophet Silas' arm was extended, hand waiting for the stone.

Atreus dropped it.

It clattered against the floor and rolled away.

Prophet Silas didn't break eye contact at first. His nostrils flared and his eyes burned, but eventually, he backed off in favor of retrieving the stone. As soon as he did, Atreus ran.

He headed for the door on the left, the one he'd seen the sunwalker come through. Prophet Silas let out a shout right before he yanked it open. Atreus shot through the doorway, running like his life depended on it.

Beyond the door was a long, narrow hallway with the same color scheme as the room, the floor black marble and the walls white. Sunstones rested overhead to light the route.

His boots pounded against the floor as commotion broke out behind him, but he didn't slow or glance over his shoulder. He didn't know what exactly he was looking for, but he would know once he spotted it.

A set of doors stood ahead, and he hoped they weren't locked. He skidded to a halt before them, breathing hard. His hands fumbled for the handle and yanked, and thankfully, the door gave.

A great gust of wind hit him as soon as he stepped through, blowing his hair back and temporarily stopping him in his tracks. The shouts behind him were louder now, and he then made the mistake of looking back. Prophet Silas was pursuing him with half a dozen enforcers.

Atreus slipped between the doors. He considered blocking them with something, but it was pointless. The enforcers would break through in seconds.

He turned, eyes seeking another path, but they widened upon seeing the space he'd run into. It was a massive vertical channel. He stood along the outside of the circular tunnel on a twenty-foot platform that wrapped around the opening in the middle. The wind in here was intense, tugging at his clothes and hair. He reached down and plucked the real stone out of his boot, holding it tightly to make sure it wasn't stolen away by the gale. He squinted against the gusts of wind that caused his eyes to water as he approached the railing near the center of the channel.

Each step was careful yet firm. The wind could probably sweep him away if he was off balance for even one moment. He peeked over the railing and an even stronger gust of wind hit him, forcing him to squeeze his eyes shut and pull back.

But he'd seen enough. The channel continued downward into a pit of black that likely extended for a long, *long* time. He opened one eye and looked up to see a tiny white dot at the very top of the tunnel, quite a distance away too. He realized, with some bizarre amazement, what he was looking at a few seconds later. The sky. He was staring at the sky of his home realm for the first time in his life.

The doors behind him broke open and he spun around. If looks could kill, he would drop dead on the spot. Prophet Silas' robes whipped in the wind. He didn't move any closer, but the enforcers did. The raging wind probably felt like a slight breeze to them.

Atreus' throat tightened. He needed to think of something. He needed more time.

"Stop!" he shouted over the wind. He held his hand out—the one holding the true stone—over the channel. He suspected Prophet Silas had already discovered the one he'd dropped was a fake. "If you come any closer, I'll drop this."

He hoped they cared enough about each individual stone to heed his threat.

The enforcers stopped, standing still in the wind. Atreus released the breath he'd been holding and looked past them, finding the prophet. The enforcers would only approach him if Prophet Silas gave them the order. And it appeared he wouldn't as long as Atreus held the stone.

"You want it so bad?" Atreus asked. "Why?"

Prophet Silas' lips twisted, eyes pure molten, but he didn't respond.

Atreus was going to see just how important this stone was.

"Call all the prophets here. And the enforcers," he said. He dropped his arm and watched in satisfaction as the prophet pitched forward, his eyes widening. "Do it or I'll drop the stone."

CHAPTER
THIRTY-SIX

As soon as Lena woke up, she sought out their guests. Aquila was ideal, but she'd take any of them.

Her prayers were answered after thirty minutes of stalking around the palace when she spotted Kieryn. He saw her the same time she saw him, and he had the nerve to turn on his heel and start walking in the other direction.

"Kieryn!" she hissed as she hurried to catch up.

He let out a heavy sigh when she finally fell into step next to him.

"I won't take up much of your time. I need you to tell me where Aquila is."

"How am I supposed to know where she is?"

Lena walked faster and turned so she was standing in front of him, blocking his path. "You'd know where she spends her time better than I would. Please. It's important."

Kieryn eyed her doubtfully but caved. "Check the libraries. She goes there sometimes to hide."

She thanked Kieryn and hurried away to check each and every library. The palace did not have a shortage of them, much to her annoyance. But thankfully, she found Aquila in the third library she searched through. It was one of the larger ones situated on the east side of the palace. She'd assumed that since their guests were unfamiliar with the palace, they hadn't yet had the time to discover the smaller, more hidden rooms, including the personal libraries. Her guess had paid off.

Aquila sat on the ledge before a window, her legs pulled up to her chest and her face turned away. Lena's feet stopped working for a moment.

She stood there, in between the towering shelves, watching Aquila. The recognition was stronger than before. An ache began in her chest, growing in intensity the longer she looked at Aquila. The tear inside of her was widening.

She stepped into the alcove. Aquila rolled her head to the side and stared at her, appearing utterly unimpressed.

"Another memory returned to me," Lena opened with.

Every time she closed her eyes, she felt like she was being tugged back to another memory. Whatever it was that kept her memories locked away was slowly unraveling.

Aquila sat up straight, her legs flattening in front of her. "Which one?" she asked carefully, her voice strained.

"Does it matter?"

The look Aquila gave her told her it did, in fact, matter.

Lena moved closer. "It was when we got split up. At the pirate ship."

Aquila's hands flexed in her lap.

"I think Julian sold us out."

The sorcerer froze and then carefully slipped down from the window ledge. "What makes you think that?"

Lena shrugged. "I remember thinking it then. That he found out who I was and decided to turn me over for the coin. And from what *little I know now*"—she gave Aquila a pointed look that was ignored—"it makes sense. The enforcers wouldn't stop until they caught me. They sent their Slayers after me . . . but they didn't bring me back to the Highlands. I was locked away for a while, but then bailed out by some lady . . ."

She cut herself off, swallowing harshly.

"How does that make sense? If Julian told the enforcers you were the runaway queen, why didn't they take you straight to the palace?"

"I don't know—"

"And he had to know before." Aquila pressed her lips together and stepped away, her eyes swirling with a plethora of emotions Lena couldn't all identify. But she recognized the anger. And the betrayal. "He had to know who you were. He knew the whole fucking time."

Aquila was finally offering up information, so Lena wasn't going to stop her. "How?"

"He's a powerful person. Someone you don't want to cross."

"Did he teach you then?" she nodded toward the gloves.

Aquila scoffed. "No. He ran off soon after you were caught. Don't you remember? *We weren't his responsibility.*"

"Is that why he took away my memories? Me being captured compromised him? Why didn't he do the same to you?"

"I don't know," Aquila said quietly, but her voice was stubborn. Torn. Lena believed her. "He's not a good man. He had his own selfish reasons for everything he did, including taking us in. When we ended up being too much trouble, he got rid of us and disappeared. But I don't think he sold you out."

"And what makes you think that?" Lena pushed.

For a second, she thought she might get something. Aquila's throat worked and her lips parted, but she sealed them shut before a sound escaped them.

Lena's hands curled into fists at her sides and a bolt of heat shot through her, heightening her frustration. "You're either scared of him, you care for him, or you're hiding something. Or maybe you take delight in my suffering. That would certainly explain why you looked like you wanted to rip my throat out when you first arrived. You found out I was alive after two years and you were what? Disappointed?"

Aquila glared at her. "I was *angry* you didn't try to find me. I was surprised at first when we stepped foot in The Lands and I heard about their young queen. Even more surprised when I spotted you in the Lowlands. And relieved . . . I thought you were *dead*."

Lena had tried to keep her identity hidden in the Lowlands. She'd cut her hair short, wore hoods, pitched her voice, and stayed out of sight. She didn't have to give a name often, but when she did, she never gave the same one twice. Why had she given Julian a name so close to her real one? Perhaps *he* had given that name to *her*. That would make sense if Aquila was right and Julian had known Lena's true identity from the start. Had Aquila known? No, based on what she had just offered up . . . Lena didn't think so.

"Two years have passed since then. You didn't make the connection in that time? You didn't see the flyers?"

Admittedly, the flyers hadn't worried Lena. Her heart seized when she first saw them a week after she ran away, but she stopped worrying when she saw how horribly she'd been drawn. Her ruler portrait hadn't been painted yet and her family didn't have any illustrations of her. The only thing the artist of the flyers had to go by was other people's descriptions, and the people who knew her the most were dead. She was convinced the Blessed who'd described her to the artist purposefully did a poor job to keep her from being found, which she wasn't mad about. The Blessed had probably hoped she would get killed in the Lowlands and they would wake to three gongs sounding overhead. The flyers had slowly disappeared with time and distance.

"I left The Lands right after you were taken, and Julian disappeared. I caught a ride on an old ship with a fool of a captain who ventured a little too far out. The waves pulled the ship under, but I managed to grab hold of a piece of driftwood. I swam to an island and was nearly delirious by the time Sorrel found me, took pity on me, and brought me back to Ouprua." Aquila flicked her eyes over Lena again, from her feet to her collarbones. Her eyes caught on Lena's Imprint. "I hadn't heard any news about The Lands' *queen* until I stepped foot back on this soil. It hasn't been easy for me either. I find out you're alive, the queen, *and* that you don't remember me all in a couple of days." She nodded toward the mark on Lena's chest. "And then there's that. I know you didn't have that before."

"And you didn't have those before either." Lena gestured toward Aquila's gloves. "Time has passed. Things have changed. For the both of us."

"Apparently so," Aquila muttered bitterly.

The two allowed the silence to swell between them. They waited to see who would break first. Aquila made it clear it wasn't going to be her, so Lena went ahead.

"Well, it's nice to know you don't hate me."

"Sometimes I do," Aquila told her.

"But not all the time?"

The sorcerer retreated to silence once again.

Lena decided to go a different route. "I need your help with something."

Aquila raised a brow.

"Look, if you're not going to tell me anything, fine, but I'm going to the Lowlands and I want you to come with me."

Aquila's gaze turned sharper, her voice harder. "What for?"

As of right now, Lena knew little about Aquila. She *remembered* little. Her suspicions could just be suspicions or there could be something tangible behind them. Maybe hidden feelings were seeping through, telling her she could trust Aquila. At least with this. And if her gut feeling was wrong, well, maybe she could convince Aquila to come anyway. Maybe returning to the Lowlands as Cal and Quil was what they both needed to repair the complicated bond between them. That would at least give Lena more insight into her hidden past if Aquila wasn't going to help her. No one could truly leave the Lowlands behind, not after being there for as long as they had.

"I have an errand to run."

And a theory to test.

~

"She's stable," Aquila said with a furrow between her brows as she pulled her hands away from the little girl. "The medicine helped. She's just resting now."

Lena took a step closer and examined the girl in the bed. Her cheeks were flushed, and she was shivering even though three blankets were draped over her. Aquila shoved her hands back into her gloves, covering her tattoos.

When they arrived at the rundown building, Lena hadn't known how Aquila would react, especially when asked to help. Lena visited these kinds of places occasionally. They technically weren't orphanages, but everyone in the Lowlands called them that because there wasn't a better name for them. The people here took in kids, put a roof over their heads, and gave them food to fill their bellies. They didn't have to, but they did. How these places got the money and the supplies had always been the question, but Lena now knew the answer: it was because of people like her. People who had the money or the skill to procure the necessities.

Lena came when she could and brought what she could. Some of the kids had come down with a cold the last time, so tonight, she'd brought medicine alongside more food, water, and clothing. But she also wanted to check something, so she'd asked Aquila if she would use her sorcery to look over the kids. Privately, of course, and when Aquila agreed, Lena had ushered the matrons of the orphanage out of the sick kids' rooms. She doubted they would rat out Aquila for her sorcery, but she couldn't be sure. They'd been patiently waiting at the end of the hall for thirty minutes now.

"Is she the last one?"

Lena nodded.

Aquila sighed, and when she saw that Lena had no intention of leaving the room, she turned toward her. "What are we doing here?"

"Helping the children."

Aquila's frown deepened. "Was this the errand you had to run? Was this"—she gestured toward the sick child—"the reason you wanted me to come along?"

"No." That was the answer to both, but Lena didn't clarify. She pretended not to notice Aquila's glare.

"I used to live in a place like this," Aquila admitted. She crossed her arms and looked around the room. It wasn't very grand. Some of these places were barely standing.

Lena hid her surprise. She didn't remember that, which . . . wasn't surprising. "Now you're volunteering information?"

"Would you rather me not?" Aquila challenged.

No.

"Come on," Lena said instead. "I still have that errand to run, and I don't want to get back too late."

The two of them left the room. The matrons at the end of the hall thanked them again for the supplies, especially the medicine.

They left through one of the back doors. Lena didn't want to run into any more kids. None of them had approached her or talked. They'd just stared, their wary and untrusting eyes following her like an unwanted shadow. She knew it was best for both them and her if she kept her distance.

She spotted Cowen at the corner when she stepped out into the red-hued night. He hadn't wanted her to go to the Lowlands so soon after the kidnapping incident, but he knew he couldn't stop her, so he'd tagged along. He had even helped her collect the supplies by taking a trip to the treasury and then the apothecary in the city for the medicine.

To her, it was all rather simple. The Cursed needed things. The Blessed had them in excess. The solution seemed rather obvious, yet the Blessed chose to ignore it, so she chose to ignore them.

"You meant it?" Lena asked suddenly, glancing at Aquila out of the corner of her eye. "The medicine's working?"

The matrons weren't sure what the kids had caught, so Lena hadn't known what medicine to get. She'd gone for something widespread and useful.

"I wouldn't lie."

Lena gave her a flat look.

"About that," Aquila added on.

"Can you . . . heal them?"

"No." Aquila shook her head. "I'm . . . This isn't exactly my skillset. This kind of sickness . . . You would've been better off bringing Kieryn."

Kieryn? Lena stored that bit of information away for later.

"Right . . . well, I wanted—"

"To badger me for answers. I know," Aquila said, turning on Lena once again. "You would've brought your husband in my place otherwise." She tilted her head to the side. "Aren't I right?"

"What does it matter?" Lena said. "I didn't bring him. I brought you."

Aquila simply stared back, her face blank.

True to her word, Lena had told Ira about this trip to the Lowlands. Maybe he'd seen the nervous look in her eyes or maybe he'd felt her apprehension through the bond, but he hadn't asked to come along. Thankfully. Aquila would accept Cowen's presence, but Ira's would likely scare her off. And something told Lena having Ira and Aquila in the same space would be a bit awkward. Ira hadn't spoken openly about his dislike of their guests, but he didn't have to. The marriage proposal only made him more agitated. He'd practically told her as much yesterday after she left the hedge maze with him. And then there was that scene at the ball.

Even though she'd been honest about sneaking out, when Ira asked who was going with her, she'd only spoken Cowen's name. She didn't need Ira's permission to spend time with any of their guests, but she didn't want him getting worked up about it either. She just . . . she needed to figure things out—the Aquila and her thing—on her own.

"And I wouldn't have to badger you if you'd just tell me." Lena held her hand up before Aquila could respond to that. "I know. For whatever reason, you're being stubborn and keeping your mouth shut about this."

Aquila scowled at her. "And you're being persistent."

"Wouldn't you be? If this was your past?"

Aquila looked away, and the shadows hid her face. "Sometimes it's better not remembering things," she muttered.

Lena paused when the sorcerer's words hit her. How many times had she wished the images of her family's bodies could be wiped from her mind? Her rough encounters in the Lowlands? But not knowing about those things—being left to wonder—could be just as agonizing.

She swallowed roughly. "Well, you don't get to make that decision for me."

Aquila didn't have anything to say to that. Lena fought off the disappointment and dropped the conversation. The direct approach didn't work with Aquila, so she would have to try something else.

∼

It had been months since she last visited Dugell, and she'd developed a lot of questions since then. Who better to go to for answers than a Secret Seller?

He'd moved houses, but she knew exactly where to find him. Like before, he had hired muscle floating around his house. They were supposed to blend in with the night's usual drunks and thieves, but someone who knew what they were looking for could see right through them. She could very well walk up and tell them to tell Dugell she was here. She could stroll right in, but there was no fun in that.

"Like old times, huh?" she said under her breath as she and Aquila climbed a nearby building.

Aquila didn't respond, but Lena didn't care this time. She had her focus on Dugell's house as they crept across the rooftops. No balcony this time, but there was always a way in.

Lena looked at the alleyway below. Two large men were hunched over buckets. She leaped across the gap and didn't bother checking to see if Aquila followed her before heading for the rear of Dugell's house. One man. And one window.

She grabbed a stick that had found its way on the rooftop and threw it off to the side. It clattered across the compact soil as it hit the ground. The man underneath her turned in that direction and then walked over to the noise.

She moved quickly, swinging herself over the edge of the roof and climbing down the side of the building with practiced hands. She held herself stable as she fiddled with the window latch. The metal that held it shut was old and nearly rusted, difficult to move, especially with one hand.

She cursed under her breath and shifted so she could grab her dagger to hack away at the latch, but as soon as she unsheathed it, the lock shattered. Lena flinched and hid her face in her shoulder to shield it from the scattering metal. She cracked her eyes open and stared at the broken lock, then glanced up.

Aquila's gaze was on the lock, but it slowly slid to Lena. Her eyes were sharp. Her fingers outstretched. Lena pulled her eyes away from Aquila's gloves before opening the window and sliding inside.

The halls were dark and silent. She didn't make a noise as she moved down them, looking under each door for a shroud of light. She stopped at the corner and peeked around it. Two men stood on either side of a door at the end of the hall. Her last meeting with Dugell must've really shaken him up. These men weren't hired muscle. No, Dugell still didn't trust them enough in his own home. These men were mercenaries—specially trained in the south, and especially cruel. She'd heard rumors about some of the stuff they were required to do as part of their "training." Alas, they were still Cursed.

She glanced over her shoulder at Aquila and held up two fingers. Then she pointed one at herself and one at Aquila. Without waiting for confirmation, she spun around the corner.

The guards noticed her almost immediately and drew their swords. Lena *really* didn't want to be here any longer than she had to, so she let her Slayer out. The hallway creaked and groaned around its size. If her Slayer was any bigger, the floors would cave and the walls and ceilings would splinter. It quickly tackled one of the guards, cutting off his scream immediately by tearing into his throat. The other guard stared at her Slayer with wide eyes before turning to her. She threw one of her daggers and he deflected it, but right after, her Slayer took off his head.

Some mercenaries.

She walked over to retrieve her dagger and then turned around.

Aquila's face was dark, but not in anger. "I didn't sign up for killing anyone tonight."

"Hardly anyone who kills signs up to do it," Lena said as she sheathed her dagger. "*You always get a choice, but if you choose wrong, you die.* Isn't that what Julian used to say?"

Aquila's face shifted, and she took a step forward. "How do you know that? Did you have another *vision*?"

Lena paused in front of the door of Dugell's study, her brows drawn down. "No . . . I don't know how I know it. I just do."

Dugell was already cowering in the corner when Lena came in, his eyes wide and his hands trembling. His bottle of wine sat forgotten on his desk.

"Really? Guards?" She called her Slayer back to her after it finished its meal, walking across the room. "If I wanted you dead, I would've had you killed already. And you can't keep me out."

Dugell eyed her distrustfully. "What do you want?"

"I want the same thing I wanted before: answers. You have them and I have questions."

She sat in one of the chairs before his desk and gestured to the chair behind it. "Go ahead. Sit. I don't intend to stay long, but you may as well get comfortable."

Slowly, Dugell moved across the room and lowered himself into his chair. He was still shaking, and his eyes didn't leave her. Not until Aquila showed up in the doorway.

"My guest. She won't hurt you," Lena assured him. "Have you heard any news about activity in the Highlands?"

Dugell's gaze returned to her. "That's a rather broad question."

"Whispers? Rumors? . . . Deaths?" she prompted.

Dugell cleared his throat and shook his head. "Nothing that you probably haven't already heard."

"Tell me."

He hesitated, looking down at the scrolls on his desk. "I've heard lots of things. I've heard that a band of wild rebels is killing Blessed. I've heard monsters are creeping down the mountain to hunt. I've heard a single Blessed is responsible for all of this . . . terror." He raised his eyes to hers again, his head still dipped low. "Someone from the palace perhaps?"

Lena kept her face impassive. "And who's saying these things?"

Dugell looked down again. "Everyone. Anyone. When people aren't told the truth, they begin to speculate."

Yes, she knew that.

She leaned forward, resting her elbows on her knees. "Have you told anyone about our meeting?"

Dugell shook his head.

"And you won't tell anyone about this one either? About me or my guest?"

Another head shake.

She wasn't stupid enough to give a Secret Seller one of her own secrets, so he didn't have much information to sell off to others, but the mere news of her presence here could be valuable to some.

"Have you heard anything about Alkus Brendigar?"

Dugell sat very still in his chair, his lips pressed tightly together.

She tilted her head. "If you tell me no, I'll know you're lying."

His lips parted and quivered, but no sound escaped them. The candles around the room accentuated the thin sheen of sweat that covered his face.

She laced her fingers together and rested her chin on top of them. "You know, I'm getting really tired of people withholding information from me. Why do you protect Alkus Brendigar?"

"I don't—"

"Is he one of your clients too? Does he pay you?" She sat up straight and snapped her fingers as if she'd just had an epiphany. "No, it runs deeper than that. Familial."

Dugell was rigid.

"You have family who are Blessed. What's their name?"

His jaw clenched. "Mahersi."

"And one of them—your great aunt, I believe—married a Brendigar. Alkus' second cousin. So what does that make the two of you?" Lena waved her hand. "I don't really care for the details—"

"It's not like that!" Dugell blurted out. "He's not—I don't care for him. I don't have a deal with him. I'm not trying to protect him—"

"Then tell me what you know."

"You have to promise me immunity," Dugell said. There was a wild look in his eyes. He was scared, but not only of her. "What I tell you . . . people can't know it came from me. Least of all *him*."

"I have to?" she repeated. "I wouldn't think a powerful man would be afraid."

"A smart man would be," he replied. "And Alkus Brendigar is *the* most powerful man in The Lands."

Lena gritted her teeth. "So everyone thinks, including him."

"Then it's true," Dugell said. "What is truth other than what most people believe?"

She took a deep breath and dug her fingers into the chair's arms. "Tell me what you've heard."

"I've heard . . . that he's gearing up for something. He's moving his pawns. He's not paying me, but he is paying others."

"To do what?"

"That I don't know. I don't even know if those he's paying know what he wants."

She knew what he wanted, but she didn't know what sort of game he was playing in order to get there. He'd surprised her with Ouprua, and he could do it again.

"Where's the money going?"

Dugell hesitated again. His eyes flickered behind her. To Aquila. She hadn't moved from the doorway. A bead of sweat trickled down the side of his face. "Lots of places. He's a rich man."

"And does he get his money from your family's orchard too?"

"No."

"Then where does he get it?"

Council members received an annual income, but it wasn't infinite. They didn't have to worry about housing since they stayed in the palace; food and medicine were provided to them free of charge too. But Alkus wasn't from a royal family. He didn't have a vault overflowing with generational wealth. But there were a number of people who would help him with almost anything he needed.

"I'm sure you know," Dugell said carefully. "Your list."

Her lips tightened. "If you don't know what he's paying for, who does? Where exactly is his money going?"

Another bead of sweat rolled down his skin. He reached for a piece of paper on his desk and handed it over to her. Lena eyed it and plucked it from his shaking hands. She read over the jumbles of numbers.

"What is this?"

"Coordinates. One of my informants followed a money trail leading . . . there."

She raised her eyes, looking at him through her lashes. "You're sure?"

He was slow to nod. "My informants wouldn't lie to me."

"And you wouldn't lie to me either, would you?"

Dugell's eyes were large and latched with hers when he said, "No."

She gave him a tight-lipped smile and pushed herself to her feet while tucking the note away. "That's a relief. I'm not going to tell anyone I got this information from you because that would be troublesome for me. I don't want you dead because you're still useful to me . . . right?" She stared down at him. "You *are* still useful to me, aren't you?"

"Yes," he said, so quietly that she could barely hear it.

"Good. And one more thing." She leaned in closer, bracing her hands on his desk. "Collect any and all information about a man named Julian Toro. He's tanned. Brown hair, brown eyes. Middle-aged. Wears gloves and a hat. Not Blessed. Can you do that for me?"

Dugell nodded.

"Much thanks. Here." She pulled a small bag of coins from her waist and tossed it onto the desk. "For your troubles."

Lena and Aquila exited Dugell's house the same way they'd come in after Aquila distracted the hired muscle with her sorcery. Cowen was a few streets away, watching the house in case anything went amiss. They'd argued earlier when she told him to wait behind. In the end, he'd stayed put but close and given her a time limit.

Aquila turned on her almost immediately after Dugell's house disappeared around the corner, grabbing her arm and pulling her back so they were face to face. "What do you think you're doing?"

Lena merely blinked at the emotions swimming in Aquila's eyes. "You've made it clear you're not going to tell me anything, so I'm figuring things out my own way."

"If Julian hears that someone is after him, he'll—"

"What? Come and find me? Good." Lena wrenched her arm from Aquila's grip. "That's what I want. Now if you'll excuse me, I have another errand to run. Alone."

"Cal—"

But she was already gone. She left Aquila behind on the streets of the Lowlands again.

CHAPTER
THIRTY-SEVEN

Lena's muscles ached when she finally got back to her room well past midnight. Her head was throbbing and her eyelids were heavy. When the door slid shut, she let out a weighted breath and swayed on her feet. She could fall asleep right there. On the spot.

"It's late."

She turned around and opened her eyes. Ira sat on the edge of her bed—*their* bed—his eyes trained on hers.

"It is," she agreed as she walked farther into her room. As much as she wanted to crawl under the covers and fall asleep, she needed a bath. "You didn't have to wait up for me."

"I did."

She trudged into the washroom and began to draw a bath. Her eyes slipped closed again as the hot water filled the pool.

Ira followed her. "Did you find what you were looking for?"

"I suppose I did . . . in a manner of speaking."

"In a manner of speaking?"

There was something off about his tone. Something that made Lena lift her head and turn to face him. " . . . Yes. I took the medicine to kids who needed it, and it's helping. Then I visited an informant of mine."

Two, actually.

"With Cowen?"

"Yes, with Cowen. He was nearby. Where are you going with this?"

Ira took a deep breath and walked toward her. He wore sleepwear. His pants were silky, as was his shirt. She bet it felt so soft against the skin. She held herself back from reaching out.

"I know it wasn't *only* you and Cowen," he said as he stopped in front of her.

She glanced back toward the pool and the rippling water inside of it. She'd known he might find out, though she'd hoped he wouldn't.

"And how do you know that?" she asked, glaring up at him. "Did you send someone after me? Were you *spying on me*?"

"I'm not spying *on* you. I'm spying *for* you," Ira stressed. "You have informants. I have mine—"

"But I've never asked my informants about *you*."

Ira pressed his lips together. His nostrils flared. "I didn't *ask* about you, but I heard all the same."

"And what makes you think—"

"I want to trust you," Ira cut her off, his voice sharp and cool. "And I do trust you, sometimes against my better judgment. You keep saying again and again you'll be honest with me and then you lie, and you promise again and lie *again*. Why?"

She bit the inside of her cheek and blinked away the burning in her eyes. She knew why. Or she would know if she took the time to look deeper, but she was afraid of doing that. So instead, she said, "Maybe I'm just a liar."

Ira stared at her and locked his jaw. The light from the candles draped shadows across his face, but she could still see parts of him. The burning in his eyes had nothing to do with the candles' flames. She had hurt him. Again. Maybe that was all she could ever do.

"I'm still here, Lena," he implored, begging her to see. "There's nothing you could do to make me leave. How long must this go on for you to understand that? Sometimes I need my space, but I'll *never* turn my back on you. Not for good. I'll always come back if you're there waiting. I swore it when we married."

She tasted blood on her tongue. "Our *marriage* is fake. Well, no, it's not fake, is it? We had the ceremony, said the vows, strengthened our bond, but it feels *fake*. Ingenuine. And I know marriage doesn't have to be *real*."

But she wanted this one to be. She hadn't wanted to get married but had been coerced into it all the same. She'd thought Ira would be the best option because she trusted him. His proposal had been convincing, but still, she'd been wary, and that feeling had only grown.

Lena batted off the faucet. "This was a bad idea."

The room was quiet now, and she realized that perhaps they were being too loud in the dead of night. She lowered her voice. "This marriage is a favor, a transaction, a deal—whatever you want to call it. Just like what happened in the cabin. It's all . . . It feels real, but it's not."

She spoke the last words softly, as if reminding herself.

It's not real. It's not real. It's not real. Even if it feels that way to you.

Her throat tightened and the metaphorical dagger in her chest dug deeper, piercing her heart and cutting away at it. All the dead weight held her down, in place. She was acutely aware of Ira's gaze on her.

She didn't want it to be like this. She didn't understand why things were unfolding this way. They were friends. Best friends. But she'd been naive to hope that nothing would change. She knew better. Of course things would change! Their marriage was too tempting. Like a moth to a flame. Her feelings were being brought to the surface and becoming harder to ignore. Everything she wanted was presented to her on a silver platter. She could touch, but that was all. Nothing could run deeper. It did for her, but it couldn't for them. Their relationship was superficial, but her feelings were not. They were drowning her.

"I'm sorry—"

"Stop it," Ira commanded. He shook his head and caught his lower lip between his teeth. "Stop. It—feels real. To me."

The tremble in his voice was so faint, but it reached deep.

She steadied herself against the pool. "It's not," she whispered.

"It *is*," he argued as he took a step forward. "If it's not for you, then fine. That's okay. But don't pretend to know how I feel."

She frowned. "I'm not pretending. You came to me weeks ago with a *proposal*. You laid out the benefits. I tried to talk you out of it because—I knew it was a bad idea, but I still said yes."

Tears began to fill her eyes much to her own horror. And the more she willed them to go away, the longer they lingered. She squeezed her eyes shut, but a single tear escaped, rolling down her cheek and dripping off her chin.

"The young woman from Ouprua," Ira said, his voice giving nothing away. "Do you like her?"

She took a deep breath and then let it out. "Does it matter?"

"It matters to me."

The least she could do was give him the truth here, especially after lying about bringing Aquila to the Lowlands. "I don't hate her. I don't love her. It's . . . complicated." And that was putting it lightly. "Sorrel said I'd marry one of them. Aquila or Kieryn."

" . . . And you're leaning toward her?"

"I don't know. Maybe. I really haven't given *who* much thought. I've been worried about other things."

She opened her eyes once she subdued her tears, knowing they could come back at any time.

Ira was solemn and still. "You don't have to marry either of them."

"The Lands needs this alliance," she said.

"There's got to be another way," Ira said urgently. He ran a hand through his hair. "Do you want to marry her?"

"It doesn't—"

"Do you desire to marry her? Do you want something else that I can't give you?"

"No."

What she wanted from Aquila wasn't a relationship. At least not the romantic kind. She wanted answers. An explanation.

Ira nodded. Her admission alone seemed to make him steadier. "Then we'll find another way to seal this alliance. You don't have to do anything you don't want to do."

Her lips parted, but she didn't quite know what to say. Ira's fists were clenched at his sides and his jaw was locked. He stood firm, both literally and metaphorically.

"Ira, I don't think—"

"I love you."

Her words dried up in her throat and her mind went blank. She couldn't speak or think. She could only stare, wide-eyed.

Ira on the other hand . . . once those three words tumbled from his mouth, more followed. "I've loved you for a while now. It came to me in pieces. The first one was right before you left, and then another while you were away. People say you don't realize what you have until it's gone, and that's true. I thought then that what I felt for you was love, but I didn't know for sure until you came back. I should've told you before—"

"Then why didn't you?" Her voice was twisted and cold, a reflection of what she felt inside.

"Because I didn't want to scare you off—not that I think you scare easily. Because I didn't want to pressure you. To make you feel like you had to do something you didn't want to. Because I was a coward. Because I was afraid that if I told you I loved you and you didn't love me back, you would leave. Or at least distance yourself from me, which wouldn't be your fault, but I couldn't bear it. Because I was selfish. Take your pick."

He took another step forward so he was only an arm's reach away. His eyes were shining, and his fingers were itching at his sides.

"When I came to you that night in your room after the ball, part of me was being selfish. The thought of you having to marry someone else . . . " He shook his head. "You're your own person. You can do what you want, choose *who* you want. But I want to keep you for myself, if you'll let me. And I can't help that. I've tried, but, as I said, there's no one else. And there never will be. I came to your room hoping . . . and then when you told me you lied and you didn't have anyone else in mind, I went for it. I saw the opportunity and I took it. I was selfish and a coward, I guess, because I didn't tell you the true reason why I wanted to marry you.

"And yes, the marriage was beneficial, and I did it because I care for you, but it was deeper than that. And I'm sorry for misleading you, but at the same time, I'm not. I've been through a lot of shit. I didn't think I could get scared anymore, but then you came into my life. And then left it, not of your own volition, but you were still gone. And then you came back again. I would do anything to make sure you—"

"Stop. Stop. Wait." She stood and looked away from him. Her mind was working again and overflowing. "What?"

"Lena, I—"

She headed into the bedroom.

"Let me explain this, okay? Don't run off without letting me—"

"Why now?" she asked as she paced the room. She wouldn't look at him. Couldn't. "Why are you telling me this now?"

"Because I can't keep it to myself anymore," he rasped. "I thought I could. I told myself I would. Because putting my feelings for you aside, a marriage between us *was* your best option. I told myself I'd be there for you in whatever way you needed. As a friend. An ally. An executioner . . . A lover."

Lena paused. She could feel the heat of his stare between her shoulder blades.

"But I was fooling myself thinking I could do that—do this—and not let my feelings get in the way."

He wasn't rambling. His voice was strained but firm. There was no doubt in his words. He spoke almost as if he dared someone to challenge him, so she did.

"How do you know?" She wetted her lips and finally looked at him. For a moment, she lost her words because she could see the truth clear as day across his face. Still, she said, "It can be confusing. The desperation and the relief can easily be mistaken for—"

"No," Ira snapped. "People have been questioning my actions and my feelings for long enough, myself included. I know what I feel. I know what I want."

Her mouth dried up and shivers spread across her skin. She bit the inside of her cheek again, *hard*, and she was still here. In her room. This was actually happening.

"You don't have to say anything. You don't have to tell me how you feel. I didn't tell you this expecting something in return." Ira took a deep breath through his nose and straightened. "I couldn't keep it to myself anymore, and I'm sorry if that fucked things up, but . . . I'm not sorry for loving you. So . . . "

The air between them was tense. She was having a hard time believing it, not because she thought Ira was a liar, but because good things didn't happen to her anymore. Not like this. The people she cared about always got hurt, and *this* felt like an admittance to a deeper level of compassion, one that would only bring more pain. For him, and for her.

His predicament was almost exactly the same as hers. She'd thought things would be fine. That she could keep her feelings shoved down. She hid them from him—and herself—because she was scared of what acknowledging her feelings would do to him and her and their relationship.

"You're thinking too much," he said, watching her carefully. "Again."

"I think something like this deserves a bit of thought, don't you?" she snapped.

Ira took a deep breath before nodding, turning on his heel, and heading for the door.

Lena stepped forward and blurted out, "Where are you going?"

"Somewhere else," he replied without stopping. "You said you needed to think about this, so I'm giving you the space and time to think about it. But don't twist my words."

She walked after him. "So you're just going to leave? After saying all of that?"

Ira let out a humorless laugh but finally stopped. She did too only a few steps away from him

He turned. "What do you want me to do, Lena? You don't want me to *leave*. You don't want me to *stay*—"

"I never said that!"

He stared at her, his face frozen and waiting. She swallowed against her dry throat and mustered up her courage. He'd already done the hard part. Ira had been the first to admit his feelings. He had no safety net to fall back on, but she did. And this was hardly the most terrifying thing she'd ever faced, but it was a completely foreign type of fear. She wasn't fighting for survival. She was fighting for . . . acceptance. Affection.

"I never said I didn't want you to stay," she muttered. "I just got you in here a few days ago . . . Do you want to leave?"

His fingers twisted together in front of him, and he said, "No."

"Then stay," she breathed out. "I want you to stay."

His eyes roved over her, slow and assessing. "Why?"

"You know why."

He shook his head. "I want to hear you say it."

He walked back and stopped right in front of her.

It was three words. They were *only* words. But they weren't, were they? Something more came with them, and it was the *more* that she feared. And what would come because of that.

She didn't have a great record with those she dared to care for. The more love she extended, the more pain that followed. Keeping it bottled up protected not only her, but them. But lately, it had begun to hurt. She'd been unsure of those feelings too. Though after the cabin—after their first night together—she was certain but still reluctant to acknowledge it. Scared.

You need to stop living in fear. That's not a life worth living, she told herself, remembering Cowen's words. *The regrets will only pile up alongside the losses. You're stronger now than you were before.*

"I love you."

The words sounded strangled and distant to her ears, but they were hers. And meant for him.

Part of her waited for the realm to cave in. For the screams to start and the blood to spill. She waited for the monsters to creep in and ruin things once again. But none of that happened.

Her heart was beating a mile a minute in her chest and her skin was buzzing.

"I love you," she said again. This one was much more certain. And still, nothing happened. It was just her and Ira.

Unlike her, he didn't question her words or her feelings. She didn't owe him an explanation, but she wanted him to *know*. To understand. She wanted to get these things off her chest so she could breathe easier.

"I had a bit of a crush on you when we were younger, actually. I thought about you a lot when I was gone, but then I stopped because it hurt too much. I didn't know if you were alive and thinking about that—about you—only endangered me out there, and I had to survive. I had to get back. If not for me or you, then for my family. So I could avenge them. But then I saw you in that council chamber and I felt like . . . I felt like everything was going to be okay. It was an overwhelming relief and it made me feel lighter and forget about all the bad things because finding out you were alive was the best thing that had happened to me in a long time. All I cared about was you. And that feeling didn't entirely leave and it scares me if I'm being honest because I don't know how to deal with love like this when—"

She was cut off when Ira stepped forward, crossing the remaining distance between them and sealing his mouth over hers. His hands cupped her jaw and his thumbs swiped over her cheeks while his other fingers angled her head farther back. He moved closer, one of his legs between hers. His lips caressed hers, gentle yet firm, drawing sighs from her mouth as she melted in his arms.

This was the first time he'd kissed her like *this*. It was tender and warm and affectionate, all things he'd been toward her before, but it was amplified now. *Real*.

She wasn't a smooth talker like Ira. She couldn't put what she was feeling into words easily. What she said never fully encompassed what she truly felt. Things still slipped through the cracks. She couldn't tell Ira what she truly felt, but she could show it to him.

She wound her arms around his neck and tangled her fingers in his hair. She kissed him back just as he had kissed her—with everything she had. This wasn't about passion and satisfying their needs tonight. This was about something that ran deeper between them. Something that'd always been there but had just taken them a while to find.

His hands moved. One was at the base of her skull. The other along her hip, his fingers under her shirt, stroking her bare skin. They stumbled back together, unwilling to separate. The backs of her legs hit the bed. She placed her hands against Ira's chest and pulled her mouth away from his, breathing heavily. Ira trailed kisses along her jaw.

"I smell," she huffed out.

"I don't care," he murmured against her. He stopped at the very back of her jaw, just under her ear, and *bit down*.

She jerked. Heat bloomed across her face and quickly spread to the rest of her.

"Ira, I—" She gasped, her words getting stuck in her throat when Ira slowly dragged his tongue under her ear, directly over the mark he'd just made.

Her skin was especially sensitive right now, so the slight scratch of his tongue nearly sent her eyes rolling back. Her underwear was slightly wet. She shut her eyes, breathing hard.

Fuck it.

She grabbed the front of his shirt and *pulled,* sending both of them falling back toward the bed. Ira braced his hands on either side of her to catch his weight and avoid crushing her, but she wished he hadn't. Part of her wanted him to hold her down and steal the air from her lungs and put her where he needed her.

Their lips met again, and this kiss wasn't like the one before. It was rough and heated. A battle, but not for dominance. Lena's elbows dug into his shoulder blades and the heels of her feet dug into his calves. She could feel him against her thigh.

"I want you," she gasped into his mouth. She was only breathing in Ira's air and he was only breathing in hers. She grabbed one of his hands, bringing it down her body and pressing it against her sex. "I want you *here.*"

Ira tore his lips from hers and groaned against her cheek. "*Lena* . . . you're killing me."

"Well, I don't want to do that." She smirked. "You have a job to do first."

He laughed lowly. It was but a puff of air against her heated skin. "I shall serve my queen . . . if that pleases her."

Oh. Her gut twisted again, and her legs quivered around him. She absently pressed harder into his hand, but he didn't move an inch.

"*Ira,*" she moaned. "Don't tease. I hate it when you tease."

"And I think you're lying."

She shook her head. "*No.*"

He ducked down and kissed her again. She responded quickly, lifting her head off the mattress to move with him.

"You're sure about this?"

"Yes." She pulled back and nodded. They were nearly nose to nose. "And I'm sorry for questioning your feelings. I know you can make those calls for yourself. I was just—"

"I know," he assured her, his voice gentle, as was their next kiss. "I know."

"I can make those calls too." She kissed the corner of his mouth. And then one of his scars. "I was still running away. I realize that now. But I won't run anymore. I know what I want. *Who* I want." She leaned forward and brought her lips to his ear. "And right now . . . what I want is for you to *fuck me.*"

"No."

Lena blinked and leaned back, staring at Ira in question.

"Tonight, I'm not going to fuck you." Ira's lips brushed over hers, so lightly that it couldn't even be called a kiss. "I'm going to make love to you. And if you want more after that, I'll give you more." He pulled back and looked into her eyes. "But let me do this for you."

"You always do things for me," she murmured. "What about you? What do you want?"

He smiled and she melted against the bed. It was an easy smile. One that unfurled unconsciously across his face. One that made him look even more stunning. "I told you what I want."

They met each other in the space between. Their kisses were slow and soft. Every time she sped things up or deepened the kiss, he pulled back. A noise of frustration left her, and he smiled against her lips.

His fingers worked at her pants, sliding them *ever so slowly* down her legs. The cool air sent shivers across her newly revealed skin, but Ira's fingers burned a path straight through her as they trailed down her thighs, then the backs of her knees, then her calves. She was practically drenched by the time he got to her ankles and threw her pants aside.

His hands smoothed back up her legs, but rather than touching her underwear, he grabbed the hem of her shirt and slid it off much like he had her pants. She lifted her arms for him when he pushed her shirt over her head. He kissed the center of her chest, right over her Imprint. It warmed and sent another wave of heat through her. Or maybe that was all Ira's doing.

He continued to trail down her body, his lips moving across her breasts and her ribs. He would pause to suck a bruise into her skin, and she would jerk every time his teeth grazed her. She would feel the curve of his mouth afterward. He was having too much fun teasing her.

By the time he reached the skin above her navel, she was trembling with anticipation and barely constrained desire. Her legs tensed, and Ira smoothed his hands over the tops of her thighs.

"Relax." His hot breath washed over the front of her underwear, and her hips shifted. Her muscles would be lax one moment, syrup under his touch, and tense the next, alerted by that same touch. But not in a bad way. "Do you trust me?"

She closed her eyes and nodded. She tried to relax her upper body, letting her shoulders sink into the mattress.

"Lena?" One of his fingers slipped under the waistband of her underwear and tugged. Just a bit. "I need words."

"*Yes.*"

He dragged her underwear off her legs, slowly again. She twisted the bedsheets between her fingers as he ducked his head and placed a soft, almost tantalizing kiss on her inner thigh. And then another, only an inch higher. She tensed, her legs automatically rising, but he placed his palms on her thighs, pushing them back down and holding them steady.

"*Ira.*"

"Hm?" He hummed against her skin, his mouth *so close* to where she ached the most.

She bit her bottom lip in an attempt to stifle the noise that wanted to crawl out of her. She forgot what she wanted to say. She forgot everything but him and his touch and his mouth. And then he finally gave her what she wanted.

He leaned in and pressed a hot kiss against her sex. She couldn't hold back the noise any longer. It tore from her throat and her hips raised from the bed. Ira removed one of his hands from her thigh to brace it across her hips as he ate her out.

His tongue swiped around her clit, and he provided just enough friction with his mouth to make tears spring to her eyes. She couldn't move. He was holding her down just like she wanted him to, and there was no trace of discomfort or panic. The heat and the tingles that spread through her were welcomed and only made her wetter. And Ira responded to that, alternating the amount of pressure and suction. The edges of her vision blurred and the coils in her gut tightened.

"*Ira!*" One of her hands came down to fist in his hair. The other one tugged helplessly at the bedsheets.

His hand slid under one of her thighs, lifting it and hooking it over his shoulder. That hand continued to slide down her thigh, his fingers stopping inches away from her sex.

"You're so wet," he murmured into her.

She moaned and dug the side of her face into the mattress, focusing on her breathing. A tear fell from her eyelashes.

"It's only for me, right, Lena?"

Her toes curled as his breath washed over her, and she bit down on her lower lip. "Only you," she cried out. *"Only you."*

He smiled against her skin before sealing his mouth over her sex again. He licked inside of her, his tongue warm and wet and firm against her inner walls. He pressed his entire face against her, the bridge of his nose brushing over her clit as his lips and tongue teased her mercilessly. He didn't let up this time, not as she writhed and gasped and tightened her fingers in his hair until she was nearly pulling it.

Ira only briefly drew back to breathe, his fingers taking over in that time. He was attentive and steady, constantly pushing her toward the edge, drawing out the storm from deep within her.

The sensations became too much. They rolled through her, leaving her a shuddering, hot, dripping mess. She could do nothing but allow herself to be caught in the feeling as it built and built and built until she couldn't hold it back any longer.

The cord inside of her snapped. Her vision whitened and she cried out. Her body quivered as the heat flooded out of her, leaving her sated, languid, and heavy. Yet she was floating. The sweetest essence coursed through her veins. She didn't want to come back down; she wanted to stay there forever.

A soft sigh left her lips, and she cracked her eyes open. Ira was leaning over her now and they were farther up the bed. His hair stuck up in all directions because of her tugging on it, and his lower face was wet, but his lips were still red and inviting. His dark eyes searched hers as he leaned in and kissed her passionately.

She could taste herself on his lips, but she didn't mind. Quite the opposite, actually. They kissed and kissed until her skin started to prickle with heat again and her stomach clenched. She was still tingling and stimulated from her last orgasm, so the pleasure she was experiencing was tinged with a bit of pain, but she liked it.

She shrugged off her bra and then tried to climb into his lap. Her limbs were heavy, but her body was waking up, still very much wanting to be close to him, wanting to *feel* him. She worked at his pants and Ira kicked them and his underwear off. Now they were both completely naked.

She slid her hands over his abdomen and chest, tracing his body once again. "I'll never get tired of this," she whispered. "*You.*"

Ira's eyes softened. "Yeah, me neither."

They moved so that he hovered above her. Their legs tangled and their lips locked. He supported most of his weight again, but he let some of it press her into the mattress, holding her still and enveloping her. She felt safe. And *alive*. Every nerve in her body picked up on every graze, every kiss, every *anything* and amplified it a hundred times over.

Gasps and choked moans escaped her as he pressed his lips over her breasts, taking her nipples into his mouth. One of his hands slowly worked her open even further. His fingers hit places his tongue couldn't, and it was quickly driving her close to the edge again.

She tugged on his hair, warning him that it was enough. The heat in her abdomen had built up more rapidly this time. She didn't know how long she could hold it if he was taking his time kissing all the way down her body. His mouth touched nearly every inch of her, and it brought tears to her eyes. She'd never thought she would be worshipped in this way.

One of Ira's hands tangled with her own and pressed it into the pillows by her head. "I love you."

"I love you," she said back.

Ira pulled away from her, just enough so she could look down and see his erect cock against his toned abdomen. She shifted for him as he positioned himself and pulled her legs over his hips. He grabbed the base of his cock and glanced at her before moving any closer.

"Have you?"

"Yes." She found no judgment on Ira's face. No darkness or jealousy or surprise. Nothing but receptiveness. "Have you?"

He nodded. "Yes."

And then he was pushing inside.

The girth of his cock was larger than that of his fingers, but it felt *so much* bigger when he pushed inside of her. He went slow, and when she tensed, he stopped, waiting for her to relax again before he continued. He did this until he was fully seated inside of her.

They both took a deep, synchronized breath.

He watched her as she adjusted to the full size of him. It was an odd feeling, but not one of discomfort. Her nerves were *singing* and she squirmed at the overstimulation, but it felt so good.

She tightened her legs around Ira, and he keenly came forward. His forearms landed on the either side of her and he began to move.

He rocked into her, slowly at first, and the drag of his cock against her walls sent tingles up her spine. Ira leaned his forehead against hers, his brows drawn together as he moved again, a bit faster and deeper this time. But he never went *fast*. And that was almost more torturous. But it felt divine. It seemed like . . . he was savoring her. Savoring *this*.

She felt each and every inch of his cock as he thrusted into her. He was being attentive and deliberate, coaxing lewd noises from her mouth. He noticed the way her face and body would react when he changed his angle or when his fingers or cock brushed over a certain spot. He picked up on what she liked and kept things that way.

"You're beautiful."

Her breath and gut twisted when he drove deep once again. Her nails dug into his shoulders as his fingers trailed across her cheeks and collarbones, her breasts and the valley between them. If he had paint on his fingers and his lips, her entire body would be covered in it. Marked. He'd seen all of her, and he was not afraid.

Ira's lips slipped past her cheekbone in a messy kiss. "I love you. Always."

Her heart was going to burst out of her chest at any moment. Their breathing was erratic and their bodies gravitated toward one another as his thrusts became uneven.

"There's nothing I wouldn't do for you."

Lena moaned shamelessly as the heat and energy building in her twisted and curled, folding in on itself. Ira gasped and his hand squeezed hers tightly. His thrusts were quicker and deeper. They were both falling together. The pressure in her abdomen reached a crescendo, as did her shouts of pleasure. Their foreheads touched and they both cried out as they came.

She was stuck in a haze. Her limbs trembled, prickling with sensitivity, yet loose and lost among the softness under her and the warmth over her. She blinked the tears out of her eyes as her body came back together.

Ira pulled out from her with another groan and rolled to the side. She moved with him, resting her head on his sweaty chest. It rose and fell under her cheek.

"I love you too," she said again, gazing up at him.

Ira's smile was bright and loose, sloppy in an affectionate way that warmed her chest. He pulled her closed and she cuddled up to his side. She was exhausted, but she didn't fall asleep just yet. Neither did Ira. His fingers twisted in her hair, gently breaking apart any tangles that had formed during tonight's activities.

"If you need something more . . . if you need something I can't give you . . . I won't fault you for seeking it out."

Lena raised her chin from his chest and looked at him, her brow furrowed.

He met her gaze evenly. "I just wanted to tell you that. I meant what I said earlier. You're your own person, so if you want someone—"

She placed her hand over his heart. "I *want* to be with *you*. There's no one else. Okay?"

He hesitated, and then nodded.

She bit the inside of her cheek, thinking and asking herself if she really wanted to bring this conversation to the table now. They *were* already on the topic. "Whether or not either of us like it, Sorrel is pushing for a marriage to seal the alliance."

His hand covered hers on his chest. "If you don't want to marry, you don't have to," he repeated.

She smiled and squeezed his hand. "Aquila was with me when I went to my informant tonight. I didn't want to ask about Sorrel in front of her, so I went somewhere else afterward."

"And you found something?"

"Maybe. It has to do with her past. The people she was tied up with. I don't know if it's anything substantial, but it could be."

"*Substantial?*" Ira repeated, raising a brow. A slow smile unfurled across his face. "Blackmail?"

"Sorrel is dead set on a marriage. I don't think anything else is going to change her mind."

Ira's fingers threaded through hers and he brought her hand to his mouth, kissing it. "My villainess."

She rolled her eyes. "I like them—our guests—but . . . "

"But you shouldn't be forced into another marriage," Ira said simply.

She nodded and rested her head on his chest again. "Alkus is planning something too."

"When is he not?" Ira huffed as his thumb stroked her hand.

"He's moving money around in the Lowlands."

Probably the Highlands too, but the Lowlands was what really stumped her. It possessed far fewer resources than the Highlands did, so what was he employing down there?

Ira stilled. "We'll figure out why."

"He has people watching us. We'll have to be more careful, especially with going to the Lowlands. We just need to catch him slipping up first."

"And we will. We'll deal with him and Sorrel."

"And then we'll get our happily ever after?" she joked, looking up at him once more.

Ira smiled again, but it was weak compared to the others.

They both knew that wouldn't happen. Those kinds of fairy tale endings didn't exist in real life.

"We'll be happy," he amended. "I'm happy right now."

Lena smiled, and this one was genuine. She leaned forward to place another kiss on his lips. "Me too. Let's keep things that way. For as long as we can."

It was a promise and a wish.

Ira's smile widened momentarily, like one of his cheeks had tugged at the corner of his mouth with an invisible string and then let it go. "Forever then?"

She laid her head down and closed her eyes, keeping a firm grip on his hand. Her body was content and lax, ready to drift. "Forever."

CHAPTER
THIRTY-EIGHT

Within thirty minutes, there were dozens of prophets and enforcers in front of Atreus. It wasn't all of them, but it was enough.

"You asked me earlier about a plan," he said, still looking at Prophet Silas. "I don't have a plan, but I know you do. I've always wondered why you sent us out. I didn't have a single clue until I started finding these stones and we were left in that realm for hours. I know we can't come back here without these stones, meaning someone else was collecting them before me. They're important. Why? What are you planning to do with them?"

"You think I'm going to tell you?" Prophet Silas scoffed.

"Maybe not you."

"Someone else then?" The prophet laughed. "None of us answer to the likes of *you*."

"You just did," Atreus pointed out.

Prophet Silas glowered at him. "And now you're extremely outnumbered."

"I'm testing something out."

His arm ached from holding it up for so long against such strong winds and his fingers were almost numb from holding the stone so tight. He was worried the stone would slip out without him noticing.

"If it's my patience you're testing then I'm afraid you've far exceeded it," Prophet Silas said, stepping forward.

Atreus shuffled back, bumping into the railing. Another gust of wind hit him, causing him to careen to the side. His other hand smacked down on the bar, holding him steady. He gasped, his heart hammering and hands shaking at the close call.

"Stop while you're ahead!" Prophet Silas called. "Like I said, you just can't win."

Atreus soaked in the prophet's words, staring down at the bottomless pit next to him. He swallowed thickly and turned around. "I saw the man you met with weeks ago. He was from above ground, wasn't he?"

Prophet Silas frowned. "I'm not playing your childish games."

"But you have us play yours! I won't do it anymore."

"You don't have a choice," the prophet hissed. "You are evil incarnate. It will not be purged from you unless you're faced with evil just as violent and wicked. Only then can you realize your sins and make amends!"

"I didn't do anything wrong!" Atreus shouted, his voice breaking and being swept away by the wind, because no one cared. He might as well be screaming at a wall. "None of us did! *You* are the crazy ones!"

"'*Didn't do anything wrong*'?" Prophet Silas repeated incredulously. "Someone hasn't been paying attention in seminar. Perhaps you need more lessons."

"How do you even know we're sin reincarnated? Maybe it's not us at all. Maybe it's you—"

"Do *not* compare me to *your kind*," the prophet spat. "We serve the Numina, acting only in their interests. We are their messengers in this realm. We hold knowledge others can't even imagine. The Numina will bring salvation to the realms through us."

Atreus shook his head. "You're crazy," he said again. "And whatever you're trying to do, I won't let you do it."

And with that, he opened his hand and let the stone fall.

"*No!*"

Prophet Silas lunged forward, but he was too late. The stone had disappeared. Atreus stared at the dark abyss that had sucked it up, and for a second, he thought about joining it.

The enforcers seized him and dragged him back down the long hall. He kicked his legs fruitlessly, trying to gain purchase on the slick tile. Their grip was harsh and unforgiving, bruising his skin. He was thrown to the ground, and he barely had time to curl in on himself before the fists came raining down.

"You evil creature!"

Hit.

"You monster!"

Hit.

"Ungrateful demon!"

Hit.

"You'll never understand what we're doing for you!"

Hit.

"You're too far gone!"

Hit.

"The soul inside of you is too corrupt!"

Hit.

"And you're corrupting the others!"
Hit.
"With your diabolic delusions!"
Hit.
"You think you've got this all figured out? That you understand everything?"
Hit.
"Well, I'll show you. I'll show you what you still have to be afraid of."
Hit.
"Maybe that will get you to fucking fall in line."

Atreus was left bleeding and bruised on the floor when Prophet Silas stepped back. He gasped for breath. Every inhale was thin, nearly a wheeze, and accompanied by a stabbing pain that made him groan and flinch. He spat out a mouthful of blood and pressed his unbruised cheek against the smooth black floor. It was so cold.

Prophet Silas grabbed the back of his shirt and hauled him up. Atreus' legs struggled helplessly under him, never finding their footing. The prophet didn't give him the chance. Atreus' shirt collar ripped, and he was thrown onto the floor again. His injured side hit the hard marble and he cried out. Prophet Silas reached down, and with one harsh tug, tore Atreus' shirt the rest of the way and pulled it from his body.

Atreus focused on his breathing.

In and out.

In and out.

In and out.

But he couldn't get enough air. Something was wrong with his side. Bruised rib, maybe. He braced his forearm against the floor as he reached his other arm down to touch his trembling skin. He hissed at the contact and bit his bottom lip, muffling the noise that escaped him.

A cracking sound caused his body to lock up. His eyes trailed to the side, seeing the tails of the whip brush the ground.

The first lash was excruciating. The tails of the whip cut through his skin like knives through butter, creating multiple cuts with only one blow. He grunted and tensed. The muscles in his forearm quivered and gave out after the next lash.

He collapsed to the ground. His mouth broke open with the next series of cuts. His cries only seemed to incite Prophet Silas, who brought down the whip again. And again. And again.

Blood trailed down Atreus' back and sides, dripping onto the floor. His raw and exposed flesh burned against the cold air. He might have been screaming, but he couldn't hear anything past the cracking of the whip.

More blood filled his mouth. Did he bite off his tongue?

His entire body had been taken over by the pain. It was so intense it was almost numbing.

He counted eight lashes before he slipped under.

~

HIS WHOLE BODY was screaming in agony from the moment he woke up. Atreus tried to open his eyes and failed. His muscles were heavy and swollen. Moving was difficult, but he turned his head to the side and groaned as his bruised cheek scraped against the rough pillow.

He forced his eyes open. Only a sliver. Finn sat on the floor next to the bed, his own eyes rimmed with red. He immediately noticed that Atreus was awake and sat up straighter.

"Atreus, you look . . . "

"Like shit," someone else filled in for him.

Two other people stepped into view behind Finn. Weylin and Vanik.

Atreus swiped his tongue over his cracked lips, feeling a deep cut in his mouth when he did so. He prodded at it again. Speaking would hurt, but he still tried. It took him a few attempts to get the full sentence out, and it was more of a croak than anything, but it was intelligible.

"What did you find?"

Vanik stared back at him, his arms crossed and his stoic expression unchanging. Dread spread through Atreus.

They hadn't found anything.

But then, Vanik grinned.

PART THREE
THE REVOLT

CHAPTER
THIRTY-NINE

Lena's eyes roved over the words on the page. She was skimming at this point, looking for one word in particular—*bond*. This was the fourteenth book she'd been through today. Or was it the fifteenth?

She'd found herself with some free time as of late. They all had. The explosions in the distance had faded, as had the murders. And the *Ateisha* were staying put.

But she still had her fair share of problems, the alliance being one of them. She'd been going out of her way to avoid Sorrel, which was somewhat difficult now that their guests had two seats in the council chamber. They didn't get to weigh in on matters, but they were present. And Sorrel was almost *always* one of the two, so Lena would more or less run out of there as soon as she ended the meeting.

Aquila was avoiding her, and it seemed that Kieryn was just indifferent about her presence. She still hadn't run into Von, and she didn't know if that was due to good or bad luck, but she'd take what she could get. She reminded herself that their guests from Ouprua wouldn't be here forever.

With each passing day, Sorrel grew more and more impatient, but Lena just needed more *time*. She'd told Ira everything she knew about Sorrel, including the lead she had on her past. Ira had offered to figure out what was going on with the list and the prisoner, but she'd pulled him back on that. It would no doubt lead to an argument with Alkus, which they didn't need right now. What they needed was to distance themselves from said councilman, especially now that they were watching him and following his moves. Perhaps it would give him a false sense of security. Whatever the case, she was glad to get rid of the headache that was him. For the moment.

Ira and Cowen had cautioned her against going down to the Lowlands too often. The more she went, the more likely she would get caught. Alkus *could* already know about her late-night escapades, and part of her wished he did. She *wanted* him to know that she was moving against him.

No news on Julian had surfaced yet either.

So for now, she was just . . . waiting.

She had spent this free time doing various things. One of them was having sex. She and Ira were having *a lot* of sex. In their bed. In the bathing pool. In their secret spot. In Ira's study. In *her* study. She had literally been to it more times for sex than anything else, instead preferring to meet someone in their own study when discussing matters or working alone in her room.

And since they were having a lot of sex, she was also drinking a lot of contraceptive elixirs. Sometimes she would fall asleep afterward and Ira would retrieve it for her. They had to be somewhat secretive about it since contraceptives were frowned upon in The Lands.

But she and Ira didn't spend every waking moment together. Ira occasionally had his own matters to deal with, and he needed his alone time. Lena understood that. She had her own personal tasks as well.

She was currently in one of the smaller libraries in the palace, researching. Not many people came here, which was exactly why *she* had come here. Their guests weren't the only people she was avoiding. Mikhail was another one. If she had to listen to him talk about children one more time, she would jam a dagger into her eardrums. Or cut off his tongue. The latter was preferable.

Mikhail had swayed to the untrustworthy side of the loyalty spectrum. He could be counted on in some ways. He was devoted to the Numina, and she didn't think that would change, but she could see him losing sight of his other obligations, namely supporting *her*. He still believed in her rulership for now, but Alkus had been whispering in his ear while she was gone.

As a prophet, Mikhail believed in omens and prophecies, yet half of such opposed her while the other half supported her. The *Ateisha*, the explosions, the murders, the potential uprising in the Lowlands—that had all happened during her time. She hoped Mikhail would turn his cheek to Alkus' words, but she couldn't count on that. She didn't care much for the prophecy, but as long as it helped her maintain her position as ruler, she would continue to use it to her advantage.

Because of Mikhail's unknown allegiance, she hadn't asked him about the bond. She'd decided to look into it herself. The smaller libraries, however, didn't have a lot of books, so she'd sought out the head librarian.

The old woman had looked at her in disbelief when she asked for the palace catalog, eventually leading her to it when she stood firm. The catalog wasn't just *one* binding. It filled an entire room.

Lena recruited the help of Benji and Andra the next day. The three of them scoured through the entire room, taking note of any text that might contain what she was looking for. In the end, she'd had a list of 1,348 books. She could already feel the headache beginning to form.

The trio had a system set up. While she was in the library, one of them stayed with her while the other found the texts she needed and brought them to her a few at a time. The librarians fussed over all the displaced books, but Lena promised they would be returned to their rightful place. And they always were.

The book she was currently skimming was called *The Ties of Time*, which was a very poetic title in her opinion. The writing, on the other hand, less so. She flipped through the pages, eyes snagging on the larger section titles.

Divine Bonds.
Firstborn Bonds.
Cursed-Blessed Bonds.
Family Bonds.
Reincarnation.

The last one made her pause. She slowly flipped through the section, looking at the subtitles. A lot of them were self-explanatory, but one she came across puzzled her.

Cornerstones

Cornerstones continue to be an enigmatic concept across the realms. Many theories surround this powerful object, but none have been confirmed. It's commonly believed that a Cornerstone is a type of support system that preserves the soul of its maker.

When a soul is reincarnated, they might have a few similarities with their past selves, trifling features that are ingrained in the soul, but most aspects of their new self are completely different. They have a new mind and personality. They don't remember anything of their past lives. Dreams may provide glimpses, but that is rare. In essence, they are a new person with a recycled soul.

However, if someone were to create a Cornerstone, it's thought that their self in that lifetime would be preserved throughout their reincarnated selves, meaning that their consciousness would be present, as well as their motivations, desires, preferences, . . .

A Cornerstone, essentially, is believed to make someone immortal.

Some scholars believe the Cornerstone loses strength over time or only works for a certain period of time. Others believe that this immortality will only end once the Cornerstone is destroyed.

Many more questions surround this phenomenon, namely, does consciousness develop normally in each succeeding lifetime or would a newborn come into this world with the mind of someone much older and wiser? How was this concept discovered or created? How does one create a Cornerstone?

In response to this last question, scholars have—

Lena sighed and flipped the page. This type of bond stretched through a single soul's lifetime, not between multiple souls, and she was looking for the latter. But it was close. If something like that could exist, then there had to be a type of bond that connected people—multiple souls—throughout time.

She carefully jumped from subtitle to subtitle until she came across one that looked promising.

Soul Bond

A soul bond links the souls of those involved in the ceremony. Soul bonds are the highest form of devotion, even stronger than marriage. As far as scholars are aware, there is no infallible way to annul it, and it lasts longer than a single lifetime. As long as these souls exist in the realms, this bond will as well—

"Kalena."

She looked up from the page and quickly closed the book. She wanted to keep what she was reading to herself.

Jhai stood a few feet away, her hands clasped in front of her. Right, Lena had asked Benji to bring Jhai to her after he finished bringing over the books.

"I hope I'm not interrupting anything," Jhai said, her eyes flitting to the stacks of books covering the table.

"No," Lena said as she placed the book aside. "You're fine. How's your family?"

Jhai had spent the last two days down in the Lowlands with them per Lena's suggestion.

Jhai's neutral expression wavered. "They're faring. My gran came down with a cough last week."

"I'm sorry to hear that. I hope the cough clears up." Lena waved at the chair in front of her. "Please, sit. I imagine a sick family member would be quite worrisome, but other than that, your time in the Lowlands was enjoyable? Did you miss the palace?"

Jhai sat. "Both places have their own sort of beauty. Not many would agree with that, but I think you would. I missed my family, though. I was glad to see them, especially during these times." Her eyes swept over the books again before returning to Lena. "Thank you for allowing me to go."

"Of course. You're my attendant, but I don't want to keep you here. If you ever need anything, talk to me first and I can arrange something. You can see your family any time you'd like—"

"Thank you, Kalena."

"—if you do something for me."

Jhai's brows rose just a fraction and her lips parted. She quickly composed herself, but not before Lena saw what she needed to see.

"I . . . don't really understand." Jhai shook her head. "I do whatever—"

"This is something different." Lena leaned forward and lowered her voice. "I need you to look out for something. For *me*."

Jhai's face was still scrunched in confusion. "Don't your guards do that?"

"They protect me. They stay by my side. I need someone who can travel through the palace discreetly and be my eyes and ears in places I can't reach. In return for your service, I can help you and your family. I can get medicine. Food. Whatever they need."

Lena could see the cogs turning in Jhai's head. She couldn't refuse the offer.

"What exactly do you need me to do?" her attendant asked slowly.

Lena fought off a smile and leaned back in her chair. "For *now*, I need you to go back to the Lowlands to be with your family. Benji will give you medicine to take to them. Tomorrow, I'll sneak into Alkus' study to retrieve a book. I expect you back in the palace the following morning so I can hand it off to you, and you can go back to the Lowlands, with your family, to keep it hidden. Do we have a deal?"

Jhai remained silent, her eyes tracing the veins of the wooden table. Her mouth twitched to the side as she worked through things in her head.

"Yes," she muttered, meeting Lena's gaze. "Yes, we've got a deal."

AFTER RETURNING all but one of the books to their rightful locations, Lena brought *The Ties of Time* to her room so she could finish reading it later. And then she took a stroll outside.

True to her word, she'd sent Jhai off right after their conversation with medicine and a few other helpful items. She hoped she could trust her, but she would have to wait a few days to see if she could.

As soon as she hit the trees surrounding the palace, she let her Slayer out. Despite the bloodbath that had been the Night Run, no statutes had been put in place to limit Slayer activity. Their behavior and everything that'd resulted from it was just . . . nature. It was how things were. It was accepted. Even in their Slayer form, the Numina still seemed to rule this realm.

"Where are you going?" Andra called after her.

Lena didn't reply because she didn't exactly know the answer to that. She was just . . . *going*, letting her feet take her wherever.

The air had gradually cooled as they moved away from the height of the warm season, so the middle of the day wasn't so stifling. There was actually a nice breeze that rustled the leaves and made shadowed patterns dance across the forest floor.

She took a deep breath, the smell of wildflowers, tree sap, and wet soil filling her nose. It reminded her of all the trips she'd taken into the forest with the others when she was younger. The games they'd played didn't exactly make up her fondest memories, but there had been moments when she bested them, moments when they made a fool of themselves, which she'd enjoyed. She had gone off on her own out here too . . . and with Tuck.

She stopped and looked around until she spotted a familiar tree up ahead. The trunk split about twenty feet up and the rest of the tree was in a twisted Y-shape. She knew where she was. She turned ninety degrees and kept walking for a few more miles until she reached her destination.

The wind picked up, blowing her hair back from her face. The leaves and branches rattled, creating their own sort of tune.

The treehouse looked the same as it had five years ago.

It wasn't rotting or covered in vines, which told her someone had been coming to this place and keeping it tidy. But only one other person knew about this treehouse, at least as far as she knew. Things could've changed. Or he could've been lying to her from the start. The latter seemed more likely. After all, this lie wouldn't have been the first, and it was smaller than the others.

The treehouse rested about thirty feet above the ground, nestled between the trunk and a thick branch. Boards, nails, ropes, and probably a bit of magic secured its position. The roof was covered in a sheet of moss, but it'd been placed there intentionally. The only way to get up into the treehouse was to climb up the makeshift ladder built out of more boards and nails hammered into the tree trunk and crawl through the tiny cut-out opening in one corner. Lena had done it dozens of times before, and she did it again right now.

"Your Majesty?" Benji called as she began to climb.

"It's fine," she grunted out.

The wood was worn and smooth with age and use, more than she remembered it being. Her fingers fit into the distinct finger grooves as she climbed.

As soon as she pulled herself inside, she looked around. A sleeping roll lay in the corner with a bag next to it, and carved wooden pieces sat on the window ledge.

She walked over and picked one up. A perfect cube. Her fingers traced the grooves. It was smoother than the ones she recalled. He was getting better. Curved lines cut through all six surfaces of the block and larger dots were scattered along them. There were other wooden cubes—at least two dozen of them—and they all had a similar design. A few were stacked next to the bag.

He'd made a . . . puzzle?

The thought of Tuck whittling a puzzle for his own entertainment was a funny one that forced a short laugh out of her throat. She set the cube back down and picked up one of the other items. The detail of the figurine was much more impressive. Did he carve these with specific people in mind, or did he just start whittling away and unconsciously replicate the features of different people he'd come across?

They all had their time-consuming hobbies that occupied their mind when they could no longer stand the thoughts that naturally plagued it.

She put the figurine down and ambled to the opposite wall of the treehouse. The thin grooves in the wall became noticeable as she approached. There were dozens of them, each one no longer than a few centimeters. She'd created a fair share of those when she was younger, when Tuck was teaching her how to throw daggers.

She pulled out the dagger she almost always kept on her and returned to where she'd been standing. The faded paint on the dagger wall was more perceptible from this distance. She lined herself up, raised her hand, took a deep breath, and then snapped her arm forward, flicking her wrist. In the blink of an eye, the dagger lodged itself into the center of the faded target. The hilt vibrated for a few seconds, creating a hum before stilling.

Lena stared at it. She snorted softly and shook her head. "What are you doing?" she mumbled to herself.

She retrieved her dagger and brushed her thumb over the large nick she'd created in the wall.

At first, she'd been horrible with daggers, but Tuck had surprisingly been a patient teacher. He wouldn't get frustrated or rush her. He would just tell her to try again and give tips when need be.

"Why are you even teaching me?" she asked one day after the dagger she threw bounced harmlessly off the wall. That had been her thirtieth throw that day.

He shrugged, and without even looking up from picking under his fingernails with his dagger, replied, *"Do you want me to not teach you?"*

"... No."

"Okay then. Go pick up that dagger."

He had been confusing—he still was—but she'd actually enjoyed his presence then. When it was just the two of them, that was. He grew nastier around other people. Or maybe it was just the other people. They were nasty—there was no question about that—and maybe she'd expected Tuck to defend her.

She shook her head again as if that alone would cast aside those thoughts. "Stop it."

Tuck didn't need any excuses made for him.

Lena climbed down the ladder and headed off, ignoring the part of her that clearly wanted to stay.

CHAPTER
FORTY

The Ruler's Treasury was based underground.

The treasury was the largest building in Solavas and one of the largest in the Highlands, so there was plenty of room for the Ruler's Treasury alongside all the other thousands of vaults above ground, but that apparently would not do. The teller who was leading her and Ira to the Ruler's Treasury had explained that it was deep underground for security reasons and because of its size.

"You are a special guest," the teller said, "so you get special treatment."

"I'd rather not," Lena mumbled.

Her voice didn't reach the teller, who was a few paces in front of them in the narrow hallway, sifting through the ring of keys he held in his hand, but Ira heard her. He huffed out a laugh and bumped her with his shoulder.

"What?" She turned to him. The hallway was underground but well lit, meaning he could see her irritation clearly. And she could see the amusement written across his face. "Do we really have to be here?"

Ira tottered his head from side to side. "Mhm, no, *but* this has to get done sooner or later."

He gave her a knowing look.

Lena had her people in the Lowlands and Ira had his. She kept hers loyal through fear mostly, throwing in money or something else they wanted from time to time, but Ira was insistent on the latter alternative. Nothing, he'd said, did the job better than money. And she could outbid anyone in The Lands.

"*I know how these sorts of people work. You do too,*" he'd told her that morning. "*We're spread too thin right now. You need a job done, so get in touch with them, keep your identity safe, pay them half upfront and the rest at the end when they've delivered. I have someone who can meet them for us."*

And that had been that.

She did know how those sorts of people worked, but her past made her prudent with her money. In the Lowlands, she'd stolen what she'd needed, and she hadn't needed much money since returning to the Highlands. Cowen had withdrawn money for her the other week before they went to the Lowlands with Aquila, but this was Lena's first time actually visiting the treasury. She hadn't grown up with money, so she didn't naturally turn to it as a way to solve her problems, but now she had more money than she had time.

She'd visited her other informant a few days ago; not Dugell. They'd only managed to get the name of one of Sorrel's victims. Edmund Sharry. A Blessed. And apparently his name had been *very* hard to find. There was no trace of the other victim, which, strangely enough, made Lena even more hopeful that she was on to something.

Sorrel had killed two people. She'd willingly offered up that bit of information to Lena, yet the details were hard to find. Why? Why say anything at all if you're trying to keep something hidden? There had to be more to the story. Something else was going on. Ouprua had buried the incident and the names and pardoned Sorrel more for their sake than hers because they hadn't wanted news of Sorrel's crime getting out. And they still didn't. But there was still the question of *why?*

Lena didn't know what sorts of connections her informants had, and she wouldn't ask because she'd be overstepping, but she would bet they'd known about Ouprua far longer than the council, meaning they possibly had people out at sea. Still, the second name couldn't be recovered. *Yet.* She was determined to get that name. It could be the missing puzzle piece she needed to sway Sorrel, or it could be the beginning of something more, something bigger that required more digging. In that case, she had more money she could spend, right?

She didn't really care about the money or hiring dirtyhands to get the information she needed. Not right now. But she *did* care about what she and Ira were doing in the meantime.

"Do we have to go house hunting?" she grumbled under her breath. She'd tried to talk him out of this twice already. "I don't even want to buy a house. We already have one."

Ira held back a grin. "Unfortunately, the council does not see it that way. A house in the Lowlands is not a proper home for the queen."

She snorted. "I'm sure some of them think that is *exactly* where I belong."

"Well, you know how much the council cares about appearances."

She looked at him again and rolled her eyes, unable to tell if he was being serious or not.

"Let's just cut this short and get the first one," she huffed. "I really don't care."

They went down in a lift, which she thought was even *more* unnecessary. The annoyance was practically simmering off of her. Ira seemed to find this whole thing rather entertaining. The teller, on the other hand, seemed oblivious to it all. He explained the architecture of the treasury as they traveled downward.

"The Blessed's vaults are on the ground level. The ones belonging to the council members are a bit underground, but stairs will take you to them easily enough. You have to take the lift to get down to the royals' treasuries, though—oh, look! We just passed that level. Yours, of course, is the deepest and farthest back for safekeeping. Some of the items in the vault have been there for centuries. The Ruler's Treasury is of utmost importance. Only a few people have access to it and know its location. One of us is always working."

Lena slid her gaze to Ira, her eyelids low and her lips flat. He grinned and mouthed, '*enthusiastic.*'

Thankfully, they reached the bottom quickly and continued through the halls, which were much smaller and colder now. It was a maze down here.

"Has anyone broken in and gotten lost?" she found herself asking.

"Oh, yes, but it hasn't happened in some time," the teller replied somewhat upbeat.

Comforting.

After about five more minutes of walking, they reached the doors. They were, predictably, large and gold.

The teller went up to the doors and moved the metal bars attached to their surface. Upon first glance, the bars just looked like an elaborate design, but they moved too easily. It was another key. And there was a certain way to position them.

When the teller finished moving all of the bars to the proper location, he took the key he'd singled out from the ring, placed it in the keyhole, and twisted it. The doors unlatched and a hum reached her ears. It wasn't loud, but it still startled her. She reached her hand up instinctively as if she were going to snatch the faint sound out of the air and hold it in her palm. But the hum had settled already, blending into the rest of the white noise reverberating through the space.

The teller turned around and smiled at her. "After you."

Lena's mouth dropped open as soon as she set foot inside the vault. It was larger than she ever could've imagined. The ceilings stretched upward for a good one hundred feet, but it was the length of the room that truly stumped her. And the contents of it. There were thousands of bags of coins and bars of gold and silver stacked on top of each other. Rare gems were piled in chests and jewelry containing glittering crystals and stones were splayed across granite tables.

Her awe quickly turned into vexation when she truly processed just how much wealth this room contained. And it just sat here.

She looked at Ira. His face was grim.

The teller smiled merrily at her. "Take whatever you need."

Oh, she would.

"This house was recently built and is quite private, which I know is something you were wanting. It also comes with a nice area of land. It has six bedrooms and five bathrooms—"

"Why would we need six bedrooms?" Lena asked as she trailed her fingers along the countertops. "There are only two of us."

The estate agent faltered and looked at Ira as if she expected him to save her. She'd been doing that a lot, much to Lena's aggravation. And Lena had been interrupting the agent's clearly well-planned pitch quite a bit as well.

"For now," the agent said, "but your family might grow soon."

Lena flashed her a flat smile. "Of course. May I ask a question? Out of the list of houses you've prepared to show us today, which one has the fewest number of bedrooms?"

"A house on the east side of Solavas next to the river. I know you wanted to stay in the capital—"

"And how many bedrooms does that house have?"

"Four."

The agent walked into the other room and continued her delivery, but her gaze lingered on Ira again.

"That's too many bedrooms," Lena grumbled once the agent was out of earshot. Most of them would just sit there, untouched, and waste away.

"The cabin has three bedrooms," Ira pointed out unhelpfully as he stepped up next to her.

"But that's much more practical than four. And *way* more practical than six. With three there's one for us . . . one for you if you annoy me, and one for a guest. What would we do with *four?* With *six?*"

"Maybe have more guests."

A drawn-out sigh left her mouth for what had to be the dozenth time that day. "Or maybe you'll just have more rooms to pick from when I boot you out of ours."

Ira grinned again. "This house is nice, and you said you wanted to get the first one."

It *was* nice, but not like the cabin was nice. In typical Highlands' style, the house was sleek, contemporary, and minimalist. There were no splashes of color or clutter that gave the place charm. It was spacious, black and white, and boring. It felt cold.

"You can decorate it," Ira said, clearly picking up on her distaste. "It doesn't have to stay like this."

"We can furnish the home however you'd like," the agent said. She had waited for them in the sitting room, right next to the white couches, which was absolutely the worst color choice in Lena's opinion. "And make any other changes. Whatever you want."

And there it was again. The agent's eyes drifted over to Ira and then *down* and back up. Right in front of her too. Lena didn't know if she should be more insulted or impressed by the woman's audacity.

"Great," Lena said, her voice clipped. The woman's gaze jerked back to her, the tops of her cheeks red. "Now if you could get out. Please. *My* husband and I would like to tour the house ourselves."

The agent's face reddened further.

Ira laughed next to her as the agent scrambled out of the house.

"What?"

"Seems like you don't share well either," he said as he stepped past her to head upstairs.

Lena was left gaping, but she quickly snapped her mouth shut and followed him. "She was practically undressing you with her eyes!" she hissed. "Right in front of me too! It was tactless."

Ira only laughed again, and it soured her mood even further.

"What's so funny?"

"You." He pushed open one of the doors and stepped inside.

Lena's eyes were burning into Ira's back, so she barely took in the room. "I'm glad you find my frustration amusing," she bit out.

Ira took his time sweeping over the space, but then he slowly turned to her, appearing calm and collected, not at all reacting to her temper and cutting remarks. He wore a small smirk on his face.

"What I find amusing," he drawled as he closed the distance between them and grabbed her hands, "is that you *still* feel threatened. I'm not interested in that woman, so it doesn't matter how much she stares."

"It matters to me," Lena said petulantly.

Ira's smirk widened.

"It's nice to feel wanted." He smoothed his hands up her arms as his eyes dropped to her lips. "Jealousy looks good on you."

She rolled her eyes and tried to pull away, but Ira's grip on her shoulders tightened, holding her still as he dipped his head to kiss her. He didn't start off soft or slow. His lips moved fiercely over her own, his tongue entering her mouth the moment she parted her lips. He stole her breath away, and then pulled back just as she was about to break away for air.

Ira turned and continued to look over the room as if he hadn't just given her a soul-sucking kiss.

She stared at his back, her lips tingling and mouth ajar.

"There are so many windows," Ira commented, his voice smooth. He didn't sound at all affected by their kiss. She, on the other hand, was trying to get her pounding heart under control. "Even in the bedroom. Don't you think so?"

He turned to her then, and she saw the glint in his eyes. It sparked the fire growing within her.

She snapped her mouth shut and strolled toward the bed. "We could get curtains," she suggested as she trailed her fingers over the bedsheets.

They were soft. Would the mattress be as well? Not that it really mattered. The estate agent had said they could change anything. Still, she wanted to try it. Maybe her opinion of this place could be altered.

Ira hummed noncommittally as he made his way over to the other side of the bed. "We could."

She raised a brow at his tone. "You don't want to?"

He shrugged. "I'm open to it." He fell back onto the bed and laced his fingers across his stomach. "But there's a certain thrill that comes with having all these windows uncovered while we fuck."

Her heart skipped a beat, and she met his darkened gaze.

"I think I saw the estate agent out there. Do you think she can see inside? Should I go down and ask her if the windows are tinted?"

Lena's eyes narrowed as the fire lining her gut flared. "Stop it."

"Stop what?" He patted the space next to him as an invitation. "It's comfortable."

Rather than lie down next to him, she strolled over to the window. Sure enough, the estate agent stood out front, fiddling with her booklet and kicking at the gravel.

Lena felt Ira's presence behind her. He slid his hands along her waist and wrapped them across her front, pulling her back to his chest. "Should we put on a show for her?" he whispered in her ear.

Lena sunk into his embrace and laid her hands over his. Her breathing sped up, just a bit, but Ira caught it.

He pressed his nose into her hair, and his lips brushed the shell of her ear as he spoke. "Do you like the idea of people watching us?"

She rolled her head into the dip of his shoulder, her eyes fluttering closed. "No, and I don't think you do either." She turned in his arms, placing her hands against his chest. "You don't like to share, remember? And apparently neither do I."

Ira's eyes didn't leave hers as she gently pushed him back, walking with him. The corners of his lips lifted slightly. "You're right. I can be a bit greedy."

She shoved him hard, and he fell back onto the bed. She quickly straddled his lap and leaned forward until her face was inches above his. "I like you that way."

Even through their clothing, sparks ignited across her skin. Part of her wondered if Blessed's enhanced senses made sex better for them. Ira always satisfied her, but when the high of sex faded, she always wanted more. She chased the way he made her feel. Maybe it had nothing to do with Blessed's enhanced senses and everything to do with Ira. Maybe he just drove her that crazy.

Ira's gaze latched onto her lips, his eyelids low. "I like you in any way," he replied slowly. "On your back. In my lap. On your hands and knees." His hands slid up the back of her thighs, stopping right below her ass. "Which one will it be today, Lena?"

His words caused her mind to become even more muddled by desire. She bit her lip and dropped herself fully onto his lap, feeling his hard length against her.

"You're sweet. I like it when you're sweet but . . . " She dragged her thumb across his bottom lip. " . . . I don't think I prefer *sweet*."

They stared at one another for a few seconds before the tense string holding them back snapped and they crashed together. Her lips cut across his and his tongue slipped into her mouth as their hands scrambled to push aside the clothing that separated them. She was already boiling, and the sweep of his hands across her skin set her on *fire*.

"Don't be gentle," she gasped into his mouth. One of his hands brushed over her trembling abdomen and she careened into him. They both moaned as they lined up just *so*. "Or slow."

He tore off his shirt as she fumbled with the button on his pants and then the ties. Her hands brushed over his jutting hip bones as she grabbed the side of his pants and tugged. A breathy laugh traveled from his mouth to hers. He lifted his hips, and she pulled back to get a better grip. She watched the way the muscles in his abdomen flexed as he moved.

Her hands slid over his strong thighs. She felt the urge to kiss them, so she did, and his breath stuttered. She worked his pants the rest of the way off as her lips traveled up. He grabbed her hands and *pulled* her up into his lap the moment her mouth touched the bottom seam of his underwear. He brushed a thumb over one of her nipples as he kissed her, his lips catching the noise that left her mouth.

"You like it when I move you around," Ira observed, his mouth curving into a slow grin.

She didn't deny it.

She sat too high above his hips, but she fixed that by bracing her hands on the bed and grinding down against him. Ira groaned and his hands tightened on her sides, smoothing down to the small of her back and under her shirt. She raised her hands so he could lift it off her.

"I also like it when you leave marks," she confessed. "And when you make decisions for us."

She and Ira had been dancing around each other for so long. They slowly opened up to one another, then they talked, and then they began to touch. It was all innocent in the beginning. Ira was touch starved. He'd sit close to her so their shoulders grazed. His foot would rest against hers or their elbows would brush at the dinner table. Upon her return, they'd picked up right where they'd left off, but their touches were bolder after years apart—still meant to comfort. They confided in one another—verbally, mentally, and physically.

After both of their confessions, she'd looked back at their relationship and realized how much they'd acted like lovers. All of the elements had been there except for the mutual agreement. A few days ago, Cowen had made some comment about them being emotionally constipated, which she'd brushed aside initially, but she often found herself returning to that.

They really were idiots. They'd wasted so much time.

"Hey," Ira said, pulling her from her thoughts. "You're thinking too much."

She pressed a weighted, searing kiss on his lips. "I'm thinking about you," she said, and then crawled down his body again.

He didn't pull her back. He watched her as she settled between his legs and fiddled with the waistband of his underwear. She maintained eye contact with him as she leaned down and gently pressed her lips against the bulge hidden under the fabric. He hissed and his hands twitched against the mattress while she smiled against him.

"Lena," he warned, his eyes burning.

She decided she liked that look on him.

"You said you didn't want slow. Or gentle. I thought we weren't doing any foreplay." His words were strained.

She kissed him again and smoothed her hands up and down his thighs. "I've changed my mind."

She wasn't sure if it was her words or her mouth or her hands that caused him to groan.

"Lena," he warned again, his voice drawn tight. His body too. He gripped the sheets, looking as if he would unravel completely if she pulled down that waistband and took him into her mouth.

"Ira," she said, her voice soft and coy. She blinked at him, her hands still trailing up and down his legs, but each time, she inched up a bit higher. "You always take care of me. Let me take care of you."

Her hands rested at the very tops of his thighs.

Ira took a deep breath. She could see how badly he wanted this, how close to the edge he really was. The black of his pupils had nearly taken over the deep, storming blue. His lips were still slick and parted as he looked down at her.

She couldn't resist the urge to kiss him again. She bit his bottom lip before pulling away, and Ira chased after her, stopping only when he saw the look in her eyes. At last, he leaned back, bracing his hands against the bed, and nodded, giving her the permission she was waiting for.

Lena pulled down the band of his underwear, tucking it under his balls so it stayed in place. She wrapped a hand around the base of his cock, her fingers not quite touching. A hiss escaped Ira's lips and his legs tensed. She traced the vein along the underside of his cock, and the rest of her hand slid up with her thumb, providing just enough pressure. Ira groaned, his hands twisting further into the covers until his knuckles grew white. She reached the head of his cock and pressed her thumb down on it slightly.

"*Fuck*, Lena!" he gasped, arching into her touch.

She smirked and licked a line up him before taking the head into her mouth. His cum was warm and salty, and there was a deep musky scent here that she wanted to just sit in. She pressed the heel of her palm against her center as she moved her head down, taking more of Ira's cock into her mouth.

The noises Ira made encouraged her. She relaxed her throat and swallowed as much of him as she could. Her hand worked at the space she couldn't reach, twisting and tightening her grip just barely until she heard Ira hiss again.

"Ah, shit," he breathed. His legs moved on either side of her and his head fell back, revealing his throat. "*Shit.* Lena, *your mouth.*"

She smiled around his cock and hollowed out her cheeks as she sucked, twirling her tongue around his head. She pulled off and pressed a soft kiss against the side. "You can touch me if you want."

She grabbed one of his hands and placed it behind her temple. When she let go, his fingers threaded through her hair. His grip turned firm, and her mouth returned to his cock. Her other hand moved faster over her center. She was throbbing and wet and *so hot*. The heat in her head and cheeks and core was making her delirious and frantic. She closed her eyes and moaned when her palm hit *just* the right spot. Ira cursed at the vibrations that coursed down his cock and his hand pushed hers aside.

"Come here," he growled, his eyes wild and his hand gripping the base of his cock.. "*Come here.*"

She didn't move for a moment, blinking stupidly and trying to clear some of the fog from her mind, but when she *did* move to meet him, he grabbed her almost immediately, tossing her onto the sheets and easily holding himself over her.

"You'll be the death of me," Ira hissed as he tore off her bra. "And I'd let you. I'd give you the knife and let you drive it through my heart if it meant we'd always be together. That we'd always love each other."

He pulled off her underwear and he finally, *finally* touched her. His fingers dipped between her folds, one sinking into her with no warning. Lena cried out and her back arched off the bed. He quickly slipped in another finger while he sucked a bruise into the side of her neck.

She grabbed his skin, her nails digging in and leaving marks of her own as she yanked him closer. "Fuck me."

"*Now* you want to go fast?" he responded breathlessly. His thumb swiped over her clit, and she choked out a moan.

She pressed her palms against his chest and pushed him back. "I want to be on top."

Ira's lips parted and he nodded. They both groaned as she settled on him, his bare skin touching hers.

Lena soaked in the sight of him below her, his cheeks flushed and his hair wild and his lips wet. She wished she could commit this view to memory. That she could never forget it.

She positioned herself right over Ira's cock, and he watched as she lowered onto it, taking it all in one go. The barest hint of pain that swept through her made the pleasure all the more lovely. She threw her head back, a ragged moan escaping her throat. She felt so *full*. So *complete*. This wasn't what sex was like with just anyone. She was certain now. It was Ira that made her feel this way.

Lena lifted herself slightly and began to move her hips. Ira's cock dragged against her walls and his fingers tightened on her skin. She raised herself until only the tip was inside of her and then dropped back down, rolling her hips. She moved against him almost recklessly, wanting him deeper, wanting more of the heat to consume her.

Ira's jaw was clenched, and his eyes were closed as he rode out the waves of pleasure running through him. He let her control this moment between them, and she took advantage of it, knowing it was only a matter of time until Ira was pushed over the edge by her teasing. He never took control entirely—not unless she wanted him to.

She dragged her hands over his chest as she moved. Her fingers brushed his nipples and the tense muscles in his lower stomach. His hands tightened on her, and in response, she moved faster. She bit down on her lower lip and tossed her hair out of her face. She could feel his cock deep inside of her, stretching her to the brink and pressing against another entrance.

Ira sat up then and *pulled* her down. A zap of pure pleasure surged straight through her. The sound of their cries and her pounding heart filled her ears. He moved with her now, his hips meeting hers and his hands placing her *just right*.

She twined her arms around his neck, her face falling forward. She stayed there, riding out the throes of pleasure. Her legs burned, so she let Ira do most of the work now.

Lena was so lost in the hot, coiling pleasure building inside of her that she hadn't noticed one of Ira's hands slide toward her sex. His fingers lightly trailed over her clit and touched the rim of her already stretched entrance, his own cock. She shuddered and moaned with each bolt of ecstasy that shot through her.

"I think you could take more, don't you?" he whispered in her ear. She sobbed at the thought of it. "You love being stuffed full. You're practically sucking up my cock. I think you could take my fingers alongside it. How many do you think? One? Maybe two?"

"*Ira.*"

He seized her lips in a heated kiss as his movements grew more sporadic. His fingers quickened.

"You'd be so *good*," he hummed. "So good for me, right?"

She couldn't find her words. She nodded. Her cheek slid against his. Sweat coated both of them, and the air was thick and hot, making it difficult to breathe.

"You'll have to show me next time," Ira growled out before pushing his thumb down against her clit.

Lena's vision whitened completely, and her mouth opened in a wordless scream as her orgasm shot through her. Ira grunted in her ear and tensed. A different kind of warmth filled her, and then he became just as boneless as she was.

She huffed against Ira's neck, slumping against him entirely. Ira collected her in his arms and dropped back against the pillows. Lena was sprawled across his chest, rising and falling with the deep breaths he took.

For a few minutes, neither of them talked. They focused on catching their breath and regaining the feeling in their limbs.

Ira broke the silence. "I like the mattress."

A laugh tumbled from her throat, and she looked up at the ceiling. "I guess this means we have to buy the house."

"We were going to buy the first house anyway," he pointed out. He dropped his mouth to the top of her head. "We already started the closing process."

"Oh, really?" She tipped her head back, even though he was too close for her to see. "And what does this closing process entail?"

"Well, we say we're getting the house and hand over the money. We'll get the keys and it'll be ours as soon as I fuck you in every single room."

Warmth stirred in her belly again as her breath caught. Now she was beginning to see the bright side of having so many bedrooms.

Ira had stilled against her, but when she turned to meet him, he kicked back into motion.

The estate agent had to wait a bit longer, but at least they had good news for her.

CHAPTER
FORTY-ONE

Ira said *'I love you'* like someone else would say *'hello'* or *'goodbye.'* Sometimes it was warm and dripping with honey. Other times it was dark and made her feel what only Ira could make her feel. Sometimes he said it softly, like it was a marvel. Like he couldn't believe he was allowed to love her. And he always lit up when she said it back. At first, he almost seemed surprised, and then pleased and honored and adoring. Sometimes he would tell her he loved her again, pulling a second confession out of her as well. And a smile.

Each time he said he loved her, a part of her broke—in a good way. She hadn't thought of something breaking as a good thing before this, but she understood now. Broken things could be fixed or altered. It allowed the bad parts to be thrown away and for something better to take its place. It *changed* you. And those pieces of her that broke off were mended again, by Ira. It sounded ridiculous, but she *felt* it. Especially in moments like this.

They were lying in their secret spot, looking at the stars through the hole in the roof. Two nearly empty bottles of wine—Ira had insisted they would both need one—and a basket that had been filled with cheese, crackers, and meat was set off to the side. Their eyes were heavy and their stomachs were full. Their heads rested on the same pillow, bodies curled toward one another. One of Ira's arms was behind her head, the other pointed up at the sky.

"That one is the Claeo constellation. It kind of looks like a flower, doesn't it? You see the center circle and then the petals surrounding it, each one with a star at the tip."

She squinted her eyes. "I guess it looks like a flower. It could be a dozen other things, though."

Ira laughed softly. "You don't have an artist's eye."

"Well, that's why I have you here with me. Show me another."

His arm moved a smidge to the right. "That one next to it is called the Leiterra constellation. It's in the shape of the tear. The star at the very top is large and bright compared to the others in the sky. That's the Guiding Star. It points north. One should find it if they're lost."

She'd picked up on that star while in the Lowlands and used it as a sort of compass, but it was only because of Ira that she'd thought to look at the sky in the first place.

"You know so much."

His shoulder moved under her head. "I just read about it."

She smiled, wondering if she'd imagined the bashful note to his voice or if it had actually been there. She tapped her hand against his chest. "Tell me more."

He pointed to another cluster of stars. "The Traimor constellation. It's kind of shaped like a cornucopia. You know what the constellations are named after?"

She nodded. "The Numina."

Like everything else in The Lands.

"Yeah. Naming a group of stars the *Cornucopia Constellation* sounds a bit silly. But they still needed some sort of common identifier, so scholars used the Numina's known names. Claeo is the Numen of Joy. Flowers are one of her symbols. Leiterra is mourning. The tear is obvious. Traimor is the Numen of harvest, hence the cornucopia."

"How many constellations are there?"

He gave a half-hearted shrug again. "A few hundred."

"And they all have names?"

"Yes, but not every star in the sky belongs to a constellation. A few of them remain nameless."

She squirmed her head further into the pillow and closer to Ira so she could better see where he was pointing. "Show me one."

He grabbed her hand and pointed her finger instead, moving closer so their heads were touching. "You see that one? The small star with the blueish tint between Claeo and Leiterra? That one's unnamed."

When Ira dropped his hand, she let hers fall with it.

"That's sad," she commented. "Not having a name."

She chewed on her lower lip and stared at it, and then the other stars surrounding it. A nameless among named. It must be lonely.

"That'll be your star," she decided. "The Ira star."

He laughed, heartfelt and full. "What? Why?"

"It's blue."

There were other reasons too, but she kept those to herself. They were both outcasts amongst the idols, deemed unimportant by onlookers, and left with the bare minimum.

Krashing, the alcohol really is getting to me.

He laughed again and tucked his face into the pillow, rolling onto his side. She turned to look at him and practically melted when he lifted his head and gave her a loose smile. There was still a glaze over his eyes from the wine.

"The stars," she asked softly in the space between them, "what are they?"

He reached out and slowly traced her face with his pointer finger, starting at her brows and trailing down the bridge of her nose. "Some people think they're souls waiting to be reborn. The brighter the star, the longer the soul's been waiting."

She traced his face with her eyes while his finger left tingles in its wake as it brushed across her skin.

"That doesn't make sense. The stars are always up there. They never change." For the most part. She didn't actually take the time to count every star in the sky every night. "So according to your theory, those souls are never reincarnated."

"I never said I believed that," Ira hummed as his finger grazed the corner of her lips.

Lena shuddered slightly.

"Cold?" Ira murmured.

"I always am."

"I know." He folded her into his arms and said because he could, "I love you."

"I love you too," she murmured. It was an involuntary response at this point. They hadn't been together for long, not like this, but Ira seemed determined to make up for lost time.

A smile crept onto her face when a certain thought crossed her mind. She peered up at Ira from under her lashes. "If you love me, you should let me see those sketches—"

He pushed her head back down, gathering her against his chest and muffling her laughter. She'd asked him about his sketches many times since their first trip to the cabin, but he had yet to let her see them.

Ira only let her back up once her laughter subsided and she said she wouldn't mention it again. Here, of course. Now. Bringing it up later was fair play.

Her gaze returned to the stars. They really were beautiful. She could understand Ira's interest in them. She thought, in some ways, not knowing everything was comforting. The unknown leaves room for hope.

As the minutes passed, her muscles loosened. She dug her nose into his shoulder and allowed her mind to wonder. "What if we're a star?" she said suddenly. "What if stars are other realms with people. Maybe we're in someone's sky too."

Ira tucked his face into her neck and let out a weighted breath. "Maybe. I hope we're always in the same star."

She smiled softly. "Me too." She carded a hand through his soft waves. "Tell me, were you always this sappy?"

He snorted. "You already know the answer to that."

"You showed me a different side of you then. You're showing me another one now. You always pleasantly surprise me, Ira Vaenyr. I feel like I'm always learning something new about you."

"Skathor."

She furrowed her brows and looked at him. "What?"

"Ira Skathor," he repeated, watching her. "I know people don't have to change their family names after getting married, but I wanted to. Mine doesn't mean anything to me. It . . . only brings up bad memories. Your family took me in. I want to carry their name—if you'll have me."

Lena swallowed the lump in her throat and pulled his head back to her neck, blinking away the tears. "Yeah." She pressed her lips to his temple. "Yeah, I'll have you."

Ira became boneless in her arms. "Even with everything I've done? Everything I will do?"

She frowned. "Why are you talking like that?"

" . . . Sometimes I wonder if this is all just a dream. If the only good things you experience are fake and one day you'll wake up to the night terror that is reality. Before the Tower, I was with a group of travelers. Dirtyhands. We did what we had to in order to survive, but *only* what we had to. That was the rule. Though not many people followed it."

"Did you?"

"I'd like to think I did. But when you're out there, it gets to your head. Honestly, I think getting caught and dragged to the Tower was a good thing."

Years ago, Lena would've said she didn't believe in fate, but now, after everything that had happened, she did. She believed in it, but only to a certain extent. *Destiny*? No, she wasn't convinced that the Numina had planned every single step of every single person's future. Maybe a few to set up their entertainment, but not all of them. And if she was wrong, if the Numina had mapped out everything for everyone, should that frighten her? Anger her? Relieve her to know that everything she'd done wrong wasn't actually her fault? What was the point? What were they all doing here?

Her chest tightened and her hand found Ira's amongst the blankets.

"We've all done horrible things to survive. The people who haven't are lucky. You're too hard on yourself. I love *you* and whatever that may entail." She took a deep breath and let it out through her nose.

No more thinking about the what-ifs.

She gazed up at the stars again, eyes finding that small, blue one. "I mourn the part of you I never got to meet."

He shook his head against her collarbone. "What you're talking about . . . I don't think he was ever there, Lena."

She frowned again but didn't say anything.

Ira's breathing eventually evened out and he slipped under. It was rare that he fell asleep before she did—even rarer that he *stayed* asleep—so she took the time to observe him until she could no longer fight off the pull of sleep herself.

~

SOUL BONDS . . . *see pages 444, 452, 470-497, 525 . . .*

. . . Cornerstones require great effort to construct. It is unknown what they look like, but many historians suggest they are made of the strongest naturally occurring minerals, such as diamonds, moissanite, and corundum, among others. A weaker material wouldn't be able to hold the high magic quantities a Cornerstone contains. A fraction of this magic comes from the creator, but the remainder is likely contributed through a Soul Sacrifice.

A Soul Sacrifice is the permanent destruction of a soul, and it results in the strongest known magical output in the realms. The energy of a soul can power nearly anything, including Soul Bonds and Cornerstones. Scholars believe a Cornerstone and its effects can be made stronger if more souls are sacrificed during the initial creation process, though that is only a theory. This type of magic is generally looked down upon because of its aberrant nature and is not advised by followers of the Divine Touch.

. . . Unlike other phenomena, we know how a Soul Bond is created. For souls to be tethered, their current bodies need to be close to death. A soul is most vulnerable and can be linked with another when it's passing between lifetimes. The closer to death the bodies are, the higher chance the bond will hold. Because of this, most people who create a Soul Bond are unable to be stabilized and die shortly after, but they find their soulmate(s) again in each subsequent lifetime.

There have been about two dozen recorded cases of Soul Bonds. Each of them described some sort of internal pull toward the person who holds the soul they're bonded with—

"Kalena."

She shut the book.

Jhai stood in the doorway of Lena's room, alone. She appeared perplexed, maybe even a bit angry if the creasing of her brows and the slight frown on her face were anything to go by. "You lied to me."

Lena hadn't met Jhai with the book yesterday as expected. Jhai could've gone back down to the Lowlands like Lena had said, sans the book, but she'd stayed.

"I had to be sure."

"About what?"

"That you weren't going to sell me out to Alkus. That you weren't on someone else's side. I gave you the supplies you needed for your family and a way out. You could've told Alkus my plan before leaving. I would be in chains before I could retaliate, and you would be rewarded. But you didn't tell. And you came back."

Jhai's face twisted as if Lena's concerns were ridiculous. "What? You think I would've turned against you? And gone to Alkus? Why? Your Majesty, I serve you—"

"Stop," Lena commanded. She shoved the book off her lap and stood up. "I know there's something more about you. Did you think I wouldn't catch on to the questions you were asking? You were pushing it—pushing *me*—and risking your position. Why?"

She didn't really expect a clear answer, and it wouldn't change what she had planned. She would appreciate it though.

"I've always pushed things," Jhai said. "That's how I survived in the Lowlands. You know what it's like. I'm just a Cursed with hope, Kalena. And *you* are the first glimpse of it we've seen for a long time."

The reminder that so many people were looking up to her for guidance, salvation, or *anything at all* made her stomach twist. But all that came with her position, did it not?

She crossed her arms and dug her fingers into her sides. "Why ask me all those things? What were you trying to achieve?"

Jhai shrugged, her mouth opening and closing as she appeared to search for the right words. "I don't know. I guess . . . I wanted to see if you were on *our* side."

Lena knew what side Jhai was referring to. And her first thought was to ask why Jhai would even think that, but then she remembered what Kieryn had said to her in the hedge maze.

"It's funny how one's mindset can so quickly shift when offered an opportunity once thought to be out of reach."

She supposed, in a way, she did want to forget about her hardships and just . . . move on. But she couldn't. She *wouldn't*. Not when the root of a lot of her problems had been caused by the people she would be mingling amongst if she left her old life behind and embraced her new one, the one the Imprint on her chest gave her. In a way, she was doing that now—mingling with those people—but she hadn't forgotten or forgiven. She was still fighting against them, even if it was slow-moving. She hadn't given up.

Jhai stepped forward. She held herself like she had in the washroom after the field games. Confident. Strong. Determined. "If you are . . . then I'm on your side. I promise."

People lied all the time, herself included. But Jhai seemed to be smart enough to know the stakes, and now she knew Lena had been watching her. It should make her all the more wary.

"Okay," Lena said at last. "Then prove it."

CHAPTER

FORTY-TWO

Sorrel wasn't at the council meeting today. Von and Kieryn took up the seats, and the latter of the two stopped Lena after she called the meeting to a close.

"Sorrel is becoming impatient," Kieryn said as he stepped in front of her before she could leave the room.

She looked around and, upon noticing multiple pairs of eyes on her, shook her head. "Not in here."

Kieryn followed her out into the hall.

"I've had a lot on my plate lately, but—"

"Then maybe you need to rearrange your priorities," he said. "We're gone in less than two weeks. Sorrel's made it clear that if we don't receive an answer before then, this opportunity won't present itself again."

She took a deep breath and glanced over her shoulder. No one was following her other than Andra and Benji, but she needed to go farther. "I understand. Why didn't Sorrel come to the meeting today?"

Though, Lena was glad she hadn't.

"She knows you're avoiding her." Kieryn gave Lena a closed-lip smile. "And she heard we hit it off the other day."

Just how much did Sorrel know about her interactions with the others? Her and Kieryn's meeting wasn't exactly a secret—their conversation, on the other hand, was another matter—but her talks and trips with Aquila were.

Speaking of Aquila . . .

Lena glanced at Kieryn out of the corner of her eye. His hands were bare and unblemished, but Aquila had said enough in the Lowlands to make Lena believe that Kieryn was some sort of sorcerer. In the hedge maze, he hadn't denied that he was a magic user.

"Aquila said something the other day," she said quietly.

Kieryn raised a brow. "You two made up?"

They were far enough away from the council chamber now. She stopped, and Kieryn stopped with her.

"Don't say it like that."

He sighed and flicked his hand in a way that somehow conveyed a *'whatever.'*

She went for the nearest door. The room behind it was empty and contained a long table with a few cushioned chairs against the wall. She looked back at Kieryn and nodded her head toward the room. Andra and Benji frowned at her. At that moment, their resemblance to Cowen was uncanny.

She flashed them a sweet smile. "Two minutes?" she bargained as Kieryn slid past her.

Benji raised a brow and looked behind her.

Kieryn barked out a laugh. "If we were doing what you think we were doing, it would take longer than two minutes."

She threw an exasperated look over her shoulder, but Kieryn did the hand-flick thing again.

"I need to discuss something important with him. Two minutes," she assured her guards. And then, without waiting for them to agree, she shut the door and swiveled around to face Kieryn. Like Cowen, Benji and Andra were probably counting down the time, so she didn't waste any. "You're a sorcerer?"

Kieryn's expression shifted into something contemplative. Though, it wasn't long before he said, "Yes."

"Where are your tattoos?"

"I'm guessing you saw Aquila's," he drawled. "They don't have to be on your hands, you know?"

Well, she knew that *now*. Her stomach twisted at that bit of information. Tattoos on one's hands were difficult to hide without drawing attention, but tattoos somewhere else . . . That was a different matter. The practice wasn't common, but she still wondered how many sorcerers she'd come across with their tattoos hidden under their clothing.

"Where are yours?"

Kieryn smirked. "If you wanted me to undress, you could've just asked."

Lena gave him another exasperated eye roll.

"No fun," he sighed. He turned around and lifted his hair so she could see the thin, dark lines that stretched up the back of his neck and disappeared at his hairline. He dropped his hair and faced her. "Satisfied?"

"So, that's your move?" She gnawed on her bottom lip, the wheels of her mind turning and placing together the pieces. The knot in her stomach twisted further.

"Sorcerers? You were reading my mind in that hedge maze, weren't you? What else can you do?"

Kieryn's brows lowered. He wasn't glaring at her, but his gaze became colder. Flat. "You're asking a lot of questions. And from what I hear, you're in debt when it comes to those. You owe Sorrel answers first."

"Fine." She cleared her throat. "I'll talk to Sorrel after the Eve of the Revival."

She was tired of celebrations, but there was no chance of skipping this one. It was a holiday mostly celebrated by the prophets, but over time, the Blessed and Cursed had begun to celebrate it as well. The Eve of the Revival was when everything changed centuries ago. The war had ended, the divisions had been made, and relative peace had started. It was the origin of how things were now. When she was younger, she hadn't thought much of it. She'd just been excited for a celebration. But as she got older—saw more, learned more, experienced more—she'd begun to question it. And other things. Though, it didn't matter what her opinion on the holiday was; as queen, Lena's attendance was mandatory.

"And you'll give her an answer?" Kieryn pushed.

She counted the days between now and the holiday, and then she counted the number of days that gave the dirtyhands she'd paid to get that information. It would be tight, but she didn't have much of a choice.

"Yeah. I'll have an answer for her."

LENA PLANNED to spend the rest of her day reading *The Ties of Time* before she had to meet with Ira and go to a financial meeting.

Most matters concerning the defense and economics of the country were discussed and decided in the council chamber, and the instruction was then given out to the necessary sectors. This meeting, however, had to do with her and Ira's personal finances. They needed to make sure everything was in order before purchasing the house.

However, those plans were foiled when she ran into Tuck on the way to her room. He looked like he'd just gotten back, covered in a long, dark green cloak and layered in mud. His boots clicked on the floor, as dirty as the rest of him. His short hair was in disarray and his mouth lacked any sort of mischievous curl.

Lena teetered to a stop and couldn't seem to push herself into motion again. She stared at Tuck, her mouth slightly ajar as if she planned on saying something. She didn't know what, though. The last time she saw him, she'd been angry and drunk. Her face heated.

Tuck stopped soon after she did and stared at her, his eyes flat and immovable. Like a wall. That look on his face didn't belong on *his* face. It sent a shiver down her spine.

"You're back." Her voice came out weaker than she would've liked.

"I am," he droned.

Andra and Benji shifted behind her.

"You missed the council meeting earlier."

"I am well aware."

"Aren't you supposed to report what you found to the council?"

"Yes."

She cleared her throat, threaded her fingers together, and then unthreaded them. "Did you find anything?"

"Anything?" he echoed as his brow quirked. His fingers remained still at his sides, devoid of any shiny rings. "Well, of course I did."

She fought the urge to roll her eyes. "Did you find what they sent you out for?"

Tuck pursed his lips slightly and tilted his head. "And what do you think they sent me out for?"

"You know what?" Her hands clenched, but she shook them out. "Never mind. I just—forget about it."

She stepped forward, planning to quickly slip past Tuck, but before she could, he shifted toward her. Benji and Andra tensed, their eyes beginning to glow. She held her hand up, halting them.

Annoyance rippled across Tuck's face, curling his lip. "I'm sorry—no, wait, honestly, I'm not. For anything, actually."

His words cut deep, and she glared at him, but he kept going before she could say anything.

"But I am confused." He touched his forehead with his dirty fingers as if remembering something, and he laughed coldly. "You say you hate me. You say you don't want to talk to me or see my face again. You hit me and glare at me and insult me. Yet *you're* the one stopping me, talking to me, staring at me. *What do you want?*"

Lena shook her head, an unpleasant taste in her mouth and something equally as disappointing settling in her chest.

"Nothing," she said with finality. "I don't want anything from you."

The smallest smirk made its way onto Tuck's face, twisted and bitter. "Yeah, keep telling yourself that. Maybe one day it'll be true, but it's not today."

A flash of heat rolled through her, and she stepped forward. "You—"

"When you finally figure out what it is you want, let me know," Tuck interrupted coldly. "I'll be sure to keep my distance in the meantime. Now, if you'll excuse me, I'm tired. I want to get some sleep so I can enjoy this fucking holiday."

And with that, he walked off.

CHAPTER
FORTY-THREE

Vanik told him everything.

Atreus' head was pounding, but he held onto every word. He needed to know that the pain he'd endured was worth it.

They had agreed before being sent out that Atreus would distract as many prophets and enforcers as he could, giving Vanik, Weylin, and Mila the time they needed. As it turned out, Weylin was as devious and stealthy as he looked. He'd been scouting the Institute over the past few months, making sure he didn't go too far and spacing out his trips to prevent anyone from growing suspicious. He'd discovered a section of the Institute that wasn't accessible to the firstborns, and its description sounded similar to the black and white room. But not quite. *There was no furniture*, Weylin had said. No two doors along the back wall—only one that he'd been unable to open. Meaning there was another black and white room. Maybe even more than one.

Weylin thought he could break through the door if given enough time, and that was where Atreus came in. Prophet Silas already had it out for him, so getting a rise out of the prophet was easy.

Weylin had wanted Vanik and Harlow to accompany him, but Atreus had wanted someone there he could trust. Too many people couldn't be sneaking around, so in the end, Mila had gone with Weylin and Vanik.

Atreus had developed a mutual agreement of sorts with Vanik and his crew. Vanik had made it clear that he was looking for a way out, but Atreus didn't think they would leave Harlow behind. He'd been betting on that when he sent Mila with them.

The three of them had broken through the door. They hadn't taken anything, but Vanik told Atreus and Finn all about what they'd discovered.

Weylin had left, but he hadn't gone to sleep. He remained close by, watching to make sure no one approached the three of them and overheard anything. The sleeping hall wasn't exactly quiet at night. Many chose to relish in the peaceful solitude rather than take their chances with the maelstrom that sleep could be. Still, they couldn't be too careful. Not with this.

"We found letters between the prophet and someone we think is from above. The sunwalker said more children would be coming as long as the prophets had stones to show for their efforts," Vanik said softly, a trace of a snarl already on his lips. He looked to the side, and the shadows concealed part of his face. "One of the letters alluded to the possibility that some of the kids being sent to the Institutes aren't even firstborns."

A soft noise escaped Finn's mouth as if he had been punched in the gut.

Atreus closed his eyes and set his jaw. The ribbons of pain woven through his muscles tightened when he dug his fingers into the sheets, but he allowed the dull pain to remain for a few seconds. It subdued his rage.

He wasn't surprised by this. Not really. But learning it was the truth, or at least very likely, squashed that tiny bit of hope he held deep within himself, the tiny bit of hope that wanted to believe things hadn't gotten *that* bad yet. Who was he kidding? In the Institute, hope was killed just as quickly as firstborns were.

"We also found a stone disc," Vanik said, his voice clipped and lined with vexation. "Mila wanted us to tell you about it. She made us swear." He turned back then so Atreus saw the roll of his eyes.

Mila was back in the girl's sleeping hall with Harlow. The enforcers didn't allow them to visit one another's sleeping halls, no matter the time of day.

"She thought it was important." Vanik's tone made it clear that he disagreed. "It's big. Maybe two feet in diameter. Blinding white. Displayed in a thick glass casing. Small circular wells are all along one side of it. Mila thought it was the perfect size for a stone to fit in."

The display case definitely implied some importance, and they already knew the stones were significant. Though, they didn't necessarily know the full extent of *how* they were important. This was only a theory, but it was another piece to this puzzle that resulted in more questions than answers.

"The stones get us out of those shitty realms," Vanik said. "Past that, who the fuck cares?"

"They can do more than that," Atreus countered. "The prophets are collecting them for something important. They care about a singular stone enough to bend to the will of whoever holds it."

Vanik couldn't argue with that, so he decided to move on. His sour expression faded quickly and a grin took its place. "We found a way out."

Atreus' heart seized, and Finn let out a heavy breath.

"The door was huge, but we didn't see any way to open it. The symbol of the Blessed was on it. And there was a tiny glass hole at the top that let in light. Sunlight, we think."

"*Think?*" Finn echoed. "Do you *think* it's a way out or do you *know*?"

Vanik glared at him. "It's the strongest lead we have. If you want to go in search of another way out, be my guest. But this is a start."

"So, you want to go back and scout the area again? How many times?" The tentative hope that had found its way onto Finn's face earlier was slipping away. He glanced at Atreus. "How many times are you going to make Atreus go through this?"

"Did you think one trip was all it would take? If it was that easy, we wouldn't all still be here," Vanik snapped as he pushed away from the metal bed frame. "We almost got caught half a dozen times. And *if* we're caught, we'll be *lucky* if all we get is a beating, solitary, and restoration. Atreus isn't the only one putting his ass on the line." He crossed his arms, staring down at Atreus in bed. "He'll just have to be smarter about his methods of distraction."

∼

ATREUS WAS STUCK in bed for three days. Miss Anya visited to give him medicine and check the wounds on his back. She would ensure the stitches were holding before applying salve to the lacerations and then redressing them. He bit into the lumpy pillow while she worked, his hands squeezing the bars of his bed frame and his back arching despite her telling him to stay still.

The swelling had gone down, and he could finally see out of both eyes. He could chew better too. The enforcers had been bringing him some type of soup or porridge for every meal, but he couldn't stomach much at first.

Finn came back throughout the days to check on Atreus when he could. They'd switched beds for the time being so Atreus didn't have to climb.

His body felt like one giant lump of aching flesh. Prophet Silas *had* bruised one of his ribs. Miss Anya couldn't do much about that since the injury was internal. And since a bruised rib would severely limit his capacity to work or fight, she had Prophet Silas unseal his Imprint for a short amount of time to help speed up the healing process.

The medicine Miss Anya had given Atreus left him fading in and out of sleep, and the haze that had coated his mind since the beating in the black and white room only made things worse. Sometimes he didn't know what was real and what wasn't, so when he saw Prophet Silas staring down at him with unfeeling eyes, he thought it was a night terror, one in which the prophet had returned to finish him off. It would be easy. Atreus was bruised and delirious.

But the prophet merely knelt down, unraveled Atreus' seal, and then left.

And despite the pathetic state he was in, two enforcers still stood guard next to him while his Imprint was unsealed to make sure he didn't summon his Slayer.

By the end of the third day, he could stand and walk, albeit very slowly. Most of his bruises had faded to a nasty green and yellow. On the fourth day, he was back on the normal schedule. Everything ached and pulled with each movement, but it was better than lying in bed all day, bored out of his fucking mind.

He wasn't surprised when he was put on garden duty again.

As soon as he stepped into the room, Judah raced up to him. He barreled into Atreus, ripping a choked gasp from the older firstborn's mouth as his side twinged. Black spots danced across his vision as a weighted heat fell upon him. He leaned over slightly, trying to regain his breath.

Judah seemed unaware of Atreus' grapple with pain. Or perhaps he was too upset to notice. He was sobbing and had his hand tangled tightly in Atreus' shirt. "They wouldn't let me see you!"

Right. Finn had told him to stay away, and Weylin had ensured he had.

"They wouldn't let me see you! I was so scared! I didn't know if you were okay!" Judah nuzzled his face into Atreus' bruised abdomen.

Atreus let out another grunt of pain, carefully peeling the kid off him. "I'm okay," he said, knowing he looked anything but. "I'm healing now, so don't . . . plow into me, okay?"

Judah nodded, teary-eyed.

He hardly left Atreus' side the entire time they worked. And then later too when they walked to the dining hall and seminar.

The prophets lectured about the wickedness of Edynir Akonah and the *wretched sorcery* he'd committed. Atreus felt Prophet Silas' eyes on him. Today's topic wasn't a coincidence.

"Edynir Akonah was a scholar," one of the prophets said. "He lived at an academy with others who pursued various subjects. It was there that the gateways between realms were discovered. The realms used to be open, free to travel between. It was a rich and prosperous time. Realms exchanged resources and knowledge, but that was soon ruined by Edynir Akonah. He grew obsessed with the realms and the possibilities they provided in his search for power. He bargained with the leaders of the other realms, asking them to join his cause. But they all turned him away, and he became resentful toward them.

"Soon, his own abilities weren't enough to satisfy his dark desires, so he resorted to sorcery, the drawing of magic from souls—a truly dark force. With it, he accomplished unnatural feats. Stories of his conquests spread far and wide, and he built himself an army. He conquered nearly all the lands of his realm. He challenged the Numina. This was when Kerrick Ludoh rose up against him. Edynir Akonah was afraid of Kerrick Ludoh's power. He shattered the realms as an act of revenge, but also as a way to ensure Kerrick Ludoh couldn't gain more allies. To this day, the realms are fractured. As are the things inside of them.

"After the defeat of Edynir Akonah, Kerrick Ludoh made it his mission to heal the realms, but it's a difficult task. Along with severing the pathways between realms, Edynir Akonah also burned all records of any research about them. He burned the academy down and killed all scholars who knew anything. He not only shook our realm. He shook all of them. He set us back centuries. All because of his desire for power."

Later that night, when they were lying in bed and everyone else was asleep, Finn said, "I think they're lying."

Atreus knew what Finn was talking about, but he didn't respond right away. He thought the prophets were lying too. Maybe about everything.

"About what?" he eventually asked. His words came out mumbled because his face was half buried in his pillow. He had to lie on his stomach until his back was fully healed.

"Edynir Akonah."

" . . . Why do you think that?"

A rattling noise came from overhead. Finn climbed down the ladder and sat next to Atreus.

"Because it doesn't make sense."

"Things don't have to make sense, Finn," Atreus grumbled. "No matter how badly you want them to."

"I've been taking notes on everything they tell us about Edynir Akonah," Finn said. He knelt on the ground and fished his journal out from underneath the bottom bed. He flipped through its pages, returning to Atreus' side. "He grew up in a small village and was loved by all, but he was eventually driven away because some grew fearful of his power."

"Finn, where is this—?"

"Just a second. I've written down notes after every seminar about him. So, according to the timeline the prophets gave us, he left the village and began studying at the academy. He was there for a few years before being expelled. Today they told us that he started making a name for himself and building his army. They said he resorted to sorcery, but before . . . " Finn flipped through the pages and squinted at the paper, bringing it close to his face so he could attempt to read his writing in the shadows. " . . . before they mentioned he used sorcery at the academy."

"So?"

"So it's different. When did he learn it? When did he *use* it? The details matter. The prophets have lectured us about sorcery before. How it's an evil, unnatural ability that takes *months* at the very least to understand. For Edynir Akonah to use it on a wide scale, he would've had to practice for *years*, don't you think? There's a gap somewhere in their story. Something they're not telling us. Their version just doesn't make sense. He had everything. Why would he risk it all?"

Atreus sighed and closed his eyes. "Because he didn't have *everything*. No one can ever have that. You're too optimistic, Finn."

He briefly thought about what Prophet Silas had told him the other day. About him never having anything.

He swallowed thickly and added, "Are you sure you aren't just biased? Maybe you've convinced yourself the prophets' story isn't the truth because you don't want to believe it is."

Atreus was well aware it sounded like he was defending the prophets, but he wasn't, or at least, that wasn't what he was trying to do. He knew they were liars. He was just trying to protect Finn and shut down these wild ideas of his before they got him into trouble.

"Maybe that's true, but it just doesn't add up." Finn paused for a while, and Atreus thought he was going to drop it and climb back into bed. Instead, Finn added, "Judah and I have been exchanging stories. It's something that calms him down. He shared with me the stories he was told at the compound before the Institute."

Atreus frowned. He'd told Judah not to repeat those. "They're just stories. Tales told before bed."

"Maybe that's not all they are. Judah knew about Edynir Akonah before coming here. He remembers a *before*, Atreus. And he thought Edynir Akonah was the *hero*. He said the stories he heard from this woman called Miss Seila are different from the stories told here. He said Edynir Akonah was *betrayed* and *framed* and—"

Atreus cut him off before he could get too out of hand. "He's eight, Finn."

"So what? He's smart. You know that. Why are there different versions of the story?"

Atreus knew that history was written by the victors. The ones in power dictated what others did, saw, and heard. They wanted to control what others thought too, but that one was trickier. In the Institute, they had lessons and a library, but all the information was biased, leaning in favor of the prophets' viewpoints. Atreus had never bought into their ideologies and their stories, but getting into this conversation was the last thing he wanted to do right now.

"I'm tired, Finn," he said at last.

"Oh," Finn said. "Right, of course. Sorry . . . I just—"

"I know."

Atreus kept his eyes closed, but he felt the bed move as Finn stood. He heard him climb into bed.

Atreus barely got any sleep that night, and it showed the following day, but no one said anything. He needed to get better sleep tonight. They were due for another Outing soon.

~

HE WAS on his way back to his bed the next day when Mila stepped up next to him. She had something in her hand. She kept it low, swaying it to get his attention.

His brows furrowed when he spotted it. "What's that?"

Mila gave him a flat look. "A book."

"I know what a book is," he said, exasperated. "But why do you have it? I thought we weren't allowed to take them out of the lecture hall or the library."

Mila leaned in close. "We're not," she whispered in his ear. "But I'm not really supposed to have this at all."

Atreus stared at her with wide eyes. He glanced around to make sure no one was looking. "You stole it?"

She shrugged.

"From where? The library?" It hit him a moment later and his eyes widened even further. He lowered his voice. "You stole it from that room you went to with Weylin and Vanik?"

Her smile was small, sweet, and not at all worrying.

"Why would you do that?" he hissed, looking over her shoulder once again. "If the prophets find out—"

"They won't," she said confidently. "I found it stuffed under all these papers in the closet. Everything was covered in dust. I guarantee no one's touched anything in there in years. No one will even notice it's gone."

"Let's hope so," Atreus grumbled.

Mila slid the book into his hand. "I've already sifted through it. The book is about the stones. You have a connection to them, so I figured you should read it."

He stared down at the book, but he didn't dare open it here. "I'm not really a reader."

It was a piss-poor excuse. And the look Mila gave him said she wasn't buying it. Atreus would be lying if he said he wasn't intrigued.

Resigned, he stuffed the book under his uniform. "You better hope no one catches me with this."

"*You* better hope you hide it well enough."

The two split as they entered their respective sleeping halls. Atreus was still sleeping on the bottom bed. He'd told Finn they could switch back now that he was somewhat healed and back on his feet, but Finn wouldn't hear it. He made an effort to beat Atreus back to the sleeping hall every night so he could take the top bed. And sure enough, Atreus saw a lump under the thin cover.

He slowly bent down, a hiss escaping through his clenched teeth. He slid the book between the metal slats of the bed frame and the bottom of the mattress, right next to Finn's journal and his own that he never bothered touching unless he was required to bring it to seminar.

When he pushed himself back to his feet and turned around, Vanik stood at the foot of the bed, his arms crossed. Atreus nearly jumped, but his sore muscles kept him from moving much. He'd barely done any physical labor today, yet he felt incredibly stiff. And sleep would only make it worse.

"What do you want?"

"To talk," Vanik said, his words clipped. He tilted his head to the side and walked off without saying another word.

Atreus' and Finn's beds were already in the corner of the room, a good distance away from the next set of beds, which was nice for privacy reasons, but it apparently wasn't good enough for Vanik.

Atreus rolled his eyes before following.

"Look, I don't fucking like it, but people look up to you here. They have ever since you started pulling your wonder boy shit and sniffing out the stones. And even though we're working together, I still don't fucking like you," Vanik said as soon as Atreus reached him.

"You could've insulted me over there."

"I don't like you," Vanik repeated. He continued as if Atreus hadn't said anything at all. "You try to do too much. Even when you're bruised and bloody and halfway to death. I saw the look in your eyes when I mentioned the disc and the stones." He stepped forward and shoved his finger into Atreus' chest. "Don't get any crazy ideas in that head of yours. Forget about the disc. We want out. That's all we've ever wanted."

Atreus pushed Vanik's arm away. "And I told you earlier that the stones are valuable. They could be our way out!"

"Or not," Vanik retorted. "We can leave without them. We already found an exit."

"So you think."

Vanik's eyes flashed. "You need to keep your eyes on the bigger picture. You get the stones to get us out of those realms so we don't die and so we can come back *here* and figure out a way to get out. That's it. Forget about the stones past that."

But he couldn't. There was something more to them. They had to have another purpose.

"The prophets will use—"

"The prophets can do whatever they want with those stupid stones after I get out. I don't give a fuck."

Atreus glared at him, his jaw set. He wanted out too. Almost more than anything. He'd spent hours wondering what this realm looked like. He wanted to see it. He wanted to prove to Prophet Silas that he wasn't stuck here under his boot. But . . .

There hadn't been a '*but*' before.

Things had changed over the past few weeks. He'd discovered pieces of a larger puzzle he hadn't even been aware of. He felt like he was finally getting somewhere after being here for *years*. He was closer to understanding the prophets' *true* agenda and learning how to tear it apart. He wanted to escape this place and the prophets' grasp, but he also wanted to destroy it. And them. They'd hurt more people than just him and they would continue to do so if Atreus and the others just *left*. It would be a larger blow if Atreus crippled them.

Revenge was the word he was looking for.

And by giving the prophets a taste of their own medicine, he could save countless other firstborns from being sent out to realm after realm.

He was close. And Mila had given him that book. They could do it all—find out the secret behind the stones, destroy the prophets, and escape.

Vanik took a step closer, dropping his chin and speaking low. "Your problem is that you always try to play the hero. It's going to get you killed one day and I won't be around to get dragged down with you," he sneered. "Drop the hero act or we're done. I mean it."

CHAPTER
FORTY-FOUR

The Eve of the Revival was more . . . orderly than the other celebrations Lena had experienced in the Highlands. The holiday was typically celebrated privately within one's home. If one wanted to take part in a more community-wide celebration, they went to the local temple. There was nothing out in the streets or at the taverns. Because of the nature of this holiday, the gathering at the palace was relatively small.

She'd thought she would prefer the smaller crowd, but it turned out to be worse than the alternative. There were no random guests to act as buffers. Nowhere to run off to or hide since the event was being held in a single room. She sat at a table with the royal families, those on the council and *their* families, the prophets, and their guests from Ouprua.

Mikhail was just finishing up his prayer at the head of the table as the waiters placed the last of the dishes along the wooden stretch.

" . . . may we pray that Amaya's soul finds peace among the Numina, and may her next life be as prosperous as this one. May she rest. May we rest."

"May we rest," they all murmured.

Lena squeezed her hands in her lap. For Amaya's sake, Lena hoped her next life was nothing like this one.

She raised her gaze to look down the table at Amaya Feydohr's empty seat. The royal had died the other day after ingesting a lethal amount of Cloud, one of the popular drugs circulating through the Highlands. That was the official ruling, anyway. There had been no signs of struggle. Only a dark, swelling bruise on her head from where she'd hit it against the table. At least that was what the guards and the physicians had assumed. It was too easy to kill some of these people.

As soon as the servers stepped away, the Blessed reached for the food and filled their plates. The room was crowded with just over a hundred Blessed all sitting at one large table. And she had the worst company around her, bar Ira, who sat to her left. Aquila sat on her other side, rigid with discomfort. After Aquila was Sorrel. Mikhail was at the end of the table, Sorrel to his left and Alkus to his right. Next to Alkus was Von and then Kieryn who sat across from her. Tuck was next to him; his gaze would periodically move over to Ira, but Ira pointedly ignored it. Ophir was to Tuck's right and then Avalon. Celine sat across the table from them, directly to Ira's left. Trynla was next to her. They were all silent as they collected food and started eating. Like one big happy family.

Lena bit into the roast and glanced around, chewing slowly.

Mikhail looked over the rest of them as well with a pleasantly neutral expression. Alkus stared stone-faced at the table as he picked at his food. Von continued to load his plate up as if he wasn't allowed to go back for seconds; he seemed unbothered by the strained atmosphere. Maybe she was just imagining it.

Kieryn caught her gaze and raised a glass to her, his lips stretching into a closed-lipped smile that immediately fell away afterward.

Tuck leaned forward with his elbows on the table. He was fiddling with his rings, twisting them around his fingers and staring at them intently. Ophir frowned at Tuck's poor posture, but before he could say anything, Avalon touched his arm and leaned over to whisper something in his ear.

Lena couldn't see Trynla, but she could hear her talking to Celine.

Ira nibbled on his food, same as her.

Aquila was still stiff, and her plate was still bare, but her knife was in her hand. Lena was glad she had Aquila as a buffer between her and Sorrel. Still, she wished the distance was longer.

"What's everyone's resolution for the new year?" Mikhail asked in an attempt to break the silence.

Down the table, everyone else was already talking amongst each other.

To kill my enemies, was the first unfiltered thought that came to the forefront of her mind. Thankfully, she had her walls up. She grabbed her glass, the one filled with wine, and took a long sip.

Everyone else seemed reluctant to share their resolution, so they stayed silent, eyes carefully scoping out their company.

Kieryn cleared his throat and leaned forward. "We don't really . . . celebrate this holiday," he said with a smooth, almost taunting smile, "but in the spirit of camaraderie, I'll set a resolution."

He picked up his glass of wine and drank it. *All.*

Lena's eyebrows continued to climb as he swallowed more and more wine. He set down his glass with an exaggerated *"Ahh."*

Sorrel let out a heavy sigh.

"I am going to start drinking less wine," Kieryn declared.

Mikhail's brows were also raised, and his mouth was opening and closing like he was trying to find something to say. "Oh. That's . . . a start."

Tuck was relaxed in his chair now and trying to hide the smirk on his face. "I think I'll spend more time away from here," he said, raising his chin. He was looking at Mikhail, not his parents. "For the good of The Lands. I can scout out any issues that may arise . . . and I have a feeling there will be quite a few of them."

His gaze slid to Lena then, quickly.

She glowered at him and shook her head minutely. *Don't.*

Tuck settled back in his chair, and Lena noticed Kieryn's arm reaching out toward him under the table. Her brows furrowed.

Ira's thigh brushed against hers. He didn't meet her gaze when she turned toward him, but he didn't move his leg back either.

" . . . Any good news anyone would like to share?" Mikhail asked, desperately trying to change the subject to something he deemed more appropriate for tonight's occasion.

A wave of silence ensued once again before someone decided to speak up. Alkus this time.

"The prisoner still isn't talking, but the killings have stopped."

"For now," Von piped up in between bites of food.

Everyone stared at him, but he paid them no mind as he continued to eat.

"Let's not talk about death tonight," Mikhail said. "Let's keep the spirits high."

'Keep?' Tuck mouthed to no one in particular.

Kieryn leaned forward again, his face one of feigned contemplation. "Didn't a lot of people die during this night centuries ago? What exactly is this holiday's history again? I know you've mentioned it before. Forgive me. I am quite forgetful."

"And he doesn't listen well," Sorrel said, her eyes burning into Kieryn, who merely shrugged and turned back toward the Grand Prophet.

"That's alright," Mikhail said, but he looked a bit uneasy. "The Eve of Revival marks the end of the War of Krashing. It marks the beginning of peace and our new age of Blessed and Cursed, and the sacrifices we all have to make."

Kieryn nodded. "Right. Sacrifices," he drawled out. "Thank you."

Mikhail's pleasant smile faltered, and his responding nod was stiff. "Of course."

Lena forced her fingers to release her fork. They were tightly clenched around the handle, her knuckles white. The silverware hit the tablecloth with a muted *thump.*

The beginning of peace? She mentally scoffed. *The sacrifices we all have to make?* She didn't want to think about this any longer, so she changed the topic back to something she *did* want to talk about.

"I'm visiting the prisoner soon," she announced.

Ira's leg tensed. Eyes turned toward her, but the only pair she cared about were Alkus'.

"As soon as I'm on the list," she added.

"List? What list?" Mikhail questioned.

Lena stared at Alkus expectantly.

He held her gaze as he said, "It's a precaution."

"Against me?"

Ira's leg was gone. A second later, his hand fell on her thigh, squeezing it slightly, but she ignored him.

"He kidnapped you," Alkus argued, but his voice remained even. There was too big of an audience.

Alkus didn't care for her safety. He knew that she knew that. And half of the people here probably knew that as well.

"Good thing he's behind bars then. He shouldn't be able to hurt me or anyone else as long as your people are doing their jobs, right?"

Ira's grip on her thigh tightened. She hadn't yet pulled her eyes away from Alkus, so she couldn't see how everyone else was looking at her, but she could feel the shift in the air.

The palace guards and the enforcers were supposed to report to and follow orders from her, but they weren't. Not all of them. Like every other group or class, in the Highlands at least, half of them were loyal to Alkus. And she had just inferred as much aloud.

Alkus' stare was carefully concealed, but not perfectly. One could make out the animosity if they looked hard enough. He was probably wishing her attacker wasn't behind bars. Or that her attacker had finished the job.

"Right," he said slowly. "If the guards do their job, you should be safe."

He was probably wishing they *wouldn't*.

"Then I don't see what the issue is."

"Your Majesty," Mikhail cut in. "I don't think you visiting the prisoner is appropriate. Perhaps—"

"You're young," Alkus said firmly. "And you didn't grow up here. There are lots of things you don't understand. We're trying to help you."

"Help—?" Lena bit her tongue before she could say something she'd regret. "There are many ways you can help me, but this is not one of them."

Mikhail tried to draw them all in again. "Perhaps we ought to change the conversation."

He was ignored.

"The man who attacked you cannot be reasoned with," Celine said sensibly in her soft, sweet voice. "He hasn't cooperated with the guards. He's a criminal—"

"So is her husband," Tuck murmured darkly into his cup.

Lena stiffened, and Ira's hand on her thigh slackened, but he didn't pull away. His touch was the only thing keeping the cold at bay.

"*What did you*—?" She snapped her mouth shut when Ira gave her another warning squeeze. She caught the reproachful look he gave her and threw her own look right back, hoping it conveyed what she was thinking. *I'm not going to let him insult you like that.*

Ira didn't budge.

"Tuck," Ophir scolded.

At the exact same time, Tuck pushed his chair back and stood. "Please excuse me," he said curtly. "I need a breath of fresh air."

Ophir scowled and looked at Avalon and Celine. The latter immediately rose to her feet.

"I'll talk to him," Celine said before excusing herself and following Tuck out the door.

Avalon, on the other hand, didn't look surprised or disappointed by Tuck's outburst. She appeared resigned. Her eyes met Lena's dead on. Then she sighed and picked up her glass of wine.

"Well, uh . . . how about dessert?" Mikhail tried again.

None of them had finished their meals, but they didn't argue with the Grand Prophet. He waved his hand and servers soon emerged with the dessert.

Lena moved her leg away from Ira's touch. His gaze burned into the side of her head, but she didn't turn to meet it. She stayed still in her chair, her hands fisted in her lap.

"Oh no," Trynla whined. "I can't have that. The baby doesn't like peaches, and they're already acting up tonight."

The *clink* on glasses sounded in front of Lena and she looked up to see Kieryn reaching for Tuck's half-empty cup of wine. He froze upon seeing everyone's eyes fall upon him and then shrugged.

"Can't let it go to waste. I've always been a bit shit at keeping resolutions." He looked at Lena then, smiling. "You might want to keep that in mind when you decide which one of us you want to marry."

She clenched her jaw and stood. "Excuse me," she said curtly before following in Tuck's footsteps and walking out the door.

∼

LENA RAN AS SOON as she set foot outside of that room. She knew Andra and Benji would be right behind her, maybe Ira too, and she didn't want to give any of them a chance to catch up with her.

She didn't slow until she was far away from everyone else and was sure no one had followed her. She sucked in a gulp of air and ran her hands over her face, likely messing up her makeup. But she didn't care. She wasn't going back.

A chilly breeze flowed past her, lifting strands of hair from her face and causing bumps to rise across her skin. She rubbed her hands over her arms in an attempt to warm herself up and spotted the deep blue curtains fluttering at the end of the hall, the night sky visible just beyond them.

She went over to shut the windows but ended up leaning her elbows on the sill instead, staring up at the stars. She tried to identify the constellations and name them, but it was difficult to do from another perspective. There must've been hundreds of thousands of stars in the sky. Maybe there were that many other realms. If that was true, The Lands was so small—*they* were so small. And their problems were too. Not to them, of course. Not to her. No matter what else was out there, what happened *here* was their reality.

She sighed and stood straight. Playing the *what-if* game was dangerous. She was just about to close the windows when a familiar voice stopped her short.

"... were you doing back there?"

"Eating. Making small talk."

Lena leaned out the window, just enough so she could see beyond it. Her gaze moved in the direction the voices were coming from until she spotted them. Tuck and Celine. They were on a balcony that must've been a few halls over. The palace curved here. Her position was the more inward one, so she could see the other two slightly in front of her quite well. She kept herself close to the edge in the hope that they wouldn't see her.

Celine frowned. She ducked her head in an attempt to catch Tuck's gaze, but he was pointedly looking away from her. "Inappropriate small talk."

He scoffed and turned away.

"Hey, hey, hey." Celine reached out to try and stop him. "Tuck, come on. Talk to me."

He didn't. He stood with his back to her, his shoulders tight as he looked out over the lawn.

"You've been upset ever since you returned." Celine followed him and rested a hand on his back. "Why is that?"

"I'm irritated," he corrected. "There's been a lot going on. A lot on my shoulders. I slipped up." There was a pause, and then, "I'm sorry."

Celine sighed and patted his back. She walked around him, facing him once more. "You were reckless." She grabbed his hands. "You cannot be reckless."

Tuck remained silent, his head dipped. Lena couldn't tell if he was looking at Celine or his feet. She could only see the side of his face.

"You're right. There has been a lot going on, and there will continue to be a lot going on. These are harrowing times." One of Celine's hands grabbed his upper arm. "But you *cannot* crumble under it and become reckless. When you're reckless, bad things happen. Don't you remember?"

He shuffled his feet and stayed silent. Lena thought she saw him jerk, as if he wanted to flee from Celine.

"Tuck," his mother admonished. In her eyes and her voice was a warning that rose the hair on Lena's skin. "Do you remember?"

"... I remember," Tuck said hoarsely.

Celine's eyes softened and she almost looked at Tuck pityingly. She let go of his other hand and cupped one of his cheeks. "I'm sorry, my sweet boy. But this realm is cruel. You must be too if you want to survive in it."

Lena shut the window then, as quietly as possible, and turned. Her balance was unsteady, and the hall curved and blackened in her eyes. She squeezed them shut and placed a hand on the wall to steady herself.

When she opened them again, Benji and Andra stood at the end of the hall, Ira right behind them. Her guards stayed back as Ira approached. He didn't say anything when he stopped in front of her.

"Why didn't you let me defend you back there?" she exclaimed almost immediately.

"I didn't want the dinner to become more tense than it already was, especially not on my behalf. I don't care what they say," Ira said simply and softly as he leaned against the wall.

She crossed her arms. The frustration that had sparked inside of her slowly fizzled out, leaving her feeling vulnerable, empty, and *stupid*. "I don't care for their opinion, but I'm not going to let them say those things about you. I know you would do the same if they said something about me."

Ira sighed and pushed away from the wall. "I *am* a criminal, Lena. I've done bad things. I don't deserve your defe—"

"We have *all* done bad things. I hate how they throw it in your face. And *Tuck* was the one to say it. Out of everyone!" His hands were as bloody as everyone else's. "Before tonight . . . I was *happy*. I've been happy for the past few weeks. I've been avoiding them . . . but it doesn't last forever. I just . . . I can't *live* with those people. I—"

"You won't have to," Ira promised. He gave her a knowing look. They had told each other a lot these past two weeks. He knew what she was doing, and she knew what he was doing. "Playing the long game will be worth it."

"I hope you're right."

His mouth twitched into a smile. "When have I ever been wrong?"

She returned his soft smile, albeit hesitantly.

Ira extended a hand. "Want to get out of here?"

Her shoulders dropped, and she let all her worries slide away. She placed her hand into his. "I thought you'd never ask."

CHAPTER
FORTY-FIVE

Ira took Lena to his study. She let the door fall shut behind her and slowly scanned the room as Ira walked toward his desk.

"... Are we going to read?" she asked as she edged farther into the room.

He snorted and sifted through his desk drawers. "You can do whatever you'd like."

"When you asked me if I wanted to get out of there, I pictured a slightly different destination," she said as she strolled around the room, her gaze scouring the shelves.

Ira had a rather impressive collection. He'd made an effort to build and personalize his shelves after getting the space years ago when he earned his position on the council.

"But I'm not picky. Though, I do suppose I sound it. Sorry. Anything away from the others is perfect. Truly. Sometimes I wonder if I'm getting too comfortable up here. It's nice, but I don't *need* it—this lifestyle. But I do need you, I think."

"You think?" Ira asked from behind her.

She smiled and pulled out a book from under an empty bottle. It was a history book. A large one at that, the pages yellow and the binding falling apart.

"I *know*," she amended. "You and baths—those are the two things I've grown quite fond of here."

Ira snorted. The noise was closer. "Don't tell Cowen."

Her grin widened as she slid the book back. "He would understand the bath part."

"Mhm, I don't know. I feel like he's accepted me ever since he pulled me aside for the talk."

She spun around, her eyes wide. "What?"

Ira was right behind her and smiling, though it was tense. Like he was trying to brush something off but wasn't quite able to. "He talked to me before we got married and then again the other week after we . . . talked about our relationship."

Before the wedding . . . That was before Cowen and Lena were on good terms again. Before she stopped ignoring him.

"What'd he talk to you about?"

Ira laughed. "I'm sure you can guess."

Before she could ask another question and force him to recall those conversations, he raised his hand between them. Held between his thumb and pointer finger was a ring.

She stared at it for a moment, then met his gaze. "What's this?"

He smiled softly again. He did that a lot around her, and she cherished every single one. "A ring. For you. I know not many people give or exchange them anymore with marriage, but I wanted to—if you'll wear it. I don't need a material reminder, but . . . I've been thinking about one for a while, so . . . "

Lena plucked the ring from his fingers and held it slightly above her face. Something was engraved on the inside. She brought it closer to her eyes and rotated it, reading the words.

May we find each other in the stars.

Her heart melted and spread through her veins, making her soft and warm. The large, goofy smile that extended across her face reflected that. "How'd you do this so quickly?"

Ira shrugged, a slight grin still on his face. "I know some people."

"You?" she said, aghast. "The king consort? Know some people?"

He rolled with it. "Only some. You're lucky one of them happened to be a jeweler."

Lena admired the ring again. It was simple—gold with a small purple gem in the band. Her birthstone.

"I am, aren't I?" she murmured to herself. And then, to him, she said, "Of course I'll wear it. Put it on?"

She didn't miss how he perked up slightly at her request. He took the ring from her, slipping it onto the same finger that wore the Ring of Rulers. It fit perfectly.

"Thank you," she whispered as she looked up at him from under her lashes. "I love it."

He was still holding her hand, and he used his grip to pull her closer, even though they were already nearly toe to toe.

Their kisses started off slow and gentle, like a caress, like the soft way Ira said *I love you* at night and in the morning. Even the tingles that came from his touch took their time spreading through her. She felt safe and loved and at home.

Home.

She hadn't thought she would ever have that again.

Ira moved forward until her back hit the shelves. She ran her fingers through his hair, tugging slightly, and his hands curved around her waist.

And then there was a knock at the door.

They pulled apart, but still stayed in each other's arms, their breath meeting in the space between them.

Another knock forced them apart.

Ira let out a huff of frustration and headed for the door. She followed him until she reached the corner of the bookshelf.

Benji's voice filtered into the room as soon as Ira opened the door. "There's someone out here who would like to speak to Her Majesty."

Ira's frown was in sync with her own.

"Who?" he asked.

"Sir Kieryn from Ouprua."

Ira looked back at her and she sighed, her shoulders sagging.

Kieryn wasn't the worst person to come looking for her tonight, but that didn't mean she wanted to speak with him. However, she didn't always get what she wanted. And dealing with him now could save her some trouble later.

"Is it only him?"

Technically the holiday wasn't over, so she didn't have to speak to Sorrel yet.

"Yes."

"Alright," she said, pushing off the shelf. She didn't want to invite him into Ira's study, and the hallway was less private. Hopefully that would limit what he was willing to say. She could see the question in Ira's eyes when she passed him. "It's okay. I won't be long."

Lena stepped through the door and spotted Kieryn a few dozen feet away, leaning against the wall with his arms behind him. She gave Ira one last look of reassurance before he disappeared. He didn't shut the door, so Benji did.

Kieryn straightened as she approached and cleared his throat. He appeared rather bored. His hair was a bit messy, a few strands pulled out of its elaborate hairstyle and falling around his face. Some of the hair toward the crown of his head was stuck up as well, as if Kieryn had been scratching or pulling there. His glassy eyes told her that he'd continued to drink after she left.

"I am here on behalf of Mikhail," Kieryn said, his words sounding as crisp as usual. "The dinner is over, but he wants you to return for . . . I don't really know what happens after, but he wants you to return."

She looked at him dubiously. "It took you a while to find us."

"My abilities do not allow me to know where anyone is at any given moment," Kieryn lamented. "And I may have taken a brief detour."

She fought the urge to roll her eyes. "I think I've had enough socializing for today."

"Haven't we all," he sighed. "But I'm afraid he's insistent."

She was unsurprised by this. "And he sent you to find me?"

Kieryn flashed her a charming smile. "I volunteered."

Lena could ignore Mikhail's request and send Kieryn on his way, but there would be consequences. Not large ones, but irksome ones. Maybe she'd follow Kieryn's approach and just drink herself silly. The celebration couldn't go on for much longer. People parted before midnight to pray.

"Fine."

When she turned, Benji met her gaze and nodded without her having to say anything. He walked back to Ira's study, likely relaying the message to him. Lena turned back around to stare at Kieryn.

He was smiling lazily at her, a fine brow arched. "You left in a hurry back there. Did what I say upset you?"

"No," she replied curtly. "Your honesty is one of your better qualities, remember? I just—I needed a break too."

Kieryn nodded and leaned back against the wall.

She continued to stare at him, thinking about the dinner, him and Tuck, and the comments. The hand. She squinted and tried not to speculate because she didn't want to spend her time thinking about Tuck, but here Kieryn was, and the question was at the forefront of her mind again.

"Did you do that for him back there? For Tuck?"

Kieryn's face remained impassive. "Do what?"

"Attract the attention toward yourself? Be loud?" she offered up. "You're not usually."

"What do you know? We've only had a handful of conversations."

"Stop messing around. I saw you reach out to him." She shook her head. "Why would you . . . ?"

Kieryn shrugged. "I like him. I think he's one of the better people here."

She nearly choked. "Tuck?"

"Yes," Kieryn confirmed, sighing heavily as if *she* was the ridiculous one.

Ira was coming up behind her, but she didn't cut the conversation off there. "Are you sure you aren't biased?"

Kieryn acted as if he didn't know what she was talking about. She gave him a look that told him she wasn't fooled. She'd seen them at the celebrations together.

Before he could say anything, someone came racing around the corner. They skidded to a halt when they spotted Lena and the others. A messenger.

"Your Majesty!" the messenger gasped, her eyes wide with something akin to panic. "You must come quickly!"

Warning bells immediately started going off in her head. Her body involuntarily tensed, and her Imprint warmed. Ira's arm brushed against hers as he stepped up next to her.

"Why? What's happened?" she asked.

"Councilwoman Trynla went into labor," the messenger explained. "Prophet Mikhail said you must meet them in the infirmary for the child's birth."

Her mind spun and she lost her point of balance for a moment. She clutched onto Ira's arm to keep herself steady. "Why?"

"He said your presence is good luck, especially on tonight of all nights. And someone else was already supposed to be retrieving you."

The messenger looked at Kieryn but then quickly pulled her eyes away.

Lena shook her head. "I don't think—"

"He told me to tell you it was not a request," the messenger said with urgency. "We must hurry!"

The alarm was beginning to seep into her. Trynla was in labor. *A baby.* Lena had never witnessed a birth before. Not really. She would come before the pushing began or after the baby was born, or she would hear the entire thing from the room over. And what luck did she have to give?

Ira's face was ashen, his eyes distant. He tried to give her an encouraging smile, though it wavered. "Go. I'll be right behind you."

"I don't—I mean, I can't—"

"Lena." He pulled her hand away from his arm, and his fingers brushed over her rings. *Their* ring. "You have to go."

She didn't understand, not really, but her feet still moved her forward after the messenger and away from Ira and Kieryn.

She realized a few seconds later that Ira's hand had been shaking.

CHAPTER
FORTY-SIX

They had one day off during the calendar year. It was the only holiday the prophets recognized.

The Eve of Revival.

All the firstborns knew everything about this historic event. The prophets made sure they knew. In the days leading up to the holiday, they had slightly longer seminars so the prophets could reiterate their history and the beginning of the purging of sin. On the day of the holiday, the prophets were nowhere to be seen.

Atreus assumed they'd gone above ground. The enforcers stayed behind to supervise and make sure things stayed somewhat orderly. It was the same every year. Atreus didn't appreciate the actual holiday or what it stood for, but he appreciated the relative freedom it gave them.

He was in the library with Mila. Judah and Finn were there too, but they sat off to the side between the shelves, currently engaged in a rather serious card game. Finn's game.

Murmurs and laughter occasionally reached Atreus, pulling him out of his book. He was almost done with the one Mila had stolen, and it *was* useful. He'd learned a lot and many of his suspicions had been confirmed. His conversation with Vanik the other day had troubled him. He'd started reading the book that night and had been reading it every day since.

He knew the stones were a gateway, but there was more to it. The passageway between realms was tangible yet not at the same time. The book described it as a flow of energy—a stream. Anyone could sense it and ride along it before the shattering of the realms. After that event, only a select few could utilize the stream. They could take others with them, but it was difficult and dangerous if not perfected. The stones were a solution to this issue, which begged the question of how they came to be. Were the stones created or had they always existed?

Atreus could accept the idea that the prophets were only collecting these stones so they could travel between realms if it weren't for the giant disc Vanik had told him about.

And what business did the prophets have in these other realms? Most of them were desolate. The only thing one would get out of the other side was a gruesome death.

And as he suspected, the stones were more than just tickets. They were concentrated vessels of energy. Magic.

Atreus wondered if that was all magic was: energy concentrated in extremely high amounts. The book didn't elaborate further on that particular aspect, but it did hint that the stones could be used for other purposes. The possibilities were endless. They were a weapon, but only if they could be controlled. The question of *why* the prophets wanted to use the stones as a weapon also had many possible answers.

A large part of the narrative was missing. The prophets only fed the firstborns what they wanted them to know, and all the books inside the Institute aligned with their philosophy, meaning they wouldn't be helpful to him. But he had to at least check it out and be sure.

So when he lost his focus due to the commotion or his own jumbled thoughts, he would tuck the book away and amble through a few aisles in search of another text that might answer the questions he'd gained. Mila would stay behind at the table to make sure no one came across the book. Atreus, unsurprisingly, came back empty-handed every time.

But when he was heading back to the table this time, a hand caught his pant leg as he walked by the group playing games. Atreus stopped and followed the arm to see Judah's pouting face.

"Why are you studying on our day off?" Judah asked.

"I'm not studying."

"You're *reading*," the kid said as if that was the same thing.

"I thought you liked stories."

Judah tilted his head toward the center of their little circle and blinked up at Atreus. "I also like games."

Atreus frowned. "I'm not playing."

"Please."

"Come on, Atreus," Finn chimed in. "One round."

The rest of the group looked up at him.

He sighed and tried to tug his leg away, but the kid's grip was surprisingly strong. "I don't even know the rules."

"I'll explain them to you," Finn said. His eyes gleamed in a way that told Atreus there was no getting out of this. "Sit. Mila! Come over and play a round. Atreus is!"

"I didn't say—"

"*This* is what you told us to meet you here for?"

Harlow, Weylin, and Vanik were approaching. The latter was the one who'd spoken, and he was looking at Finn with skepticism and annoyance.

Finn appeared unperturbed. "It's a holiday. How do you spend a holiday?"

"Sleeping," Weylin replied.

"Not doing this," was Harlow's response.

"However the fuck I want," Vanik said.

Atreus sighed. Judah tugged on his pant leg again, and he finally gave in, sitting next to the kid.

Everyone shuffled outward, making room for the new players. Mila took her place in the circle wordlessly. She caught Atreus' eye and nodded. The book was safe. He didn't know where it was, but he trusted Mila.

Finn patted the spot next to him, peering up at the trio.

"I'm not playing a game," Vanik scoffed.

He went to leave but stopped in his tracks when Finn said, "I have wine."

Vanik paused.

Today was *also* the only day they were given wine. A small celebration of sorts. Finn was managing the two bottles he'd snagged from the dining hall earlier.

Atreus didn't care for the alcohol. He'd grabbed a few pieces of fruit for himself. *Real* fruit, not that gray mush. They weighed his uniform down, but he didn't take them out, worried that someone else would steal them if given the chance.

Vanik begrudgingly sat down, not in the circle, but Finn seemed to consider it a win. He passed over a bottle. Weylin sat down too, though Harlow took a bit more convincing.

"Okay, I'm going to explain the rules quickly again," Finn said. "Each person has four cards. Your goal is to get three cards in a row anywhere in the suit or to collect five pebbles. You can do this by trading or stealing. If you want to trade, you ask another player if they'll take one of your cards. You have to identify the card with the number and suit. They can accept or deny this trade. If they accept it, they have to give you one of their cards, but you have no say in which card. That's their choice. *Or* you can choose to steal. Each person has two pebbles in front of them. If you want to steal from someone's hand, you have to give them a pebble. You can choose from their entire hand. The first person to collect five pebbles or get three cards in a row in the same suit wins."

Vanik leaned forward and rested his elbows on his knees. "What kind of game is that?"

"It's fun!" one of the younger firstborns chirped. Others spoke up in agreement.

They were being genuine, practically vibrating with excitement, and based on the dumbfounded look on Vanik's face, he had no idea how to respond to that.

He pulled back and took another sip of wine, then grimaced. "This shit's gross."

"Then stop drinking it," Weylin said easily as he picked at his fingernails.

"Can I have a taste?" the same kid asked.

Vanik shrugged and went to hand it over, but Finn stopped him. "What are you doing? Eli's ten."

"If they're old enough to be sent to another realm to die, don't you think they're old enough to drink?"

He ... had a point.

Finn seemed to think so too. He was frowning, but he pulled his hand back. "Fine, but we're monitoring them."

Atreus glanced at Harlow again. She sat with Weylin and Vanik away from the circle, but she'd distanced herself from the two of them as well. Her knees were pulled to her chest, her arms wrapped around them. She stared at nothing in particular, her mouth flat, but when she caught Atreus' gaze, she scowled and angrily pushed herself to her feet. Before he realized what he was doing, he stood and followed her.

"Atreus! We were just about to start."

"I'll play the next round," he told Finn before slipping between the shelves.

He caught sight of Harlow disappearing around the corner of a shelf. She was walking quickly, perhaps even *running* from him. He sped up his step and turned into a larger aisle.

"Harlow."

She didn't stop. She turned down another aisle, escaping his line of sight again.

He blew out a heavy breath and jogged after her. Grabbing the corner of a shelf, he swung his body around and—

—ducked as something flew for his face.

He turned to look at the now motionless object on the floor as he raised himself to his full height again. She'd thrown a bookend at him. It was made of iron.

He rounded on her. "What the fuck?"

Harlow crossed her arms, completely unconcerned. "Don't get sloppy now just because it's the holiday."

Atreus strode forward. "You could've killed me!"

She scoffed. "Oh, *please*. Don't be so dramatic."

A short, low laugh rumbled from Atreus' throat as he took a step back. "*Clearly* you're still upset with me."

"Grudges are stupid."

"Then maybe you're being stupid." Then quieter, more to himself, he said, "Maybe we're both being stupid."

"From what Vanik tells me, it's only you."

"You listen to everything he says, do you?"

Harlow's frown turned more severe, but he was used to her glaring at him.

"I wanted to talk to you about our conversation in the dining hall," he said quickly before she could walk away from him again. "I ... might've handled that poorly, but ... "

Atreus stopped and really thought about what he was doing. About why he'd chased after her.

These past few weeks had felt like an extended night terror. He was overwhelmed, and things just kept happening. He didn't have time to process it all. Not until today. So when he saw Harlow, the first thing he'd thought of was their last conversation and the past two Outings.

When she approached him in the dining hall, he'd all but derided her concerns and their implications. He'd brushed her off, and that had hurt her. Tensions were high during that time. He was stressed. But he mainly reacted that way because he was trying to convince himself alongside Harlow that those ideas were ridiculous. He didn't want to think about why that *Te'Monai* had left Harlow alone in the volcano, why it'd changed course right after he screamed. He tried to convince himself that it was some freaky coincidence, that it had nothing to do with him, and in order for him to start believing that, he needed to shut Harlow down. So he had.

But then the next Outing happened, and he ran into that *Te'Monai* underground and had no choice but to face that forbidden topic. He'd hoped his . . . *role* in all of this began and ended with the stones, but it didn't. He was wrong. There was no ignoring anything about that *Te'Monai* turning its back on him and leaving. He didn't know what to do with this information, and he didn't know exactly why he was coming to Harlow with it instead of Finn or Mila, but here he was.

Maybe part of him felt like he owed it to her in some way. She'd thought the *Te'Monai*'s behavior in the volcano was weird, and it *was*. It was unnatural because Atreus had controlled it, just like he'd controlled the one underground in the last Outing.

Logic had been one of the first things to go when he started getting less sleep. And tact.

"During the last Outing, I came across a *Te'Monai* under the hill. I was face to face with it, but it turned around and left because I told it to."

Harlow's expression slowly shifted into one of disbelief, but it wavered, like she was having some internal battle.

"You told it to?" she repeated slowly, processing his words.

"I thought it," he corrected. "Judah was there."

The boy was new to the Outings, so he didn't exactly understand the importance of this as much as Atreus, Harlow, and the others. Still, Atreus had tracked down the kid after getting back and made him swear not to tell a soul what had happened.

"So . . . under the mountain—"

"Volcano."

Harlow's eyes cut sharply to his. "Who cares? Under the volcano—the same thing happened. So you . . . control the *Te'Monai?* How—?"

"I don't know." He scratched the back of his head and started pacing. "I don't know the full extent of it. It's only happened twice, and one-on-one. I don't know if it would work on a group of them. I don't know why it's happening *now* and I— there are too many things I don't know."

Harlow grabbed his arm as he moved past her, stopping him in his tracks. "Well, what we *do* know is that you can help. In some capacity."

He snorted. "If we don't know in what capacity, is it really that much help?"

"*Yes.*"

An uproar of laughter sounded a few aisles over. It wiggled its way into his chest and loosened the strings that held it tight. He noticed the tension seeping out of Harlow as well.

"We'll talk about it another day," she whispered. "We can't do much but speculate right now. The only way to understand this . . . ability of yours is to test it."

Her words passed through him because his mind was elsewhere, confronting another concern. "What if it was a fluke? It's never worked before, so there must've been some sort of catalyst. And guidelines."

Harlow looked around. "And did you think you were going to find a guidebook inside here?"

She was mocking him, but she was right. As she'd said, there was nothing he could do about this now. There were no *Te'Monai* set aside for him here.

His friends' laughter reached his ears again. He sighed and nodded. Harlow returned it, a harsh downward jerk of her chin, and then whirled around.

"Wait."

She paused, and Atreus fumbled for the words. He'd called out to her before he knew what he wanted to say. No, he *did* know what he wanted to say, but he didn't know how to say it.

The bags under her eyes were still prominent, but she wasn't the only one haunted in this place. They all had their demons, even Judah.

"For what it's worth . . . I'm sorry for . . . writing off your feelings like that."

He remembered the look on her face when she told him she was prepared to die. He could see it clearly behind his eyelids if he let them fall. Her survival unsettled her, not because she'd lived, but because she didn't know *why*. He hoped that what he'd told her would put that haunting to rest. But he knew it wasn't as simple as that.

Harlow's shoulders were tense and hunched forward, her hands clenched at her sides. Had she meant to shield herself or had she done that unconsciously? Her gaze swept over him gingerly. "Thanks."

"What are you two talking about?" Vanik came around the corner, his eyes narrowed and his hands slipped into the pockets of his uniform pants.

"Nothing," Harlow said smoothly, turning away from Atreus.

The cynical look on Vanik's face made it clear that he didn't believe her, but he didn't push back. He might have if Atreus had been the one to say it. Instead, Vanik sniffed and looked back in the direction of the others.

"Didn't enjoy the game?" Atreus asked.

Vanik turned his glower on him. "I said I wasn't playing any stupid games and I meant it. I don't know how any of them can. None of this is a game."

"They know that, but not everyone can keep forging on without a break, especially the younger ones." Atreus had seen the light in Judah's eyes. He'd smiled genuinely for the first time in a while. No thoughts of monsters or bloodshed filled his head. "This is good for them."

Vanik scoffed and looked at Harlow, but she held her hands up, signaling that she was staying out of this.

"None of this is good for them," Vanik muttered. "It gives them false hope. A false sense of security. They need to realize that every day here is shit, even today."

"Why?"

Vanik shook his head. "It's what will keep them alive."

Atreus couldn't argue with that, but he didn't want to agree with Vanik, so he remained quiet.

Harlow scratched at one of the book's spines, her face hidden by her hair.

"We should leave today," Vanik said all of a sudden.

Atreus whipped his head around. *"What?"*

"The prophets are probably gone. The firstborns don't have to follow any schedule, so they're scattered about. We know where the exit is." Vanik marched forward, stopping only an arm's reach away. "We should leave now."

They'd discussed this before, but Atreus and Mila had quickly shut it down. They didn't know the layout well enough. They knew where the exit was, but not how to open the door. There were other reasons Atreus didn't want to leave so soon. He didn't say them aloud, but Vanik knew them. They were why he'd confronted Atreus the other night. They only had one shot. If they were caught, that would be the end.

"*No*. We already talked about this," Atreus hissed. "We're not ready."

"You mean *you're* not ready."

Vanik stuck his finger in Atreus' face, and he felt the overwhelming urge to smack it away.

"No, I mean *we are not ready*," he reiterated. "And you know it. Don't get sloppy just because you're desperate."

Rage rippled across Vanik's face. Atreus knew Vanik was going to swing at him, but he didn't try to dodge. However, Harlow saw the hit coming too and ran forward to intercept it.

"Hey!" She shoved Vanik back before his blow could land and followed him, a hand braced on his chest. "What's wrong with you?"

Vanik threw his hand out, eyes still blazing. "We can't keep waiting. We don't have that luxury. If you see an opportunity, you have to take it. That's how you survive."

Harlow set her jaw. "He's right about this, and deep down you know it. We can't leave today."

Vanik took a step away from her, but Harlow grabbed his sleeve, holding him in place. She ducked her head, trying to catch his eyes. "*Soon.*" She didn't let go of him until he nodded.

Atreus released a breath and watched Vanik in case he decided to lunge at him again.

"Excuse me."

A fourth voice made them all stiffen.

A firstborn around their age slowly slid around the corner, the bookend Harlow had thrown in his hand. Brown hair. Brown eyes. Pale skin. He blended into the crowd down here, but Atreus recognized him. Tolar was his name.

"What?" Vanik snarled. He'd made it no secret that he didn't want others in on their plan, and there was no telling how much Tolar had overheard.

Tolar didn't back down under Vanik's fury. In fact, he only hardened under it. He stepped forward, a frown tugging at his lips. "What were you saying? About leaving?"

None of them said anything. Ice filled Atreus' veins and the cold dripped down his spine.

Tolar's gaze moved between the three of them. "You're trying to escape, right? That's what you're talking about?"

"Don't be stupid," Vanik growled, but it was a weak rebuttal.

None of them could say anything to turn this around.

"I'm not," Tolar snapped. "I know what I heard. Denying it isn't going to change that."

"So what?" Harlow said.

The intensity in Tolar's eyes faded a bit when he turned his attention to Harlow. No one in the Institute got along with Vanik, save for Harlow and Weylin. Vanik had a reputation for himself.

"So I want in. Or *out*, I guess."

"No," Vanik said immediately.

"*No?*"

"You heard me. Now *fuck off.*"

Harlow placed a hand on Vanik's shoulder, pulling him back. They were beginning to grow too loud and would soon attract much more attention than they wanted—than they already *had*.

"What's wrong with you?" Tolar fumed. "I'm not staying here."

"Then die. I don't care, but you're not coming with us."

Tolar appeared taken aback by Vanik's lack of empathy. His mistake. He swallowed thickly and looked over his shoulder. "If you want this plan of yours to remain a secret, I suggest you let me in on it."

Vanik's eyebrows rose so high they nearly disappeared under his hair. "You're *threatening* us?"

"I wouldn't have to if you'd just do the decent thing."

"I don't have any decency left." Vanik sneered. "But I do have plenty of rage."

Tolar eyed him distrustfully, wrapping his arms around his stomach. "Yeah, whatever." He looked at Harlow and Atreus. "How many of you are there?"

Neither of them responded, but Tolar didn't seem put off by their hostility.

He nodded. "I'll find you tomorrow. I'm assuming you talk about the plan in the sleeping hall, away from the prophets' and enforcers' ears."

Once again, no one confirmed anything, but Tolar seemed fine with that too. He set the bookend on a shelf and then left.

As soon as he disappeared, Vanik spun around, visibly seething, his eyes wild and his hands shaking.

"How many people?" He directed his words at Atreus. "How many people are you trying to save and bring along? Because this plan only works for so many. We'll all crash and burn because of your fucking hero complex!"

"This isn't my fault!" Atreus threw back. "I didn't invite him over here."

But Vanik was hearing none of it. He'd already left, and with one last unreadable glance at Atreus, Harlow followed him.

Atreus stood there for a moment, everything calm except for his heart. It rattled his bones, weighing him down with each thump. His legs moved quickly, and his hand swiped out.

The bookend clattered onto the floor again, and this time, a piece broke off and slid into another aisle. He realized then what exactly the bookend was. A prophet. Or more specifically, Kerrick Ludoh. The piece that had broken off was his head.

CHAPTER
FORTY-SEVEN

The trip through the halls was a blur. The next thing Lena remembered with clarity was being pushed into the infirmary. The screams immediately flooded her ears and she stopped moving. The messenger turned when she noticed that Lena had stopped.

"Your Majesty?"

Lena's gaze moved over the cots. Most of them were empty. Trynla lay in none of them. The screaming was coming from farther back. Her eyes returned to the messenger, who stared at her in concern.

"Your Majesty? Are you alright?"

Her head felt too heavy and too slow, so it was slightly delayed when she nodded. "Yes. I'm fine. Where—?"

"This way."

The messenger led her to the back of the infirmary and down another hall adjacent to the large room. Doors lined the left wall. One of them was open toward the end of the hall. A group of people was huddled outside the doors, most of them prophets. They talked amongst each other as if they didn't hear the screams at all.

Lena suddenly stood in the doorway. Physicians shuffled around the bed, clad in their white gowns. Mikhail was in the room. Other people she didn't recognize moved quickly, grabbing blankets and sharp tools that gleamed under the bright sunstones. Trynla lay on the bed, fidgeting and crying out every few seconds.

There was too much going on. Too many people and sounds and instruments. What were they even going to do with those?

Mikhail spotted her then and said something, but she couldn't make it out over the commotion in the room and the fuzz in her ears. He walked over and led her to where he'd been standing.

Lena's eyes latched onto the bed, onto Trynla. Her flushed cheeks remained the only splashes of color on her otherwise pallid, sweaty face, and strands of her light brown hair were stuck to her forehead. The dress she'd worn earlier had been mostly stripped from her, and the thin gown that was its replacement didn't cover much.

"You're just about there," one of the physicians told Trynla from between her legs. "The baby is coming soon. You're doing great."

Trynla let out another sob. One of her hands fisted into the material of a blanket. A physician held her other. Both of their knuckles were white, faces contorted with pain.

"Why did you call me here?" Lena asked, turning on Mikhail.

The prophet merely smiled at her. "Because this is a momentous occasion, and a great opportunity for you."

"It's the birth of a child, and not any child I would care about." She had to raise her voice to be heard over all the commotion. She pretended she didn't notice the slightly hysterical edge to it.

Mikhail frowned. "Children are the important pillars of our society. We cannot continue and grow without them, especially firstborns."

Lena's eyes moved to the doorway again, to the prophets waiting outside.

"It doesn't make sense for you to go to every childbirth. It's impractical," Mikhail continued, seeming completely oblivious to everything around him. "But this one—everything aligned perfectly. The child will be destined for great things. They are very lucky. Trynla is as well."

Trynla was red in the face, screaming on the bed as the physicians told her to push.

"Can't I wait outside the room? I can see the baby—"

"No, you must be here." Mikhail sounded and looked truly perplexed as to why she would want to leave.

She flinched again as one of the physicians yelled, "I can see their head! Keep pushing!"

Trynla shook her head. Her chest rose and fell rapidly. "No, no, no, no, no. I need space. I can't breathe—"

"You're doing great! Now push. *Push.*"

A scream tore out of Trynla's throat as she did what the physicians told her to do, what her body told her to do. The physician beside her flinched.

Lena saw red on the white bedsheets and stumbled back. Into Mikhail. His hands caught her shoulders, steadying her.

"Easy there. Do you need to sit down?"

Did *she*? She wasn't the one pushing out a baby.

Lena took a deep breath and then immediately regretted it. The room was drenched in sweat and blood. A heaviness came with it, one that draped over her and held her still as Trynla screamed again and pushed. The constant reassurances likely went unheard. Lena barely processed them, and she wasn't even yelling.

"The head is out. One more big push for their shoulders."

Lena couldn't see the baby, which she was grateful for. She didn't want to see it. She didn't want to be here. She felt like she *shouldn't* be here, but everyone else was making themselves at home. The people in the hall were still talking amongst one another as if there wasn't someone giving birth only feet away.

"Is it always like this?" she heard herself asking.

But she already knew the answer. No, it wasn't supposed to be. It *shouldn't* be. She'd heard the yelling before, and she'd seen the blood *afterward*. Seeing everything in real time . . . the screaming and tears and blood . . . How was that a momentous occasion? Some of the births were quieter and quicker, never easy but *easier*. And what came after was sometimes just as difficult.

"Every birth is different," Mikhail said. "Some prophets believe the length and difficulty of a birth indicate the child's potential."

Her brows furrowed. *That* was how they looked at it? It was such . . . a shallow understanding. " . . . Do you think that?"

"Almost there. Push! *Push!*"

"I do," he said, almost proudly. "One day you will understand. When you have your firstborn."

Lena flinched as a particularly loud shriek sounded, and then the baby was out. A cry pierced the air, and the physicians took the baby to the other side of the room, cleaning them off and swaddling them.

Trynla looked utterly exhausted, but she still leaned forward, wincing as she did so. "Let me hold them. Please," she panted, reaching her hands out.

Her pleads were ignored as the physicians handed the baby immediately off to the prophets. Mikhail smiled down at the bundle while Trynla called from the bed.

"Calm down," one of the physicians told her with a smile. "You did well. Congratulations. He's beautiful."

"He?" Trynla whispered, her eyes filling with tears. "Can I hold him?"

The physicians shushed her gently and carried on as if the question had never been asked. They crushed something up using a mortar and pestle, and then dumped it into a nearby cup of either water or tea. Lena watched the physicians give it to Trynla, coaxing her to drink it.

"You've done amazing."

Lena's feet were rooted to the floor, her body too hot yet too cold, too light yet too heavy. She felt like she was here but not. Everyone moved around her. The noises were far away, echoing in her cotton-filled head.

"Your Majesty." Mikhail waved her over. "Come see the baby."

When she refused to move, they brought the child over to her. It was a small, red, ugly thing that fussed in its blanket.

"He is a very blessed child to have the ruler present during his birth."

"You're just . . . taking him?" Lena pulled her eyes from the baby. "Why can't Trynla hold him? Name him? Can't she spend some time with the baby before he's taken away?"

The babies in the Lowlands weren't immediately picked up by prophets. They were with their parents for a few hours to a day.

Mikhail looked at her sympathetically. "I'm afraid not. The bond between them will only strengthen and separating them will be a much more difficult endeavor. The prophets try to get to the firstborns as soon as possible to prevent that."

"More difficult than this?"

For the first time she could remember, Mikhail gazed at her with arrant disapproval, dipping his chin.

"This is *hard*," he agreed. "But this is the sacrifice that must be made to keep the peace in this realm. Everyone knows this. Trynla knew this while she tried for a baby. Now she has done her part in serving this realm. *That* is what one should take away from all of this. It might be hard—the process and the letting go—but it is for the betterment of our kind. This should be viewed as a great achievement. A *positive* experience." He shook his head when he saw the unwavering doubt on her face. "One day you will understand," he said once more.

With the baby still in their hands, the prophets stepped away from Lena and Mikhail and left the room. She'd never seen someone take away someone's baby before. And certainly not with a smile on their face.

Trynla was nearly asleep now. The physicians were wiping the blood and sweat off her and tucking her in comfortably.

"I need to go," Lena muttered.

And then she was out the door too, weaving between the people outside the room and marching down the hallway.

Her dress was too heavy. Too constraining. Her skin clammy, especially where it was hidden under fabric. She tugged at her sleeves, wishing she'd left her arms bare.

Images of the birth she'd just witnessed flashed through her mind. She'd been the only one freaking out—other than Trynla, but she had been pushing a baby out of her. Everyone else had acted like this was *normal*, and she supposed it was. Children were born every day. And all of the firstborns were taken away by prophets. Lena *knew* that. She'd just never *seen* it before.

She wasn't particularly thrilled by the idea of having kids, but she'd always known she would have to have them. At least one. She didn't particularly care for kids. She'd been nice to her siblings and cousins of course, but not nurturing. Not like Zahara had been. People would tell her she would grow out of it. One day she would want a baby, and she would understand the bond parents had with their children. She'd experienced it from one end—the child's perspective. She knew it was real, and yet the desire to experience that connection from the other end had not surfaced. And even if it soon did, she would have to go through this twice just to keep one of them. The babies . . . They were too young to know what was happening, or to remember it, but the parent wasn't. To carry a child for nine months only to have them taken from you the moment they were out in this realm . . .

It left a bitter taste in her mouth.

But this was how things were. This was how things had been for *centuries*. Her parents had four children. She had an older sibling who'd been taken away before she was born. She knew nothing about them except that they'd come first. And then Torryn. Then her. Then Zehara. *Everyone* here had an older sibling who'd been taken, and maybe they'd had a firstborn too.

It was . . . normal. It was talked about of course, but not in a way that indicated anything was wrong with it. People mentioned it just as they did the weather or dinner or the day's plans. That was how it had always been. Those were the words and thoughts that had surrounded her from day to day. After her family was killed, her problems had multiplied and become her focus.

This was the first time in her life she'd actually thought about it, like *really, really* thought about it—at least in this sort of way. In a dangerous sort of way. A doubt that was deeper than the childish curiosity she'd displayed before grew and grew. Like everyone else, she'd just accepted it because this was how things were. It was comparable to paying your taxes or abiding by the law. One did it, and it was in their best interests; it kept *relative* peace.

But the exact same thing could be said about the Cursed-Blessed dynamic, and she'd recognized the wrongness of that. The *it-had-always-been-this-way* excuse was shallow, and it didn't hold up. With anything. Once that was pushed aside and she *really* thought about it . . .

She tripped over her feet and caught herself against the side of the hall. Her sweaty palm slid down the smooth wallpaper and she slumped forward, resting her blistering forehead against the cool surface.

Maybe she was having this sort of reaction because of all the other things that had happened tonight. Maybe this was how everyone reacted the first time they saw something like that.

Mikhail had said the prophets tried to get to firstborns as soon as they could. That would explain why those in the Lowlands got to spend more time with their babies. And maybe he was right. Maybe it was a mercy to take the child immediately. She didn't know anything about being a mother, but she knew enough about losing people. The more connected you were to someone, the more painful it was to lose them.

She pushed herself away from the wall and hurried back into the main room of the infirmary. Her breath caught when she spotted Ira sitting on one of the cots. His elbows dug into his knees and he was hunched over, but his head was up, eyes watching the prophets as they left the infirmary with the baby.

She slowly approached Ira, her limbs still feeling a bit off, like they weren't properly coordinated with the rest of her.

His gaze snapped to her and he quickly pushed himself to his feet, but he didn't speak a word. He merely watched her, his face grave and troubled.

Benji and Andra were across the room, standing next to the entrance.

Lena swallowed thickly. "I need to go to the Lowlands," she said as she moved past Ira.

He furrowed his brows and stepped in front of her, stopping her short. "Now? That's all?"

"What do you want me to do, Ira? What do you *expect me* to do?"

He took a step closer and lowered his voice. "This isn't right," he hissed. "They just took away her baby—"

"Stop," she said softly, her eyes stuck on a point beyond his shoulder. Her limbs had melted, and her insides were seconds away from coming up her throat and becoming *outside*. Her mind was riding on the ocean waves, missing every other thought and word as it went up and down. Up and down. Up and down. "Stop. Just . . . let it be."

"Let it be?" he repeated, rearing back.

"Yes." And then she walked away from him. She didn't turn around. She had to keep moving.

Cowen took over for Andra and Benji before Lena left the palace. They must've told Cowen where she intended on going because he came into her room as soon as he arrived.

"You shouldn't go down there tonight."

"I have to," she said simply. "There are people I need to meet. Information I need to retrieve."

"Someone else can do that for you."

"*No*," she snapped. "They can't. I *need* to go. I *need* to leave."

Cowen didn't push her any further. He remained silent until she finished adorning herself with daggers, tying her hair back, and throwing on a cloak.

"I'm coming with you then."

She'd expected it, but his words still made her pause. "Okay."

Getting to the Lowlands was easy. They had both made the journey more than enough times, and no one was outside the palace preventing her from leaving. Her safety was supposed to be the Sacred Guard's job. And they were keeping her safe, not trapped. There was a difference.

The streets were more empty than usual because of the holiday, which meant there weren't many onlookers. Still, she was careful about covering her tracks. She met with her informant first. Not Dugell. The other one. The more reliable one. Though, she would never fully trust someone in this profession. But they were supposed to have information on Sorrel by now.

Lena could try to blackmail Sorrel with what she currently had, but there was the possibility that it wasn't enough. She would have to talk with Sorrel soon now that the holiday was nearing its end.

Luckily, her informant had found something. They gave her a single name written on a piece of paper. The name of Sorrel's second victim.

Rhys *Feydohr*.

A royal Blessed.

Lena truly couldn't give a shit that Sorrel had killed a royal, but others likely wouldn't share her sentiment. If the royal families banded together, they had more than enough influence to turn favor against the alliance with Ouprua.

This was all she had, so it had to be enough.

Cowen had likely picked up on the fact that she was a bit . . . *off*. He followed her around silently like a dutiful shadow, as always, but his gaze was especially attentive tonight. It crawled across her skin, pulling it tight. She wanted to snap at him, but she didn't even have the energy to do that. The recent events had drained her.

But she realized Cowen's hypervigilance was caused by something else when they were about to head back to the palace. He was being conscientious for her sake, yes, but he was also distracted. N*ervous*. Which was atypical. He'd always been a proud person, though he'd mellowed out over the years.

She stopped and stared at him strangely. "What's wrong?"

Cowen's gaze snapped to hers as soon as she spoke. His face twisted, and for a second, she thought he was going to deny it. But then he cleared his throat and said, "There are some people I'd like you to meet."

She blinked. That was certainly not the response she was expecting.

Like everyone else in the Sacred Guard, Cowen was Blessed. She knew he'd gone into the Lowlands looking for her, but she didn't think he had any personal ties to anyone down here. This was important to him though—these people were. He wouldn't have brought it up otherwise.

"Here?" she asked, just to be clear.

"If you're up to it," he said as he shifted his weight. His eyes would meet hers and then move away. "I know it's been a long day . . . "

Had Andra and Benji told him what had happened in the infirmary too? It didn't take an expert in body language to figure out she was on edge. It had been more than a long day. Cowen knew that, even if he didn't know what *more* entailed.

"No, it's . . . If they're important to you, I want to meet them."

Lena and Cowen had been in the Lowlands together a few times, just the two of them, but he hadn't mentioned this before. She didn't question why he'd chosen to bring this up *now*, nor did she doubt his loyalty. She was surprised he was keeping secrets from her, but not insulted. More than anything, she was curious.

Cowen took her to Silohn, the next town over, which was less than a ten-minute walk. He kept glancing over his shoulder, like he was checking to make sure they weren't being followed.

They walked into a tavern that at first glance, she thought was closed due to the holiday, but it had a singular customer. She and Cowen kept their hoods up as they strolled past the bar and into a side hallway. The barmaid's eyes followed them as she cleaned mugs, but she didn't say anything.

It was quieter back here. Dimmer and tight too. There were dozens of rooms on either side of the hall that she assumed were rented out to travelers who needed a place to stay for the night.

Cowen stopped at the last door on the right. He knocked in a pattern. Four. Pause. Two. Pause. Three. And then he waited. He glanced over his shoulder again before the door opened. Only a sliver.

A woman peeked through the crack, and when she spotted Cowen, she opened the door wider, a smile breaking out across her face, excitement wiping away the apprehension.

Cowen lit up at the sight of her too. The tightness and nerves drained from his form as he stepped into the room and swept the woman up into a hug.

Lena stepped in after him, closing the door behind her. There was another person in the room. Her eyes widened when she got a good look at them, and their eyes widened too.

It was her informant—the one she'd seen less than an hour before.

She didn't know what to do. But running away wasn't an option, so she stayed put, waiting to see what would happen. Her informant did much of the same, watching her warily.

Selling out your informant or client was bad for business, so she had no intention of saying anything. She could only hope they didn't either. Thankfully, their initial surge of shock happened while Cowen and the woman were embracing, so neither of them noticed a thing.

When they pulled apart, Lena and her informant had collected themselves. She was back to being a curious observer. Her informant, on the other hand, had warmed. There was a gentle smile on their face and their body was loose. When Cowen approached and pulled them into a hug, they went easily.

Lena watched the three of them interact for a bit. Watched as Cowen placed his hands on the woman's cheeks and kissed her lips. Watched him clap a hand on her informant's shoulder and murmur something in their ear. It was an intimate interaction, one that made her feel like she was intruding.

These were the important people in Cowen's life who he'd kept hidden. The people who warranted several weeks of deep thought before letting an outsider meet them.

Something full and warm filled her chest and she smiled, choosing to look away from them and around the room instead. It was small but had all the necessities. A bed. A connected washroom. Books, blankets, and clothes were littered around the space. It looked like they had been here for a while.

The three of them stepped apart, so Lena could get a better look at the woman. She appeared to be in her mid-thirties and was quite pretty with warm hazel eyes, copper hair, and freckles that covered nearly every inch of her pale skin. She wore a long shift dress, which wasn't tight but wasn't exactly loose either, so the rounded protrusion along the woman's midsection was noticeable.

Lena's suspicions were confirmed when Cowen's hand brushed over the woman's stomach. She was pregnant.

Lena's eyes widened, but she tried to school her features as Cowen turned toward her, smiling tentatively. "Kalena, this is Cora and Nell."

Nell. She looked at her informant. Light brown skin, dark hair, and dark eyes. Tall but not too tall. They had an ordinary face, one that could be easily forgotten. Everything about them made for a good informant because nothing about them stuck out. They blended in easily. At least now she could put a name to the face. Did the other two know about Nell's skillset?

"It's a pleasure to meet you," Cora said, striding forward and extending her hand. "Cowen's talked a lot about you—nothing bad or incriminating, but I've been looking forward to meeting you."

The smile that spread across Lena's face came a few seconds too late and was too stiff, pulling at her cheeks. She shook Cora's hand while shooting Cowen an accusatory look. "*Oh?* Has he now?"

"I assure you, it's all good things." She took a step back, out of Lena's immediate space, but she still stuck close. "I've pestered him about meeting you, but I never thought he would bring you here."

Lena caught the glance between Cowen and Nell.

Cowen cleared his throat. "Yes, well, we happened to be in the area and I thought it was about time she met my family," he chuckled, flashing a smile of his own, but there was something weighing it down.

Cora caught on to it and she frowned slightly.

Family. Lena marveled at the word Cowen had used. Her mind supplied another a few seconds later: *Home.*

"I didn't know you had anyone special." Lena tried to keep her voice light, but it fell flat. She was acutely aware of every passing moment. She didn't want to be here, but she *did*, for Cowen. "Honestly, I'm a bit relieved. I'd feel bad if you spent all your time and energy on me."

There was truth in that—in all of it. But especially in that last bit. Most people who served her or worked in the palace had somewhere or someone to go back to. They could separate their work life from their personal life. But the members of her Sacred Guard weren't supposed to *have* a personal life. They had taken an oath to protect her and that was supposed to be a full-time, never-ending job. They knew what they were getting themselves into when they signed up for it, but it didn't stop her from feeling guilty. She felt like she was taking something away from them. But sometimes she had to be selfish, and she felt guilty for that too.

Cowen huffed out a laugh at that. "Well, I do still spend a considerable amount of time with—"

"Uh, none of that," Lena cut in quickly, laughing uneasily. "How'd the three of you meet?"

Cowen's smile widened and Cora laughed. Nell's face softened yet again. They had stayed back near the far wall.

Cora immediately launched into the story, explaining how she'd run into Cowen five years ago when he was in the Lowlands searching for Lena. He was being rude to a messenger boy who was unsure if he'd seen the runaway queen while on his route. The boy was stuttering and cowering while Cowen nailed into him relentlessly, quickly becoming impatient. Cora witnessed the exchange and instead of walking past like so many others had, she went over and gave Cowen a piece of her mind. Cowen was taken aback to say the least. The annoyance didn't properly set in until he was back in the Highlands. He was put off by her, but at the same time, he couldn't stop thinking about her. He convinced himself that he wouldn't run into her again . . . but he did. And this time Nell was with her. The two were together before Cowen came along. Nell thought Cowen was a bit of a pretentious ass as well, but they didn't get *impassioned* as easily and greatly as Cora did.

The three of them continued to have small skirmishes with Nell being the peacekeeper of sorts. At some point, the genuine insults turned into flirty banter. Nell was the only one who realized this at the beginning, and it drove them crazy. It took a while for the other two to realize and accept that they had feelings for each other—feelings other than annoyance and animosity. Tensions grew between the trio until things grew too taut and exploded. Navigating the relationships between the three had been tricky, but they'd all come out of it together and stayed together.

Lena caught the sly smiles, exasperated looks, and loving glances they secretly gave one another as they told the story, but her gaze kept returning to Nell.

They weren't as revealing as Cowen and Cora when it came to their emotions, but she could tell they cared. The way they carried themselves and the fond look on their face was leagues more expressive than what she was met with when visiting them for secrets. It was a bit odd—thinking about one of her informants and one of her Sacred Guards being in a relationship together.

"So I'm the reason you three got together?" The words left her mouth rather bluntly, but thankfully Cora spun it into something comical.

She laughed and leaned against Cowen. The two of them had sat on the bed sometime during the story. Lena had planted herself in the armchair in the corner.

"There were times when it could've gone either way," Cora said. "You could've been the reason I met the biggest pain in my ass."

"You *are* the reason I met the biggest pain in my ass," Nell said.

Cowen rolled his eyes. "Enough of that. From both of you."

He sobered up a bit, looking back at Lena. Unlike the others, he'd picked up on the strain in her voice and on her face. That was part of his job, wasn't it? Detecting when something was wrong, especially with her.

Lena shook her head, telling Cowen and trying to tell herself that everything was fine. She needed to get over it. Snap out of it. Whatever. The muscles in her cheeks pulled again, her mouth splitting open into a polite smile.

She couldn't stop thinking about Cora's pregnancy. How far along was she? Was this Cora's first child? If so, would the baby be taken away like Trynla's child? Would it be immediate and *difficult* and require Cora to down a calming elixir? Whose child was it? On one hand, it didn't really matter. If the three were together, the baby was all of theirs. Lots of people had more than two parents. She was an odd one out in that sense. Her parents hadn't been in serious relationships with others while together.

But the biological parents of the baby did matter in the legal sense for record-keeping purposes. Firstborns were determined according to their birthing parent because that was apparently the most accurate way to account for firstborns. It kept the numbers consistent but put pressure on those who were able to have kids, because those who *weren't* couldn't do their part in upholding society, couldn't be purged of evil, until they had a firstborn child to show for their efforts.

Lena tried to keep her mind away from the topic of firstborns and pregnancy and keep her eyes away from Cora's bump, but both kept slipping. And eventually Cora caught her.

Much to Lena's horror, Cora beamed and rubbed her freckled hands over her stomach. "You must be wondering about this..."

That was one way of putting it.

"I think I'm around sixteen weeks, but I'm unsure. We only found out recently."

Four months. Almost halfway there.

Cowen's face was grave. She didn't know exactly what he was thinking, but she had some guesses. Pregnancy could be overwhelming. Becoming a father was a lot. If this child was a firstborn . . . well, they would have to prepare to part with it. And if it wasn't, they would have to prepare to raise it.

The Lowlands wasn't the most ideal place to raise a baby, but many people did it just fine. However, she was almost positive that Cowen, with his upbringing in the Highlands, wouldn't like the idea of them being down here. He'd grown up in comfort, and he likely wanted the same for his child. But it wasn't like he could just move his family into the Highlands, especially not with his position.

"I've been putting things in order," Cowen explained. "For when the time comes."

Nell shifted against the wall and Cora's eyes saddened. She placed a hand on Cowen's knee. "Maybe now isn't the time . . . "

"There won't be a better time," Cowen argued.

Lena's eyes narrowed and she looked between the three of them. "For the baby?" she clarified.

Nell's jaw clenched, and their eyes latched onto Cowen's back. Cora looked about ready to cry, which really threw Lena off. Rather than explaining anything with words, Cowen stood and unbuckled his pants.

Lena's brows shot up. "Um, what are you . . . ?"

Her voice faded as Cowen dropped his pants to the ground, revealing the Imprint on his thigh. Her lips parted in shock as she took in the sight of it. The Imprint looked . . . infected. Only the center still had its true golden color. Dark, nearly black, branches extended from it, cutting through his swollen and red skin. It wasn't a pretty sight, and it looked painful.

She jumped to her feet, but she couldn't bring herself to move toward him. She snapped her mouth shut and tore her gaze away from his Imprint. He looked so tired. Had the change been immediate, or had he looked this way all night?—pale and a mess, eyes rimmed with red. Had she been too concerned with herself to notice?

"What's wrong?" Her voice came out far too fast and high. "Are you sick? Why haven't you seen a physician? Is it Slayer Sickness?"

She hadn't seen it before, so she didn't know what it looked like when your Slayer started poisoning you. But it could happen for a number of reasons, and it was usually treatable.

Cowen shook his head. "No. Lena, it can't be cured."

She stared at him, not understanding.

"This is what happens when you break an oath."

She shook her head, taking in the sight of his Imprint again. "You didn't break an oath."

"I did. According to the Numina. I took an oath to protect the ruler of The Lands with all my strength and undivided loyalty. I took an oath to give up my life for the ruler's. I'm not supposed to have other . . . distractions."

She knew that. She *did*. But she hadn't thought . . .

"That's not fair! You didn't break your oath. *You didn't*. There must be a way to fix it. To talk to the Numina. You didn't betray me—"

"I don't blame you, Lena," he said solemnly. "This isn't your fault. I knew what kind of life I was signing myself up for when I took that oath."

Lena clenched her jaw, trying to suppress the tremors spreading through her. "We'll find a way to reverse it. There must be ways!" She thought of sorcery and all the other possibilities in places they didn't yet know about. "Breaking an oath isn't always deadly. I can try to—"

"No, Lena."

"You are not dying!" she snapped, throwing her hands out. Her lips quivered as she stood there, and she felt like her fifteen-year-old self again, seeing her family's corpses laid out across the furniture. Cowen was one of the only people she had left. "You have a relationship—a *family*—and a child on the way. Why are you so *resigned*—?"

"I waited too long," Cowen sighed. "The signs started showing up years ago. It was meant to deter me, but I ignored them. I didn't stop seeing Cora or Nell. I wouldn't. I read up on oaths and tried to find a loophole. I took medicines and visited *many* physicians—even some sorcerers. I've exhausted every possible remedy. And over the past few months it's only been getting worse. Nothing can stop this, Lena. It's too late."

Tears blurred her vision. She looked at Nell, who appeared to have placed their informant mask on their face. She couldn't detect a single emotion. They were just . . . unfeeling. Blank. Empty.

Cora appeared much more distraught. Her head hung low, and her copper hair hid her eyes but not the tears dripping off her chin. One of her hands lay lifelessly in her lap, her fingers trembling. Her other hand was pressed over her stomach, as if to console her unborn child. *Cowen's* unborn child.

Lena glared at the giant *red-black-golden* scar that was his Imprint. Tears spilled from her eyes. "You're not even *trying*," she cried. The tremors had taken over. "You can't do this!"

The walls of this room were closing in on her, pushing her ribs up against her lungs and her heart. Her anger swelled and her Slayer slammed against its confines. She couldn't be inside right now. She needed some air. She needed—

So much.

Too much.

"Lena—"

She ripped open the door and ran from the tavern.

CHAPTER
FORTY-EIGHT

The first day of the new year was a bad one. Ira was nowhere to be found. He hadn't been in their room when she returned last night or when she woke up this morning. He didn't make an appearance at the council meeting either, so she had to make up an excuse for him.

Trynla was absent as well. She wouldn't get out of bed. The council seemed more concerned about her absence than *her*. They still had more than enough people to reach quorum, but the four empty seats glared at the remaining fifteen. However, Sorrel and Von made the room appear fuller than it really was.

Tuck came into the council chamber once the meeting started. As it turned out, he *had* found something while he was gone. Something that was supposed to be impossible: a path through the Kubros mountains. He said the path didn't appear to be naturally formed, not entirely anyway, meaning people had been using it.

Some of the council members wanted to send Tuck back out, but the council as a whole ultimately decided against it. They had no leads. Sending him out there empty-handed would be pointless.

After the council meeting, a day full of trials awaited them, as was custom during the first few days of the new year. In Lena's opinion, it was a shitty way to mark the beginning of the year, but most of the council seemed to think it was a good way to set an example—to set standards for the year to come. Because of this, the trials were open to the public and held in the throne room.

Tables had been dragged in and positioned before the sweeping staircases for masters of the law. They offered counsel during the trial, but it was ultimately the High Council who decided the verdict.

The matters brought before them weren't black and white, and she disagreed with others on the council many times, but she was always outnumbered. They were growing annoyed with her, as she was with them. Before she knew it, they were on the last trial of the day.

Mikhail called for the defendants to enter, and the guards let them in. One guard walked up to the table of law masters and handed them a scroll that detailed the defendants' crimes. One of them read it aloud.

"Kaini Denab and Sharaena Tunova are accused of the following crimes: fraud, refusal to cooperate with the law and Numina's will, theft, assault, and endangerment."

Two women stood in the center of the room, their heads down and their hands bound in front of them. Sniffles came from the one on the right. Both were shaking, though Lena suspected it was for different reasons.

"These accusations are based on the following series of events, collected and recorded as accurately as possible by witnesses, the defendants, and enforcers of the law: Kaini Denab did not disclose her pregnancy at any time. Sharaena Tunova helped her hide it and the firstborn after they were born. The women kept the child hidden for two months before enforcers tracked them down. Both Denab and Tunova ignored the enforcers' orders to surrender the child. They sent their Slayers after the enforcers, but they, and the child, were eventually safely secured."

Lena furrowed her brow and sat up straighter in her chair. Surely something must have been recorded incorrectly. Or read wrong.

Fraud? Refusal to cooperate? Theft? Assault? Endangerment?

The master of the law set aside the scroll and asked the women, "How do you plead?"

"Please," the woman on the right begged. "We were just doing what we thought was right. We tried to protect our baby."

Lena glanced at Mikhail even though she could only see the back of his head. He sat in the closest seat to her left. Alkus sat to her right. Just like in the council chamber.

"What you thought was right was against the law," Mikhail said not unkindly. "The child is not in any danger. There is nothing you need to protect them from."

The other woman raised her head then, her eyes filled with bubbling fury. "Is the unknown not something we should be protecting our children from? What happens to firstborns when they're taken? We never hear or see from them again. It worries us! And we're not the only ones who've grown skeptical."

Murmurs trickled through the crowd. One of the law masters banged the gavel against the table, silencing the spectators.

"Us mortals are not meant to know everything. The Numina have plans—plans that involve the firstborns—and it is our job to be their faithful servants," Mikhail said smoothly. "The unknown can be frightening, I understand, but you must trust in the Numina. All will be well as long as you do not turn your backs."

Mikhail didn't waver, she noticed. Even in this situation, he didn't doubt his beliefs. She'd always wondered how and how *much* the Numina spoke to the prophets. She wanted to know what it was that made someone so devout.

"We sympathize with you." Mikhail raised his hands, gesturing toward the rest of the council. "You are lost. Perhaps you can be found again. However, you did commit a grave crime, one that cannot be easily forgotten."

The woman on the right began to weep again, while the other stared at Mikhail and the council with something akin to hate. "I held him in my belly for *months*. He is my child and you people want to take him away from me—"

"He is not your child," Mikhail said matter-of-factly. "The laws are clear. A firstborn belongs to no one but the Numina. They are servants to the realm. This sacrifice allows us to prosper instead of perish."

Lena frowned, her fingers digging into the arms of her throne until her nail beds stung.

Servant? Prosper? The only ones *prospering* were the Blessed, but not all of them. Trynla was despondent in bed because of her child. Cowen was dying because he wasn't allowed a life of his own. Ira had been imprisoned and hunted down. The women in front of them were mourning and in chains.

Was *this* what the firstborns were sacrificed for?

"Your Majesty, please!" the impassioned woman called out. "Be merciful. They already took our child. We know there's no getting him back. And we know a punishment will be given, but I ask that you leave Sharaena out of this. I made her keep it a secret. I told her I would hurt her if she told. She has nothing to do with this."

"No." The woman on the right—Sharaena—looked at her female companion and shook her head, her eyes wide and cheeks wet. "No, that's not true. I—"

"*Quiet,*" Kaini hissed.

"*No,*" Sharaena cried, reeling toward her partner. "No, I won't let you—!"

The guards yanked her back before she could touch Kaini. She cried out when she hit the ground. Kaini clenched her jaw and moved to help her, but the guards stopped her too.

Lena leaned forward in her throne, ready to tell the guards to step back, but they did so on their own. She looked at Mikhail to find him already looking at her, waiting.

"What punishment does the court call for in a matter such as this?" she asked.

"The offenders receive a life sentence," Mikhail said.

"*What?*" she blurted out, her eyes widening. "Life in prison? For hiding their baby for two months?"

The amiable expression on Mikhail's face wavered for a moment. "Yes, with the chance of early release if they behave. They stole something very important—"

"They didn't *steal* anything." People had to realize how this sounded. The punishment didn't match the crime. "They just wanted more time with *their* child."

"Your Majesty," Mikhail said with great restraint and patience. "That child was never theirs to keep. The moment the baby was conceived, it was marked for the Numina. You know how this works, and how important it is to keep this tradition." He sounded as if he was trying to remind her of such. Quieter, he said, "If we let them off lightly, what message does that send? It tells the public that we've become more tolerant of these sorts of crimes. People will question our traditions and break our laws, and where does that lead us? To ruin."

"A lifetime is a long time for a Blessed," she said, holding his gaze. "*Too long* for this."

The firstborn was in the custody of the prophets now, and no one had been seriously hurt.

"*This*, Your Majesty, could lead to our downfall," Alkus pitched in softly. "These are dangerous ideas, and when you let them run free, they spread."

Her first instinct was to say that those ideas weren't dangerous, and they weren't, not *now*, on a small scale. But Mikhail and Alkus were looking ahead. Any idea that went against the government was dangerous if it grew large enough. Revolts and disorder could quickly follow. Yet that wasn't a bad thing, was it? To them it was, but to her . . .

Kaini was openly pleading with Lena. Sharaena was still on the ground.

They hadn't done anything wrong. They had only . . . kept their child. It was against the law, but it was *their* child. No one had been hurt. And the law wasn't always right. Or just.

What was right and wrong? Was it subjective or was there some widespread, preeminent truth that determined these things? Was it both? Did the government determine right and wrong? The Numina? But they were unjust, so everything they created was too.

The matter of firstborns was something many of them didn't fully understand. According to the prophets, that was okay. Mortals weren't *meant* to know everything the Numina know. This was the Numina's will, so the people of The Lands had to carry it out. And people did. They followed blindly.

Even though she hadn't given up a firstborn, she had participated in the system. The system that had prophets ripping newborns out of their parents' arms with smiles on their faces and condemning anyone who rebelled against this tradition to life in prison.

"Lots of people have dangerous ideas. Is this how you treat all of them?" Lena asked Alkus.

"Yes," he said simply. "This is how we set an example."

She scowled. No, this was how they kept themselves in power. Anyone who opposed them was locked up for life.

Mikhail looked at her with something akin to disappointment. It was much clearer than last night. And it lasted much longer.

Strike two, he was telling her.

She could physically see the bars slamming down between them and his hand extending toward Alkus, ready to reach an agreement. She'd opened her mouth, opposed traditions Mikhail held dearly, *publicly. Again.*

Ira wasn't here. There was no one keeping her from being rash and saying exactly what she felt.

She'd tipped the scales out of her favor. She could see that too.

" . . . I think Her Majesty has had enough for the day," Mikhail said softly. "Please escort her back to her room."

It was a dismissal at best. A punishment at worst.

"I'm fine," she said sharply, but guards were already heading her way. Not Sacred Guards, of course. They answered to her. At least they had to act that way in public.

Benji and Andra stepped up to stop the guards from coming any closer. Everyone seemed to hold their breath. Mikhail stared at her, his eyes narrowed.

"I am offering my—"

"The trials have almost concluded for the day. The council will finish deciding these matters without the help of Her Majesty. She needs rest."

Mikhail was still looking at her, but he spoke to the room at large as if it was already decided. Some of the council members squirmed under her gaze, but they didn't speak up for her. Of course not.

Mikhail's mind was made up. If she argued, she'd only be digging herself a deeper hole. No ground would be made. Not for her at least. Or those two women. Only for those who wished to see her stumble. If she made a scene here, she'd be proving their point that she was *young, inexperienced,* and *troublesome.*

See, she is not yet ready for this position, they would say.

The guards shifted again. She wordlessly stood and made her way down one of the long stairways, trying to hold herself with dignity as everyone watched her, including the two women.

She'd seen the smirk on Alkus' lips when she left her throne.

∽

Lena walked down to the dungeons. The guards at the door stood straight when she approached, their faces already twisted with dread.

"Don't bother. I won't turn back," she said before they could so much as open their mouths. "You can report to Alkus all you want, but the only way you'll be able to stop me from going in there and talking to the prisoner is if you restrain me."

The guards exchanged nervous, almost frustrated glances. She waited a few seconds before marching forward. The guards' shifted, but they didn't stop her as she opened the door and stepped inside. They didn't stop Benji or Andra either.

It was even colder on this side of the door, which was likely intentional. The frigid temperature in the dungeon was meant to be a discomfort to any occupants. Luckily, she had thought to wear a coat this time.

All but one of the cells should be empty, but she still peered into each one as she walked down the passageway. The palace rarely held prisoners. This place was, after all, a palace and not a castle, despite the dungeon. The palace—and the people living in it—weren't designed for fighting and protection. Not only was holding prisoners a risk, but it was also an eyesore and required much more effort than many were willing to put in. Criminals were usually held in local jails in the city and, if found guilty at their trial, shipped off to faraway prisons.

She paused when she came across the occupied cell. Her attacker sat on his bed, his back to the wall and his legs bent in front of him with the heels of his feet digging into the edge of the mattress. His arms rested on his knees while his fingers fiddled with a piece of paper, folding it and then unfolding it again and again. His brown hair was parted down the middle and tucked behind his ears. As soon as he spotted her, he smiled. For someone who had been stuck in a dark, freezing cell for weeks, he looked considerably . . . well.

"The queen has finally decided to pay me a visit," he announced, his voice lofty with feigned wonder and his breath a small cloud in the air. "To what do I owe the pleasure?"

"I have some questions for you."

Her attacker sighed and leaned his head back against the wall. "Everyone does."

She could see what Ira meant when he said the prisoner had a penchant for dramatics, and she could imagine how difficult it was to interrogate him.

"You're a popular guy," she muttered. "Now earlier—in the forest when we first met—you said, '*you're her.*'"

Her attacker smacked his lips together. "Was there a question somewhere in there?"

"You were looking for me?" she asked clearly, her voice sharp.

"Mhm, not exactly. You're the queen. Don't you think that's a normal reaction for someone to have when they see the queen for the first time?"

"So you didn't come to the ball or the festival then?" she clarified. "You're Blessed, meaning you very well could've attended both. Why didn't you?"

He shrugged. "Was busy."

Not only had the ball marked her return. It'd also provided people with the opportunity to become her intended. The possibility of marrying the ruler of The Lands was an enticing opportunity for many. Because of these two things, the palace had been packed with guests from all over the Highlands.

She pressed her lips together. "What's your name?"

"You can call me whatever you want to call me." A lecherous grin made its way onto his face, but his eyes were still fixed on the piece of paper. It was soft and flimsy after being folded so many times.

"That's not what I asked."

"But, alas, that is the answer I gave."

She bit the inside of her cheek and forced herself to take a breath. "Without your name, it's much more difficult to find your family in the Highlands. But we've developed a theory of sorts. Well, I have. I don't think you're from the Highlands at all."

"Interesting theory," he murmured. "So you think I'm from the Lowlands then?"

"Maybe."

There was no law saying Blessed couldn't live in the Lowlands, though not many chose to reside there for obvious reasons. The Highlands was the better option comfort-wise, but if someone had something to hide—if they'd committed a crime or wanted someone else to commit a crime on their behalf—they went to the Lowlands.

He finally glanced back at her then. His hair slipped from its hold, falling in front of his face, but he made no move to push it back. "You think I'm from somewhere else entirely? Isn't there nothing outside of The Lands?"

That had been the traditional understanding for years. She'd always thought there was more out there, and now, with Ouprua making themselves known, she was more certain than ever that there were other civilizations just beyond their reach.

"Many believe that, but we've come across new revelations recently." She watched him for any sort of reaction. "We've sent people out to explore the realm beyond The Lands. I'm sure they'll find something."

"You think so?" He flicked his hair out of his face and lifted his chin.

"I do. I also think it would be wise on your part to confess before our people return with this information."

Tuck would be sent out again sometime in the near future. As soon as they had a lead. She hated the idea of asking him for a favor. And after their last encounter, she didn't think he'd do anything for her.

He tilted his head. "Confess to what, may I ask?"

Shivers danced up her arms as the cold seeped through her coat. Something about his eyes unsettled her. They were . . . vacant. He was the one in the cell, but she felt trapped under his gaze.

"That you're not from here. That you're the one behind the murders. That you were sent here for some reason related to me. That you took me from my room and tried to kill me in the forest."

His upper lip curled to show more of his teeth. "You really don't remember what happened that night, do you? You think *I* took you out there?" He laughed loudly, dropping his head back again.

She faltered and drew her coat tighter around her. He could very well be lying to mess with her, but . . . he could also be telling the truth.

"Did someone hire you to kill me?" she asked quietly.

He huffed and returned his attention to the flimsy piece of paper.

"Have you been hired to kill me before? My family?"

He folded the paper again and again and again, and then unfolded it. And began folding again.

"Are you going to answer?"

"No," he said simply. She didn't know which question he was answering. "Something tells me you don't really want to know the truth."

"Of course I do."

"You're like them," he said. "They say they want the truth, but they're looking for a certain answer. They don't really want to hear anything if it doesn't fit their narrative."

At that, she took a step back. How realm-shattering could his answers possibly be? He was fucking with her. Obviously. Still, she kept silent in fear that he *would* tell her something she didn't want to hear. He was in the dungeon. He wasn't leaving anytime soon. She could figure her shit out and come back. She had other matters to deal with in the meantime.

"When you find out what you really want, come back and I'll tell you the truth." He flicked the piece of paper away. "But don't expect it to be pretty."

CHAPTER
FORTY-NINE

In her state of depression, Trynla had sent everyone away. Her attendants no longer visited her, saying she was refusing the dress or bathe. The servants left Trynla's meals in the hall because she wouldn't open the door. The platters of food went untouched. Trynla wouldn't accept any company, not even close friends and family.

So it was very easy for Lena to sneak into her room and kill her.

Lena stood over the bed. Trynla was awake and under the covers. She had certainly seen better days. She hadn't taken a bath since giving birth three days ago, so she did smell. A faint sheen of sweat covered her dull skin and dark circles sat under her eyes, telling Lena she probably hadn't slept recently.

"You're a sorry sight."

Trynla merely blinked, staring straight through Lena.

"Are you going to say anything?"

"You're here to kill me, aren't you?" Trynla murmured.

Lena was taken aback by her bluntness, but she quickly recovered, ignoring the question. "You're hurt," she said matter-of-factly. "You've been like this ever since you woke up after giving birth. Why?"

Trynla remained silent, so Lena answered for her.

"You're mourning your child. You've been trying for one for years, and you finally got one, and you loved them. And then they were taken away before you could even hold them. Your child isn't dead, but you still *lost* them." Lena cocked her head, staring down at the lump under the covers. "Before this, have you ever lost someone important to you?"

Once again, no response.

Lena gritted her teeth and crouched so she was eye-level with Trynla, only inches away from her face, yet the faraway look in the councilwoman's eyes did not change.

"If you have—if someone's been taken from you before—then how could you do the same to others? How could you take their loved ones away from them—*good people*—forever, when you know what that pain feels like? How it carves out room in your chest and just *sits* there. You can try to patch up that hole, but it'll never heal. It'll always be there as a reminder of what happened. I *remember*. I know why you did it, but I still want to ask—*How?*"

Trynla was silent for a moment. Then she opened her mouth and droned, "It was really quite easy."

A wave of fury rippled through Lena. She took a deep breath, silencing her Slayer and pulling her hands away from her daggers. Not yet.

"You felt threatened, right? So to make yourself feel better, you took out four defenseless Cursed. You arranged them on the furniture in front of the fireplace like some sort of fucked-up theater scene. You ripped out their hearts for what? What kind of message was that supposed to send?"

Trynla furrowed her brow, and her eyes sharpened for a few seconds, but then she relaxed again, sinking back into the mattress. "How is what you're doing any different from what we did?"

"Because *I* am not killing innocent people. *I* am not acting out of fear and striking first. I'm acting out of revenge." Lena leaned in closer. "You're a sickness. You, Alkus, Ophir, Avalon, Celine and all the other Blessed who think the way you do. Your child is better off without you. You're not stupid, so you should realize that at the very least."

Trynla merely blinked, back to looking past Lena like she wasn't even there. "Go ahead and get it over with then."

Lena stood up. "That's it? You're not going to fight back? Scream out for help? Convince me that I shouldn't kill you?"

"No," Trynla said simply.

"Why not? Don't you want to live?"

"...No."

Lena stared down at Trynla with a frown. "Really? This is it?" she genuinely asked. "This is what it took to break you?"

"I'm tired," Trynla muttered. "The baby was Alkus', you know? He told me he was going to protect them."

Lena stilled, her eyes widening slightly.

"You wanted your revenge, didn't you?" Trynla rasped, closing her eyes. "Hurry up and get it over with."

Lena's hands hovered over her daggers, waiting. She'd expected things to be different. She'd never . . . killed someone who wasn't fighting back.

"Are you sorry?" she asked.

Trynla didn't open her eyes as she answered for a third time, "No."

Lena's lips quivered as she looked down upon Trynla Hybraeth, the woman who'd looked down her nose at Lena more times than she could count. What she felt wasn't pity. It was disgust.

Her hand closed over her dagger. She wasn't sorry either.

CHAPTER
FIFTY

A messenger knocked on her door two days after she visited the prisoner. They told her that Councilman Alkus had invited her over for tea. She knew he knew about her trip to the dungeons. And by now, news of Trynla's suicide had likely circulated through the palace. Rejecting his invite wasn't proper, but that wasn't what stopped her from doing so. She had some things she needed to discuss with him.

She arrived at his study in the afternoon, thirty minutes later than the time that had been given to her. A woman opened the door—his assistant. Lena took her in as she walked past.

Alkus sat in an armchair positioned amongst other pieces of furniture to the left of his study. The open balcony doors in front of him revealed a fine view of one of many palace courtyards. Pastries and fruits filled one of the trays on the table next to him; the other smaller tray held teacups.

"Evanna, who is—?" Alkus stopped mid-sentence when he turned his head and saw Lena. "Your Majesty," he said smoothly, still with that slight hint of mockery in his voice, "I thought you had declined my invitation."

"Yes, I realize I am late. I had some rather important matters to attend to. I do hope you understand."

Matters more important than you, she was saying.

He gave her a tight smile. "I understand perfectly. Please, sit." He gestured to the sofa next to him. "I'm assuming one of those matters involves Trynla. I heard she killed herself last night."

Blunt right from the start.

Lena stayed standing. She didn't intend on staying long. "Yes. I met with Mikhail and her loved ones. It's quite unfortunate."

Trynla had been found late in the morning. A servant had decided to check on her after seeing yet another meal untouched in the hallway. She'd been met with the sight of Trynla lying in bed, her throat and wrists slit and the dinner knife on the bedsheets. It had looked like a suicide, and because of the way she'd been acting, people believed it.

Lena watched Alkus carefully for any sort of reaction to her following words. "She was in a state of mourning after losing her child, and she couldn't beat it."

"She didn't *lose* her child," Alkus corrected. His voice was gentle, but his body language gave nothing away. He picked up a cup of tea. His hands were unclothed and bare like Kieryn's, but that didn't mean he couldn't have tattoos elsewhere. The thought of Alkus possibly being a sorcerer had crossed her mind a few times. She had no proof other than the fact that he seemed to gravitate toward power. "They are doing very well. Definitely better than her."

"The baby's a boy," she said. Alkus paused. Only for a split second. "It's a tragedy nevertheless."

"Yes, yes," Alkus agreed as he sipped his tea, staring at her from over the rim of the cup. "The council is growing smaller by the day. Some might think we're being targeted."

She didn't falter under his gaze. "*Most*, I think. If they're smart. The killings started shortly after the Ascension, and as far as we know, they stopped when we captured the man sitting in the dungeon. All the victims were Blessed. There are no more corpses being found with their hearts ripped out, but council members are falling quickly."

Alkus set his cup down. "You think the same person is behind all of these killings?"

She shrugged. "Perhaps. The man in the dungeon could be a distraction or only one of the people responsible."

She was still convinced Alkus or one of the other council members who opposed her had connections with the people responsible for the murders. The resemblance of the killing style couldn't be ignored. She did believe that the prisoner was from somewhere far away, but he still could've easily been hired. Now and *then*. If he was good at his job, he wouldn't tell her anything useful about his customers or him. And much to her chagrin, he hadn't. Yet. If he had played a part in her family's death, she would find out.

But she needed to consider all possibilities. Maybe her attacker wasn't connected to anyone on the council. Him working independently or with someone outside of the palace was still troublesome. She still didn't know his agenda. She would've been less worried if it was just him that she had to worry about, but she was certain he was working with others after speaking with him since he kept referring to a *they*.

"Ah, right. The man in the dungeon." Alkus drummed his fingers on the armrest. "You went to visit him last night."

"I did."

"Even after the guards told you that you weren't allowed."

"I am the queen," she reminded him. "I don't need to be *allowed* to do anything. You are on the council. You give me counsel. You do not give me orders, Alkus."

Yet that was exactly what they had done at the trial. And she'd listened, and she hated herself for it.

He laughed faintly, a quick puff of air that left his nose. He pushed himself to his feet, smoothing his hands over his vest. "It wasn't an order. Only a recommendation."

Her eyes narrowed slightly. They both knew that was a lie.

"I stand by the statement I made at the holiday dinner. You are young and inexperienced. You will make mistakes. But it is the council's job to keep you from making too many."

"And who keeps you from making mistakes?" she challenged. "Your secretary?"

Alkus narrowed his eyes right back, the corners of his lips tugging up. "Very good, Your Majesty. You *are* learning."

"I am a quick study."

"Perhaps." He moved around the chairs and tables. "So you understand then that some things must be done, even if you do not wish for it."

"Of course."

He leaned back against his desk. One ankle crossed over the other and his hands laced together. "That's good," he murmured. "Because I've told our guests from Ouprua that we've agreed to move forward with this alliance. You're to marry one of them. The blond or the brunette. The engagement party will occur before they leave."

Her mouth dropped open and she swayed on her feet. "You did *what?*"

"I made a decision for us since you didn't show any interest in doing so. They're leaving soon. I did what had to be done for The Lands."

Her mouth snapped shut and then opened again. Her words tumbled over one another in her throat, fighting to make their way out first. "I was going to talk to Sorrel—"

"After the holiday, yes. But days had passed, and you hadn't yet met with her."

How did he know about that? Did he have someone following her? Had Sorrel told him?

"You can't make decisions regarding The Lands—regarding *me*—without first consulting me *and* the council," she seethed. "You went behind our backs when you first invited them here, and then again with this!"

Alkus was once again treating her like a figurehead. A face of The Lands who held no power. Her Imprint seared on her chest as fury rolled through her. For a moment, she considered unleashing her Slayer. But there would be no going back. There was no way she could cover this one up. She had to be patient.

"I did what had to be done then, just as I did what had to be done now." He pushed himself to his full height and took a step closer. The click of his shoes echoed through the room. "Let me ask you this—who fights for you, Your Majesty? You've been so concerned with welfare that you haven't invested enough time into the people who already have it. *They* are the ones who have the power, but they always want more. They want people who promise them more. You haven't promised those people anything."

"And you have?" she goaded. She wanted to hear him say it. She wanted him to admit that he'd turned people against her for him and his agenda.

"Not directly. But the people know where I stand." He took a step closer. "With tradition. And tradition brings comfort, especially to the people up here. It brings comfort to the guards outside of your precious Sacred Guard. It brings comfort to those sitting on the council. It brings comfort to the royal families. It's about finding what people want and giving it to them. And you know what our guests from Ouprua wanted? An answer. And I—not you—gave it to them."

He was too close. Close enough that she could hit him. Or stab him.

"Ira is loyal and holds influence, but he's one man. Your Sacred Guard is sworn to your position, not you. Who knows how long they'll uphold that oath. The Cursed? They're weak. What can they give you?"

Her smirk was nearly a sneer. "The Blessed don't have all the power," she said simply. "You think you do, and that's your biggest weakness."

Alkus looked at her as if she'd said something both absurd and bold. "You're wrong. We *are* power. You don't understand this realm or this position. You think you're bringing about some sort of revolution, and you are, but not in the way you think. You're naive. You should've taken my advice from the beginning. Marrying Ira was a mistake—"

"It wasn't," she snapped.

"It *was*."

She gave a short, bitter laugh. "And who would you have picked? Your nephew? *You?*"

His icy smile was somehow condescending. "Ira is a sinking ship. The day you chose him, you chose to drown. And if left on your own, you'll drag this country down with you. I will not let you ruin everything we've built here."

The heat inside of her flared up. "Was that a threat?"

His callous eyes remained locked with hers. "That was a promise, Your Majesty."

The doors slammed open, and Lena jerked away from Alkus.

The man who'd run in was red in the face and out of breath. "I apologize, councilman, Your Majesty, but more bodies have been found."

CHAPTER
FIFTY-ONE

"Killing him is the easiest and quickest way to fix this mess," Vanik told Atreus after having pulled him aside. The two were pressed into a small alcove in one of the corridors as the group of firstborns made their way to morning seminar.

"*What?*" Atreus' eyes darted to the firstborns walking past them before returning his attention, and his glare, to Vanik. "We're not doing that."

Vanik's eyes flashed, and his face turned stone cold. "Then it's your problem," he sneered before shoving past Atreus and disappearing into the crowd.

And Vanik had meant that. Later that day when Tolar found them in the sleeping hall, Weylin and Vanik were nowhere to be seen. They'd left Finn and Atreus to keep things from falling apart. There was no telling if Tolar would uphold his threat, but Atreus didn't want to push him and find out. If word reached the wrong person, it was over. Vanik *knew* that, but he was too stubborn to compromise.

Atreus didn't know what to do. Tolar had started following him around like a shadow to make sure nothing was going on that he didn't know about. Vanik and Weylin, and Harlow by extension, had distanced themselves shortly after. They'd been at a standstill for days.

Atreus could only appease Tolar for so long, especially when there was no new information coming in. No meetings or moves that inched their plan forward. And Vanik, Weylin, and Harlow were partly to blame for that. Their skillset was needed to pull this plan off. He'd realized just how valuable they were once they were gone. But he knew he was valuable too. They were playing the waiting game, seeing who would break first, when they didn't even have any time to gamble away in the first place. Vanik couldn't be reasoned with, and he doubted Weylin would listen to him either. Maybe he could get through to Harlow. Him or Mila.

"You're not lying to me, are you?" Tolar asked five days after the holiday when he cornered Atreus in the corridor on the way to lunch.

"No."

The skeptical look on Tolar's face didn't let up. "Why haven't you been having meetings? What are you waiting for?"

For you. For Vanik. For me. For everyone.

Atreus took a step closer and lowered his voice. "Getting out of here isn't easy. If it was, someone would have done it already. We're being careful. Things are coming along."

That seemed to placate Tolar somewhat. "It's not like we're living a life of luxury here and can afford to sit back and wait. Any day could be our last. Shouldn't we be moving with more urgency?"

We? How quickly he had adopted that.

"We know what happens if we get caught. We don't know what happens if we wait," Atreus explained. Tolar was still frowning, so he added, "You'll know if there's news."

That apparently was the wrong thing to say. Tolar's face hardened and he stood straighter. The uncertainty from moments ago morphed into something threatening. "Good, because like you said, you know what happens if you're caught. And I really don't want to tell the prophets."

Oh? Back to you, *is it?*

That was roughly how his interactions with Tolar went every time. He would push down his simmering anger, and only reassurances would leave his mouth in response to Tolar's threats. But that was already starting to grow old—for him and for Tolar. Every time a prophet appeared or Tolar disappeared, Atreus immediately thought the worst. But nothing had happened. Yet.

Days passed without an Outing. They worked harder in the mines. Their shifts lengthened and the explosions started up again, resulting in more injuries.

Ten days after the holiday, they received a visitor.

They didn't get any sort of warning. They were at dinner when Prophet Silas stepped into the room through the second pair of doors only the prophets had access to. Like the doors the firstborns used, it was on a platform, but there were no stairs connected to it, only a door likely leading into some secret hallway the firstborns had never seen. Prophet Silas looked down at all of them and announced that they had a visitor.

Atreus' chest tightened. They never had visitors in the Institute—or at least they never *saw* them. He knew there were people and supplies coming in and out periodically.

But if they were getting a visitor now . . .

Atreus looked over the dining hall, his gaze settling on Tolar and his group.

Are you responsible for this?

Tolar had threatened to tell the prophets, but he appeared just as shocked as the other firstborns.

The door creaked open and the visitor stepped onto the platform. It was the sunwalker Atreus had seen in the black and white room. As he stepped up to the railing, Prophet Silas stepped back. The man was smiling, practically beaming down at them.

"It is so good to finally see your faces. Before I say my piece, I must commend you all for your hard work and dedication. We wouldn't be able to do this without the effort you've all put forth."

Atreus' lip curled and his grip on the fork tightened. Finn covered his hand, momentarily stealing Atreus' attention. His friend's face was pallid, his eyes swimming with uncertainty. Mila's expression gave away nothing.

"You all have been doing so well recently. With that assessment and Prophet Silas' . . . input, I think it's time we move you to the next stage."

The next stage?

Whispers rose, filling the room, but the visitor waved his hand, and everyone quieted.

"You will be sent out tonight," he announced. And after one last sweep over the crowd, that sick smile still on his face, he left.

Prophet Silas followed him, leaving the firstborns and enforcers in the room alone. No whispers started after they left. Not for a while. The entire room was frozen, their food forgotten. They usually got *at least* a twenty-four-hour notice before being sent out. Today, they had gotten *hours*. And *the next stage*? Again?

Atreus didn't know what to expect on the other side of that portal, but he knew something would be different, like before. He hated the unknown.

He forced himself to eat more of his food. Judah followed his lead, his hand shaking the entire time. They hadn't been given knives for dinner, so they had no way to defend themselves.

This thought filled his mind as they moved from dinner to seminar and then to the cavern. Time passed quickly yet slowly.

If they had no weapon . . . did that mean they didn't need one? The prophets were cruel, but they wouldn't send everyone out without *something* if they needed to defend themselves . . . right? Then again, he'd thought they wouldn't send the kids out, but they had. There was no telling what lengths the prophets would go to now.

More people than usual crowded together in the cavern. Miss Anya was there along with others Atreus had never before seen in the Institute. More sunwalkers?

But he understood exactly why they were there and why knives hadn't been provided at dinner when one of the visitors said, "Blessed, please create lines on the right side of the cavern so we can tend to your Imprints. Cursed, stay where you are."

Atreus' feet were anchored to the ground. So this was their plan? The prophets *were* weeding them out. They were unsealing the Blessed's Imprints, letting them fight with their Slayers—*if* they could summon their Slayers—and leaving the Cursed to die with no means to defend themselves.

The impending doom that fell over him made his knees weak and his chest tight. He raised his head and watched as the realization hit everyone else. Watched as the horror spread across Cursed's faces. They had survived against the odds so far, but now . . . they were preparing to die.

He was Blessed. As were Mila and Finn. Vanik, Weylin, and Harlow were too. Conveniently. Atreus' eyes found Tolar. A brutal thought crossed his mind—one in which he hoped Tolar was Cursed so they could rid their hands of him before he could be any more trouble. But the lack of panic on Tolar's face told Atreus they wouldn't be getting that lucky.

People slowly began to move, creating lines. Atreus went to follow, but something held him back.

Judah was looking up at him, confusion and dread written across his face. "What are they doing?"

Atreus' heart stuttered to a stop. How could he forget? *Judah. What about Judah?* He was terrified to ask, but he had to. He dropped to his knees and gripped Judah's shoulders. "Are you Blessed or Cursed?"

Judah paused and then slowly shook his head, as if he feared he'd get in trouble for his answer.

Atreus could barely breathe. Claws held his heart hostage in his chest. "Okay. Okay. It's fine. It'll be fine," he said, trying to convince both himself and Judah.

The kid wasn't stupid, though. The tears slowly welled in his eyes. "Did I do something wrong?"

"No," Atreus said quickly. He pushed himself to his feet. "No, you did nothing wrong. *Nothing.*"

He looked around the cavern for the others. They had been split up somehow during the walk from seminar to here. But instead of finding his friends, he found Prophet Silas. The man stood at the front of the cavern, his hands behind his back and his eyes already on Atreus. The sunwalker's words echoed in Atreus' head.

"With that assessment and Prophet Silas' . . . input, I think it's time we move you to the next stage."

The prophet's input? Atreus just knew he had something to do with this change. Perhaps his defiance came at a greater cost than he'd thought.

He spotted Mila and Finn enter a line in the middle of the cavern. He'd wait for them to get back before he left Judah.

"Remember the conversation we had before the first Outing?" He looked at Judah intently, urging the kid to pick up on the gravity of his words and this situation.

Judah nodded.

"You need to be brave like that. Even braver. *Strong*. And you need to listen to me, do you understand?"

Judah nodded again, but he didn't look brave or strong or confident.

Atreus didn't have it in him to give an inspirational talk right now, so he merely bent down and told Judah, "Fight like the heroes in your stories, okay?"

Judah stiffened, and panic flashed across his face when he realized he'd been caught. But when he saw that Atreus wasn't mad at him for sharing his stories, his eyes brightened. Confidence and conviction livened him. Atreus hoped it wasn't only for show.

He didn't like it, but Judah held onto these stories, to his pieces of fiction, just as Finn did. They were what kept him afloat during these dark times, but he needed to be careful with them. Atreus told him as much, told him to only share these stories with Finn in private, and Judah nodded a third time.

Atreus' eyes returned to Prophet Silas. This wasn't Atreus' fault. This wasn't any of their faults. This was just another fucked-up manipulation tactic. He couldn't stop fighting the prophets, even if that meant putting others' lives on the line. If he stopped, nothing would change. For anyone.

His stomach turned over on itself until he thought he was going to be sick. He didn't want to play with fate. Who was he to decide the future of those in this room? He wasn't a hero, but he was tired of lying down and letting the prophets walk all over him.

Mila materialized at his side, and Atreus left Judah with her while he entered one of the lines. When he got to the front and the sunwalker told him to reveal his Imprint, he prepared himself.

They unsealed it, and the effect was immediate.

Atreus stumbled away. Heat spread through his body, surging outward from his Imprint. His vision blackened and his ears rang, but he stayed on his feet. Any aches and pains disappeared now that his Imprint was functioning fully. He felt like he was being reborn. It was pleasant, yet also painful because his Imprint had been suppressed for so long. The power was making room for itself once again, pulling his muscles and pushing at his bones. Reforming him. His movements were lighter, each breath reaching deeper.

The bond between him and his Numen snapped into place, opening entirely, and it scraped the inside of his mind. He fisted his hands in his hair and pulled. The bloodlust seeped through his veins, and then gushed, filling every crevice in his broken body. For a moment, he debated releasing his Slayer here and letting it tear apart the prophets.

When his vision cleared and he became steady on his feet, he made his way back to Finn, Mila, and Judah. As soon as he reached the three of them, someone shoved their way through the crowd and stepped up to the group.

"We're sticking next to you," Tolar said, leaving no room for argument. "You have a plan, right?"

Atreus stared at Tolar and then the three guys behind him. Had Tolar told them what he'd overheard in the library? If he had, there was nothing Atreus could do about it now. And if he hadn't . . . well, Atreus wanted to keep it that way.

He nodded slowly. "Yeah. Yeah, I have a plan."

Tolar nodded back, as if they had reached an understanding. Before anyone could say anything else, the portals opened, and the enforcers ushered the firstborns forward.

Judah held onto Atreus' shirt as they approached the white floating pools. The fully unsealed bond was *so loud*. He could barely think. He had no idea what they were walking into. He needed to be calm and focused.

Atreus dug his fingers into his Imprint, trying to silence everything rushing toward him. He sucked in a breath as he stepped up to the portal and moved through it.

At first, he saw nothing. Only darkness. But then he felt the breeze and the presence of other bodies around him.

They'd made it to the other realm, but they must be underground somewhere. He stomped his foot. They stood on a firm but uneven surface. Rock? He moved blindly, not wanting to get caught in the initial bloodbath. But there was none—no bloodshed. It was quiet. *Too* quiet. Anything could be lurking in the darkness, but minutes passed and no screams filled the air.

He should be glad, but all he felt was unease.

He forced one foot ahead of the other. The ground under his feet slowly started to slope upward. After a few minutes of walking, their surroundings slowly became visible. They were in a cave. Other firstborns inched forward around him, appearing just as confused and troubled as he felt. He saw the source of light a few seconds later—the exit. Atreus quickened his pace, only to stop short as soon as he stepped out of the cave.

Because they were no longer alone.

But instead of being met with raging *Te'Monai* at the cave entrance, they were met with humans.

CHAPTER
FIFTY-TWO

The explosions in the distance resumed the morning the council told the public about the murders. They knew the people would react badly, but they couldn't hide it any longer. The bodies had been found in the Lowlands even though all the victims were Blessed. News spread quickly. By the time the enforcers had collected the bodies and notified the council, hundreds of people across The Lands knew about the murders.

Death was an everyday occurrence in the Lowlands, but the people had seen how the enforcers had reacted. They knew the victims were Blessed. And they knew there was something bigger going on.

It wouldn't matter what the council told the public. The complete truth or white lies—the outcome would be the same.

Those delicate rumors of revolts? They weren't rumors anymore.

The friends and families of the victims began to talk to one another. They were upset at the lack of progress and transparency. They decided to band together and take matters into their own hands.

Up until this point, no one had known where the bodies had been found. The guards and enforcers had managed to find the earlier bodies quickly enough to keep word from getting out. But the same couldn't be said about the most recent round of killings, and since those bodies had been found in the Lowlands, the families assumed *all* the bodies had been found in the Lowlands. The Blessed quickly blamed the Cursed and then the council for covering for them.

The storming of the Lowlands was brutal. Buildings were torn to shreds and blood coated the streets before the waves of reinforcements showed up to help the enforcers end the dispute. The Blessed eventually returned to the Highlands, but their mutiny continued. And the Cursed began to strike, as well, angry that the council had let them be the scapegoat yet again.

Every guard and enforcer the palace could afford to spare was sent out to keep the peace, but the state of things was so fragile right now. The people wanted answers and actions taken. And the council needed to give it to them quickly if they wanted to keep things from growing worse.

They had another council meeting. The four empty seats continued to taunt them. Lena still didn't know where Ira was, but he wasn't the priority right now.

The people were angry, but their anger would fade overtime. At least the Blessed's would. That was what Alkus said, and many agreed with him.

Keeping information hidden during a criminal investigation was standard, and the Blessed would see that. For the time being, the council needed to tell the Blessed what they wanted to hear: that they were doing everything in their power to find the remaining offenders and that the public would be notified as soon as they were in custody.

A curfew was also issued. Pairs of enforcers would patrol the city streets from sunset to sunrise, keeping an eye out for any signs of danger. Messengers were sent to the victims' families with personalized letters signed by the council members and a hefty monetary compensation for their troubles.

Alkus ended up being right. The Blessed had calmed overnight. They didn't do well outside the comfort of their fancy homes. They couldn't create and maintain an uproar like the Cursed could. But the council was considerably less concerned about the Cursed. Money had also been sent down to the Lowlands to compensate anyone who had lost something or someone during the initial riots. That was it.

Most people would agree that now wasn't the best time to go to the Lowlands, but Lena wasn't most people. Everything and everyone, *especially* the enforcers, was in disarray. It was the perfect moment to move.

She'd pinpointed the coordinates Dugell had given her weeks ago. It was the house of a fucking town head. Alkus was transporting loads of money to the person in charge of Dram, a decent-sized town south of Tovaah, and she was going to find out why.

But she had something else to do first.

She caught up with Jhai in the attendants' hall that connected to her antechamber. She made sure the coast was clear before leaning in and murmuring, "Tonight. I want it done."

Surprise flashed across Jhai's face, but she quickly shoved it down and nodded.

"Prove to me that I was right to trust you," Lena said quietly before leaving.

She found Aquila next, in the same alcove in the same library as before. And like before, Aquila sensed her almost immediately.

She sighed and turned toward Lena. "Whatever you've—" Her voice died when she saw the determined look on Lena's face.

"I need your help. Again."

It took Lena five attempts to successfully fasten the clip at the top of her cloak. She slammed her hands down on the windowsill. Her palms throbbed against the splintered wood, but she only pressed down harder until her hands ceased their trembling.

She couldn't afford to be distracted. Not tonight. Not with everything going on. She had a means of dealing with Sorrel. Now she needed one for Alkus. As far as she was concerned, he'd confessed to making a grab at her position. He would never be ruler, but there were other ways he could be in control. She needed to get rid of him before that happened.

"You're going to break the wood if you squeeze any harder."

Lena relaxed her hands, pulling them away and turning once she had herself under control.

Aquila stared at her oddly, like she knew exactly what had been racing through Lena's head and didn't buy the calm and collected look on her face.

"Are you ready to go?" Lena asked before Aquila could say anything.

Aquila's eyes narrowed, but she nodded. She was wearing an outfit similar to Lena's: something dark that covered a lot of skin but wasn't heavy.

Lena heaved open the window, and the cool breeze of the night drifted inside, fluttering the curtains and the few strands of hair that had escaped from her braid. She flipped up her hood, securing it to make sure it wouldn't fall before climbing out of the window and setting foot on the roof. It was patchy and steep, but she wasn't worried. This was like second nature to her.

Aquila followed, her hood up as well. Lena purposely kept her back to Aquila, but she could still feel the sorcerer's heavy and questioning gaze, trying to pick her apart.

"Just like old times, right?" Lena sighed, her eyes roving over the horizon. The sun had set a half an hour ago, and The Lands was now painted in red. She allowed herself to return to her time on the run. Just for tonight. "Let's go, Quil."

She sprinted forward and leaped off the edge of the roof. The wind sailed against her face and rippled through her cloak as she flew through the air. Her body tightened, preparing for impact, and when her feet hit the roof tiles, none of them broke. She grinned and took off again, pumping her arms and legs to move faster. She jumped, waving her arms through the air to propel her forward. As soon as she hit the flat roof of the next building, she was rolling and popping up to her feet, scaling the next house. She kept moving. She needed to. From building to building she traveled, running and jumping and climbing, until she was near her destination.

She looked over the town, breathing hard but feeling so light. She found the house they were looking for, the one that belonged to the town head. It wasn't hard to find because town heads typically flaunted their abundance. They were still Cursed and weren't on the same level as Blessed, but they had more comforts, money, and privileges than any other Cursed. Each town had a town head put in place by the Blessed. They were typically hated by most because they weren't just assholes; they were traitors. They understood how difficult life was down here, but they still hoarded resources and accepted bribes from Blessed instead of helping the people they oversaw.

It was difficult to get a town head replaced. The Blessed hardly listened to the Cursed, and the town head used their money and influence to gain the support of prominent gangs and bribe enforcers to look the other way. And if they were replaced, the next one would probably be just as bad. Like everything else in the Lowlands, the political system—if you could even call it that—was corrupt and lacking. It made perfect sense that Alkus' money was going here.

The house was at the end of the street. Tall and wide. There was a second-story balcony from what she could see. Risky. She'd bet the town head had guards, and not just for-hire street muscle. She would also bet that there were locks on all the windows and doors. Blackout curtains too. Also a chimney—potentially their way inside.

She'd given Aquila a quick run-down as they were traveling to the Lowlands. She'd told the sorcerer that the paper Dugell had given her contained coordinates that led to a town head's house. They knew Alkus' money was going there. They didn't know why. So, tonight they had two objectives: to find out why and to steal proof of the money transfers. As long as they had the latter, Alkus' days were numbered. *Proof* was the main issue. She didn't have any proof of the past, but she would get proof for this. And this time, she would make sure it stuck. He wouldn't just get a slap on the wrist as punishment.

Cal moved closer, keeping her eyes out for any threats. She was *flying*. The ice in her lungs thawed and her chest burned with exhilaration. She didn't really care if anyone saw her. If they did, all they'd see was a dark blur anyway. No one could touch her like this. She was in control.

A hand snatched her wrist, dragging her to a halt and yanking her around.

"*What* is your problem?" Aquila snarled.

Cal tried to pull her arm away, but Quil wouldn't release her. Her lips curled into a snarl. "Nothing, but you'll become one if you don't let go of me."

Quil didn't listen. Did she ever?

"You're running away like a mad man is chasing you. You're being reckless. You know we can't."

"If you're reckless, you're dead."

Cal's brows furrowed. She didn't know where that memory had come from.

"Something's clearly bothering you."

Yeah, a lot of things, but that's hardly new.

"If you can't do this, say so."

"I can do this," Cal snapped. "I'm fine. I don't have a problem, and if I did, why would you care?"

It was a low blow, and maybe she would admit to herself that she wasn't in the best head space if she was in a better head space, but she wasn't, so she didn't.

Quil recoiled. For a moment, her expression was open and vulnerable, laid bare for Cal to see. But Cal's words didn't shut Quil up. They only spurred her along. Quil shook Cal using the hold she still had on her wrist.

"Why would I care? *Why would I care?*" She kept her voice low, but it cracked, allowing the frustration and disbelief to seep through. "Tides, I don't know why I keep coming down here for you—"

"Yes, you do," Cal interjected. "You know exactly why, but you won't tell *me* why."

That shut Quil up, which Cal had anticipated. Anything relating to her forgotten past seemed to do that.

Quil's grip loosened, and Cal pulled her wrist free, immediately turning away from her and toward the house.

"That's where we're going." Her voice sounded strange to her ears, too flat and forced. "We'll get in through the chimney, grab what we need to grab, and get out. There are likely guards inside. We need to take them out quickly and quietly to avoid drawing attention."

"Okay," Quil said easily. "So no Slayers?"

All the heat and emotion from moments ago had disappeared. She sounded focused and professional. But for Cal, the heat lingered.

Cal nodded. "No Slayers."

They moved quickly and carefully to the town head's house. Cal checked to make sure there wasn't a fire kindling underneath her before taking a deep breath of fresh air and lowering herself down the chimney. She tried to breathe as little as possible as she inched down the cramped, dirty flue. She got stuck once or twice and told herself not to panic.

When she finally reached the bottom, she was covered in soot, though it wasn't noticeable on her dark clothing. Quil climbed out after her, her face coated in a fine layer of the same black powder. They cleaned the soles of their boots and shook off any excess soot before moving through the house.

Quil took the lead while Cal dragged behind. Even though they were out of the chimney and away from the fireplace, the heat in her only grew. She rested her hand over her Imprint. It was no warmer than usual. A piece of soot got in her eye and when she rubbed it away, a lingering ache remained. Quil looked over her shoulder, but Cal waved her off.

Quil removed her gloves when they reached a corner, revealing the fine, dark lines along the back of her hand. Semi-transparent wisps of magic appeared in the air, swirling about Quil's fingers before shooting around the corner.

A moment later, Quil nodded. The coast was clear.

They slipped around the corner. The first footfall sent crippling tingles up Cal's legs and a wave of dizziness washed over her. She squeezed her eyes shut and shook her head. Only the throbbing behind her eyes remained.

They stopped at another corner and Quil held up two fingers. Two guards in the hall. Cal was surprised there were so few. Perhaps the town head had grown too comfortable.

Tendrils of magic danced around Quil's fingers again before slithering down the hall. A door flew open, and Cal peeked around the corner. The guards were walking away from them to investigate the sound. Cal and Quil saw their chance and moved quickly.

Cal snuck up behind one of the guards, but he sensed her before she could dig a dagger into his neck. He swiped out and she ducked, stepping in closer and head-butting him, which was the quickest move but not the best decision. The throbbing in her head immediately intensified. The guard staggered back with blood dripping from his nose, clearly not expecting that sort of hit.

Cal fought off the black spots that littered her vision and lunged forward. She slid right around the guard, aura flame licking over her arms and chest. He couldn't hold her back without getting himself burnt, so sealing a hand over his mouth to muffle his screams was rather easy. She stabbed him in the heart, and as soon as he stopped moving and making noise, she lowered his body to the floor.

She looked over at Quil who took out her own guard right then. Cal was about to make a comment about beating her when she felt something drip down her face. She touched her aching forehead, expecting to feel a bruise or some blood from head-butting the guard—that *really* had been stupid, though old habits die hard—but she only felt a bruise. No blood. That was coming from her nose. Her vision blackened again, and her balance faltered with it. Cal teetered to the side and caught herself on the wall. She barely rested her head against it, but it felt like she was banging her head on stone. A groan escaped her lips as she squeezed her eyes shut, trying to alleviate the sudden build-up of pressure behind her skull.

"Cal?" Quil called. Her muffled voice echoed in Cal's ears, like it was traveling through water to reach her. "Are you okay?"

She pinched the skin between her pointed finger and thumb, even though it had never worked, and it didn't work now. The ache in her head only grew. It was going to split her open. A high-pitched ringing pierced her eardrums. She tried to push herself up, but her body was heavy and uncooperative.

"*Fuck*," she breathed out.

Hands smoothed up her arms. One gripped her shoulder, the other her chin. The pain intensified when her head was tilted back and the cap of her skull pressed against the wood. A small cry escaped her lips.

"Shh, shh, shh." Quil placed her palm over Cal's lips. "You have to be quiet. Talk to me. Come on. Tell me what's happening."

She sounded almost panicked. Or maybe that was Cal; she definitely felt the panic. She didn't know what was wrong, and that only made everything worse. Her lips parted and she tried to say something, but any pressure, any movement, any change, multiplied the pain deep within her head.

She gritted her teeth. *You've dealt with worse. You're fine. Get up. Get up!*

She wouldn't let herself be beaten by a fucking headache. She was only faintly aware of noises down the hall as she reached for Quil's arm. Her eyes cracked open, only slightly. It was dark in the house and outside, but it was still too bright.

Quil cursed and then pulled Cal to her feet. The most violent wave of vertigo washed through her, and vomit rushed up her throat.

"Don't throw up. We need to move. Come on," Quil hissed.

She swallowed the sick back down. "No," she gasped, her raw throat screaming. "The ledger!"

She wouldn't leave without it, but she couldn't fight Quil in this condition. The sorcerer easily dragged her to a nearby window. The lock broke immediately under Quil's influence and the night air washed over Cal's face. It felt nice.

"Go!"

Quil all but pushed her out. It was only thanks to those survival instincts that had been instilled in Cal over the years that she didn't tumble off the roof and smash into the ground. Her hands grappled at the roofing, but she didn't move farther away from the window.

"What are you doing?" she hissed, ignoring the unpleasant pangs each word sent through her. "We need to get—"

Quil's hand snagged her collar, pulling her close until they were nearly nose to nose.

"Go, you fucking idiot," she snarled before pushing Cal away once again. And this time, she slammed the window shut.

Cal tried to yank it open, but Quil had repaired the lock so that it was perfectly latched on the inside. She cursed before climbing to the top of the house. The adrenaline had forced the worst of the pain to the back of her mind, but she still felt like she was wading through thick honey instead of air.

She ran to the chimney and was just about to climb back down it when a pool of light became visible at the bottom. A fire had just been started, likely Quil's doing to keep Cal from coming back. A noise of frustration left her throat.

You better fucking make it, she thought before turning her back on the town head's house and running.

She'd lost track of how many buildings she had leaped over, but she stopped a safe distance away and heaved herself over a ledge, dropping down behind it. Her body trembled from exertion and her headache returned in full force. She closed her eyes because keeping them open burned a path through the front of her skull. She might've fallen asleep. The next thing she remembered was Quil next to her.

Cal became alert as soon as she sensed her. A dagger fit into her hand, and that reminded her of the three she'd left behind.

"My daggers—"

Quil was already dropping them in front of her. "I'm used to cleaning up after you," she said.

Cal reached for her daggers and tucked them away with trembling hands. Sweat dripped down the back of her neck. "I don't . . . I don't know what's wrong," she admitted, wincing when another bolt of pain split through her head. Her vision darkened again, and this time it didn't return.

"Can you make it back?"

Cal grasped at her Imprint. It burned against her palm, even through all her layers of clothing. Her nose started bleeding again, and iron soaked into her tongue. The pain blooming in her skull spread, shoving aside her muscles and attacking every nerve in her body.

"*No*," she moaned.

Soft tendrils brushed over her, and for a second, everything felt better, as if the rubble that smothered her had been lifted.

But then it all came crashing down. The pressure was more than before. It squeezed her mind and her heart and her bones. She couldn't hear anything past the roaring in her ears. She couldn't see anything. She could only feel, and it was unbearable.

Her body gave into the pain, and Cal collapsed.

CHAPTER
FIFTY-THREE

Atreus was frozen in the mouth of the cave. He couldn't tear his eyes away from the humans. Was his mind playing tricks on him? He blinked and bit the inside of his cheek, but the figures in front of him didn't disappear.

A voice cut through the air. "What the *fuck?*"

Vanik stepped forward first, his face twisted, his abrasiveness masking his apprehension. "Is this some sort of sick joke?"

About a dozen people stood in front of them. They didn't appear shocked to see the firstborns, but when Vanik approached, they all shuffled and reached for the swords at their hips.

Atreus moved then and their attention snapped to him, almost all at once. Judah tightened his hold on Atreus' shirt and slid behind him.

"Easy," Atreus said, holding up his hands. "We're . . . not here to hurt you."

The words sounded odd, but they were genuine. He didn't *want* to hurt people, or things, but he would. Sometimes he *had* to. His Imprint heated in preparation. He hoped he didn't have to use it. There would be no going back if he did, and his Slayer could be difficult to control. He'd only let it out twice before.

One of the people said something, but in a language Atreus couldn't comprehend.

He shook his head. "We can't understand you."

And it was possible they couldn't understand him either.

Eventually, the people gave up trying to speak to them and simply turned around, looking over their shoulder before walking away. Atreus took that as an invite to follow.

He was aware that they could very well be walking into a trap, but what were they going to do if they stayed behind? He didn't want to wait for the *Te'Monai* to appear, and as far as he knew, they still needed to find the stone to get back. Maybe these people knew where it was.

"We're just going to follow them?" Vanik asked when Atreus took a step forward.

"Do you have a better idea?" Mila shot back.

Turned out he didn't because he moved after grumbling something under his breath.

They trailed behind the people of this realm, maintaining a safe distance from them. The tall and thick trees they walked through provided a perfect hiding spot for any attackers. Compared to the firstborns, the people of this realm were small in number. There had to be more of them somewhere.

The trees soon became sparse and then eventually disappeared. Nothing and no one jumped out at them. A gray castle sat on the edge of a cliff ahead, stretching toward the skies. Atreus couldn't look away from it, but it wasn't the castle's beauty that enraptured him. It was the stone's hum. He heard it clearly when he looked at the castle. The stone was up there.

The group brought them up the winding path of the cliffside and then inside the castle. They were taken to a circular space where four long halls met. A chandelier dangled over them, twinkling crystals draping from it. As suspected, other people were already there, waiting for them.

"Who is your leader?" a woman asked as she stepped forward. Based on her elaborate attire, how she carried herself, and how everyone else regarded her, she appeared to be the one in charge.

Atreus looked around. He was the only one who did. Everyone else was staring at him. Even Vanik.

"Look, I don't fucking like it, but people look up to you here."

After a few seconds of silence, Atreus cleared his throat and stepped forward.

The woman's eyes focused on him. "Come with me," she said and then disappeared down the hall to the right.

He hesitated before following, and like earlier, he stayed a few feet away, watching her, waiting for her hand to slither out from underneath her dress and grab something.

"You must be confused."

He didn't respond.

"I want to show you something."

Many hallways branched out from the one they walked down, but the two of them kept going straight until they reached a dead end. There were no doors at the end of the hall. No escape. Only an oval mirror with gold trim hanging on the wall, slightly smaller than him. She beckoned him closer.

He approached cautiously and stopped in front of the mirror, not quite understanding what she was trying to show him. He rarely saw his reflection. He rarely got the *chance* since there were hardly any mirrors in the Institute, but even when he did, he avoided looking. He wondered now, as the scream caught in his throat, if he avoided looking because, deep down, he knew what he would see. Staring back at him wasn't a human. It wasn't anything close. In the mirror, all he saw was a monster. A *Te'Monai*.

Atreus moved and the image in the mirror moved with him, the grisly features shifting.

"What . . . ?" His voice was barely a whisper.

What stood in front of him?

What kind of sorcery was this?

"It's you."

He shook his head. As did the image in front of him.

No. It can't be . . .

"It is. You've been afraid to look at yourself because you've always known what would greet you—the truth. You can't be afraid anymore, Atreus."

"What are you doing?" He forced the words out. They came straight from his chest. Strangled and weak. "How do you know my name?"

"Everyone knows your name."

He blinked, unable to look away from the monster in front of him. "What kind of sick game is this?"

"It's a game we've all been forced to play. For centuries. We're all just hopeless pawns. But *you*, Atreus, are the key."

Ice traveled up his arms and legs, settling somewhere deep in his chest. "That can't be true."

"It is the truth," she said. "Whether you choose to believe it or not is another matter." She stepped up behind him. Her reflection in the mirror was *her*. Tall, regal, and completely human. "I know you've been told many things. You don't believe all of them, but I wonder which truth you *will* believe."

Slowly, his reflection started to change. The *Te'Monai* in front of him grew shorter and skinnier until its form started to resemble that of a human's. A man's. He was older than Atreus and had different features, but when Atreus raised his left arm, so did the man in front of him.

"Who is that?"

"That's also you."

His brow furrowed and he cocked his head to the side. The man did the same. He was strong and hardened. He'd seen a lot and been through a lot. The soul resided in the heart, but many said the eyes were the windows to the soul. And the look in the man's eyes made Atreus take a step back.

Bells rang from overhead.

He jerked away from the mirror. The trance broke. A few seconds later, a scream pierced the air.

His heart dropped. No. *No.*

He spun around, glaring at the woman.

"What did you do?" he demanded. Heat unfurled through his body, spreading out from his Imprint. *"What did you do?"*

The woman appeared unperturbed by the fury lacing Atreus' voice and the violence occurring nearby, and that nearly sent him over the edge. He would've let his Slayer out there if she hadn't turned her back on him.

"I have not done anything that hasn't already been done," she said as she walked away. "You will meet my sisters soon."

He stared after her, debating if he should chase her down and force answers out of her. He quickly cast that thought aside. His friends were more important.

He ran down the hall. The woman was already gone. She must've slipped into one of the connecting hallways or the dozens of doors. The hallway she'd taken him down was so long that he couldn't even make out what was going on at the end of it even though it was a straight shot. The dread grew exponentially the closer he became, especially after he saw the blood.

Atreus skidded into the main hall. The fighting was in full force. The people of this realm had their swords drawn and were cutting down the firstborns. Slayers were out, racing across the space in bright blurs of color, adding to the bloodshed as they ripped people apart. And not all of their victims were of this realm. After being dormant for so long, the Slayers were harder to control. They wanted blood, and they didn't care who they got it from. But not all the bloodshed could be blamed on them. Humans were killing humans.

His trembling hands hovered over his Imprint. Was he really about to do this? There were no *Te'Monai* here, no monsters . . . right?

He caught sight of Finn. He was still with Judah, holding onto him and protecting him.

Something out of the corner of Atreus' eye stole his attention. He twisted out of the way right as a sword sliced through the space he'd occupied only a moment before.

Atreus quickly regained his balance, and his gaze locked onto a human from this realm. Their slate gray eyes were filled with determination as they charged at Atreus again, the blade of their sword flashing under the chandelier lights.

Stop! Atreus screamed. *STOP!*

But it didn't work.

Panic descended upon him as the sword cut through the air, aiming for his neck. That was all Atreus saw. Because after that he just *reacted*. Whatever had held him back earlier evaporated. He didn't even have time to think. He just did.

He let it go.

When his Slayer tore out of him, he couldn't breathe. The sensation was distinct, like it had taken one of his limbs with it, something important, but everything was still there. He stumbled, his balance off, his throat pinched, and his vision blurred.

This all happened in a split second, and as soon as his Slayer was in this realm, it tackled the person about to impale Atreus with their sword.

They immediately started screaming as their flesh melted, and Atreus wasn't quick enough to pull his Slayer back before it sank its claws into the person's chest. Atreus closed his eyes in defeat. His Slayer could have that single prize, but no more. He couldn't let it lose control.

His Slayer finished its meal in seconds. Its anticipation raced through him when it smelled the blood in the air, but he held onto it, even when it fought against him, pushing at the boundaries he'd set up. The ache behind his eyes strengthened alongside his grip.

Attack only *the people of this realm,* he commanded. *Don't kill anyone. Only incapacitate.*

His Slayer snarled in displeasure. They hunted to kill. They didn't leave survivors. It was more difficult for them to do so, against their nature.

Do not kill anyone, he repeated, his voice unyielding. *Anyone* else.

When he was sure his Slayer would obey, he loosened his mental grip and took a figurative step back. He could feel the tether that linked them together. The scale was balanced. All was well.

The ringing in his ears stopped and the discomfort afflicting his body settled, morphing into something intoxicating. His hands shook for an entirely different reason now.

Atreus wasted no time in running through the thick of the battle to get to Finn and Judah. He spotted a discarded sword on the ground, a severed hand still wrapped around the hilt. He grimaced and kicked aside the warm appendage, snatching the sword for himself.

Finn had his Slayer out and seemed to be in control. His Slayer kept anyone from getting too close, but it let Atreus pass.

He latched onto Finn's arm. "Mila?"

"I saw her just a second ago!" Finn shouted over the noise. "She was fine. She had a grip on her Slayer."

Atreus looked around, but he couldn't see anything past the barrage of Slayers, bodies, and swords.

He pulled Finn and Judah down a hall, farther away from the battle. He knew Mila could take care of herself. She was the most resourceful of the three, but he didn't like the thought of leaving her behind. He told his Slayer to find and help her.

"I need to find the stone," Atreus told Finn as soon as they were in the clear. Nowhere was safe, but the hallways were considerably less busy. Anyone who approached them was interceded by Finn's Slayer.

Finn nodded. "Go."

Atreus took off running, not knowing exactly where he was going. He tried to focus and find the hum he'd heard earlier. He picked up on it a few seconds later.

The familiar buzzing washed over him, guiding him down the winding halls. It grew stronger the closer he got.

After taking too many turns to count, he skidded to a halt in front of an ordinary door. The humming sound was at its crescendo, so loud and powerful that it was nearly disorienting.

He ripped the door open and stepped inside and was faced with . . . his reflection. Dozens of them. It was the human one. The person that was not him was staring at him from a hundred different angles.

It was a room full of mirrors. And somewhere in the middle of this all sat the stone.

The door slamming shut behind him was what forced him to move. The firstborns were fighting for their lives out there. He needed to hurry.

The eyes of the man in the mirror moved with him as he looked around the room, so he was always looking himself in the eye. To say it was unnerving would be an understatement. So he kept his eyes low as he shuffled farther into the room. He slid his feet along the floor and outstretched his hands to feel around for any obstructive objects. He inched himself around the mirrors that way for a while until the door was out of sight when he turned around. All he saw were more images of himself. No, not him.

Focus. You have to focus.

His heart hammered against his ribs. The thought of getting lost here crossed his mind, as did drowning among his harrowing reflections. But he had a way out, an invisible string that connected him to the stone.

He tried to push the anxious thoughts aside and *listen*, but then he accidentally caught sight of the man in the mirror watching him with his dark, weighted eyes.

What do you want? he nearly asked aloud. *What do you want with me?*

The woman's words from earlier made no sense, but he couldn't reflect on them now.

The man in front of him disappeared as Atreus turned a corner. In the man's place stood a pedestal with the stone sitting on top.

He sprinted forward. His hand closed around the stone and suddenly he was back in the Institute, sprawled across the cold floor of the cavern. His Imprint was a hot brand on his skin, and his Slayer was locked behind it, back in its realm.

Prophet Silas stopped in front of him, his shiny boots only inches away from Atreus' face. He looked down at Atreus with a stoic yet severe expression. "Do you get it now? Did you see what you wanted to see?" His words were both flat and patronizing.

Atreus clenched his jaw and dropped his head to the ground, thinking of the view that had greeted him in the mirror.

No. No, he didn't.

CHAPTER
FIFTY-FOUR

Lena woke up to a pounding headache and a stiff body. She winced as she slowly opened her eyes and took in the dim room around her. The familiar wooden walls and colorful, soft decorations told her she was in the cabin and not the palace.

She sat up, hissing between her teeth as she did so. She checked all of her limbs, and then her Imprint. As far as she could tell, there was nothing wrong with it.

Her latest memories resurfaced—her and Aquila sneaking into the town head's house, the pain, and her passing out on a roof.

She didn't know what exactly had come over her and how it'd taken her down so quickly. It'd felt like the worst migraine imaginable and affected her entire body. She still felt its lingering effects. Her fuzzy mind and heavy limbs forced her to move slowly as she tossed the quilt aside and pushed herself to her feet. She wore loose pants and a long sleeve shirt, and she smelled fairly decent, all signs of sweat and soot gone from her skin, meaning that someone had bathed and dressed her while she was unconscious. An insatiable itch began to build under her skin.

It was probably someone you knew. You're at the cabin. You're safe. You're fine.

She scratched at her neck as she left her room. The cabin was quiet. Ira's room was dark, his door closed. She ventured downstairs, keeping her hand on the railing for support. With the state she was currently in, stumbling was a possibility, and if she tripped, there would be no catching herself.

Soft voices trickled into her ears. Male voices. Two of them. They were coming from the back of the house. A breeze flowed toward her as she reached the bottom of the stairs and turned around the corner. The back door was open. She brushed her fingers over her Imprint as she quietly approached the doorway, her feet rocking from heel to toe. Her Imprint heated as per usual, letting her know that she could rely on her Slayer if she needed to.

" . . . just needs some rest."

"Her Majesty needs more than that. She's sick."

She stopped a few feet away from the doorway. The voices belonged to Cowen and Mikhail.

"The physicians didn't understand her affliction. That doesn't make her sick. She'll be back on her feet soon. There's no need to keep her here."

Keep her here? Physicians had seen her? Then she'd been out for a while.

Mikhail sighed. "I don't doubt that Her Majesty will recover quickly, but . . . there are other matters regarding her to be concerned about . . ."

"What are you implying?" Cowen asked stiffly.

Mikhail lowered his voice further. "I saw what she was wearing that night. It begs the question of her whereabouts and what she was doing. And why you weren't with—"

"I knew where she was," Cowen cut in, his voice steel. "So did my guards. She was safe."

Liar. Even now, after she ditched him *again*, he was protecting her.

"With the recent activity in the Lowlands and the killings starting back up, I was only worried—"

"As was I, Grand Prophet. But she is safe and sound. There is no need to worry."

"She may be now," Mikhail agreed. "But what about when she finds out about her attendants? These past few days have been stressful for her. This news will be as well. She should take her time recuperating down here. Ira will keep things in order until she returns."

Lena chose that moment to step out onto the porch.

Cowen's face shifted in mild surprise when he spotted her. "Kalena."

Mikhail turned around, looking even more startled to see her.

She held his gaze. "What happened to my attendants?"

Mikhail and Cowen exchanged a glance, which only irritated her further.

She stepped forward. "Tell me."

"They were killed," Cowen said before Mikhail could. He looked back at her, his expression apologetic. "Their bodies were found in the servant's hall. I'm sorry, Kalena."

Her legs weakened under her. "All of them?"

"No. Jhai is well." Cowen glanced at Mikhail again, as if he was worried about what he might say.

She took a step to the side and rested her hand on the back of a chair for support.

They were dead. *Killed.* Eloise. Louelle. Odette. Devla. Renetta. All dead. Because of her.

"When did this happen?"

"Two days ago," Cowen supplied.

Two days?

"How long was I unconscious?"

"... Two days."

They'd been killed the night she went to the Lowlands with Aquila. Jhai hadn't been at the palace then, out doing what Lena had instructed instead—getting rid of more of Lena's enemies. Indirectly.

Lena had more questions, but she couldn't ask them while Mikhail was here. She looked between the two of them and stood straighter. "We need to go back."

"Back?" Mikhail raised a brow and pulled his hands from his robes. "You need to rest, Your Majesty."

"I spent two days resting," she said impatiently. "I need to return to the palace. As queen, that's where I belong."

Mikhail's smile was lacking. "You need more rest. The council has discussed this matter and agreed. With the killings of Blessed, those on the council, and now your attendants, it seems likely that you are the next target. We were discreet in moving you here. Not many know of this place. The Sacred Guard and additional palace guards have been placed around the perimeter for your safety."

"I can protect myself—"

"You are to remain here," Mikhail said swiftly as if he anticipated her reply.

They'd already made their decision. Again. They had the steel bars in place and the key was miles away.

"Five days," he insisted. "Take this time to mourn and recover. Return as queen."

No more mishaps, he was saying. *No more fits. Or we'll lock you up again.*

Alkus had something to do with this—her attendants. She just *knew* it. He had threatened her in his study. And then disaster had unraveled, and she'd been dragged under by some mysterious cause. She hadn't touched the tea in his study. She hadn't touched anything. Nonetheless, she was exactly where he wanted her: out of the way but still alive, so he could still rule in her place.

Mikhail had said that Ira would keep things in order until she returned, but she hadn't seen him in days. Had that been another lie told in an attempt to appease her?

Whatever the case, it was abundantly clear that Mikhail had chosen his side.

~

COWEN TOLD her she'd spent the past two days sleepwalking and battling nightmares. She had been in and out of consciousness ever since Aquila dragged her back to the Highlands. Cowen had found them quickly, already having been out in search of her. He took control of the situation while Aquila unwillingly fled so the enforcers and guards wouldn't know of her involvement. Lena's attendants' bodies had been discovered only an hour before. In those moments of stress and uncertainty, she was moved to the Lowlands after the palace physicians looked at her. They didn't know what had happened to her. No one did, including herself.

And her attendants hadn't been the only deaths as of late. Jhai had done her job and gotten rid of members of the Lorrantoa and Spevkov family. Nell had helped Lena with this. It'd been in motion before she found out about their relationship with Cowen and Cora. Her attendants' deaths had looked like an attack from someone on the outside, so they blended in with all the others, sans the missing hearts. But that didn't matter. The council was juggling too many things at once, and with these recent deaths and her absence, they barely reached quota.

"I need to get word to Jhai. She isn't safe in the palace."

Cowen nodded. "She was given a leave of absence. She's back with her family."

Home wasn't necessarily safe for her either, but it was better than the palace.

"Ira?" she asked hopefully.

The gradual fall of Cowen's face was answer enough.

She shook her head before he could say anything. "Forget it."

She slipped off the kitchen stool and headed for the stairs. She didn't know what she was going to do during house arrest for the next *five days*, but she wasn't going to stay downstairs with Cowen. She wasn't ready. Not yet.

Cowen didn't say anything as she disappeared up the stairs. She stopped at the top, unsure of where to go, what to do. There weren't many options. Her room or the small sitting room. When she looked in the direction of the latter, she was reminded of Ira, so she went into her room and buried herself under the quilt again.

She didn't think she was tired, but sleep took her quickly.

DEAD BODIES LITTERED *the ground at her feet. About half a dozen of them. Cal had been staring at them for the past ten minutes ever since she removed their masks. They were just kids. Younger than herself.*

It wasn't supposed to be this way. This run was supposed to be in and out. They had entered the tavern, paid off the barmaid to point them in the direction they needed to go in, waited it out, and then slipped into the adjacent room to collect their target.

They didn't expect the extra hired guards.

Cal did what she was trained to do: she protected herself first and secured the target second. That had led to the death of the six kids at her feet.

She felt something over her shoulder. Her heart skipped a beat as she spun, aiming her dagger at the attacker's throat. A hand caught her wrist and legs trapped hers so she couldn't kick. The hand squeezed her wrist until she was forced to release the dagger, but by then, she'd recognized her attacker and relaxed slightly.

"You're going to hurt yourself with the way you're swinging knives around," Julian said. *"What have I taught you?"*

Cal yanked herself out of Julian's grip. He wasn't involved in this run. He hardly ever got involved, but he was almost always available during them. Cal couldn't see Quil, so she suspected that she had run off to get Julian after seeing the mess Cal had made.

"I killed them," she said, her voice dull. "All of them. I don't know why I didn't knock them out. I was just reacting and—"

"And you did exactly what you should have," Julian said. He nudged one of the bodies with his boot. "It's a cruel realm out here. You steal or you starve. You kill or you're killed. These kids knew the risk."

"It doesn't matter!" Cal exclaimed while swiping her arm out. "Things shouldn't be this way! I didn't—I don't want my first kill to be like this!"

She wouldn't forget it. Julian had told them that too. Their first kill would stick with them decades later. Their faces would haunt them, and the memory would always be crystal clear.

"Cal," Julian said slowly, brows creased under his hat as he watched her face carefully for any sort of reaction, "this wasn't your first kill."

She frowned and glanced at the bodies, shaking her head. "No, it's . . . "

Her voice died when she saw the look on his face. It was the look of someone who was treading carefully. Not quite pity. But it was him throwing something out there, testing her, and waiting. He'd never looked at her like that before.

∾

LENA WOKE SWIFTLY, scrambling up in bed. Her throat twisted, a strangled scream trying to rip its way out. Her heart slammed against her ribcage and her skin was on fire. She threw the covers off and looked down at her arms and legs. No blood. Her shaking hands slid over her body. No injuries either. Her pulse was thrumming, but it was fine. She was fine.

The door swung open and Lena tensed, reaching for the dagger she'd hidden under her bedside table, but she stopped when she realized it was only Cowen in the doorway. He had a dagger in his hand, night clothes on, and was looking around the room for any sort of intruder.

The tension seeped out of her body. She slid back on the bed and drew her arms close. Cowen quickly realized there was no one else in the room and that her panic had come from a nightmare.

So this was what he'd meant. These nightmares . . . they were too real. Too specific. They were memories. Were all of them? Was that what she was battling? She imagined what she must've looked like while sleepwalking—caught in a panic but up on her feet. Cowen had seen that and dealt with that. With her.

"I'm fine," she said. Her voice sounded feeble and scratchy, her throat sore—as if she'd been screaming while she was asleep. Surely not. Cowen would've come sooner. "It was just a bad dream."

Strain no longer lined Cowen's form, but he still looked troubled. "Okay. Do you want to talk about it?"

She shook her head.

"Do you want some sleep elixir?"

She shook her head again. "Go back to your room. I'm going back to sleep."

She pulled the covers over her head and curled up on her side. Her door closed, and a few seconds later, a door down the hall opened and closed. She sat up and scooted back until her shoulders hit the headboard. She glanced at the spot next to her, empty and cold.

Going off like this without any sort of warning wasn't like Ira. He could take care of himself—she knew that—but it didn't stop her from worrying.

COWEN UNDERSTOOD her and what she needed, so he gave her space. He had to stay in the house for her *protection*—to make sure someone didn't break in and she didn't sneak out—but he kept to the guest room or the library for hours at a time so she could roam the house.

She sat at the dining room table, nibbling on a cracker since she'd been too sour to actually cook lunch, when she heard the creak of a floorboard behind her.

The tightening of her muscles was involuntary, but she quickly relaxed when she heard the shuffling. She figured it was just Cowen trying not to disturb her as he quietly moved through the house.

That was until the presence moved directly behind her.

She stood quickly, her chair scraping against the floor. The butter knife fit into her palm easily and she turned on the intruder, ready to jab the blade into their—

"Ira?" Her grip on the knife loosened and she looked over him, noting the blood and the bruises. "What happened?"

She naturally careened toward him, her hands hovering in the space between them. His hair was in disarray, the waves falling forward to shield his eyes. She ducked her head, trying to catch his gaze, but Ira kept his chin down, his shoulders slumped. Though, the purple bruise on his jaw stood out starkly.

"Shhh. Just . . . bring me to bed," he requested softly.

For a moment, she didn't move. She could only stare at him in suspended disbelief. She'd never seen Ira this . . . worn down. In her mind, he always seemed invincible, which was a ridiculous thought because he was mortal too. He'd been hurt before.

"Yeah," she said, her voice equally as soft. She nodded and stepped toward him. "Yeah, of course."

She took one of his hands and wrapped his other arm across her shoulders. Scrapes littered his knuckles and he hissed when her fingers pressed against his side. The questions could wait until she got him in her room.

She lowered him onto her bed and hurried to shut the door. When she turned back around, his elbows were on his knees, his fingers knotted in his hair.

"Ira . . . ?" she called out carefully.

He didn't show any sign that he heard her. He didn't move or make a noise.

The horrible feeling that had gripped her when she first spotted him was only growing, as was her list of questions.

Where have you been?
Why did you run away so suddenly?
Why didn't you tell me where you were going?
What happened to you?
Why are you here now?

"Ira?" she said again, her voice stronger.

Nothing.

She bit the inside of her cheek and headed for the washroom. There was a med kit somewhere in here. Ira was lying on his side when she stepped back into her room.

"Get up. Take your shirt off."

He rolled over slightly so she could see one of his eyes. The dark smudges under it told her he hadn't been sleeping well, or at all.

"I'm not in the mood," he murmured.

The panic rolling through her did nothing to calm her nerves, and the mystery of the situation didn't help.

"Get up," she said again. Then pleaded, "Ira."

He sat up and took off his shirt. His movements were stiffer than normal, likely due to the scattering of bruises across his chest and abdomen. She looked him over in his entirety, taking note of every injury or sign that screamed *wrong!* His eyes were dull and tired, knuckles split and bloody. He had a bruise on his cheek, a busted lip, and a bruise on his jaw. The skin stretched over his ribs contained the worst of the bruising. All of his injuries must be fairly recent, or they wouldn't be bothering him this much.

Her lips parted, a dozen questions perched right behind them, but she snapped her mouth shut and got to work. She sat next to him on the bed and opened the kit. One of his hands covered hers.

"Don't. They're just bruises. They won't even bother me in a few hours."

He was right, but she wanted to do something to help. She brushed his hand aside and sifted through the kit.

"There's salve. It'll make you feel better."

"Save it for something more important—"

"No," she said sharply, cutting him off. "*You* are important."

He stayed quiet then, choosing not to argue with her further.

She grabbed the jar of salve and looked over him. "What's comfortable for you?"

He wordlessly lay down on his back and stretched his legs out in front of him, his movements slow.

Lena moved just as carefully as she straddled his hips. "Okay?"

He nodded, his eyes fixed on her face. They remained there as she unscrewed the lid, dipped her fingers into the salve, and began to spread a thin layer of it over his bruises.

None of his injuries were serious, but that hardly soothed her concerns. There were too many other things that worried her. Like the fact that he'd shown up out of the blue, wounded and muted, after days of absence and silence, *after leaving with no warning whatsoever.*

"What happened?" she finally dared to ask again as her fingers gently swiped over his discolored skin.

"I got into a fight."

The corners of her lips tugged downward. "Obviously."

Silence fell between them again, and she couldn't take it. Was this how he'd felt at the beginning when she kept shutting him out?

"Ira . . . talk to me. You're worrying me," she said honestly. "You left without a word. I heard nothing from you *for days*, but I still covered for you at the council meetings, at the trials. I thought . . . "

She'd thought he would've at least come back once he found out about her incident in the Lowlands. But he had . . . hadn't he? He was here now, nearly three days later.

"I had no idea where you were, and so many things happened while you were gone—"

His hand covered hers and she realized she was pressing down too hard on his skin.

She went to pull her hand back. "I'm sorry. I didn't mean—"

But she swallowed her words when Ira held her hand tighter and yanked her forward. He twisted out of the way so they lay next to each other, their heads ducked in close.

His eyes slipped closed. "I know," he said simply, quietly. Every word he'd spoken since arriving sounded like it was taking more energy out of him than he had left, and part of her felt bad for drawing out these answers, but another part of her needed to hear them. "I heard about everything that happened. I came back as soon as I could."

"Where were you?" She raised herself on an elbow. "What happened?"

"I tried," he said, his voice cracking. He whispered so quietly she almost thought he was talking to himself. "I tried to fix things, but it didn't work."

Alarmed, she moved closer to him and ran her hand through his hair, trying to pull him in.

Ira pushed her away.

She sat there, unsure of how to react. He'd never pushed her away before.

He curled further in on himself, his face nearly disappearing into the pillow. "They hurt."

"What?"

"They hurt," he exhaled, his body sagging against the sheets.

"What hurts?" She sat up further, looking over him, wondering if she'd missed something.

"My scars."

Her shoulders lowered, and she slowly looked over him again, more closely. Under the bruises, hidden by the shadows and the stretch of skin over his muscles, were his scars. Some were small and a few shades lighter than his skin. Others were much larger and cut across the bends of his body like an angry burn.

She swallowed the lump in her throat and slowly reached a hand out. He tensed when her fingers brushed over his forearm, over the handful of tiny scars that rested there. She paused, waiting, but he didn't say anything. He melted as her fingers traced his scars. She closed her eyes and tried not to count the lines of raised skin. She drew shapes between them, connecting one scar to another like stars forming constellations in the night sky.

"I'm right here, Ira."

He mumbled something.

"What?"

"No," he said louder, his voice rusty. "You should go."

Her fingers paused again, and she opened her eyes. She didn't want to disregard his wishes or push his boundaries, but she wanted him to know she wasn't going to give up on him this easily. Even if they weren't married, she would choose to spend the rest of her life by his side. She grabbed his hand with hers—the one that had the rings on it. She made sure he could feel the cold press of them.

"I'm not leaving you," she whispered. Her breath washed over his hair. From this close, she could see some dried blood on his waves. Her eyes stung, so she squeezed them shut again.

"Let me stay." Her voice cracked and her chest split open. "You're safe here."

He mumbled something again that she wasn't able to make out. But he didn't push her away or tell her to leave. He let her hold him as her fingers brushed over his scars.

∼

THEY HAD FALLEN asleep in each other's arms and slept for nearly twelve hours.

Ira was already moving better in the morning. He smoothly slipped on his shirt without so much as a hiss of pain.

"You don't have to leave," she told him as she sat up in bed.

He paused on his way to the door, his shoulders tight and his hands flexing at his sides. He spun on his heel and came back to her, dipping his head to press a firm kiss against her lips.

"I'm sorry," he said once he pulled away. "For leaving so suddenly without saying anything and not being there when you needed me." His jaw clenched and his eyes flashed up to hers. "I want to be there for you, and it's tearing me up inside because right now that means being up in the Highlands, in the palace, instead of being down here with you, in our home."

She deflated. Right. Ira had to hold down the fort up there. She put a smile on her face, hoping it looked somewhat genuine. Ira's expression told her otherwise.

"You have to go back because you're the only one in the palace I can trust. According to the laws, you rule in my stead. Without you there, Alkus will start calling the shots. He's managed to convert Mikhail to his side."

Ira was still staring at her intently. When she caught his gaze again, he kissed her once more, long and slow. He pulled away but stayed close. Then, smooth and unflinching, he asked, "Is it time to kill him? Alkus?"

Her eyes were still on his lips. "Maybe."

"I could do it for you. If you want," he murmured.

Rather than answer, she leaned forward and Ira let her kiss him. She kept it soft. The night before was still fresh in her mind. He didn't break easily, but he still deserved to be treated with care.

"You have to go," she repeated. "But not right at this moment."

She ended up convincing him to stay for another hour.

CHAPTER
FIFTY-FIVE

Lena softly knocked on the door with her bruised knuckles.
The rustling on the other side paused momentarily, and then a low voice spoke. "Who is it?" Her voice was tinged with pain, the syllables of her words broken up.

Lena rested her forehead on the rough wood of the door. "It's me."

The rustling resumed and then the telltale click of the lock sounded. She opened the door and took in the scene in front of her. Bloody washrags were strewn about the cramped washroom, and streaks of blood painted the sink basin. A poorly stashed med kit was balancing on the ledge that was too thin to be called a countertop, its contents spread out wherever they would fit. Aquila leaned against the sink, her shirt off and her expression twisted in discomfort. She held a white bandage over a wound on her side.

Lena did a quick sweep of the rest of Aquila's body. Minor injuries. She wasn't at risk of bleeding out. The state of the washroom made Aquila's wounds appear worse than they were.

"Let me help," she said as she closed the door behind her. They had done this enough times—patched up each other's injuries—so Aquila didn't argue.

Lena inched forward in the tight room, trying to avoid the bloody washrags. Aquila shifted, giving her enough space to stand in front of her. Lena took over holding the bandage from Aquila, who hissed when it was pulled back.

"It's not even that bad," Lena teased.

Aquila sneered at her. "How about I give you a matching one and you can tell me how much it doesn't hurt."

Lena smirked but didn't respond. She worked silently for the most part. Aquila didn't like to be talked through these sorts of things. She'd snap and accuse Lena of coddling her, and then she'd later grumble an apology into her pillow.

"Is there anything else?" Lena asked as she finished tending Aquila's upper half.

"Only one on my thigh," Aquila said, and she shifted again.

She looked more comfortable now that Lena had dressed some of her wounds, and the furrows between her brows were almost gone. Very rarely did they all completely disappear. Aquila scowled more than anyone Lena knew.

Lena spotted the patch of blood on the outside of Aquila's thigh. She slapped her hand against Aquila's other leg gently. "Strip."

Aquila smirked at her and pushed away from the sink, forcing Lena to take a step back. They were close in height, so with Aquila only inches away, Lena was forced to stare directly into her eyes. They were dark, but not as dark as hers. Sometimes, when Aquila stood in the light, Lena could see the lighter threads of gold in her eyes. She wanted to reach out and push Aquila's hair out of her face. They both had the same horrible boyish haircut, but it was becoming overgrown, falling over their ears and into their eyes and nearly reaching the base of their neck. Julian would make them cut it again soon.

"If you wanted to get me naked, all you had to do was ask," Aquila said.

The grin stayed on Lena's face as Aquila bent down to remove her pants.

The wound on her thigh also wasn't anything severe. She'd gotten nicked in the leg by a dagger with a nasty blade while they were out running an errand. Lena disinfected it first. With alcohol, because that was the only antiseptic Julian cared to keep around. Aquila's thigh tightened at the burning sensation.

"Easy," Lena murmured as she laid her hand on Aquila's bare skin.

Aquila didn't bite her head off for it this time.

Lena quickly applied any appropriate ointments they had before dressing the wound as she had with the others. By the time she was finished, Aquila's eyelids were drooping. Lena sent her to bed and stayed behind to clean up the mess. She'd gotten off much easier on this errand, and she knew Aquila had something to do with that. Lena also stayed behind because she needed a bath. Aquila had washed up before. Lena didn't bother trying for hot water. They almost never had it. She thoroughly washed herself, scrubbing off dirt and blood.

When she stepped out of the tub, she wrapped one of the clean towels around her and went into the room across the hall. It was small and cramped—but hers. Dropping the towel, she quickly slipped on underwear and a large shirt that nearly fell to her knees. When she turned toward her bed, she was unsurprised to find Aquila curled up in it. They each had their own room, but they didn't like to stay in it alone.

The events of the day began to weigh on her. She was ready to sleep, even though that sometimes wasn't too pleasant either. But it was better with Aquila. She crawled under the covers and drew her knees to her chest.

Aquila's eyes were closed, but she must've felt the movement. "Cold?" she murmured into the pillow she'd brought over from her room.

Lena didn't say anything, but a moment later, Aquila turned around. She wrapped her arms around Lena, pulling her close. Their foreheads touched, and their warm breaths mingled in front of their faces. Lena allowed herself to close her eyes.

"You always run cold," Aquila huffed.

"Maybe I run at a normal temperature and you just run hot," Lena retorted, snuggling deeper into Aquila's arms. Aquila hadn't bothered putting clothes over her undergarments.

"Mhm, is that what you think? Regardless, how convenient for you," Aquila said quietly. "I'm starting to think you're using me for my body heat."

Lena laughed softly. "You caught me. It's your warmth, not your personality and life skills, that enamored me."

Aquila was silent, but Lena could feel the tension in the air. She opened her eyes, looking at Aquila in question.

"It's nothing," she said, her eyes looking anywhere but Lena's face. "I was just thinking."

Lena knew exactly what Aquila meant. She was thinking about before. The past. How different her life would be now if things hadn't unfolded the way they had. Lena only knew this because they'd both had these thoughts before. They had agreed it was a dangerous path to go down. A path filled with what-ifs that could pull you under, into a realm of gloom, before you even realized what was happening. They had also agreed that if one of them did chase it, the other was supposed to pull them back.

Lena raised one of her hands and cupped Aquila's cheek, forcing her to meet her gaze. "Stop thinking. It's not your strong suit."

Aquila scoffed and brought up her own hand, knocking Lena's aside. "Fuck you."

Lena laughed and rolled over onto her other side. Aquila followed her, pressing her front to Lena's back. Aquila's arms were still wrapped around her. Lena threaded her fingers through Aquila's and brought their linked hands to her mouth, pressing a kiss against Aquila's knuckles.

"Have you thought about it lately?"

Lena was glad Aquila couldn't see her face. She considered herself a decent liar, but not around Aquila. She had thought about it lately. She still had nightmares about it. Even years later. She kept seeing her family's bodies on the furniture and Ezra's panicked face. She saw Tuck and the rain and the Slayer. She thought about Ira too. About what had happened to him. It ate away at her.

Hope was a dangerous thing down here. One had to use it sparingly, or it lost its power. She hoped Ira was still alive. And if he was, she hoped he would keep fighting like she was. Would this ever stop? Would she ever not think about it?

"Sometimes, but it doesn't matter." She swallowed the bitter taste on her tongue. "Thinking about it is pointless. It won't change anything."

Lena gripped Aquila's fingers tighter. Lips pressed against her shoulder. Neither of them said anything else about it. They stayed silent until they fell asleep in each other's arms.

CHAPTER
FIFTY-SIX

"What did you think of the book?" Mila asked when they met after he finished it.

He shrugged and handed the book back to her. "It was useful, but it raised more questions than it answered."

So had the last realm. Atreus didn't know what to make of it. He thought about it every night before bed, but he didn't get any closer to figuring out this *next stage*.

He resumed the nightly meetings, mostly because he could tell Tolar was close to the end of his rope. The last Outing had spooked him too, and he wanted to get out as soon as possible. His threats had become more worrisome. Atreus didn't have any news—not any that he would share with Tolar, at least—so they essentially reiterated what they already knew and threw out new ideas at their *meeting*. And by *they*, he meant him, Finn, Judah, and Tolar. Vanik and Weylin were still throwing a fit.

Vanik was in an even worse mood than before. During their last Outing, someone's Slayer had gone for him. It'd clawed his face, leaving behind a wound that ran from his temple to his chin. If he hadn't twisted away in time, the claw would've ripped through his skull. But he'd walked away from that encounter after his own Slayer got involved, which wasn't something many people could say. Slayer attacks were quick and ruthless. Shortly after their return, Miss Anya had told him his injury would scar. Vanik walked into the sleeping hall later that night, the left side of his face bandaged, and demanded to know which weak-minded idiot had the Slayer that had maimed his face. Unsurprisingly, no one answered. Everyone had been giving him a wide berth since then, save for Harlow and Weylin of course.

Atreus didn't want to face Vanik's wrath either; it would be harder to talk some sense into him while he was this worked up. But he needed to get over himself soon and come back. That was the only option. He had to see that. Ditching Tolar would only endanger them.

"You haven't told anyone else, have you?" Finn asked Tolar during one of their meetings after a lull in conversation.

Tolar's head jerked up, and he looked at the three of them, blinking slowly. "No," he said. "No, I haven't told anyone."

Finn nodded but caught Atreus' eye when Tolar looked away.

There was no way to tell if Tolar was telling the truth.

The days passed by slowly with no announcement of another Outing. They had longer breaks, which was nice because that meant they spent less time fighting for their lives.

However, Atreus felt like he was wasting this added time. He'd scoured the library from one side to the other and hadn't found anything useful. The questions in his mind about the stones, the prophet's plan, and the realms haunted him at all hours of the day, but his thoughts were especially loud at night, which was another reason why he'd resumed the nightly meetings.

Judah had taken it upon himself to step up lately. He was nimble on his feet and small, so he could get from place to place much quicker than any of them, which was useful when they needed information relayed to Mila.

When Judah first told him that he wanted to help, Atreus felt . . . *wrong*. His stomach sank and alarms blared in his head. Everyone had to fight to survive, and that didn't begin and end in those other realms. Judah was growing braver and smarter with each Outing. He was maturing and realizing the stakes. Judah wanted to do his share of the work and learn and *live*.

Part of Atreus was relieved and proud, but another part of him was angry that Judah had to grow up so quickly to survive. Worry was also there, and that scared him. He had no reason to deny Judah's offer aside from his own feelings, but even those were conflicting. In the end, he'd said yes because he hadn't been able to face what saying no meant. But there were conditions. Judah could relay information, could cover for them, but he could *not* sneak around and spy on the prophets like Weylin had. That was a logical line drawn in the sand. A sensible limit that one could say was made without the involvement of feelings.

Nothing looked promising. They were at an impasse. Atreus was being stretched thin, forced to stand still and take the punches. And if he snapped, everything he was holding together would crumble.

He really needed to get some sleep, but his night terrors had become more frequent. So instead of being in bed, he sat in the corner of the sleeping hall again with Finn and Judah.

Tolar would appear soon.

Finn leaned over, his shoulder touching Atreus'. "You need the sleep elixir tonight."

Atreus hid a yawn in his other shoulder. "I'm fine."

"It wasn't a suggestion."

"I don't need coddling."

"No," Finn agreed, his green eyes strangely bright in the dim room. "You *need* sleep."

"I *need*"—Atreus tested the word on his tongue—"Vanik to stop pouting and rejoin these meetings. I *need* to know what this stage entails. I *need* answers to the dozens of questions floating around in my head. I *need* Prophet Silas to get off my back. I *need* to get out of here—"

Finn placed his hand on Atreus' knee and he stopped, realizing he was ranting.

Tolar walked up to the group shortly after. He pulled something out of his waistband as soon as he sat down.

Atreus frowned. "What's that?"

Tolar smiled at them, waving the folded piece of paper in the air. "A letter. I stole it from the prophets."

Atreus' eyes widened, but it was Finn who spoke.

"You did *what?*"

"I know, I know. But I wanted to help. I've just been . . . sitting and listening. I decided to do something. I snuck off while working in the mines and tailed one of the prophets. It wasn't that hard. The enforcers have a blind spot, you know? They have poor peripheral vision because of their helmets."

Atreus hadn't known that, but he stored away that bit of information for later. How had Tolar figured that out? Lots of trial and error? Seemed pretty stupid, but desperation could produce that.

"What if you were caught?" Finn pointed out.

"Well, I wasn't."

"What if they find out the letter is missing?" Atreus asked. The panic was there, but faint, resting in the pit of his stomach.

Tolar shrugged. "They'll probably think they misplaced it, but I doubt they'll be looking for it. I found it in a pile of opened letters in the bottom drawer of the desk. This one had the most recent date."

Finn and Atreus exchanged uneasy glances.

"I can help," Tolar said. "I *can*. I want to contribute. I don't want to be deadweight."

" . . . What's it say?" Judah asked.

Tolar's grin returned. He handed the letter over. "See for yourself."

∼

THE LETTER CONTAINED information about the next shipment of kids: when they would be arriving at the Institute, how many there were, and where they came from. The firstborns stayed in a different sort of facility until they were about nine or ten, and then they made the transition to an Institute where they were eventually sent out. At least that was the way things *had* been before all these changes.

Atreus knew of all the large compounds where the firstborns were raised. The numbers coming from those were consistent. But there were about two dozen kids who all came from separate places. Not compounds. Towns, perhaps? Were these kids stolen from their homes?

But it was that first piece of information that caught Atreus' eye. The when.

The letter contained the exact date and time the shipment would be arriving at the doors. In three days, right after dinner. The letter also outlined how many enforcers would be accompanying them. Nine. That wasn't that many for over a hundred kids.

This shipment's arrival was the closest thing to an opportunity they'd received in a while.

Atreus planned to share this information with Vanik, Weylin, and Harlow the next day, in hopes that it would mend their relationship and get them to work together again, but the trio was nowhere to be seen. He grew worried as the day passed and none of them made an appearance, and that feeling intensified when Prophet Silas pulled him aside after seminar and brought him to the black and white room.

Had the prophets found out about the missing letter? Had Tolar told someone else and they'd snitched on them? Or was this about Vanik and the others?

He didn't want to give anything away, so he stayed quiet.

"What do you think you're doing?" Prophet Silas asked.

It was a vague question, one that still didn't tell Atreus exactly why he was here, so he didn't answer it.

Prophet Silas leaned back against the desk. "I told you to drop it—your little plan. So tell me why we caught your friends trying to break out."

Atreus kept his face carefully neutral, not showing an ounce of the emotion he was feeling. So that was what happened. They had— *What?* Gotten scared after the last Outing? Their frustration with him and Tolar had grown too great? Part of him wanted to laugh at them. The other part of him wanted to curse them for being so *stupid*.

Atreus feigned confusion. "Who?"

Prophet Silas threw him an exasperated look. "Vanik, Weylin, and Harlow."

"I'm not friends with them."

They were careful about interacting in front of the prophets and enforcers, only meeting and talking in the sleeping halls. The next day, Mila would fill him and Finn in and they would do the same for her. Harlow, Vanik, and Weylin had the same system, so nothing looked out of the ordinary to anyone who happened to be watching. The only way the prophets would know their two groups were friendly was if someone *told* them, but even still, it was a he-said-she-said situation.

"I don't believe you."

"Well, I don't know what to tell you."

The prophet's eyes narrowed, and he hit Atreus' cheek. Not hard. But enough to make him wince. "Watch your cheek, boy."

Atreus bit his tongue, clasping his hands behind his back to keep himself from reacting.

"They're in solitary until the next Outing, reflecting over this crazy idea they've got in their head. Escape?" The prophet laughed lowly and shook his head. "You firstborns will never see the light in this realm. Not while I'm here."

Atreus took a deep breath, his nails digging into his palms.

"You're free to go." Prophet Silas waved his hand in Atreus' direction as he took a seat behind the desk. "I hope you remember this, Atreus, whenever you try to fight back."

Blood smudged his hands when he left the room.

ATREUS STARED at the bottom of the bed, his mind heavy and clouded.

Finn had given him the rest of the sleep elixir after Atreus told him what happened to Vanik and the others. Atreus *did* laugh then, and Finn shushed him and dragged him to bed. Judah looked over the edge of the top bunk, asking if Atreus was okay. Finn replied for him, saying he was just tired and that Judah should go to sleep. Thankfully, the kid had listened.

That was thirty minutes ago.

Since then, Atreus had calmed. He lay flat on his back on the bottom bed, his shoulder pressed against Finn's. He'd never moved back to the top bed after he healed. He found that his night terrors lasted longer if he opened his eyes and saw the fathomless dark above him. On the bottom bunk, his eyes found the bed, so he realized where he was and calmed quicker. It only helped his night terrors, which had become more frequent as of late; it didn't *prevent* them. Hence why Finn no longer stayed on the top bunk, and Judah had moved closer. Finn had been crawling down often, either to help Atreus through a night terror or to convince him to sleep, so he'd just stayed down here. Finn's presence, however, *did* prevent night terrors. At least Atreus told himself it did. It certainly soothed him while he was awake. When he felt cold and detached, Finn's warmth dragged him back.

"What are you thinking about?" Finn whispered.

Atreus blinked slowly at the bottom of the bed, debating if he should answer honestly. "The last Outing."

Finn shifted next to him. His leg bumped Atreus'. "We all made it out. That's the only thing that matters."

Atreus used to think that, but things had changed. He'd tried to forget about his interaction with the woman and what he'd seen in the room full of mirrors, but he couldn't. Every time he closed his eyes, he saw his reflection. He saw the monster.

"The woman I went off with," Atreus began. He hadn't yet told anyone what'd happened. "She said some things about me. Showed me some things."

He could feel Finn's eyes on him even though he was still staring at the bottom of the bunk.

"Like what?"

"She showed me what I truly am."

"And what is that?"

Atreus couldn't say it. He didn't believe her—not fully. But he was worried that if he said it aloud, he'd be accepting it. Speaking it into existence. Facing the truth he had been running from.

"I'll tell you what you are. You're my friend. And you're a good person. Despite everything, you still care for others. You're trying to keep everyone together. You're *saving* us. Whatever she told you was a lie."

Finn didn't know that, but Atreus decided he didn't want to talk about this anymore.

"Tell me about your stories."

"I thought you told me my stories were dangerous and not to be repeated."

Atreus sighed and moved slightly into a more comfortable position. "I don't care anymore."

Finn was quick with his response. "Don't say that."

Atreus didn't say *anything*, so Finn pushed himself up on one elbow to look down at him.

"Atreus, you can't say that," Finn implored. "That's not true. You *do* care."

"I do care," Atreus agreed.

Finn let out a breath and sagged against the bed again. "Promise me you'll keep fighting."

". . . I promise," he said.

A few beats of silence passed between them.

"Why do you want to hear a story?"

He shrugged. "They're important to you. And Judah."

They help you keep a grip on this realm, this reality. Maybe they will help me too.

They could just be stories for the imagination, but maybe there was more to them. Atreus could understand Finn or Judah creating and exchanging these stories, but for a prophet to share those ideas . . . ideas about Edynir Akonah being the hero . . . There had to be a reason for it. Perhaps he should be asking about Miss Seila instead of the stories.

"Is that really why?"

That was one of the reasons, even if it wasn't *the* reason. "I'm tired," was what he said. Yet he couldn't fall asleep.

After a moment, Finn sat up and rolled off the bed. He returned to Atreus' side with his journal in his hands.

"You can't read it."

The sleeping hall was too dark for that, especially tonight. Everything had been gloomy lately.

"Yes," Finn agreed, "but I put something in here."

Atreus heard the fluttering of pages before a piece of paper was pressed into his palm, over the crescent shaped marks from earlier.

"What is it?"

"You'll have to wait and see when you have light. Do you have a specific story request?"

Atreus rubbed the paper between his fingers before tucking it away. "One about Edynir Akonah."

∼

ATREUS KNEW something was wrong the moment he woke up because he was being yanked from his bed by an enforcer. His grogginess was swept away in an instant and any self-preservation he still had was screaming in alarm.

Finn was on the other side of the bed, hair tousled and eyes wide but still layered with sleep, dried drool on his chin. Enforcers had a grip on him as well.

The rest of the male firstborns were bunched together at the far side of the room. Judah stood at the front of the crowd. Tolar thankfully had a grip on his shoulder, keeping him from doing something stupid like running toward them.

Prophet Silas walked up to the bed and pulled the blanket aside, revealing the journal they'd left between them when they fell asleep.

Atreus' heart sank as the prophet picked up the book and flipped through it. There was no hiding it. There was no going back. He'd never been more grateful that they didn't write their name inside the book.

He surged forward. "It's mine!"

"No, it's not," Finn said a split-second later. "I wrote it. That's my handwriting."

Atreus' gritted his teeth. *Fuck you, Finn.*

"It's mine," he said again. "I wrote that because I don't believe in your bullshit for one second. As far as I'm concerned, what you tell us in seminar is just as real as the words I write on those pages."

Come on, he goaded. *I know you hate me. I know you want an excuse to hurt me. Take it!*

"Atreus—"

"*Shut up!*"

Prophet Silas turned to him now, his face cold as ice.

Atreus leaned forward, as much as he could in the enforcer's grip, and stared straight into the prophet's eyes, so he could see the truth and the rage deep within Atreus' own. "I won't stop fighting back. I'll *never* stop fighting you."

And then he spat right at the prophet's feet.

Finn inhaled sharply. Atreus didn't take his eyes off Prophet Silas. And Prophet Silas didn't take his eyes off him as he ordered the enforcers to take him away.

Atreus was growing used to the black and white room. He was growing used to the cold floor. He was growing used to the hateful words, the vile promises, and the pain. He was growing used to seeing his blood bathe the ground. And he was growing used to meeting a realm of black.

CHAPTER
FIFTY-SEVEN

Lena remembered everything now. Her memories came back to her in the form of vivid dreams. They sucked her in and didn't let her go easily. Sometimes they were horrific, but they were also clarifying. She didn't understand how such a large volume of memories could return to her so quickly yet quietly. But it hadn't been quiet, had it? The whole thing had been rather dramatic. The start of her getting her memories back—that was what had incapacitated her at the town head's house. Days of splitting headaches, aching muscles, crippling nightmares, muddled thoughts . . . And now she had access to her hidden memories.

She was far from an expert on sorcery, but Julian would surrender bits of information, which she could now recall. Complex sorcery—like blocking one's memories—must be comprised of intricate spells. Another one of Julian's mantras was that *nothing lasts forever*.

The spell had unraveled. It'd been stretched like a rubber band, and when it snapped, the backlash had hit her like a ton of bricks. *That* was why she'd collapsed and why she'd been riddled with nightmare-memories. It was why her head still throbbed and she went through the day with a foggy mind. It was why the palace physicians hadn't been able to tell what was wrong with her.

Fuck you, Julian, she thought for at least the dozenth time as she woke up from yet another frightful memory.

The gaps in her timeline were quickly filling. Before, when she reached back, her hand would meet something solid that she couldn't pass, something useless and hollow. Now the wall was gone, and memories were in its place. So many of her questions had been answered. She knew why Aquila looked at her with contempt yet still helped her. Everything finally made sense. Except it didn't.

Because with her memories—with the scenes and the people and the dialogue—came her emotions. They were heavy yet delicate, intimate yet shared, and it made her sick that something so strong and treasured could be stolen. The waves of emotions would bombard her, pulling her this way and that, changing quickly. She was unable to manage the onslaught and would go from angry to upset to hopeless within a minute.

She needed to talk to Aquila, but she didn't know how to reach her. Cowen might be able to get a message out. If she asked him. But even if she did, it would be difficult for Aquila to come to her with all the guards surrounding this place.

Cowen didn't trust the entirety of the Sacred Guard. The palace guards had to be reporting to Alkus, so she knew she wouldn't be getting out of here until he decided to let her out. Mikhail had said five days, but she wouldn't be surprised if Alkus found a way to extend her stay. If he had his way, she'd probably be here forever—trapped in her cage like some sort of exhibit.

She could only imagine what kind of bullshit he was spewing at the council meetings, about her and everything else going on in The Lands. He was probably convincing the others that they needed a stronger leader who wouldn't cave under the pressure or have public outbursts or challenge their traditions. She could see the others agreeing. There was no one left in the palace to support her name but Ira. He was better than her at all the politicking. She had to just be patient and trust that he could handle things up there. This too would pass. Right now, she needed to turn her focus to the more immediate issue and make sense of the outpouring memories and emotions that emerged from somewhere deep inside of her.

Even though her memories came back to her while she was sleeping, the entire process of reclaiming one's mind was exhausting. She found herself sleeping more and more because those hours of extra sleep made her more fatigued. So it was no surprise that she slept in.

When she eventually ventured downstairs, Cowen had already been up for a few hours. She found him in the kitchen, washing dishes. It was an odd sight, a domestic one that made her pause and think about her first time at the cabin. She stood there in the doorway long enough that he eventually caught sight of her.

"Breakfast is on the stove," he said before going back to drying off a pan.

She wordlessly slid her gaze over to the stove where a covered plate sat. Her appetite had been rather weak lately. She knew Cowen was trying to respect her wishes and give her space while also making sure she was taking care of herself. He wasn't that discrete. He would leave food in front of her door or on the table, most of it being sweets because he knew she couldn't deny that. But perhaps her appetite was returning because the smell of this food alone made her stomach grumble.

"Be careful. It's hot," Cowen said as she walked over to the stove. He grabbed two oven mitts and handed them to her.

Using the two mitts to take the plate off the stove, she removed the metal cover and gazed down at the meal Cowen had made. Smoke salmon, toasted bread, soft cheese, and tomatoes. Her mouth watered. It was an unusual assortment, but it was her favorite.

She'd been introduced to a lot of new foods when she moved to the palace, and this combination had quickly become her favorite meal. It wasn't one you could get in the Lowlands. At least not entirely, but there were still pieces of it that reminded her of home. She would request this meal from the palace chefs day after day. She was surprised that Cowen remembered it. They hadn't been on the best of terms then. They hadn't disliked each other, but he was younger, less mature—as was she—and had always poked fun at her. But he too had sobered up after the events that led to her family's death and Ezra's exile. She supposed they weren't on the best of terms now either. But he was trying. This breakfast was another olive branch of sorts. He was giving her space and being kind and patient and she was giving him the cold shoulder.

"Thank you," she murmured, and Cowen nodded.

Lena took the plate to the dining room, slipping one of the mitts under it so it didn't burn the table. A glass of water and silverware had already been set out. She stared at them for a moment before sitting down and digging in. She cut and stacked the salmon and tomatoes and smeared the cheese over the toast. A moan nearly escaped her as the delicious flavors slipped down her throat.

From her seat, she could perfectly see Cowen in the kitchen. He was now putting the dishes away. The dish towel was slung over his shoulder as he reached up to situate the cabinets' contents. When he finished putting everything away, he tugged the towel off his shoulder and began to wipe down the countertops.

It was odd seeing him like this. She was used to seeing him as a soldier. He was obviously more than that, and she often felt guilty that he couldn't explore those parts of his life because of the oath. Because of her.

But he had.

He had fallen in love and started a family. A family that would go on without him because of the backlash he faced from breaking his oath.

Her grip on the fork tightened.

She had reflected on the falling out in the tavern a bit since it happened. She hadn't necessarily wanted to. She didn't want to remind herself that Cowen was dying, but she couldn't ignore it either. To say it haunted her—especially now when she was stuck down here with all the time in The Lands to just *think*—would be appropriate.

She was frustrated with him. But more than anything, she was frustrated with the situation. Cowen deserved to have a family and be happy. Doing so didn't make him any less loyal or capable of protecting her. But she knew it would be easy for some people to argue the opposite. And those people would no doubt be the ones sitting in their comfy chairs in the Highlands. People who had never had to give up anything before. People who acted like they understood suffering and sacrifice when they hadn't even gotten a lick of it.

"Kalena, are you okay?"

She blinked and pulled her eyes away from her half-eaten plate of food. Her hand was shaking, her knuckles white from holding the fork so tightly. She released her grip and the fork clattered to the table.

Cowen stood in front of her. He had swapped out his towel for a jar of jam and was looking down at her with the same look he'd given her all of yesterday. That frustrated her too, but she couldn't blame him. She was kind of . . . out of it.

"Yeah," she murmured. Her eyes swept over the label of the jar. *Bumbleberry jam.* Also her favorite. It wasn't in stock at the cabin. She had looked.

He held the jam out to her. "I thought you might like this."

She carefully took the jar from him. "How'd you get it?"

"I asked for it to be brought down."

Her brows rose slightly as she gazed down at the jar in her hands. She brushed her thumb over the label. "The last time I had this, my parents were alive."

Cowen didn't respond to that, and she didn't blame him.

She set the jar down on the table and laughed. It was short and twisted, more like a bark than anything. Her elbows dug into the wood as the heels of her palms dug into her eyes. She laughed again, but this one was more broken.

"Kalena?"

"I'm sorry," she said, her voice soft yet hoarse. It was sandpaper and shards of glass tinkling across the floor. It cut her throat open. She swallowed to make sure she wasn't actually bleeding. "I'm sorry."

She hoped he understood, because right now, she wasn't able to say more. She couldn't even look at him. She squeezed her eyes shut tighter, pressed her palms harder into her skull until she saw black spots and her headache reemerged.

"It's okay," he said, his tone warm and soft, a sharp contrast to her own.

A sob escaped her throat and her shoulders sagged. She kept her face covered as she wept over the jar of jam.

It wasn't okay. She had been horrible to him, and he was dying.

A hand rested on her shoulder. It was a comforting weight that punched right through her chest.

"It'll be okay, Lena."

She didn't cry for much longer. She hated crying. Almost as quickly as it broke out, she sucked it back in and pushed it away. When she was certain no more tears were going to come, she pulled her hands away from her face and wiped it clean.

"I think . . . I'm going to fix up the house—my family's house." She sniffled, unscrewed the lid of the jar, and slathered a generous portion across the bread. "And visit their graves . . . if you'd like to join me."

She took a bite of the toast. While she was chewing, a traitorous tear trailed down her cheek.

The hand on her shoulder tightened. "I'd be honored, Kalena."

"And . . . can you do me a favor?"

~

She ducked into the tavern, lowering her hood once she stepped into the narrow hallway. Rivulets of water ran down her cloak and dripped onto the wooden floor, creating small puddles in her wake. She needed to clean that up. Jess hated when they left the hall wet.

The bar doors swung back and forth as she slipped through them and into the back room. Julian was sitting at the bar, as usual, but there was a book next to him instead of a mug of ale. She stopped in her tracks.

"Recognize this book, do you?" He tapped the cover and sat back in his chair. "Where did you get this, Cal?"

She'd snagged it while on a run. She and Quil had been tasked with stealing jewelry. Only *jewelry*. But that book had caught her eye. It was foolish, yes, and against the rules, but she'd been frustrated, and that rule was stupid.

She didn't tell Julian that. Any of that. If he cared enough to pick up a book and start questioning her about it, that meant he already knew.

"You know better than to take things for yourself when on a run—"

"It's just a book. I'm sure the people we stole it from care more about the missing jewelry than they do a book."

Julian arched a brow at her sharp response. "The jewelry is safely hidden away. This book"—he tapped the top again—"is not. Imagine if someone found it—someone other than me. If it gets into the wrong hands . . . well, then those people we stole from would know exactly who the culprits are."

"That's not going to happen," she said defensively.

Julian held up a gloved finger, and her voice tangled in her throat.

"I'm disappointed in you, Cal. You broke the rules for *this*? For a *book*?" He pushed it off the bar and it clattered to the floor, the pages strewn open. She flinched. "These stories aren't real. They don't matter. The only thing that matters is the here and now. If you wander around with your head in the clouds instead of in reality, you're going to get yourself killed. Do you want to die, Cal?"

Her fists clenched at her sides. She wanted to speak, but her lips were sewn together. Her voice swelled in her throat, having nowhere to go.

"Well?" Julian looked at her intently, inciting her further even though he was the one holding back her voice. "Do you?"

The pressure in her throat and at her lips vanished and she finally opened her mouth. But before she could say anything, she was yanked away from the scene. It was a sudden jerk that came from her chest, like an invisible string was threaded around her heart, squeezing the air from her lungs as she was flung through the room. Her feet weren't moving, but her body was. She flinched and closed her eyes as she quickly approached a wall, but she went right through it without feeling a thing. Her surroundings blurred until they were indistinguishable streaks of color smeared across the landscape she was being thrown through by some powerful force.

Her chest burned and her eyes watered as the wind whipped against her skin and her hair.

And then she screeched to a halt.

She grasped at her throat, sucking in mouthfuls of air that had evaded her only seconds before. Darkness enveloped her now. It took a few moments for her eyes to adjust. When they did, she recognized where she was.

The shrine.

She whipped her head around, looking for the Numen, waiting for it to seep out from the shadows and reveal itself. Her body appeared to be released from the hold of time—it was like a snapping sensation in all of her limbs. She was free to do and say what she wanted because this was not a memory. This encounter had never happened before this moment. It reached through the cracks of time and created a space for itself.

"Why did you bring me here?" she dared to ask. "Is this... real?"

Silence sat in the dark shrine for a few passing beats, and then there was a loud *whoosh!* that rumbled in her ears and shook her body.

"Of course this is real," the booming voice of the Numen said behind her. "Must you ask such foolish questions?"

She hesitated before turning to face it. She couldn't see the Numen in detail, only a faint outline, but as soon as her eyes fell upon it, its presence and power draped over her like the stifling heat of the warm season. It burned your skin and stole your breath and sucked you of all energy. Her knees trembled, but she was unable to fall. Or take her eyes off it. Most of it was dark, but there were times when she caught a glimpse of its bone-white face and the dark red pits that were in the place of its eyes.

"I heard you," it said. "Crying out for strength. For power."

She shook her head. A coldness crawled up from where her feet touched the ground. "I wasn't..."

"You were," it hummed. "You forget we are connected. I can feel what you feel. And right now, you feel trapped."

She tried to take a deep breath, but the overwhelming pressure surrounding her forced her to remain still.

"You should never feel trapped. Not with my power." The voice grew softer and closer until it caressed her ears, the inside of her mind. The darkness surrounding her was replaced with images of her past and the past of thousands of others. She saw heartache and bloodshed and anarchy. "Show them our strength. If you do what I say, no one will be able to stop you."

"... How?"

She could feel it smiling next to her.

"Follow the pull. Find the well of darkness. Pledge yourself to me and you'll have the realm at your fingertips."

"I don't want the realm," she said. The chill had risen from her feet, now engulfing her entire body. Only her lips could move. "I want... power."

"I can give you both."

And then she was falling.

Black ink spilled around her, coating her skin, staining her hair, filling her nose and ears and mouth. She couldn't breathe. She couldn't see. She could barely even think.

She plummeted deeper into the dark abyss. The cold had paralyzed her completely. She heard a hum. A voice calling to her. It wrapped her body in warm silk and sang. The lovely tune spun through the air, whispering her sweet nothings.

"Come to me."

"I can protect you."

"I can give you what you want."

It was one voice, coming from a hundred different angles, curling over itself in her head.

"We can win."

"Come to me."

"Save me."

"Wake up."

It grew in volume, fighting to be heard. She flinched as the pleas assaulted her eardrums.

"I can give you anything!"

"We'll escape together!"

"You need to wake up!"

The words scraped against the inside of her mind.

"Find me!"

"You need to—!"

"—WAKE UP!" a voice hissed as she was shaken roughly.

Lena's eyes snapped open and were immediately met with darkness. A blind panic took hold of her, and she lashed out, her knee hitting something soft. A grunt sounded next to her and the pressure on her shoulders disappeared. She stumbled back and hit something coarse that dug into her shoulder blades. Her hands grappled against the surface at her sides. Tree bark. At about that time, her eyes adjusted to the darkness enough so she could see where she was.

She was outside. In the forest. In the *Highlands*. The treehouse was right over her head, and Tuck stood a few feet away, scowling at her, a hand pressed against his side.

"What was that?" he gritted out, his green eyes glowing in the dark.

She blinked again and looked around. She didn't know how she'd gotten here. The last thing she remembered was lying down after dinner. Before that, she and Cowen had spent all afternoon and evening at her old house. She still wore her sleep clothes. The clouds overhead concealed the moons, so the forest was coated in a red so dark it almost looked black. How had she made it up here? How had she gotten past the guards?

"You were sleepwalking," Tuck said, watching her carefully. "Your eyes were open and glowing, but you wouldn't respond to me."

Her Imprint was hot too, but her Slayer was where it should be—tucked away.

What's going on? she asked it.

She'd been talking with her Numen before she woke up. It was a real talk, not a figment of her imagination. She was sure of it. But no voice reached back out to her now, not her Numen or the mysterious warm voice that had sung to her as she fell.

"That . . . happens sometimes," she said lamely.

Of *course* Tuck would be the one to find her at a moment like this, when she was unguarded and her mind was too muddled.

"Really?" he drawled, raising a brow. "So this isn't the first time this has happened? And yet you still managed to get this far?" He looked around. "No guards in sight. Maybe you need better ones."

She scowled. "That's none of your concern." She crossed her arms and looked up at the treehouse. "What are you even doing out here in the middle of the night?"

Like her, he wore comfortable clothing. His unlaced boots looked like they'd been shoved on haphazardly, and he hadn't bothered tucking the bottom of his pants in, so the fabric was bunched up or falling over his boots.

Her eyes narrowed. "Were you . . . *sleeping* out here?"

"No."

"So you were just visiting then? In the middle of the night?"

"I could say the same to you," he fired back. "Not enjoying your vacation in the cabin?"

"It's not a vacation," she retorted, her voice tight.

She didn't like that he knew about the cabin, but she wasn't surprised he *knew*, given who his parents were.

It's a punishment.

But she wouldn't admit that to him, even though he probably already knew that.

She switched the topic and gestured toward the treehouse. "Is this your vacation home? I would've thought you'd go for something more . . . flashy."

His smile was grim. "It holds sentimental value. And I know I'm not the only one who thinks that."

She frowned.

"I know you were here while I was gone. Why?"

She could deny it, but it would be a piss-poor rebuttal. "How do you know that?"

"Because you made a mess—"

"No I didn't—" She snapped her mouth shut.

He gave her an unimpressed look and inclined his head. "The blocks. You messed with them."

"I put them back exactly how I found them."

Tuck shrugged.

"Fine, sure. I came back," she huffed. "I don't even really know why, but I did." She ran her hands down her bare skin, beginning to regret sleeping in short rather than long sleeves.

"And then you came back tonight," he added as he stared at her strangely.

She didn't want him telling anyone about this . . . incident. While sleepwalking had been a normal occurrence for her over the past few days, she hadn't, as far as she knew, made it out of the cabin before. So why now? And *how?* None of the council members needed to know about this sleepwalking incident. That would only give them more of a reason to extend her stay in the Lowlands.

But she couldn't *tell* Tuck not to tell anyone. For one, she didn't trust him to listen. And she'd be giving him leverage by telling him just how much she wanted this to be kept a secret.

"What are you getting at? And *why?* I thought you were done with me?"

"Yeah, well I was irritable then and a liar always. Maybe a bit of a masochist as well."

Lena rolled her eyes and tried to keep her heart calm as she said, "Okay, well, I'm leaving." She gave him a wide berth as she pushed off from the tree and went to walk past him.

He didn't move or turn toward her, but he did open his mouth. "I'm sorry to hear about your attendants."

She stopped.

"I know you didn't know them for long, but I assume you must be feeling somewhat responsible for their deaths. After all, they were killed because of you."

Her hands tightened into fists at her sides. "What do you know about that?"

Tuck ignored her question. "A lot of important people have been dying lately—no, sorry, that's misleading. A lot of important people have been *killed* lately. The council knows they're being targeted. They suspect there's a spy hiding in the palace, so they've put together new safety precautions. New intel is being pumped out every few hours by different sources. There's no pattern to the guard rotations and no schedules are given out in advance. The council members are moving constantly and they're only all together during the meetings, which are heavily guarded and at random times. Nothing is to be put in writing. News is only spread verbally. I think they're even confusing themselves."

If this was affecting the council, Ira had to know about it. Why hadn't he told her yet? Maybe he couldn't risk sending a message, but he could come down to see her himself.

Then again, this could all be a lie. Tuck could be messing with her.

She turned around, facing Tuck again. "How do you know this?"

His eyes were locked with hers as he shrugged. "It's what I do. I sneak around. I investigate. I watch. I listen."

"If the council is purposefully trying to confuse people by giving out false information, how do I know the information you're giving me isn't false?"

"You don't."

She scoffed and turned away. Of course. She didn't know why she even tried with him anymore.

"Just like you don't know if Alkus' study will truly be empty and unguarded three days from now in the early morning while he's residing in a private room in the north wing."

Her lips parted and she mulled over the information. " . . . You're right. I don't know if that's false, but how can it be true? You said yourself no schedules are given out in advance. Three days is a long time away."

"It could happen."

Yes, she thought, her head filled with nothing but chaos and caution, *it could.*

She almost asked him why he was telling her this. The question was at the tip of her tongue. This information was . . . oddly specific. There was something in his voice she couldn't place. Part of her felt ridiculous for even entertaining the idea that maybe . . . just maybe there was some truth to what he was saying.

She shook her head, clearing those thoughts from her mind. This was *Tuck*. He thought of everything as a joke. And *he* was not one of her friends. This whole interaction could be one of the pieces the council had put in place to further confuse her and keep her away.

She started walking. It was going to take a while to get back to the cabin.

"How are you going to sneak back in without anyone noticing?" Tuck called after her.

She didn't respond.

"You know, if you ask nicely, I might help," he sang.

She gritted her teeth and muttered under her breath, "I'd rather get caught than ask for your help."

CHAPTER
FIFTY-EIGHT

She *was* caught when she tried to sneak back into the cabin, but thankfully, it was by Andra and Benji. With their help, she managed to get back inside without drawing any more attention to herself.

Cowen was stunned to find out she had snuck away, but she quickly explained what had happened before he could get even more upset. Sort of. She didn't tell him everything. She left out most of the details of her dream and the fact that she'd run into Tuck. All he knew was that she'd had a weird dream with her Numen that was somehow related to her sleepwalking. He appeared just as concerned and perplexed as she felt.

But no matter how long they stayed up mulling over this mystery, they weren't making any progress. She was practically useless; her mind was on its last leg and her eyelids wanted nothing more than to slip shut. Cowen eventually sent her to bed, and she went without protest. She didn't hear his door open. He was probably staying up so he would notice if anything else happened with her. She wanted to tell him to sleep, that his body needed it, but she knew he wouldn't listen to her. Not tonight. And she was already in bed, and it was so warm and cozy. Sleep took her quickly, and as far as she knew, there were no more mishaps that night.

The next morning while Cowen caught up on sleep, Benji took over. Now that Lena had some rest under her belt, she could finally focus on everything that had happened the night before. And what Tuck had told her. She lowered the barriers in her mind and extended a message to Ira, telling him to come down tomorrow night.

They would make their move the next day.

She contemplated Tuck's information. Three days. Less than two by the time

Ira arrived. Tuck's information could be completely fake. Regardless, they had to act soon. She wouldn't wait much longer.

∽

Lena wondered when Aquila would stop by. *If* she would stop by. Cowen had gotten the message out, but Aquila could've ignored it. Or the message could've been intercepted. It was a risk reaching out to Aquila at a time like this, but Lena needed to speak with her. She knew that Aquila coming *here* was a risk too. Alkus' guards still swarmed the woods. She saw them every time she went outside, and she hated it.

Fortunately, she didn't have to wait long for Aquila.

It was late and Lena was putting off sleep. She was tired of the memory-dreams —tired in general—and now she was worried about wandering off. Earlier, she'd snapped at Cowen when she stumbled out of her room after a nap and nearly tripped over his legs. Later she'd apologized, and they'd ended up compromising. Trusted members of the Sacred Guard would be told about her sleepwalking episodes and placed on night watch in case she fell under this trance again and snuck out. And Cowen would sleep *in his room*.

She knew he was only doing his job, but she hated the hovering. And the way she saw it, if a Numen wanted something, no one could stop it. So he might as well get some rest. The pallor of his skin and the bags under his eyes had worsened over the past few days. She hoped it was due to the stress of this situation and the little sleep he had been getting, not his health, but deep down she knew it was probably all three. As soon as Alkus was dealt with, she would look into a way to save Cowen.

A rapt on the window yanked her from her thoughts. One of her hands whipped out to grab the dagger under the bedside table while the other touched her Imprint, but then she caught sight of the person crouching on the roof. She sighed. The dagger stayed in her hand as she reached forward to unlock and open the window.

"You look like a mess," Aquila said as she crawled into the room.

Lena wore loose pants and a shirt again. Nothing fancy but nothing unusual. It had become her daily attire down here with the approaching cold season. Her hair was pulled out of her face in a low knot.

She closed the window and crossed her arms. "I haven't really been sleeping well." She wasn't defending her appearance—she didn't have to—but it sure did sound like she was.

Aquila hummed distractedly and walked past her to survey the room.

Lena turned with her. "I remember. Everything."

Aquila became rigid, like the string along her spine had been pulled. "Well then," she said after a few beats. "I was worried you would. I used my sorcery to try and help—after the town head's house—but I'm really no good at healing . . . that sort of thing." She turned toward Lena slowly as the cogs turned in her head; her eyes revealed as such. She was unguarded, trying to decide where to trek. "My specialty lies in manipulating larger, *tangible* things. That's why my tattoos are on my hands. Kieryn . . . he deals with the details and the intangibles."

The tattoo placement was beginning to make a lot more sense.

"I had to try, though," Aquila continued. She cleared her throat. "But I thought it might . . . trigger something. Or make things worse."

"I don't think you made it worse," Lena offered. "But I don't think you could've stopped it. Kieryn either. Julian's spell was going to unravel no matter what."

Aquila mulled over that, her eyes moving over Lena's room again with great focus.

A flush rose in Lena's cheeks. "Why?" she demanded, trying to regain Aquila's attention.

"Why what? Why would I try to help you?" Aquila scoffed and shook her head. Her eyes were still on the walls, her jaw tight. "Sometimes I ask myself that too. But I just can't seem to help myself when it comes to you."

Facing Lena seemed to take a lot of effort. Aquila's eyes were dark and wavering when they met hers. Open. Scared. Lena had seen that look before. In a memory.

"Why didn't you say anything?" Lena's voice was quiet, but it seemed loud in this room. "About . . . us?"

Aquila laughed, short and empty. "Because I'm sure that would've gone over well. I show up here, see you *alive* and on the *throne*, you don't seem to remember me at all, and I tell you that— *What?* We used to be lovers?"

"Obviously not at the start," Lena fired back. "But there were moments where you could've. I came to you time and time again asking for clarity and you shot me down! Don't blame the circumstances for your cowardice!"

Aquila surged forward, her eyes flashing. "Just because I was scared does *not* mean I was a coward. It didn't matter if you came to me asking for answers. It's not my job to *fix this*. You can't ask me to relive it all for *you*, after you got the power, the position, and the *person you love*." She sneered at that last part. "What was I to do?"

Lena took a step back. She wouldn't have reacted exactly like Aquila had if their roles were reversed, but she couldn't deny that it was a tough situation to be in. Reliving the past could be . . . difficult. She couldn't blame Aquila for putting herself first.

"I've regained most of my memories, but not all of them," Lena said instead of answering the question. "I still don't know why Julian would do this. Maybe to save his skin if either of us got caught, but this never happened to you."

Aquila shook her head. "I don't know. He was a secretive man, always speaking in riddles. It wouldn't surprise me if he put this type of spell on both of our minds as a failsafe—a way to protect him and us in a bad situation—but like you said, nothing happened to me. I wasn't captured, but I never saw Julian again after the ship." Her brows creased. "Whatever spell was placed on your memories—it was complicated. He must've created it himself because there's nothing like it out there, as far as I've heard. Sorcery of that power . . . is not circulated. Maybe he could only perform this spell on one of us. Maybe he messed it up with me. Maybe he didn't place spells on our minds before and he visited you after you were captured."

"But wouldn't I *remember* that?"

Aquila shrugged.

Lena gritted her teeth in frustration. "And the spell just happens to be unraveling now after only two years?"

"It's a difficult spell," Aquila said again. "Something like this is unheard of. Perhaps other sorcery wore it down. Or your newfound power. There are a lot of variables that affect the length and strength of a spell. Spells are made of magic, but they exist away from the sorcerer for periods of time. They're trickier. More . . . " Aquila waved her hand in the air, searching for the right word. " . . . unbalanced than immediate bursts of magic like me changing that book into a dinner plate."

She pointed to the desk, and Lena turned, frowning when she spotted the plate instead of her book.

Now that everything was coming back, no part of her past was spared. Memories that she wished had stayed hidden resurfaced. What she experienced when she remembered those things was akin to what one would feel if pushed off the side of a cliff. That panic that jumped up your throat and choked you when you first began to fall, when you realized there was nothing under you and that death was imminent . . . *that* was what she'd felt for days and days.

But she didn't get to pick and choose. She'd said she wanted them all back. She didn't want to be in the dark any longer. She wanted to be in control. But it hurt more than she'd thought it would.

She eyed Aquila. Regaining her memories—she supposed it didn't only hurt her.

Aquila stiffened, immediately turning defensive. "Why are you looking at me like that?"

"Like what?"

"Like you feel sorry for me. Don't . . . *don't* look at me like that."

"I'm not. I just—"

"It's not your fault." Aquila's eyes mapped out the room again, tracing the lines of wood. "It wasn't like we were in love or anything. We were both just lonely and wanting to feel . . . *something good*. We were each other's only options."

Lena didn't know why that hurt, but it did. While it might be true—that she didn't love Aquila, *hadn't* loved her—it might not. She was confused and overwhelmed. The emotions that had returned with her memories were too much for her to deal with right now. She had so many different parts of herself. So many different lives. Each involving different people and motives and memories. But they were all her. And what she did know was that she cared for Aquila to some degree.

"Why'd you come here?"

Lena *had* sent her a message, but Aquila had chosen to respond to it. And she'd admitted that she'd been worried Lena's memories would come back, so why come here and have to face that?

Aquila turned back to her, a single brow raising at the hardness of her voice. "I got the ledgers."

Lena's face slackened. "From the town head's house?"

Aquila nodded. "I snagged two before chasing after you. They have the signatures and everything."

"Alkus' secretary? Evanna?" she clarified.

Aquila nodded again.

Lena bit the inside of her cheek, her mind working. She had already sent word to Ira to come to the cabin tomorrow. Cowen was already here. But three wasn't enough. And she wouldn't reach out to Jhai right now.

"Can you come back here tomorrow? In the evening?"

"I can try," Aquila said. "But the guards are swarming the woods like crazy. It's easiest to sneak past them at night."

"I'll handle the guards." She'd talk to Cowen later. "Can I count on you to be here?"

The urgency in her voice was notable. She was grasping at something that was slowly moving away, out of arm's reach. She needed this to work, and she needed it to work *soon*.

Something in Aquila's eyes softened. Her chin dipped.

Lena breathed out a sigh of relief. "Good. Bring the ledgers . . . and Kieryn."

∼

Lena spent the next day in the library. She didn't really know what she was doing there other than killing time.

She scoured through books and scrolls about the pact between a Blessed and a Numen and read every account she could find recording a strange interaction between the two. Nothing about sleepwalking, but strange dreams, it seemed, were actually very common. So that wasn't helpful either. She quickly grew irritated when she got nowhere, so she switched over to reading up on politics, customs, and the law. And when she could no longer stand that because her mind grew numb, she pushed away the urge to go into Ira's study and instead sat in an armchair, allowing herself to drown in her thoughts.

The ledgers *should* be enough, but Alkus was resourceful, and other Blessed were lenient with punishments when it came to their kind, especially those in high positions of power. She couldn't say for certain that he didn't have a card up his sleeve that would allow him to get away with this. The break-in to the town head's house had happened days ago, so Alkus already knew the incriminating ledgers had been stolen. Meaning he was probably preparing a safety net in the event that the ledgers resurfaced and were used against him. But there were other ways to get rid of Alkus. Less legal ways but they were also less foolproof.

"We're not . . . killing him," Cowen said the evening of their meeting.

It wasn't a question, but the words came out of his mouth sounding stiff and uncertain. His eyes flickered between Lena and Ira, the former of which sat at the dining room table. Ira stood at the head of the table, his arms crossed. The two of them exchanged a look.

They had talked briefly when he first arrived thirty minutes ago. She asked him about the council's safety protocols. He said they were changing things constantly, but other than that, he didn't seem to know any of the details, confirming her hunch that he had purposefully been left out of this plan because of his relation to her. Had other people on the council, those who hadn't sided with Alkus, also been left out of the loop? Or had Alkus managed to convince them in her absence? Did she have any potential allies left?

Neither of them confirmed nor denied Cowen's statement, which only made him appear more troubled. "How would you even do that?"

"Kill someone?" Ira clarified. "There are many ways to do it."

Cowen sighed heavily and looked at her imploringly.

Lena avoided his gaze and looked over her shoulder. "We're waiting for two more."

Aquila and Kieryn couldn't very well just walk in through the front door. They should be able to make it. Aquila had given Lena her word. She would come. Lena had talked to Cowen about thinning out Alkus' guards today. They couldn't say anything to them that would raise alarm, so Cowen had members of the Sacred Guard pair up with the palace guards so they could distract them if need be and create small gaps in the perimeter. That was all Aquila needed.

Lena moved her gaze back to Ira. She hadn't told him Aquila and Kieryn were coming, but she hadn't *kept* it from him either. He'd only arrived a half an hour ago, and there were many other things on both of their minds. He probably knew now. There weren't many people she would invite to a thing like this. But maybe she should tell him outright. She didn't think Ira *hated* them, but she knew he didn't like them. And she was pretty sure Kieryn didn't like him either. She didn't know what Aquila thought of Ira.

He was staring at her now and she wondered if he was reading her mind. That would be the easiest way to tell him. She let her mental barriers drop and the knowledge of Kieryn and Aquila joining them float to the forefront of her mind. The exact nature of their mental bond was still a mystery to her. She'd paused her research on it since it wasn't a pressing issue, and lately, she hadn't had much time to dwell on issues that weren't pressing.

Entering Ira's mind was still something she couldn't do. She'd attempted to reach out to him a few times when he disappeared, but she'd received no response. No feeling. Nothing. And he could still only reach into her mind when she let him.

Her mental barriers were up almost all the time, not only because of him though. Once she found out that Julian had messed with her mind and not all sorcerers had tattoos on their hands, she'd grown a bit more paranoid about her mind being invaded. While Ira had said he wouldn't use this ability on her, Kieryn had made no such promise.

She didn't know if Ira picked up on what she was trying to tell him. His face didn't change. He looked exhausted. She supposed the whole lot of them did. His eyes were gloomy, and they got this far-away look to them sometimes before he caught himself and pulled up his mask of neutrality again. The smudges under his eyes hadn't improved since he came to the cabin days ago, bloodied and bruised.

His dreadful appearance was part of the reason why Lena hadn't told him about the sleepwalking incident the other night. She didn't want to worry him further. Not now. She would tell him once Alkus was dealt with and they had the time to worry about other matters.

Aquila and Kieryn arrived five minutes later, the sound of faint footfalls overhead announcing their entrance. It was a bit too loud to be covert, which told Lena it had been intentional, their way of letting others know they were here.

They appeared a few moments later, coming down the stairs. Both were wrapped in cloaks and Aquila had a bag slung over her shoulder. Kieryn pushed his hood off, his bright blond hair immediately catching the light. He looked less than enthused to be here. Aquila already seemed irritated, which wasn't great. Her face was closed off as she took in the scene.

"Fun party," she muttered as she walked to the other end of the table.

Kieryn trailed after her but chose to stay near the wall so he could survey the group in its entirety. He caught Lena's eye and said drily, "Thanks for the invitation this time around."

She sighed, already second-guessing her decision to call him here. Maybe he was the reason Aquila was so cross.

She turned toward Cowen and Ira, the latter of who stared coldly at the newcomers. Not glaring. She had seen that before and this was a few degrees warmer. Just a few. She looked at him pointedly, but he wouldn't meet her gaze.

Cowen appeared exasperated yet apprehensive. He looked between the four of them, raising his eyebrows at her as if to say *well?*

"Did you bring the ledgers?" she asked Aquila as she wrung her fingers together. She had forgone naps for the day, even though her body had requested them, so she needed to stay moving in some way if she wanted to remain attentive.

Instead of responding, Aquila swung the bag around and dug her hand in it. She dropped two large, leather-bound books onto the table.

Cowen frowned and stepped forward to open them.

"Aquila snagged it from the town head's house we raided in Dram."

Cowen's brows rose high on his forehead, and Kieryn merely hummed at that bit of information.

"We knew Alkus was funneling money there, but we wanted to know *why*. And we needed proof of it if we wanted to use this against him. The signatures in these ledgers lead back to Alkus."

"They're not his signatures though," Cowen said as he flipped through the pages.

"No, but they're as good as," Aquila said. "Evanna Levorri is an influential Blessed member, but she holds no political station. She does reside in the palace and is essentially—"

"Alkus' secretary," Ira interrupted, appearing deep in thought. "I've seen her around his study and by his side in public, especially recently."

Cowen shook his head and stepped back, his mouth pinched. "Even if we brought this to the prophets' attention, who's to say Alkus won't blame it all on Evanna? It'll definitely reflect badly on him, but that's not enough to get him locked away."

"There has to be a trail," Lena said. "Officially, that funding is coming from Evanna, and I doubt she'll work with us, so we have to find proof that she's getting that money from Alkus. There *has* to be something in his study. I doubt it would be in the treasury's records. He must've bribed someone there to cover for him. And if we can't find anything about the money transfers to the Lowlands, then there must be *something else*. This can't be the only illegal thing he's done."

She *knew* it wasn't.

"It's not about what he's *done*," Kieryn said. "It's about what you can *prove*. Do you think a man like Alkus leaves trails?"

"I think he's overconfident," Lena said as she sat up straighter, meeting Kieryn's eyes. "And that can make him sloppy."

"Okay, but how are we going to get into his study?" Cowen asked, drawing them all back to the main issue.

All four of them stared at him blankly.

"We're going to break in," Aquila supplied after a few beats of silence passed.

Cowen rolled his eyes. "And *how* are we going to do that? I'm sure its well-guarded. And I've heard of the changes they're making in the palace. It won't be easy."

Lena thought about Tuck's cryptic words once again. She couldn't rely on them.

"People panic in moments of disarray," she said.

Kieryn seemed intrigued. Aquila's face shifted in confusion, but it was Cowen who let out a warning, "Kalena."

"Nothing crazy." She'd thought about how they could make an opening for themselves to sneak in hours ago while in the library. "No one will get hurt."

Cowen still looked unsure. He sighed and leaned back. "You are the queen," he said. "You need to think about what you're doing—"

"Do not belittle me," she cautioned.

"I'm offering my advice," he said. "This does not have to be a battlefield for you."

"It does!" she snapped vehemently, slamming a fist down on the table. The wave of emotions she'd been holding back over the past few days had swelled and then crashed suddenly, surprising even her. She pulled her fist back and stared at the crack it had created across the tabletop. Heat spread across her cheeks, and she could feel everyone's eyes on her. "I've always had to fight. To survive. To prove my place here. Do you think I enjoy it?" She didn't look at any of them as she sagged in her chair. "Believe it or not, I'm trying to do what's best for The Lands, but I can't do that if I play by the rules."

She glanced at Cowen now, waiting for him to object. He still appeared troubled, but after a long stretched of silence, he nodded. "I'm with you."

She nodded back at him, grateful for his support.

Aquila inclined her head when Lena looked at her, saying all she needed to with her eyes.

Kieryn still appeared uninterested, leaning against the wall with his arms crossed, but he didn't protest, so she took that as a win. She would need his skillset.

Ira was already watching her, his face showing her what she already knew.

Lena told them her plan.

CHAPTER
FIFTY-NINE

A spiking pain shot through Atreus, and he hissed, flinching away from the pressure on his sensitive skin.

"Sorry, sorry," a familiar voice croaked. "Atreus? Hey, come on. Come back to us."

His eyes fluttered open, and he immediately squinted against the light overhead. It was too bright to be the Institute. And too cold. "Where are we?"

"In another realm." This voice belonged to Mila. He realized the other voice must've been Finn's. "Atreus, you need to get up."

He forced his eyes open entirely, blinking slowly to adjust to the light. The bleary gray sky and the tops of pointed green trees filled his vision when his eyes focused, as did three faces. Judah's red-rimmed eyes and quivering lips brought forth an ounce of guilt from within Atreus, so he looked away from the kid, focusing on Mila's anxious face instead. She gave him a reassuring smile that didn't quite meet her eyes. Finn appeared just as worried as the others, but Atreus' attention was immediately drawn to the fading bruise splashed across Finn's temple.

His arm moved on its own accord, fingers hovering over the discolored skin, but he didn't touch it. The pain that came with his movement was secondary to his concern. "When did that happen?"

Finn shook his head. "You missed a bit while you were out."

Finn and Mila helped him sit up. Atreus groaned as his sore muscles shifted. He moved his arms and legs, testing everything out. Nothing was too badly injured, much to his surprise.

"How long have I been out?"

"A few hours," Mila said.

That wasn't enough time for him to heal naturally. Prophet Silas could've had Miss Anya patch him up before the Outing. They also could've unsealed his Imprint again to allow him to heal faster. He must have gone somewhere because someone had swapped out his sleeping wear for his uniform.

Atreus brushed his hand over his Imprint, then stilled. He couldn't feel his Slayer. Or the extra rush of power. His Imprint was still sealed.

The other firstborns surrounded them. Vanik, Weylin, and Harlow were here too, standing a few feet away and staring at them mulishly. Vanik's uncovered scar was nasty, blistered, and red, standing out drastically against his ivory skin.

No one had knives.

Atreus looked back at his lap and said under his breath, "I can't feel my Slayer. Something's wrong."

"I know," Finn said uneasily. "My Imprint is still sealed too. I fought the enforcers after they took you away, so they put me in solitary. Miss Anya gave me some sort of elixir. I just woke up minutes before you did. They did the same to Vanik, Harlow, and Weylin."

Atreus stared at him in shock and then looked at Mila.

She shook her head, eyes glassy. "I was conscious. I found Judah in the cavern. They didn't unseal *anyone's* Imprints this time."

A cold seeped through him, and it wasn't caused by the frigid air. They had no Slayers. No knives. No way to defend themselves. There were no *Te'Monai* surrounding them, which was good, but he was sure people would come, like before. And eventually, they would attack.

"Help me stand," he said. He bit the inside of his cheek as they hauled him to his feet. Their hands remained under his arms as he found his balance.

"Can you walk?" Finn asked.

"Yeah." Atreus shifted his weight from leg to leg. "It's not that bad."

He ached, but it was the kind of ache that could be overcome if he kept moving. Finn and Mila dropped their hands. And as soon as they did, Finn was rounding on him.

"Why did you take the blame for the journal?" he demanded. "You shouldn't have—"

"Drop it," Atreus said. "It's done."

But he knew better than that. Prophet Silas would continue to hold this over his head, and there would be consequences, not just for him. For everyone.

Thankfully, Finn did drop it, but he wasn't *over* it. The tension lining his body was apparent. Though now wasn't the time to argue. They had much bigger issues to worry about.

Atreus fully took in the realm they'd been transported to. The terrain was harsh and barren. The wind chilled him to the bone and ice or snow covered nearly every surface.

"Why would they do this?" Tolar asked as he stepped forward from the crowd.

He twisted his hands together in front of him. "Why would they send us here to die?"

Vanik rolled his eyes. "You can die if you want, but I'm not."

Atreus stared at the trio. When Vanik met his gaze, Atreus narrowed his eyes.

I know what you did, you asshole.

Vanik didn't back down, but Atreus didn't expect him to. He was an asshole, after all, and he was stubborn. Regret wasn't in his repertoire of emotions.

They started walking, and within a few minutes, people appeared. Although they were wary, they still followed when beckoned. The people took them to a town, and the firstborns were split into groups almost immediately, which sent alarm bells off in Atreus' head. It was eerie how everyone's eyes swept toward him.

He wasn't placed in a group. Another female stepped forward, who he assumed was the leader. Meanwhile, the people of this realm tried to direct each group into a different house, which sent the alarm bells off once again.

"Oh, no, I don't think that's necessary."

But he was ignored, and everyone was ushered into the houses anyway. Atreus stood stiff in the snow, his eyes darting around for some sort of threat. It used to be so obvious before. There were humans and there were *Te'Monai*. He *knew* who the enemy was. Or so he'd thought. Now . . . he didn't know what to expect.

He caught Mila's eye. Judah was in her group, thankfully. Finn nodded at him, Tolar at his side. Even Vanik watched Atreus. The two certainly didn't see eye to eye, but they weren't enemies here, in foreign territory. They were all with him. None of them were taking any chances this time. They'd act at the slightest hint of danger. The firstborns might not have their Slayers, but they were still fighters.

Atreus followed the woman into what he assumed was her home, which was a good distance away from the rest of the houses.

"You're injured," she observed.

He frowned at her back. "Uh, yes. I . . . get injured quite a lot." He really didn't want to spend more time here than necessary, so he cut to the point. "Are you one of the sisters?"

The woman smiled over her shoulder. "I am. My name is Nepara. You already met my sister Elwa."

So that was her name.

"Er, yes. I had the . . . pleasure of meeting her."

"What did you think?"

"Of her?" he clarified.

"Of what she revealed to you."

Atreus frowned. " . . . It was crazy."

He felt like that was better than saying *she* was crazy.

"Was it?"

"*Yes.*"

"You will soon understand. It will come to you."

Nepara wandered farther into her house, leaving Atreus even more confused than he was moments ago.

He strode after her, entering another room. "*What* will come to me—?" His eyes widened as he took in his surroundings. "Woah."

They were in a house—that much he was sure of—but this circular room had no ceiling. The walls stretched upward for what seemed to be forever. Shining azure tiles covered the walls, but they were mostly concealed by rows upon rows of books.

Nepara took a book off the table in front of her and handed it to him. There was a runic language on the cover, which he didn't recognize.

"Are you familiar with this?" she asked.

"No."

"Depending on who you ask, some will say it's history. Others will say it's a fairy tale."

He flipped through the book. Every page was filled with those strange symbols. "What's it about?"

"You."

His head snapped up. "What?"

"It's about you. About the martyr Edynir Akonah. The one true hope we have left—"

"Stop. Stop, stop. *Stop*." He waved a hand in the air, closing his eyes and the book, thinking. Or trying to.

Nepara hummed sympathetically. "The truth can be difficult to hear—"

"It's not the truth!" He flung the book aside and a wild laugh escaped him. "So this is what the prophets meant by the next stage, then? You're working with them to . . . What? Mess with us? With *me?*"

She didn't seem offended by his outburst. She took a step closer and looked at him clearly. "Do you think your prophets know everything?"

"They know what the Numina tell them," he said, repeating the mantra they were often told in seminar.

Nepara nodded in agreement. "Exactly. And the Numina lie."

She went to retrieve the book, leaving Atreus to think about what she'd said. The Numina could *lie*. They weren't just. The prophets tried to purge all the books that showcased them or the Numina in less than favorable light from the Institute, but a few had slipped through the cracks. Years ago when Atreus first arrived at the Institute, a handful of firstborns stumbled across them, and word spread. Eve was one of those firstborns. The books were thrown out, but the damage was done. The prophets' perfect story, their grip, was fractured now. When the prophets were forced to address the Numina's nature during seminar, they tried to spin it to their advantage. Atreus hadn't bought it. He still didn't buy it. He didn't buy anything the prophets said. If the Numina were unjust, then so were the prophets.

Nepara handed the book back to him. "Your prophets don't know we're here. Their reach only goes as far as their realm."

"That's not true. If it was, we would be free of them here, but we're not."

"You could be. You mortals are so narrow-minded. You look into the future and only see one possibility. You're like sheep blindly following your shepherd."

He frowned. *You mortals?* "That's not true. Every day we're fighting for our freedom. For another choice." He threw his arm out, pointing in the direction he'd come from. "That's what we're doing here. Now."

"Then listen to me," Nepara said, her voice deepening and becoming more serious. "Listen to me when I tell you that *you* are Edynir Akonah—"

Atreus was already backing away. He scoffed. "I can't be. He's dead!"

"The soul never dies," she said simply. "His passes on, generation after generation, in the hope that one of his selves will be capable of breaking the cycle and restoring the realms to the glory they were before."

He stared at her, truly bewildered. "Do you hear yourself? Edynir Akonah was the one who *shattered* the realms. Why would he want to fix things?"

She shook her head and sighed. He couldn't help but feel scolded in some way.

"People lie," she reminded him.

"*I know.* That's why I have such a hard time believing what anyone says, especially people who tell me I'm a war criminal reincarnated."

"You're smart, Atreus. I know you doubt the prophets—as you should. And I know this must be a lot to hear, but you saw him. You saw Edynir Akonah as your own reflection, yet you still deny it?"

Edynir Akonah . . . as his own reflection?

He took another half-step back, shaking his head. "No."

The floor began to crumble under him and his legs trembled with the effort it took to keep him standing. He searched through his mind for something, for solid proof that would allow him to push back against her words, but he came up empty. He didn't know what to believe. Everything was either crazy or hopeless.

"That man in the mirror . . . you're saying that was Edynir Akonah?"

She smiled. "Just as he is you."

"No."

"*Yes.*"

"He's a murderer!" Atreus exclaimed, his hands shaking. His heart rattled inside his chest, banging against his ribs. He recited what they had always been told because for once, he was scared of it being a lie. "He grew greedy and challenged the Numina! He slaughtered thousands!"

"Lies," Nepara repeated, calm and collected. "Spread and preserved by Kerrick Ludoh and his followers. Little did they know they only won the battle, not the war. Edynir Akonah is fated to return and show the realms the truth."

"Which is what?" Atreus snapped. "Since you seem to know so much, what's the truth?"

"You must figure that out on your own."

Her answer was predictable yet vague, and it made Atreus want to scream and pull his hair out. He took a deep breath, collecting his thoughts and reminding himself that he couldn't let his emotions control him. They could attack at any moment. She was trying to confuse him, make him vulnerable.

"Where's the stone?" he demanded.

"In a rush to return to your cage?"

A bell sounded from overhead just like before, but he couldn't find out where it was coming from. And like clockwork, a scream rang out a moment later.

"It appears my time is up." She turned away from him.

Atreus looked over his shoulder at the doorway, feeling conflicted. He still had questions, but his friends needed his help.

"Wait!" he called out, whipping back around to face Nepara. "The stone! Where is it? Why are you attacking us?"

She ignored his questions. Instead, she said, "The truth is hard, but it is the truth, Atreus."

She touched one of the shelves and it slid back, revealing a secret passageway. Atreus couldn't follow her even if he wanted to. His feet wouldn't lift from the ground.

"Be careful of the people you surround yourself with. You do have many choices ahead of you, but you can't run from your destiny, Atreus."

She stepped forward and the shelf began to close behind her.

"*The stone*—!"

But the bookcase was back in its original position and the sister was gone.

Atreus stared at the shelf in shock. The invisible force that had been sticking his feet to the floor disappeared. He took a step forward, wondering if he could get the shelf open and chase after her, but then another scream split through the air. He turned on his heel and sprinted out of the room.

The snow was steadily coming down now. Humans from this realm and firstborns flooded the main street of the town. Most of the firstborns had armed themselves with something they'd found—knives, fire pokers, axes, hammers, metal pipes.

Atreus spotted a pitchfork next to a pile of hay at the corner of the house. That would do.

As soon as he grabbed the pitchfork and spun around, a man ran from around the corner, stopping right in front of him. The bloodied shovel in his hand sent Atreus' stomach reeling. Which firstborn did that blood belong to?

"You don't have to do this," he said as he extended his arms in front of him. The man appeared a bit out of his element, his face pale and his arms trembling. "You can drop your weapon. You all can. We don't have to be enemies."

Before the man could respond—either by setting down his weapon or by swinging it at Atreus—a large, bright yellow figure zoomed around the corner of the house, tackling the man to the ground.

The man shrieked and withered in the snow as his skin burned, but he grew silent and still once the Slayer bit his head off.

CHAPTER
SIXTY

Lena and Cowen left the cabin right before sunrise. Evading the palace guards who roamed the woods required assistance from other trusted members of the Sacred Guard. They created a distraction during shift change, which threw everyone into a scramble long enough for Lena and Cowen to slip past.

To get to the Highlands, they snuck up the cliffs using a not-so-secure pathway that wasn't really a pathway in case their usual route was being monitored. Most of the ascent they had to climb, and the high winds that always blew at the cliffside tugged at her clothes, but they both made it to the top without injury.

Aquila met them in the forest a quarter mile away from the palace.

Lena took in her jaded appearance and the way her feet dragged slightly. "Everything go okay?"

Aquila's brows twitched, but she nodded. "The rumors should be spreading through the servants' corridor like wildfire, and more than a handful of prophets were approached by concerned Blessed who wanted to know what their plan of action was for an issue of this severity."

Since their meeting in the cabin two days ago, they had all been doing their part to make sure this plan ran smoothly. Yesterday, Ira had made sure the enforcers and prophets had received a few anonymous tips regarding Alkus' illegal activities. Even those on Alkus' side could only ignore people's concerns for so long, especially if they received public pressure.

Aquila had just finished stirring up trouble in the palace. Since manipulation of tangible things was her sorcery specialty, she could shift her and others' appearances. Doing so was tricky and took a lot out of her, especially when she had to change forms multiple times to replicate about a dozen nosy servants and apprehensive

Blessed *on top of* shifting Kieryn's appearance so he could move through Solavas to drop vague reports about a show happening at the palace. And now she had to do the same for Lena and Cowen so they wouldn't be recognized on their way to Alkus' study.

"That's good." Lena nodded and stepped forward, so she was within arm's reach of Aquila. "What do I need to do?"

"Pull down your hood, for one," Aquila said, one side of her mouth tugging up and then quickly falling back down.

Lena did so and Aquila raised her trembling hands to her face. The sorcerer's cold fingers brushed over Lena's cheekbones, the bridge of her nose, the shape of her mouth, the arch of her brows, and her jawline. The chill Aquila's touch brought lingered, sinking into Lena's skin and dancing across her bones and muscles and tissues, stretching and pulling them slightly. It was an odd sensation but not painful.

Lena didn't take her eye off Aquila as she worked. The wrinkles between her brows and the shadows under her eyes were deep, her skin too pale apart from her flushed cheeks.

"You should rest," Lena said as soon as Aquila stepped away.

The sorcerer's mask of concentration cracked, and she glowered at Lena. "Done," she announced flatly, ignoring Lena's request. "You look strange enough."

Lena frowned when Aquila stepped past her and moved on to Cowen. She reached up to touch her face, feeling her altered features: her button nose, her thinner lips, her slightly extended brow bone. The changes were subtle. She could only notice the difference because it was *her* face, but she couldn't literally *see* the changes, not like she could with Cowen when his features began to shift. It was strange—witnessing the pieces of his face expand or shrink. The end product was him, yet not. She recognized him as Cowen because she *knew* he was Cowen, but if she walked past him on the street, she couldn't say for certain that she would pause.

"It won't last forever," Aquila said as she pulled her hands away from Cowen. "So you better get going."

"You should rest," Lena said again as she walked over to Cowen's side.

Aquila looked as if she might collapse any second now. On top of shapeshifting and spreading rumors, she had also visited Dugell last night for Lena. Aquila had met him before and knew how people like this operated, but that didn't mean she'd been happy to do it, especially when she found out why Lena wanted her to visit him. Dugell was going to take the fall for them if something went wrong. Well, not *him*, but whoever he decided to supply as the scapegoat. In the end, Aquila had gone to ensure they would have a safety net.

The sorcerer let out a mirthless laugh. "If you think I'm going to disappear while you're in there, you really don't know me at all."

Lena saw Cowen frown out of the corner of her eye, but she ignored it, keeping her attention on Aquila. "Wait around if it makes you feel better," she told her. "But I'll be fine."

Aquila appeared unconvinced.

"You've done your part. Thank you," Lena said genuinely. Executing this plan would be much harder without Aquila's help. Maybe impossible since they wouldn't have the ledgers.

Right before Lena turned to head toward the palace, she caught sight of the unveiled distress on Aquila's face, and her traitorous mind went back to the pirate ship at the dock. She knew Aquila was thinking the same.

It wouldn't be like that this time.

Once she and Cowen arrived at the palace, they swapped out their clothes for oversized servants' uniforms and stuffed the ledgers and the letters underneath them before slipping into the servants' corridor. Lena pulled her hair down around her face as a precaution, even with her altered features. Cutting through the palace using the servants' corridors allowed them to travel quickly without running into any influential figures, *but* there was nowhere to hide in the small passageway. Hence, the need for the shapeshifting. Servants were notorious gossips; if they caught sight of her *and* Cowen, word would get out, and their plan would crumble.

She caught pieces of hushed conversation as she walked down the passageway. Everyone was talking about something happening outside the palace, which meant Kieryn and Ira were doing their jobs of drawing in the crowd and delivering the show, respectively.

Something twisted in her chest at the thought of Ira risking his life for a distraction. She'd been surprised when he said he would duel Alkus given his bad experiences with duels in the past and the way he'd reacted when she challenged Cressida.

"*That wasn't necessary,*" Ira told her when she mentioned her duel, appearing and sounding confident but also somewhat detached. Cold. "*This is. We have a day to set things up and lay a trail, which should work, but that's not a lot of time. This is a surefire way to get Alkus out of the palace and create a big enough spectacle that will attract the public, the prophets, the enforcers, and the guards.*"

She'd been a bit put off by his initial comment, but that wasn't her most immediate concern.

Blessed lived to be entertained. The more dramatic and scandalous the event, the better. There was something about having so few problems that made people want to create more for themselves. So they would undoubtedly come to an encounter like this, especially with the recently circulated rumors.

But she wasn't worried about whether the spectators' showed; she was worried about Ira. Not only him having to fight, but him having to relive his past trauma. Though, the former was nothing to overlook either. She trusted his judgment and his abilities, but she didn't know what strengths Alkus possessed, especially if he was messing around with sorcery like Ira claimed. His informants had uncovered such recently.

This information hadn't shocked her when Ira revealed it at the cabin. Alkus was ambitious and power-hungry, so it made sense that he would grab hold of any power he could, even if he condemned that power and called it "rotten magic" in public. Ever the hypocrite.

But at least they were using this against him.

She and Cowen slipped out of the servants' corridor around the corner from Alkus' study and were immediately met with a wave of noise. She fought to keep from flattening against the wall when four guards ran past them.

You're supposed to be blending in. Act like you're supposed to be here.

They stayed closed to the wall and walked quickly, stopping at the corner before the private hall that housed Alkus' study. It *should* be guarded, even with all this commotion. Alkus would have told the guards to stay no matter what. She knew what logic told her, but Tuck's voice clashed with it. He couldn't have known the schedule three days ahead of time, not when the timetables were constantly being changed, and yet . . . she considered it. She wavered.

When the others asked her how she was going to get into Alkus' study without running into the guards, she'd told them she had it figured out. They hadn't bought it that easily, and to be honest, she hadn't either. She didn't have a *plan* for getting in per se, but she was testing something. And if guards still stood watch outside of Alkus' study, she and Cowen could take them. Probably.

"What's the plan?" Cowen whispered.

Lena took a deep breath before spinning around the corner and striding down the hall with purpose.

Two Blessed passed her, but they didn't give her a second glance with her uniform. She willed her heart to calm and hugged her front tighter, her fingers biting into the ledger. The heat from her Imprint spread through her and tingles began at her fingertips. She didn't want to use her aura flame if she didn't have to. The purple aura flame wouldn't exactly be telling in any other situation, but if someone caught sight of it, they would be more likely to believe Alkus when he insisted that she'd set him up. And she didn't want to kill any guards today, especially not around Alkus' study, as that would also look suspicious.

She was close. If she looked up, she would see the door.

So she did.

And no one was there. The hallway was empty.

Her shoulders lowered, and her grip on the ledger loosened as her step sped up. She glanced over her shoulder as she reached the door. Cowen was the only person she saw. To her astonishment, the handle gave easily. She and Cowen quickly slipped inside, locking the door after them. They exchanged a look of thinly veiled disbelief.

"Why are you surprised?" he breathed out. "This was your plan, right?"

"Right," she said slowly, her mind working as she asked herself why Tuck had given her this information and what that meant. "Yeah, my plan."

Was this a trap? Should she expect guards to break down the door at any moment? If that was going to happen, what could she do? Not run. They were already here with the ledgers and the letters. The plan was in motion. They needed to get this done.

"Let's move quickly," Cowen said, snapping her out of her stupor as he removed the ledger from under his clothes.

She slipped out the ledger she'd carried and looked around.

During the meeting in the cabin, the five of them had decided to plant something in Alkus study to ensure that he was arrested, just in case they couldn't find anything linking "Evanna's" payments to Alkus. It needed to be something big and incriminating *enough*, something his buddies in the palace guard and council couldn't ignore or make excuses for, which meant they needed to make this spectacle immediate and public.

Ira had suggested the killings.

And that was where Alkus' sorcery came in.

There was an old superstition in The Lands that anti-sorcery individuals, including Alkus, used to villainize sorcerers. It was the belief that since sorcery wasn't a magic granted by the Numina, it was unnatural and drew from a wicked power source: death. Particularly, souls. Many history books stated that human sacrifices were what fueled the dark and powerful magic known as sorcery. So they could tie Alkus to the killings by utilizing that widespread belief. In theory. They still needed to tie in a few more pieces, which was what they were doing here.

Cowen had initially been against painting Alkus as the killer when the real one was still free, but they'd eventually swayed him. More killings would happen regardless. And if Captain Haveers was smart, he wouldn't let his guard down just because one person had been locked up. And Alkus very well *could* be involved in these murders. She still hadn't written off that possibility.

Upon first thought, killing Blessed might not seem like something he would do, but if he could somehow justify it as a means to an end, a stepping-stone to power and the betterment of the Blessed as a whole, then it seemed *exactly like* something he would do. And if he was involved in the killings, then he likely knew all the victims. Therefore, he would also know all the deaths he wasn't responsible for. And if he were to look at that list of deaths, it would be pretty easy for him to deduce *who* had killed them. After all, no one had wanted them dead more than her.

So she was getting to him before he could get to her by leaving the ledgers in his study as a gift. He might still be able to talk when he was locked up, but his influence and what he could do with it would be limited. And him pointing fingers at her *after* he'd been locked up would seem a bit . . . insincere?

Those ledgers directly linked Alkus to the robbery that had occurred at the town head's house, and once they were found alongside the letters, well . . . Alkus would deny he had any part in it of course, and the town head he'd been paying would likely try to cover for him, but the councilman would still have to be locked up. And if things went in her favor, he would *stay* locked up once the other news broke. And if things didn't go in her favor, well, that was what the scapegoat was for.

The ledgers couldn't be in plain sight, but they needed to be somewhere they would be found when the study was searched. And somewhere believable. Alkus wasn't a fool, but he was also rarely under scrutiny. He didn't necessarily have to be secretive in his own space if no one else was ever allowed in without his permission.

"Check for a locked drawer or a secret compartment. Something guarded."

If they found one, whatever contents it contained would also be useful in incriminating Alkus, and they could dump the ledgers and letters inside and leave things a bit disordered to ensure it caught the enforcers' eyes.

Lena rummaged through his desk while Cowen combed through the bookshelf. Every drawer was unlocked and filled with neatly organized stacks of paperwork and supplies like seals, wax, and ink.

"Here."

She turned as Cowen heaved a huge marble statue away from the wall. He knelt and reached behind it, removing a piece of its calf. Inside was a compartment filled with papers. Of course. Alkus would hide important documents in a hollowed-out portion of a marble statue.

Cowen handed the papers over, and she sifted through them. One in particular caught her eye. The crisp, cream paper wasn't timeworn, and on it was a broken wax seal of an emblem she didn't recognize. She assumed it belonged to a town head because all their emblems were slightly similar and less elaborate than those of Blessed. And Lena had suspected that Alkus was working with more than one town head.

A groan of frustration left her lips as soon as she unfolded the letter.

"What's wrong?" Cowen asked.

"It's in code." She dropped it onto the desk. It used the characters of the common language, but they were scrambled, making the entire letter completely unintelligible. "If this is how he communicates with the town heads in every letter, then the documents Aquila forged are useless!"

The ledgers contained most of the information needed to convict Alkus, but they weren't necessarily connected to him yet, nor did they tell the entire story. There were gaps that Lena would rather fill ahead of time than leave open and allow Alkus to use them to tear the story apart. So, Aquila had forged letters between Alkus and two town heads—the one they had visited and another who seemed like the type to align themselves with a Blessed—which explained the nature behind the money transfers: Alkus needed Blessed's souls, but he couldn't kill those people himself. He was looking for skilled outsiders to do his work for him, but growing up in the Highlands his whole life, he didn't know where to find these kinds of people—dirtyhands—so he outsourced this job to the town heads, who had their own networks of dirtyhands already established. In return for the town heads finding Alkus the best of the best dirtyhands—Blessed who had gone rogue and could kill other Blessed—he would ensure they stayed in power, and a cut of the money he sent for hiring the killers would be theirs to keep.

And of course Aquila had mentioned that Evanna would be sending the money. The lot of them hadn't had time to get into the treasury's records, but they'd agreed the letters and the ledgers should be enough to convince the enforcers to pay the treasury a visit themselves. And once the enforcers requested Alkus' and Evanna's records, they would find the money transfers, and everything would fall into place.

Aquila could use her sorcery to replicate anyone's handwriting as long as she had a reference, and the ledgers had provided just that for the town head. Ira had brought down a document with Alkus' handwriting, and a few hours later, they'd had two letters, stamped and signed, one written and about to be sent out by Alkus and another he'd supposedly received from Dram's town head. Both filled in the holes to their story.

And now they were worthless.

Lena chewed on her bottom lip. Aquila was somewhere nearby, but they didn't have time to go find her. Maybe they would need to make time.

Cowen appeared next to her and dropped the two letters Aquila had crafted onto the desk.

Lena looked between them. "Well . . . she got the handwriting down."

But the difference in style was too obvious. They wouldn't just stop communicating in code. This would only give the enforcers and prophets more reason to believe Alkus when he would inevitably deny ever receiving or writing the forged letters.

Cowen grabbed a blank sheet of paper from a drawer and a pen from the top of the desk. He began to write out the alphabet. She watched him curiously, but she perked up when he started writing the alphabet backwards directly under the first line, matching up each letter with its reverse counterpart.

"It's a simple code—"

"Which is exactly why he used it," she murmured.

A simple safety precaution but not one that was too complicated. Alkus couldn't be bothered. And in his mind, he didn't need elite protection. His status already did that for him.

"The handwriting doesn't matter," she decided, which wasn't exactly true, *at all*, but the code was more important, and they couldn't get to Aquila right now. Lena decided they didn't have time. "At least you figured out the code, so we can rewrite it correctly. And add the emblem. We'll try to replicate the handwriting as best we can."

It needed to be close. Without solid evidence, this situation was just a he-said-she-said case. The public pressure would help once said public received word of Alkus' link to the murders, but still, the evidence needed to be good to stick. Then again, if the enforcers looked into the letters and the trails deep enough, they would probably uncover more incriminating evidence against Alkus, so it wouldn't necessarily be a bad thing. Hopefully.

"I'll copy them over," Cowen said. He grabbed a blank paper and then paused before he began to write, as if realizing what he was about to do.

Lena looked at the sheet and then the pen resting in his still hand. "I can do it—"

"No," Cowen said, blinking hard and leaning down over the paper. "No, I've got it. I . . . I've actually forged Alkus' handwriting before. Not for something of this degree, but still . . . "

Her lips parted. That was news to her. "For what?"

One of Cowen's shoulders raised in a half-hearted shrug. "When I was looking for you, sometimes the council didn't always grant my requests. Sometimes I accepted it . . . and sometimes I forged documents so I could get my way." He glanced at her. "But like I said, nothing this big. I did it sparingly for small things, so I wouldn't be caught. And I wasn't."

"And you won't be now," Lena assured him. She cleared her throat to rid it of the tightness that she felt and then stepped forward to grab a sheet of blank paper for herself. "I'll decode this message."

And then she set to work. The coded letter and the key sat between them.

She kept an ear out as she worked through the letter in case anyone came back this way. They would have some time to clean things up and escape since they'd locked the door—unless the guards simply busted it down—but the whole point was to go in and out *unnoticed*. She wasn't sure how much time they had left, but she hoped it was longer than they needed.

When she finished decoding the message, she straightened and looked down at it in disbelief.

The scrawl of Cowen's pen stopped. "What's it say?"

She skimmed over the code again to make sure she had translated it correctly. "He . . . was paying the town heads to incite riots."

"What?" Cowen stepped closer and read over the decoded letter himself. "Why would he do that?"

Lena didn't answer. Her brows furrowed as she stared at the letter. She counted back the days just to be sure. This letter spoke about the riots that had happened when the news of the killings was released to the public. The town heads had taken care of the revolts in the Lowlands and Alkus must've had others stir up unrest in the Highlands. Did that mean he *was* tied to the killings? Was this all one big, interconnected plan?

"I have to go," she said suddenly, snatching up the message she'd written out.

"Go where? I'm not done with the letters."

She stopped in her tracks, conflicted and spurred on by questions and a ticking rage. She took a deep breath and glanced at the doors before turning back to Cowen. "Hurry. We need to leave."

He looked like he wanted to say something, but he didn't. She assumed he was thinking the same thing she was: they could talk later.

She hurried over to the statue and slipped the ledgers and the original coded letter inside. They barely fit. Cowen finished up the first forged letter, the one from Alkus, stamp and signature and all, and she slid that in too. The second letter was trickier because Cowen hadn't replicated the town head's handwriting before, and they didn't have the stamp, but his forgery skills were still extremely helpful as he copied and encoded the writing with practiced precision. The signature was the sloppiest bit and he had to touch up the stamped emblem by hand to get it to match the one Aquila had made, but it was the best they could do with what they were given.

As soon as the second letter was done and put in place, they sealed up the statue and pushed it back toward the wall, but they left it angled just enough so that it would catch someone's eye.

"You take the servants' corridor and get out of here," she told Cowen as they cleared off Alkus' desk and put everything back exactly as they'd found it. "I have something to do first, but I'll meet you at the cliffside."

Cowen's head snapped up and he looked at her as if she'd told her she was going to call for the guards. "*What?* No, I'm not leaving you."

"Cowen, please." Her eyes flashed to the door again. "I need to do this on my own."

"I can't—"

"You serve me!" she snapped. She closed her eyes and took a deep breath. "You're supposed to listen to me. So please . . . "

"You can't ask me to leave you up here, unprotected, while you're still sick—"

"I can and I am." She opened her eyes and glared. The letter crackled as her hand tightened around it. "I'm capable of taking care of myself. I'm not unprotected, and I'm not sick, not like you. I don't need you here!" She snapped her mouth shut and froze. "Right now," she added. "I don't need you for this."

Hurt flashed across Cowen's face before he shoved it away, his expression becoming distant and neutral. "Is this an order?"

She fought to keep her own face blank. "It is."

"Fine," he said stiffly. "But if you're not at the cliffside within an hour, I'm coming back."

"Fine."

When they left the study, they went their separate ways without so much as glancing at each other. Her heart dropped, but the heat slithered in to take its place.

She lowered her mental barriers and reached out to Ira. *Where are you?*

She moved through the hallways quickly but not so quickly that she drew attention to herself. Though, not many people roamed the halls, and those who were would hardly pay attention to a servant.

She gasped as she turned a corner and the hallway disappeared. A barrage of images flashed through her mind, taking over her sight. Her balance wavered, and she put a hand on the wall. Trees surrounded her. Some were snapped in half and littered the ground. A flash of blue filled the corner of her vision. She was seeing through Ira's eyes like she sometimes saw through her Slayer's. It was only for a few seconds, but it was enough. She soon found herself blinking at the pristine halls of the palace again. She didn't know they could do that.

The band of guards around the exits didn't look twice at her as she left the palace. She spotted the crowd almost immediately. Most of the people who'd flocked to the palace after hearing promises of a fight were chatting amongst each other now that the duel had moved out of their line of sight. Because of the rules, they couldn't chase after the participants.

Her facial features began to shift back as she scuttled around the palace, in the direction she knew Ira was in. The string that tied them together acted as a guide. Her Slayer materialized beside her, and she sent it ahead, but not too far. Walking into the middle of a Slayer duel certainly wasn't one of her brighter ideas.

She looked through her Slayer's eyes for a moment. Its gaze zoomed forward through the destruction surrounding it. Trees had fallen. Holes and mounds of misplaced dirt and branches covered the ground. In the middle of it all were two figures, one standing over the other. Their Slayers were nowhere in sight.

Her consciousness snapped back to her own body, and she picked up her speed, sliding into the newly-made clearing in under a minute.

Ira still stood over Alkus, saying something in a voice too low for her to make out.

She marched over, pulling the letter out. Ira straightened and looked at her over his shoulder. His dark eyes assessed her as he wiped the blood off his face, but he only managed to smear it further. Alkus looked worse for wear, which greatly pleased her.

"What is this?" She shoved the letter in his face. "Why did you do it?"

Alkus' eyes raked over the piece of crumpled paper and then slid up to meet hers. He remained silent on the ground.

Her hands trembled as she shoved the paper closer, and her Slayer growled alongside her, prowling a few feet away. *"Answer me!"*

"You know why I did it," he wheezed. "I did it for the same reason you did *this.*"

"No, you attacked first! You *always* attack first. I'm defending myself—!"

"You're making bad decisions. Over and over again." Alkus laughed, showing his bloody teeth, and then winced. "And they'll come back to haunt you. Eventually."

Lena sneered and punched him in the face. He groaned, and she dropped onto her knees next to him. Aura flame coated one of her arms from the elbow down, and she rested that hand inches away from his neck. With her other arm, she jerked the letter forward again, this time too close for him to read, but she was sure he didn't need to read the letter to remember its contents.

"Explain this. I won't ask again."

"You were in my study," he observed.

"*Explain this!*" One of her fingers touched his jaw, just for a few seconds, but it was enough to cause a second-degree burn.

"Fucking *bitch!*" he hissed, ripping his face away. He raised one of his hands, as if to strike her, but Ira's boot slammed down on his wrist.

"Watch your mouth," he growled, blue eyes blazing once again even though his Slayer remained locked away.

She assumed both he and Alkus had nearly depleted their energy.

Alkus' laugh was dark and curling, coated with pain. "I knew the moment the prophets came down from the temple with your name that you would be this country's downfall. Some people didn't want to believe it, so they turned to the prophecy and justified your choosing." He scoffed. "They're lying to themselves. The people all believe in signs—good and bad ones—so I just had to show them that for you, the bad outweighed the good, which was easy enough when you came back during the explosions and the *Ateisha* migration. The killings started too, and then the riots . . ." He clicked his tongue in mock sympathy. "Things aren't looking good for you right now. The people, sooner or later, will see this. They'll understand why a Cursed should never sit on the throne."

Lena narrowed her eyes and restrained herself from driving her hand through his throat. "Well, it looks like things didn't go according to plan, did it?"

Alkus tilted his head and stared at her challengingly. "Did it?" He winced when Ira's boot pressed down harder on his wrist.

"I know you don't want to die," she said. "You want to live and rule, right? Tell me why I shouldn't kill you right here so that you're no longer a problem for me."

Alkus' face twisted and he sneered up at her. "I won't beg. Not to you." He spat and a glob of blood hit her cheek. Ira kicked him in the face, drawing a cry from his mouth and more blood from his nose. "Kill me if you must. Just like you did all the others."

She stared at him, her heart beating calmly in her chest. Her aura flame was only inches away from his skin, not quite burning him . . . but almost. If she ended it here, she wouldn't have to worry about him again. He would be out of the way, so she could tackle her other problems.

But that would be too easy. For him.

She pulled back the aura flame and pushed herself to her feet. "I hope you enjoy your cell," she said before walking away.

∼

LENA FOUND XAVIEN EASILY.

Amid the brewing tension, he'd decided to take a trip to the hot springs located a few miles into the forest, about equal distance from the palace and Koseria, the easternmost city in the Highlands. Of course, with all the killings and riots and the event at the palace, the hot springs was nearly empty. He and two other women had the entire place to themselves, but his company ran off to grab more food or wine. Or drugs.

Lena had been waiting nearby long enough to see them sniff white powder from a tray. Cloud. And by the looks of it, they had taken quite a bit. He was making her job too easy.

Once the naked and giggling women disappeared between the trees, heading for the lodge nearby, Lena made her appearance.

Xavien was lounging in the hot springs, his eyes closed, body lax, and legs floating in front of him. "Forget something?" he called, cracking one eye open.

She channeled all her strength into her arms and yanked him out of the water, throwing him onto the grass. He stared up at her, wide-eyed.

He tried to call his Slayer and summon his aura flame, but the former was easily taken down and eliminated by her Slayer and the latter fizzled out as soon as she sealed her own aura flame over it. He was too high to do anything other than soak in his own panic.

She didn't give him a chance to scream or scramble to his feet. Her aura flame stretched to form a thin, sharp blade. She placed it at his mouth as she pinned him down. "Shh, don't talk."

"What are you—?"

She pressed her knees harder into his thighs until he cut himself off with a choked gasp. "I said *don't talk*. I know you're not very bright, but you're not *that* stupid. You know why I'm here, don't you? Nod yes or no."

Fear coated his hazy eyes as her aura flame dagger rose. The purple crackling energy was reflected in his dilated pupils. Ever so slowly, he nodded.

"I'm going to kill you. Do you know why I'm going to kill you? Nod yes or no."

He didn't move.

She twisted her hand so the dagger pointed down, directly over his eye. "You were in on the plan to kill my family. You and the others tormented me. You spied on me and my parents and my siblings. When Tuck led me out into the forest, away from my family, you *knew*, didn't you?"

Xavien shook his head. "No, we—"

She cut his eyebrow. Skin burned and blood spilled. "*Shut up.* I don't want to hear your excuses. You haven't changed. You've only gotten worse. You showed that to me at the ball. You don't regret a thing."

None of them did.

"You're wrong," Xavien garbled out, trying to inch away from the ever-approaching dagger and the blistering heat. "Please. *Please!* I was just a kid."

She cocked her head to the side, her eyes narrowing. "So was I."

So were her siblings.

She slid the blade into his skill.

CHAPTER
SIXTY-ONE

Atreus staggered back into the side of the house.

That was a Slayer. What the fuck was a Slayer doing here? Mila had said the prophets hadn't unsealed anyone's Imprint.

Roars filled the air. The snow was coming down harder now, so it was difficult to see the town streets. But the Slayers were bright enough to cut through the haze. At least half a dozen of them littered the streets, and they tore into people left and right. Slayers had better eyesight than Blessed, but something in Atreus' gut told him they weren't making exceptions for firstborns. Like before, they took down every person they saw.

He pushed away from the house and ran toward the thick of the battle. All he could think about were Finn, Mila, and Judah.

If things weren't so dire, he might've laughed when the snow picked up even more, falling from the sky in sheets of cold gray gossamer. The visibility went from shitty to nonexistent in a few seconds. The wind picked up with the storm and it the whistled in his ears. The screams blended into it far too well.

Atreus stopped, breathing hard. He looked around, only seeing gray and the occasional flash of bright colored light.

What are you going to do?

What are you going to DO?

If he went anywhere, he'd essentially be traveling blind. His enhanced sight was useless in bad weather like this.

But *he* wasn't useless. In every realm, his job was to find the stone and get them back to the Institute. As many of them as possible. The others relied on him. To act. *Quickly.* He couldn't afford to let anything affect and distract him here.

Push it aside. Push it aside. Push it aside.

He didn't need to rely on his eyesight to find the stone.

Atreus took a deep breath and closed his eyes. He visualized his location in his mind and then *expanded*, stretching out from that point in search of the hum that always seemed to find him.

Cries and inhumane screeches filled the air, making it difficult for him to pick up on any other noise. Each scream peeled away at his armor of concentration and made him want to curl in on himself, but he forced his body to relax and allowed the cold to numb him. The sounds soon mixed and softened, creating a static that filled his ears.

And then he caught it.

The tingles hit him first, spreading through his body and coaxing it to turn toward the source. The hum came a few moments later, almost clicking into place.

It was there.

He didn't know where *there* was. He couldn't see past a few feet in front of him, but he moved forward anyway.

Small ice pellets rained down at an angle, scraping against his face and biting into the back of his hands. He gritted his teeth and tucked his chin close to his chest, careful of the occasional patch of ice. Thankfully, their uniform jackets were somewhat thick. Atreus was freezing, but he wouldn't *freeze*.

He could see his connection to the stone behind his eyelids. Real but not tangible. A stream leading him forward. When the sound around him shifted, he opened his eyes and took in the forest before him. The needle-covered tree branches caught most of the current snowfall, but mounds of accumulated snow from the previous blizzards remained under the trees. The wind kicked up the top layer of snow already on the ground and it briefly danced in the air before falling back down, creating snow drifts.

Atreus yanked his feet out of the snow and picked up his speed now that he could see better. The humming grew louder, the buzzing stronger. His thighs ached at the effort it took to move through the snow, but he still wasn't going fast enough. He gritted his teeth and pushed harder.

He ran as fast as he could, trying to home in on that magical string leading him to their ticket out of here—

His skin prickled with something that had nothing to do with the stone or the cold, and before he realized what was happening, his body involuntarily tensed in preparation for the force that rammed into him a split second later.

He stumbled back, his hands grabbing the shoulders of his assailant. Better a person than a Slayer. Using his momentum, he spun around and shoved them away. He steadied himself right as the other person fell back against a tree trunk.

"Harlow?" His shoulders dropped as he stared at her in surprise.

Unlike him, she didn't lower her guard for even a second. Her wide eyes searched over Atreus' shoulder as she fought to regain her breath.

"We've got to go," she panted, reaching out to grab him.

A chilling laugh danced through the trees, and they both immediately froze. There was nothing human about that sound. He didn't spot any glow between the trees, but it was close.

A branch cracked and they took off running.

"This way!" he shouted as he leaped over a snowbank. "The stone is this way!"

He didn't look back to see if she was following him. Fear gripped him tightly, preventing him from doing anything that would slow him down.

A Slayer had set its sight on Harlow and was hunting her, and she had led it straight to him. The Slayer wouldn't stop, so neither could they. If it caught up to them, they were dead. But they couldn't outrun it. His only hope was that they reached the stone before the Slayer reached them.

The trees started to thin and the snow had let up, so he could see beyond the forest. A large, open field began where the trees stopped, with a giant white wall at the other end.

Tree branches snapped and groaned behind him. The Slayer shrieked this time, and Atreus' heart skipped a beat. It was close. So close.

Icicles dozens of feet tall hung down from the rocky edges of the huge cliff. There had to be a cave hidden somewhere in there. Some place for the stone. Or at least some place they could hide. But he didn't know if they would even make it to the wall.

He broke out of the forest and the wind slammed into him, howling in his ears. He got about forty feet out before he began to slide. His legs locked and he threw his arms out for balance. The snow moved under his feet, revealing the ice beneath it. He spun around right as Harlow slipped, falling forward on her hands and knees a few feet away. They made eye contact, a silent message passing between them right as the Slayer broke from the treeline.

It was an electrifying white, which was why he hadn't been able to easily spot it earlier. Its screech chilled his skin more than the cold ever could.

"Now would be a good time to test that theory of yours!" Harlow shouted.

His eyes darted to hers. "What?"

"We can't outrun it!" She pushed herself to her feet. "There's no getting away now unless you do your thing and call the fucking *Te'Monai!*"

He stared at her stupidly, eyes wide.

The Slayer charged toward them.

Harlow stared back at him, waiting. "*Atreus!*"

"I don't—I can't—"

The Slayer was closing in fast. It moved over the snow and ice like they were nothing.

"*We're going to fucking die if you don't do something!*"

Everything slowed around him. All sounds faded. Looking at the Slayer directly from this distance was nearly blinding. It was so close. So frighteningly close. All he had to do was close his eyes and count to five and things would be over. He wouldn't have to fight anymore.

But he'd promised Finn, and he didn't want to die. He wanted to live.

I don't want to die.
I don't want to die.
I don't want to die!

The Slayer lunged toward them, jaws open and claws outstretched. Atreus stared into its dark eyes, and for a split second, he saw his reflection.

He blinked. The ice shattered and the Slayer was seized in midair.

Atreus and Harlow stumbled back, trying to outrun the cracks in the ice that spread toward them. The ice snapped and groaned as it split. Atreus heel came down to meet nothing but air, but Harlow grabbed his arm and yanked him forward before he could fall. They both went sprawling onto the ice as the cracks slowly crawled to a stop only inches away from their feet. Atreus looked up just in time to see the giant serpent crash back against the ice, sinking under the water with the Slayer still in its jaws.

He winced as frigid water rained down on him and stared aghast at the giant hole in the ice. Water sloshed over the sides and chunks of ice bobbed in the rough waves.

Chest heaving, Atreus turned toward Harlow.

She slowly looked at him. "Was that . . . ?"

He nodded.

"We've never come across them in the water before."

He shook his head and swallowed roughly. "What the fuck was that? Not the *Te'Monai*. The Slayer. I thought everyone's Imprints were sealed."

Harlow's face turned grave. "I thought so too."

Flashes of light in his peripheral vision caused him to turn back to the forest. At least a dozen more Slayers stepped out from the trees. They all let out exciting shrieks when they caught on to his and Harlow's scent. They were predators celebrating finding their prey.

His eyes roved over the Slayers in horror. Just how many firstborns had their Imprints unsealed? Had they *all* lost control? Was there even anyone still alive back at the town?

The Slayers sprinted toward them, kicking up snow in their wake.

"Atreus! Do the thing—"

"I know, *I know!*"

The issue was that he couldn't *see* the *Te'Monai* in this realm. Before, he would see one and direct his intentions, and they would act. Now they were below. He felt like he was grasping at empty air.

Help. We need help. The Slayers—get rid of them. Kill them.

His chest tightened, as if forming into a knot. The string that extended from him, connecting him to some transcendental source, was yanked. Something expanded inside of him, and then under him. The ice shook. And then it cracked. *All of it.*

Atreus was thrown to the side. He took a deep breath before plunging into the freezing water. The sensation of thousands of tiny needles pressing into his skin was immediate, and he gasped without thinking. Water flowed into his mouth, and he rapidly swam up toward the light above him, his chest burning for air. As soon as he broke the surface, he began coughing up the water he'd inhaled. He greedily drew in all the air that he could as he blinked the iciness from his eyes, kicking his legs to stay afloat.

Screeches and deep moans filled the air around him. Slayers were being swallowed and dragged into the water by the *Te'Monai*. A slippery, gray tentacle raised from the water right next to him. Something crashed behind him, sending him under the waves again.

Atreus opened his eyes under water, trying his best to swim away from the thick of the fighting, but it surrounded him. All he could see were large, withering limbs and fading light and the deep, dark water. He threw his arms out in front of him and began to swim, only resurfacing when he could no longer stay under.

By the time he reached solid ice again, he was exhausted. His legs ached because he'd refused to ditch his boots, knowing it would be all but impossible to walk in this terrain without them. He had swallowed several mouthfuls of water and was shivering. So when a hand extended in front of him, he didn't think twice before grabbing it.

The hand hauled him back onto the ice and Atreus collapsed against it, coughing out whatever water remained in his lungs. He raised his head to find Tolar standing over him.

"Thanks," he breathed out, pressing his forehead against the ice. It didn't feel good, but he needed a moment. He slowly pushed himself to his feet, taking note of the ways in which his body protested. "Did you see Harlow climb out—?"

His words were sucked back down his throat when he caught sight of a knife heading straight for him. Atreus twisted out of the way, but his reaction speed was delayed. He couldn't dodge it completely. The knife cut right through his uniform and into his forearm. Blood immediately poured from the wound.

Atreus stumbled away, pressing a hand against the ice to brace himself. He regained his footing right as Tolar came at him again, but this time, he was better prepared.

He spun with Tolar's lunge, sliding in close so his back was against Tolar's front, and grabbed the wrist with the knife. He elbowed Tolar in the face with his other arm. Or tried to anyway. Tolar somewhat blocked it, so Atreus hit near his temple instead of his nose. Tolar staggered back, and Atreus squeezed his wrist, trying to get him to drop the knife, but Tolar blindly reached out and grabbed onto Atreus' arm. Right over the wound. And then he *squeezed* back.

Atreus screamed. His vision darkened and a surge of heat coursed through him when Tolar dug his thumb into his flesh.

He wasn't sure what exactly happened in the next few seconds. When his vision returned, he was several feet away from Tolar. And the knife was on the ice between them.

"What the fuck are you doing?" Atreus snapped. "You're trying to kill me?"

Tolar was nursing his wrist. Atreus had dug his nails in, so there were deep grooves in Tolar's skin.

"I'm *going* to kill you," Tolar sneered. His eyes glowed green and his Slayer materialized next to him.

His Imprint was unsealed. Fantastic.

Atreus eyed the knife. It was useless against a Slayer, but he had his own way of fighting those things now. He inched back toward the water. Slowly.

"How'd you get the knife? They're under lock and key at the Institute?"

"It was given to me," Tolar said. His Slayer took a step forward, its feet melting the snow, but the ice under it was too thick to thaw completely. "I'm not the only person who wants you dead."

Despite his pounding heart, Atreus fought to keep the smirk off his face. Right there. That was what he'd wanted to know.

"Prophet Silas is finally sick of me, is he? Are you a snitch, Tolar? Did you go running to him because you didn't feel included? He decided I was too big of a problem. He gave you a knife and unsealed your Imprint. Your buddies' too. Did he give you that letter as well? I take it that all the information it contains is fake then."

Tolar stared at him a bit oddly before saying, "No. He gave me the letter, but its contents are true. None of it matters though."

"How does it not matter?"

"Because you're not going back to the Institute. You're dying here."

Atreus' face tightened, a scowl pulling at his lips. "Tell me, what did he offer you in return?"

He was close to the water now. Only a few feet away.

"Whatever it was, it's a lie. And if you believed a single word he said, you're even *stupider* than I thought."

"Shut up!" Tolar snapped. His Slayer snarled with him.

"*Think about it,*" Atreus stressed. "He's got you doing his dirty work for him. You've turned against your people, and for what?"

"Vanik was right about one thing," Tolar said. "You can't take everyone. I knew you didn't want me on board. I knew you were pretending. *I knew you would turn on me.* So I did it first. What did you think was going to happen to the rest of us if you got out? *You* would no longer be around for the prophets to blame."

Most of that was true, but not all of it.

"The prophets can't kill all of the firstborns. They won't—"

"And that makes it okay?"

"*Nothing about this is okay!*" Atreus' heels teetered on the edge. "That's why we're trying to get out."

Tolar's eyes darkened. "*You.* That's why *you* are trying to get out. You would leave the rest of us to rot."

The Slayer slowly prowled toward Atreus.

He shook his head. "That's not true."

He had nowhere left to go. He took his eyes off the Slayer to plead with Tolar one last time.

"You don't have to do this. *Think*, Tolar. The prophets are the real enemy and they're *using* you. If you do this, you will accomplish *nothing*. You're siding with *them*, not us."

Call your Slayer back, he begged. *Come to reason. Don't do this.*

Tolar scoffed and followed his Slayer. His brows were drawn together, a frown tugging at his mouth. "There's never been an *us*, Atreus. You can only afford to look out for yourself, right? I'm not siding with them. I'm siding with *me,* and the other firstborns who will get left behind."

"You're killing the only hope they have!" Atreus exclaimed. "If we get out—if *anyone* gets out—there's a chance for *everyone!* How can you not see that?"

Tolar didn't respond. He stopped before the knife and bent down to pick it up.

Bright blurs raced past in the distance as howls filled the air. More Slayers had arrived. Just how many firstborns were in on this plot? How many firstborns wanted him dead?

Te'Monai's tentacles broke the ice around him, dragging the Slayers under. Water shot dozens of feet into the air. Slayers burned on land but underwater their aura flame was practically useless.

Tolar wouldn't listen to logic. He had already made up his mind. He wanted Atreus dead. He was too far gone.

"*Be careful of the people you surround yourself with. You do have many choices ahead of you, but you can't run from your destiny, Atreus.*"

"For what it's worth, thank you for trying," Tolar said. "Even if it was all an act."

"I did try," he agreed, looking back at Tolar. His blood trailed down the back of his hand and dripped onto the ice. "I *tried*. I always *try*, and it doesn't work."

If Vanik were here, he'd be laughing at him. But Atreus didn't even know if Vanik was alive. Or Weylin. Or Harlow. Or Finn or Mila or Judah.

Atreus pointed at Tolar, his eyes cold. "You're going to try to kill me," he clarified. "And it's not going to work."

Tolar narrowed his eyes, and his Slayer stopped approaching.

"You're going to die," Atreus said softly, *brokenly*. Because that was the truth. Atreus needed to keep going, and he couldn't if Tolar was alive. The wind carried his words, delivering them to Tolar's ears. "I tried . . . but you wouldn't listen."

For a few moments, everything seemed to slow. Tolar's Slayer stood only about twenty feet away.

Back away.

It didn't.

The Slayer sprang forward with a single silent command from Tolar. The heat from its form washed over Atreus, but before its claws could sink into his flesh, tentacles shot out from the open water behind him and wrapped around it. The blazing aura flame worked to burn the threat, but the tentacles were thick and armored and there were too many. The water was too close.

Atreus dropped to the ice to avoid the Slayer as it was dragged into the frigid depths, but he quickly popped back up and ran.

Another massive tentacle rose from the water and slammed down on the ice only a few feet behind Tolar. The traitor let out a cry and stumbled forward to avoid falling into the water. Maybe he couldn't swim.

The strike from the tentacle had cut off the slab of ice from the rest of the solid sheet, so Atreus and Tolar were floating, at the complete mercy of the waves.

They met in the middle.

Tolar straightened right as Atreus lunged. In a blind panic, Tolar shoved the knife forward, but his grip was weak, and he was still clearly startled by what he'd just seen—and *experienced*; his connection to his Slayer had been severed abruptly, which always left people feeling a bit off-balance.

Atreus knocked the knife out of Tolar's hand and tackled him to the ice. He grabbed the front of Tolar's uniform to lift him up only to slam him back down.

"You tried to kill me!" Atreus raged. "After I only tried to help you! Vanik wanted to kill you after you overheard us in the library, but I told him not to! *I saved you!*"

He slammed Tolar down against the ice again and again and again.

The traitor merely laughed, which set Atreus' blood *blazing*. "You didn't do shit—!"

Atreus punched him in the face. And then again. And again.

"You're not the hero," Tolar slurred, spitting out blood. "Everyone thinks you are, but they're wrong." He lifted his head, leaning it in close like he was about to share a secret. Softly, he said, "I see you for what you really are."

Atreus saw his reflection in the mirror. The monster. The *Te'Monai*. And while it scared him, the thought of someone else seeing it absolutely *terrified* him.

He stared down at Tolar, frozen and unfeeling. His hands loosened in Tolar's uniform. "That's not me," were the words that escaped his numbed lips.

It isn't.

"It is," Tolar spat. "You can't be a good guy and survive. Not without loss. And *you?* You haven't—"

He choked on his own blood when Atreus grabbed the knife sitting on the ice and plunged it into Tolar's chest. He did it again and pressed it in farther, leaning down.

"*You* did this!" Atreus said between gritted teeth.

Tolar stared up at him, eyes wide and mouth open. He was finally panicking. He looked so surprised. Why was he surprised?

"*You made me do this!* I tried, Tolar! *I tried! You* ruined this!"

He didn't remember if he said more or what he said. He only remembered the moment Tolar *stopped*—stopped moving, stopped breathing, stopped making noise.

Atreus pushed himself off him and took a half step back. The knife was still in Tolar's chest. He left it there as he dragged Tolar's body to the edge of the ice and then pushed him into the water. Tolar sunk beneath the waves, his hands outstretched above him. Atreus watched until his body disappeared in the depths.

He turned around and stared at the blood stain on the ice, unsure of what to do. The cold went right through his frozen uniform and aching bones.

The humming finally broke past the barrier he'd built around his mind, coaxing him forward once again. He put one trembling leg in front of the other, stopping only when he reached the edge of the ice again.

A small clear chunk of ice bobbed on top of the waves. Atreus dropped to his knees haphazardly and reached out to grab it. He pulled it into his lap, and in the center was the stone. Its song lulled him like the waves, returning his heart rate to normal.

I've made my choice.

He carefully smashed ice against ice until the stone was free. The light blue jewel rolled across the snow.

I want to live.

Atreus scrambled after it.

∼

WHEN HE RETURNED to the Institute, he didn't put up a fight when handing over the stone. He was actually rather compliant.

He pushed himself to his feet despite his sore body and marched right up to Prophet Silas, who, despite typically having a secure hold on his emotions, looked rather surprised to see him.

You're going to have to try harder, asshole.

Atreus lifted his chin as he stopped before the prophet. He slapped his bloodied hand with the stone against the prophet's chest. "Add it to your collection."

Prophet Silas clenched his jaw but took the stone from him wordlessly. Atreus turned his back on him and walked out of the cavern. The enforcers stepped in front of him, blocking the exit.

"Let him go," Prophet Silas said.

And they did. Atreus went back to the sleeping hall, and for the first time in a long time, slept peacefully.

∼

He was sent to Miss Anya later. The cut on his arm didn't need stitches, so she only cleaned and dressed it. She then applied some sort of ointment to the bruises that littered his body after checking to make sure he had no other serious injuries.

"Did Prophet Silas have you heal me earlier?" he asked as he tugged his shirt on. She stopped what she was doing over by the medicine cabinets. "After he punished me and before I was sent out?"

She began moving again, carefully setting glass vials onto a shelf. "No. He didn't have me do anything."

Atreus caught how she'd worded her response and thought about what that meant. He lifted his head when she walked up to him again.

"Here." She pressed a vial into his hands. "You've got to be running low."

She went back to sifting through the medicine cabinets, her back to him—a clear dismissal.

Atreus climbed off the bed and left the infirmary. Once he was in the hall, he unfurled his fingers. In his palm was a vial of sleep elixir.

∼

They were sent out again almost immediately. The remaining firstborns stood silent and still in the cavern, like soldiers about to be sent to a war they'd never wanted to fight in. They were resigned. Yet angry.

"In the past few weeks, we have made great strides, but we are being urged to advance faster," a prophet announced. "Because of this, there are three realms targeted for today's Outing. A third of you will be sent to each realm. I will read out the names of those in each group, so listen closely."

The room shifted before him. Everything became silent, but the prophet's words didn't reach Atreus' ears. He couldn't hear anything over his thoughts.

They are splitting them up.

His eyes immediately found Prophet Silas'.

Of course.

Divide and conquer.

Prophet Silas' first attempt hadn't worked, so he was trying again.

Atreus listened to the names being called, latching onto each familiar one.

Finn, Weylin, and *Judah.*

Vanik, Mila, and *Harlow.*

Atreus.

He would be alone.

PART FOUR
THE RAVAGE

CHAPTER
SIXTY-TWO

Within twelve hours of breaking into Alkus' study, a band of guards came down to tell Lena that she could return to the Highlands and resume her duties.

Whispers about Alkus' defeat and the documents that had been found in his study surrounded her as soon as she set foot in the Highlands. While awaiting trial, Alkus was in close company with the man he'd had guarded so heavily. She hoped they had *great* conversations.

Evanna had apparently been unwilling to sell Alkus out, so she'd also been imprisoned in the meantime but not in the palace dungeon. There was plenty of room down there, but the enforcers had chosen to send her to a holding cell in Solavas for the duration of the investigation.

No one rushed to greet Lena when she stepped into her room, reminding her of the deaths of her attendants. That thought held her still for a while. It crept through her, leaving nothing but a cold, consuming ache. She longed to crawl into her bed, but before she could sit down, someone knocked on her door.

She sighed but called, "Come in!"

Andra stepped into the room, a wrinkle between her brows. "There's a physician in the hall. They've come about Ira."

The cold completely dissipated, and she straightened. "Where is he?" she asked urgently.

She hadn't gotten a good look at him during the duel. She'd been a bit narrow-sighted and short on time. He'd won and been on his feet, but that didn't mean he hadn't been hurt.

She hurried out to the hall and a physician led her through the palace, stopping in front of Ira's study.

"He's not in the infirmary?" she asked. So it couldn't be that bad.

The physician shook their head. "Councilman Ira refused to go. He said his injuries weren't serious, and they're not, but they're nothing to dismiss either. We treated him here and left him some medicine."

She entered the room to see Ira standing, hunched over his desk with his head dipped. The hand splayed across his forehead hid his face from her. He wore a black silk button-up, but it was completely open, revealing his sharp collarbones and the planes of his chest. And white bandages.

She strode toward him. He didn't lift his head to acknowledge her presence until she rounded the desk and stopped at his side. He had a bruise high on his left cheekbone, right under his eye, which had a splash of red in the corner due to a burst blood vessel. Bandages covered his right hand and shoulder, as well as his abdomen.

"The physician said the injuries weren't serious," she accused.

"Because they're not."

"You always underplay things, Ira."

He pushed himself away from the desk and sat in his chair, moving smoothly without wincing. "Most of it is superficial and already healed. I walked away from the duel. Alkus did too, but I'm sure inside he was *crawling*." Ira's upper lip curled as he stared off into space, recalling the incident.

She bit the inside of her cheek and took a step closer. "Are you okay?"

"I'm fine, Lena. I said—"

"I don't mean physically."

A harsh breath left his lips and he pushed himself back to his feet. He walked over to a liquor cart by the bookshelves and poured himself a glass, downing it in one go. The picture of sanity.

She believed him when he said he wasn't seriously hurt. He was moving well, but his motions revealed his agitation. He'd volunteered to duel Alkus, and he'd done his job by providing a distraction. He'd won. But maybe she shouldn't have let him do it at all.

"Ira, don't shut me out."

"Oh, you want a glass too?" he asked, his back still to her.

"No."

He shrugged and drank the glass he'd poured for her. When he went to make a third, she walked over and grabbed his wrist before he could. His eyes snapped to hers.

She stared back calmly, pushing down on his arm until he finally set the bottle of liquor down. She then placed her hand on his bare chest, right over his heart. "Talk to me."

His lips twisted. "What do you want me to say?"

"*Anything*. I'm here, alright? I'll listen."

So much weight and emotion rested behind his stare.

"Okay," he said, quick and sharp and cold. "I'm not seriously injured. I'm fine. I've certainly had worse, but I walked away from that fight *hurting*—more than before. And it won't stop. Nothing will make it stop. No medicine or sleep or alcohol or time. And I hate it and I hate them and I hate the Numina for making it this way—"

She grabbed his other hand and pulled him completely toward her.

"It'll get better," she told him. "It *will*."

Some of the emotion broke through and something akin to anguish clouded his eyes. "You can't know that."

No, she can't. But she has to hope.

"I have a Flair," Ira suddenly said. "I haven't told you. I don't know why. I wasn't trying to keep it from you. For most of my life, I didn't even know I had it. But I can be persuasive. Most people don't even notice the effect I have on them. It's not flashy, but it's useful, even though it doesn't always work."

He ripped his hands away from her and she let him.

"I tried to use it when I was arrested. I tried to use it during the attack and when people challenged me for a duel. And. It. Never. Worked." Ira ran his fingers through his hair, tugging at his strands. "Nothing ever works when I need it to work."

"You have a Flair?" She'd heard everything else, but she couldn't get past *that*. "Why didn't you bring it up sooner?"

He was right about it not being a showy Flair, but it sounded pretty fucking useful. She thought about all the ways they could've *tried* to use it. All the hassle it could've saved them.

"I don't know, Lena. I don't know. I just said that." He turned back on her, throwing his hands out. "Maybe I didn't tell people because I didn't want to use it. Because that's what you were thinking right—how useful it could be?"

She frowned, suddenly overcome with guilt and annoyance. "You're in my head?"

"Your walls are up," he said, but that wasn't an answer.

"Have you ever used it on me?" she blurted out. The thought came to her suddenly, refusing to leave her mind until she addressed it.

He flinched, and she immediately regretted asking.

"*No*," he said darkly, almost glaring at her. "No, I've never used my ability to manipulate you. Did you hear anything I just said? You told me you'd listen, and—"

"I am," she said hurriedly, stepping forward. "I am. I will. I'm sorry. I—"

"Do you know what happened the first time I dueled Alkus?" His voice dropped in volume again, a secret staining only the space between them. "Alkus put me in a coma. The physicians didn't think I'd wake up. But to spite them all, I did. I avoided him after that. Until I was strong enough to *beat* him. And I did. Beat him. I should've put *him* in a coma."

Her lips parted and whatever she was about to say died in her throat. She slowly walked toward him, and he didn't back away. Her fingers slipped into the space between his and she gently tapped the bandages on his hand.

"Maybe I should've killed him," she whispered.

It was an offer to take part of the blame. Not that Ira should blame himself, but if it was self-pity or self-hatred he felt, she would dampen it and take on whatever he would let her.

"We should leave," he said suddenly. "Right now. We can run away and forget our problems—"

"What?" She stepped back but didn't let go of his hands. Her brow furrowed as she looked over his face. "Run away? Now?"

His face crumpled. It was slow, but he didn't seem disappointed or surprised.

"I have responsibilities here, and so do you." She shook her head. "I already ran away once. I won't do it again, especially not after all the progress we've made. We're so close to being *done.*"

No, not done. They would never be, not while they remained in their current positions, but the hard part would be over. They could rest.

"You're right," Ira said, his voice flat and his face impassive once again. "Running isn't an option. How silly of me. Then you would have to leave behind your new friends."

Although his words were dull, they cut deep. She gave him a disapproving look. "You know that's not why."

"Do I?" he countered. "You didn't tell me about going down to the Lowlands with Aquila the first time. You didn't tell me about her and Kieryn joining our meeting in the cabin."

"I did—"

"At the dinner table, minutes before they arrived!" He took a deep breath and turned.

For a moment, she thought he was returning to the liquor cart, but he only moved back behind the desk a few steps away, adding more distance between them.

"You have no right to be upset with me. Not when you disappeared for days with no warning, and I still don't know where you—"

"You're right." He spun back around, his shirt fluttering. "We've both been dishonest with one another."

Her shoulders slumped and she sighed. Sometimes he was so blunt with the way he said things, and it just made the situation worse.

"I know that I love you," she began. "I want to be with *you*. I want to make it work. I know I can be difficult and frustrating, yes, but things *will* start getting better now. Mikhail can't hold the fort down on his own." She moved forward, but the desk sat between them. "We can't let them win. Not when we're so close."

"I want to be with you too," he said simply, his eyes on her but not quite *seeing* her. "I said I wouldn't ask for anything you're unwilling to give, and . . . if you need something that I can't give you—some*one*—I wouldn't fault you for seeking it, or them, out. I couldn't. I've said that before. You're your own person. And so am I, but I don't think . . . I don't think I'm that impressive of a person on my own." He exhaled heavily and looked at the far wall. "I'm my best with you, so I don't like to think of myself . . . otherwise. I know how it sounds, but I won't apologize for my feelings. Or the fact that I want you all to myself."

The last of his words came out in a low rasp. His gaze flickered to her, dark and heavy, and heat slowly prickled through her.

"Ira—"

"I'm not good at sharing," he said as he smoothly moved around the desk while maintaining eye contact. "You know that."

She felt drawn to him, her feet unconsciously gliding over the floor, bringing her to him and erasing the distance between them. For now. She couldn't help the way she reacted to him. If she was *fire*, he was both air and oil, something she needed to *breathe* to survive and something that incited her.

Her eyes slipped closed as Ira's hands brushed over her arms and shoulders. She sunk into his embrace. Logic was holding on by strings—he was hurt, and they were in the middle of discussing something important. But he made her insatiable, and it had been a while since they'd done anything like this. The moment his lips grazed her cheek, she abandoned all thoughts other than him.

A soft sound involuntarily escaped her lips. Ira must've taken that as a sign of encouragement because his lips trailed down her jaw. She automatically arched into him. One of his hands tightened around her elbow, the other snaked behind her, fingers fanning across the small of her back, supporting her as he spun them around and walked them forward.

"Ira," she said again. She wasn't quite sure why. Maybe in an attempt to regain his attention so they could go back to the conversation at hand. Maybe she just liked saying his name.

He nipped under her ear, drawing a gasp from her. She ran into something that cut into her hips. The desk.

Ira's hands moved and then she was in the air. She grabbed the front of his shirt, used to him moving her around like this by now. He set her on top of the desk and was quick to move in between her legs. She opened them wider so he could press against her and *oh* she felt so warm. They could dance this dance with their eyes closed.

He kissed her like a starved man, rough and intense, and she was forced back under the pressure. He moved forward with her, unwilling to let an inch of space develop between them. She wished it was this easy all the time.

They sucked in small gasps of air when they could, but they were willing to compromise full lungs for a full heart. The heat surging through her focused in her lower abdomen, coiling and pulling tight when Ira's hands swept down her thighs. He grabbed the end of her dress and hiked it up so her legs were bare to him.

They moved fast and almost frantically. Her hands shook and her vision blurred as he knelt before her, slipped off her underwear, and pressed his mouth against her sex.

Krashing, she had missed this. It had been too long. She would come any second. His blazing tongue was soft yet firm as it curled against her clit. A loud moan escaped her when he added his fingers.

"Lift your hips, Lena," he murmured against her.

The vibrations of his voice shot through her, causing the knots in her abdomen to tighten further. She drew her legs up around his head, but he pushed them back down.

She planted her shaking hands next to her hips and lifted. Her arms shook and she could barely hold her weight for more than a few seconds, but that was all he needed.

One hand clamped down on the flesh of her hips and he pulled her forward, thrusting his face farther into her folds. She cried out and fell against the desk, her back flush against the cool wood for only a split second before Ira's tongue pulled at the string along her spine. She arched until only her ass and shoulders touched the desk. Her knees came up, framing his head, and this time, he let them. He released her hip to drape his free arm across her pelvis to keep her still. She smothered her moans with her fist while her other hand scraped uselessly against the desk.

The building pressure and blistering heat sent tingles through her, making her feel light, like she was floating. The burning coil constricted as she neared the edge. And then he pulled away.

Lena lifted her head, a curse at her lips. Ira was already looking at her from between her legs, his lips wet and red. Her mouth dried up at the very sight.

"Remember . . . " He placed a kiss on the inside of her thigh, maintaining eye contact. " . . . only I can make you feel this way."

She nodded and reached out. He grabbed her hand, weaving his fingers through hers.

"We're bonded." He pressed his lips to her fingers, to the mark on the center of her palm. "There's no going back from that."

"I would never want to," she breathed out, falling back and staring up at the ceiling. There were stars. Of course there were stars.

Ira's mouth returned to her core, sucking and licking until she squirmed against him and the desk. She was taut and trembling, tears blurring her vision, her head thrown back and lips parted as obscene moans filled the room.

The heat intensified as the tingles spread over her skin and deep inside of her in tandem with his tongue. She was right at the edge again, but Ira didn't stop this time. His hand returned to her, his thumb pressing down on her clit to create a delicious friction that had her shuddering. He repeated that movement a few times with his finger and his tongue and that was all it took to finish her.

When her vision returned to normal, tremors still ran through her body. Her sweaty skin stuck to the desk, and she had no intention of detaching from it anytime soon, at least not on her own. Her legs were too heavy and uncooperative right now. Ira's forehead was pressed against the inside of her thigh, and he was breathing just as hard as she was.

"Do you need—?"

"No," he huffed out. "No, I'm good."

He stood up and she saw that he was, in fact, taken care of. Another rush of heat went through her at the thought of him getting off on getting *her* off. He leaned over and she sat up to meet him. Their kiss was softer than the ones they'd shared just minutes ago, but it was just as passionate. Her hand traced the lines of his jaw as she held him close.

"Is your hand okay?" she asked after pulling away. His injuries had escaped her mind.

"It's fine," he said, kissing her again.

He moved back to give her room to slide off the desk, which she did slowly, making sure her legs would support her. She felt like a mess. And the desk was just as untidy as she expected it to be when she turned around to look at it.

One of the stray papers caught her eye, and she grabbed it without thinking. It was an invitation to a ball in the palace two days from now. They were celebrating Lena's return and good health, but the large, sprawling letters at the bottom of the invite snagged her attention. The ball also served as an engagement party for the marriage that would unite The Lands and Ouprua.

The high the sex had provided faded away then.

Right. The engagement. They had to deal with that.

She could feel Ira hovering over her shoulder. "I didn't—"

"I know," he said quietly. "I know Alkus answered for you."

His silence was loud, so she felt like she had to further explain herself.

"I wouldn't have said yes. I was thinking about it, but that was before we got the information about Sorrel." She turned around to face Ira. "Now we just have to see if she cooperates."

He eyed her while he buttoned up his shirt. "And if she doesn't? What then?"

"Then *we* will figure it out. We're good at improvising."

His lips curved up slightly.

She left his study shortly after. A messenger passed her as she walked down the hall. Lena stopped around the corner and overheard the messenger telling Ira that Prophet Nya needed to see him.

∼

"I'm surprised you requested to meet with me. You haven't shown any interest before," Sorrel said. "In fact, I would say you've gone out of your way to avoid me."

"I will admit, I've been . . . apprehensive. Time does not change the gravity of this decision," Lena said as she sat down on the other side of the small circular table.

"But time itself does change. And the less time you have, the more desperate you become. I assume that's why Alkus came to me with an answer instead of you."

They sat on a screened-in balcony overlooking one of the courtyards in the palace. The courtyard was empty. Lena had made sure of it. Picking a less popular courtyard certainly helped, but Andra and Benji were scouting the halls nearby, keeping people away. They'd agreed to monitor the halls only if she called another Sacred Guard to take their place, so Tammin, another trusted guard, was on the other side of the balcony doors, keeping an eye on her while also letting her and Sorrel have their privacy.

Lena wasn't worried about Kieryn or Aquila using their sorcery to overhear this conversation. And even if they did, she didn't think they'd do anything with this information. Von, on the other hand, was another story. She had Ira dealing with him today, keeping him far away.

Sorrel rested her legs on a wicker footstool as she picked at the fresh fruit and small cakes. She had no interest in tea. Lena hadn't touched hers either.

Her smile was too bitter to be genuine. "He shouldn't have answered for me."

"You should've answered sooner," Sorrel replied easily.

"Why *are* you so set on marriage?"

Sorrel finally looked at her, eyes narrowed slightly and sharp. "Does it matter? You already agreed to it."

"*Alkus* agreed to it."

Sorrel waved her hand. "Same thing. An agreement was reached. Our alliance will happen, as will a marriage between you and whoever you choose: Kieryn or Aquila." She popped a chocolate covered raspberry into her mouth. "If you invited me here to try and talk me out of this marriage, you can forget about it. The deal is done. You should feel at ease knowing you're doing a good thing for your country. Perhaps you don't see it that way, but the others do. Alkus did." Her fingers snatched another raspberry. "Pity what happened to him."

Lena didn't share that sentiment. "Actually, I did invite you here to try and talk you out of the marriage, but I think you'll want to listen to what I have to say."

Sorrel paused, her lips parted and another raspberry halfway to her mouth.

Lena spilled everything her informant had found. "You told me you killed two people when you were younger and that prevented you from gaining a title, but you didn't tell me who those two people were."

Sorrel set the raspberry down.

"But I found out. Eventually. And they were *important* people, which was why Ouprua covered for you. The repercussions would affect them as well, and they didn't want that. I'd be willing to bet they *still* don't want that."

"Yes," Sorrel said slowly, watching Lena with careful eyes as if seeing her for the first time. "They don't want that. And you don't want this marriage. So you want me to waive it? Come up with another agreement to safeguard this alliance? And in return, you won't release the names of those I killed?"

Lena's silence answered her question.

Sorrel's legs dropped to the floor, and she leaned over the table, resting her elbows on the tablecloth. "How do I even know you know the names?"

"I can say them if you want." She wouldn't lose anything if she did. "The men weren't from Ouprua. I'm sure their families would be glad to learn what really happened to them."

Sorrel blinked. "Fine," she said simply, flat. "No marriage. You despise them both that much?"

"I don't *want* to be married." That was reason enough.

"Again," Sorrel added. "You don't want to be married *again*. Unless that's not what you meant."

Sorrel was picking at a scab, trying to make it bleed.

"I want to work with you, with Ouprua," Lena said honestly. "Kieryn and I reached an understanding when we met after the festivities." An understanding that she hoped wasn't compromised by this conversation and her actions on this balcony. If what Kieryn had said was true and Sorrel didn't agree with The Lands' division of class, she wouldn't throw away working with Lena just because of this. "We both want to change things here, and they *can* be changed. We can make them change, but not if our partnership starts with me being forced to marry."

She knew Sorrel was trying to trap her with this marriage, draw her in close and make it difficult for her to turn against them if she ever decided to. Lena didn't take well to being ensnared.

Sorrel tapped her fingers on the table and pursed her lips. "May I cash in my questions now?" she asked abruptly, throwing Lena for a loop.

"Sure." She might as well get rid of this debt while she could. "You have four."

"Have you grown to like Kieryn or Aquila?"

Lena kept her expression neutral. "I've spent a bit of time with both. I wouldn't consider them friends, but . . . I don't dislike them. I still don't know them very well."

"Really?" Sorrel grabbed the raspberry she'd set down earlier. "I know Aquila grew up here, in the Lowlands. She doesn't like talking about her past. I don't blame her. I'm sure you kids had it rough."

Lena's brow twitched.

"Did you know her?" Sorrel's eyes were on the table, allowing Lena a brief moment of privacy to sort out the emotions that raced through her.

"Aquila?" She didn't have to force the disbelief. "Not everyone who grew up in the same place knew each other. I'm not sure you understand how large the Lowlands is. I hardly left my family's property."

They'd been lucky to live a decent distance away from others and be on good terms with their neighbors. Still, dirtyhands and all sorts of people could've cut through their property, so they hadn't been allowed out past dark or to go into town without one of their parents.

"What about after?" Sorrel asked, eyes watching Lena now. "After they were killed? You went to the Lowlands but where? Back home?"

Her fingers curled in her lap. "I went wherever I had to. So no, not . . . home. That would've gotten me killed."

Sorrel raised her brows but didn't comment on that.

"Last one," Lena reminded her.

Sorrel smiled, but it wasn't nice. "Do you believe everything these people are spouting about you and the prophecy? That you're the *Arawn?*" The word rolled off her tongue. "Their savior?"

Lena clenched her jaw. "No," she said a few seconds later. "No, I don't believe everything."

The smile was still on Sorrel's face. "Well, you're not the only one."

CHAPTER
SIXTY-THREE

Lena wanted to run to Aquila immediately, but that was probably exactly what Sorrel expected her to do. She didn't want to walk right into a trap. What had provoked Sorrel to ask Lena about Aquila? About *her* and Aquila? Did Sorrel know something? Did she know about Aquila going to the Lowlands with her? Or about Aquila *and* Kieryn's role in Alkus' takedown?

She went back to her room to think. The first sign that should've made her pause was the fact that Trent and Kilvar stood guard at her door. She knew the name of everyone in her Sacred Guard now. Cowen made sure at least one trusted member of the Sacred Guard was always on duty, meaning she'd gotten to know a particular group more than the rest. Trent and Kilvar were not in that group.

The second warning sign greeted her as soon as she walked into her room.

Jhai waited for her in her antechamber.

Lena immediately drew to a halt. "Jhai . . . What are you doing here?"

"I was called back upon your return," Jhai said, a pleasant expression on her face despite everything she'd endured. Her hands were tightly clasped in front of her.

Lena opened her mouth, but Jhai quickly added, "Grand Prophet Mikhail thought it might be a nice surprise for you."

Jhai's eyes darted to the side and that was when Lena realized they weren't the only two people present. Mikhail strolled around the corner a second later, looking relaxed and completely at home in *her room*.

A surprise indeed.

Her expression and voice hardened as she asked him the same question. "What are you doing here?"

He gestured toward Jhai. "I made sure your attendant returned safely. We can call upon more ladies if you wish—"

"No," she cut in. "I don't need anyone else." She didn't need to put anyone else in the line of fire. "Jhai's been returned safely." *Against my wishes.* "So you can go."

"I wanted to talk to you about another matter." He continued without waiting for her permission, "Our council grows small, but the issues we face only seem to grow larger."

"New representatives will be chosen soon. The royal families can fill their absent seats," she responded impatiently. "Why haven't they brought their candidates before the council?"

"They're . . . apprehensive."

She raised a brow. "About?"

"The council is being targeted, Your Majesty. They're worried that whoever they place on their chair may be the next corpse we find."

"Good thing we have the killers locked away then."

Mikhail gave her a look that was less than pleased. "You know as well as I that Alkus is not one of the killers we're looking for."

She almost laughed. Almost.

Mikhail's eyes flitted over to Jhai. He lowered his voice as he took a step closer. "There is something bigger going on here. Something . . . sinister. I can feel it. The Numina have been distant lately. They know it's coming."

She frowned. "Matters will be sorted soon. The alliance has been secured. Ouprua will aid us in our struggles, just like we will for them. This is a good thing."

He still seemed unsure. His eyes moved around the room as if he expected something to come crawling out of the walls.

"Things are changing for the better," she told him.

He shook his head. "Change isn't anything good."

Of course he thought that. He was Blessed. A traditionalist, even if he had once cast his vote for her.

"Mikhail," she said, regaining his attention. "You need to rest. These past few days have been stressful on you."

He looked weary and confused. Did he remember those words?

Muffled noises rang out from outside her bedroom, too faint to make out. A few seconds later, the doors opened and Cowen strode in. He stopped short, the tension bleeding out of him when he spotted her and the other two occupants in the room.

"Your Majesty," he said a bit stiffly, nodding to her. "Grand Prophet Mikhail. Lady Jhai."

Mikhail was much shorter than Cowen, and slighter, but he seemed to be looking down his nose at the captain of her Sacred Guard. "What's the meaning of this intrusion?"

"I believe," Lena cut in, "it's time for you to go, Grand Prophet. You've said your piece. Now get out of my room and rest." Mikhail gaped at her. "Please."

He looked around as if he expected someone to save him, but Lena, Jhai, and Cowen only stared. She'd displeased him further—she could see that—but she didn't really care. He grumbled as he left her room, still having the grace and manners to nod at her in parting.

And then there were three.

She ignored Cowen for now, turning to Jhai instead. "I'm sorry he retrieved you. He had no right—"

Jhai shook her head. "He had every right. I may not be a member of the palace staff anymore, but I *am* still a member of the queen's staff."

Her voice faded near the end. She was now the *only* member of the queen's staff.

"Well, I can release you and you can go back—"

"No!" Jhai said suddenly, her eyes widening. "No, you can't release me. I . . . have worked very hard to get here." She glanced at Cowen, and then back at Lena. "I've proved my worth."

"You have," Lena reassured her. Jhai's hands were stained with Lena's mess. "And if you wish to stay . . . I won't release you."

She wouldn't quite say she trusted Jhai, but her attendant had been faithful. Whatever Lena, Ira, and Cowen—and to an extent, Aquila and Kieryn—had done, *were doing*, Jhai was a part of. She couldn't betray them without incriminating herself.

"I'll ensure that your job is kept, but you can return to the Lowlands to be with your family."

"It's okay, Kalena. Really." Jhai smiled gently. "I want to be here."

Lena didn't understand that. If she were in Jhai's position, she'd choose her family over anything. But she wasn't in that position.

"Okay." Lena tried for a somewhat comforting smile. "Let me know if you need anything."

"I'm your attendant. You're supposed to let *me* know if *you* need anything," Jhai said.

"Right." Lena laughed nervously and looked at Cowen. He was avoiding her gaze. "Jhai, if you don't mind, could you give Cowen and I some privacy?"

Jhai nodded and left through the door in the antechamber that led into the attendants' hall. Maybe Jhai would want to stay somewhere else. Somewhere she wouldn't be surrounded by the empty rooms of her now-dead coworkers and friends. Lena would bring it up to her later. For now, she had to deal with the mess she'd made of her and Cowen's relationship. Again. She was beginning to lose track of how many times she'd fucked up her relationships.

"I'm sorry," she admitted almost immediately. "I had to visit Alkus. Alone. I had to get answers for the letter."

Cowen didn't say anything.

"He was paying people to incite riots in the Lowlands so the Cursed would lose faith in me. So they would slowly turn away and not bat an eye when the Blessed finally decided to get rid of me." She scoffed, shaking her head. The thing was, she really did think the people's support was that fragile. The core of their beliefs was hard to budge, but everything surrounding that wasn't. They would still believe in the savior the prophecy foretold, but they would no longer think it was *her*. They would cast her aside. "I shouldn't have said what I said . . . then. I was stressed and we had a time limit, but that's not an excuse. You didn't deserve that. I . . . It was cruel—what I said. And untrue—"

"It's not."

"It *is*." Her hands flexed at her sides. "I do need you. And you may be sick, but you just need some help. I'll find someone who can cure you—"

"It's impossible, Kalena," he said, sounding tired. He looked it too, but his eyes were hard and clear. "I need you to understand that. There is no recovery for me. Things are only going to get worse."

"No. Cowen—"

"Kalena, *yes!*" he snapped, startling her. He closed his eyes and took a deep breath. "We keep having the same conversation over and over again about trust. I am not having it again. *Listen*. I need you to listen. I'll be dead within the month. I can feel my body declining. And before you say anything, no, I will not take time away. My fa—" He stopped. They should be safe within the confines of her room, but he evidently wasn't willing to risk it. "They both know how I feel about my position. They know I would never leave, and they know not to ask that of me. So don't—ask that of me.

"I was out looking for you nearly *every day*. I will not disappear now that you're back. No matter how nasty you are to me, okay? I made a promise to Ezra, but that's not the only reason I'm staying." He took another deep breath, his eyes shining. "We should've stopped it. We should've been there with your family, but we weren't. We lost you and them because we were careless. In a way, the council was right to blame us. We failed you. I vowed to make sure that didn't happen again and serve you in whatever way I could, as if that could make up for everything I did. Everything I didn't do. I don't expect your forgiveness, but I need you to understand that I would *never* betray you or turn away. You don't have to hide anything from me, let alone anything to do with Alkus. Or anyone else." His eyes sharpened slightly, and he pitched his voice lower. "I followed you the other day when you left the study."

Her eyes widened as she processed his words. "What? No . . . I ordered you to leave—!"

"Yes, and I ignored those orders."

She was still trying to wrap her mind around what he'd said. And what that meant.

"I would've . . . " *Sensed you*. But she wasn't so sure of that. She'd been wrapped up in her own head, her attention solely on the letters and Alkus. She could've missed Cowen. It was possible. Had Ira noticed him? She dared to ask, "How far?"

"The entire time."

His words were a weight in her chest, and her shoulders slumped under the forced of them. *The entire time* . . .

She shook her head, still unwilling to look at him. "No, you were waiting for me at the cliffside—"

"I followed you up to a point. When I was sure you were in the clear, I parted and took a shortcut back. I know the Highlands better than you, Kalena. I arrived a minute before you did."

"So you saw—?"

"Everything," Cowen confirmed, his voice and expression unwavering. "And I can't say I agree with it, but . . . I understand. And I feel responsible for it, for this pain you feel. I . . . Your family wouldn't have wanted this for you."

Her heart plummeted, so suddenly that she became nauseous.

"You don't have to hide from me or do this alone. You can hate me all you want and try to push me away, but I will remain here, by your side." He took a step closer, his eyes imploring. "Please, *let me* spend the rest of my short life protecting you. I can't bear the thought of failing you again."

She blinked away the tears in her eyes. "You didn't fail me. And you're already forgiven," she whispered. "Few people have shown me loyalty in the way you have. I'm sorry to have ever questioned it."

"It makes sense that you did," he said hoarsely.

"Still, I want you to know that I'm sorry. And I never told you how much I appreciate what you did—searching for me. It was a long shot, but it means something that you tried, that you fought for me."

Not many people had. Or would.

And not many people accepted her as she was—broken and angry but *trying*.

"Of course. It was the least I could do."

She bit her bottom lip. "And I understand if you're upset, but I—"

"You're forgiven," Cowen said before she could even finish her sentence. "My life's too short to hold grudges over things as small as that. I know you didn't mean it."

"Can you not talk like that? Like you don't care about your own life?"

"I've come to terms with it," he said simply. "You need to."

"I'm not giving up on you," she said stubbornly.

Cowen didn't fight her on this again, even though she'd expected him to. "I have a favor to ask of you. I know it's not proper, but . . . it's about my . . . *them*. When I'm gone . . . can you make sure they're all right. I know they can take care of themselves, but still . . . I want—"

"Of course." Her voice was thick and choked but determined. "Of course I'll look out for them. *All* of them."

He smiled at her. "Thank you, Your Majesty."

He's too kind, she thought. *Too good. And that's why he's dying.*

∽

LENA WENT in search of Aquila. She couldn't wait any longer. The small library on the east side of the palace was her first stop, and she nearly started running when she saw Aquila's legs from around the corner.

"We need to talk," she said as soon as she stepped into the alcove.

Aquila was already sliding off the ledge, her expression serious and shielded. "Yes, we do." She looked over Lena's shoulder at Cowen who'd stopped a few feet away.

Lena turned back at him and tilted her head. He looked between the two before disappearing amongst the shelves, though she knew he was still somewhere close. She could sense him. And only him. No one else was nearby.

"Sorrel found out I've been going to the Lowlands with you," Aquila said quietly as soon as Cowen left. "I don't know how she found out, but I'm not surprised that she did. She grew suspicious of me being that cooperative that quickly and asked if I had any relationship with you prior to our arrival."

Lena's eyes widened. "What? If she knows about that, do you think she knows about your and Kieryn's involvement in taking Alkus out?"

"I don't think so," Aquila said, but she looked unsure. "There's no way to know with her. She only shows what she wants you to know. I told her I didn't have a relationship with you before, but she *knew* I was lying."

Aquila took a deep breath and straightened. She tried to smooth out her face, wipe the emotions away, but it didn't quite work entirely. Her mouth or eyebrows would twitch, or her eyes would narrow slightly.

"Sorrel's sending me back early. I'm leaving tomorrow." Aquila was unable to look at Lena as she said that last part. Her gaze drifted to the side; her hands curled into fists.

"She's sending you back?" Lena repeated, dumbstruck, unable to do anything but stand there and stare.

"Tomorrow morning."

That was so soon. *Too soon.*

She shook her head. This must be some kind of punishment. It was Sorrel's way of getting back at her for the blackmail.

For a brief moment, Lena thought about going back to Sorrel and adding conditions to their agreement, but she realized quickly how foolish that would be. The terms of their alliance and Ouprua's aid, particularly concerning *her* agenda, were fragile right now, after the meeting. Would Lena allow it to break for this? For her?

"I'm being sent back only a few days before everyone else," Aquila said as if that made the situation any better, but her tone and body language spoke of how she really felt about this.

"Why? Why make a show out of sending only *you* back early? Won't that look odd?"

"Not enough to bother Sorrel apparently. She thinks this *lesson* is more important. She said I shouldn't be meddling in the affairs of another country, especially before the alliance is instated," Aquila recited. She paused and looked away again. "And she said someone of my status should be making decisions with my head, not my heart."

"Fuck her!" Lena blurted out. "She's a bloody hypocrite."

Aquila looked at her in surprise.

Lena hesitated and then took a step closer so they were nearly toe to toe and whispered, "I met with her earlier today. I wanted this alliance to work, but I didn't want to marry. I knew Sorrel wouldn't change her mind unless I forced her hand, so I found some dirt on her. I blackmailed her to get out of the marriage and this is how she's retaliating."

Aquila frowned and jerked back. "You hired dirtyhands to dig something up on Sorrel?"

Lena merely stared back, unblinking.

"What did you find?"

"She killed two people when she was younger. They were Blessed. One of them was a *royal* Blessed. Ouprua covered it up because they knew The Lands wouldn't like it. And it seems like the same is true today because Sorrel quickly agreed to throw out the marriage."

"And to throw me out to sea," Aquila grumbled under her breath. "Was it really a good idea to piss her off?"

"I wasn't going to be forced into another marriage," Lena hissed. "I will make all of my own decisions regarding my relationships."

Aquila stared at her, eyes softening. "Yeah," she agreed. "You should have that right."

Lena looked at her, really *looked* at her. "Why didn't you tell me about us?"

"I was scared," Aquila said, her brow creasing. "For a lot of reasons, but . . . " Her throat worked and she shifted farther back. "I was mostly scared of you. What you could say, and how those words could hurt me."

"So you hid it? To protect yourself?"

Aquila shrugged helplessly. "I'm tired of getting hurt. If I can do something to prevent it, I will. And I was doing it for you too."

Lena saw that now, but she hated it.

"If you . . . wanted me, you needed to come to that conclusion again on your own terms. Someone didn't need to tell you what you felt."

Her nose burned as her chest constricted. "I just got everything back," she said quietly, mostly to herself. And then to Aquila—and to an even deeper part of herself—she admitted with much more hesitancy, "I wanted the chance to get to know you. I wanted—" Her breath caught, and she swallowed thickly. "I wanted *time*. I thought we'd finally have it."

We meaning her and Ira and Cowen and his family and Aquila. All of them.

Aquila's eyes glistened under the dim lights, but she stayed put, many feet away. "It doesn't matter what you do. Sorrel has made up her mind."

Lena shook her head again, at a loss for words. Nothing she could say or do would change this. She'd thought she'd had power over Sorrel by forcing her to agree to the alliance without a marriage pact, but she'd only shown her hand while leaving Sorrel with all her cards at her disposal. And because of Lena's actions, she'd decided to use them.

"But we will see each other again," Aquila tried to assure her, but once again, her words fell flat.

"When?"

Aquila didn't answer that question. She probably couldn't. "I wanted to let you know," she said a few moments later, "before I left. I wanted you to know that it wasn't my choice."

She slipped past her. Lena's heart jumped in her throat, and she jerked her hand out to grab Aquila's.

"Wait." The strangled word came out of her mouth quickly. She didn't even know what to say past that. She just wanted Aquila to wait. To stay. There had been no time for her to make sense of all the memories and emotions she'd recently reacquired. She needed to figure things out and give Aquila an answer to this unspoken question between them. Maybe not a definite answer but *something*. They needed to make some progress.

She understood now what Aquila had meant when she said sometimes it was better not remembering things. It could save you the hurt.

"It's okay," Aquila said. She squeezed Lena's hand. And while Lena slackened her grip, it was Aquila who let go.

This time, when she walked away, Lena didn't stop her.

CHAPTER
SIXTY-FOUR

"Kalena," a voice beckoned, sifting through the dark to reach her. "Come here. Kalena, come find me."

She turned, trying to seek out the voice, but it was impossible to tell which direction it came from. She couldn't see anything but herself. Her limbs cut through the suffocating dark as easily as the smooth voice did.

"Where are you?" Her voice was loud but scratchy to her ears. "What are you?"

"I am the beginning. I am a creator and a prison. I am what you seek."

A warmth draped over her, and a weight settled on her shoulders. Claws.

"Follow the voice," the Numen said. "Go to it, and you shall find the power you seek."

Her feet shuffled forward on their own accord.

"Come on. A little bit farther," the voice coaxed.

She reached her hand out but felt nothing.

"Find me," it sang.

"Save me," it pleaded.

"Free me," it hissed.

She was suddenly yanked forward. The wind cut at her face and the darkness swallowed her whole.

∼

LENA'S EYES snapped open as she sucked in a breath of cold, crisp air. She stood . . . outside, and a hand was wrapped around her arm. She blinked up at Tuck. He immediately released her and took a few steps away, holding his hands out in front of him in a placating gesture.

"We need to stop meeting like this."

She looked around, taking in the trees and the treehouse. "What the *fuck?*" She whipped her head back around to glare at Tuck. "Did you bring me out here?"

The look he gave her was one of disbelief and irritation. He waited a few seconds before saying, "*No*, I didn't bring you out here. You were sleepwalking again."

The last thing she remembered was lying in bed, worrying about Aquila. Ira had been in his study, and Benji and Andra had taken over watch from Cowen. She remembered her strange dream as well. Her Numen had been in it, and the hypnotic voice. Just like a few days before.

Twice this had happened—the strange dreams and sleepwalking and ending up *here*. And she didn't understand why. Why *now?*

"I heard you were sick."

Tuck wore comfortable clothing. He must've been staying in the treehouse again. She didn't understand that either.

"I'm not."

"Really? So what would you call this then?" He waved his hand at her. "I didn't realize it was completely normal for people to sleepwalk into the forest in the middle of the night. You were mumbling something too. Said you were going to find something. Maybe you still have a fever."

"I don't have a fever," she said between gritted teeth. "The council lied. I was never sick or crazy."

"I didn't hear it from the council." Tuck scrutinized her further. "Maybe you have Slayer Sickness."

She opened her mouth to immediately argue with him but paused when she actually processed his words. "What?"

"Slayer Sickness," he repeated, looking far too casual for what he was suggesting. "You gained your Imprint fairly recently. If you or your Slayer still haven't adjusted completely, it would make sense. I saw you scratching at your chest. Your reactions are delayed too, did you know?"

Lena touched her Imprint. It was warm, but that wasn't abnormal. She didn't have Slayer Sickness. She would've gotten it earlier if she was going to get it at all.

Slayer Sickness wasn't uncommon and was relatively easy to treat, but no singular "cure" worked for all cases. If left unresolved, it could lead to death, but many people noticed the symptoms before then. However, finding a "cure" wasn't always easy due to Slayers' erratic natures.

Lena knew that, which was why she'd spent so much time and effort establishing her relationship with her Slayer at the beginning. She'd needed to keep her guard up. She'd been vulnerable then in a way that she wasn't now, and her Numen had known that.

It could pick up on her internal conflict, sniff out her weakness, and attack. It could challenge you and make you play its game. And if you couldn't keep up, you'd get sick. Overworking or underworking your Slayer could lead to Slayer Sickness. And the repercussions didn't only start and stop at the Blessed. Slayers could go into Blood Frenzies if they had too much blood, and that made it harder for the Blessed to control it. Sometimes something as simple as . . . *change*, on the Blessed or the Slayer's end, could infect you.

"I don't have it," she said with much more conviction than she currently held. "Slayer Sickness or any sort of sickness. I'm just . . . " She didn't owe him an explanation. Right now, she didn't even have one. "Where did you hear that I was sick? If not from the council."

"Around," he drawled.

She glared at him.

The corners of his mouth twitched. "I heard you were sick while floating in the clouds. That's all."

Cloud? She blinked. "While you were high? And you believed it?"

"The symptoms are there. You can't ignore them—"

"I don't have Slayer Sickness," she said *again*. She was somewhat new to this, even after two years, but Ira wasn't. He was with her nearly all the time. "Ira would've told me."

Tuck's expression twisted into something cross and cruel. "Sure," he muttered curtly, yet she could still hear the disbelief in his voice.

The flame inside of her spiked. "We don't lie to each other."

He barked out a laugh. "You still believe that?"

She took an intentional breath, trying to stamp out the heat in her chest. She didn't need to let her Slayer out here.

On second thought . . . why not? This was a golden opportunity. They were out in the middle of the forest at night. Alone. No one knew where she was, and she was willing to bet no one knew where Tuck was either. He was on the list.

Her Imprint became hotter the more she thought about releasing her Slayer, as if it was trying to convince her that she should follow through on her idea.

Tuck was a good fighter. He'd gained a formidable reputation. He had taught her how to throw a dagger. She'd beaten him during the field games, but part of her still wondered if he'd done that on purpose, knowing it would piss her off. At the moment, he wasn't distracted or at a disadvantage. If she wanted to take him down, she needed to be strategic about it.

"I believe *him*," she said slowly, baring her teeth, "more than I'll ever believe *you*."

Tuck stared at her in disappointment. "He's still got you under his little spell, huh?"

She smiled bitterly. "You'd like to think that, wouldn't you? Funny thing is, I could say the same thing about you. Why'd you tell me about Alkus' study? You couldn't have known the schedule. It was too early. Which means you must have *made sure* that no one was there. You cleared the guards yourself." Since returning to the palace, she'd thought about this a lot too. "*Why?* Why help me? Was it all part of some larger plan? You open the door for me only to lock it once I step inside? Act like you're doing me a favor, but really, you're messing with me again, right? And now you're going to run off and report this to your parents?" She scoffed and strode forward. "No, you probably already did that, didn't you? So what's next? What can I expect? Are you going to tell them I'm sick too? That now's the time to finish me off because I'm *vulnerable?*"

He glowered at her, and the muscles in his jaw moved. "You think I'm just a spy for my parents, do you?"

"Of course you are! Why else would you do what you did? You showed me your true colors years ago."

"I told you that—" He stopped and took a deep breath. His fingers flexed at his sides. "I don't subscribe to everything my parents believe. I'm sure you'll be delighted to know we actually have tiffs quite often."

"Oh, how horrible for you," she mocked. "Is that why you're out here?"

"Maybe." He stared at her intently now, his green eyes too bright at night. "But I haven't told my parents anything, and I didn't tell you that information to trick you. I did it to help you. Lena, I'm not your enemy."

That was what lit a fire in her veins. She gritted her teeth so hard her jaw ached. "Don't call me that," she hissed, lunging forward to shove him back. He went easily. "And I don't believe you."

"I'm telling the truth."

She shoved him again, harder. "*I don't believe you.*"

Another laugh bubbled out of his throat as he stumbled away. "What do I have to do to get you to believe me?'

"*Nothing*. Because I won't ever believe you! I can't. You shattered my trust once. I won't let you do it again! *You*—"

She snapped her mouth shut and wrapped her arms around herself, forcibly making herself take a step back before the rant turned into a breakdown. She put more distance between them. It was becoming too similar. Low visibility, high emotions, out in the forest, with him.

"I could only save one."

She turned back to him. "What?"

"I could only save one." His face was open for once, his eyes imploring.

Her heart lurched, but she didn't look away. She pried her lips open and ignored the complicated feelings his words sparked inside of her. "I don't believe you," she repeated slowly.

Tuck walked toward her but stopped when she stepped back.

"I want to help you again," he breathed out. He appeared earnest, and sounded it too, but that was what he did best. He played the part people needed him to play. "You said you don't need it, but you do. Something's wrong, and I guarantee it traces back to your Numen. This has happened twice, right? The sleepwalking and the dreams, and both times you came *here*. Where are your guards? Where's Ira? What happens if someone doesn't wake you up? I'm out here. I'm *here*. Let me help."

She stared at him, her face giving nothing away because she didn't even know what she was feeling. *Conflicted.* That was the best way to describe her current state. She shouldn't be conflicted about anything involving Tuck. He had betrayed her. But he had also helped her. But the betrayal and the favor were not of the same magnitude.

"I don't want or need your help."

He didn't follow her when she left. She didn't know exactly where she was going. She just had to get away from him. Her strides lengthened as tears blurred her vision. Why was she crying? Over him? Over this . . . *thing* that was happening to her?

She wiped at her eyes before any tears could fall. Rustling from ahead alerted her, and she instinctively reached out to her Slayer.

Cowen came into view and her shoulders slumped.

"Benji and Andra checked your room and said you were gone. What happened? Were you taken? Are you alright?" he blurted out as he stopped in front of her, his wide eyes looking her over for any sort of injury.

A fresh wave of tears sprang to her eyes, and she shook her head. "Cowen, something's wrong with me."

· CHAPTER

SIXTY-FIVE

The entire terrain was a wasteland. The strong wind pasted his clothes to his skin and yanked his hair around his head. He squinted against the scorching gale and tried to spot a notable landmark, but all he could see was the orange sky and the red rock that stretched on for miles and miles. There weren't even any hills or trees. The ground was flat, the sky monochromatic and cloudless.

Atreus looked around at the few dozen people who had been sent to this realm with him. They were hunched over due to the wind and shielding their eyes, but they slowly turned toward him.

Right. He found the stones. He got them out. He knew that everyone relied on him, but the strangeness of their current situation reminded him of that even more. He had no plan, no allies here. The weight was all on his shoulders. So he had to put on a brave face and trudge forward. He had to hope that the others would be able to find the stones in their realm without him. They were resourceful and had made it this far. They were survivors.

And so was he.

Rule number one: keep moving.

Atreus walked with the wind across the red rock. He walked and walked and walked. The scenery didn't change. At all. The sun didn't move. No clouds filled the sky. He didn't see one person or animal or land formation or any ounce of nature. The others behind him were the only thing that told him he was actually covering ground.

The howling wind burned his face and made it difficult for him to hear anything, which was why he kept walking as normal when a faint crack resounded from below him.

A shout rang out and then he was falling.

Everything became dark in the blink of an eye. He was weightless. His mouth opened in a soundless scream as he plunged into the depths of this realm. He fell for what had to be several minutes, and he could only think about how hard he would hit the ground.

But then he started slowing.

Maybe he was only imagining it, but the force of the wind lessened, and his body started to grow heavier. This continued until he was being softly lowered.

Light filtered upward, illuminating the jagged red rock around him. He was in a tunnel. When he looked down, he could finally see something below him. The tight tunnel opened up and the wind subsided. He now floated in a much larger space that stretched for miles in every direction. It was . . . another layer of this realm.

His feet touched the ground and he stumbled, his legs unsteady after the drop.

Down here was . . . strange. No wind. Not even a slight breeze. The still air was almost sweltering. The red rock had a thin layer of sand over it, but it wasn't disrupted by his footsteps. He dug his boot into the ground and lifted it away and —nothing.

"Edynir Akonah."

Atreus jerked and spun around. A woman stood a few feet away. She hadn't been there moments before. Dark blue robes were draped over her, the sleeves so long they covered her hands. She stared at him, a pleasant expression on her face. The third sister.

"It's nice to finally see you in the flesh in this lifetime. My name is Zosia."

"Edynir Akonah is not my name."

"It is."

Lately, everything had been happening too quickly. He hadn't had time to catch a breath, and he certainly hadn't had time to process everything that'd been revealed to him during his meetings with the sisters.

"How do you know?" He tried to recall what the other sisters had told him, but his mind was racing too quickly for him to backtrack. "How can you be sure?"

"The flame grows bright inside of you, just as it did him. You share the same gifts. And you have the same demeanor. He challenged Kerrick Ludoh just as you challenge the prophets. He had a way with people and a loyal following just as you do. The realms spoke to him. Power gravitated toward him. The creatures listened to him. Does that sound familiar? It's not a coincidence."

"How do you know all this? About him and me? You've been watching me?" he accused as he walked parallel to her.

"I am the only one of my sisters who met Edynir Akonah before he died. And of course we've been watching you. We're not the only ones. We had to be sure you were the one."

"... And you're certain?"

"Yes," Zosia said confidently. "His work remained unfinished upon his death. He was always fated to return." She tilted her head toward him. "Tell me, what do you know about Edynir Akonah?"

"I know what the prophets told us. And I know that one of your sisters said it was all a lie."

"Not all of it," Zosia said, but she waved her hand as if to say *go on*.

Atreus watched her warily. "I was told that he became greedy. He challenged the Numina. When his power wasn't enough, he resorted to sorcery. The leaders of the other realms rejected the invitation to join his cause. He burned the academy down. He shattered the realms because he grew paranoid that his enemies would overpower him. He was blind to the threat at his side. Kerrick Ludoh, his childhood friend, killed Edynir Akonah when he realized he was too far gone. Kerrick Ludoh was labeled a savior and those on his side became Blessed. Those on Edynir Akonah's side became Cursed. Kerrick Ludoh was the first prophet and he vowed to heal the realms and serve the Numina. He ... gave up his firstborn child as a sign of good faith." Atreus recited all of this, his voice monotone save for the slight bite at the end.

Zosia nodded. "Very good. Now I'm going to tell you the truth. Some things are the same. Half-lies are easier to tell. They're more believable.

"Edynir Akonah was the first Blessed. He had always been favored by the Numina. He and Kerrick Ludoh were childhood friends, but Kerrick Ludoh grew jealous of Edynir Akonah's abilities. He convinced the village Edynir Akonah was an evil spirit. A bad omen. Edynir Akonah took it upon himself to leave when he heard the whispers that followed him, and he gained entry to the academy soon after. The same academy where the pathways between realms were discovered.

"Years later, Kerrick Ludoh found him and apologized. The two became friends again and studied and trained together. They traveled the realms and learned from their leaders. And one day, Kerrick Ludoh went missing. It was thought that he got lost between realms. He turned up months later, shaken and confused. It was all an act. While missing, he'd been gathering the information and the power he needed. *He* was the one who studied sorcery first. *He* was the one who had this grand, ambitious plan for this realm—how society should be and how people should act in it. Anyone who defied his ideas wouldn't be a part of it. His plan didn't involve any of the other realms. He was only interested in their power. Once he got what he needed, he turned on all of them.

"He burned the academy first. And then he began killing leaders in the other realms. The fighting started and the pathways were monitored and then shut down completely. But the War of Krashing spanned across all the realms. Kerrick Ludoh and Edynir Akonah weren't born in your realm, but it *was* where most of the fighting happened. Both had Numina and mortals on their side, and both were very strong. The war was bloody and devastating for everyone and everything involved.

"Kerrick Ludoh was smart, and he knew Edynir Akonah well. He knew his friend had a weakness when it came to others. To put it simply, he cared too much about the people close to him. Kerrick Ludoh exploited that and then killed him. Afterward, he used his powers to shatter the realms. The lines connecting them were already unsteady due to the shockwaves of the war, but it still took nearly everything out of Kerrick Ludoh to break the realms apart completely. Yet that only helped him lie. He was too weak for the Imprint to hold, so he told the people he gave it up to become a prophet.

"He and his followers shared their side of the story, the one you have heard, and as victors of the war, people believed them. There wasn't another perspective. The Numina knew the truth, but they didn't care for justice. The divide between Blessed and Cursed isn't as clear-cut as the prophets would like you to believe. Blessed and Cursed predated the war, but they became more common after it. They were on both sides. However, anyone who still followed Edynir Akonah and knew the truth was quickly and quietly killed. It was during this time that Kerrick Ludoh found out Edynir Akonah wasn't really gone.

"Souls are reborn every day, but they're essentially wiped clean after each lifetime. One typically cannot tap into one of their past lives and their past lives typically cannot tap into their current self. However, it is possible with a phenomenon called a Cornerstone, which Edynir Akonah created in secret. He wanted Kerrick Ludoh to know that even if he did triumph during this war, he hadn't really won. There would be more wars to fight between the two of them. Edynir Akonah told his most trusted generals to relay this message to Kerrick Ludoh should the latter win and hunt them down. He told them to tell Kerrick Ludoh that his plan would never come to fruition.

"When Kerrick Ludoh realized what Edynir Akonah had done, he panicked. He had no way of getting to and destroying the Cornerstone that granted Edynir Akonah immortality because he had shattered the realms. It was after this that he insisted upon the firstborn program. He told the people that the Numina had come to him with a solution. One that would protect them and allow them to atone. The evil, he said, would be sucked from the realm so it couldn't poison the people any longer. The firstborns would bear the burden. It was a price they all had to pay for the part they played in the war. Kerrick Ludoh gave up his eldest to show his compliance, and the others followed suit. These children, in a way, were keeping the prophets' oath to heal the realms. They were searching for a way to reconnect the pathways so Kerrick Ludoh could finally kill Edynir Akonah. And firstborns are still doing the exact same thing today."

Atreus stood still and silent for several minutes, his lips parted and his mind mulling over this influx of information. It certainly wasn't simple. She had the details. But who knew how long she'd been waiting here for him. She'd *met* Edynir Akonah. Supposedly. She could've been knitting together and rehearsing this story for *centuries*.

He tended to follow his gut. It was what kept him alive in matters of life and death when his mind didn't have enough time to react. And his gut had always told him the prophets were bad news and that there was more to the stories told in seminar. Finn thought so too. As did Judah; he'd been *told* stories where Edynir Akonah was the hero. And now these sisters were telling Atreus practically everything he knew was an outright lie or twisted with one, that he was Edynir Akonah reincarnated, destined to . . .

"Where do I fit into all of this?" he asked quietly, his mind still whirling. "Say you're right and I am Edynir Akonah reincarnated and there's this . . . Cornerstone thing—so what am I to do? Kerrick Ludoh is dead."

Unless there was some weird immortality thing going on with him too.

Zosia's eyes searched him. She raised her chin again. "Even if he is dead, his philosophy certainly isn't. It's still carried on every day. His vision isn't complete, but when it is, you can believe it won't only be firstborns who are living the way you are."

That was already happening.

He waded through thick sludge trying to process every one of her words and any one of his thoughts. Nothing clicked. Everything was sand slipping through his fingers.

Atreus shook his head and tugged at his hair. "So you want me to do what? Kill all the prophets? Even if I did manage to do that, the idea would still exist. How do you kill an idea?"

"With time. And power. That was how this idea came into existence in the first place. You kill the flowers and the pollen will eventually cease to exist. It's not immediate, but it's possible."

That was what he wanted, wasn't it? He didn't want anyone else to go through this. It was why he struggled with the idea of leaving everyone behind. It was why others said he had a bleeding heart that was going to get him in trouble someday.

And it already had. With Tolar.

"You're not the hero. Everyone thinks you are, but they're wrong. I see you for what you really are."

He took a step back. "No, I can't do that. I'm in a *prison*, fighting to *survive*. Find someone else who has more freedom and time on their hands—"

"There is no one else," Zosia said strictly. "You are one of a kind. *You* are the person we've been waiting centuries for."

"If I am Edynir Akonah and Edynir Akonah is me, or . . . whatever, then why didn't you find him earlier? In a previous life? Or later? Why *now?*"

"Because now is the right time." She made it sound simple when none of this was really simple.

He so desperately wanted to brush this aside and say it wasn't his problem, but his hatred toward the prophets grew every day. He wanted to escape but also make them pay. He wanted to hurt them and stop them from hurting other people. And it sounded like this was exactly what Zosia wanted him to do, but this wasn't the only thing she wanted from him. No, he wouldn't be that lucky. If he agreed to . . . whatever this was, there would be many more matters, one right after the other, that he would have to deal with as . . . Edynir Akonah. It sounded insane, but his life was insane. The Outings, the stones, the *Te'Monai* and his control of them . . . and now these sisters who were adamant that he was some . . . *chosen one.*

He didn't want to be. He didn't want to be noticed. He wanted to escape this all. But then the question of *'And do what?'* circled back around.

"You do have many choices ahead of you, but you can't run from your destiny, Atreus."

He had nowhere *to* run. And this wouldn't stop. The sisters. The Outings. The deaths. It would all continue to haunt him even if he did get out and got away from it all. The prophets wanted him dead. They weren't hiding it anymore. Without this . . . guidance, this insight, this plan . . . he might be dead before the next shipment arrived. He didn't have many options if he wanted to survive, so he couldn't afford to be picky.

Atreus sighed and raised his eyes to meet Zosia's. "What do I have to do?"

She smiled. "Keep collecting the stones. It's the only reliable means you have of traveling between realms, but they can also be used—"

"As a weapon," he cut in. "Yeah, we figured that out. But a weapon for what?"

"For anything. We don't know for certain. But those stones contain immense quantities of magic, and lots of magic means lots of power, tangible and not. If the prophets wanted to use them to cause immense damage, they could, which is *why* you can't allow them to complete the weapon and use it."

"We can't steal the stones they already have. They've been onto us lately. They're trying to get me killed. Our Imprints are sealed, so we can't use our Slayers. We've made some risks, and we've paid for them."

With bruises and blood and bodies.

"You don't need to steal all the stones now. The opportunity will come," Zosia assured him. "We're in no danger of them using the weapon any time soon, but at the pace they're making, it'll likely be ready within the next decade."

Decade? That meant there was time, which was good, but . . . a decade? That was a long time to be wrapped up in this. He hadn't really thought about anything past escaping, about what his life would be like out of the Institute. He couldn't afford to. He had to focus on the now. On surviving. But what would he do after he got out? Would he fight for the rest of his life? It seemed like that was the only thing he knew how to do.

"I can't do any of this from inside the Institute, so how do I escape? How can I fight back? Like I said, our Imprints are almost always sealed—"

"Your Slayer isn't the only beast you can call upon."

Her words were a grim reminder of his newfound . . . ability. He looked down at his hands. They were clean now—literally speaking. Not metaphorically.

"I'm . . . still new to that. I don't really understand—"

"They listen to you. They'll come running when you call. That's all you need to understand."

"I've called them while in their realm. I've never tried to summon them from their realm to mine," he argued.

"So try," she said simply.

"That's your advice? Just *try?*"

"Let me put it in another way you may better understand." She took a step forward and lowered her chin, holding his gaze. "*Fight*. That's what you know. That's what you're good at. If you're trapped, find a way out. Survive, and not only for yourself. Other people are depending on you—"

"I know that," he gritted out. "I'm reminded of that *frequently*."

"Then I'll remind you again," Zosia said sternly. "You have more enemies than you know, but you must focus on the task in front of you first."

She moved her arms and her sleeves slipped away to expose her hands. She unfurled her fingers to reveal *two* stones, one in each palm.

"You will need both. You are strong, but you need allies to support you. Choose them wisely. Always keep one stone with you and give the other to a trusted companion. You can meet here in this realm to discuss anything you need to keep private. And I will always be here to guide you and answer your questions."

Atreus swallowed the thickness in his throat and stepped forward, reaching for the stones, but she pulled back before he could grab them.

"One last thing," she said. "The prophets have fooled many people and some of those people have allied themselves with the prophets. Their reach extends much further than you may think, but what's important for you to know now is that they have someone who is magic-sensitive working with them. Someone who's in the mines. Someone like you."

He stiffened. "A firstborn?"

She nodded. "Before the shattering of the realms, anyone could sense and travel through the pathways. They were concentrated streams of magic, and, once you knew where to look, extremely noticeable. When the realms shattered and the pathways were severed, some of that magic was sucked away. The remaining traces of it floated in the space between realms, their signatures much fainter than before, but still there. We call it the Stream and only certain people, those who are magic-sensitive, can pick up on this trace and use it to travel. Due to the oaths prophets took centuries ago to give up their magical abilities, they cannot be magic-sensitive. This person, whoever they are, is a Blessed firstborn. They have been the one sending you all to these realms, and they were the one bringing the stones back to the prophets before you."

He tried to wrap his mind around this. The portals and the Outings weren't the prophets' doings? They needed someone else—a fellow firstborn—to initiate it?

He knew a firstborn had been helping the prophets find the stones. Nev had seen someone who'd looked like a girl being led away by the prophets, but that was it. He hadn't been certain, so he could be wrong. It wasn't like Atreus could go around asking. With all the shit that had happened recently, the questions about who'd been collecting the stones in the first place had been forgotten. They knew it was a firstborn—there wasn't really another option—but to find out this person was *also* the one responsible for sending them to these bloodcurdling realms . . .

"And they're still alive?" he asked. "You're sure of it?"

"Yes."

So it hadn't been Tolar then. Maybe it was one of his buddies? One of the dozens of firstborns who'd seemed to be fighting for the prophets in the last realm?

"Why would they do that?"

Perhaps for the same convoluted reason Tolar had sided with the prophets. Atreus didn't understand it.

None of the firstborns stayed behind in the Institute. Not anymore. So whoever was working with the prophets wasn't only sending other people to die, they were also sending themselves, knowing that they possibly wouldn't make it. Unless they had some sort of immunity. He couldn't think of one good reason to cooperate with the prophets. If they came to him, he would tell them to fuck off.

The prophets were the executioners, but this firstborn—this *traitor*—was the knife. Without them, this whole operation wouldn't work.

"What about the enforcers? Could they be magic-sensitive?"

His stomach plummeted as she shook her head.

"We can't know their motives or what the prophets have promised them," Zosia said. "But every one of these programs has at least one magic-sensitive individual. They blend into the crowd, report anything if necessary, and keep the operation going. If they die, there's usually a long break between Outings while the prophets find another magic-sensitive individual."

"What if they already have one on standby so there doesn't have to be a break?"

Zosia shook her head again. "They won't. It's too risky, especially in the long run. They can't provide privileges to too many people without others taking notice. They're already taking a risk on trusting a single firstborn who could turn on them at any moment. The more magic-sensitive individuals they have, the higher the risk but not the reward. Not to mention those magic-sensitive firstborns could separate the group and ruin the prophets' schedule. They've always just had one."

"We were split up today. There are three groups. How could one firstborn do that?"

"Your seal," Zosia said simply, nodding to his Imprint even though it was hidden under his clothes. "It's a signature. This magic-sensitive firstborn knows it, so they're able to send each of you down a stream to another realm even if they're not with you."

So there was no way of telling what group they were in. He tried to recall if there had been any long breaks since he was moved to the Institute years ago. He couldn't think of one, which meant this traitor had been at the Institute for at least as long as he had. So they were around his age or older. And alive. And they maybe looked like a girl.

"You need to incapacitate this person," Zosia said. "They're dangerous in more ways than one. Not only can they sense magic and take you to other realms, but they can also call upon the beasts in these realms."

He snapped his head around and threw her a wide-eyed glare. "Why didn't you say that before?"

Zosia continued, hardly phased, "It's a threat, yes, but you can counteract it. Whoever this person is, they can only call on the beasts, not control them. You could use this to your advantage, but *only if* the timing is right. Only if you're ready."

"I . . . I'm not!"

If the letter Tolar had given him *did* in fact contain true and accurate information, then the new shipment of firstborns would arrive soon. Atreus hadn't even had time to discuss it with Vanik, Harlow, and Weylin. And now there was the whole Edynir Akonah thing and the disc-weapon and this traitor who could drop them off anywhere and call *Te'Monai* to attack at any moment.

"I'm not ready!"

"I know that," Zosia said gently. "But you may not have a choice. If you want to keep that from happening, find this person and get rid of them."

His limbs locked. "You mean kill them?"

"Yes," she said, unflinching.

The first thought that came to mind was a protest.

I don't kill humans!

But he did. He had. And humans could be just as wicked as the *Te'Monai*, but he couldn't control them. Everything he knew was being rewritten and flipped around. But killing someone else . . .

Tolar had attacked him first, and he would've kept coming. Atreus had protected him. It'd been self-defense. This, in a twisted way, could be considered self-defense too. He was looking out for himself, and the others. This person was hurting them. This person was responsible for countless deaths alongside the prophets. If they were gone, he and the others would be safe, at least for a while. They would have time to breathe and figure something else out.

"How do I find out who it is?"

"Have you ever noticed anyone's absence? Maybe they receive special privileges or protection. The prophets wouldn't want to lose them."

They were all sent out. If anyone stayed behind, someone would eventually notice. There weren't *that* many of them, even fewer firstborns left close to his age. The thought of the traitor being someone in his shipment made him sick. He wasn't civil with everyone around his age, but he still felt like they had some sort of connection due to the time they'd spent in this wicked place.

He went over the criteria again. Someone alive. Around his age. Probably a girl. They always made it out of the brawls alive and probably better off than most. They got special privileges. Maybe they weren't always present. They could get away with more things if they were out of sight. But they weren't too withdrawn. That would bring forth suspicion. They must play the part well if they'd managed to survive all this time without drawing attention to themselves. They were smart and sneaky and—

A sense of foreboding came over him as the blood drained from his face. *No.* For a second, he thought he might actually be sick. Once his mind latched onto the face, it couldn't let go. He wanted to throw that option out, say it was ridiculous, and hit himself for even thinking it could be her, but the more he thought about it, the more it made sense.

"Mila?"

"I don't know. We were separated."

They always got split up in the other realms, even when they made plans to stick close. And when she did make an appearance, she was never hurt badly.

"I saw her just a second ago! She was fine. She had a grip on her Slayer."

The book she'd given to him was all about the stones. He'd been trying to figure out their true purpose at the time.

"*The book is about the stones. You have a connection to them, so I figured you should read it.*"

That was why she'd picked out that book for him. *And* insisted that Weylin and Vanik tell them about the disc. She was the only one of them besides Judah who hadn't been locked up before their previous Outing. She'd said the prophets hadn't unsealed *anyone's* Imprints. A blatant lie. Dozens of Slayers had been running around.

Atreus had been so caught up in killing Tolar and the target the prophets had painted on his back that he hadn't thought to question Mila about that before being sent off to the next realm.

Krashing, it's right there! All the evidence!

But it couldn't be her. It just couldn't. She wouldn't . . . She was his *friend*. One of his only friends.

Regardless, he couldn't shake the dread that had latched onto him the moment he thought of Mila as the traitor. He hoped he was wrong. He really fucking hoped he was wrong. He hoped this was a big misunderstanding or coincidence or *something that didn't dismantle the very thing that kept him sane through all this*. But he needed her to tell him this herself.

"I have to go," he said suddenly. His voice sounded wrong to his ears. Far away and muffled. "I have to go right now. Give me the stones."

Zosia handed them over. "Remember, you can summon the beasts if—"

Atreus vanished.

CHAPTER
SIXTY-SIX

"We've managed to secure the alliance and . . . deal with the killings. And Her Majesty is in better health." Mikhail sent her a rather weak smile that she didn't return.

The council chamber was so bare. So quiet and tense.

Mikhail cleared his throat and continued. "Now that those matters are dealt with, we should switch our focus to the *Ateisha* and the explosions. There have been more sightings of the *Ateisha* over the past few days, meaning they're venturing lower once again. If we can't push them back naturally, we'll have to build some sort of barrier. And the explosions are closing in, but we have no way of knowing what exactly is causing them. It would be ideal if someone could go and scout out the situation for us."

Mikhail's gaze swept over the room, landing on Ophir.

"My son?" he asked as he ran his hand over his chin. He sounded almost amused.

"He would be the best option, Ophir," Mikhail said. "He's the only one who's made it through the mountains. During the holiday, he volunteered—"

"He's unreliable," Ophir interrupted. "Last time he had to find a trail. This time you want to send him on that trail and into the land beyond the mountains to investigate explosions that have been going off for over a decade? He wouldn't return—at least not until he needed something. Tuck is like a child in that way. He acts out. Makes messes and then leaves others to clean it up for him."

A bell chimed above them, telling them they'd reached the top of the hour.

"That may be true," Mikhail said carefully, "but we don't have many options."

His gaze flickered around the half-empty room. "We can resume this another day to let everyone think about our next course of action."

~

"Aquila's gone."

The cool wind ruffled the leaves of the neatly trimmed hedges, but it didn't reach inside the gazebo at all. Lena didn't know if that was Kieryn's doing or not, but she appreciated the bubble of privacy that seemed to envelop them.

"That she is," Kieryn said as he tapped his index finger against the wooden railing. His ring made a dull *thunk* each time. His unfocused eyes were trained somewhere past her. He appeared solemn, which she'd like to say was uncharacteristic of him, but she was beginning to see it more and more. "Everyone seems to be . . . *leaving*, one way or another."

There were a few things he could be getting at with that.

"Are you afraid she's going to send you away too?"

He shrugged. "Afraid? No. Will she? Probably not. Sending Aquila back early was already enough hassle, and we're all set to leave soon anyway."

Lena chewed on her bottom lip. "Sorrel's upset with me," she admitted. "I . . . talked her out of the marriage."

Kieryn raised a single brow. "Did you find out Aquila was terrible company too?"

He didn't know about her and Aquila's past. No one did. Though Aquila thought Sorrel had a hunch, which Lena didn't like. But Sorrel couldn't know anything for certain. Unless she'd hired someone to dig up the past, just like Lena had done with her.

She and Aquila had been discreet but not completely invisible. If Sorrel had the tenacity and the money and connections, she could figure out the truth. Or part of it anyway.

"I won't let someone else dictate my life."

"Dictate?" Kieryn looked at her, unimpressed. "Really? Did you think you wouldn't have to make sacrifices being in the position that you're in?"

She responded with an unimpressed look of her own, but there was a bit of hostility there as well. "You sound like Alkus."

Kieryn didn't respond to that. A minute of silence passed before he said, "What's done is done."

She nodded and went back to chewing her bottom lip.

Her and Aquila's relationship, then and now, was . . . extremely private and personal. It was something they both kept close and quiet for many reasons. She'd just gotten those pieces of her life back. A silly part of her was worried that if she shared those important moments, they would be taken away again. Or used against her. Or Aquila. Sorrel would likely pull the same card and use it to blackmail her.

Kieryn... She'd trusted him by extension because she'd trusted Aquila to keep him under control. But Aquila was gone now.

Something about Kieryn told her he was the more calculative of the two. Aquila was burnished bronze and rough edges and stormy on the outside, softer on the inside. Kieryn was sparkling silver and smooth stones and eloquent. Their first conversation at this exact spot had showed her that he understood politics and strategy. He truly seemed like he was on her side, but he'd known Sorrel longer, and if she decided to turn against the ruler of The Lands...

Lena still trusted him somewhat but not with her and Aquila's past.

She stood and walked across the gazebo, dropping next to Kieryn. "Do you think that Sorrel knows about you and Aquila helping me?"

Aquila had said that Sorrel knew about her accompanying Lena to the Lowlands. About her helping *the queen of The Lands before the alliance was instated*. Lena didn't know if Kieryn knew about that, but he'd probably assumed something was going on between her and Aquila. She'd asked him about Aquila enough times, and while she didn't know what Aquila had said to him when recruiting him to take down Alkus, that must've been another obvious indicator.

"Maybe." He didn't sound worried, just resigned. "If she knows, or if she finds out, she'll be more upset with the fact that we did it behind her back than the actions themselves."

Lena angled her body toward him slightly. "Why did you help me? You could've turned Aquila away and not gotten involved... saved yourself from all of this... uncertainty."

He shrugged. "I took a calculated risk."

"Do you think this will affect the alliance? The aid you promised *me?*" Not The Lands. Not the Blessed. *Her.*

"Maybe, but I don't think it'll be detrimental." He stretched his legs out in front of him. Today, he wasn't dressed in his usual attire. He wore no earrings or makeup, though his skin was smooth and clear without it. He had his rings on and his hair simply pulled back. The color of his clothing was more muted than normal. "Sorrel isn't a fool. One squabble might upset her, but it won't change her morals. I assume she'll be more difficult from now on, but you'll get your aid." Kieryn paused. "You ask a lot of questions when you're nervous."

"I'm not nervous," she said almost immediately. "I'm just..."

Nervous wasn't the right word, but it wasn't *wrong* either.

A weight had fallen over her shoulders when she returned to the Highlands, and it dragged her down everywhere she went. It darkened everything. She didn't want to acknowledge it. Things would get better, not worse. This period of silence was peaceful. It wasn't the quiet before the storm. Nothing was brewing.

"Just?" Kieryn prodded.

She pursed her lips and decided to change the topic altogether. "I need to ask you something."

"You mean to say you haven't already?"

She ignored the clear snark in his voice. Her mind was already on someone she'd sworn not to waste any time thinking about. She'd seen entirely too much of him lately. He was invading her mind.

What was his angle? Alkus' study; her sleepwalking incidents; him offering her his help—Why was he involving himself? Why *now*?

She went back and forth with herself.

He's a liar. He's hurt you before, and he'll do it again. You're a fool if you believe otherwise.

He cleared out the hall for you. He helped you get rid of Alkus. He wants to help more.

The small, weaker part of her that wanted to believe in Tuck ran off emotion. The larger, stronger part of her that was convinced Tuck was not to be trusted ran off experience and logic. But that small part of her was still hanging on, and she couldn't seem to shake it off.

She'd been pulling the petals from the flowers on her desk, alternating between perspectives.

He's lying and wants to hurt me.
He's telling the truth and wants to help me.
He's lying.
He's telling the truth.
Lying.
Truth.

She would always end on truth, and that small part of her conscience would swell.

She'd decided it was time to discuss her . . . troubles with someone else, and Kieryn was the best candidate. She honestly didn't know what she was looking for. Sometimes it felt like she didn't know much of anything anymore.

"Tuck was the one who told me about Alkus' study," she said quietly. "He cleared the guards."

She paused, but Kieryn didn't say anything. He didn't react, still tapping his index finger on the railing.

"We keep . . . running into each other. He says he wants to help, but I know him and—Can you please say something?" she hissed, turning on Kieryn completely. Her cheeks warmed. She didn't even know how to piece together her sentences anymore. Tuck made her nonsensical in every way.

"What do you want me to say?"

She stifled a groan. "You've defended him before. During the holiday. You said he was one of the better people you've met here. Why?"

"Why did I say that or why do I think that?"

"*Kieryn.*"

He took his hand off the railing and straightened. "I like him because I like him.

Unlike the others here, I don't think he's fake. Or bad. I don't think he's necessarily good, but who can be in this realm? He lies to protect himself or others. He does act out sometimes, but only to get attention, and I like a flare for dramatics. He hides in plain sight, and he's able to because so many people have already made up their mind about him due to the way his parents present him to the public. So he feeds into it, and sometimes he hates it. I hate it too. He could run, but he always comes back. Why do you think so?"

She was taken aback by the length and depth of Kieryn's answer. Had he and Tuck spent more time together than she realized? But even if they'd spent every second together since Kieryn's arrival, that wasn't enough time for Kieryn to understand Tuck so . . . fully. Or at all. Kieryn's assessment must've been off. But that thought was lackluster, faltering even as she conjured it in her mind.

"He always comes back because why wouldn't he? He has everything he could ever want here. There's nothing beyond the mountains."

"That's what they tell you, but that's not what you believe."

No, not anymore.

"Still, he has comfort here. He's a royal Blessed who's expected to take his father's seat on the council one day. He has food and money and shelter and whatever else he wants."

"It's not that simple. What do you want? More than anything?"

Her lips parted and stilled. *More than anything?* Anything. The word rang in her mind. " . . . My family back."

Aquila wasn't always here to pull her back from the dangerous game of *what-if*. Lena would leave this all behind for her family in a heartbeat.

"You're the queen. You would now identify as Blessed. Why can't you have that?" Kieryn asked.

She glared at him. "You know why."

"So you understand that *wanting* something isn't that simple, even if you are Blessed? I'm not excusing their privilege," he said before she could argue. "*But* they can't have everything they want."

"What's the point of this?" she asked bluntly. "Are you trying to make me feel sorry for Tuck because he can't get everything he wants? His family killed my family. He lives a better life than hundreds of thousands of others—"

"And currently, so do you."

Lena shook her head. "What are you—?"

"I'm answering your question," Kieryn said, stretching his legs out in front of him again. "I defended him because I like him, and I sympathize with him. I don't think he's like the rest."

"And after a few weeks you're suddenly the expert on Tuck, are you?"

He shrugged, unbothered by her frustration. "You asked for my opinion. I gave it."

She could throw his opinion out, but she'd come to him for a reason. He was an observer. He sat back and smiled and said what he needed to say while sucking in all the information he could. He was doing that right now. She knew their meetings were transactions. He gave her information because she gave him information, but she made sure it was information she was okay with giving out. Since finding out about his sorcery, she'd kept her mental barriers up around him at all times.

"He stabbed me in the back once."

"You know, I haven't heard the full story of that tragic incident." He rolled his head to the side, blinking at her.

"I'm not in the mood to relive the past," she said coldly.

He took her refusal easily. "Neither am I, Your Majesty. Neither am I."

Lena was afraid to sleep.

Cowen had set up more guards around her room in case she slipped into another sleepwalking trance and tried to escape. She wouldn't let him into her room, and he hadn't push back.

Ira had been spending most nights in his study, pouring over documents and matters that Alkus had been responsible for before.

The safety precautions were more for peace of mind than anything—Cowen's. Not hers. She didn't have Slayer Sickness, but something *was* off. And a mortal was no match for a Numen. If it wanted something, it would get it. But she hadn't told Cowen that, of course. She wasn't sure how her Numen had gotten past all the guards, not once but twice, but she was certain it could happen again. And the only way she could prevent that was if she didn't sleep.

Benji and Andra were on shift tonight so Cowen could rest. Jhai had said she would like to remain in the attendants' hall, so Lena had told her to lock her door and not come out. Lena didn't think anything *bad* would happen per se, but she didn't want to get anyone else involved.

She sat at her desk and read. She had a full teapot next to her at the start of the night. Whenever she grew tired, she paced her room.

Focusing was difficult. Each time she sat down to read, she found herself halfway down the page without having picked up a single thing. She would start over only to get distracted once again.

She dug out her list and read over the names she had left.

Prophet Bianca
Hiram Lorrantoa
Lyle Lorrantoa
Sohan Lorrantoa
Merrick Spevkov
Arden Spevkov
Ophir Vuukroma

Avalon Vuukroma
Celine Vuukroma
Alkus Brendigar
Cressida Veranos
Vix Civerr
Crane Dhalygen
Tuck Vuukroma

Fourteen people left. She and Jhai had gotten rid of eight so far.

But killing was the easy part. Change on the other hand . . . That was where the real challenge lay. She couldn't commit to change with these people here.

She stared at the last name on that list.

Tuck had tricked her. His betrayal had hurt the worst. She was furious with him and the rest of the Blessed, but she was almost equally as furious with herself for putting her family in that position when she knew it was all too good to be true.

Tuck was at the forefront of this all, but his name was the last one she'd added to the list. Why?

She knew why, but she wouldn't admit it. Still, to this day, she wanted there to be an explanation. An excuse. Something that would make things seem better than they were. But sometimes there were no justifications, and life and people were just shit.

You'll only hurt yourself again, thinking like this.

"Fuck you."

Lena pressed her fingers over his name, so hard that the paper nearly ripped. She quickly shoved the list away and went back to her book, pacing when her mind still couldn't absorb anything.

She wasn't quite sure how she fell asleep.

SHE WAS CLOAKED in darkness once again, caught in a dream. The same dream. She existed in a quiet void. The only tangible thing was the darkness she stood on.

"What's happening to me?" she called out. "Why are you doing this?"

She knew her Numen was here, hiding in the shadows. It took its time responding.

"I'm bored," its deep, powerful voice grumbled. "I've waited and waited. I've never waited on a mortal *this long.*"

"Waited for what?"

"For you to listen! I do not understand why you ignore the voice and power that calls to you. It's time for you to seize it!"

There was a pressure behind its words that forced her to her knees. She flinched under its power as it came at her from all sides, squeezing her into a tight ball.

"You were Cursed when you came to me. You were never supposed to have an Imprint," the Numen spat.

"But you granted me one!" she blurted out. "You gave me power."

"Yes." Its voice sounded heavy and worn now, tinged with a bubbling rage that came from somewhere deeper. "I made a pact with you, but you weren't the first."

She couldn't move her head to look around. She couldn't rise from her knees. She was subservient in her own mind.

"The first what? The first Cursed?" The pressure in her head grew, but her thoughts were clear. "Have you given a Cursed an Imprint before?"

The history books didn't mention any situation like hers, but that didn't mean that something like this hadn't happened before. Maybe the Blessed had hidden it.

"Of course not!" the Numen boomed, and she cried out as its power slammed down on her again, forcing her into a lump on the floor. "The Cursed do not get this Touch. Once the soul is reborn, their fate is supposed to be sealed."

"Supposed to be," she gasped out, struggling against the Numen's hold. "But it doesn't always happen that way, does it?"

A sharp wail escaped her lips as her bones contorted and her blood burned. Her mind enlarged, pressing against her skull with such intensity that her vision momentarily disappeared.

"Mind your tone, mortal," the Numen snapped.

"Please. Please. I just need to know why I was chosen for all of this. It keeps happening over and over again."

Her being named ruler. Her receiving an Imprint. Her strange dreams and sleepwalking.

What was so special about her?

"What's special about you," the Numen said, its voice coming closer, wrapping around her, "has nothing to do with you."

And then she was being flung away. Light flooded her vision so quickly that her eyes burned. She feared for a moment that she might go blind, but she didn't. She was outside now, on barren terrain.

On the horizon, a cloud of darkness spread.

∼

LENA'S EYES snapped open when she felt a gust of breeze hit her face. She was greeted with icy wind and darkness and a feeling of weightlessness. Her hips dug into the marble railing of her balcony and her upper half was almost completely horizontal.

She stared at the ground fifty feet below her.

CHAPTER
SIXTY-SEVEN

A scream caught in her throat, and Lena scrambled back, but the movement only sent her farther over the edge. She swung her arms behind her, her nails scraping helplessly over the smooth marble. She locked her legs around the railing pillars and tried to pull herself back. Slowly, she stopped tipping.

If she had woken a few seconds later or been slightly slower, she would've fallen.

She took an unsteady breath and used her legs to lean herself back. Her hands grabbed onto the railing as soon as they could. When she was fully vertical again and no part of her was hanging over the edge, she stumbled back into her room.

What the fuck! She reached out to her Numen as she paced before her bed. *Do you want me to die?*

Her Numen was immortal; she was not. If she died, they'd find another Blessed to make a pact with. Incidents like this reminded her of how erratic the Numina were. To them, this was all a game. If they weren't entertained enough, they would wipe the board and start over.

What did it want? Why was it torturing her like this?

I want power, she told her Numen. *I'm not trying to fight against you. Show me the way.*

It was slightly terrifying giving into her Numen, especially with what had just happened, but that'd been a warning. It wasn't done with her yet, and she wasn't done with it. She still needed its power, and if it was trying to show her *more*, then she needed to listen. If she didn't . . . then perhaps Slayer Sickness wouldn't be *that* implausible.

Once she calmed her nerves, she crawled into bed and tried to fall back asleep. She slipped into her dreams rather quickly, but the only thing that greeted her was the barren land and the massive storm cloud on the horizon. Her Numen wouldn't come or answer any of her questions.

She was able to leave and wake at will this time.

Had she pissed it off? Was it busy? How could it be busy? What did Numina even *do*?

She quickly got out of bed and changed into something more suitable for the weather.

When she opened the door to her room, Benji looked surprised to see her. She ignored the other guard and pulled Benji into her antechamber.

"There's somewhere I need to go."

◦

THE FAINT GLOW shining through the treehouse window greeted her as she approached. Did Tuck ever sleep in the palace?

Benji stayed at the edge of the clearing as she climbed the treehouse ladder.

Tuck's weary eyes and tousled hair told her that he'd been asleep on his lumpy sleeping roll. A small piece of sunstone sat next to him, illuminating the interior of the treehouse.

She immediately cut to the chase.

"I don't trust you. I don't like you. I don't want to be friends with you, so don't get the wrong idea about this. You offered to help me, and I'm taking it. I'm not going to owe you one bit. If anything, this is you paying *me* back. You will help me figure out what's wrong with me, you will help me fix it, and then we will go our separate ways. That's it. That's the extent of our relationship. Do you understand?"

Whatever this sleepwalking-dream thing was—it was dangerous. She didn't want to put the people she cared about at risk. So, in a way, it was rather convenient for her that Tuck had volunteered. Part of her *wanted* him to get hurt in this process.

He blinked at her, his eyes becoming more aware as the drowsiness drained away. And then ever so slowly, he nodded. "Okay," he rasped. "You couldn't have waited until morning to tell me this . . . ?"

She was surprised but pleased that he'd agreed to her terms so quickly. "No." She sat down. "We need to start now."

"Now?" He wiped a hand over his face. His shirt sleeve fell down his arm, revealing small yellow bruises that were almost healed.

"It's not Slayer Sickness." *Not yet.*

His face twisted in a way that said he didn't quite believe her.

"What are you even doing out here sleeping in the cold?"

Tuck yawned into his fist and sat up straighter. "I visit the treehouse sometimes after floating in the clouds. The palace is warm, but I find this place cozier."

She leaned forward, squinting her eyes. "Are you high right now?"

Tuck ignored her question. "Why do *you* keep coming out here? Can't stay away?"

"I'll go away. Right now." It was a shallow threat but dealing with him in general was difficult enough.

"No, you won't."

She glowered at him but stayed still. "I have a few questions for you."

He swept his hands out and settled back against the wall. "Fire away."

"I want the truth, if that means anything to you."

"Will it matter what I say, truth or not?" He pulled his sleeves over the palms of his hands, holding them with his fingers as he crossed his arms over his knees and rested his chin on top of them. "If you don't want to believe it, you won't."

Maybe not, but she still wanted to hear his answers. "Why are you being so helpful all of the sudden? It's . . . confusing."

"Maybe I'm tired of you hating me. Maybe . . . I'm finally daring enough to try."

That was impossibly vague.

"To try what?"

He sighed. "Explaining myself? Breaking away?" He shook his head. "I don't even know. You needed help, so I offered mine, and you're asking why?"

"Of course I am," she said, raising her voice slightly. "Need I remind you what you partook in five years ago?"

"No, you don't need to remind me," he said coldly. "So you still think I want to kill you? Seriously?"

"Well, don't you?"

"If I wanted you dead, I had the perfect opportunity not once, but twice, when you came stumbling here, asleep. I could've driven a dagger through your chest, and you would've been none the wiser."

"Maybe you were waiting for something."

He rolled his eyes. "Like what? By your logic, the end goal is killing you, so why would it matter how or when it happens?"

"I don't know!" she exclaimed. "That's what's so frustrating. You're not acting like you're supposed to, so I don't know what's going on anymore. I don't know what to think."

Especially after visiting Kieryn. He'd spoken of Tuck highly, and it had made her feel out of place, like she and Kieryn were living two different realities.

"Tell me," Tuck mocked, "how am I supposed to act?"

"Like the asshole who betrayed my trust five years ago, who turned his cheek when the other Blessed said nasty things about me. I know he can't be far."

His smile was brittle. "Right, well that asshole is still here, speaking to you. In fact, you voluntarily sought him out."

"Right." She angled herself better toward him and gestured between them. "This thing. It's a transaction—"

"You've said that before, and I get it. You need to set your trust issues aside and—"

"*Trust issues?*" she raged.

He raised a single brow. "Yes, trust issues. You have them."

Clearly. But she didn't appreciate him pointing that out.

"Maybe I have a hard time trusting people because so many of them ended up stabbing me in the back. I place my trust in those who have earned it. *You* lost that trust years ago."

"Then tell me how I can gain it back? I can't revive your family, but there must be another way."

The words lined up behind her lips slipped away at his question. No snarky or scathing comeback could be found. The bubbling heat residing under her skin melted away so that only a bone-deep tiredness remained. She rubbed at her face, trying to soothe the ache that rested in her temples.

"Stop it," she said firmly, but her voice wavered. "Stop messing around."

Tuck seemed to sense the shift in the air. He softened just a fraction. "I'm not. Not right now."

She looked to the side, mortified when her eyes began to sting. She clamped her lips shut and her chest burned with the effort it took to hold herself together. And of course, as soon as she acknowledged the burnout, everything became worse.

"I'm so tired," she whispered. She didn't know why she was admitting that to him, but the words were already out of her mouth. "I'm tired, Tuck, so please just . . . not tonight."

"I'm not looking for a fight."

She scoffed.

" . . . I'm sorry, Lena." His voice was soft and sincere.

That was all it took for her to crumble, and it was pathetic.

She turned away and thought about tumbling through the opening of the treehouse. Her legs were weak, but she didn't need them to fall. She leaned her head back, resting it against the wall. She half-expected to see stars above, but there wasn't an opening in the ceiling.

Her eyes drifted closed. It wasn't the smartest thing to do in the presence of someone who'd hurt her before. But she was tired. And if he came at her . . . let it happen.

"I know you don't believe me and you hate me, but I think about what happened five years ago every single day."

She didn't move.

"I overheard people saying some things. About you and your family. My parents were in that room, in that meeting. They caught me spying. They always said I stuck my nose where it didn't belong. They still say that. But then, since I'd already heard their plans, they wanted me in on it. They thought . . . this was an opportunity for me to prove myself, as their heir. They've given me many *opportunities* throughout the years, but I just can't seem to meet their expectations. I've failed every time."

She bit down on the inside of her cheek to hold back her retort. Did he want her to feel sorry for him?

"I was supposed to isolate you so they could take out your family. And then I was supposed to deliver you to them. But I couldn't. I let you go. Twice."

"*My hero*," she sneered.

"I don't expect you to thank me for it," he said, his voice hard. "It was a shit thing to do. I'm not trying to excuse it, but . . . I want you to know the truth. I couldn't go through with it. I panicked. After I let you go the second time, my father locked me in a wardrobe and sealed my Imprint so I couldn't go after you, or help you. My parents didn't come back to let me out of the wardrobe for quite some time, so I—" His voice caught in his throat, and he swallowed thickly. "It doesn't matter."

She opened her eyes, watching him intently. "Why didn't you tell anyone? Why didn't you tell *me?*"

"We didn't talk anymore. We grew apart. You stopped looking my way as soon as you broke Ira out of prison, remember?"

"Because you and your friends were *horrible* to me."

"They weren't my friends—"

"No? You just hung around them for fun then?"

"You don't understand," he said between gritted teeth, leaning forward. "You didn't grow up here. You don't know what the expectations are like. We didn't have a say in who we wanted as friends or what we wanted to do when we were older. That was already decided for us. My parents wanted me to spend time with you at first, and then they changed their minds, but I didn't stop seeing you. They had always written me off as a troublemaker, and since I could never meet their wild expectations, I swore to meet that one. So to answer your question, no one would've believed me if I told them what I'd overheard. You were avoiding me. More people wanted you gone than not. The only Blessed who would've supported you wouldn't listen to a single word coming out of my mouth. So tell me, *what could I have done?*"

"Said *something!* To *someone!* Pulled me aside? Warned my Sacred Guard? *Not* lead me out into the forest *while my family was being slaughtered?*" she seethed.

She wanted to hit him and scream, but she also wanted to cry. She'd been angry for so long. She was always running to catch up. Her family still hadn't received justice. She had the highest station in The Lands, yet she wasn't able to get what she wanted. Just as Kieryn had said.

Tuck winced and receded in on himself. Just a bit. "I'm sorry," he said hoarsely. "I'll keep saying it because I *am* sorry, but I . . . They were *everywhere*."

She didn't know who *they* were, didn't really care, but she could guess.

Tuck's parents left a lot to be desired. She'd never thought of them as good people, so it made sense that they wouldn't be good parents. She saw the way they acted and heard the way they spoke about their son, like he was nothing but a nuisance. Incompetent and childish. They were all bad news, even Celine with her sweet words dripping in poisoned honey. Tuck was hardly ever with them in public. They were constantly having to find him and reel him in, like at the ball and the holiday dinner.

"Your father said something about you earlier."

Tuck's laugh was low and bitter. "I'm sure he did."

"He said you're unreliable. That you make messes and act out and expect others to clean it up for you."

He hummed. "That's rich."

"Do you think it's true?"

"Sometimes," he murmured, his eyes on the floor, his eyelashes brushing the tops of his cheeks. "But we're all a bit of a mess." He plucked one of the wooden cubes off the floor, then added, "I was especially so after you ran. I acted out even more. Everything you find aggravating about me—imagine that tenfold. No one could stand me. Well, *almost* no one. I purposely created issues. I would disappear for long periods of time without telling anyone. Eventually, my parents had enough. They shipped me off to Ironwave Academy when I was sixteen. The school on the east coast." He let out a heavy breath. "It was pretty shit. I got expelled after a year and came back here."

Lena wasn't foolish enough to believe everything Tuck had said. Forgiveness was out of the cards, but her temper had cooled, perhaps chilled by the night breeze and tampered by her exhaustion.

"I *can't* believe you. I *can't* forgive you," she said slowly, hoarsely. The words scraped her throat as they came up.

"Okay."

"Then why try?"

"Like I said, I'm tired too."

She shook her head and brought her arms and knees up to her chest, forming her own little bubble. "I did consider you a friend once, I think. You were better than the others, but that's not saying much."

"Xavien's dead now," Tuck commented.

"Yeah. Guess he got what was coming for him."

The silence wasn't comforting. It only allowed time and space for unwanted thoughts, private thoughts that Tuck didn't deserve to know. Like how she was more upset with herself than anyone. She'd convinced herself and her family that it would work, lied to herself, even though she'd known better—her parents had taught her better—because she'd wanted that life for them, wanted *more*. She'd been selfish and naive, and it had gotten her family killed. She wished she could go back and be the daughter, the sister, they deserved.

She could outrun her hate for Tuck and people like him by avoiding them or hurting them. But her hate for herself? She couldn't outrun that.

"One day," Tuck said, his voice soft and slow, his face hidden in his arms again, "we'll all get what's coming for us."

CHAPTER
SIXTY-EIGHT

Only a few dozen people were in the cavern when he returned, and none of them were prophets.

"Atreus!"

He spun around. Finn was striding toward him. He looked like he'd been crying, his cheeks blotchy and his eyes red. Judah was at his side, and while he appeared visibly upset and shaken up, he didn't look nearly as distressed as Finn.

Atreus' eyes swept over their figures, searching for any injuries. He didn't find anything major—only scratches and dirt.

Finn lunged forward only a few steps away, squeezing his arms around Atreus, clutching onto him as if he was going to slip away at any moment. "You're okay," Finn wept into his shoulder. "You're okay. You're okay. You're okay. You're okay . . ."

Atreus was taken aback by Finn's reaction. He glanced at Judah, but as soon as he met the kid's wide and glassy eyes, the younger quickly looked away, wringing his fingers into his pant leg.

The air shifted around them, becoming heavier and sullen.

Atreus pulled back from Finn and stared at him strangely. "What's wrong?" he demanded, his voice muted by his thudding heart.

Finn's lips quivered and a fresh wave of tears filled his eyes. "Mila . . . she didn't make it."

He shook his head almost immediately, denying Finn's words. His brows and lips turned down. "No."

"Yes," Finn said, voice thick and wet. "Vanik and Harlow said . . . the people they met helped them find the stone, and then they . . . turned into monsters. They shed their skin and became *Te'Monai*. One of them tackled her and there was a steep hill nearby. She disappeared. And when they found the stone and returned . . . she didn't."

The people . . . turned into Te'Monai? As shocking as that was, Atreus focused on something else.

Disappeared. Not *dead.* They hadn't *seen* the *Te'Monai* kill her.

The bad feeling in his gut persisted.

"Where are Vanik and Harlow?" he asked.

"The prophets took them away as soon as they returned. They took Weylin too. Said they had to go back to solitary."

So it was only the three of them. The cavern was still relatively vacant. This couldn't be *everyone*. The other two groups had gotten back before he had, meaning they'd found the stones rather quickly without much trouble.

"Where is everyone?" he asked urgently.

Finn opened his mouth to reply, but another voice cut him off.

"Atreus."

He tensed and turned to face Prophet Silas. Four enforcers stood silently behind him. The prophet's eyes were cold, but he was smiling.

Atreus' stomach twisted further. Something was definitely wrong. He couldn't ignore the voice that screamed in his head, telling him to run, but there was nowhere to go.

"I need you to come with me," Prophet Silas said.

"Where is everyone?"

The prophet folded his hands behind his back. "They didn't make it to the next stage. You know how this goes."

Atreus tightened his fists, the stones pressing into his skin.

"Come now, Atreus."

If he fought, it would still end with him being dragged away. He stepped forward, but a hand on his wrist stopped him. Judah gazed up at him with worry. Atreus turned, putting his back to the prophet and enforcers.

"It's okay," he said as he turned his palm, discreetly passing the two stones to Judah. He squeezed Judah's hand around the stones, sending him a silent message. "I'll be back soon, okay?"

Judah's eyes widened. He looked past Atreus at Prophet Silas and then nodded, taking a step back to Finn's side.

Finn shot Atreus his own apprehensive look, one Atreus returned with the slight shake of his head and the barest tilt of his chin. Finn's expression shifted from concern to confusion and then realization, but he quickly masked it.

Atreus' message might not have been clear to someone else, but Finn understood it.

Get out of here, Atreus wanted to tell him. *Hide.*

He went with Prophet Silas.

Their steps echoed through the corridor, reminding Atreus of how empty the Institute was now if what Prophet Silas had said was true.

According to him, over half of the firstborns were gone. Dead. Just like that. Had the people killed them? Or had the *Te'Monai?* Why were the *Te'Monai* suddenly appearing again? No, not appearing . . . transforming? Regardless of who or what had killed the firstborns in another realm, the prophets were the ones to blame. And the traitor firstborn.

His eyes bored into the back of Prophet Silas' head. Hatred coursed through him. He already knew the prophets were frauds, but now he knew exactly *how*.

He noticed that they weren't heading in the direction of the black and white room and stopped. The enforcers behind him stopped.

Prophet Silas walked ahead a bit before slowing his step and turning. He didn't look surprised by Atreus' antics. "Another act of rebellion?"

Prophet Silas wanted him dead. He was separated from his friends. Hundreds were dead or missing. It was now or never.

"Which firstborns are working with you?"

Prophet Silas blinked but gave nothing away. "Enough of this.

He waved his hand, but Atreus dodged the enforcers when they went to grab him. He knew he couldn't outmaneuver them entirely, but he wouldn't let himself get dragged away so easily.

"I know the truth," he hissed. "I know about the tyrannical philosophy you prophets preach and follow. I know that we're used as sacrificial pawns because you are too cowardly to even fight for your own beliefs."

The prophet's eyes flashed. "Shut your mouth, boy. Didn't I say you wouldn't be getting another warning?"

"I don't give a *shit*," he spat. He retreated another step, moving closer to the wall. There was no going back, nowhere to run. If he was going down, he was going down fighting. "I'm not scared of you. You're weak and *pathetic*. You have the blood of *thousands* on your hands, yet you still tell us *we* are evil. I didn't know exactly how to fight back before, but I do now."

The prophet's face warped with fury, but rather than snap at Atreus, he laughed. It was low and acrid, draping over Atreus like the callous darkness of the Institute, sending shivers down his spine.

"You stupid boy," he chuckled. "You think you know everything, do you?"

"I know enough," Atreus said, his body angled, eyes darting between the motionless enforcers and the manic prophet.

The laughter faded and Prophet Silas wiped a hand down his face, pausing over his eyes and shielding them from Atreus. A malicious glint flickered within them when he dropped his hand, dark amusement now splayed across his face.

"You're sick," the prophet sighed, almost pityingly. "You don't even realize it, but you would have. One day. Unfortunately . . . you won't make it that far."

Prophet Silas nodded at the enforcers, and they stepped forward.

Atreus instinctively moved back, but he hit the wall. He was cornered. The enforcers' large hands reminded him of the *Te'Monai*'s bloody claws.

Now was the time to call them.

Zosia said he'd know how.

He gave into the panic and called out to the *Te'Monai* with everything he had, just like he had in the realm of ice and snow.

Come! Help me! Kill them! Kill the prophets and the enforcers!

But nothing happened.

He ducked under the enforcers' hands, crouching against the wall.

He tried again, his chest burning with exertion, his head throbbing. Nothing.

He tried to run, but an enforcer grabbed the back of his uniform and threw him. His head hit the rough stone and a choked groan escaped his lips. He leaned forward, his vision fuzzy.

He hoped Finn had listened to him and was somewhere else. Somewhere safe. Not that there was such a place in the Institute.

Atreus reached deep inside himself, trying to find that cord that linked him to the realms, to the *Te'Monai*. It was faint, but it was there. He could feel it, like the thrum of the stones.

He wrapped his hand around it, making sure he had a good grip, and then he pulled with all of his might, calling to them, ordering them to come and *fight*.

A roar sounded through the Institute.

His eyes widened. The enforcers stopped. Prophet Silas looked down the corridor in the direction the roar had come from, unadulterated terror clear on his face.

The *Te'Monai* had come. They were here in the Institute.

But the cord inside of him was still taut. It had not moved. His cry hadn't reached another realm.

The *Te'Monai* were responding to someone else's call.

CHAPTER
SIXTY-NINE

Much to Lena's aggravation, Tuck was still a good teacher. She was much more insolent now than she'd been before, but he still responded to her jabs with patience and reason. He didn't raise his voice. He would grow irritated sometimes, but it was short-lived. He was always the first to collect himself and steer them back on topic.

She told him about her odd and dark dreams. Her Numen was always there, and oftentimes this alluring voice was too. It beckoned her closer, and her Numen encouraged her to follow it, promising her power when she reached it.

Tuck wore a puzzled expression and fiddled with a dagger as she told him all of this.

"And when you follow the voice, you keep ending up here?" he clarified slowly.

She nodded and looked out the treehouse window, her eyes finding the tops of the city buildings over the trees. Solavas wasn't far from here. Perhaps a five- or ten-minute walk. Most of the tall buildings she passed over with little care, but her gaze caught on the top of the treasury. The steeple at the front shot high into the sky and was covered in gold to display the treasury's magnificence and riches. It winked against the setting sun as if waving goodbye. That signal had tormented her every single day recently. It said *try again*.

Try again. See you tomorrow. Try again.

They couldn't figure it out. Each time they met, they went over every detail of her dreams. She didn't have much material to go off of, and it didn't help that her Numen had been giving her the silent treatment as of late. It probably wouldn't speak to her until she found this power. She didn't even know what *this power* was. All she had to go off of was a voice and some ominous, vague descriptor.

"I am the beginning. I am a creator and a prison. I am what you seek."

Lena worried more about Slayer Sickness as time passed. She made sure to note any odd symptoms she had.

After about a week of meeting and walking away without any answers, Tuck suggested that she sleep in the treehouse. "You keep coming here, so this location must be special somehow. You said you haven't had any more dreams lately. Maybe you'll have one here."

It was worth a try. They didn't have any other leads. But the thought of Tuck watching her while she slept didn't sit right with her for a number of reasons.

Her lips parted but she stilled. Tuck picked up on her hesitance soon after the suggestion left his mouth.

"I'm not going to kill you," he said dully, clearly tired of having this conversation.

"I don't like people watching me sleep," she said defensively.

"I'll stay outside of the treehouse and sit at the base of the tree. If anything happens and you try to go somewhere, I'll follow. Hopefully whatever it is your Numen wants, you can find if you're not interrupted."

That sounded better. She still didn't like it, but that didn't really matter. They'd exhausted their options. She was desperate, and if she went without answers any longer, her health could be at risk. When she agreed to work with Tuck, she'd been prepared to do things that would make her uncomfortable if it meant getting to the bottom of this issue that plagued her. Sleeping in the tree house wasn't the *worst* thing she could do. She would never admit this to Tuck, but sometimes she just needed to face her fears to find out some of them were, maybe, just a *bit*, irrational.

When she arrived the next day, Tuck sat on the ground with his long legs extended in front of him, lounging against the large tree that held the treehouse. He grabbed a nut from the bowl next to him and tossed it into his mouth. "Good evening, Lena."

She crossed her arms and scowled at him, but she didn't correct him. She didn't have the energy today. "Let's just get this thing over with."

"Anxious?"

"*Annoyed*," she corrected.

Tuck ate some more nuts. "Well, go on then. I'll be here."

That's no comfort, she nearly threw back.

She took a deep breath and climbed into the treehouse. It looked the same as it had the night before. The only items inside were Tuck's sleeping roll, his pack, a sunstone, and the wooden blocks and figurines. With how much time Tuck seemed to spend out here, she would expect it to be a bit homier.

The sleeping roll would be more comfortable than the hard floor, but she wouldn't use it. She felt like she was proving a point as she lay down in the opposite corner, even though Tuck had no way of knowing what she was doing.

She rested her head on her arm, closed her eyes, and tried to relax her body, but the tension was knitted into her bones. Her heart was a steady but powerful drum in her chest, startling her awake every time her mind began to drift.

Be alert.

Danger.

You can't sleep.

Lena tightened her grip on the dagger she'd brought with her and pushed away the warnings, telling herself that she was safe. She was fine. She could sleep.

She repeated that mantra to herself again and again, speaking over the other voices that tried to tell her the opposite.

Eventually, she did fall asleep.

Her dreams were empty. It was only her amidst the inky blackness.

And when she woke, she was no longer in the treehouse. She was directly under it.

Tuck stood near the base of the tree a few feet away, watching her, his mouth and eyebrows downturned.

"Did you wake me up?"

"No. You climbed down yourself and then just . . . stopped. You were staring at the ground for ten minutes before you woke up."

"What?" There was nothing but soil and leaves and tree roots under her feet. She shook her head. "I was dreaming, but . . . I was alone. Nothing or no one spoke to me."

"But you were dreaming," Tuck said as he came closer. "That's not nothing. Subconsciously you were pulled into it, toward something."

"Something in the ground?" she said skeptically.

Tuck crouched next to her and stared at the soil intently as if it was going to reveal what they were looking for.

"Maybe," he muttered under his breath. "The only way to be sure is to start digging." He pushed himself to his feet. "Back up."

She did. The words in her mouth dried up after he summoned his Slayer.

The green glow of it washed over her and clashed with the red from the moons, making the area even darker and muddier than before. She was several feet away from it, but the heat still reached her, peeling at her face.

She took another step back, her own Imprint flaring. Tuck's Slayer paid her no mind as it immediately began to dig, shooting streams of dirt behind it in her direction. She grimaced and moved aside, avoiding the soil.

"A little warning would be nice!" Lena hissed as she willed her heart to calm.

At first, all she could see and think about was the darkness, the trees, and the green Slayer so close to her.

You have your own now, she reminded herself. *You have protection.*

"Sure," Tuck said, not even paying her any attention. His eyes were on the hole his Slayer was creating. It was moving quickly, having already created a large pit nearly ten feet deep.

For her own peace of mind, Lena called her Slayer. Part of her worried it wasn't going to show when she called it, so she was relieved when it did. It was nice to know her Numen wasn't *that* upset with her.

Tuck finally acknowledged her, raising a brow at her Slayer's appearance, but now it was her turn to ignore him.

His Slayer paused momentarily at the arrival of the new Slayer, but after a silent command from Tuck, it continued its digging. Her Slayer stayed at her side. She could feel its desire to run and taste blood, but she kept it close.

"There's nothing there!" Lena shouted over the commotion.

After another minute, Tuck called off his Slayer. It had disappeared so far into the ground that she could hardly see its green glow anymore. When it crawled back out of the hole, she walked forward to look into the pit.

"Just dirt." Under her breath, she sighed, "Obviously."

"What's your Numen?"

Lena looked up at Tuck, startled by his question. "What?"

"Your Numen," he repeated. "What's its title? Or name?"

Her mouth opened and then closed again. "What does it matter?"

He gave her an odd look that lingered. "Their title says a lot about them. It can explain why they act the way they do, and since you're having problems with your Numen, it's important."

She'd known from the start that she would be more prone to issues with her Numen because of its title, especially because of how late in life she'd received a pact, but she'd hoped things wouldn't become this problematic. On the bright side, things could still get much worse, but that was exactly why she was trying to deal with the issue now.

If she refused to answer, Tuck would grow ever more suspicious and become even more determined to find out her Numen's title. No one knew. Not even Ira. He hadn't asked, so she hadn't told him. Admittedly, she did feel a little bad about that. It wasn't trust that was the issue, or judgment. She didn't have to worry about that from Ira. It was the pity.

Numen of Calamity. Oh how that makes sense for Kalena Skathor.

"Lena?" Tuck was still looking at her strangely. "Your Numen?"

This information could be used against her, and telling Tuck this was arguably more dangerous than spending time with him.

"What's yours?" she asked instead.

"Numen of Stealth," he gave up easily. "Deivikos."

There was a bated silence between them that she was obviously supposed to fill with her Numen's title. She swallowed thickly. Her Slayer felt her discomfort and growled. Tuck's Slayer then picked up on the growing hostility and growled back.

Tuck wordlessly dismissed his Slayer, and it disappeared. "You don't want to share?"

"It's not a secret," she lied. "Your father knows. I told the council."

"So what did you tell them?"

"That the Numen I made a pact with is the Numen of Fortune."

His own expression was unchanging, but his eyes shifted with this new information. "Fortune," he repeated to himself. To her, he asked, "Was that the truth?"

Her heart lurched to a halt.

At first, she thought it was because of his question, but she realized a split second later that her reaction had been caused by her Slayer. Something had caught its attention. A threat. It perked up and turned, its muscles wired with tension as it stared into the trees, preparing to take off at any second.

Hold, she told it.

She waited for her Slayer to relax and turn back toward her, but it never did. Another low growl permeated through the air as its body remained low to the ground.

It wouldn't let up.

It smelled blood.

She blinked and her Slayer took off. Leaves and dirt flew into the air. The underbrush and branches hissed as the Slayer tore through them.

"Don't call it back," Tuck said quickly, suddenly at her side. His eyes were fixed on her Slayer in the distance. The purple glow was fading quickly. "We need to follow it."

Lena could feel what her Slayer felt, *see* what her Slayer saw. She was the first one to run after it, but Tuck quickly caught up. She lost sight of her Slayer soon after—it was too fast for them—but she was still able to sense it. The tether that linked them kept her on its tail. She took the lead for the most part, but whenever she switched over to her Slayer's eyes, Tuck moved to the front.

In her Slayer's head, she could better smell the blood it hunted. The scent was strong and becoming stronger by the second. Nothing looked out of the ordinary. Her Slayer was still racing through thick lines of trees.

When she snapped back to her own body, she was surprised to see how quickly Tuck was moving. He'd caught onto her Slayer's trail. He was agile and silent as he moved, blending into the shadows and never hesitating about where to step next. This must be how he was when sent on a mission as *The Wraith*. It was different from the Tuck she usually saw.

She stumbled to a stop. Her breath caught in her throat when her Imprint gave a sudden, harsh flare. The heat seeped into her lungs and burned away the air.

Tuck whipped around at her gasp. "What's wrong?"

She touched her burning chest with wide eyes. "My Slayer . . . it just . . . disappeared."

She could feel it back in its other realm, trapped behind her Imprint. But she hadn't called it back. Had it returned on its own volition?

"Did you—?"

"No."

Tuck's expression hardened. "Let's go."

They continued following the path her Slayer had made. By the time they reached the end, they too could smell the blood.

They slowed and dropped closer to the ground as they advanced forward, unsure of what they might find. She didn't recognize this part of the forest. The trees extended for dozens of miles in the Highlands.

She froze when she heard a groan and then a whimper. Ice replaced the blood in her veins, and her eyes latched onto the thick underbrush that obscured her view. The sounds and the smell were coming from just ahead.

She peered through the branches and vines, taking in the small clearing in front of her. The red moons made the carnage laid out before her appear bloodier. The grass was stained with red and littered with bodies. Some were still, and some stirred weakly.

A man stood over them all. He moved without any hesitation, trailing after another man who was trying to crawl away. Pitiful whimpers left his mouth, and when he realized that he wasn't escaping, he turned on his back to face his soon-to-be executioner.

"Please. *Please!* Don't do this," the man begged. "I can give you anyth—"

Lena watched in horror as the man leaned down, dug his hand into the other man's chest, and ripped his heart out in one swift move. He turned, holding the fluttering, bloody organ under the moonlight like it was some sort of sacred prize.

She gasped. It was quick and quiet, barely there, but still audible.

Tuck shot her a reprimanding look, but her eyes were stuck on the man. He'd heard her. He stared straight at her.

Blood trailed down his arm as the heart puttered to a stop. Black covered him from head to toe, but his face was left bare. The night was dark and he stood several feet away, but she would be able to recognize him anywhere. His glowing blue eyes betrayed him.

It was Ira.

Tuck reached for her, but she darted away from him, unwilling to be touched right now. She had just seen Ira kill that man. He'd probably killed the others in this clearing. And not only them.

"Lena," Tuck hissed in warning, trying to grab her again.

She stepped away, tensing.

But it was too late. They were already surrounded.

CHAPTER
SEVENTY

A few seconds after the initial roar, the screams began. Just like an Outing. Atreus remained still for a moment as snarls and cries echoed down the dark halls. The *Te'Monai* were here. Summoned by someone else, someone who didn't have control. The Institute was being attacked.

He scrambled to his feet and stepped away.

Neither the enforcers nor Prophet Silas reacted. They weren't used to this—the immediacy of danger. He didn't think the enforcers felt much of anything, fear included, but they only obeyed prophets' orders, and Prophet Silas looked frozen in a state of shock, so Atreus used that to his advantage.

He ran.

In the direction of the *Te'Monai*.

Prophet Silas shouted after him, which Atreus ignored. He needed to find Finn and Judah. And Mila. He didn't believe that she was dead.

Carnage was already strewn on the ground of the cavern. None of the firstborns had weapons and their Imprints were sealed. They didn't have much to fight with.

Atreus reached inside of him for the cord, but the moment he did, a piercing screech rang out close by. He turned and braced himself just as one of the *Te'Monai* emerged from the shadows and pounced on him.

Atreus raised his arm to protect his face, ducking to avoid the fast-approaching *Te'Monai* at the same time. It overshot and the very ends of its claws scraped over Atreus' forearm. A grunt of pain escaped his lips and he fell forward. He spun around quickly, kicking at the stone floor to get himself back on his feet.

The *Te'Monai* tried to do the same, scrambling to gain its balance on its long spindly legs.

This one was particularly ugly—gray, sickly skin stretched tight over its form, showing the pointed bones that made up its skeleton. Its bright blue eyes wouldn't leave him, and it roared, revealing rows upon rows of tiny, razor-sharp teeth. Its chest was concave, and its thin, curved claws tapped against the rock as it chattered, watching him.

The *Te'Monai* darted toward him again and Atreus stumbled back, snatching up a rock from the ground. Adrenaline pumped through his veins as imaginary claws gripped his throat.

STOP!

The *Te'Monai* halted, its blooded claws only inches away from Atreus. He stared at the talons, his eyes wide and chest heaving. He half-expected them to jerk forward and plunge into his gut, but they didn't. He had a grip on it. He cocked his head to the side. The *Te'Monai* followed his movement.

Attack the other Te'Monai, not the firstborns, he ordered.

He held his breath as the *Te'Monai* took a hesitant step back and then dashed into the shadows. He focused on extending his reach to the other *Te'Monai*, telling them the same thing he'd told the other one.

Don't hurt the humans.

But the screams persisted.

Was there some sort of limit to this? A rulebook? He'd discovered his abilities recently and had only tested them *once*.

He took a deep breath and squeezed his eyes shut. Finn and Judah were his priority. Everyone else . . . that wasn't on him.

He turned to run farther down the corridor but skidded to a halt when he saw a familiar figure.

Mila.

He tensed as she approached. She stared at him evenly, no panic evident in her body language or written across her face despite what was going on around them.

He didn't know how many warning signs he'd come across since returning to the Institute, but this was the last one. No words had been exchanged between the two of them, yet he knew. Everything fell into place smoothly and silently. The dark void in the center of his chest grew. Bit by bit, it was always growing.

"Finn told me you were dead," he said tonelessly.

Mila dipped her head, staring into his eyes intently. "But you knew that wasn't the truth."

There wasn't a scratch on her. The way she was acting, the look on her face . . . she knew that he knew.

"Tell me the truth," he said, his voice growing in volume. "I want to hear it from you. Tell me you're not working with them!"

He flinched when another scream rang out from down the corridor.

Mila's silence was her answer.

"Why?" he demanded fiercely, taking a step forward. His Imprint was sealed, but his skin was *burning*. "Why would you betray us for them? They send us to our deaths!" He paused, glaring at her. "Actually, it's *you* who does that. All the blood that has spilled is on *your* hands." He shook his head, wanting to tear his hair out. "This whole time . . . when I was figuring out the stones and the *Te'Monai* and my connection to them, you *knew* and you didn't say *anything*."

None of his words seemed to phase her. "There's more to this than you understand. Sometimes sacrifices need to be made."

Atreus scoffed. He'd been told that far too many times. "Get rid of the *Te'Monai*."

"I can't. Only you can."

But he *couldn't*. It wasn't working.

"You're distraught about something. Distracted," Mila observed. Her dark hair slid across her shoulder as she tilted her head. "You better figure it out. People are dying, Atreus."

He clenched his jaw. "Because of you."

"No, because of you. I saved you earlier. Now it's your turn to be the hero."

Hero. Hero. Hero.

The word mocked him. He wasn't a hero. He was just trying to survive.

His throat tightened. "Get rid of them."

"I can't—"

Atreus surged forward, grabbing Mila by the collar of her uniform and yanking her close. He held the sharp edge of the stone against her neck, pressing hard enough that a bead of blood welled. *"Get rid of them!"*

A laugh sprang from her throat, so dark and wild that it startled him. Mila had always been so reserved.

"You're pathetic," she said. "Even now in the crux of danger, you can't do anything. Are you scared of your power? It's okay. I was too."

He stared at her in disgust and disbelief and tightened his grip on the stone, but he wasn't able to push it any farther. He couldn't.

"No? I can see you need some motivation," she mused.

Mila moved her hand, and something flashed between them. Atreus pulled back, grabbing her wrist and twisting her hand so she was forced to drop whatever she was holding. The knife clattered to the ground, but she was already out of his grip and running away.

"I'm going to kill one of them!" she called over her shoulder. "But I'll let you pick who. Finn or Judah, Atreus?"

"Mila!" he roared after her, but the shadows had already swallowed her up.

He cursed and grabbed the knife, then bolted after her, following her laughter through the dark, twisting halls.

The way she was acting *frightened* him, but it also fueled the rage bubbling in his veins. How could she be so . . . detached yet playful? And to threaten Finn and Judah like that?

The rage only heightened his power. Whenever he came across a *Te'Monai*, he redirected them with a single thought. It was like there was some proximity rule to this ability of his.

After a few minutes of chasing her, he realized where she was leading him. The garden. The door to the room was already open when he turned the corner.

He hesitated before striding forward and shutting the door behind him, sealing them both inside. He scanned the room, but the tall plants and plots of soil blocked his view.

"Mila! Come out here!" he yelled. "I'm in no mood to play games. You owe me an explanation!"

Silence.

He edged around the boxes of plants, carefully scouting out every inch of space, but there were too many places to hide in here—the cracks in the walls, the dark corners, behind the plants, *in* them. He'd been in here enough times to know just how much of a maze it could be if you weren't familiar with it.

"Mila!" he shouted again, frustration seeping into his tone. And despair. "How could you do this? To your . . . *friends?*"

It was a dangerous title he'd only given to two people, and one had betrayed them.

"I'm trying to make you understand."

Atreus spun around, latching on to her voice. He stepped up onto a box and swatted the tall plants aside as he moved through them. His boots sunk into the soft soil and the sunstones shot blinding light and blistering heat down on him.

"You wouldn't have listened if I talked to you. So I had to *show* you."

He emerged from the plants, still surrounded by other raised plots full of greenery, but Mila was nowhere in sight.

"You have to show me by *killing people? For years?* Or maybe even longer. How long have you been working for them, Mila?" She was quiet now. "*Answer me!*"

"One thing you need to learn," she said, and he chased after her voice again; it was everywhere yet nowhere, "is that you can't be everyone's hero."

He knocked the stalks aside and kicked at the vines tangling around his feet, dragging him down.

"I *do* consider you a friend, Atreus, but there are things bigger than just us, here, in this place, at this moment."

"I thought you were my friend too," he said. "But I was wrong. We're not friends."

"We are," she said with certainty.

Atreus stumbled out of another garden. He couldn't find her, but her voice sounded so clear to his ears. Where the fuck was she?

"Remember that."

The air around him quieted, as if all the noise had been sucked out. The hair on the back of his neck rose as a laugh trickled through the room. It wasn't anything human, but it wasn't a *Te'Monai* either.

He slowly turned, noting the faint, yellow glow from between the plants. She'd called her Slayer, meaning her Imprint wasn't blocked.

Of course it wasn't. Had it ever been?

He couldn't control someone else's Slayer, and he couldn't fight one himself, not without *his* Slayer.

"Call them, Atreus," Mila sang.

A bead of sweat trailed down his temple as he slowly moved forward, keeping an eye on the glow. He reached inside, finding the cord again and tugging.

Nothing answered his call.

"You're not trying hard enough."

He gritted his teeth and tried again, desperate and furious.

The Slayer slithered through the rustling plants. Hunting.

His heart pounded in his chest and his palms were slick with sweat, slipping on the handle of the knife that was useless in this fight.

The Slayer darted forward. The plants hissed and whipped as it sprinted through them.

Atreus tensed, his heart leaping into his throat. A shockingly bright Slayer sprang from the plants, lunging at him. He dove to the side, but Slayers were more agile than any of the *Te'Monai* they'd faced. It changed direction quickly, already on him before he could scramble to his feet.

It was the same Slayer that had attacked that man next to the sister's house in the realm of ice and snow.

It screamed in his face, claws pinning down his shoulders. He yelled back, struggling under its crushing hold as its blazing talons dug into him, drawing blood and burning his skin. The sweltering heat that enveloped his face stole the breath from his chest. His heartbeat was deafening in his ears, the aura flame melting his nerves. One of the Slayer's teeth dug into his collarbone, and he screamed, tears prickling the corners of his eyes.

"*Call them!*" Mila shouted.

The panic and adrenaline squeezed him tight, locking his body and flooding his brain. It built in his chest until he could do nothing but let it go.

His hand wrapped around the cord and tugged.

This time, the cord gave, and the rebound hit him violently, making him feel like he'd smacked into a wall after being thrown across the room.

The immense rush of power that responded to his call threw him off center, away from this situation momentarily. He felt weightless yet heavy. Euphoric yet in pain.

When his vision cleared, he was still on the ground in the garden, but the Slayer had been ripped off of him by another *Te'Monai*. One that *he* had called.

CHAPTER
SEVENTY-ONE

The guards had forced them to give up their weapons before taking them back to the palace.

Lena's mind was reeling, but she did think about calling her Slayer, even though the guards surrounded her and Tuck, outnumbering them six to one. When she reached inside her Imprint, her hand closed around empty air. She couldn't summon her Slayer. The panic clogged her throat.

She looked at Tuck, wide-eyed. He tried to fight the guards to get to her, but they were able to restrain him. The guards ushered him along as they cut through the forest, being firm but not harsh. It was like they were trying to reason with Lena and Tuck. Coax them into cooperating.

Tuck tried to catch her eye, but she wouldn't look at him then. She was trying to make sense of what she'd seen.

Ira had killed those people. All of their hearts had been ripped out. By Ira. He was the one doing it? He was the one responsible for these killings from the start? He could have a partner. Was it her attacker? Someone else? Which killings was he responsible for? The ones after their honeymoon? The ones during the Night Run? The ones after the holiday? How far back did this go? Was he responsible for her family?

The trip was a blur, and everything happened so quickly once they set foot inside the palace. They'd used a secret side entrance to get inside, one that led to Lena and Ira's wing.

She hadn't even known about it.

Tuck was separated from her, and they wouldn't tell her where they were taking him.

Ira appeared shortly after, cleaned of any blood. The guards passed her off to him without question.

"Don't cause a scene," he told her as his hand sealed around her arm and he steered her away. "Be quiet so you don't wake anyone up."

"Get off me!" she yelled, pushing him away.

Ira clenched his jaw and only held on tighter to the point where his grip became uncomfortable. "Stop yelling," he hissed. "Please."

"Are you serious?" Her words came out in short huffs as she struggled against his iron grip. He'd never used his strength against her before. She'd always trusted that he wouldn't. A sourness coated her throat. "Ira! Let go!"

He opened a door and shoved her inside. She stumbled a few feet into the room and looked around.

It was clearly lived in. She recognized some of the items around the room, on the desk and the bookshelves, saw the canopy of stars over the bed, the paper figurines, and concluded that this was where Ira slept when he didn't want to share a space with her.

It burned a bit, deep in her chest, and the heat only grew as she turned to face him.

"What the fuck? You don't yank me around like that!"

Ira stepped away from the door once he made sure it was securely shut.

"I'm sorry," he said softly, "but you were going to make things worse if you drew attention to us."

"Make things worse *how*? Want to explain to me what I saw out there?" Her voice remained loud and sharp.

He sighed and set his shoulders as if preparing for a fight. Hers immediately rose in response. "I never wanted you to see that."

"Well, I can guess why!"

Her mind kept replaying those moments over and over and over again. It blurred with the other bloody scenes—the bodies strung up after their honeymoon, the bodies she'd seen in the Lowlands, the Covaylens, Trynla, her family.

Lena closed her eyes, unable to look at him, and said slowly to keep her voice from trembling, "Tell me I'm wrong. Tell me you haven't been the one killing Blessed this entire time. Tell me you didn't lie to me, especially after all the lectures you gave me about trust in our relationship! Tell me this is one big misunderstanding!"

"This is a misunderstanding."

She scoffed and turned away to distance herself from him. She wanted that to be true, more than anything, but it couldn't be. She'd offered the excuse, and he'd taken it. But she'd *seen* him.

"Wait, wait." Ira blocked her path, holding up his hands in front of him. "I know how it looked—how it *looks*—but those people were not good people—"

"I don't care about that! I don't care about them! I care about you lying to me about something this big!" She sucked in a mouthful of air, but only a fraction of it reached her chest. "You had plenty of opportunities to tell me the truth. You didn't say *anything* after suggesting we frame Alkus for the killings. You didn't say anything to me while the guards were interrogating my attacker about the killings! *Why?*"

"I'm sorry—"

"No, that's not good enough." Her voice trembled, but it was raw and yanked from somewhere deep within her chest. "You can't say you're sorry, you'll do better, and then end it there. Not for *this*. I want an explanation this time." Her mind was a useless jumble. She tried to grasp at straws. Anything. "Is someone making you do this? Are you being threatened?"

The killings had started shortly after she returned. Before then, Ira had been on his own up here, strong but outnumbered. Maybe one of the other Blessed had forced him into this. But even she realized how weak that rationale sounded.

Ira shook his head. "Lena, I can't—"

"You're still hiding things from me! *Why* are you doing this?"

Tears sprang to her eyes, blurring her vision and only adding oil to the fire. Her Imprint seared. A molten handprint wrapped around her throat, burning her vocal cords as she continued to scream and pour her heart out, begging him to see reason, to see *her*. How he was hurting her.

"It was brutal," she added, soft and choked.

" . . . Do you think they didn't deserve it?" His fingers itched at his sides. The limited light in the room cut across his sunken cheekbones, making him appear colder and estranged.

Lena lunged forward and shoved him, a snarl at her lips. *"Deserved it?"* she raged. Her arms came up in front of her, curling and shaking with unrestrained emotion. She shoved him again as she pitched forward, her voice coming out a hoarse scream. *"Did you kill my family?"*

She finally got her first real reaction out of him. His eyes widened and the remaining color in his face was wiped away.

"No, Lena, no." He stumbled over his words, holding his hands up now as if to defend himself. "No, I would never—"

She knocked his hands aside. "You ripped out that man's heart! I saw you! All the victims had their hearts ripped out, just like my family five years ago! Swear on it! Swear on their lives that you didn't!"

Through the tears, she could see the shock splayed across his face. The whites of his eyes stood out, and his lips were parted. It was a genuine reaction. He hadn't known. He really hadn't known about her family being mutilated. His face filtered through all the different emotions—shock, heartbreak, pity, realization, horror, and then anger. Resignation.

"I didn't . . . " Ira shook his head again. Torment twisted his face. "I didn't hurt them, Lena. I swear on their lives. I would *never*. They were good people. I cared for them. They—*You* fought for me when no one else would. And they accepted me. *Please stop crying.* They were *kind* to me when no one else was. I wouldn't—"

"Then who did?" she demanded.

The seams that held her together were splitting. Everything was tumbling down. Every*one*. They were showing her their other face and ripping the fabric of her reality out from under her feet. Even Ira.

It had taken her a while to regain her head after the attack. The first few months she spent in the Lowlands were a grief-stricken, panic-inducing blur. She worried about the threats in the Lowlands and the Blessed sending someone to finish her off. She was constantly having to *move* and *react* and *fight*. She wasn't able to sit with her feelings and contemplate the idea of revenge until she got a hold of her Slayer. That was when she started building her list. She already had a few people in mind, and a few more found their way on there. All Blessed of course, but she'd missed something. Because now . . . Ira was connected to this.

"I don't know," he whispered. "I don't know. I'm sorry. I promise I would tell you if I knew—"

"That's the thing," she said coldly. "I don't know if I can trust you anymore. You're lying or keeping things from me entirely and disappearing and not explaining *anything*—"

"I'm sorry. I've apologized before and I'll keep doing it," Ira said softly, but his face was stern once again. "But don't act like you weren't doing this very same thing months ago. And you're still doing it too! You shut Cowen out when it's convenient! And *Tuck?*" His eyes flashed.

Was he trying to turn this on *her*?

"He's been helping me figure my shit out since you haven't been around!" The words tumbled out of her mouth, lined with spite, before she could think them through.

"Really?" he chastised. "Tuck Vuukroma? I thought we agreed he was dangerous?"

"We're all dangerous! I just saw you rip someone's heart out with your bare hands! We've all killed people! We have the power of a Numen on our side! We're all pretty fucking dangerous!" She sucked in a breath. "The only reason we were out there was because I've been having these weird dreams and sleepwalking and he's trying to help me determine the cause of it before it gets worse—"

Confusion and concern were visible under the hostility, softening his features. "Weird dreams? Sleepwalking? What's—?"

"You'd know if you were ever here! I feel like I haven't seen you in weeks! We were apart when I was stuck at the cabin, and when I was able to come back to the palace, you were *still* always gone. And I had no idea where you were. What happened?" she lamented, drifting closer to Ira again. She hated that she still leaned toward him even when furious with him. "Everything was fine. *More* than fine! We were happy and comfortable and then the holiday happened . . ."

And he'd disappeared.

She waited for an explanation, but the only thing she got was a blank stare.

"You have to stop," she begged, realizing that she sounded much like he had, much like Cowen had, when speaking to her months ago, weeks ago, days ago. "No more secrets. No more disappearing. You can't do it if you want me to trust you."

Silence sat between them. It grew heavier with each passing second, pressing down on her shoulders. The tears stubbornly persisted.

"Ira," she pleaded, her voice and resolve weak. "Don't do this to me."

She loved him so much. So, so much. That was terrifying on its own. He was her foundation. She'd thought everything she knew and believed about him was solid, but now it was slipping. Slowly. And the repercussions of that were even more horrifying.

"Shhh." He glided toward her and cradled her face. She tried to pull away, but her attempt was half-hearted. It was pathetic how quickly and willingly she sunk into his embrace, and his warm, familiar touch only made her cry harder. "I have never done something without your best interest in mind. You can ask me anything that will make you feel better." He smoothed his thumbs over her cheeks, smearing her tears.

"And you'll decide if you want to answer it honestly or not."

Ira frowned at her, as if she was the one causing the problem.

"Why the hearts?" She swallowed thickly. "Why are you taking out the hearts?"

"I need them," he said simply.

"Why?"

Ira opened his mouth and then closed it. He was unwilling to give her the answer she wanted.

A noise ripped its way out of her throat, and she pushed his hands aside, taking a step back. She wiped away the rest of her tears herself. "Who's Prophet Nya?"

Ira barely reacted to that name. "She's one of the prophets I've been talking to about reform programs. She doesn't come down from the temple often. I can introduce you to her next time."

"What reform programs?"

Ira tilted his head slightly. "The ones you mentioned to me, about the Lowlands. With the paperwork and legislation I've been drafting, I needed some input from the prophets. They have a better understanding of the law. But I needed to ensure it was a prophet we could trust."

"You trust this Prophet Nya?"

Ira nodded. "I do."

"And who were those guards in the forest?"

She hadn't recognized any of them, but there were hundreds of guards at the palace. What concerned her more than their identity was what they might do now after seeing the mess Ira had created.

"They're our guards, Lena. They work for us, not Alkus." Ira dipped his head. "You don't have to worry about them saying anything."

Her? Ira was the one who had been caught red-handed, quite literally.

"Did you pay them off?"

He tilted his head from side to side. "Something like that."

"I want a straight answer. I don't like repeating myself. You're a fool if you trust that they'll keep their mouth shut. We have our fair share of enemies here, and a lot of them could outbid you. If the guards weigh their odds, they're not sticking with us."

This would be a golden opportunity for someone like Avalon or Ophir.

"I have it taken care of," Ira said. "They won't tell anyone anything."

The first thing she thought of was exactly what had gotten them into this mess in the first place: murder. Killing them would silence them.

"How can you know that?" she demanded.

"Since I can't give you the full truth about everything else," he said. "I'll give you this."

He took a few steps back and breathed deeply. The room around them slowly melted away. Trees sprouted in place of the wallpaper. Grass replaced carpets and the arched ceiling was now the red sky. They were standing in the middle of the forest.

"What the fuck?" she breathed out, taking a step back in alarm.

"It's an illusion," he quickly assured her. "A spell placed on your mind that makes you see what I want you to see. I cast one every time I go out."

"To kill," she added on.

His face tightened, but he nodded. "To kill."

Lena looked around the room. "But I still saw you. *Tuck* saw you."

Ira's expression soured again at the mention of Tuck. "His mind is a bit more difficult to tamper with than the guards'."

"But not mine? You didn't try to illusion me?"

"No. You said you don't want me in your head."

She faltered. He was confusing her.

"So you're a sorcerer now then?" *You too?* "This is another secret you've kept from me."

Ira's sorcery could've come in handy so many times, just like his Flair. She'd had a hard enough time convincing Aquila to help her, and there had still been things she couldn't tell Aquila. But she could've told Ira. Her plans could've been easier if he'd confided in her about this.

"Where are your tattoos?"

She'd seen him naked multiple times. There wasn't an ounce of ink on him. The only permanent dark mark on his skin was his Imprint.

"First off, I wouldn't call myself a sorcerer just because I engage in sorcery. And no one needs tattoos to practice sorcery. They're more symbolic than anything, but it can help store the magic."

"And the *why?*" she snapped as she crossed her arms tightly. "Why did you keep it from me?"

"It's illegal—"

"We've both done plenty of *illegal* things." She threw her arm out. "Need I remind you *again* that you just killed people!"

A ragged groan left her throat, and she scrubbed her hands over her face. She needed . . .

. . . *needed, needed, needed* . . .

Her mind searched for the word after.

For now, she just needed a break. A breath.

She turned on her heel, heading for the door.

Ira jerked after her. "Wait. *Wait.* Don't leave."

"You don't get to ask that of me," she ordered, her voice thick. "Not when *you* are the one who's been leaving me."

"You're right!" He scrambled in front of her. His eyes were shining again, and it made her want to cry. "You're right. I'm unfair. I'm horrible. I'm sorry."

"You've said that already—"

"I love you," he said, his voice low and unsteady. "I don't know how many times I have to say it for you to understand what you mean to me. For you to understand what I would do *for* you. I don't know if you ever will because I don't think I'm able to express it—the full extent of what I feel for you. Words and actions aren't enough. But it's only been you. I don't want anyone else, and I never will. And I need you to know that." He paused, his eyes slipping shut.

"I told you I'm not good at expressing what I'm feeling, but I'm trying. For you. Because that's what you deserve. You deserve someone who cares and someone who will make you feel *safe*. And I want to do that. I hope I do that, even if I do have to lie to you in order to achieve that. I *need* to keep you safe. And I hope . . . I can be better for you. Before the Tower, I told myself I wouldn't let anyone get close, but then I did, and now I walk around with this overwhelming fear that, sooner or later, I *will* lose you. In some way. And I don't want to, so I'm doing what I can to keep us safe."

"And that involves lying to me?" she asked him seriously. "About all of this? How do I know these are the only things you've lied to me about?"

"I suppose you don't." His eyes were still dark, but up this close, she could see the fine details, the light blue crystals near his pupil. The scars. The past. The hurt. "But I swear to you—I'll even make an oath—that I am not lying about my love for you. And everything I do . . . is with you in mind—*Us*."

For a moment, she was tempted by his offer. But then she thought of Cowen.

Ira's heavy eyes searched her face. "Do you doubt that I love you?" he asked hesitantly.

"No," she said honestly. She was a fool in love. "I've lost too many people I've cared about in my life. I'm not going to walk away from the few people I have left. I love you and only you."

Her words ended awkwardly. It sounded like there should be a *'but'* at the end. They both waited for it. It didn't come.

"I'm tired of fighting," she exhaled. She was tired in general.

"I hate fighting with you."

"Then tell me the truth. No more secrets."

She expected the silence, but its arrival still hurt.

"Let's rest," he suggested a few beats later.

Lena was worn to the bone. It was nearing midnight, and her lack of proper sleep and the events of tonight had drained her.

She was upset with Ira, but she loved him. She wouldn't walk away, and to a certain extent, she hated this hold he had on her. She hated that he was unknowingly exploiting her fear of abandonment, but she was to blame for this attachment, this perhaps unhealthy codependency, just as much as he.

He reached out, offering his hand, but she ignored it. She walked over to one side of the bed and slipped under the covers, turning her back to him. Her body sank into the mattress and the heaviness of sleep weighed on her almost immediately, coaxing her under. But she stayed awake long enough to feel the bed dip as Ira lay on the other side. He didn't try to move closer to her.

Just as she was about to fall asleep, she heard him whisper, "I hope you understand."

She might've imagined the tremor in his words. And the way his voice sounded thick and wet. Like he was crying.

She squeezed her eyes shut tighter. A single, stray tear trailed across the bridge of her nose and onto the pillow. She fell asleep soon after.

CHAPTER
SEVENTY-TWO

Lena didn't sleep for long. The nightmares started almost as soon as her eyes closed. They were different from the others she had before. In these nightmares, she kept seeing Ira ripping out that man's heart. She saw all the victims of the killings at Ira's feet. She saw him tearing through the dozens of Blessed like they were nothing more than weeds in a garden. Sometimes the recent victims were replaced with her family. Her body wouldn't move and her mouth wouldn't open. She could only watch as they were slaughtered again and again.

She woke in cold sweat, her body locked. Ira's deep breaths told her he was still next to her, though his breathing wasn't even enough for him to be asleep.

The scenes replayed in her head even when her eyes were open.

The canopy of stars over Ira's bed did little to distract her. She couldn't stop seeing the viciousness in which Ira had acted, the snarl on his face, almost like it'd been personal. And maybe it all was.

She didn't know the details of his life before the prison. Or while she was away, just like he didn't know everything about her life during that time.

All the thinking and worrying made her nauseous, so she brushed Ira off when he offered to have breakfast delivered. He asked about the weird dreams and sleepwalking incidents, and he seemed disappointed when she refused to talk to him about it. What had he expected?

Ira left occasionally, but he always told her where he was going and how long he'd be gone. His gaze lingered every time, but the tenderness from the night before had been wiped away. His mask was back.

She stayed in his room for the first few hours of the day, unsure where to go from there, both literally and figuratively. She took the time to look around his room. It was dark, charming yet practical, orderly in a chaotic way. Just how she would expect his space to be. She noticed all the empty bottles. They had been artfully placed around his room, just like his study. Some were stuffed with flowers by the window. Others held quills on his desk. Even more functioned as book stoppers on the shelves. You wouldn't notice how many littered the space unless you sought them out specifically. They blended in with everything else.

She wandered into his washroom. It was like hers but smaller. And darker. And like his washroom in the cabin, there were no mirrors and little decor.

A little after noon, Cowen came storming into Ira's room.

"Where have you been?" he hissed without so much as a hello. "I've had guards out searching for you all night! Andra and Benji told me you've been going out into the forest every day, and that you snuck away from them last night. None of us knew where you were! Do you have any idea how worried I was? How worried we all were? You can't just disappear like that! Not after everything that's happened! I thought we had an understanding. What you did was reckless and—"

"I'm sorry," she said, her voice low but sincere. "You're right. I was being reckless and selfish, and I shouldn't have snuck away." She'd been almost . . . ashamed to meet with Tuck, for a multitude of reasons, but she'd thought it would be easier if fewer people knew. Like she could forget about it. Now she realized how stupid that sounded. But she was glad Benji and Andra hadn't been there last night. They wouldn't have backed down, and the whole encounter would've ended . . . much worse than it had. "I have no excuse. I won't . . . be doing it again."

She would no longer be meeting with Tuck. She had decided that on her own. They hadn't made any progress together, and after the shit show last night, she was done.

Cowen seemed momentarily taken aback by her apology, which made her feel even worse because she *should* be apologizing. Again. Cowen, Andra, Benji, and the others deserved it. She was racking up apologies she had to give out.

"Good," Cowen said, nodding once. "You shouldn't. I don't know why you bothered with him in the first place."

She didn't really know either.

He sat at the foot of the bed. The sunlight streamed into the room through the gaps in the curtains, illuminating his hair and making it look like spun gold. "What's going on, Kalena? I serve you, but I cannot do that properly if you don't tell me what's happening."

Ira was right again—she was doing to Cowen what Ira was doing to her. Guilt seeped into the cracks of her skin and weighed her down, causing her to sink farther into the mattress.

Her Slayer had smelled the bloodshed from miles away and led her to it. To Ira. Part of her wished she'd never snuck out last night. Ignorance was bliss. But that was what the Blessed thought, wasn't it? She couldn't ignore what she'd seen. What she knew. What she felt. She knew what she had to do. Deep down she did. She was the queen. Even though she didn't always act like it. She tended to only use that to her advantage, but she had other duties. She had a job that she was utterly failing at. Everything was slipping. The cornerstone was crumbling.

"Okay," she said as she swung her legs over the side of the bed and stood up. "We're going to talk to the prophets."

Cowen pushed himself to his feet with her and frowned. "Mikhail?"

"No." She was still trying to avoid him. "The apprentices. We're going to the prophets' temple."

LENA HAD NEVER BEEN this close to the mountains before. From a distance, they appeared to hug the back of the palace, but in reality, they were still a few miles away. The temple sat relatively low on the mountains, only about a hundred or so yards up, too low for the *Ateisha* to be an issue.

The gates leading up to the temple extended from the base of the mountains. Another safety precaution, but it was also a way to ensure privacy for the prophets and the apprentices who resided at the temple.

Two apprentices stood at the gate when Lena and Cowen approached, both younger than she was. They straightened when they saw her.

"Your Majesty," the girl said quickly, bending at the waist to give a full bow. She did that quickly too, and her twin blonde braids flopped over her head. She smoothed them back, her cheeks red. The boy stayed silent next to her.

Lena smiled at them, trying to appear casual and relaxed. "Hello. I'm here to speak with one of the prophets."

The girl's mouth opened, and her eyebrows shot up in surprise, but she likely would've taken Lena's word for it if the boy hadn't cut in.

"The Grand Prophet didn't tell us anyone was visiting," he said, eyeing her distrustfully. "We're not allowed to let anyone in without his approval." He shot a scolding look at the girl. "You know it's been this way since the break in."

Lena frowned. She hadn't heard of any sort of break in at the temple.

The girl flushed once again. "But she's the queen," she said quietly, though since Lena was only a few feet away, still loud enough for her to hear.

The boy opened his mouth, likely to argue further.

"You can bring the prophet out here if I'm not allowed to go in," Lena suggested. "Please. It won't take long."

The two apprentices exchanged a look, appearing to have a silent conversation. After a few seconds, the boy sighed. "Who are you looking for?"

"Prophet Nya."

The boy slipped inside the gates. The girl smiled at them and shuffled awkwardly.

"What's your name?" Lena asked. The girl's smile dropped, and Lena added, "I'm not asking so I can get you in trouble. You've been helpful."

"Oh. My name's Layla," she said shyly. "And the boy—his name is Rafe. He's really not that mean most of the time. He just takes this job very seriously."

Lena was struck with a sort of sadness, a wistful nostalgia, when she saw Layla and Rafe interact. It reminded her of simpler times.

A few minutes passed before Rafe came back with a woman who appeared to be in her mid-to-late twenties. Her fiery red hair stuck out to the eye even though most of it was concealed, pulled back under the hood of her robes. Her skin was pale and youthful, only a few shades darker than her white attire. Bright green eyes widened when she saw who was waiting for her, but she composed herself quickly.

"Your Majesty," she said evenly, dipping her head in respect and greeting. "How can I help you?"

Lena turned toward Cowen and tilted her head. A request. He nodded and tried to steer the apprentices away from her and the prophet, but Rafe made a fuss and refused to leave the gates, so she and the prophet ended up walking away.

"I have a question. I apologize for calling you out here only for this, but I . . . " She didn't want to raise alarm—with Prophet Nya or with Ira if the prophet told him about this interaction, which Lena had to assume was a possibility. "I was curious. My husband Ira tells me that he's been meeting with you."

She let those words hang in the air, watching Prophet Nya's face for a reaction.

Recognition flashed in the prophet's eyes. "Yes. Councilman Ira and I have had conversations occasionally."

Lena smiled and looked away. So he had been telling the truth about that.

"Is something wrong, Your Majesty?"

"No, no," she was quick to say, keeping her voice light and casual. "What do you talk about? I've been meaning to have this conversation with him, but we've both been so busy lately with everything that's going on. I'm sure you've heard. But he suggested I just come up here and talk to you myself."

"Oh." Prophet Nya faltered. "Really?"

Lena nodded, watching her out of the corner of her eye, waiting.

"Well, we spend most of our time talking about spiritual matters," she said. "Most people turn to the prophets for those sorts of things, but also about the prophets' roles in the council. I only go down to the palace on occasion, so we meet when we can. I realize it might not be the best timing. I apologize."

"No," Lena said. "No need to apologize." She laughed softly. "I really should've guessed that's why he's been meeting with you. One's spiritual affairs are quite private. I don't wish to pry, so I think I'll cut this conversation short and mention it to him, see if he's willing to speak with me about it." She turned toward the prophet fully and smiled. "Thank you. I really appreciate you taking the time to answer my question."

Prophet Nya dipped her head again. "Of course, Your Majesty."

Lena's pace was swift as she and Cowen headed back to the palace.

"Did you get what you needed?" Cowen asked.

"Yes."

Ira and Prophet Nya had given her different answers. At least one of them was lying. She didn't know who or why, but she had her suspicions, and that made everything even worse.

∼

Jhai had argued when Lena told her to go back home to her family for the foreseeable future, but in the end, she'd given in because Lena had refused to budge. Jhai accompanied her and Cowen down to the Lowlands since they had somewhere to go themselves.

They parted with Jhai close to her home, and Lena and Cowen went on their way to the tavern in Silohn, but Jhai called out before they got too far.

"Wait!"

Lena turned. Jhai stopped a few feet away and her eyes moved past Lena to Cowen. The captain of the Sacred Guard got the message and distanced himself a bit so they could have privacy.

"Stay safe up there," Jhai said. Her mouth twisted and she rocked on the heels of her feet.

"I'll try. You too. I know the Lowlands can be . . . "

"I can take care of myself," Jhai said not unkindly.

Lena smiled. "Of course . . . And I want to thank you, for what you did. You've been loyal—"

"Of course, Kalena," Jhai said, mirroring her and smiling, but it fell a bit flat. Her lips twitched again, and she looked around before taking a sudden step closer.

Lena startled but barely had any time to process the invasion of her personal space.

"Look for where the green silk glows," Jhai whispered in the air between them.

And then she stepped away and headed off, waving goodbye at Cowen.

Lena stood there for a few moments, perplexed, and she watched Jhai disappear around a street corner.

"Kalena?" Cowen was back at her side. "Are you ready to go?"

She nodded, shoving away what Jhai had told her.

Lena dragged her feet as they walked to the tavern. She did want to see Cora and Nell, but things had ended badly between them last time. Not to mention that had been Cora's first impression of her. And even though Nell had met her before, she wasn't proud of showing that side of herself to them. Cora and Nell deserved an apology just as much as Cowen, and she wanted to make sure it was delivered sooner rather than later.

The barmaid gave Cowen a knowing look as they walked past but barely looked at her, which made her feel even worse. Her shoulders slumped and she tugged the hood of the cloak farther over her face.

Cora, though, didn't seem to hold anything against her. She smiled genuinely at Lena after embracing Cowen, no tight lips, judgmental eyes, or tense shoulders.

Lena still hesitated in the doorway. She had an odd relationship with Cora. She'd only met her once, but she cared about her relationship with her because she cared about Cowen. It was the same with Nell too. Lena had never really been in a situation like this before.

"I'm sorry," she blurted out, her eyes flitting between Cora and Nell, who sat in the chair in the corner. "I'm sorry for how I acted last time—"

Her mouth snapped shut when Cora crossed the room and pulled her into a hug. She froze at first, not expecting the contact, but Cora's hands were warm against her back. Her embrace was supportive, not constraining. Lena melted into Cora's arms.

"Don't apologize," Cora murmured. "I reacted just as badly when I found out about Cowen. Worse even."

She pulled away, giving Lena another encouraging smile, but this time, it strained and the pain in her eyes was visible. She had come to terms with it. She knew one of the people she loved was going to die. Nell had the same resignation on their face.

Lena had been putting the thought aside. She couldn't accept it. She'd seen plenty of death in her life. She knew how easily it swung down its sword, but she was still in denial. This was yet another reminder of how cruel the Numina were. She'd lost too much. But she wasn't the only one losing someone.

For Cora's sake, she hoped her smile was convincing.

Her gaze dropped to Cora's stomach. It was noticeably larger than last time, even though it had only been a few weeks.

Cora followed Lena's gaze and placed both hands on top of her belly. "They're getting big, aren't they? We're starting to think we miscalculated. Seven months seems more accurate now."

Lena's eyes widened. The baby would arrive in only a few months. But it was a firstborn, wasn't it? So it would be taken. *If* the prophets and enforcers knew about it.

She could see the excitement and wonder on Cora's face and the adoration and concern on Cowen's. Nell wore a mix of those emotions, but they kept them muted as if they were worried about revealing too much.

Lena held her breath as she watched the scene before her, wondering when it might be the last time she saw it.

∼

She visited her family afterward. She needed their guidance now more than ever.

Lena picked some flowers from the garden and laid them in front of each grave before kneeling.

"I'm back in the Highlands now, so that's why I haven't been able to visit you every day anymore." She twisted her fingers in the grass. It was starting to brown. The change of seasons always hit the Lowlands first. "But . . . even though I'm back, things aren't better."

Her voice caught and she swallowed thickly, but that didn't help to improve the tightness in her throat. Each word had to weasel its way through, coming out small.

"Ira and I are fighting. I think. He's keeping things from me. I was keeping things from him too. I still am. I'm not proud of it, but it's different. What he's . . . "

The scary thing was that she didn't know why he was doing what he was doing. Did she want her family to know this about him? Eventually, they had all accepted him, but they'd been wary at first. *Concerned*, not disgusted and blatantly disapproving like the Blessed. She didn't want her family's image of him to be tainted.

"I don't like fighting with him. I don't know what to do." She reached out and began to trace her father's name on the rough stone. "He feels so distant. So . . . different. But he's not. He's still the Ira I know. He has to be."

The things he'd said to her, promised her, the things he'd done—they couldn't *all* be lies.

The pad of her finger traced across a particularly rough spot and the stone nicked her skin. She pulled her hand back, watching as blood welled at the tip of her index finger. Tears rose to her eyes.

"I wish you were here. All of you," she confessed quietly. "I tried to keep going and fight like you said. I've done it so far, but it's so hard doing it alone." She sniffled and wiped at her cheeks. "I guess I haven't been alone, not for all of it, but lately I've been feeling more lonely."

Aquila was gone. Ira was out of reach. She had Cowen, but she felt bad for taking him away from his family. He only had so much time left. And she didn't even know what to call her relationship with Tuck.

"Father, mother, tell me what to do," she pleaded. "I have this horrible feeling that something bad is about to happen and I can't shake it. Cowen told me that's just my paranoia speaking . . . I hope that's true. I hope things return—"

To normal. That was what she'd been about to say, but that wasn't right. She didn't want things to go back to how they'd been. She wanted things to change, but she also wanted peace. She'd known from the beginning that she likely couldn't have both, not at the same time, but she hoped that, for once, she would be lucky.

"Please," she croaked as tears slid down her cheeks. "I need you."

Lena didn't expect them to answer. At the end of the day, they were dead. And that reminder only added to the horrible feeling she'd been carrying with her for days.

As she walked to the cabin and then her room, she acknowledged that the paranoia had lived within her for much longer. *Years*. But it shifted with the times. Lately it had been high.

She was back in the Highlands. Ira was alive. She was avenging her family by crossing off names on her list. Alkus was out of the way. The alliance was secured. Yet she still felt it.

What good was this power she'd gained from a Numen when she didn't know how to use it? In some ways, she was just as helpless as before. And Imprints came with their own difficulties. That was the price of the power. Some might question if it was worth it.

Lena looked at the Ring of Rulers on her finger. It sat right under the ring Ira had given her. She'd gotten so used to both of them that she often forgot they were there. She hadn't understood what the deal with the Ring of Rulers was at first, but she'd grown to realize just how important symbols were. And how important it was to keep those symbols preserved.

She wanted to make sure nothing happened to the ring if she went on another sleepwalking adventure, so she hid it under her bedside table, telling herself she'd come back for it when things were over. She would slip the ring back on her finger when she truly felt like a queen, and not the scared little girl who was still fighting to keep her chin above the water.

CHAPTER SEVENTY-THREE

Lena went back to Ira's room instead of her own. She was partly disappointed in herself. This felt like she was crawling back to him, but she was scared that if she left, he would too. Again. And she couldn't let that happen.

Ira had told her earlier that he wouldn't be back until after midnight, so she waited up for him. She collapsed on his bed and stared up at the starry canopy. She thought about what she should do.

She was lost and in love and scared of losing more than she already had.

But she needed to make a decision, or one would be made for her. There were many things she could do or say, but the question was, would Ira listen?

He had lied to her about countless things. *Important* things. And for a long time too. There were apparently reasons for his lies, but he wouldn't tell her those either. She had even caught him in his lies when she went to visit Prophet Nya. Even if she called him out on it, she doubted he would tell her the truth.

He'd assured her with promises of protection and flatteries of love, but that wasn't what she needed. She needed trust. She and Ira wouldn't work without it. But she couldn't leave him.

Her chest ached and she rolled onto her side.

She had a right to be upset, even if she was being a bit hypocritical. She'd kept secrets from Ira, yes, but not for long, or not secrets of this degree. That would be like her keeping her Imprint from him. No, not even that was comparable.

The door opened and Lena rolled over and sat up straight. She locked eyes with Ira and he halted, his hand still on the door handle. He looked exhausted.

He'd told her he had a meeting with Mikhail and Kimbra Nai'Estor, one of the council members. The fact that she questioned if that was the truth was painful enough. Would she be questioning everything he told her now?

The relief that came across his face when he spotted her ate through the exhaustion, and it made her chest tighten in an entirely different manner. He closed the door and moved to the folding screen next to his wardrobe, but he didn't bother stepping behind it as he stripped his outer shirt.

"How was your day?" she asked carefully.

He took off his undershirt so his chest was bare.

"Draining," he said. "Long. Frustrating."

"None of those things are good."

"Well, it hasn't been a good day."

She snapped her mouth shut. He was in a mood. Well, so was she. "I want you to answer one of my questions. Just one. Truthfully."

She heard the heavy exhale, but she ignored it.

"Who killed my family?"

His back was to her as he undressed. He kicked off his boots and tore off his socks, but he paused at her question. He knew that she wasn't asking about the people on her list.

"I told you, Lena. I don't know. I swear it—"

"Then you're going to help me find out who it was."

He sighed again and raked his hands through his hair.

"Yes," he said. "Yes, of course."

Ira pulled his pants and underwear off in one go so he stood completely naked in front of her.

She sat back against the pillows. Her surly mood faded gradually as she sunk into the bed and admired his bare form. The muscles of his back and shoulders flexed under his skin as he reached down to snatch up his clothes. She watched his strong thighs shift, his toned abdomen twist as he turned. His pale skin was smooth, save for the raised lines of his scars. They were mostly on his back, but a few were scattered around his body. One wrapped around his hip, another at the hollow of his throat. There was a larger one on his thigh.

Her chest ached with the knowledge that Blessed did not scar easily.

She didn't see his scars as flaws. She had her fair share of them that she'd gotten while she was Cursed. Still, she had fewer than Ira.

Scars were a testament to their bearer's strength. What they'd gone through. What they'd survived. Ira was a fighter. But those experiences changed you, physically and mentally. The pain of *then* stuck with you. She could see it in Ira's shoulders, the shadows under his eyes and the bruises on his hand, in the scars on his skin.

He headed for the washroom. Lena stood from the bed and caught his hand as he passed. He stopped and looked down at her, watching and waiting. She wordlessly tugged him back toward the bed as she sat down.

He tried to pull away from her. "Lena . . ."

She dropped his hand as if it'd burned her and tried to ignore the nasty feeling sprouting in her chest. "You don't want to?"

"It's not that." He sighed. "We shouldn't. Not when we're fighting."

She tucked her legs under her and leaned back. "*Are* we fighting?"

He gave her another reprimanding look that certainly wasn't helping this situation.

"I *know* that I love you. I *know* what I feel for you. I *know* what I want."

But there are so many things that I don't know.

He stared down at her, his lips flat. She held his gaze for a few seconds before crawling farther onto the bed. She could sleep. But a moment later, she felt the mattress dip as he followed her.

Lena reached a hand back, and when he took it, she pulled him toward her, twisting them so his back was to the headboard. She let go of his hand and pressed down on his shoulders, and he took the hint and sat, moving back when she ushered him to do so. She knelt at his side, her face only inches away from his.

Ira's eyes finally left hers to flit down to her lips. She swallowed thickly and placed a hand on his chest, feeling his strong and steady heartbeats. Ira lay flat on the bed when she pushed, his waves fanned out on the pillows, and she ran her fingers through the dark strands as she straddled his waist.

Ira didn't touch her. He only watched.

She gently twisted his hair between her fingers. So soft and dark. In the sun, it gleamed the deepest, darkest blue rather than brown, a drastic contrast to his pale skin. He was beautiful.

She smoothed back the rest of the hair from his forehead, her fingers softly scraping against his scalp. His eyes slipped closed, and only then did she allow herself to reveal what she was feeling.

Her thumb traced his brow bone as his eyelids fluttered and his long lashes brushed the tops of his cheeks. She counted his small freckles and smoothed her finger across the tiny scar on the bridge of his nose. His bottom lip was fuller than his top and red and torn like he'd been chewing on it. He must've picked up that habit from her. She trailed her fingers around his jaw, feeling days-old stubble he'd yet to shave.

She leaned toward him, and her hair fell forward, creating a dark curtain around them. She kissed him softly on his lips.

Ira opened his eyes when she pulled back slightly. They stared at each other for maybe a few seconds or a few minutes, having a silent conversation with their eyes. But she couldn't understand him. Still. Even like this.

Her eyes began to sting, so she kissed him again. He responded to her this time, kissing her gently and lovingly, coaxing her mouth open. Neither of them were in any hurry. They wanted to savor this moment.

His hands smoothed up her calves until they rested below the backs of her knees. Their tongues touched lightly, not unlike the soft brush of his fingertips over her heated skin. They kissed until her lips tingled and her chest tightened from lack of air.

He never took in these situations. Not really. He read her, with his eyes and his hands. He always knew what she wanted, and more importantly, what she *needed*. Even when moving her abruptly or holding her tight enough to leave bruises, he was so considerate. He *saw* her. He was one of the few who cared enough to *see* and *listen* and *respond*. It was basic decency, and it shouldn't cause her to tear up, but it did.

Her heart was strong and fast and about to burst.

She couldn't lose this. She couldn't lose him.

When faced with the fear of a loss like this, she understood what Ira had said yesterday about protecting her. She was scared to think about what she would do. For this. And him. To keep and hold and settle.

One of her hands left his hair to touch the scar in the hollow of his throat. It was darker than his skin and flashed silver under the light. The wound must've been deep. It was at such an important spot too. She imagined blood on his skin and pressed her lips over his scar.

"They don't hurt anymore," he said.

She closed her eyes. A stray tear escaped, hitting his skin and trailing down his chest.

He gathered her into his arms and kissed her like he would never get the chance again. Like this was the last kiss she had to remember him by.

She pressed herself flush against him and let go of everything, pouring it into him. He sat up straight to better position her, and she corded her arms around his neck, bringing him closer to her with her elbows, fingers carding through his hair again. One of his hands snaked under her robe, gripping the bare flesh of her hips and dragging her against him.

She moaned into his mouth as his lips made their way down her neck, teeth scraping against her flushed and sensitive skin, littering her with dark marks.

She did the same to him, but her lips were gentle and attentive when brushing over his scars and the bruises from days before. He pulled her up once her mouth skimmed his hips, and she cradled his face.

Please, she wanted to say. *Please. Remember this. Don't throw this away. Don't do this.*

She continued to sing the words into his mouth as it met hers again and his fingers slid down her body. The heat grew around them as the space between them decreased. They gasped into each other's mouths, grabbing and pulling at hot, sweaty skin.

They were too close but not close enough. The hot air that enveloped them made breathing difficult, but she didn't dare pull away. He didn't either. Perhaps they would become one. Maybe they could be forced together, forever connected.

Like the tides and the moon. She responded to Ira and Ira responded to her, pushing and pulling against the other until they met just right along the horizon.

She cried as she came. The fabric stars overhead twinkled. She tucked her face into Ira's neck, chanting in her head, *Please, stay.*

Stay. Stay. Stay. Stay. Stay.

⁓

He didn't.

When Lena woke up, he was gone. This hadn't been the first time, but it hurt more than the others.

She dragged herself out of bed, ignoring the note he'd left for her. Andra and Benji were on duty since Cowen had gone back to the Lowlands last night. They waited for her outside Ira's door, and if they noticed the bruises and haphazard way she'd thrown herself together, they didn't comment on it.

"I'm going to talk to Tuck," she announced.

They also didn't comment on that.

"Oh," Tuck said as soon as she crawled into the treehouse. His eyes were hazy and bloodshot, and his shirt was fastened one button off along the entire front as if he'd hastily put it on. "Her Majesty has graced me with her presence. *Finally.*"

He pushed himself to his feet and attempted to bow, but it was half-assed. He nearly stumbled into the wall, but he was still nimble enough to catch himself, spin away, and slump down onto his sleeping roll.

She didn't see any bottle, but that hardly mattered.

"You've been out here every night?"

His lips twisted like he'd tasted something sour. "Why do you say it like I've been out here waiting for you? You'd like that, wouldn't you? Having everyone wait on *you?*"

She wasn't going to let him get a rise out of her. She only came for two things. "Our deal—agreement, whatever—is off. We tried, but it didn't work. I'll figure things out on my own—"

"You mean with *Ira—*"

"*Don't,*" she said quickly, her head snapping around.

It was a precarious situation they were both in. They'd seen Ira do something terrible. She loved him and would protect him. Tuck hated him and would do anything to ruin him, but maybe she could convince him not to. Tuck was hard to read sometimes. One slip from him and it was over. That was the other reason why she'd come.

Tuck stared back testily, his cheeks flushed. "I'm surprised he let you out of his sight. Unless he left you first."

Her fingers curled and she took a deep breath.

"I don't even know what you're doing here, visiting me when you have him back. That was the only reason you came to me in the first place, right? Ira wasn't available. Don't you have more pressing matters to deal with?" He waved his hands around in the air while he talked. "Like the fact that your husband is a murder—?"

"Shut up," she hissed as she took a step forward.

She looked around instinctively, even though they were in a small wooden box thirty feet off the ground in the middle of the forest. She doubted Andra and Benji would be able to hear something whispered inside the treehouse, but Blessed could hear well, and she still didn't want Tuck saying such things aloud.

Tuck's eyes flashed and he leaned forward. "Did I strike a nerve? Are you worried someone may overhear and your *perfect* husband's image will be ruined?"

Lena glared at him. "You don't know everything, so you're going to keep your mouth shut."

He reared back and laughed. "Really now? Do you think you know everything? He's got you under his spell. He *killed* those people. Ripped their hearts out. You can't pretend that didn't happen. Do you realize how hypocritical you're being?"

She clenched her jaw and ignored his question. "Tuck," she said firmly. "Promise me that you won't tell anyone what you saw."

"Why should I?"

"Because . . . I'm asking you," she finished awkwardly.

He laughed again and it was far too loud and unrestrained.

"Please?"

He tapped his finger to his bottom lip and pretended to think about it. "Hmm, no."

Her heart twisted. "Tuck, you can't—"

He pushed himself to his feet again, but he was much steadier this time. "Actually, I can. And I will."

She closed her eyes and tried not to let the panic she felt seep into her face and her words. "Please. Just . . . give me a few days, okay? I'm trying to figure some things out—"

"What's there to figure out, Lena? He. Killed. Those. People. Ripped. Their. Hearts. Out." Tuck scoffed. "Wake up. You're the queen first. You can't protect him because you love him."

The fire rekindled in her chest, and her eyes snapped open. "Now who's being the hypocrite?" She strode closer, but he stood still, blinking down at her. "I know your parents were involved in my family's murder, but you won't give them up, just like I won't give Ira up, because you love them! You're still holding onto the hope that they'll wake up one day and start loving you instead of pushing you around and telling the other Blessed how much of a nuisance you are!"

The only sound that filled the air was the rustling of the leaves and the creak of the wood against the wind.

Tuck smiled bitterly. "Well, it looks like I stand corrected," he said, his voice hoarse. "You *do* seem to know everything."

She clenched her jaw. "I shouldn't have—"

"Don't apologize," he jeered. "You meant it."

Her stomach twisted. She didn't even know where that had come from. "I'll do what I have to do in order to protect my people."

He raised a brow. "Meaning . . . Ira? And the Cursed? Everyone knows you hate the Blessed, even though you are one now. That's part of the reason they want you out. If The Lands started burning tomorrow and you could only run in one direction, you'd run to the Lowlands without a second thought. Those people Ira killed were Blessed, weren't they? Would you be as subservient as you're being now if they were Cursed?" He leaned down until he was only inches away from her face. His eyes were still bloodshot and dilated, but he accessed her with clarity. "That's what I thought."

Tuck took a step back and grabbed his daggers and the sunstone on his way to leave.

"Don't say anything about Ira."

"I'll think about it," he said brusquely as he brushed by her.

She turned with him. "Tuck—"

"What are you going to do?" He paused and looked at her with morbid curiosity, taunting her. "Are you going to send your husband after me? Will I be his next victim?"

She bit the inside of her cheek as her Imprint burned. It was a harsh reminder of what her Slayer had discovered. What Ira had done. And by extension, what she was allowing to be done.

"The longer you wait, the more blood you'll have on your hands."

LENA FLOATED amongst black ink clouds.

"I'm trying to listen," she lamented to the darkness. "I'm trying to work with you and find this . . . power." She needed it now more than ever. "Why are you working against me?"

Nothing.

"What happened the other night? With the Slayer?"

Pissing off a Numen was an extremely bad idea, but at this point, it was the only way to get any sort of response out of it.

"I didn't call you back, yet you came back. Why? Were you scared?"

Of Ira? Of a simple human?

She expected a boom or a rush of wind or a realm of pain, but she got none of those things.

Instead, the Numen appeared slowly and smoothly, power crackling in the breath between the syllables as it spoke. "Scared?"

The scenery around her shifted, and suddenly, they were back in the depths of the shrine.

"What reason do I have to feel scared? I do not experience weak mortal emotions."

"Then why did you come back?"

Why had it reacted the way it had? Slayers craved blood and violence unlike anything else.

"I was called back."

"I didn't call you—"

Lena paused. She hadn't called it. But someone... had.

No, it couldn't be...

"Before you said, 'I made a pact with you, but you weren't the first.' You didn't mean the first Cursed."

She'd immediately assumed the Numen had been talking about lifetimes outside of her own. In the past. But that wasn't the case.

"So what do you mean by the first? Did you... make a pact with someone before me in this lifetime? While I was alive?"

She didn't even know how that would work. According to the history books, Blessed and Numina had found out after the War of Krashing that creating multiple bonds ended in disaster. The Numina remained unscathed, of course, but some didn't like that their "champions" were falling ill so quickly. Maintaining multiple pacts with multiple Numina drove the Blessed insane. There was no way to meet all the Numina's needs. Slayer Sickness set in quickly and the Numina were merciless, each grabbing one limb and yanking in an attempt to get what they wanted. And they didn't know when to stop. Or they didn't care to. From that time on, it'd been greatly advised that Blessed make a pact with a single Numen, and that was now the norm. But for a Numen to make a pact with multiple Blessed... no one should get hurt, right? The stress was put on the Numen. But Ira had a pact with another Numen too.

"I made a pact with him."

That made her pause.

Him.

She opened her mouth and dared to ask, "Ira?"

She hoped the Numen would deny it, but it didn't. It issued no verbal confirmation either, though the silence was clear.

"I don't understand. How did you make a pact with him? Blessed and Numen aren't supposed to have more than one pact—"

"No," the Numen cut her off, its voice harsh and... angry. "The pact is not of the usual nature. He called upon me with his darkness and trapped me. A mortal trapping a Divine!"

A boom sounded then and the ground shook. She fell to her knees as debris rained from above.

"We made a deal, one that resulted in me extending an offer of power and protection to you."

"Ira trapped you for that reason?" she clarified.

The Numen scoffed. "Humans are such emotional beings. He worried for your safety. I could sense the boy's panic."

She'd always wondered how she'd stumbled upon the shrine, how a Numen had taken enough of an interest in her to offer up the power she would need to survive. The Divine Touch.

It was Ira. Everything went back to him.

"What did he have to give in return?"

Nothing that powerful could be free.

A dark laugh echoed in her mind. "I only take deals made in blood and being."

She straightened as another piece fit into place. "Are you the one making him kill all those people?"

The wind in the shrine picked up. Within seconds, it was howling. Her hair whipped around her, and she closed her eyes as they began to water.

"I think you've overstayed your welcome," the Numen hissed.

A pressure built in her chest and then she was yanked back.

LENA JUMPED out of bed before she was even fully awake. Her mind was still foggy, but she finally had something substantial. And she wouldn't wait to bring it to him.

She ripped open her bedroom doors but paused when she saw Andra and Benji in the hall talking with another member of the Sacred Guard, Zaltain. All three of them immediately stopped when she stepped out and their expressions shifted, settling on troubled.

Anxiety wound its way through her chest. "What's wrong?"

All three of them exchanged glances, but it was Andra who stepped forward, her eyes shining with sympathy and distress.

"It's Cowen."

CHAPTER
SEVENTY-FOUR

He watched, disoriented, as the *Te'Monai* and the Slayer fought, snarling and clawing deep.

"Atreus!"

He jerked at the muffled voice ringing out next to his ear. He was yanked forward, and a wave of dizziness came over him at the sudden movement.

"Come on, you need to get up. Let's go."

It was Finn.

He wrapped an arm around Atreus' waist and draped one of Atreus' arms over his shoulders before standing. Atreus stumbled into Finn's side. Pressure immediately started to build in his head. He squeezed his eyes shut, trying to push the aches somewhere to the back of his mind and regain focus, but the strain of calling the *Te'Monai* was a knife digging into his skull. He hoped it was temporary because right now, he barely had enough energy to walk.

"Atreus, come on," Finn grunted, hiking him up as he half-dragged him along. "I need your help here."

"Go," he muttered.

"What?"

"*Go.*"

If any of the *Te'Monai* came after him, he could save himself. He still had enough energy and adrenaline to redirect the *Te'Monai*—at least that was what he told himself—but he wasn't sure how long his ability would last in his weakened state. He was already slowing Finn down. He could give Finn a head start and catch up with him later.

"Don't be stupid," Finn snapped, his voice firm. "I'm not leaving you."

Two *Te'Monai* came at them. Finn grabbed the knife he must've picked up by Atreus and held it out in front of him.

Atreus narrowed his eyes at the *Te'Monai*.

Leave us alone, he ordered, ignoring the throbbing in his head. *Kill the Slayer and any Te'Monai trying to kill a human.*

And they did.

Finn looked at Atreus in shock, but he quickly got them moving again, likely realizing that now wasn't the time. Atreus' head lolled against Finn's shoulder as his vision darkened.

"Atreus?" Finn grunted as he was forced to carry more of his weight.

"Judah?" he rasped, forcing his feet to stay under him and move forward.

"He's fine," Finn said curtly as he dragged Atreus toward the exit. "We need to go—"

The ground beneath their feet exploded and they were ripped apart. Atreus was airborne for a few seconds before he crashed against the wall and landed on the floor.

He coughed and rolled onto his side, gasping for air. His ears were ringing and the thick taste of copper slid down his throat. He blinked to clear his blurred vision, but he still couldn't see much of anything due to the dust and debris in the air.

A yellow glow cut through the gray haze.

Panic forced him to his feet.

"Atreus!" Finn shouted, his voice strained and hoarse, but he was okay. Okay enough to yell, that was. "Where are you?"

He needed to move faster, but his body wouldn't let him, his limbs seconds behind every thought that crossed his foggy mind.

"Mila?"

Atreus jerked his head up and started running, or trying to, ignoring the trembles and aches of pain.

No, no, no.

"Finn, run!" he shouted, but his throat was sore, and the sound barely traveled. He coughed as the dust was sucked into his throat and covered his nose and mouth as he stumbled through the settling debris.

"You're alive?" There was an air of skepticism and relief in Finn's voice.

Atreus sped up even though his muscles screamed in protest. "Finn! Get away from her!"

"Atreus?"

Stop her. Stop her. Stop her, he chanted to anyone and anything that would listen.

Atreus waved the dust away and Finn's form was finally visible in front of him, moving toward him. A look of relief flashed across Finn's face, and then, he froze, his eyes widened, his lips parted. Atreus mirrored him, watching as Finn collapsed to his knees and hunched over. The hilt of a knife stuck out of Finn's back. Mila stood behind him, appearing mournful.

"*No!*"

A *Te'Monai* soared over his head and tackled Mila. She struggled with it and called her Slayer to her aid. Atreus didn't pay any more attention to her or that fight. He dashed over to Finn's side, all pain forgotten.

"No. No, no, no, no, no," he moaned as he crouched down next to his friend. "Hey, Finn. Hey. Look at me."

Finn's eyes were still open, but unfocused and twisted in pain. He reached back around him, but Atreus caught his arm, stopping him. The dagger had been shoved in all the way to the hilt. And right over his heart. Atreus knew Finn's fate when he coughed and blood tainted his lips.

He swallowed the lump in his throat and eased Finn down on his side.

"She stabbed me," Finn said in disbelief. "Why would she do that?"

"Shhh, don't talk."

"I'm dying, aren't I?" Finn asked. His throat bobbed as he tried to catch his breath.

Atreus clenched his jaw. They didn't lie to each other, especially not about death. "Yes." His voice cracked.

"Oh," Finn said, thin and delicate. "*Oh.*" Tears flooded his eyes and Atreus' own began to sting. "I expected it eventually, but I just . . . There's something tucked into the back of my pants. Get it."

As gentle as possible, Atreus wrapped his arm around Finn's shoulders and tilted him forward. He spotted the item in Finn's waistband. His journal.

"How'd you get it back?"

"Miss Anya. She's . . . not with them."

Atreus frowned and shook his head, but Finn spoke up before he got the chance to.

"I want you to have it—my journal. And read the stories I wrote."

The pressure in Atreus' chest, in his throat, grew. "I will," he said, his voice deep and wet.

"Edynir Akonah," Finn said in wonder. He let out another wet cough and blood dribbled down his chin. Atreus held him tighter, ducking his head. "I do believe he was a hero. I wrote stories about him. And us."

Atreus squeezed his eyes shut. "You were right. You were right all along."

And Atreus should've listened to him sooner. He should've confided in him after meeting the first sister.

Finn took a shallow, unsteady breath. Atreus got a full view of Finn's bloodstained teeth when he smiled. "In another life, we're heroes and we all make it. You, Mila, and me. I even gave us names. I split up Edynir Akonah's name. Not very creative, I guess," he wheezed.

"Finn, you don't have to—"

But his friend kept going, his eyes usually so bright and full of life trained somewhere in the distance, unfocused and darkening with each passing second. His bloodied lips kept moving, telling the stories only he could tell. "I was Edyn. You were Ira. And Mila was Konah. It's silly."

"No, it's not," Atreus said automatically. "I like it."

"You can read more," Finn said, his eyes fluttering closed.

A grip of panic squeezed Atreus' heart again and his throat tightened. "*Finn*," he said desperately, leaning over his friend.

Finn's eyes opened again, but he looked so tired. He was so pale, and it made his freckles stand out even more. He raised a trembling hand slowly and touched Atreus' cheek.

"Don't cry," he pleaded, his breath catching in his chest. He hiccupped and more blood bubbled past his lips. "Don't cry. You're making me scared. I don't want to die. I thought . . . we'd make it out."

"We will," Atreus said vehemently as he reached a hand up to hold Finn's fingers. "In the next life, in your stories, we will. I promise." He squeezed his eyes shut. Tears ran down his cheeks despite Finn's request. "I'm sorry. *I'm sorry.*"

"It's . . . not your fault." Finn coughed.

Atreus opened his eyes and saw that Finn was fighting to stay awake, to stay here with him. Atreus didn't want him to leave, but he didn't want him to fight more than he already had.

It's my fault. I should've been stronger.

"You should have left me behind." The words tumbled from his mouth without much thought.

"I would always come back for you," Finn rasped, yet he sounded so certain, so strong.

"Your next life," Atreus said through the tears and the thickness in his voice, "is going to be *so* much better than this one. You don't have to fight and you can write all the stories you want."

A smile crossed Finn's face. One last time. "You'll read them?"

"Of course."

"I'm glad," he said, now struggling for air, his words garbled, "I had you . . . here. Don't—forget me."

"I won't," Atreus promised fiercely, tears clouding his vision. "I could never. I promise."

Finn's fingers squeezed his briefly and then his eyes closed and his hand fell limp. He took his last breath as he slackened and became dead weight in Atreus' arms.

Atreus could do nothing but stare at Finn's lifeless body. He was dead. And it *was* Atreus' fault.

No.

He lifted his gaze to where Mila was.

It was hers.

He carefully moved Finn and slid the knife out of his back. He laid his friend down on the ground and pressed his palm against his still chest.

"You were too good for this," he said before rising to his feet and tucking the journal into his waistband.

Mila's Slayer was gone, likely having disappeared when she grew too weak to sustain it. She was still alive, but the *Te'Monai* that had attacked her was dead, and it was heavy enough to keep her pinned to the floor. She didn't struggle as Atreus approached.

"Do it," she sneered. "Kill me."

He stopped a foot away from her.

"Why?" he asked tonelessly.

"Because sacrifices must be made."

She had the audacity to appear sad, as if she hadn't been the one to bring this reckoning down upon all of them.

He stared down at her, at someone he would've called his friend hours ago. She had the blood of thousands on her hands. She'd killed one of her only two friends. And she wasn't going to stop. Just like Tolar.

Driving the knife in was easy.

Mila's eyes widened. A choked gasp left her lips as Atreus plunged the blade into her heart. She died within seconds, her lips turned up peacefully.

He didn't take the knife out until he was sure she was dead, and then he looked around at the remains of the garden. The plants were flattened or destroyed or torn from the soil. Chunks of rock littered the space from the explosion. All the *Te'Monai* were dead or gone.

He caught sight of a figure near Finn's body and immediately tensed before realizing it was Judah who knelt at his friend's side, his shoulders shaking with the force of his sobs.

Atreus moved to stand behind him and placed a hand on his shoulder, but Judah quickly spun around and smacked the hand away as a sob escaped his lips. He stared at Atreus then, eyes wide as if he'd been caught doing something he wasn't supposed to do, as if he expected something bad.

Atreus clenched his jaw and took a step back. "We need to go."

"We can't just leave him here!" Judah cried.

They couldn't bury him here either. Atreus thought for a moment. "Do you still have the stones I gave you?"

Judah sniffled and nodded. He dug them out of his pocket and handed them over. Atreus knelt next to Finn, wrapping one arm around him. "Hold on to me," he told Judah.

The kid did as he was told. Atreus closed his hand around the stones and focused on the pull he felt. His eyes slipped shut and there was a click. The cool air of the Institute turned still and hot. When he opened his eyes, he was greeted by the realm he'd just come from.

Zosia stood a few feet away, not appearing at all surprised to see him. She looked at Finn's body with pity. It made Atreus want to yell at her.

"Take care of him," he said instead, his voice rough. "Give him a proper funeral. Bury him. Protect him."

Zosia nodded.

Atreus took one last look at Finn and committed him to memory. When his eyes began to itch, he closed them and grabbed Judah, speaking to the stones again.

He thought it was fate, really, when they arrived back in the Institute and Prophet Silas stood in front of them. He was miraculously still alive and appeared uninjured despite the blood and grime that covered him from head to toe. Atreus had to believe that the Numina had left the prophet for him.

"*You*," Prophet Silas spat like a curse once he spotted Atreus. "You did this!"

"Actually, *you* did," Atreus said matter-of-factly. He strode forward, taking great delight in the way the prophet stumbled back. There were no enforcers around to protect him. They'd likely all been killed. Everyone *truly* seemed to be dead. "Or more specifically, *Mila* did."

Prophet Silas backpedaled until he tripped over a piece of uneven stone and fell.

Atreus advanced and placed his boot on the prophet's chest, keeping him pinned to the ground. He rested his arms on his knee and leaned down, eyes burning. "Do you remember when you told me I wasn't going to win? That I'd never see the light of this realm?"

Prophet Silas stared at him with genuine fear for the first time. Atreus relished the sight.

"You were wrong about a lot, but maybe you got one thing right."

He looked at the man who had abused him, physically and mentally and verbally, who led this operation that slaughtered tens of thousands of kids every year. He really looked at him.

"Maybe I am the monster," Atreus whispered before shoving the blade into the prophet's stomach.

He'd been injured enough times to know what places hurt the worst without being completely fatal. He wanted the prophet to suffer. He wanted him to panic and hurt and fight for his life only to realize, as life was draining out of him, that he had failed. It would only be a taste of what he'd put the firstborns through every day.

Atreus watched with a strange sort of satisfaction as blood and life drained from the prophet.

"Another thing," he said as he removed the knife and stabbed the prophet in the thigh. Right next to a major artery. It was a nasty wound. The prophet's scream was shrill and strangled. "Atreus the firstborn is dead. My name is Ira now. Remember it."

Prophet Silas glared at him, lips trembling and dripping with spit and blood as he tried and failed to manage the pain.

The blade lodged in one of the prophet's eyes. His cry ricocheted off the cavern's ceilings and he reached his hand up to claw at the knife, but Atreus easily batted it away.

"Don't *look* at me like that. *You* don't deserve it. The only thing you deserve is this."

The next stab was in his shoulder, right in the dip. The noise that came from the prophet's mouth was too weak to be a scream. He whimpered and might've tried to say something, but his cries for help went ignored.

Ira stabbed him again. And again. And again. And again and again and again and again.

Blood splattered onto his face. Into his eyes. His mouth. He didn't let up even when Prophet Silas stopped moving and was just a vessel of meat spilling blood across the cavern floor.

Ira didn't stop stabbing it until something hit him across the back of the head and his vision went black.

CHAPTER
SEVENTY-FIVE

Zaltain didn't know everything. The physicians had only told him that other guards had brought Cowen in after an incident, and he'd immediately rushed to relay the information to Lena.

As the four of them headed for the infirmary, she couldn't help but imagine the worst-case scenario. Cowen had been with Cora and Nell earlier tonight. Had they seen him like this? With everything that had been going on—Alkus, Tuck, Ira—she hadn't been able to look into oath-breaking. The guilt weighed her down. Cowen's condition was serious and only getting worse.

"Zaltain, Andra," she said before they reached the infirmary doors. "I need you to do something for me."

She pulled Andra aside, unsure if she could trust Zaltain with something of this magnitude. "Find someone who is knowledgeable about oath-breaking. Someone who can *fix it*. A scholar or physician . . . You'll probably have to go to the Lowlands."

She let that statement speak for itself but gave Andra a pointed look. She realized what she was admitting, but it couldn't be helped. The potential benefits outweighed the possible drawbacks. They were running out of time.

Andra's lips parted slightly in realization before she snapped her mouth shut. Her eyes hardened and she gave Lena a sharp nod. She and Zaltain disappeared quickly.

Lena and Benji entered the infirmary.

A breath of relief escaped her when she spotted Cowen in a cot. He was sitting up and talking with a physician, an exasperated expression on his face as he took the vial being pushed into his hands. He looked tired and pale. The bags under his eyes had darkened and she just now noticed his cheeks appeared sunken in, only slightly. He was losing weight too.

Cowen spotted her when she was only a few feet away.

"I'm fine," he said before she could say anything. "I was walking across the grounds and felt lightheaded. I fainted for only a moment, but the other guards insisted upon bringing me here for a check-up."

Lena moved to his side. Benji had stayed back at the doors, so when the physician disappeared, it was only her and Cowen.

"Good," she said firmly. "Because you and I both know this is more serious than you're making it out to be."

"I *stumbled*, Kalena. I was tired. It was—"

"Don't say it was nothing." She grabbed one of the nearby chairs and dragged it closer so she could sit. "A few days ago, you were trying to tell me how serious this is—"

"Because I wanted you to understand that there's no coming back for me." His dull eyes met hers. "But I mean it when I say this was nothing. I'll know when things get bad."

"You will tell me?" It was more of a demand than a question.

Cowen nodded, a lackluster smile stretching across his face. "Of course."

"Has this happened before? Do you have any other symptoms?"

The exasperation came back, but it was a mild case. "No. I'm fatigued and my muscles ache occasionally. I get migraines. As I said, nothing out of the ordinary."

"But it is getting worse. You wouldn't be here if it wasn't."

He let out a light laugh and deflated against the pillows. "Well, it's certainly not getting *better*."

She frowned and looked in the direction the physicians had disappeared into. Only a few were working since it was so late at night. "They don't know, do they?"

It sounded like Cowen had been coherent when brought in, so she wouldn't think he'd let the physicians get a look at his Imprint. Lena wasn't sure what would happen if someone saw it. Would they immediately know that he'd broken his oath? Would they try to lock him away?

She wouldn't let that happen.

"No," Cowen sighed. "They're treating this as exhaustion. They've only checked my heart rate, asked me questions, given me medicine."

His legs shifted under the blankets and the tension seeped out of his muscles. He did look awfully tired.

"I'll let you sleep," she said as she began to stand from the chair.

"Wait."

She paused and then sat back down.

Cowen frowned at her, looking at her attire. She wasn't in sleeping clothes even though it was well past midnight. "You weren't sleeping?"

"No, I was." Even if falling asleep had been an accident.

His frown deepened and he surveyed her face, looking for that crack that only a few people were able to detect. "Are you still having trouble sleeping?"

Lena tried to smile. "Don't worry about me."

"It's my job."

"Well, you're off duty now. So just focus on . . . " *On getting better,* she was going to say, but as Cowen had pointed out earlier, there was no getting better. But she hadn't tried everything. She'd hardly tried at all. "Just rest so you can get back on your feet."

The look he gave her was delicate, as if she was the one in the infirmary cot and not him.

Tears born from stress filled her eyes, coming about so suddenly that it startled her. She leaned forward to place her elbows on the edge of the cot and covered her face with her hands.

"I'm not ready for you to leave," she confessed quietly, her voice but a rasp.

"I know," Cowen said, kind and soft. "I'm not ready to leave either."

She sniffled. "I'll take care of them," she said, reminding him of her promise.

"I know you will."

She stayed by his side, even when he fell asleep. Her chin rested on her palm, but as time passed, her eyes grew heavy, her head slipped, and she no longer had the energy to catch herself. As soon as her head touched the thin mattress, she drifted off.

LENA WOKE UP TO SHOUTS.

She sat up, groaning at the stiffness in her neck and back. Light filled the room, so vivid and plentiful that she had to squint her eyes as she looked around to pinpoint where the noise was coming from.

The grogginess left her quickly when the doors to the infirmary burst open and Avalon Vuukroma stormed in, followed by another member of the Sacred Guard, Piper.

Benji was wide awake and stepped in front of Avalon before she could get too close to Lena. When Avalon tried to get around him, Benji moved with her, red aura flame licking across the hand he placed on his sword.

Avalon narrowed her eyes, but she didn't try to move past him again. She looked over his shoulder, her eyes burning as they met Lena's. *"Where is my son?"*

Cowen had been woken up by the racket too. He tried to sit up, but Lena placed her hand on his arm.

Her eyes remained locked with Avalon's. "What are you talking about?"

"My son," Avalon hissed. "He's missing. He was supposed to meet Ophir this morning, and he didn't."

Lena stood up, taking her time to allow the last bit of lethargy to seep out of her.

"It's Tuck—*your son*—and you're surprised he's missing an early morning meeting?"

With his parents, she almost added.

Avalon narrowed her eyes. "He wouldn't miss this," she said with absolute certainty. "And I know he was with you last night."

Silence coated the infirmary. Piper barely concealed her shock before Lena caught sight of it. Benji stood straighter. She didn't look at Cowen, but she could feel his gaze. She could imagine the rumors coming out of this place if the physicians had overheard.

Avalon raised her chin in response to Lena's glare. If Avalon had marched all the way here for Lena, then she must have been pretty sure of her involvement. The question was *how much did she know*? And how did she find out? Was Tuck truly working with his parents? But why would he tell his parents where he'd been only to disappear on them later? Was his disappearance just another ploy? That didn't seem to make much sense.

"We ran into each other and talked," Lena said evenly. "Don't insinuate that anything else happened. We parted ways shortly after. I don't know where he went. Maybe you should figure out why your son is avoiding you instead of pestering me with your family problems."

"Kalena," Cowen warned.

Avalon's gaze sharpened further. "Do you think I don't know my own son?"

Lena did her the favor of not answering.

Avalon took a step closer, now nearly toe to toe with Benji, but she didn't even spare him a single look. "People are disappearing. *Dying.* And don't think I haven't put together the timeline. The deaths started when *you* returned. I don't have proof of anything, but if you start messing with my family," she warned, her voice steel, "I'll know. If he doesn't show up soon, I will be paying you a visit again."

And with that, she turned, her shoulders back and chin high, and left the infirmary.

Avalon's words weren't quite a threat, but they were meant to be. If Lena's three guards hadn't been present, perhaps Avalon would've been less careful. Nevertheless, the weight of her message was delivered. But it confused Lena. Avalon's words didn't match her actions. If she cared for her son, she had a strange way of showing it.

Piper left the room and Benji returned to guard the door. Any physicians that had been peeking around the corners scattered.

"You met with Tuck Vuukroma last night?" Cowen asked quietly, his voice almost free of judgment. Almost.

Lena gritted her teeth. The way he'd said it reminded her of Ira. *Ira.*

Sunlight cut through the infirmary, glaring down from the skylight. It was morning. Hours had passed.

"Yes, and you know why," she grumbled. She stepped away from Cowen, and her feet carried her to the infirmary doors, after Avalon. "I have somewhere to be. Rest up. I need you in top shape."

"Kalena!" Cowen called after her.

But she ignored him and slipped out of the infirmary, the doors booming behind her when they shut.

"Where are you going?" Benji asked as he stumbled after her. Piper was nowhere in sight.

"I'm tired of waiting. It hasn't done me any good."

Everything was crumbling apart, and she was just *waiting*. As much as she hated to admit it, Tuck was somewhat right. She was being a fool. A sad, idealistic fool.

Time clearly wasn't waiting for her. Ira wasn't going to tell her the truth voluntarily—not the entirety of it. He was a smooth talker, always had been, and she'd let him talk his way out of everything because she wanted to believe him. She wanted it so bad. Any excuse within reason she clutched to her chest and *hoped*. But it wasn't enough for her anymore.

The guards on duty at the dungeon let her through with little fuss, and she picked up a sunstone by the entrance. Once again, the shift in temperature was immediately notable as she stepped down into the dark vault. She shuddered and tightened her grip on the sunstone even though a piece of this size hardly emitted any warmth.

"We'll need the keys," she told the guards, holding out a hand expectantly.

They exchanged wary glances. "Uh . . . neither prisoner is set to be released—"

"I'm not releasing anyone. I'm simply relocating one of them, or rather, Benji is. That's not against the rules, is it?"

"Um, no, but—"

"Great. Then, keys," she ordered sternly, extending her hand farther. When they still hesitated, she added, "How do you think the council would react to finding out about your allegiance with Alkus, the man currently imprisoned on multiple serious charges, *including* the gruesome deaths? How do you think the public would react? Maybe they'll do nothing. Maybe they'll think you two were his accomplices? Should we see which it is?"

They handed over the keys rather quickly after that.

Benji closed the door, cutting off all sound from the outside, and the two of them ventured down the hall between the cells. Chills spread over her skin as the light from the entrance disappeared behind her, but the cold was only somewhat to blame. She wasn't scared of who she was facing. She was scared of what they might tell her.

Despite spending months in a cell, her attacker looked well. His skin was a bit paler than before, pulled tighter across his face, and his hair was more tangled, but his eyes were clear. A bit red, but he hadn't succumbed to the cold, the dark, or the solitude.

He smirked when he saw her and sat up from lounging on the dirty cot. "I wasn't sure you'd come back. I was getting lonely." His gaze moved over her shoulder. "You were kind enough to give me company I suppose, but he's been very *poor* company."

A familiar voice scoffed behind her. "I don't converse with criminals. I wasn't placed down here for your entertainment. I shouldn't have been placed down here at all."

Lena turned and looked into the cell across from her attacker's. Alkus sat on his cot, his knees pulled up to his chest. Even though he'd only been in the dungeon for a few weeks, he looked thoroughly disheveled, worse than her attacker.

His greasy hair was a mess around his head and the bags under his eyes were so dark they appeared bruised. Her eyes were drawn to his short, uneven nails as he picked at them, and his chapped lips pulled back into a sneer when he noticed her staring. A thin sheen of sweat covered his pasty skin, despite the cold. He wasn't used to environments like this. He'd always had a silver spoon in his mouth.

Her attacker sighed. "We've been through this before. You are *also* a criminal. That's why you're down here. Might as well make the most of it."

Alkus ignored him, focusing entirely on Lena instead. "I know what you did." His voice shook, and his eyes were wild. "Your husband is a *monster!* We should have killed him when we had the chance. Did you plan it all from the very start? To sacrifice The La—?"

"I'm not here for you," she said stiffly as she turned her back on him. The heat from her Imprint was welcoming amidst the chill. "Say what you want, but you can't convince me you don't deserve to rot down here."

"What is your goal exactly?" Alkus continued. "Whatever it is, it won't work. You'll ruin this place—"

"Shut up, Alkus! You've lost. Nothing you do or say will change that."

"I'll be out soon enough."

"Maybe," she conceded. "But not without a trial." She turned to Benji then, ignoring Alkus completely. "It seems the councilman isn't enjoying his company and would rather have solitude. Move him farther down where he can obtain that."

Alkus protested, but with his Imprint sealed, he was no match for Benji. The guard was easily able to wrangle him deeper into the dungeon.

Lena waited for Benji to come back, not saying a word to her attacker in the meantime. And he didn't say anything to her, but she could feel his gaze burning into the side of her head like a brand. She fought to keep still under his heavy scrutiny.

Benji returned a few minutes later, with the keys but without Alkus.

"Wait for me by the door," she told him.

He frowned and opened his mouth to likely protest, but she'd anticipated it and cut in before he could utter a complaint.

"They're both behind cages with their Imprints sealed, and I won't be here long. Give me ten minutes."

She'd come here for answers, and as soon as she got what she needed, she would leave.

Benji didn't seem happy about it, but with one last glare at her attacker, he strode back toward the entrance.

She stared after him until the shadows swallowed him completely and she could no longer hear his footsteps echoing in this cold prison. And then she turned on her attacker.

"I know what I want now," she said, standing tall in front of his cell. "I want the truth, however dangerous it may be."

He smirked. "Really?"

The sunstone bit into the soft flesh of her palm as she squeezed her hand around it. She was tired of people questioning her decisions as if she was incapable of making them herself. She'd thought about the bad things this truth could unveil, and it worried her. She could be unlocking a beast. But *she had to know*. This anticipation had been building inside of her for days, choking her and flooding her mind.

Ira was gone.

Tuck was gone.

Aquila was gone.

Cowen was dying.

She took a few steps forward until she stood right in front of the bars of the cell, close enough that he could grab her if he darted forward.

"I'm done playing games," she said. "And I'm nearly out of patience. I'm a spiteful person. I hold grudges for a long time. Ask Alkus. I won't bat an eye at leaving you down here to rot alongside him if you don't tell me what you know. You have one chance. Are you involved in these murders?"

His hair fell in front of his face as he tilted his head forward, keeping his eyes locked with hers. "I haven't killed any of the victims if that's what you mean."

"I want a straightforward answer—"

"And I'll give you one, but don't say I didn't warn you."

He pushed himself off the cot and walked toward her.

She didn't back away.

"First," he said as he stopped right in front of her and reached a hand between the bars, "let me introduce myself. My name is Weylin."

Her brow furrowed. She ignored his hand. He then told her everything.

He told her about Atreus.

LENA NEARLY RAN through the halls on her way to Ira's study. It was empty, and it looked like no one had been there for days. Empty bottles littered his desk and shelves. The curtains were drawn closed, making the room appear darker and smaller than it actually was. Even the air seemed stale. Old. *Wrong*.

She reached out to him. *Ira. Ira, come back. I know everything. Come back now. We need to talk.*

She ran to his room. Her heartbeat was too loud. Black blurred the edges of her vision when she took the corners too fast.

His room was empty as well. Dirty too, which was unlike him. But there had been so many signs lately, so many things he'd done that were unlike him. Where was he?

Lena walked across his room and searched through the papers on his desk. Her vision blurred, and she swiped at her cheeks with the backs of her trembling hands.

Ira, come back! I know the truth. I know about Atreus.

Silence greeted her. Solitude and sorrow.

She stalked into his washroom and swept her gaze over the space. Something was different. The air was hot and smelled faintly of pine. Someone had been in here recently. Someone had drawn a bath.

She noticed the dirty clothes and towels that had been haphazardly thrown into a bin in the corner. She went over and pulled the items out, looking over each piece of fabric carefully and bringing them to her nose. She stopped when she spotted a stain of blood on one of the shirts. It was long and thin, as if Ira had been cut, and relatively fresh.

Lena pulled out more clothes and towels until the bin was nearly empty. When she went to pull out the last item, she paused. It was heavier than the rest and lumped together. She tried to shake it out, but it wouldn't budge. Frowning, she leaned down farther to grab the fabric wad in its entirety and lifted it from the bin. The piece of clothing was carefully folded, too much so for it to be a coincidence.

She carried the bundle to the vanity and began to work apart the deliberate wrappings. And when the fabric fell away, there, in the center, was one of Tuck's silver daggers.

It was different from the one Tuck had left in her room all those months ago, and Tuck wouldn't be careless enough to leave one lying around for anyone to take, meaning Ira had stolen it.

She glanced at the empty laundry bin and all the clothes and towels strewn across the floor. She picked up the dagger and tilted it. Light reflected off the blade, revealing a cracked emerald.

Tuck cherished his daggers like no one else. If one was damaged, he would get it fixed.

For Ira to have a flawed dagger of Tuck's...

That meant there had been a fight.

The pieces lined up in her mind as the dread settled in her stomach.

Ira had been missing for nearly a day. She hadn't seen Tuck since last night.

It could very well be a coincidence. Ira could be elsewhere, and so could Tuck. Ira had been keeping his distance more and more ever since she came across him in the forest. And if she were Tuck, she probably would've skipped out on the meeting with his father too. Maybe he was acting out. He wasn't too happy with her at the moment either.

But she couldn't shake off this feeling of *wrongness*.

What if she was mistaken? What if something had prevented him from coming back? What if he'd been attacked?

It was no secret that Tuck and Ira despised each other. And Ira knew that she'd been spending time with Tuck. But surely, he wouldn't have gone after the royal.

How would you know? You just found out he's been lying to you. About everything.

Not about everything.

"What are you going to do? Are you going to send your husband after me? Will I be the next victim?"

Both Tuck and Ira had lied to her. She could only trust herself and her gut right now, and it was telling her something was off. The knife; the fresh, bloodied clothes; Tuck's disappearance—it wasn't pure happenstance. Not at all.

"The longer you wait, the more blood you'll have on your hands."

Lena cursed and ran out of the room. She hoped she was wrong.

CHAPTER
SEVENTY-SIX

I ra had a pounding headache when he woke up. He was lying on the ground and covered in a viscous substance. His entire body ached, even his fingertips and his eyelids. He groaned when something nudged his side.

"Wake up," a familiar voice ordered.

He squeezed his eyes shut tighter and tried to fight off the wave of vertigo that swept through him as he sat up. He rubbed his hand across his face, and when he pulled it away, red covered his palm. Blood—Prophet Silas' blood. He was covered in it. Some of it had dried, while some of it was still congealed.

He was in a room with Vanik, Weylin, Harlow, and Judah. The latter was huddled in the back of the room, his eyes fixed on the floor. The other three stood closer, staring down at Ira with various expressions of severity. Other emotions were thrown into the mix, but he was too tired to decipher them. And he didn't really care.

"I thought you three got locked away."

"They tried," Harlow said. She stood closest to him, and Vanik stood the farthest, the knife held tightly in his hand. "We put up a fight when they tried to shove us in solitary. By the time they dragged us back, the *Te'Monai* had shown up."

They also had splatters of blood on them, not as much as him, and likely from the *Te'Monai*. Not humans.

"Was that you?" Weylin asked cautiously.

He shook his head. "Mila." *At first, anyway.*

Harlow took a step back, face gray under all the gore and grime. "What?" She turned to look at Judah and he withered under her gaze.

The two of them must've been close since the boys and girls were separated at night. While he, Vanik, Weylin, Finn, and Judah had been planning, so had Mila and Harlow. And now Mila was dead. So was Finn.

"She was working with the prophets. I don't know why, but she wouldn't stop."

Harlow turned back to look at him. "You killed her?"

He nodded, his head heavy, but everything else light. Empty. "She killed Finn."

Weylin stepped forward, pulling Ira's attention toward him. "Are you with us?" he snapped.

"He's in shock," Vanik said.

Weylin looked over his shoulder at Vanik. "Well he needs to snap out of it if we want this to work."

"Want what to work?" Ira asked.

Weylin's face tightened as he stared down at him. "You're getting out."

Ira looked around. "We're all getting out."

Nothing stood in their way now. The enforcers and prophets were dead.

Vanik scoffed and stormed forward, his face twisted in irritation. "The door only opens from the outside, meaning we can't leave until someone else comes in. And no one is going to accidentally come across the entrance."

Ira thought about the letter. The incoming shipment. It could come at any minute. He opened his mouth to tell them as much, but Vanik beat him to it.

"We know about the firstborns and enforcers coming. Finn told us before we were sent out." His face hardened. "We don't have the strength to take them down, not when there are so few of us left. We're exhausted and injured, and our Imprints are sealed. The best we can do is hold them off while one of us escapes."

"Then send Judah," Ira argued. "He's the youngest."

"And the most inexperienced," Vanik shot back. "If one person is getting out, it needs to be the one who has the best chance at survival. The one who knows the most and can do the most."

Ira stared at Vanik, momentarily at a loss for words. "Then you go." He pushed himself to his feet, stumbling as the room tilted for a moment, but he steadied himself against the wall. "You've wanted to since the very beginning."

"You're not listening. It *has* to be you." Vanik clenched his jaw and looked away like it irritated him to say this. "It's always been you. With the stones and the prophets and the *Te'Monai*. You're the best chance we have."

Ira shook his head, glancing pleadingly at Harlow and Weylin, but of course, they backed Vanik. He could see how much they wanted to argue, how much they wanted things to be different. They wanted out. They were the closest to escaping they'd ever been.

Weylin had done all the spying and sneaking around to prepare for this. He and Vanik had found the door. They'd tried to escape, and now they had to stay behind. Ira couldn't live with the guilt. He wanted everyone to get out.

"Someone else can do it—"

"No, they can't," Weylin said, sounding frustrated and resolute at the same time.

"I can't just leave you all behind! What do you think the reinforcements are going to do once they arrive and find this bloodbath? They'll blame *you*."

Flashes of the whipping filled his mind, and that had only been for talking back and losing one stone. He couldn't imagine what the punishment was going to be for something like this.

"We'll get solitary and maybe a beating, but that's it." Vanik almost sounded casual. "They'll get this operation up and running again and send us off."

"And that's a better alternative than trying to escape?" Ira asked incredulously.

"We've survived so far," Harlow said.

"Yes, and you've been lucky! We all have! One day that luck's going to run out."

"Then get us out before that happens," Vanik hissed.

A noise of pure frustration left Ira's mouth. "What about the stones?"

"I think we can manage," Harlow said. "We found them without you this last time, didn't we? Your group was the last one back."

"We've thought about this, and we've already voted," Weylin added before Ira could say anything more. "If someone's getting out, it's you."

"You can't ask me too—"

Vanik grabbed his ruined uniform and slammed him against the wall. "Wake up!" He shook him. "This isn't for you. This is for *us*. All of us. We all want out, but that *can't* happen right now. Do you understand? The only way we can all get out is if *you leave*. Today. We're wasting time right now. We don't want your fucking pity! We want your word."

Ira tried to grasp the fleeing wisps of anger but came up empty-handed. He sagged in Vanik's grip, swallowing the bitter taste in his mouth. Vanik was right. He was wasting time. They needed to get to the door before the reinforcements arrived and they missed their opportunity.

"It has to be me," he whispered, finally getting it as the pieces clicked into place. Lately, everything had just been him.

Vanik nodded, loosening his grip. "It has to be you," he echoed. "Don't forget about us. You want to be the hero, then come back and get us out."

"You can't be everyone's hero."

Still, Ira told them what he'd told Finn. "I won't forget about you. I'll get you out. I promise."

Promises were expensive in their life.

Vanik released him entirely and took a step back. "Let's get to the exit. It's just up ahead."

"Wait," Ira said as everyone went to move. "The stones—"

"No," Weylin said. "We're not wasting any more time retrieving them."

"No, not the others. I came back with two stones."

Judah was already looking at him, and when the kid met Ira's gaze, he shrunk under it. Judah had been there, he realized, when he stabbed Prophet Silas until he was nothing more than a bloody pulp. Judah was scared of him. Not for the first time.

"I picked them up," Judah said in a quiet voice.

He fished them out of his pocket and held them out. He flinched back slightly when Ira came forward to take them from his hand, and Ira acted like the slight movement wasn't a punch in the chest.

You've gotten too attached, a voice in the back of his head said. *The best thing to do now is run.*

Ira turned toward Vanik. "I met another woman. One of the sisters. She told me . . . a lot. We can talk about it later." He shook his head, not wanting to get into everything she'd said. He still needed to make sense of it himself, and he didn't have the time or energy to do it now.

"Later?" Vanik barked, irritation seeping into his voice again. "There won't be a later—"

"The woman also gave me these two stones," Ira cut in, uncurling his fingers to reveal the stones in his palm. "She said I'd need allies. We can meet in that realm as long as we both have a stone."

And discuss anything that needs to be discussed.

Vanik eyed him and then the stones before grabbing one.

"Let's go," Harlow said impatiently.

Weylin was nowhere to be seen, but neither Vanik nor Harlow seemed surprised or concerned by his absence.

"One more thing—"

"Talk and walk," Harlow snapped.

Ira followed them blindly through the halls as he told them that *Mila* had been the one sending them to the other realms, not the prophets. He tried to explain everything about the magic-sensitive individuals quickly but thoroughly, adding any other piece of information that might be helpful.

He still wanted to discuss his conversations with the sisters later, but he thought the others needed to know *how* they were traveling to different realms in the first place. Since Mila was gone, even with the new shipment coming, the firstborns would be sitting around in the Institute for weeks while they waited for the operation to start up again. Maybe longer since they had to wait for prophets too. It would give them time to collect themselves and make a plan. And if they needed extra time in the future, they just had to find and kill the magic-sensitive firstborn, which he realized was easier said than done.

Both Vanik and Harlow were skeptical about this new information, and Ira admitted that he had no way of guaranteeing it was true, but he believed it was. Even if there was another magic-sensitive firstborn in the incoming shipment, nothing could be done without prophets present to regulate things.

Ira had been too busy talking to pay attention to their surroundings as they walked, so he didn't look around until they stopped. A huge metal door stood in front of him. He squeezed his fist tighter around the stone. As soon as he was out, the stone would be his only lifeline to the others. To Finn.

Someone stepped up next to him. Vanik held out the knife and said under his breath, "Will you attack me if I give this to you?"

Ira took it slowly. "Only if you give me a reason to."

"When that door opens, we won't be able to hold everyone off. Weylin went to find others, but we'll still be outmatched. You'll need to fight too. Fight for your life, because other people are relying on you." Vanik jabbed a finger into his chest.

"I understand," he said, his voice far away and flat. Everything seemed somewhat removed. A completely unrelated thought cut through the haze of his mind then. "Have you seen Miss Anya?"

Vanik frowned at him. "No. Why are you asking me that? Why does it matter?"

"Finn said . . . she wasn't with them. She got him back his journal and gave me sleep elixir. She patched me up without the prophets telling her to." He didn't trust her. He didn't even know if she was still alive, but if she was and if what Finn had said was true, she could help them. She had before. "If you need something, go to her."

Vanik's frown deepened, but he didn't say anything.

Weylin came back with a few dozen others. Ira didn't know if they'd been waiting for a long time or not. With each passing minute, the tension grew. They waited for a noise on the other side of that door. They knew what to expect, and he couldn't decide if that made things worse or not. He knew Weylin probably hadn't told the other firstborns the plan. They all thought they were getting out, finally, after everything. But they were sacrificial pawns, bleeding for *him*.

His chest collapsed further, making it difficult for air to reach his lungs. Numbness coated his skin and sunk deeper until his muscles relaxed. His mind. The wounds from before had healed or were now at least bearable. The adrenaline hummed under his skin like the songs from the stones.

Judah was still avoiding him and had planted himself against a wall on the far side of the space. Ira watched him for a while before going over to him, stopping when Judah shifted away. He was looking at Ira like . . . he was a *Te'Monai*. A monster.

Does he see your true reflection too?

Can they all see it?

Ira wouldn't apologize for killing Prophet Silas. He'd deserved it. Every second of it. But Judah didn't understand. Judah had only seen Ira stabbing the prophet to death. He didn't see the bigger picture. He hadn't been there for years.

"Don't stop fighting. You hear me?"

Judah bit his lip and stubbornly stayed quiet. Ira sighed and stepped away. Harlow stood off to the side, watching them out of the corner of her eye.

"Take care of him," Ira said to her as he passed.

A noise echoed through the room and all of them froze. Another bang sounded and then a whirring noise. The door clicked and then ever so slowly inched toward them.

He adjusted his grip on the knife and the others readied themselves. As the door opened farther, he saw the enforcers. And the kids behind them.

"Go!"

He wasn't sure who said it, but they all moved forward, charging at the enforcers before they could even process what was going on. The two sides clashed in a flurry of metal and flesh. Grunts and screams rose quickly. On both sides.

Ira flinched with each one he heard, wondering if it had been Judah or Harlow or Vanik or Weylin. But he did what Vanik had told him to do and kept barreling forward. He pumped his legs and swiped out at anything and everything in front of him.

He quickly realized that there were more firstborns than the letter had stated. More enforcers too. *Double* even. And a lot of them remained near the back of the crowd—dark, large, imposing, and covered in armor.

Ira faltered.

More cries rang out behind him. Ira gritted his teeth and blocked out the noise. "Come on!" he raged.

Two enforcers approached first. Ira ducked under one of their arms and took a stab at the next one. They had spaces between their armor near their joints. They were small and difficult to hit, but Ira had good aim.

The enforcer reeled back, still silent as ever when Ira's blade sunk into its flesh. It wasn't a fatal wound, but it created an opening.

A rock sailed past him, hitting one of the enforcers in the head, temporarily disorienting it. His eyes widened and he looked back.

Vanik glared at him, another rock in his hand. "Go!"

Ira bolted. Vanik had stolen the attention of a few enforcers, but most of them still moved to stop Ira, closing in around him. Their large shapes loomed over him, cutting off what little light he saw.

Panic sprouted in his chest, and something tightened in his gut. The cord. He yanked on it, fighting off the reaching claws. A flash of dizziness overcame him as a screech sounded, but he was able to stay on his feet.

He'd only summoned one *Te'Monai*, and this one was smaller than the others, but it was fast and had wicked claws. It climbed up the enforcers' tall bodies, too quick for them to grab, and sank its claws into the juncture between the enforcers' backs and necks.

Slowly, one by one, the enforcers sank to the ground, but one of them managed to grab the *Te'Monai* while it was on another enforcer. A horrible shriek filled the air as the enforcer squeezed it.

Ira didn't wait to see its end.

He dove under the closest enforcer's legs and scrambled to his feet. He dodged a pair of outstretched hands and then there was nothing standing between him and the rest of the realm.

Sand started to coat the rock below him, making his movements slower, so he pushed harder. He was in a cave, running up an incline. The exit was ahead, a clear bright circle.

His blood thrummed in his veins as he sprinted as hard as he could away from the clash behind him, afraid that the moment he let up, something would drag him back.

He couldn't let that happen. Not when he'd gotten this far. Not when he had people who were relying on him.

The circle of light grew larger and brighter as he drew closer, and then suddenly, he was charging through it. Just like a portal. Except this time, he wasn't transported to another realm. This time he caught the first glimpse of his own.

Ira stopped, breathing hard, and looked around. Blue sky and golden sand. That was all he saw for miles. And the sun. He saw the sun. Ira stared up at it mesmerized, but only for a second. It burned his eyes and he needed to keep moving.

He ran and ran and ran until he could no longer feel his legs. And then he forced one in front of the other, screaming at them to move even when they felt disconnected from his body.

He needed to escape. He needed to get somewhere safe.

His pace eventually slowed down to a stumble. Any faster and he would collapse. The scenery hadn't changed. Gleaming golden sand stretched as far as the eye could see. There were no landmarks in the distance. The horizon shimmered and the sun beat down on him like it wanted to see him fail.

Ira made himself keep going.

He thought of Finn and Mila.

He thought of Judah.

He thought of Vanik and Harlow and Weylin.

He thought of all the others who had died in another realm or in the Institute and those who were fighting for him, those he had left behind.

IRA DIDN'T KNOW how long he'd traveled before his legs finally gave out. He collapsed to his knees in the hot sand. His skin burned and his lips were so chapped it hurt to move them. He had no tears to cry, too dehydrated to even summon saliva. Cotton filled his mouth.

Still, he screamed.

He threw his head back and let go of everything he'd kept inside. He screamed at the sun until he lost his voice too.

He didn't remember what happened after that. He must've passed out because the next thing he knew, he was being shaken awake.

A hand slapped his cheek. His eyes fluttered open, and he gazed up at the people standing over him. They were all covered head to toe in tan clothing.

"Well, well, well," the one kneeling over him said. He pulled his mask down so Ira could see the nasty smile that spread across his face. "What do we have here?"

Ira was too tired to do anything but let his eyes close again.

CHAPTER
SEVENTY-SEVEN

Lena slipped out of Ira's room and the palace before anyone could notice. With Cowen in the infirmary and Andra and Zaltain away, her Sacred Guard was shorthanded. They filled the holes quickly and smoothly, but this next round of guards didn't know her as well as Benji did, so she was able to evade them without too much trouble.

There were several guardrooms around the palace. She went to the closest one and fastened a cloak around her. The weapons were locked away, and she couldn't afford to spend any more time behind and risk getting caught, but she at least had Tuck's dagger.

She fortified her mental barriers as soon as she set foot outside the palace. She'd been reaching out to Ira for the past hour, and he hadn't answered her, so she cut him off to return the favor. She wouldn't give him the chance to find her when she didn't want to be found.

As soon as she was sure she wasn't being followed, she let her Slayer out.

Sniff out the blood.

Tuck's scent on the dagger had likely been smothered by Ira's and was, therefore, hardly noticeable, if at all, but a Slayer's nose was practically designed for following a faint, distant trail of blood. Whatever had spilled last night would still be relatively fresh, just like the bloodstain on Ira's shirt.

Her Slayer led her to the top of a hill that looked like it had been brutally cut in half. A hundred-foot cliff stretched on for half a mile on both sides.

Marks in the soil indicated a struggle. Some of the grass was uplifted, like the heel of a boot had dug in and pulled. A few other scruffs like that littered the area. One of the trees had a broken branch up ahead, and she hurried in that direction, pausing only when she heard a crack of thunder. Overhead, storm clouds were rolling in. The air was swelling around her and crackling with energy. Soon it would rain and any clue about Tuck's whereabouts would be washed away.

She could go back to the palace. This wasn't her problem. *He* wasn't her problem.

But she kept going, picking up her pace in hope that she might be able to outrun the rain.

There were three possibilities.

The first one was the worst: Tuck was dead.

The second one was that he was alive but too injured to do much more than get away. If that was the case, he was probably somewhere in the forest still.

The third option was that he was somewhere else entirely, which meant he was well enough to travel. '*Well*,' however, could mean a lot of things.

If Ira *had* attacked him, then Tuck could be pretty badly hurt. Ira had fought for most of his life, though not voluntarily. And now, after finding out about Atreus, she was even more worried. Tuck was a fighter, but he didn't have the experience or the tenacity Ira had.

There was nothing in the forest, no clues. She considered going back to the hill, even though it was raining at a steady pace now, but then she came upon an old, faded sign. One poll had been nailed deeper into the ground than the other, so the sign sat crooked at the base of a steep hill. A weathered stairway trailed up into the mist next to it. The sign read: *float in the clouds.*

Lena frowned and stopped to stare at it. That was an odd saying, but it sounded familiar. She'd heard it before.

"*I heard you were sick while floating in the clouds. That's all.*"

Tuck had said that to her in the treehouse. And he'd brought it up more than once.

"*I visit the treehouse sometimes after floating in the clouds.*"

She'd always assumed Tuck had been talking about being high, but maybe . . . it was an actual place.

She moved forward, scaling the stairs as fast as she could without slipping. The rain picked up and lightning flashed across the sky. She jolted and nearly slipped as her heart jumped into her throat. She tried to calm her. It was only some water and some noise, she told herself. The last thing she needed was to be panicked in this situation.

Her legs ached by the time she reached the top, and she was completely soaked. Her clothes and cloak stuck to her like a second skin, and her breaths were fast and shallow.

Lena could make out the outline of a building up ahead. She pushed her hair out of her face and ran toward it, slipping under the overhang to get out of the cold rain. She moved toward the back of the building, hugging the side to stay dry. There was a shed a few dozen feet away that she thought about dashing to, but it looked to be on the verge of collapse. She glanced back at the building, wondering if she would be received kindly if she snuck inside.

A bloody handprint was next to the door.

It was dry and the handprint was larger than her own, likely a male's.

Without further thought, she opened the door and slid into the house. The sound of the thunderstorm was immediately muted. It was quiet inside the building, but she didn't think it was empty. She crept down the hall, studying the layout of the house as she moved.

The hall opened up to a larger room that looked like it belonged inside a pub or inn. Was that what this place was? She couldn't imagine this as a busy spot with it being out in the middle of the forest, old sign and slippery stairwell and all. She hadn't seen any other buildings either—the rain was to blame for that—but maybe this place was located near a popular path for travelers. That would explain how Tuck had come across it.

To the left was a fireplace with chairs and sofas arranged around it. A bar stood on the right side of the vacant room, and tables littered the space in between.

Lena walked forward, wiping her finger along the top of a table. It wasn't dusty. Someone was keeping up with this place.

Her Imprint warmed right as a bang sounded off to the side. She spun around, hand immediately unsheathing Tuck's dagger and holding it out in front of her.

The noise had come from the shutters outside. They were flapping wildly in the wind, hitting the window frame. Her shoulder's fell, but only for a moment. Something moved behind her.

She turned on her heel, dagger tearing through the air. Aura flame began to seep out, but she stopped short when a sword kissed her throat. Her eyes widened when she took in the sight of the wielder. A man, old and thin, about her size. He held the sword like someone who knew how to use it. The blade didn't waver at all, and neither did his severe expression.

He nodded at the dagger in her hand. "Where'd you get that?"

Lena swallowed and eyed the sword again, speculating how quickly he could move. Would he stick it through her throat before her Slayer killed him?

He must've seen the wheels turning in her eyes, or maybe she was silent for too long. "Don't even try it," he warned as he pressed the blade firmer against her skin. "Just answer the question."

"I found it."

"You mean you stole it?" he corrected.

"No." It wasn't *her* who had stolen it. "I found it. I swear. I just came to find shelter because of this storm." She slowly raised and opened her hands to show she meant no harm.

The man frowned, and his scruffy gray beard sunk with it. He leveled the sword with her eye. She tensed as he moved the blade forward, the point snagging on the wet fabric of her hood, pushing it down. He studied her face and then moved the sword down to pull aside her cloak, taking in her clothing.

"You picked the wrong day to wear a dress."

"Clearly." Her eyes flitted up to the ceiling. She hadn't heard anything overhead yet. "I'm sorry for breaking in, but if I could just stay here until the storm dies down, I'd be grateful."

He glanced up at the ceiling too, having caught her gaze.

"Sorry," he said, not sounding very sorry at all. He pressed the blade to her chest and walked forward, forcing her toward the front door. "But we don't have any room here."

Well, that was clearly a lie.

"You're going to kick me out? In this weather?"

"Something tells me you can survive it."

Lena gritted her teeth and glanced past him at the stairs. She needed to get up there. She couldn't leave without seeing for herself. Her grip on the dagger changed, and she flicked it at the old man, throwing up a small shield of aura flame right as she lunged back out of the blade's range, ducked, and darted for the stairs.

"Hey!"

She took the stairs two at a time. The old man's footsteps thundered behind her as he growled and huffed.

"Tuck!" She reached the top of the stairs and looked at the many doors on either side of the hall. "Tuck!"

Her Imprint flared and shivers raced down her spine. She listened to her gut and dropped, narrowing avoiding Tuck's dagger sailing over her head. It lodged into the wall at the end of the hallway, vibrating slightly.

Lena looked over her shoulder, her lips parted in shock.

Okay, so he wasn't kidding about throwing her out.

She shot up and made a reach for the dagger, calling her aura flame to protect her, but a voice stopped her cold in her tracks.

"Lena?"

She turned around. Peeking out of a door down the hall was Tuck. He leaned heavily on the door frame as if he needed it to support him.

"Tuck," she breathed out.

The sword was thrust in her face again. "Get out!" the man barked. "I won't say it again."

"Eldon," Tuck rasped. "It's fine. "

The man—Eldon—glanced at Tuck out of the corner of his eye. She observed their interaction. They knew each other somehow.

At last, Eldon drew the sword away. "Yeah? And what if this one tries to finish the job?"

Tuck's eyes were on her as he said, "I'd probably let her."

Eldon scoffed and looked between the two of them suspiciously for a few seconds before marching back downstairs.

"What are you doing here?" Tuck asked. His voice was thin, his skin sallow.

She slipped into the room, and he backed up—stumbled back, more like it. He was shirtless and covered in a thin sheen of sweat. One of his hands held a bandage to his side while the other supported him, clutching the nearest surface to help him stay upright. A pile of bloodied bandages had already accumulated on the floor.

"I came to find you." She grimaced when she realized how that sounded.

Tuck scrutinized her. "Really?" he asked, his voice heavy with disbelief. "You came to find me? *Are* you planning to finish the job Ira started? When he attacked me, I thought you had taken my words the other day as a challenge."

She pursed her lips. "I didn't send Ira after you. And I'm not here to kill you or . . . tell Ira where you're at." Her mental block was still up and secure. Ira hadn't tried to bypass it. He was absolutely silent. "I already told you, I—"

"Came to find me," Tuck interrupted.

He walked over to the round table in the corner of the room. On it was a knife, clean bandages, a needle and thread, and a bottle of alcohol. He grabbed the bottle and collapsed into one of the chairs, taking a swig and then wincing.

"How sweet," he drawled.

Lena's eyes widened at the sight of his injury when he pulled the bandage away from his side. Tuck had already stitched it up, but the wound was still ghastly, red, and angry. It consisted of two deep cuts nearly half a foot long. The skin was puckered around the cuts, and irritated, red lines stretched across Tuck's abdomen.

Lena took a few steps closer and noticed another scratch under the other two; it was smaller but still nothing to overlook. Tuck had deemed stitches unnecessary for this one, even though it was still bleeding.

Why was it still bleeding?

Blessed's enhanced healing stopped bleeding and sealed up most wounds quickly. He shouldn't still be bleeding, unless the wounds had been *much* worse initially. These looked like they would scar.

Tuck poured alcohol on the cuts and hissed. "It clotted, but I keep pulling it open," he said as he grabbed a fresh length of bandage to dab over the wound.

"You need to stitch it then," she said as she approached. "Let me help."

"I'm fine," Tuck grunted.

"Your stitching is acceptable at best. Seriously, how'd you survive when you got hurt during your missions?" The angle at which he'd had to stitch up the cuts was less than ideal, and he'd likely been in pain the entire time, resulting in the stitches being crooked. At least he'd had the alcohol. "Why didn't you ask that man for help?"

"I'm used to patching myself up. And I do just fine at it, thank you," he bit out.

A handful of scars littered his abdomen and chest, far fewer than Ira. While Tuck's . . . line of work was considered dangerous, he wasn't constantly on the run, having to fight. The rest and relaxation provided to him gave his wounds time to heal and him time to recuperate.

"Eldon's making medicine."

"How do you know him?"

Tuck took another drink from the bottle. His head lolled back, and he stared at the ceiling. He was a bit tipsy—his eyes red and unclear—which had likely contributed to his shoddy stitching job.

"Eldon crafts my daggers."

Her brows rose in surprise. She'd assumed some popular blacksmith in Solavas made Tuck's specialty daggers, not an old man living on a secluded hilltop.

Tuck's eyes shifted to the dagger she held. *His* dagger. "Where did you find that?"

"... In Ira's room."

Tuck scoffed and held out his hand. Lena hesitated. She still had her Slayer and aura flame. He was drunk and injured. If he was stupid enough to attack her, she could hold her own.

Wordlessly, she placed the dagger into his hand.

"You'll find it in his back next."

She tensed. "Tuck—"

"He tried to kill me," he said darkly. A muscle in his jaw twitched. "I got away, but I won't give him another chance."

"How did you get away? The tracks in the forest just disappeared."

Tuck took another sip and wiggled his fingers in her direction. "It's a secret. Can't go spilling those to the enemy."

She crossed her arms. "So you still see me as the enemy?"

"Don't *you?*" he shot back, leaning forward. He winced as the movement pulled on his stitches. "And why shouldn't I see you as the enemy, especially now? I'm just going by what you've said. We're not friends. You still think I'm going to betray you at any moment because of what my family did to yours, so why shouldn't I think the same after your husband tried to kill me? Am I supposed to believe that after all the yelling and the insults that you're suddenly being friendly?" He laughed and dropped his forehead to his hand. "Really convenient timing. Honestly."

"Now you understand how I felt—how I *feel!* You've always been difficult, but you've been especially so since my return. What about sneaking into my room? The duel? The field games? The ball? You were rude and obnoxious, and I'll admit I was too, but I had to be because of Blessed like you. What's your excuse? Why are you acting so agreeable and helpful lately? Don't you think that's suspicious? *Really convenient timing.*"

He shook his head but didn't say anything. She smacked his arm, pushing it out from under his head. Tuck looked up, glaring at her.

"I'm not here for Ira." There was more she wanted to say, but she couldn't form her thoughts into words.

In a sense, she was lying. She wasn't here for Ira in the way that Tuck believed. She wasn't here to finish what Ira had done or tell Ira where he could find Tuck. She wanted this to end—the secrets, the killings, the way Ira walked around as if he carried the weight of the realm on his shoulders. So when she found out that Ira could be responsible for Tuck's disappearance, she'd run after them to stop things from becoming worse. If Ira had killed Tuck . . . She didn't doubt that the Vuukromas would stop at nothing to find the true culprit and ruin them. They would immediately suspect her and Ira. She'd been careful with her crimes and her trips, but the chances of surviving under such scrutiny was low. And even if they did survive, it would be at what cost? The target on her back would grow larger, and her and Ira's relationship would strain. They needed to be strategic with how they took out the Vuukromas.

Right now, both she and Ira were already in hot water.

So she'd come out as damage control. She was relieved that Tuck was alive *because* it meant that Ira had dodged a particularly hard blow, one that she wasn't sure they could recover from. And now that she'd found Tuck, alive and somewhat well, she wanted to make sure he wouldn't talk. She wanted to be the first person to reach him.

This was all because of Ira. Because of her and him. Them. Not Tuck. The panic that had grasped her in Ira's washroom when she came across the blood and the chipped dagger was for Ira and the possible repercussions that could come from this. Tuck was . . .

A traitor.

But even the malicious voice in her head was lacking today. The words fell flat.

Tuck was right about one thing, though she wouldn't admit it to him.

"You can't protect him because you love him."

She would try to protect Ira just as he had her, but only if he stopped with the lies and the disappearances. She'd told him as much. She'd also once told him that she didn't care about what he'd done in his past, and that was still true. Everything before this moment she could forget about. She could live happily with him for the rest of her life, *if* he stopped. She couldn't excuse or accept what he did after this point.

She was being selfish. She didn't care about the murders or how his actions affected others. She cared about how they affected *her* and their relationship. She couldn't reach him like this. He was drifting away. Her perception of him was changing, but her love for him wasn't. And that scared her more than anything.

She was still trying to wrap her mind around everything Weylin had told her.

Ira was a firstborn. Atreus had been his name then. And he, like every other firstborn, had lived in an underground Institute. They'd never seen the light of day in this realm. She knew what firstborns were, what they represented, but she'd never seen them as evil. They were . . . necessary sacrifices. That was what she knew. What she'd been taught. But some teachings were lies, disguised as something less harsh and more tolerable so that people accepted it.

She remembered Ira's ashen face and his disappointment when she suddenly left the infirmary without doing anything. And then he'd left. Had that moment been too much for him, as a firstborn? She'd wondered why he'd been so stricken when he hadn't even been in the room.

Weylin hadn't gone into the details, but she'd seen the shadow that'd crossed his face when talking about their horrible lives, the seminars, the Outings. Her mind had gone to her time fighting for her life in the Lowlands, but she and Ira had been facing very different monsters. She knew what she was heading into to some extent and the monsters she fought looked like her. Ira, on the other hand, was going in blind and the monsters on the other side showed no mercy. He'd been condemned for something he had no control over.

He deserved something better. He'd lived a much harder life than she had. Wasn't he tired of fighting? He was so much more than a criminal and a murderer, but she knew that was all he would be painted as if the Blessed found out what he was doing. She wouldn't let that happen.

"Let me help," she said again, her voice softer this time.

Tuck didn't argue. He watched her closely as she crouched at his side. When she grabbed the alcohol bottle and pulled, he let her take it. She doused a clean bandage in booze and dabbed it around his open wound. The muscles in his stomach contracted at her touch, but he didn't make a peep. He took the bottle back after she readied the needle and thread, making sure they were sterilized too.

"Hold still," she murmured as she leaned forward and touched around the wound.

His skin burned, which was only worrisome if it stayed that way. His body was working to heal his wound, so it should be significantly better in a few hours and his fever should be down. His side twitched as she worked the needle under the skin and back through, making sure the loops were tight to seal the cut. She'd stitched up Aquila plenty of times. And herself. Even though it had been years, the technique came back to her easily.

"I didn't expect anyone to come after me," Tuck said, "least of all you."

"Don't talk," she said without stopping her work.

The storm filled the silence until she finished stitching. She cut the thread with the dagger and stood.

"Your mother came to me this morning, demanding to know where you were. You missed a meeting with your father apparently, and she was sure you wouldn't do that." She still had the dagger in her hand. Tuck was hunched over, his neck and shoulders revealed to her, but she set the dagger down onto the table. "She knew we were meeting," she said slowly. "So naturally, she blamed me for your disappearance." She waited a few seconds. "How did she know we were meeting, Tuck?"

Someone knocked on the door then, and Tuck moved to answer it, but not before Lena caught a glimpse of the stormy look on his face.

"Here's the salve," Eldon said from the other side of the door. " . . . Is everything all right?"

"Fine," Tuck bit out before shutting the door.

He went to the bed and unscrewed the lid, dipping his fingers inside the jar to grab a fair amount of salve. He nearly sighed in relief as he spread it over his wound. Once his cuts were evenly covered, he sealed the jar and tossed it onto the bedside table.

"My parents don't give a shit," he said, his voice carefully monotone, "even if it seems like they do. So congratulations. You hit that one on the nose. Pat yourself on the back." He braced his hands against the bed and leaned back. "But I know you don't care about my parents. Or me, for that matter. And you say you're not out here for Ira." It was clear by the way he said it that he didn't believe that. "So you're out here for yourself then? What does searching for me in the pouring rain give you?"

"I don't know. Does it matter? I'm here—"

"Yes, but *why*?"

"I don't know!"

"Were you disappointed when you found me alive?"

"No."

Tuck gave her an insincere pout. "It's almost as if we're friends."

"I don't want—"

"To be friends. I know," he snapped. He reached forward for another bottle of alcohol that sat on the bedside table. "I don't think you *ever* wanted to be."

Lena's mouth fell open. "You were an ass and then you helped people kill my family. What about that sounds like friend material?"

The smirk on his face was lifeless, hanging on by a mere thread. "You'll never pass up the chance to bring that up."

She thought, for a second, that perhaps it was unfair to keep dangling that in front of his face, digging the dagger deeper, especially after what he'd told her. He'd tried to help. He'd alluded that he'd been somewhat trapped in his position, that he hadn't wanted to hurt her or her family. It was hard to believe because it had come from him, and for five years, she'd believed the exact opposite was true. It made up her truth, the fabric of the realm around her.

Tuck had betrayed her. If that wasn't true and she threw that stone aside, everything she knew would fall along with it. She would begin to question *everything*.

But that was already happening, wasn't it?

"Let me ask you something," he said. "If your parents told you to kill someone, what would you do?"

She scoffed. "My parents would've never told me to do something like that."

Tuck sent her a wry grin with tired eyes and took a long swig from the bottle of alcohol. "Well, lucky you."

"Lucky me?" Lena advanced on him and ripped the bottle from his hands.

"Yes," he spat. "Lucky you. Lucky Lena who had a family who loved her, even if it was only for a portion of a lifetime. Lucky Lena who had a family who followed and accepted her no matter what. But there's no luck left for me. No Luck Tuck."

He was laughing by the end of it, and she shoved his chest. He fell back onto the bed, still laughing.

"And *you* ruined it," she hissed. "Maybe the reason you don't have a good relationship with your family is because you don't deserve it."

Tuck clutched at his chest, right over his heart. "Ouch."

"You're arrogant, infuriating—*horrible!*" Her words tumbled over one another, adding to the flames, and it didn't help that he was looking at her the way he was—like she was throwing an unreasonable tantrum and he was just waiting for it to be over. "I can't believe I came out here looking for *you!*"

A boom of thunder outside emphasized her last word, and the building shook slightly.

Tuck pushed himself up onto his elbows, a smirk on his face. "Makes you feel crazy, doesn't it? Me?"

"I would say murderous is more accurate."

"Taking after your husband then?"

"Stop bringing him into this!"

Lena closed her eyes and pressed her lips together to prevent them from trembling. It was too much. Her mind, her heart, her Imprint, the burning energy radiating through her limbs. She needed space and fresh air and silence, but she couldn't get that right now, so she took a deep breath and fought to remain in control.

"You can't ignore it."

Rain pattered against the building.

He was being so persistent. *Why?* She was fighting for her and Ira's relationship, but what was Tuck fighting for? Why did she continue to entertain him? She didn't know what it was about him that made her lose all sense and fall into these heated arguments.

Lena slumped forward, sitting on the mattress beside him. She brought the bottle up to her mouth and took three large mouthfuls before pulling it away. She shuddered. "Sometimes I wonder how different my life would be if the Numina hadn't chosen me."

That would mean no palace. No fancy clothes. No delicious foods, no soft beds, and no warm baths whenever she wanted. But she wouldn't have to put up with the Blessed, and her family would still be alive. There would be no Cowen, no Jhai, no Tuck. No Ira either. But maybe she could be wishful and believe that they'd meet another way.

"It's no use thinking like that," Tuck said. "It'll only hurt you."

She frowned at that familiar sentiment.

"Maybe I want it to," she found herself saying. Her free hand covered her face. "It's mostly my fault—my family's death."

She'd finally said it aloud, and now that she had, she couldn't stop talking. The guilt poured out of her.

"I . . . I *knew* something bad was going to happen. I knew it was too good to be true, but I wanted to . . . " An unsteady breath left her lips, and she ran a hand through her wet hair. "I wanted to think it would be different. I *hoped* . . . It was stupid. And it got them killed. And I don't even know why I'm telling you this."

"It's not your fault for wanting things."

"But I *knew*—"

"So did I."

Her mouth snapped shut. *What could I do? What could he do?*

"You couldn't have known. Not completely," he said. "You were scared."

Six years had gone by, and she still was.

"You can't fix what happened in the past, but you can influence what happens in the future."

Lena shook her head. "I love him." The crack in her voice went so much deeper.

A disgusted sound left Tuck's throat. "You say that but—"

"Have you ever been in love before?" She whipped around to face him.

Tuck didn't give her an answer, but him not denying it surprised her.

She swallowed thickly. "Then don't ridicule me."

"You were apart for five years and you so easily went back to his side. You didn't stop to think that maybe he'd changed?"

"No, I knew he'd changed," she shot back, glaring daggers at Tuck. "He told me all about the duels and how he had to fight to survive until he finally gained a respectable position. Were you one of the challengers? Did you line up to see him bleed?"

Tuck's eyes darkened and he leaned forward, now only inches away. "No, but I wish I had."

CHAPTER
SEVENTY-EIGHT

L ena's veins sparked and she shot her hand forward—to shove him, slap him—she didn't know. But she wanted to hurt him.

Tuck saw right through her. He'd laid the trap and she'd taken the bait. His hand snatched her wrist before she could touch him. His skin was blazing hot against her own. She tried to pull her hand back, but he tightened his grip.

"Let go of me," she ordered between gritted teeth. She'd give him five seconds before she unleashed her aura flame and burned him.

"You'll try to hit me again."

"It's well deserved. Would you rather I burn you instead?"

Tuck's lips twitched. "Try it and I'll burn you back."

Lena yanked her wrist again, but he held firm.

"How do you know how I acted around Ira? You don't know *anything*." A thought came to her, and she narrowed her eyes. "Unless you were spying on me? Did you sneak into my room more than once, you *freak?*"

He narrowed his eyes right back and his grip tightened just a fraction. "You caught me. I'm *burning* with bitterness. Ira wants you all to himself, and that's just not fair." He spoke it with casual indifference. A drawl that was baiting.

"Let go of me," she said again, her voice low. A warning, but he didn't heed it.

Lena shifted her weight and swung her other hand around. The alcohol spilled and poured all over Tuck. He cursed and his grip on her wrist loosened just enough that she was able to roll to the side.

His arm whipped out and grabbed the back of her cloak. She wiggled out of it and slid off the other side of the bed, but he was only seconds behind her. His hand wrapped around her thigh and *tugged*. She fell forward onto the ground, catching herself on her palms, and kicked her foot back, a fierce satisfaction rushing through her when it met his shoulder.

Despite the groan that left his lips, he was still able to maintain his hold on her. He let go of her thigh to grab her ankle, which was closer. Using this grip, he pulled her back while lifting himself. She swung her body around, elbowing him across the face.

"*Shit!*"

Tuck veered away by the force of her hit, but her lower body was still trapped by his legs.

Lena bucked while reaching out for the leg of the chair. Her fingers swiped through the air, only inches away. She gritted her teeth and squirmed in an attempt to lengthen her reach. Her shoulder *screamed*.

Tuck got up and kicked the chair away from her, breathing hard. He stood between her and the dagger on the table. Lena pushed herself to her feet, her chest heaving.

The bed was to her left. The wall behind her and to her right. Tuck was in front of her.

"You need to listen," he huffed, wincing as he shifted from one foot to the other. A large, muddy bruise was already forming on his skin where she'd kicked him. "If you go back and let Ira continue to do what he's doing, unchecked, as queen . . ." He breathed out heavily and shook his head. "He'll come for me again. He won't stop until I'm dead, which you're probably delighted about, but if you can't control him now, what makes you think you'll be able to control him later? He's testing you, and you're doing exactly what he wants you to do. He killed those people on the council. The Covaylens. Trynla. That was him."

Tuck thought . . . *Ira* had . . .

Lena shook her head. "No—"

"*Yes*," Tuck beseeched, lurching forward. His eyes were hard, but he was pleading with his words, his body language. "Lena, please . . . *listen*. Put your love for him aside and use your head. You can't tell me what he's doing is okay."

Tuck was genuinely worried about the atrocities Ira was committing, both the ones in the past and the ones that hadn't yet happened. The murders. The anarchy. She had contributed to those things. What did that say about her?

But those things were a part of life. If controlled, they were fine. But could she control him?

"There's a reason you found him in a prison—"

And there it was.

"He's not dangerous!" she snapped. "No more than any of us are. Since the first day he arrived, you Blessed have been trying to make him feel like he doesn't belong when, in reality, he was just dealt a shittier hand in life than the rest of you!"

And now, knowing his backstory, she felt this all the more strongly.

Tuck's laugh was cruel and startling. "Are you serious? It's like he's planted these excuses in you."

"What about yours then?" She took another step forward so they were within arm's reach again. "Go ahead. Give them to me."

His mouth twisted. "I already have, and you didn't listen to them either."

"I hate you," she spat with all the venom inside of her. Their relationship—her feelings toward him—was complicated. She had a hard time putting it into words, but those three worked. They might be as close as she would get. She said it again, convincing herself, wishing it was truer than it was. More genuine. "I *hate* you."

Tuck's eyelids lowered as he looked down at her, his muscles lax even though they'd practically been screaming at each other for the past ten minutes. "I know," he murmured. "But how much?"

"Not enough."

"I can give you a reason to hate me," he said, hushed. "More, that is."

He took a step closer. The heat radiating from him caressed her skin.

"I have plenty of reasons to hate you."

"Then what more do you need?"

Need? Or *want?* Because her answer would be different.

"I *need*," she drawled, placing her hand on his chest and trying to push him, "for you to back up."

But he didn't budge. His fingers wrapped around her wrist again and tugged. "I don't think we'll ever be friends. It was never an option for us, was it?"

"Because of *you*."

"Maybe," he agreed, looking down at her lips now. "But I taught you how to climb, how to throw daggers, and then you ditched me as soon as Ira showed up."

"Jealous?" she shot back, picking up on that painful thread and pulling.

"Maybe," he said again. "I wish I could hate you too. It would make things easier. We just use each other when it's convenient, don't we?"

Her resolve began to burn away. Because she was weak. Still. "How does it feel knowing you'll always be the second choice?"

Tuck narrowed his eyes. "Like this."

Suddenly, his mouth was on hers.

It took her a split second to register what was happening and push past the shock, but as soon as she did, she kissed him back just as fiercely. Her mouth opened under his and her hands clutched his shoulders, his neck, the back of his head, anywhere she could reach to bring him closer.

She dug her nails into his skin, sucking up any hisses of pain. She wasn't even sure if what they were doing could be called kissing. It was all teeth and tongue and blood. The iron mixed between their mouths, overpowering the taste of alcohol.

Tuck's hands tightened around her hips as they stumbled to the side. His legs hit the bed and he fell back. Lena followed, settling in his lap, gravitating toward his lips. His skin burned under her hands and through the layers of clothing between them.

She moved closer to the heat, sinking lower, gasping into his mouth when his hands slipped below her hips and hauled her up. She ground down as their tongues brushed. Their breaths were short and blistering and mixing in the space between them, making her lightheaded.

One of his hands came up to her neck. His fingers weaved through her wet hair, gathering it in his fist and *pulling* hard enough for her to feel the sting on her scalp. His thumb pressed into her jaw, pushing and guiding her right where he wanted her as he dragged his lips over hers again and again until hers were raw and tingling.

She matched him, pouring everything into it. All the *burning*, which was a compilation of the rage and the fear and the hopelessness and the frustration and the confusion. Everything. She just wanted to fall. To not think. To forget.

Lena rotated her hips, and a low growl came from the back of Tuck's throat. Something unfurled in her chest, dropping lower into her gut and blooming there as she slotted her lips against his. She felt a sharp sting on her lower lip and the taste of blood smeared over their tongues again.

She rose up, brushing her lips across his cheek. He kissed along her jaw, rough and open-mouthed. When they crashed back together, he shifted over and she moved a hand to brace herself—

Tuck cursed and jerked away from her, half rolling onto his side, and she quickly slid off him, almost tumbling off the bed. She managed to get her trembling legs under her just in time to avoid falling completely onto the floor, but she couldn't find her balance. She stumbled against the wall. One of her hands slid against it. A thick gel covered that hand.

Tuck was still hunched over and breathing heavily through his nose, one of his hands hovering over his wound. He pushed himself up and winced. She froze when they locked eyes.

"That was a mistake," she blurted out. She raised her hand to her lips but stopped midway.

His chest rose and fell as he tried to catch his breath. She was having much of the same problem. "Was it? It didn't feel like a mistake."

Lena swallowed and pushed away from the wall. "It was. We were both . . . angry and—as you said . . . we just use each other when it's convenient."

Her words sounded so loud in the room, and she realized it was because the storm was dying down. Good. The sooner it let up, the sooner she could leave.

She'd done her part. She'd found Tuck and made sure he was okay.

"Right. So we're just going to pretend like you weren't kissing me back—"

"I need to wash up."

She marched past him, heading for the door, and slipped into the hallway before he could say anything else. She didn't know where the washroom was, but there must be one behind one of the doors in the hall.

Once she found it, she stepped inside and looked at her reflection. Her lips were swollen and red, her hair wet and tousled. There was a smear of blood next to her lips and along her jaw.

She turned on the faucet and wiped off the marks. And then she drank a few mouthfuls of water, trying to wash away the taste of him and the memory of what they'd just done.

What the fuck was I thinking?

But she already knew the answer to that. She hadn't been *thinking*. She'd been *feeling*. The rage, resentment, and tension had led her to that.

Tuck had certainly managed to make her hate him more, but not for the reason he'd intended.

She braced her hands on either side of the sink and dipped her head.

What was wrong with her?

She and Ira had an understanding about going to others for . . . needs. Ira didn't like it; he'd made that very clear. Still, she could have another partner, just as he could, but they hadn't because there was no one else. She didn't even *like* Tuck. That'd happened in a fit of passion. It didn't mean anything. She was overwhelmed, and he'd been there, and that was it.

Lena didn't look at her reflection again, afraid that she'd see the truth written across her face.

She stayed in the washroom until she talked herself into going back out. Finding an empty room was easy enough.

She searched through the dresser and only found a larger shirt that smelled like it hadn't been washed in ages, but it was still better than nothing.

She took off her boots and damp clothes—her cloak was still in the room with Tuck—and hung them over the foot of the bed. After slipping the shirt over her head, she curled up on the old bed and listened to the waning storm.

Her heart was still pounding in her chest. It took her nearly thirty minutes to fall asleep.

~

LENA WOKE to the sound of a bell ringing.

She sat up straight, momentarily dazed and confused as to where she was. But everything came flooding back to her quickly. Tuck being attacked by Ira. Her searching for Tuck. Them arguing. Their kiss.

She scrambled out of bed and reached for her clothes and boots. She noticed that her cloak was now draped over the railing of the bed frame. Tuck had obviously come in here while she was sleeping . . . in nothing but a shirt. Lovely.

Lena changed quickly. It was still light outside, meaning she'd only slept for about an hour or well over twelve. With all the jitters coursing through her, it was hard to tell.

She raced out into the hall as the bell in the distance chimed again. She recognized it now as the palace bell. Two gongs signaled the start of a trial. An important one. The entire council was supposed to be present at these trials, but no one had told her one was happening today.

Tuck was already up and fully dressed in a cloak of his own, tucking daggers away when she came down. He spared a glance in her direction, and her chest tightened when his eyes met hers, but she quickly pushed any feelings aside.

"Do you know who the trial is for?" she asked as she walked up to him.

"I have an idea."

Alkus.

"Did you know it was happening?"

He shook his head, and she frowned. She could've accepted the fact that maybe she'd missed the announcement because of everything she'd been dealing with, but Tuck always seemed to know what was happening around the palace. They needed to move.

Eldon walked up to Tuck and patted him on the shoulder. "Stay safe. I don't want to see you back here in that condition again."

Tuck smiled softly. "It's part of the job."

Eldon gave him a pointed look as if to say *don't make me repeat myself*. He glanced at Lena again before he walked off. Yeah, he still didn't like her.

"You're okay to travel?" she asked Tuck.

"Sure."

When they stepped out of the building, one of Tuck's arms emerged from his cloak. He held out his hand to her, and between two fingers was one of his daggers. She looked at him in surprise.

"For your peace of mind," was all he supplied.

As soon as she took the dagger, he strode forward. She stared at the weapon for only a moment before concealing it under her cloak and hurrying after him.

The sky was stormy, and a few inches of water flooded the ground, which led her to believe that she'd only been asleep for an hour or so.

Now that it wasn't pouring, she could see the surrounding area and the additional four buildings that occupied it. This type of place was too small to be considered a town and something she would expect to see in the Lowlands, but she knew they were still in the Highlands. She'd seen the base of the mountains behind the hill earlier before the rain began falling in sheets. And it didn't take them long at all the reach the palace. The golden spires came into view after about twenty minutes of traveling.

Lena paused when they approached and she saw just how many people were lined up in the front lawn, waiting to be let inside. Trials in the palace were open to the public, but she was surprised that many people had shown up on such short notice.

"Let's go," Tuck said, nodding to the side.

She jogged after him and they easily slipped through a hidden side entrance.

"We're not going to make it to the throne room without someone stopping us," she whispered.

"That's why we're taking the servants' corridor."

They came across a few servants in the hallway, which was inevitable, and the staff's eyes lit up in surprise when they saw Tuck and Lena together. They had their hoods up, but no sorcery was involved this time to conceal identities. The rumors from the infirmary had likely already spread, and she recognized that this did nothing to quell them, but gossip wasn't her top concern at the moment.

The corridor didn't lead all the way to the throne room, so they had to exit and move into the public halls, which were flooded with spectators from the city. Guards stood up ahead before the doors leading into the throne room.

Tuck inched his way through the crowd, and she followed closely behind, moving into the space he'd cleared out.

"The throne room is full," one of the guards said. "No one else can enter."

Tuck stepped in front of her. "I need to get into that room."

The woman turned, nearly rolling her eyes. She opened her mouth, likely to reiterate what she'd just said, but her eyes widened when she caught sight of who stood in front of her. Seemed like Tuck was recognizable among *all* the staff. The guard hadn't even looked at her.

"Ah, of course, sir."

They were quickly ushered around the throne room to an entrance strictly accessible to royal Blessed and those on the council. The two of them slipped into the room unnoticed. The trial had already begun, and Prophet Mikhail was speaking at the front of the room.

Lena moved forward, squeezing past people until she found a spot right next to a pillar that allowed her to see the floor. Sure enough, Alkus knelt before the towering stairs the council members sat on. So many seats were empty, including Lena's own. Ira's was too, but he was present, much to her surprise. He stood next to her throne at the top of the platform.

"Do you understand the severity of your crimes?" Prophet Mikhail asked Alkus.

Ira's eyes rose, immediately finding hers from across the room. There was a dark resignation in them that made her heart stop.

No. Ira, no.

"I'm being framed," Alkus hissed, "by the outsiders. Neither of them belong here. They'll ruin The Lands."

Murmurs rose across the room. A law master banged their gavel on the table to silence everyone.

"Alkus," Prophet Mikhail scolded, but the expression on his face gave away how he truly felt. He was slipping. He was putting on a show. This was what was expected of him, but he didn't agree with it. "How do you plead?"

"Innocent—"

"I have a question," Ira cut in, his voice smooth and low, yet it traveled across the room. He began to make his way down the stairs, slowly.

Prophet Mikhail frowned at the interruption. "Councilman—"

"Did you poison our queen?" Ira continued. "When she fell ill suddenly and was confined to our home in the Lowlands, was that your doing?"

Lena's eyes widened. *Poisoned?* Ira had never mentioned such a thing to her.

"I want the truth," he said coldly, his gaze firmly fixed on the councilman kneeling below him.

He reached the bottom of the stairs right as Alkus answered.

"No." The word sounded like it had been ripped out of him. Short and strained. Alkus inhaled sharply. "But I should've."

Gasps erupted and the crowd began to shift. The woman next to her stepped on her boot, but Lena barely noticed. Her eyes were stuck on the scene in front of her.

Alkus fought against the binding that restrained his arms behind his back and went to stand, but one of the guards next to him shoved him down. Lena recognized the guard as one of the dozen who had found her and Tuck in the forest.

"My biggest regret is letting her live for this long!"

Tuck's hand touched her elbow.

"This place would be better without her. You'll all see! But by then, it'll be too late."

Silence fell over the room. Even Prophet Mikhail seemed at a loss for words. Ira stared down at Alkus with a cold gaze that made shivers rise across her skin. Tuck's hand tightened on her elbow.

A second later, the stained-glass window on the right side of the throne shattered and an *Ateisha* jumped in. It dashed across the marble floors, stopped right in front of Alkus, and took off his head with a single bite. His body remained upright for a few seconds before slowly tilting over and smacking against the floor.

CHAPTER
SEVENTY-NINE

Screams quickly filled the room and everyone scrambled for the exits. Lena was flattened against the pillar as people rushed past her. She could hardly move as she stared at the *Ateisha* in the middle of the room with Alkus' lifeless body next to it.

The pool of blood spread across the marble floor. The *Ateisha* didn't finish its meal. It immediately screeched and ran forward to attack its next victim, which just so happened to be the fleeing Grand Prophet. Mikhail's strangled scream was cut off as the *Ateisha* pounced on him, completely ignoring the other people around it.

Tuck tugged on her arm. "Lena! Let's go!"

Her eyes moved across the room, latching onto Ira, who still stood center stage despite the chaos unfolding. He appeared completely calm as more *Ateisha* crawled through the stained-glass windows. None of the monsters attacked him. They moved past him as if he wasn't there at all, tackling and tearing into anyone within reach, especially council members and anyone of high station.

Slayers were summoned, but the Blessed were more focused on escaping the danger than fighting it. Most of them had likely never faced a threat like this in their life and the fear had taken over.

For every Slayer that appeared, two more *Ateisha* entered the throne room. And without level-headed Blessed to control them, the Slayers ran wild.

Ira's eyes weren't on hers, but she felt him in her mind.

Don't run.

"Lena! We need to move!" Tuck growled. He pulled her back now, not waiting for her to snap to her senses.

The *Ateisha* were getting closer. Blood coated the floor.

Lena ... don't—

She fortified her mind and shoved Ira out. She ran along with Tuck. The exits were flooded with people trying to get to safety, but all the panic and disorder forced the flow to a near standstill.

She looked over her shoulder. Her Imprint heated and she prepared to release her own Slayer, but then Tuck squeezed her arm, and her skin began to tingle. There was a crack and her body felt both weightless and like it was being stretched from a million different angles. Then she was somewhere else.

A startled noise escaped her throat and she stumbled to the side, but Tuck kept a firm grip on her, making sure she stayed upright. They were still in the palace but in a less busy hall now.

She turned on Tuck. "What was that?"

His eyes were glowing, meaning his Slayer was out. Not here but somewhere else. He let go of her arm. "*That* is how I got away from him."

He had a Flair like Ira. Teleportation, or something like it. A Flair like that would certainly be useful during espionage.

"He's attacking The Lands," she breathed out, turning back toward the screams and the direction the hordes of people were running from.

He'd killed people. Lied to her. He was taking this too far, just like Tuck had said he would. She'd never thought Ira would go to these lengths. He was taking over The Lands. He was taking it from her. This wasn't a random attack. This was planned and calculated. This was a coup.

"You shouldn't be surprised."

She remained frozen in the middle of the hall, waiting for the moment when the screams and the people running around her would disappear and she would wake up in the building on the hilltop. She had to be dreaming. This was another nightmare.

"Lena!" Tuck yelled, causing her to jerk out of her panicked thoughts. "We need to keep moving."

She felt Ira banging against the walls in her mind, demanding to be let through, but she shook her head and lurched forward when someone roughly knocked into her while running past.

"And go where?" It came to her a split second later. "The bell."

"What about it?"

"We need to warn the others. Send out some sort of alarm."

Lena didn't know how far the *Ateisha* had gotten. The Cursed were defenseless in the Lowlands. Jhai was down there with her family. Cora and Nell too. They deserved a warning.

Tuck hesitated. More people ran past them. Her chest clenched with each scream she heard and with each smear of blood she saw.

She was the queen. She'd always wanted the power but not the responsibility that came with the position. Though she'd known what coming back would mean.

What would be expected of her—to a certain extent. Most of these people wouldn't do a thing if they saw her or any other Cursed starving on the street, but she was expected to protect them all the same.

She had failed at protecting them, at doing her job. She'd turned her back on The Lands twice—once when she stayed away and again when she came back only to do nothing in the short run but serve her own interests. She knew she wasn't cut out to be queen, but she'd thought she could pretend, and maybe, after all this, when she had time to rest and learn and listen, she could be better.

Was this fate? Were the Blessed getting what had always been coming for them? Was she?

She shoved those thoughts aside. Now was not the time to drown in self-hatred or self-pity.

"You've been telling me to act like a queen and do my job, so I am," she told Tuck. "I'm going up to the bell. I don't care if you come with me."

She turned but stopped when she saw the person at the other end of the corridor. For whatever reason, Blessed were no longer running down this hall, so it was nearly empty. The only people in it were her, Tuck, and Kieryn, who walked toward them at an unhurried pace. He dragged a sword behind him, the bloodied blade scraping against the ground. He didn't seem to see them at first, but as soon as he looked up, he stopped. His hair was messy, falling around his face, and blood coated his clothes.

For a moment, no one moved. And then Kieryn marched toward her.

"Kieryn—"

He swung the sword up and pointed the blade at her. She snapped her mouth shut. His blue eyes were ice-cold, and they didn't divert from her face even when Tuck stepped forward.

"Tell me why I shouldn't cut you down right here?"

"Kieryn," Tuck said next to her, his voice strained. "She didn't know."

If a sword wasn't pointed to her throat, she might've turned toward Tuck. Not only was he defending her, but he was also lying for her. She hadn't known Ira would do this, but she had known a lot.

Kieryn waved his hand, and the sword moved dangerously along with it, slicing through the air under her chin.

"How?" he demanded. "How did she not know when her *husband* is the one behind all of this?"

"I should have," she admitted, keeping still. "But I was blind and . . . I should've paid more attention, but I'm not on his side." Not with this attack. Not with *this*. "Please, believe me. I wouldn't support this. He's . . . taken this too far. He needs to be stopped."

Her heart plummeted to the bottom of her stomach. The words echoed in her head.

He needs to be stopped.

He needs to be stopped.

He was the enemy now. *Her* enemy.

Kieryn stared her down, assessing her. A muscle in his jaw flexed. "He sent guards to our rooms earlier—Sorrel's, Von's, and mine—and they turned into those . . . *monsters*. Sorrel and Von didn't make it. They're dead."

Lena felt the blood drain from her face. Ira had attacked their guests? He'd had Von and Sorrel *killed*? What the *fuck* was he thinking? The alliance . . .

There were other matters at hand that were more important right now. The alliance wouldn't matter if The Lands didn't make it out of this.

"I'm sorry—"

"Don't apologize," Kieryn snapped. He looked over her, eyes still cold, and then Tuck before lowering his sword. "You say you're not on his side? Prove it."

A sense of foreboding came over her then, and she tensed right as a Slayer came through the wall and leaped at them. Tuck's Slayer crashed into it a moment later in midair, causing the two to skid down the hall in a flurry of tangled limbs and claws.

The walls rushed at them, breaking away from the beams and surfaces they were attached to. Lena dove out of the way, but she wasn't moving fast enough. She threw her arms out and aura flame unfurled over them, melting through the walls and protecting her when they collapsed over her.

There was dust in the air, making it hard to see. She looked around at the piles of rubble surrounding her for Kieryn and Tuck. Tuck's Slayer was still standing, which meant he was okay. She saw him a moment later, kicking the rubble away with a snarl on his face. Kieryn stood at the side of the hall.

"Fucking Frawley," Tuck sneered.

When the dust settled, she saw a group of people standing at the other end of the hall. Prophet Nya was at the front, and next to her were two people wearing council robes. One of them was Gael Frawley. He was an elected council member. So was the other one, Lorelei Heine. They were the council members Ira had been trying to sway to their side. Except now, Lena supposed it hadn't been *her* side. It had been his. Behind the three of them stood dozens of guards.

"Your Majesty," Prophet Nya said, "if you could come with us that would be greatly appreciated."

Lena glared at the prophet and didn't move an inch. "So this is what you and Ira were meeting about then? Taking over The Lands?"

Prophet Nya hardly blinked at the heavy accusation. "He's waiting for you, and he will explain everything once—"

Lena laughed harshly. "I've heard that one before. What did he promise you? Power? Money?" She gave the prophet a feral grin. "He's a sweet talker like that. He can make you agree to almost anything."

Out of the corner of her eye, she saw Kieryn inching his way toward her. Tuck was still behind her. The guards were watching the three of them, and Frawley had his gaze on Tuck.

Something flashed in Prophet Nya's eyes. Looked like Lena had hit a nerve. But the prophet smoothed down her ruffled feathers quickly enough. "Don't make things harder than they need to be."

"You're attacking The Lands," she said between gritted teeth. "You expect me to throw my hands up in the air and surrender?"

It was clear by the silence that the prophet did.

Lena narrowed her eyes and took a step back, grabbing the dagger Tuck had given her earlier. The guards behind the prophet shuffled as if preparing to attack.

"I'm not going anywhere with you," she said before throwing the dagger at Prophet Nya.

Everything snapped into motion.

A piece of rubble rose and collided with the dagger, throwing it off course. Lena unleashed her Slayer as others were summoned, and the guards charged forward.

But then everything stopped as quickly as it had started. All the Slayers but hers and Tuck's disappeared.

Everyone in front of her appeared stuck, almost like they were trapped in an invisible hold. They tried to break out but couldn't. The panic in their eyes was visible.

Kieryn stepped forward, his hands raised. He brought them down, slowly, and the swords fell from the guards' hands. She looked at him, eyes wide and mouth agape. He glanced over his shoulder at her and Tuck, a bead of blood trailing from his nose.

"Go," he told them. "I'll hold them off for a while so you can get a head start."

There must've been five dozen people Kieryn had under his influence. She could see the strain it was causing him, so she wasn't going to waste his efforts.

"Thank you," she said sincerely as she backpedaled.

"Kalena, one more thing," Kieryn said. His breath was already coming out shorter. "The barriers in your mind. They don't work. Maybe they do for amateurs, but anyone knowledgeable in sorcery can bypass them. If you want to block people out, you need something stronger. A rune or a spell or something."

Lena frowned. "So this whole time—?"

"*Yes*. Now go."

He'd been able to get inside her head. And Ira?

"What about you?" Tuck asked him.

Kieryn smirked. "Give me some credit. I can take care of myself."

"You're being foolish—"

"*I'm* not the one being foolish," Kieryn barked. He turned back to the others as the blood dripped off his chin. "Go!"

Tuck appeared conflicted. "Stay safe," he said at last before wrapping his hand around her arm.

A tingling came over her skin again and then she was weightless and aching for a moment. A snap sounded and she stood in the bell tower at the very top of the palace. Tuck released her and leaned against the wall.

She turned with him, eyes raking over his body. "Are you okay? Tuck?"

Were his injuries still bothering him that much? Using a Flair could be tiresome, and a Flair like Tuck's seemed like it would require a great deal of energy. And he'd used it multiple times, while already not having a lot of energy to spare.

He straightened and took a deep breath. "I'm fine."

Lena had to trust that he was telling the truth.

She spun and gazed up at the huge golden bell that hung in the middle of the bell tower.

Four gongs for danger.

She stood at the edge of the tower's center and grabbed the thick rope under the bell, pulling it toward her and away. *One. Two. Three. Four.* She paused, letting out a heavy breath. And then she did it again. And again. And again.

"Shit," Tuck breathed out behind her.

She dropped the rope and followed his gaze. Smoke was rising from the north part of the palace closest to the mountains. But that wasn't what had caught his attention. In the distance, *Ateisha* sprinted down the mountainside in droves. There must've been thousands, maybe even tens of thousands of them, and they were heading for The Lands.

Lena had seen how they'd acted in the throne room. How Ira had acted. He seemed to be . . . controlling them. Calling them here.

Why was he doing this? What could he possibly be thinking? At this rate, there would hardly be any survivors.

She raced across the bell tower and looked at the other side. The Lowlands still looked relatively untouched, but it wouldn't be for long. She could only hope that her warning had saved some of them.

There were hundreds of thousands of innocent people out there. No one could outrun the *Ateisha*. Few would be able to fight them even with a Slayer because they were simply outnumbered. The Lands, in a matter of hours, would be coated in blood if things continued this way.

Her legs threatened to give, but she clutched onto the railing for support. Her eyes stung as she lowered the barriers in her mind, now unsure if they'd ever even done anything. He'd lied to her about that too.

Stop. Stop this. I'm coming.

There was silence. And then relief. It coursed through her, alleviating the dull ache she felt in her skull.

I'll be waiting, he said.

She took a deep, unsteady breath. "I'm going to talk with Ira."

"What?" Tuck spat, looking at her as if she'd lost it. Maybe she had. "No, you're not."

"Yes, I am. That's the only way this can end."

It was the truth, as much as it pained her to say. If Ira was controlling the *Ateisha*, the bloodbath would only stop if he got what he wanted. And he wanted her. And she would be lying if she said she didn't want answers.

"You think it will end after a chat with him?" Tuck fired back. "He's made his choice. This won't end unless he's dead."

Her stomach lurched violently, and her throat constricted. "No," she said quickly. "He'll see reason. Eventually—"

"There is no reasoning with him—"

"You don't know him like I do!"

You don't love him. You don't understand. Ira isn't a bad person.

Tuck shook his head. "He'll only confuse you further. He needs to go—"

"I can think for myself."

But Tuck had no reason to believe that, did he? He thought Ira was controlling her. She just had to believe that there was a way to get through to Ira. She wouldn't . . . She *couldn't* accept that losing him permanently was the answer.

"Can you?" Tuck challenged.

"Let me take care of him." She wasn't asking permission. She was telling Tuck to *back off*. "*Please*."

His eyes bore into hers. "Fine."

She was surprised but relieved that he'd agreed. He had to see that this was the best way. Ira wouldn't cooperate with anyone else.

Tuck slid something out of his sleeve and held it out to her. A blade about the length of his index finger. "But if you can't persuade him to end this, you need to end him."

She recoiled. "What? No."

"You despise the Blessed for what they've done. Ira will do the exact same thing if you allow this to continue."

He wouldn't. That was on the tip of her tongue, but she couldn't speak it aloud.

A coldness wrapped around her as she took the blade and tucked it away in her sleeve. "It won't come to that."

Tuck still watched her skeptically. "Remember what's on the line. Don't let him control you."

She nodded and went looking for Ira.

CHAPTER
EIGHTY

Lena could feel where he was as soon as she left the bell tower. Their bond drew her toward him. It was a strong pull in her gut.

She ended up on the second floor in the main hall. At the end of the corridor was a dancing hall if she remembered correctly. Her stomach flipped when she saw the smear of blood on the floor that trailed through the cracked doors. She hesitated before entering.

This was Ira she was seeing. She shouldn't be scared, but she was. She was scared of what he would tell her, yet that was what she wanted—the truth, no matter how fearsome it might be. She was scared for him, but *of* him? Ira wouldn't hurt her. Parts of him she knew were slipping away and new parts she'd never met before were taking their place, but she was certain about that. He wouldn't hurt her.

Lena repeated that to herself as she stepped through the doors and into the room. Ira stood in the middle of the space, right under the chandelier. He was dressed for a ball, not a slaughter.

He turned to her, his expression solemn.

"Why?" she demanded.

"This realm . . . this way of living . . . it's *wrong*, Lena."

"But mass murdering an entire country isn't? That's your solution?"

Ira walked forward but stopped when she took a step back. His eyes wavered as if it hurt him to see her like this. She could say the same.

"I don't want to kill," he said slowly, *earnestly*. "I don't. Believe me. But . . . " His jaw clenched. A brief flash of torment rippled across his face. "You know about Atreus."

She hesitated, and then nodded. "Weylin told me."

"He told you what he knew, but it wasn't everything. And even still . . . you can't understand. Because you weren't *there*. Life in the Institute . . . was anyone's worst nightmare. And Weylin's explanation certainly didn't do it justice." His eyes were glazed over, a far-away look filling them. "We were forced to fight to survive. We worked in the mines and attended seminar where the prophets told us we were sinful beasts—*abominations*—with smiles on their faces. They looked down on us. They said *we* were the monsters while sending us to other realms to fight the *Te'Monai* with nothing but a knife. And we were expected to just *carry on* each time after that. You had to keep moving—*fighting*—or you died. And the Numina that had made pacts with us weren't there to protect us. Our abilities were useless with our Imprints sealed. We were all alone. No one cared. Not the prophets. Not the people—the Blessed or the Cursed. We were *kids!*"

Her chest ached. "But you're *murdering* kids."

"Not them," he said, shaking his head. "They're innocent in all this."

She felt a small ounce of relief, but it was quickly squashed by the perpetual dread that seemed to reside within her. "Children aren't the only innocents. You're attacking hundreds of thousands of guiltless people!"

"They'll get a chance. The *Ateisha* aren't going after everyone. Only those in power. Those likely to resist."

The terror inside of her only grew, blooming in her chest. "Resist what?"

"Change. That's what you want, isn't it? How did you think it was going to go? You kill those who played a part in your family's murder and then what? Ask nicely? These people won't change voluntarily. That's not how it works. All you will accomplish is gaining more enemies. When they realize you won't back down, they'll come after you again. Even the Cursed. They're using you because it's convenient. They may claim to want change, but only change that they're comfortable with. What about the rest? What about the firstborns?"

"We can stop it—"

"Only like this."

"No." Her voice trembled. "*No! This*"—she swung her arm out behind her—"is not the right way—"

"You're wrong," he said, his voice cold, his face a mask of silent fury. "This is *exactly* how you enact change when people won't listen!"

"*This is slaughter!*"

"*This is healing!*" His voice boomed through the room. "Not now, but it will be for future generations. The longer we avoid this change, the longer children will suffer. The longer the *people* will suffer. We were forced to live that life in the Institute, fight for our lives as *children*. *We* were tortured and slaughtered because of this ideology that those in power support and everyone else perpetuates. No one questions it! Not even you! I saw the hesitation in your eyes in the infirmary, the horror, and you turned your back on it. *You* walked away first. I only followed suit. In what realm is it okay for a newborn child to be ripped away from their bearer's arms and raised in a place where they are hated? It's normalized, and that's the problem. The only way to get rid of an ideology is to destroy all traces of it. The temples. The books. The people."

His words sparked something in her. "That was you? The break-in at the temple?"

Ira stared at her evenly, answering her question without having to say anything.

"You killed Sorrel and Von," she choked out. "You obliterated all chances we had at forming an alliance with Ouprua. How will that help future generations?"

"We don't need them."

"We do!"

"We won't," he said resolutely.

Lena wanted to scream. "Not everyone supports the way things are." She thought of the women at the trial. "I'm sure if you talked to the people, shared your experience, and told them what life for firstborns was really like, then they would back you—"

"That's naive. And why should I do that? Why should I display the horrors of my past so they can decide if they want to change? It's not enough. They would rebel against me just as they would against you." He took another step closer. "These people are brainwashed. They see giving up their firstborn as a necessary sacrifice. They don't ask questions. They might say they care, but they still hand over their child all the same. And if they don't, they'll be hunted down and thrown in prison while their child is taken anyway. And guess what? The *baby* is blamed for the parents' rebellious actions, because surely the evil of the child must've been what convinced the parents to do such a thing. And then that child is marked, ostracized, tortured more than the rest—"

"Stop."

"Does it make you sick?" he goaded, his eyes electric. "It should. Most people truly believe this is what they must do to keep the peace and prevent another war. Some of them even think this is their way of repenting for their sins. They think they need to give up their child to keep the Numina happy." He took another step forward, his eyes softening slightly. "This is the only way. Everyone is looking at *me*."

"So that's your plan? Wipe out the leaders and take their place?" She swallowed roughly and then asked, "Are you going to get rid of me too?"

"No," he said quickly, shaking his head. "No."

"Call off the *Ateisha*," she pleaded.

"I can't. Not yet."

"You *can*." She dared to move closer, now within arm's reach. "We can find another way. *Together*. I know the truth now. Or part of it. You can tell me the rest. I'll stay. I'll listen. *I promise*. And then we can figure this out."

"It's going to end the same way. If I agree, all we'll be doing is wasting time."

How could he be so set on *this*? So casual about it? He must've been planning it for some time. Before she even came back.

"So, it's true then? You're controlling the *Ateisha*?"

He hadn't denied it seconds ago, and he didn't deny it now.

"How?"

He remained silent.

Why was he still hiding things from her? She knew about his past, about the lengths he was willing to go to.

"You're targeting *everyone*. Even if they're not killed, what's going to happen to them?"

"They get to choose," he said. "Leave or die."

Tears flooded her eyes. "That's not a choice."

"It is. That's what it's down to now. They had centuries to make a choice to turn things around, and they didn't."

Lena tightened her fists, but her whole body was trembling. "What about my people?"

The look he gave her was mournful. "Those people are not your people—"

"They are," she insisted. "I grew up down there. For a time, I was scared and helpless just like them."

"But you're different. You're special. The Numina *chose* you."

"*What's special about you has nothing to do with you.*"

The memory came back to her sharply, digging its claws into her mind.

"*I made a pact with you, but you weren't the first.*"

"*I made a pact with him.*"

She took a step back. "No. I'm not. I know about a lot more than Atreus. I know that the Numen I made a pact with made a deal with you first. It said you trapped it and forced it to help me in exchange for something."

Ira's face was carefully blank once again.

"Why? How would you even do something like trapping and threatening a Numen?"

"The Numina like to pretend that we and our desires are beneath them, but they *crave* just as we do," he said. "It's just a matter of finding out what they want."

"It said it only takes deals made in blood and being," she murmured. "Is that why you're killing people? Is that the sacrifice it demands for extending a pact to me?"

That would make sense. The numbers. The brutality. The secrecy. It would all make sense.

But he said, "No."

"So what did you give it? Why did you make the deal—?"

"Because I was scared for you!" His eyes flashed as he leaned forward. "Your family had just been killed. You were gone. I was being attacked, but at least I had a means to defend myself. I knew how difficult it could be—surviving; fighting—

without a way to defend yourself, but I didn't know what to do. I couldn't find you, but I knew the Numina could. The strongest weapon doesn't belong to us. It belongs to them. So I researched. *For years.* And eventually I found a way."

"Sorcery," she filled in, the word slipping from her mouth.

He nodded. "So I switched my focus to that. The only reason I learned was so I could help you. And it worked."

"At what cost?"

His smile dried up, turning acrid. "At a cost most are unwilling to pay."

"But you paid it?" she said hotly, fuming internally.

"Yes. And I would again. Without hesitation."

"How can you say that?"

And then do this? He was soft yet hard. Warm yet cold. These different sides of him pulled her this way and that. She didn't know what to believe.

"I know that you can bypass my mental barriers too," she said, watching his expression slowly unravel again. "You made me think that you couldn't easily get in my head, that I was in control, but this whole time you've been able to read my mind, haven't you?"

He didn't answer right away.

"*Tell me.*"

"It's not that simple. I can't always bypass them—"

"But you're able to? Sometimes?"

"Yes."

Her face crumpled and she took another step back.

He followed her. "But it's more complicated than you're making it. I didn't try —I *don't*. I swear to you. I wouldn't invade your mind like that, not unless I had to—"

"*Not unless you had to*? Why is that for you to decide?" She took another step back. How deep could he go inside her head? What all could he see?

"I'm sorry," he said, his face twisted and his hand out as he approached, like he was trying to calm a wild animal. "You're right. I'm sorry. But just know I'm telling the truth about this. I didn't invade—"

"I can't know that!" she shot back. "You've lied to me about too many things. I *can't* believe you!"

"Yes, you can," he urged, his eyes shining. "Everything I've said to you in this room is the truth."

"That doesn't make it any better," she cried. *"Look what you're doing!"* To The Lands. To the people. To her. "You're tearing things apart. You know what it's like out there when you're alone and defenseless, so how can you not see what you're doing to these people is exactly what those prophets were doing to you?"

His gaze darkened. "I'm not like them. You can't make comparisons to something you never knew."

"You're sentencing those people out there to die!"

"I told you they have a choice."

As a last attempt, she pushed down the walls she had built around herself, the ones that kept her somewhat whole and together and on her feet, and let everything pour out. Her voice was the weakest yet when she pitched forward, grabbing the front of his shirt. "I love you."

She had said it before, as a gentle reminder. But lately, she had only been using it as a plea.

Ira's face softened. She watched the stern lines melt away into the kind and loving person she knew. He raised his hands to cup her cheeks ever so gently. "I am on your side." His voice was hushed, his breath fanning across her face. "The question is: are you on mine? I will change the realm for you. Whatever you wish. I'll show you I can if you stick by my side."

Lena shook her head, but his hands held her still. "You can't. You're not listening to me—"

His grip tightened, not enough to hurt. "I *am*. There are things you don't understand. Not yet. But you will."

"Then make me understand," she cried. "You keep saying that—"

"I'm afraid," he admitted suddenly, his face crumpling as if he'd uttered a terrible secret into the realm. "I'm afraid if I tell you everything, I'll lose you."

"Ira," she lamented, her voice wet and ugly. "You can't change the realm. Not like this."

Not now.

"I *will*."

"You'll burn it down first."

"And I'll build something greater from the ashes." He rested his forehead against hers. "With you."

No, not with me.

Her lips trembled and her chest split at the thought alone. She was too weak to speak it aloud, but she supposed she didn't have to. He could read her mind. He knew. Tears flowed freely down her cheeks, and she couldn't stop them.

"Don't cry," he begged.

"You don't get to tell me that!" She wished she couldn't cry over him. "How did you expect me to react?"

Her home was being ripped from her again. Her people. Ira. Cowen. Her allies and friends were gone or fighting. She was going to be on her own. She couldn't do it again.

"I hoped it would be better," he said tonelessly.

She knocked his arms aside and stumbled back. "*Better?* You're killing everyone! You're overthrowing the current regime. *My regime.*" She spun to the side, her breaths coming out in heavy, short gasps. She wiped at her face. "This whole time you've been playing me, haven't you?"

"That's not true."

"It *is!* If you trusted me, why didn't you confide in me? I thought it was us against them?" She didn't dare turn back to him as she asked the question that she feared the most. "Do you even love me? Or was that all a lie too?"

"*No!*" Ira yelled with such conviction that his voice bounced off the tall ceilings. "That was never a lie." He paused. "You still doubt my feelings? What do I have to do to assure you that my love for you is *real*?"

Lena turned back around. "Call this entire operation off. Send everyone and everything back."

His shoulders slumped. He was looking at her like she was breaking his heart, which wasn't fair. He had broken hers first.

"You know I can't do that."

"Then I guess you don't love me as much as you claim," she said. She knew it was a cruel thing to say, but she didn't care.

Ira lurched forward. She stumbled back, but he caught up with her easily. She instinctively grabbed his wrists when he raised his hands to cradle her face. "Lena." He said her name pleadingly, his eyes wide and imploring. "*Please*, I—I'm sorry for lying. I don't like doing it, especially to you, but I'm trying to keep you safe."

"I didn't ask you to do that," she said, her voice loud and flat. "And right now, you're hurting me more than you're helping me."

"You're only saying that because you don't know everything."

"Then tell me and let me decide for myself."

She didn't expect him to give in. She'd asked him many times to tell her everything and he'd always met her with silence, brushing her off. But this time she saw a flicker of hesitation in his eyes as they searched her face.

"If you want me to explain, you have to let me finish."

Her eyes widened a fraction, and she nodded.

"I love you. That is not a lie. I need to start with that. I . . . thought the Outings were just a form of punishment at first. The prophets' way of keeping us in line and weeding us out, but I soon discovered it was more than that. The prophets had a plan."

He wasn't even looking at her anymore. He'd dipped his head, lost in his memories.

"I started coming across these stones in other realms. They . . . spoke to me, and when I touched them, they took the firstborns back to the Institute. They were gateways between realms, one of the only ways to travel since the shattering of the realms. And the prophets were collecting them. For a *weapon*. They were pure magic —*energy*. One alone has a great amount of power. Dozens . . . We didn't even want to think about what they were planning to do with it.

"I was curious about the stones and the prophets' agenda. The others prioritized getting out. They thought I would jeopardize the escape plan. That I was trying to play the hero." He gritted his teeth and a frustrated noise tore from his throat. "The prophets caught onto us. It was against their way to kill us directly, so they sent us to more dangerous places, hoping to get rid of us. We were advanced to new *stages*, and each stage brought a surprise, a change. And it was almost never good.

"I began to run into these sisters. I didn't understand what they were saying at first. It made no sense. It went against everything we had been taught in the Institute about the War of Krashing, Edynir Akonah, and Kerrick Ludoh. And it . . ." He laughed callously. "It sounded ridiculous. They told me that *I* was Edynir Akonah reincarnated. Unfortunately . . . it was the truth. Sometimes I hear him. In my head."

Her mind was barely wrapping itself around everything he was saying. "How's that possible?"

"A Cornerstone. He collected enough magic to preserve his consciousness in all his reincarnated selves."

Cornerstone. She remembered reading about that.

"I have a destiny to fulfill." He said that phrase like he had heard it a thousand times. "I'm the only one who can do this. People are counting on me, but . . . I can't be everyone's hero."

Lena released his wrists so she could lift his face. He was crying, she realized. She instinctively moved her thumbs to wipe away his tears. She'd never seen him cry before.

"The prophets lied about so much. *They* are the most dangerous of us all. The people listen to their words, believing that everything they say came from the Numina, but it doesn't. The prophets realize the power they hold, and they abuse it. The realms need to heal."

"No, Ira. No." Her cheeks were wet. Because of him. His torment. She could feel the ache in his voice. It came from somewhere deep in his chest. "You don't have to fix that—"

"I *do*. Don't you understand? I'm the only one who can. But the prophets —*Kerrick Ludoh*—cannot be alive when I do," he urged. "This is bigger than just us. I need the stones, so I can fix things."

Her hands fell from his cheeks. "You mean so you can power that weapon? How do you know it won't cause just as much damage as the War of Krashing?"

"Because I'll be in control of it."

Lena laughed cruelly and took a step back, out of his reach. "Is that supposed to reassure me? That *you*, the man attacking The Lands and overthrowing me, will be in charge of a weapon of this scale?"

His face fell. "You know me, even if your mind has been telling you something else, *you know that you know me.*"

"Get out of my head," she hissed.

"I'm not in it," he said honestly. "I just know you. Just like you know me."

She bit her lip, holding back a sob or a scream. "The man I loved wouldn't have done this."

"He did."

She closed her eyes. "My family?" she blurted out. "Their deaths. Their hearts. Did you—?"

"No, I promise. I wasn't lying about that. I wasn't involved."

"But someone you know was?" She opened her eyes again so she could see his reaction.

It was careful, as always. "Yes, but she's dead. I killed her."

"So you did lie to me," she said, venom coating her words. "You swore on their lives, and you *lied!*"

"Lena—"

"You don't deserve their name!" she hissed. "It doesn't matter what we are. *You will never be a Skathor!*"

His eyes were heartbroken. "I am," he argued. "I found a place. A family. You said—"

"I changed my mind. Or maybe I lied. It doesn't feel so good, does it? To be on the receiving end? How do I know you aren't lying to me about this person who killed my family?"

"Because I cared for your family too. I care for *you*. She hurt you, heavily. I couldn't let her live." His eyes glistened as he looked at her, *begging* her to understand. "And the people left on your list? They're dead too, or they will be soon. I made sure the *Ateisha* went after them first. For *you*."

She glared at him with tears in her eyes, hoping he could see everything, *feel* everything—her betrayal, her heartbreak, her disappointment, her rage, her finality.

"I'm sorry," he said quietly. "For what it's worth . . . I'm sorry."

She couldn't stop the tears. And the silence, the distance between them, only made things worse.

"Dance with me." He extended his hand. "You promised to save me a dance."

On the night of the first ball after she returned.

"I understand. You have responsibilities."

"Promise to save me a dance at the next ball?"

"I promise."

There had been more parties and events after that, but they hadn't gotten their dance. She realized with a heavy heart that this would be their first and their last.

She should reject him, but she didn't. A tear dripped off her chin as she took his hand. His fingers closed over hers and he pulled her into his arms, sweeping them away to the middle of the floor.

"Where's your other ring?" he murmured as his fingers squeezed hers.

"I took it off. It was heavy."

There was no music, but they were dancing. Both of his arms looped around her body, holding her close, hands settled just below the small of her back, warm and supporting. His chin rested on the top of her head. Her own arms were wrapped around his waist, cheek pressed against the hollow of his shoulder. Despite everything, his heartbeat was steady under her ear. She squeezed her eyes shut and swayed with him.

"I did try," he said softly. Each exhale fluttered her hair. "I fought for you. I always have and I always will."

He sounded so earnest, but his actions revealed more than his words ever could.

"Tell me about the Institute and the realms."

And he did.

Ira's account was much more detailed than Weylin's. He spoke of the time before the Institute. He had little memory of then. Part of that he attributed to the conditions he'd lived in. It was better that he didn't remember much, he said. He only wished it was the same for the time he'd spent in the Institute. He was moved there when he was nine, almost ten. He observed and worked in the mines for a few months before being sent on his first Outing. He would seclude himself and just watch. That was how he survived at first. He miraculously made it through the first Outing. Physically he was fine. Mentally? He didn't talk to anyone for days, not until one of the older firstborns came up to him and gave him some tips. Eve, her name was. He hesitated to call it a mentor-mentee relationship because it wasn't that. Everyone could only afford to look out for themselves in the Institute, and that idea was proven when the older firstborn was killed in front of Ira's eyes when she tried to save him in another realm.

He held on to that advice—that you could only afford to look out for yourself—but it kept slipping through his fingers. He fought against it constantly. He finally decided he'd help when he could, but he always put himself first. And that led to him witnessing more deaths than anyone else. Yet death never came for him. She could resonate with that.

He told her about the hatred Prophet Silas had held for him, what the prophet would scream at him in private. He told her where the scars on his back had come from. A whip. Her hands tightened around his waist and smoothed across the back of his shirt. It was thin, so she could feel the ridges of his scars.

He told her about Mila and Finn—the only two people he'd considered his friends. They'd wiggled themselves into his life pretty early on. One of them had died while the other had betrayed them all. He didn't go into detail about Finn's death, but she felt him tense. She heard the strain in his voice.

He mentioned Judah too and how he'd broken his rule for the kid thrown into this mess much too young. There was Vanik and Weylin and Harlow. They hadn't been his friends then, but they'd reached a mutual agreement and then soon relied upon one another. They'd saved him even though they'd disagreed with him on who to save and when to leave. In the end, only one of them could get out, and they had chosen him. He owed them.

He told her more. He told her about the Outings and the mines. The way he spoke about violence and death and the things the prophets would say to them with such indifference tore her apart. She'd known his life before had been difficult, but she hadn't known *how* difficult.

She didn't want to let him go. She wished they'd had this conversation earlier. She wished the realm was kinder and people didn't have to endure lives like this.

By the end, her tears had dried. The dread had settled, numbing her. She carefully removed the small blade in one quick flick. Ira's muscles remained relaxed. His breath was soft and even above her head. She took a deep breath and squeezed her eyes shut.

She wanted to wait. She wanted to believe that with just a few more minutes, he could be convinced, even though she'd been trying to get him to stop and understand for days now. There was still a chance. But after finding out all the lies and truths. After knowing what he believed and the scale of his plans. After hearing him speak, voice toneless at some parts, raging at others, full of conviction, she knew there was no going back. She couldn't hold out for him any longer. As he'd said, this was bigger than them.

"Are you going to stab me, Lena?"

Her breath escaped her all in one rush and she fought to keep from tensing. Was he in her mind?

"Do it. Carve open my chest and cut out my heart if you must so you can see it only beats for *you*."

Her hands began to tremble. He pulled back so he was looking down at her. If she moved her hand forward, drove the blade into his back, his life would end, but would his attack? He'd planned this. He had allies that might continue to carry out this onslaught. And what would happen to the *Ateisha* if he was gone? Would they return to the mountains or continue to carry on their slaughter? Would killing him achieve anything other than sending a message and breaking her heart permanently?

He moved back farther, grabbing her hand that held the dagger. He brought it in front of him, and she let him because she was weak. He made her that way.

His eyes darkened when he noticed the design. "Him?" He said the word like it was the ultimate betrayal. He ripped the blade out of her hand and threw it across the floor. And again, like an utter fool, she let him. "You're choosing him?"

"Choosing him?" she echoed. "As opposed to you? It doesn't work like that."

His jaw clenched. "You forgive him so easily?"

"Easily? Forgiveness?" Lena narrowed her eyes. She didn't owe him anything past what she'd already given him. She lowered her voice. "Do you think I'll forgive you so easily?"

His brows furrowed. "You have to," he said, his voice strained.

"No, I don't."

And then a series of events happened in a matter of seconds.

A crack sounded and then a blade was heading right for Ira's neck. He ducked out of the way and drew his sword. When he swung it around, he clashed blades with Cowen who had teleported alongside Tuck.

Tuck surged forward to grab Lena, but a body materialized between them. She instinctively reached for the other dagger she still had tucked away on her, but the person moved quickly. In the blink of an eye, they were out of reach and attacking Tuck. Anyone else would've been too slow to deflect that blow, but Tuck made it. She realized a moment later that the newcomer was Weylin.

"Oh?" Weylin said, his eyes lighting up with intrigue as he looked at Tuck. "You're fast."

The hairs on the back of Lena's neck stood. She released her Slayer just in time for it to collide with the one rushing up behind her. She turned, seeing the Slayers tumble away out of the corner of her eye, snarling and scratching at one another.

A woman stood several feet away. She gave Lena a feral grin, spinning the axes in her hands.

"You're mine," she said before leaping at her.

CHAPTER
EIGHTY-ONE

The dagger wasn't going to hold up against the woman's dual axes. Aura flame covered Lena's chest and arms, licking out from her Imprint. She shot out one hand, sending a wave of aura flame toward the approaching woman, but she countered it with her own golden one. The purple and gold swirled together violently before shooting up into the air and disappearing.

Lena threw up her other arm, creating a wall of aura flame. The woman snarled and took a step back, her golden aura flame spreading across her hands and arms to protect her. It gave Lena enough time to create more distance between them, but the woman was ruthless.

They clashed together again, gold and purple meeting, axe and dagger colliding. Lena gritted her teeth and pulled back, her hands and arms momentarily numb from the impact. She blocked the woman's attack with aura flame, but the woman did the same, pushing her back farther and farther until she was nearly retreating from the barrage. A noise of frustration tore from Lena's throat, and she surged forward suddenly, slipping past the protective barrier her aura flame shield provided and sliding in close to her attacker, which might not have been a bright move, but she fought best when she fought wild.

Her aura flame canceled out the woman's, creating a big enough opening that allowed her to swoop in close. She barely felt the heat gliding across her feet and head as she switched her grip on the dagger and dodged an axe swing, but she wasn't able to dodge the knee that shot up and smashed against her ribs. She grunted and stabbed her dagger down toward one of the woman's hands as she *roared*.

The woman reeled back as the cloud of aura flame headed directly for her face. Golden aura flame shot up to meet it, but she was caught off guard, just as Cressida had been. Lena's dagger skimmed over the woman's fingers. She might've hissed—Lena couldn't hear over all the noise—but she did what Lena wanted her to do and loosened her grip, allowing Lena to take the axe for herself. Though the woman recovered rather quickly and was coming back for her.

The other axe cut through the air horizontally, aiming for Lena's neck. She moved with the blade, ducking and scrambling back. By the time she was swinging her head up, the woman was in her face again. The axe came down. A wave of purple aura flame and a twin axe met it. They were on even ground now. Axe and axe. Aura flame and aura flame. They were locked in a struggle, going nowhere.

Her gaze flickered away for a second. Tuck was battling Ira. They both had snarls on their faces, but Tuck was straining. Cowen had a nasty gash on his forehead and still was pale and worn. They were both fighting hard, but they couldn't keep this up for much longer.

"*Harlow!*" Ira's voice thundered across the room, causing the woman she was battling to hesitate.

Lena moved in, gathering up all the power she had and letting out a cry as she shoved against the woman's axe.

Harlow's eyes widened as she fell back.

Lena's aura flame expanded. Everything seemed to move in slow motion as purple wisps of pure power covered the room. And shattered it.

The walls fell, the ceiling crumbled, and the floor caved. Her chest seized as she became weightless, and she called out in blind panic. Her Slayer came to her, cushioning her fall when she hit the rubble below. Dust and debris rose into the air. Coughs racked her throat as she slowly raised herself on uneven legs, stumbling over the remnants of the ballroom and swiping away at the dust that clouded the air, searching for Cowen and Tuck.

She didn't know what had just happened. That was . . . that was her. She'd done that, but she didn't know how. And she didn't have time to fathom how. They were still in the middle of a fight.

The dust in front of her was sucked away and Ira came through. Her heart skipped a beat and she reached for the dagger only to realize it was gone. So was the axe.

He looked furious, and it was directed at her. But before he could grab her, he was swept away. By an *Ateisha*.

Lena stared after him in shock but quickly snapped out of it and scrambled to find the others. Luckily, the next person she found was Cowen. He had another gash on his head that stained some of his hair and face red, but he was standing.

She looked over the rest of him. "Are you hurt anywhere else?"

He shook his head, shielding his body with hers.

She was already turning. "Tuck!"

"*Lena!*" Ira roared, fury and warning coating his voice, making her freeze. "*Where is the ring?*"

The ring? What did he want with that?

Tuck appeared next to them a moment later.

"The cabin," she rushed out. With Tuck's snooping habits, he had to know where it was. "Take us to the cabin."

"Not yet," he said, and she looked at him in confusion.

Weylin was only a few steps away, but before he could reach them, Tuck grabbed both her and Cowen, and the three of them disappeared.

Ira's scream of frustration echoed in her ears as she left the palace behind.

∽

LENA HIT the floor hard enough to bruise, and she immediately knew they weren't in the cabin. The space they were in was too imposing. She recognized the grandeur covering the walls around them. Gems and precious metals littered the marble trim and pillars. They were in the treasury.

She whipped her head around, glaring at Tuck as she climbed to her feet. "What are we doing here? I told you to take us to the cabin!"

Tuck pushed away from the wall he was leaning against and wiped the sweat off his forehead with the back of his hand. He ignored her question completely. "I figured it out—your weird dreams and the sleepwalking—while you were with Ira, ignoring me. *You're welcome,* by the way."

She ground her teeth together, a headache already brewing. "Tuck—"

"You were in the right spot. What you were looking for was under the treehouse. *Deep* under. I asked myself what could be that deep underground? How could it get there? And then I remembered what was close by, and what keeps valuable items underground."

Lena unclenched her jaw when she picked up on what he was getting at. "The treasury."

Tuck nodded.

They stood in the hall leading to the vaults. If they went right, they would end up back in the lobby. If they went left, they would reach the vaults and eventually the elevator that took them down to the Ruler's Treasury.

"We don't have time for this," she said reluctantly. She wanted to follow the voice and find this power, so her Numen would stop tormenting her at the very least, but they were currently under attack. "Ira is after the Ring of Rulers. It's at the cabin. He'll figure it out and be heading there soon. We *need* to get there first."

"We also *need* you to have your head screwed on right," Tuck argued.

She shot him an affronted glare. "Do you see what's happening outside—?"

"Yes," he snapped. "Yes, I do. And I warned you about this, but you ignored me because when it comes to him, you can't think straight. I knew you wouldn't be able to go through with killing him, which is why I was there. You're welcome, *again.*"

She opened her mouth, but he held up his finger. "No, you're going to listen to me this time. If you want to get to the cabin soon then you better find whatever the fuck is haunting you, *quickly.*"

Cowen stepped forward then, coming into her peripheral vision. She startled slightly. She'd forgotten Cowen was here alongside them.

"Your queen ordered you to take her somewhere."

Tuck rolled his eyes. "Yeah, okay, well, I'm ignoring that order. I'm thinking long-term here. So . . . " Tuck leaned forward, his eyes locked with hers, and enunciated clearly, "What do you need?"

Lena scowled at him. Arguing further would only waste more time. He'd made his decision. They weren't leaving until she found what she needed, at least not by Tuck's way of travel. And running to the cabin from here would take nearly thirty minutes. That was too long. Ira would get there first. They were reliant on Tuck's ability, and he knew that.

She had twenty minutes to find what she needed.

"A key," she said, holding his gaze. "Someone up front will know where it is."

Tuck nodded and ran down the hallway to the right.

Lena turned back toward Cowen. "The others?"

His eyes dimmed. "There were guards and monsters waiting for all of us. I assume they targeted us first. Like before—"

Cowen fell silent, but the grief that twisted his face spoke volumes.

History repeats itself.

"Are you sure?" she asked, her voice thick. "Did you see them?"

The Sacred Guard consisted of over a dozen people, and they were well-trained.

"I didn't see everyone, but I saw enough. Benji and Andra . . . I saw their bodies."

Lena turned away from him and squeezed her eyes shut. Her lips quivered as she struggled to rein in her emotions. "You should go to Cora and Nell."

"I have a deal with the barmaid if anything goes south, and Nell and Cora can take care of themselves. My duty is to remain here."

"You should be with your family."

A couple of seconds passed. "I know where I'm needed most. I took an oath, Kalena. And I intend to honor it."

She thought it was horribly ironic and cruel that he was dying because he'd supposedly broken his oath to her, yet he was the only one left to fulfill it at the end.

Tuck reappeared then, marching down the hall and dragging one of the tellers with him.

"Let's go," he said as soon as he reached them. He wrapped his arm around her shoulder, tugging her toward him and grabbing Cowen with his extra hand. Her cheek was squished against his chest and before she could protest or push away, that tingling feeling came over her and they snapped to a different location. Right before the giant door of the Ruler's Treasury.

Tuck let go of them all and turned to the teller, who appeared taken aback by this rushed confrontation. "Unlock it."

By some luck, the teller Tuck had grabbed was the same teller who'd taken Ira and her down here weeks ago.

She stepped past Tuck and the teller's panicked gaze moved to her.

"I'm the queen," she assured them, shooting Tuck a glare. He should've started with that. "You've taken me down here before. With . . . my husband, Ira. Weeks ago."

Recognition seeped into the teller's eyes. "Your Majesty!" he exclaimed. "What's happening? The *Ateisha* stormed the lobby. We had to barricade ourselves—"

"You can unlock the doors while you talk," Tuck pointed out.

She couldn't even get annoyed at him because he was right.

"We're under attack," she told the teller as he hurried to move the bars and place the correct key into the lock. "Your best bet is to hide in here. The vaults are probably one of the safest places in the Highlands."

The doors opened and she was greeted with the sight of piles of coins, gems, and precious metals. The vault was huge. Simply walking around would take too long, and she didn't even know exactly what she was looking for.

She took a deep breath and tried to come up with a plan.

"Hurry it up," Tuck unhelpfully supplied.

"Will you shut up!" she snapped, whirling on him. "You're the one making me do this. I can't focus with you breathing over my shoulder."

He raised a brow.

She turned back around, looking over the large piles once again. Her stomach dropped. "What if you're wrong and we're just wasting our time here?"

"I'm not wrong. Try to focus. You won't be able to fall asleep—we don't have time for that. But maybe if you can get into a meditative state, the voice will lure you toward it."

"What if it doesn't—?"

"*Krashing,* Lena, just *try* it."

She bit her tongue and took another deep breath, letting her eyes slip shut. Adrenaline was still thrumming through her, subdued now that she wasn't fighting, but not gone. It crawled under her skin, distracting her. She tried to push all that aside and focus on the voice, on her Numen. She brushed her fingers over her chest.

Please, listen. Guide me. I want to hear the voice. I want the power. I'll give in.

It was a dangerous thing to say to a Numen, but she was desperate and out of time.

Her Imprint heated as everything else slowly faded away. She tried to recall the voice, the smoothness of it, the allure. She wanted to return to it.

Where are you?

I want to find you. I want to save you. Free you. Let me find you.

Her feet moved forward, slowly at first, but then she began to pick up the pace, walking through the Ruler's Treasury blindly. Darkness greeted her, much like her dreams.

I'm here. I'm right here.

Please, let her have this.

And that was when she felt it—or heard it.

It was a strange hum, one that appealed to her. Low and faint, but she caught it right away. It wrapped around her limbs, pulling her near as its whispers filled her head.

"*Come closer,*" the voice said. "*Come and take me from this place.*"

Her legs moved faster, but her eyes remained closed. She relied on her other senses to direct her. She followed the hum, and after a while, she *saw* it. The noise was a visible, colorful stream winding its way through the clouds of darkness. When she reached out to grab it, her hand went right through it.

"*Free me and I can free you.*"

Her brow furrowed as she followed the path and the connection. Her feet moved on their own accord, like her body and mind knew what she sought even when she didn't.

The stream disappeared, and she stopped and opened her eyes.

She'd traveled far into the Ruler's Treasury and stood near a wall. Mounds of jewels were on either side of her, but her gaze was stuck on the table immediately in front of her, pressed against the wall. The table was littered with many things—a jewelry box, a pipe, a bracelet—but it was the ordinary black pot that stole her attention. It was no bigger than the palm of her hand and was the darkest black she'd ever seen, so dark that it reflected no light. The pot almost looked like a void in the middle of the space. It reminded her of the inky blackness in her dreams.

It looked quite dull, but it *felt* . . . captivating. The hum was coming from it, drawing her closer. She went willingly, maneuvering around the stacks of silver plates and giant pots of sapphires.

When her hand closed around the black pot, the humming stopped suddenly, and a jolt went through her. Everything was silent and still, but in a way . . . the pot was still speaking to her.

Lena hurried back to Cowen and Tuck, turning the pot over in her hands, trying to look for anything special or telling. But it was completely blank. No nicks or patterns or identifying marks. She couldn't tell if this was a year old or a century old. What about *this* could be so powerful? If she hadn't felt the allure, she would doubt that this object was the item she sought.

"That's it?" Cowen asked skeptically when she approached.

She nodded, still looking down at the strange object.

Tuck stepped up to the two of them. "Great. Now let's go."

Lena stuffed the pot away, and when Tuck extended his hand to her, she took it.

CHAPTER
EIGHTY-TWO

Lena bounded up the stairs as soon as she regained her balance in the cabin, leaving Tuck and Cowen behind in the dining room. "I'll grab the ring and be right back!"

There was nothing cozy and warm about her room today. Chills skirted down her arms as she knelt beside her bedside table. She felt under the wood for the ring and plucked it free, holding it up. The light glistened off the purplish-white gem and the gold band.

She squinted and brought it closer. She swore she saw patterned swirls moving within the gem, as if it was alive. Was this one of the stones Ira spoke of? Was that why he wanted to get his hands on the ring so badly? How many stones did he have? And how many more did he need to use that weapon?

The golden ring on her finger shined brightly, reminding her of its presence. Reminding her of him. Them.

She slowly slid it off her finger, reading the words engraved on the inside.

May we find each other in the stars.

A single tear trailed down her cheek. She quickly wiped it away and slid the ring Ira had given her onto another finger. The Ring of Rulers returned to her middle finger. Now it was alone, but it was safe. No one would be able to take it off but her.

She grabbed the extra dagger under the table too and tucked it away before leaving the room. She hurried down the stairs, opening her mouth to call out to Tuck and Cowen, but she paused.

It was too quiet.

She listened for any noise or movement. Nothing. She took out the dagger and continued down the stairs. Tuck and Cowen weren't in the dining room. To her right, flames now licked the hearth.

He was here.

She knew it. She could feel him.

Her footfalls were silent as she moved toward the back door. She reached for the handle only to run into an invisible wall. She bounced back and looked closely at the space in front of her. The barrier was slightly visible. Waves radiated in the air like ripples on the surface of a pond. She touched the wall again and pushed, but it didn't give. And the barrier stretched out on either side of her, probably wrapping around the entire perimeter of the house, keeping her inside.

Lena banged against the barrier, brought her dagger to it, her aura flame, but it stayed solid and unmoving.

"You can't get out."

She spun behind the stairwell, pressing her back against the wall.

"The barrier won't drop until I want it to," Ira said. He sounded like he was on the first floor toward the front of the house. Where she'd just been. "Make it easy for yourself and come out, Lena."

She crept along the back of the stairs and peeked around the corner. When she didn't see him, she moved silently across the hall and down the one leading to the library.

"What's your plan?" he called out to her. "You're going to get the ring and what? It's just you and me in here."

His voice came from the kitchen this time. She could only go so far. The cabin was spacious but not huge.

"I can sense you, you know? It's the bond between us."

She tucked herself into the shadows and tried to think of a plan. Her heart was beating so loudly in her chest that she worried Ira would hear. She winced as his boot scraped the floor. The barrier kept out all sound, making the cabin eerily quiet. Every noise was ten times louder than it would be normally.

"You think I'm your enemy, but I'm not."

Lena slipped into the library and stood behind one of the shelves.

"There's one thing I didn't tell you in the palace. About us. About why I would go to such lengths to protect you. It explains some of our feelings and this bond between us, the way we've always felt drawn to one another, but it doesn't explain everything. And I need you to understand that too. I *chose* to love you."

His voice was getting closer. She looked to the side and saw the door that led into his study. Before she could think twice, she moved inside the room and started to sift through his desk. When she found what she was looking for—the worn leather journal—she stuffed it into her dress pocket alongside the pot and ran out of the study before Ira could trap her inside.

"But you and I—our souls—are connected. I didn't understand why I was so drawn to you at the beginning. I searched for answers, and when I finally found the truth . . . it made so much sense. The bearers of our souls nearly a millennia ago, during the War of Krashing, were lovers. Edynir Akonah and Rhouzara Hellanthe."

Lena bit down on her lip as she slid around the shelves. There was a window, only a few feet away, but she could see the barrier in front of it. Still, she dared to inch closer.

"They loved each other so much that they couldn't bear to be separated in their subsequent lives, so they performed a ritual that bound their souls together for all eternity. They would be drawn to each other, and nothing could keep them apart."

She'd read about that too. The Soul Bond. She'd thought that fit their case, but hearing it was completely different. He was trying to distract her. She couldn't let him succeed.

Outside, two figures stood near the treeline. They looked younger than her. If they were here, they were probably on Ira's side.

"You wanted to know earlier what I had to give up for the Numen to agree to make a pact with you."

Her guesses were all horrifying, but his answer, the truth, was worse.

"Part of my soul."

She froze.

"When I said I would rip myself apart for you, I meant it. I already have. The Numen has a pact with you, but it—and *you*—will always carry a piece of me. Our souls were already intertwined, and this only strengthened our bond. Do you know what that means?"

Lena slowly took a step back from the window and hugged her hands around her middle. He'd given up a part of his soul for her, and still she couldn't trust him. He might protect her, but everything and everyone else . . . Ira would tear them down without hesitation. And she couldn't live like that. She couldn't be trapped, and that was what she would be with him, like this.

"Even if you run and escape today, there is nowhere you can go in this realm—in any realm—where I won't be able to find you. And I won't stop looking."

She ran to the other door in the library, the one that led back to the hall below the stairwell. The door creaked. Footsteps thundered behind her.

She ran for the sitting room at the front of the house, scooping up the quilts and swiping them through the fire until the flames consumed them. She threw the quilts onto the floor, watching as the fire spread to the sofas and carpet and curtains.

It was up to Ira. This house—*their* home—was going up in flames. He said the barriers wouldn't drop until he wanted them too. So he either let her go or let the both of them burn, together.

She ran toward the back of the house before he could catch sight of her.

"Just give me the ring, Lena!" he growled.

She faced the direction Ira was coming from and held the dagger to her neck. When he came around the corner and saw her, he hesitated, eyeing the blade digging into her skin.

"Drop the barrier," she ordered.

She was relying on his love for her, wagering that against his desire for the ring, his desire to fulfill his plan, his *destiny*. She wished she could say with certainty which one he would choose.

Ira prowled closer, keeping a careful eye on her. "You won't do it," he said softly.

Lena pressed the dagger more firmly against her neck, gritting her teeth in pain as blood trailed down her skin.

He tensed and took another step toward her but stopped when she dug deeper.

"Fine," he said, holding his hands up. "Fine, Lena. I'll lower the barriers." His eyes glistened, and the look on his face was one she would remember forever. "I want you to remember that I did fight for you. For us. They wanted me to kill you. They said you made me *weak*. They're not wrong." His voice was melancholy. "But you also gave me something I thought I would never have."

The first thing she thought of was The Lands, and she flinched at the implication. She'd basically handed the country over to him when she refused to see the bad parts of him. He made *her* weak.

The barrier behind her disappeared and she stumbled back. The noises from outside—the screams and roars and clashing of steel—filled her ears. Her free hand grappled at the door, and she pushed it open, moving onto the porch. Ira followed.

"I would stand by you through almost anything," she admitted with some horror. "But not this."

His eyes hardened. "You can't evade me. Do you really want to spend all your life fighting and running?"

She bared her teeth at him, eyes brimming with tears. "Of course I don't, but you've left me no choice."

"I've given you plenty of choices! The exceptions I've made for you—" He snapped his mouth shut and the rage tightening his face disappeared. His eyes went empty and dark as the exhaustion ate at him again. "They haven't changed a thing. They don't mean anything to you."

"I look around and *this* . . . " She gestured to the flames here, the smoke in the distance, the screams and the roars echoing from far away. " . . . is what your actions have done."

She couldn't support him.

She lowered the dagger from her neck and worked Ira's ring off her finger, letting it fall to the ground.

"I wished things were different," she told him before throwing the dagger at his head.

Her Slayer materialized next to the two figures near the treeline, and she took off running.

"*Judah!*" Ira yelled behind her.

Lena pushed her legs faster, heading for the woods. The sun was already setting. The trees cast shadows onto the ground that concealed her further. She needed to find Tuck and Cowen. They had to be around somewhere, likely fighting with Ira's cronies.

A hand shot out from behind a tree, grabbing and pulling her toward them. A noise slipped from her mouth as she struggled in their grip, turning and slamming her elbow against their nose. Their grip loosened and she spun around, aura flame at her fingertips.

"Fuck! Kalena, it's me!"

Cowen.

She breathed out a sigh of relief and her aura flame disappeared. When he went to pull her back to his chest, she let him.

"Thank the Numina," he said, his voice uneven. "I'm sorry. I'm sorry. Are you okay?"

She nodded, still fighting to catch her breath. They didn't have time for apologies.

She stepped back, ready to keep moving, but halted when she noticed the black veins spreading up Cowen's neck. Blood stained his clothing and skin, and the side of his head was a mess of coagulated blood.

He gave her a half-hearted grin. "Looks pretty bad, doesn't it?"

It took her a bit too long to respond. She ripped her eyes away from his injuries and the black veins. "We'll get you help, after we get out of here. Come on. We've got to look for Tuck."

Cowen huffed and shook his head.

She said more urgently, "Come on!"

And thankfully, this time, he didn't fight her.

Cowen's pace was slower than usual as they moved through the woods. She didn't comment on it, only keeping an eye out for anyone or anything else. The longer they were out there, alone, the more paranoid and concerned she became.

She heard a slight groan behind her and looked back. Cowen was leaning heavily against a tree, spitting blood onto the ground. It was too dark. It almost looked . . . poisoned.

"That doesn't look too good," a new voice observed

Lena spun around, shielding Cowen with her body and calling her Slayer back to her.

"Woah there."

The man in front of her held up his hands. He was grinning slightly, and the look in his eyes sent shivers down her spine. *Dangerous,* her mind supplied.

All Blessed were dangerous and a handful of Cursed were as well, but the man in front of her reeked of it. His eyes were blood red, glowing because his Slayer was out. His pale skin was devoid of blood, as was his hair. A large scar made up one side of his face, but it was old. The blood splatters on his clothes, however, were not. A telltale sign that he'd been fighting. Did that blood belong to Tuck?

"You look pretty exhausted," he noted.

Her Slayer was swiped off its feet before it could reach him by a larger, red Slayer. She was exhausted, so her Slayer wasn't manifesting at its full potential. The red one was able to pin it down without much struggle.

Cowen was barely staying on his feet behind her. Summoning his Slayer would probably use up the rest of his energy.

"Why don't I take you back to the palace, Your Majesty?"

"*Fuck you.*"

She couldn't leave Cowen behind, but she needed an out. Ira's allies were *good* fighters, and she had a feeling that the man in front of her was better than Harlow. She didn't want to engage in a fight, but she would if she had to. But then Cowen would be left defenseless. He couldn't fend for himself like this.

Tuck, please. Where are you?

The scarred man's eyebrows rose as his grin widened. "Alright," he said easily. "I never turn down a fight. I'll tell Ira I tried."

He moved so quickly. Her tired muscles were barely able to react even with the adrenaline, but she'd fought on her last leg before.

Right before they collided, a crack sounded and there was another body next to them. A green Slayer tackled the scarred man before the purple and red aura flame clashed. Tuck reached for her, but an axe sailed through the air between them. Lena jumped back to avoid it and caught sight of someone else in the corner of her eye.

Harlow.

She had a sword. Lena knew that sword. It was the one Kieryn had wielded.

Harlow seemed to notice the moment Lena recognized it because a sinister grin spread across her face, and she charged. Any fatigue Lena might've felt was wiped away by the wave of fury that engulfed her. She gritted her teeth and threw her hands out, a scream leaving her throat as aura flame soared toward Harlow, slowing her down momentarily. Lena used those few seconds to scoop up the axe that rested a few feet away.

The scarred man had turned his attention to Tuck, and Tuck's Slayer was busy with Harlow's. It was two on two now.

Lena glared at Harlow, aura flame coating her body like battle armor. Harlow followed suit and lunged toward her. The sword cut through the air. Lena prepared to block it, but another sword met Harlow's before she could.

Cowen slid between them and pushed Lena several feet back as he shoved his blade forward. He shouldn't have been able to contain Harlow with how sick he was, but he did, pushing her back inch by inch. Aura flame covered both of their arms, meeting in the middle in a whirlwind of fiery colors.

He dared to glance over his shoulder for a split second, his eyes finding Lena's. "Remember your promise."

Her eyes widened when she realized what he was going to do. She reached out for him, but his Slayer materialized between them, snarling at her and forcing her farther back. It then tackled the scarred man, keeping him pinned momentarily.

"Go!" Cowen shouted as he struggled with Harlow.

Tuck appeared next to Lena, his fingers curling around her shoulder. She yanked herself out of his grip and lunged for Cowen.

Time moved slowly and her body weighed her down. She could see it happening. Cowen stumbled and Harlow didn't let up.

Lena had only taken a few steps before Harlow's sword speared through Cowen's chest.

"*No!*"

Tuck's arms curled around her again as her legs gave out. The axe slipped from her fingers, and the ground around them broke. It flew away from the two of them in an explosion of wind and fury. Harlow and the scarred man flew back as the trees groaned and snapped in half.

It was over in seconds, but the area around them was in wreckage. She let out a sob, eyes seeking out Cowen, but he was lost among the destruction. Tuck pulled her in tighter. Then the scenery around them disappeared.

CHAPTER
EIGHTY-THREE

Tuck teleported them to the hill he'd fought Ira on. Lena shoved him away and took two steps before collapsing to her knees and sobbing. She wrapped her arms around herself, shaking from exertion, and cried so hard she threw up.

Tuck's hands gently pulled her to her feet. "I'm sorry."

One look at Cowen had told her his time was up. The broken oath had killed him before Harlow had.

Lena pushed away from Tuck again and ran a trembling hand over her face, wiping off the tears. She took a few deep breaths, continuing even when she crumbled and began crying again. She rubbed at her cheeks and eyes until her skin felt raw. The rest of her had numbed by the time she turned to Tuck. He surveyed her face, his jaw tense.

"We need to go back," she croaked.

He shook his head. "We can't."

"We have to!"

I made a promise.

But his face remained set. Tears filled her eyes again and she turned away, holding her breath and hoping that everything else stayed in with it.

"Then what do we do?" she gasped out. "Where do we go?"

Ira would search the entirety of The Lands for her, and they would just become more trapped the farther south they went. He couldn't make it to Ouprua, but neither could they.

Tuck's gaze moved over her shoulder. She turned and drew an unsteady breath when her eyes fell upon the mountains.

They scaled down the side of the cliff when they found a less steep section and walked to a cavern underneath. In it, Tuck grabbed the bag he'd stored there in case of a short notice or emergency. They changed into warmer clothes and collected as much water as they could from the nearby spring. It was all they could do.

In the distance, the *Ateisha* were returning to the mountains, which was good for the people of The Lands. Whoever was left. But it was bad for her and Tuck, who were heading in that same direction.

The sky darkened and it began to rain. Just like that night.

Tuck teleported them to the base of the mountains to give them a good head start. He still wasn't fully recovered, and each leap wore him down further. But they didn't stop by Eldon's for rest or supplies because they didn't want to drag anyone else into this. And they didn't have the time to stop.

Ira would be after them soon. After *her*. And the ring. He wouldn't follow them up into the mountain range. Not right away.

The bond between them was quiet and still. If she didn't know better, she would question if it was even still there. But she did know better now, and she knew this wouldn't be the end of him.

When they hiked a few miles up and the rain turned to sleet, she turned around to stare at The Lands. The Highlands had taken the brunt of the attack. The beautiful and colorful countryside had been ravaged. It appeared brown and dead. It was on fire.

Wherever she looked, she saw destruction. Calamity. Maybe she'd brought it. If she had, then perhaps she was taking it with her. The people of The Lands deserved peace. Some of them, at least. But they wouldn't be getting peace, would they? She didn't know the entirety of Ira's plans, but she knew his intentions weren't as pure as he'd presented them. This was only the beginning. In more ways than one.

Nothing had changed.

She was right where she'd started—running away with no home to return to. Except it was worse now. She could only go forward.

Lena turned her back on The Lands for the third time and followed the hum that lured her into the mountains.

EPILOGUE

Ira stood in the grand library at the very top of the palace, a room that every Blessed had needed special permission to enter. Not anymore, of course. It was his study now. The room was vast and well-fortified. It also had a large balcony with an excellent view of the mountains. He was currently leaning against the wooden desk that he'd lugged up there, staring at those mountains. Lena was crossing them right now. With Tuck.

He gritted his teeth in distaste and turned around, looking at the other four people in the room.

"How are things?"

Weylin snorted from where he rested against the wall.

"As well as can be expected," Vanik said. There was a bite to his voice that Ira also ignored.

"No rebellions?"

"Not yet."

"The casualties are nearing 20,000," Weylin said then, pointedly, "but we're not even halfway done counting the bodies."

Ira stilled, staring straight ahead. "Then count faster. What about the one from Ouprua?"

"He's locked up," Harlow said.

Kieryn had put up a good fight. Ira had planned to kill him, but he'd changed his mind after the sorcerer survived the initial attack on him. Kieryn had his uses, and those uses had become much clearer after his capture. He'd taken down nearly fifty Blessed on his own. Yes, he would be of some use later.

"We need to bury the bodies," Ira continued. "I don't want anyone burned unless I specifically say so."

Cowen's burial had been earlier today. He'd fought against Ira, but he'd protected Lena with his life, and for that, Ira was grateful. He had placed the captain of the Sacred Guard where he belonged, next to Lena's family.

The others were silent. Harlow wasn't looking at him, and neither was Judah. They were all still nursing their injuries from the attack. Weylin and Harlow had gotten the worst of it.

"What is it?" he asked bluntly.

The three of them exchanged glances while Judah stayed quiet and still in the corner. He had grown to be a very brooding teen.

Harlow was the first to snap. "What the fuck are we doing?" She pushed herself out of her chair and stared at him defiantly. "You got us out after we got you out. We fought by your side. We helped you dismantle the temple and prophets. We helped you get what you wanted. We understand that you have this Edynir Akonah destiny shit to work out, but where are we at? What are we doing *here*?"

"Helped me get what I wanted?" he echoed. "I wanted three things: The Lands, the ring, and the queen. I only have one of those things."

Harlow rolled her eyes.

"I saw that you tried to kill her," he said, his voice darkening. "Even when I told you not to. Multiple times."

"She's a threat," Harlow argued. "I'll say it if the others won't. She clouds your judgment, and you know better than anyone that we can't afford that."

He sighed and stood to his full height. "We need her for this to work. I doubt she'll take the ring off now knowing that I need it, so the only way we can get our hands on it is if we can *convince* her to give it up."

"Or we can cut off her hand," Weylin offered.

Ira threw a dark glare in his direction.

"Or just her finger," Weylin negotiated.

"I thought you already tried to *convince* her and that failed?" Vanik asked. "You've known her for years. If you haven't managed to convince her by now—"

"We haven't been *together* for years," Ira responded, irritation creeping into his voice. "And she's only been in possession of the ring for a few months. I didn't know where it was before then. I couldn't sense it like the other stones. She didn't hand over the ring because she was upset—"

"You knew she took off the ring, right?" Weylin asked. "You could've gotten it. Why didn't you?"

He turned back to Weylin, his jaw tight.

"You didn't want to take it? You wanted her to give it to you . . . as if that would prove something?"

"It would."

"She told me she holds grudges for a long time."

Ira would like to say Tuck had been whispering in her ear, saying bad things about him and that had influenced her decision making. He knew the Vuukroma had been doing exactly that, but he had to believe Lena couldn't be so easily swayed, not against him. He'd seen her face all those times he had to deflect or leave or lie. She'd been more hurt than anything. And that was all him. He'd hurt her even when trying to protect her.

"She'll come to her senses," he said. "Once things settle, she'll realize—"

"No, she won't," Judah interrupted. He had a nasty look on his face as he stared down Ira. "She won't understand because she's not a firstborn."

"Kid's got a point," Weylin said.

Judah's glare turned on him. "Stop calling me kid."

"What's the ultimate goal, Ira?" Harlow asked, bringing this conversation back on track. "If this is the means, then what's the end?"

Part of him wondered that himself. Over the past year, he'd discovered that Zosia hadn't been exactly honest with him. At all. He'd uncovered things that she was unwilling to tell him and acquired even more questions.

"I don't entirely know," he admitted. "Healing the realms? Ending the prophets and the temple and their philosophy? Permanently."

When did it stop? When did he stop?

He'd eventually told Vanik what the sisters had told him, especially Zosia, when they met in the desolate realm. He'd had to make sense of it himself first. He asked Zosia questions and did his own research and self-discovery, but it was difficult doing that when he was with a bunch of dirtyhands. In the Tower, however, he had all the time in the realm.

Vanik and the others were working with him. They were keeping Judah safe. They were protecting the firstborns. They had let him go and stay behind to fight. He owed them. It wasn't fair to keep them out of the loop, not when they were risking their lives *for him*. And they couldn't truly work together to shut down this operation if they didn't have a free flow of information between them. They had to be honest if they wanted to live. They were already fighting against the odds. And unlike many of the unfair parts of this reality, he had a say in this one. So he'd told Vanik the entire truth, and Vanik had told the others. It had taken them a while to accept it, just as it had him.

"Whatever it is, it's got to be close. I'm fighting for it. What I do know is that we need all the stones. The shattering of the realms didn't only break the realms, it cursed them. And the people in them." The corner of his lip curled up at the word choice. They were all cursed in some way. "But this realm is the most important. It's a crux of sorts. That's why it has three stones. This place was the beginning, and I intend for it to be the end."

"But you don't know how to achieve those things?" Weylin drawled.

"If you want to read through these books with me, be my guest."

"Isn't that lady—Zosia, or whatever—supposed to be helping you with that?" Harlow asked.

He and Vanik made eye contact. "Yes, she is."

"Then where is she?"

"Outside."

Harlow straightened, her eyes going to the door.

He swept his arm out, motioning for them to leave, but the four of them stayed put.

"If you want to walk away and live the rest of your lives in whatever relative peace you can find, I'm not going to stop you," he snapped. "But I have shit to do. Get out."

He looked at Vanik especially, but the blond didn't put up a fight. None of them did as they left the study. He hoped they would still be there the next time he called for them. But he had to speak to Zosia. Now.

She wasn't outside the room like he'd implied. She was in this realm somewhere and would be in his presence relatively soon, but she'd made it clear that she didn't wait on anyone. Though, she liked to keep him waiting.

He walked over to the balcony. The doors were pushed wide open so he could experience the full extent of the magnificent view. He sat down on one of the plush chairs positioned before the window and reached his hand out to touch the base of the sword that had been sheathed and hung on the golden frame earlier today. His fingers traced the delicate designs, and he waited, staring at the mountains.

Ira wondered how far she'd gotten and if she'd run into any *Ateisha*. He could still *feel* her, but she was blocking him out. Their bond and her mental barriers were more complicated than she understood.

He only had a rudimentary understanding of sorcery. He'd learned it for her, for capturing the Numen, though Zosia wanted him to learn it more formally. Since his knowledge was limited, he could only slip past Lena's defenses at certain times, not indefinitely.

He reached into his pocket and pulled out Lena's ring. He stared at it and the words engraved on the inside.

May we find each other in the stars.

A sad smile tugged at his lips, and he clenched his fist around the ring.

He was alone once again.

He had done everything in his power to protect her, but he'd still lost her. With Lena, he had *something*, and he wasn't *nothing*. Someone had chosen *him*. If he was truly and purely evil, that couldn't have happened.

"I told you that girl would confuse you."

Ira continued to gaze at the mountains and trace the sword. "She didn't confuse me. If anything, she helped me *see*."

Zosia scoffed behind him. "See what? You should've grabbed the ring when you had the chance, but you waited because you were scared of losing her. And in the end, you lost both."

For now, yes.

"You gave up a part of your soul for her. Do you realize what you've done? You cannot run around and do whatever you please. You have—"

"A destiny to fulfill. Yes, I know. But she's special."

"She's just like every other girl."

"I love her."

"You're *obsessed* with her," Zosia corrected. "You never had anything just for yourself, so when she came along, you latched onto her. You convinced yourself that your relationship with her was something more than just some boy wanting to be wanted."

Ira abruptly stood and turned on her. "You don't get to lecture me on relationships. I found something quite interesting while I was here. Being the king consort, I had access to things I didn't even know existed. And I made an agreement with a prophet who could get me what I needed from the temple." He leaned forward. "You and Edynir Akonah knew each other *much more* than you let on."

Zosia didn't falter. "And look how that turned out. Relationships are a weakness."

"Is that why you tried to kill Lena in the Lowlands? Poison? Really? You think I wouldn't notice?" he raged.

"And I told you sacrifices had to be made, Atreus."

He paused. "I'm Ira."

"You will always be Atreus."

He reared back, barely concealing his flinch. Zosia's expression had not changed once during this conversation. She'd been by his side for years, a mentor of sorts, in more ways than he'd realized.

"You lied to me. You told me I needed souls to power the tablet—"

"You do. The prophets used the souls of the firstborns who passed. Now that the weapon is in your possession, you need to keep it stable by feeding it souls. I told you that you could choose anyone—"

"You told me," he said, fighting to keep his voice even, "that I was the one making the decisions. So tell me why you decided to kill Lena's family?"

Zosia's facade slipped momentarily, but she quickly and artfully pieced it back together.

"Are you not going to take responsibility for it because you had another name then? Another skin?"

It was a tactic she used often. He didn't know everything about her—far from it—but he knew she was divine. Not a Numen, but something else. She defied all reason and law.

"Who were you then? *Tell me.*"

"Maeve," she said softly. "My name was Maeve."

He recognized the name almost immediately as one of the Sacred Guards. She'd been one of the few guards Lena had spoken highly of. They'd been close. Too close. Because all that time, Zosia had been . . .

He looked back up at her, heat consuming him.

"I told you I would always look after you, one way or another. That guard—Andy—was useful enough—"

"Andra?" he corrected, his voice sharp. "You were Andra too?"

"No, but she was working for me." Zosia clucked her tongue at Ira's confusion and looked almost disappointed. "Did you *really* think the Sacred Guard was naturally that inept?"

"You planted Andra . . . to endanger Lena . . . "

"That girl was so willing to run headfirst into danger, and that Andy guard was softer than I would've liked. She wouldn't kill the girl—"

"You don't *touch her!*" Ira snapped.

Silence coated the room. His hands trembled and his Slayer roared, sensing his rage and wanting to feast upon it, to taste flesh.

"She was distracting you," Zosia said. "Her family was distracting you. I wanted to get rid of the distractions, so I may have left an opening for the assassins, but *I* didn't kill any of them. That was truly the work of the council. I merely . . . reaped their usefulness."

"You mutilated them! They were good people! People *I* cared about! They accepted me! They taught me things—"

"Did they make you feel normal?"

He blinked and his words dried up in his throat.

Zosia shook her head. "You aren't normal. You aren't expendable. You aren't nothing. You will never be. *They are. She is.* You've elevated her in your mind. Made her appear more special than she really is."

"She *is* special. You didn't see what she did in that room. She ripped it apart. She controlled the *Ateisha*. She is calamity. She plays a part in this. I know it."

She would come back to him.

"If you continue to chase her, the only part in this she will play is your downfall."

The frustration inside of him was bubbling over. He took a deep breath and collected himself. Then, in one swift movement, he unsheathed the sword and swung it through the air and Zosia's neck. Her head toppled to the ground, and then her body collapsed. Blood spilled across the white marble as he pulled a piece of cloth from his pocket and cleaned the sword. He sheathed it again and stepped over the body.

Prophet Nya waited for him in the hall. She dipped her head in acknowledgement. "My lord."

"There's a mess in my study," he said. "Make sure it's cleaned up."

She nodded and snapped at the guards nearby. They entered the room behind him.

He kept his eyes on the prophet. "Did you bring what I asked for?"

She nodded again and moved to the side as she pulled someone out from behind her. The girl was young—she couldn't be any older than four if Ira's math was right—but she was still considered small for her age, which was normal for firstborns. Spending time underground had drained some pigment from her light brown skin, and her long and unruly black hair was desperately in need of a cut for the same reason. Ira would see to that soon.

The girl looked at him shyly, her bright green eyes causing Ira to hesitate for a moment. There was no question about it. Those were Tuck's eyes.

Ira smiled and knelt before the girl. "Hello," he said gently. "What's your name?"

The girl shifted from foot to foot, scrutinizing him with eyes much too wise for a child her age. "Emry."

"Was that name given to you or did you pick it?"

The girl scowled at him. It was a look that had been directed at him many times by an older and leaner version of this face. "I picked it," Emry said, standing tall.

Ira smothered his smile. "Good," he said. "My name is Ira. I also picked that name for myself." He stood and held out his hand. "Come on then. I have some things I want to show you."

After a few seconds of hesitation, Emry's small palm slipped into his.

ACKNOWLEDGMENTS

Wow. So you reached the end, huh? I honestly don't really even know where to start the acknowledgments because, admittedly, I often don't read the acknowledgments at the end of the book, so I'm kind of just winging it in true Faith-style (although some of my friends may say I don't wing things and that I am a meticulous planner; nevertheless . . .). This book would not be where it's at, and I would not be where I'm at without the people who had a hand in this year-and-a-half-long process, so I would be remiss if I didn't mention and thank them.

I started plotting *Cursed and Crowned* and taking it seriously in February 2022, and now, in May 2023, it's being published. I can't believe I'm actually writing this, preparing for my book's upcoming release. It's been a journey, to say the least. It feels surreal, even though this is only the beginning (hopefully) of my long career as an author. There will be many more journeys and publications to come, but I imagine the first one will always hold a special place in my heart.

With that being said, I want to thank my family members who stood by my side through this process, namely my parents. While they may not fully understand my desire to write and operate in this industry, they believed in me and supported me nonetheless, step by step. Thank you to my mom for being someone I could vent to about business decisions, plot points, and just the general stressors that come with writing and publishing your debut book. Thank you for staying up late with me or researching on my behalf. Thank you to my dad for helping me with my technology issues and being a silent but strong supporter throughout this entire process. I cannot imagine going through this journey without the two of them.

I also want to thank my cover artist Rachel McEwan. You were so amazing to work with. Being a newbie author, I had a lot of questions and wasn't quite sure how everything in this business worked, and you were so helpful and patient with me while I figured everything out. You perfectly captured the vision I had for the cover: dark, alluring, eye-catching, and absolutely *gorgeous*. I'm truly obsessed with the cover, and I fall in love with it a little bit more every time I look at it.

Thank you to my editor Chelsea Terry who combed through all 260k of this book to fix my mistakes and offer suggestions that helped improve this story. The sweet comments made me feel like I was doing something right as a writer. Seriously, thank you. My eyes and my brain could only handle so much. Like Rachel, you were so patient, kind, and flexible as I figured out my schedule. Thank you to both my cover artist and editor for making the publication of my debut book easier for me.

Next, I want to thank my beta readers, who were the first people to see the story that is *Cursed and Crowned*. Thank you for taking an interest in my book and choosing to spend your free time leaving helpful comments that helped me improve my craft. Thank you especially to Casey Hayes, Kyare Betzing, and @maddylilley on Tiktok for your thoughtful and detailed notes from start to finish and for working with my schedule. Casey, thank you for all the support and love you've shown me and this book. I appreciate you early readers so, so much, and I hope you enjoy this polished version of *Cursed and Crowned*.

Thank you to my writing friends, David Kang and Carly, for hyping me up about this story from day one. Thank you for the helpful suggestions and the serotonin-boosting messages. David, thank you for being my listening ear. I need to run everything by someone, and that person is almost always you, which unfortunately means you get spoiled for nearly everything I write (sorry about that), but I so appreciate your feedback. Thank you for being there, and I can't wait to read your stories when they're published.

Thank you to my other reader friends, Shannon and Triniti. You were also always there to listen and hype me up when I inevitably went on a tangent and started talking about my book and dreams of becoming an author.

I want to thank my three college creative writing professors as well. They don't know about the existence of this book, but each of them has helped me build my courage and skill as a writer. Dr. J, thank you for being amazing and for all the time and publishing advice you gave us.

Thank you to everyone interested in my story and those willing to be sent a copy. Thank you to anyone and everyone who shares my book or spreads the word about it. Thank you to anyone who buys it or posts a review. Thank you to all my readers for taking a chance on me and my debut book. Thank you for helping me get one step closer to achieving my dreams as an author. I see you all, and I appreciate you all. As I said, this is only the beginning of my career as an author. I hope you will stick around for the rest of it.

ABOUT THE AUTHOR

Faith Fray is a fantasy writer who lives in her head and other media more than she lives in the real world. She has loved reading and telling stories since she was a child, but she didn't start taking writing seriously until a few years ago in college when she wrote her first draft. Since then, she has come up with dozens of (heart-wrenching) story ideas that will keep her busy for the next decade or two, so she hopes her readers will stick around for them. When she's not writing, she's either reading, hanging out with her dog Remi, watching TV shows, or *thinking* about writing. She's an introverted coffee addict and nerd with an intense sweet tooth and a love for zombie media, traveling, food, and making her readers emotional.

You can find her at faithfray.com and
@authorfaithfray on Instagram, TikTok, and Twitter

Made in the USA
Monee, IL
08 June 2023

34995867R00374